THE HAVILFAR CYCLE I

The Dray Prescot Series

THE HAVILFAR CYCLE I

Kenneth Bulmer

writing as
Alan Burt Akers

Published by
Bladud Books

First published in 2007 by Bladud Books.

Originally published separately by Daw Books, Inc., as:
Manhounds of Antares (1974)
Arena of Antares (1974)
Fliers of Antares (1975)

This First omnibus edition published in 2007 by
Bladud Books, an imprint of Mushroom Publishing, Bath,
BA1 4EB, United Kingdom

www.bladudbooks.com

ISBN 978-184319-554-2

Contents

Manhounds of Antares

A note on the Havilfar Cycle

With this volume of his Saga, Dray Prescot is launched headlong into a brand-new series of adventures upon the planet of Kregen, that marvelous and beautiful, mystical and terrible world four hundred light-years away beneath the Suns of Scorpio.

Dray Prescot is a man above medium height, with straight brown hair and brown eyes that are level and oddly dominating. His shoulders are immensely wide and there is about him an abrasive honesty and a fearless courage. He moves like a great hunting cat, quiet and deadly. Born in 1775 and learning about life in the inhumanly cruel and harsh conditions of the late eighteenth-century wooden navy, he presents a picture of himself that, the more we learn of him, grows no less enigmatic.

Through the machinations of the Savanti nal Aphrasöe, mortal but superhuman men dedicated to the aid of humanity, and of the Star Lords, he has been taken to Kregen many times. In his early years he rose to become Zorcander among the Clansmen of Segesthes, and Lord of Strombor in Zenicce, and then a member of the mystic and martial Order of Krozairs of Zy. Against all odds Prescot won his way to the attainment of his single highest desire upon Kregen and in that immortal battle at The Dragon's Bones he claimed his Delia, Delia of Delphond, Delia of the Blue Mountains, as his own. And — Delia claimed him, in the face of her father, the dread Emperor of the Empire of Vallia, and before the rolling thunder of Prescot's men and comrades in the acclamations of Hai Jikai.

As Prince Majister, Prescot sailed aboard the Emperor's airboat back to Vondium, capital of Vallia, and his eyes and imagination were filled with the glories to come, for he has no need to tell us that he felt all his dreams had come true. Under his old scarlet and yellow flag, standing proudly at his side, with him sailed Delia, Princess Majestrix.

Thus ends "The Delian Cycle." This volume, *Manhounds of Antares*, opens "The Havilfar Cycle," and, as you will discover in the following pages, a new life does open for Dray Prescot on Kregen beneath the Suns of Scorpio; but that new life is cruelly different from all he expected and dreamed, hurling him into fresh adventure and danger among peoples and places far removed from those he knows and loves.

Alan Burt Akers

One

Delia

Delia and I were married.

Delia of Delphond, Delia of the Blue Mountains, Princess Majestrix of Vallia, and I, Dray Prescot, were married.

If that sounds to you like the end of the story, then you are as deceived as I was. Many and many foolish young lovers have imagined, on Kregen no less than on Earth, that in the merry ringing of wedding bells lies the happy end of their adventures.

Oh, I knew the shadowy presence of the Star Lords might again manifest itself in the scarlet and golden shape of a mighty raptor, the Gdoinye, or the Savanti might decide out of their mortal but superhuman wisdom to make use of my services again.

But that was of the future, the might-be. Who reckons of the future when he is in love and newly wedded and all of Kregen glows and beckons before him?

But, just before we could be married, there was one other item of unfinished business. All the way back to the capital I felt strongly that I was moving into a new era of my life. That this was so, although not in the way I expected, you shall hear.

After we had returned from that immortal battle at The Dragon's Bones and life took its new turn, I felt I might be able to relax. The idea that Dray Prescot could ever relax may strike you as strange. But sometimes I can, and occasionally I have been able to throw off the cares of the world for a short time and follow my own inclinations. My relationship with the Emperor would remain on a strange footing, and I know that for all his own intemperate hauteur and pride, he feared me a little, even with armed men of his own choosing about him.

We flew down to land in the square before the Emperor's palace. So impatient had he been to return that he had driven his airboat ahead of those following. I jumped down onto the hot stones of the square and looked about, surprised at the absence of people where normally one could see chattering citizens, Koters about their business, strings of calsanys, zorca chariots with their tall wheels flickering, all the brilliant hurly-burly of everyday life in Vondium.

A group of men rushed from the open gateways leading into the outer palace courtyards.

They wore garish green and purple rosettes pinned to their buff leather tunics, and flaunting green and purple feathers in their wide-brimmed Vallian hats.

With a curse I ripped out my rapier and dagger and thrust myself forward to stand before Delia.

She pushed me aside in the shoulder, and stepped up to stand boldly alongside me.

"Third party!" she said. "So there are more of them."

"Aye, my love," I said. "And you get back aboard the flier and take off — you and your father."

"If you think just because we are to be married I will meekly take orders from you, Dray Prescot, you hairy great graint, and fly away and leave you in peril—"

"Delia!"

"Come away, daughter! Let the warriors fight—"

"Yes, my father. Here is one warrior who will never run away, and I will never run from his side."

Well, that is my Delia. I had no time to argue with her. The men of the third party who had in secret infiltrated the other political parties of Vallia and sought to overthrow the Emperor rushed down upon me.

With a breath-wasting shout — for I wished to draw all their attention to me — I leaped forward, brandishing my weapons. You who have listened to my story this far will know I ordinarily never shout in action, and as for brandishing weapons, that is a waste of energy. But as I ran headlong at these oncoming killers I knew I must meet them and keep them in play well away from Delia until the remainder of our fliers arrived bringing with them my men of Felschraung and Longuelm, of Strombor, and Delia's Blue Mountain Boys.

Footsteps and the rasp of weapons at my back told me the handful of men aboard our flier had run to join me.

That made the odds a little better, but it was still something like a hundred to twenty.

That we should be thus caught up in this petty struggle right at the end! We had been victorious and had crushed the third-party conspiracy and now Naghan Furtway, Kov of Falinur, and his nephew Jenbar, who had aspired to Delia's hand, had fled the country. And now this! Truly, I cursed at the stupid and senseless danger my Delia had run into here in the great square outside her own palace.

In a screech of blades the two parties met.

I fought. I had been fighting on and off for many burs past. I had been wounded — slightly, it is true — and now despite all those years of Earthly sailor training, the years with my clansmen of the plains, and as a swifter captain on the Eye of the World, I felt that I was tired.

But while hostile men sought to slay Delia, tiredness in my rapier arm and fatigue in my dagger arm and rubbery feebleness in my legs were sins, all sins, mortal sins!

So I fought and my rapier slashed down faces, and spitted guts, and my main-gauche weaved its silver net of protection, and I held the front cluster of whooping men racing in for the kill. The crew from the airboat joined in, and, for a space, we halted that fierce onward surge.

But I knew we could not hold out very much longer.

These men attacking us with their flaunting green and purple third-party colors wore in banded rings about their sleeves the colors of yellow and blue.

Now blue is a most unusual color to be found in insignia in Vallia, for blue is the color of the nations of Pandahem, and between Pandahem and Vallia lay an old enmity.

4

But I knew these colors of blue and yellow belonged to a certain Kov of Zamra, one Ortyg Larghos, a relative of Nath Larghos, who had tried to suborn me into the ranks of the third party, and whose eye I had put out with a stone, and who had now, presumably, run overseas with his accomplices.

I could see Ortyg Larghos leaping about at the rear of his men, urging them on. He was a fat paunchy man, with a saturnine face in which all the healthy brown hair had fallen away to leave a greasy ring of fuzz around his head and a face as smooth as a loloo's egg.

There was no opportunity for me to bring my great Lohvian longbow into action, which was a pity, for I fancied if I feathered the rast his men might run away. As it was, they looked to be a bunch of mercenary desperadoes, fighting for money. Among them there were Rapas and Ochs, a Brokelsh, even a Womox, but I saw no Chuliks. From this I took heart. It is notorious that the Chuliks, regarding themselves as the most expensive of mercenaries, are choosy as to their employers.

"Hai!" I yelled, and pressed, and nicked crimson drops from my rapier across the faces of a bunch that sought to rush me together. They blinked as the blood splashed them, and in that blinking I spitted them, one, two, three, and the fourth took my dagger through his heart.

A screaming lifted at my back.

Letting the Kov of Zamra go hang I swung about, jumping agilely the while in a frantic zigzag, and stared back at the flier.

A group had brushed past the Emperor's bodyguards, those few men who had descended with us on the bloody ropes from the shattered tower in the circle of The Dragon's Bones, and were carrying him off. I could not see Delia. My heart thumped so that I had to fight for breath.

Not now! Not so close to the end!

The way back lay over spilled blood and cumbering bodies.

At the flier I saw Delia.

She stood with a sword in her hand, a Rapa at her feet coughing his guts out, with his beaked bird's head all twisted askew. She waved the sword at me.

"My father! Dray — they've taken my father!"

"Stay here, Delia!" I yelled it at her with a force that drove her back as she started to run with me. "Go back!" Now I could see, slanting down into the square, the welcome sight of fliers planing in. "Here come Seg and Inch! Get them, my heart, for the sake of your father!"

She knew exactly what I meant.

I did not mean that she would run to the fliers and fetch Seg and Inch and Hap Loder and Varden and Vomanus for the sake of her father the Emperor at all. I meant that she should run there for my sake, for our sakes.

She would have none of it.

I couldn't stop.

The descending fliers had been spotted by the men of Kov Ortyg of Zamra, and they yelled in fear, and scattered, and ran. The group with the Emperor hared off away from the palace, and running with them, angling in from the side, ran Ortyg Larghos himself.

5

I ran.

That faintness overpowering me must not be allowed to interfere now. I loved Delia and Delia loved me, but if her father died now and my aid proved ineffectual there would be a shadow between us, a shadow never mentioned, never alluded to, but a shadow nevertheless.

The hot stones of the square burned up at me.

I caught them easily enough, for the Emperor was struggling. He was still a powerful man, and well-fed, and filled with the innate majesty of his position, so that he gave them some trouble. I truly believe that this manhandling with its attendant physical exercise changed something about that man, that dread Emperor, the father of Delia. He had never been handled so for years. So that when I caught them and laid about me, he could snatch up a sword and stand at my side.

He was no great shakes as a swordsman, and I had my work cut out to guard him as well as myself, but he kept pressing on, shouting fiercely, through his teeth: "Vallia! Vallia! By the Invisible Twins!" and, when a deflected lunge from me toppled a hapless wight into his path and he could slash down, he yelled: "Opaz the all-glorious! Vallia! Vallia! Drak of Vallia!"

Kov Larghos shrieked at his men.

'Take him, you fools! Cut down the barbarian! Take the Emperor!"

I could understand what Kov Larghos must be thinking. He had been a party to the plots hatched by his relative, Nath Larghos, the Trylon of the Black Mountains, and I guessed Naghan Furtway had promised him the position of Pallan of Vondium itself. Now, with no knowledge of the utter defeat of the third party, he sought to capture the Emperor and use him as a bargaining counter.

"Keep behind me, Majister," I said. "I'll spit you by mistake if you insist on skipping out ahead of me."

I did not speak overpolitely to this emperor.

"This is warm work, Dray Prescot—" He slashed at an Och and the little four-armed halfling interposed his shield and the rapier bounced and clanged. The Och thrust with his lower right arm wielding a spear and I had to skip and slice and jump to avoid the sweep of the sword in his upper right. But he went down, screeching.

"By the Black Chunkrah!" I said. "Emperor, get back or I'll drag you back by your hair!"

"By Vox!" he yelped, swishing his sword about. "I haven't enjoyed myself so much in years!"

He had no idea of the number of times he ought to have been killed. Left to his own devices he would have rolled on the stones of the square with a half dozen rapier thrusts in his belly or his head hanging off by gristle. I beat down a fresh attack and reached out my left hand, thrust the dagger all bloody as it was between my teeth, and took a good grip of the Emperor's hair.

I yanked.

He yelled, as much in pain and injured dignity as fear, and toppled back, whereat I pushed myself in front of him, took the dagger back into my left hand,

6

smashed away a fresh developing attack, and so flung forward with my rapier nickering in and out, very evilly, like the tongues of risslaca.

The Emperor was growing annoyed,

"Just like all my Pallans, Dray Prescot!" he shouted at my back. "Denying me any fun in life."

I had time to yell back, most savagely: "If you think fighting and killing is fun, then you're still a child!"

Ortyg Larghos, Kov of Zamra, had not given up.

He made a last and as he thought final effort to take the Emperor. A solid wedge of his remaining men hurled themselves upon me. I had to use all my skill with the Jiktar and the Hikdar to fend them off. Two Rapas there were, very fierce, with their predatory beaked faces leering down upon me, who hurled themselves forefront of the others. They were not to be dismissed and spitted as easily as those who were coughing their guts out on the dusty stones around the fight.

While engaged with them I saw the Emperor, with his rapier up and out in a most ungainly stance, run at the bunch of men from the side. His face looked then — and Zair forgive me if I felt a tiny spark of joy — very much as my Delia's looked when she stood by me, shoulder to shoulder, against ravening foemen.

Larghos saw his chance. His final chance.

"Take him!" he screeched.

Green and purple feathers bobbed above the Emperor. Yellow and blue arms reached out for him.

I yelled.

The Rapas before me whickered their rapiers about in most professional passes, making me use skill and strength on them, and I could feel my strength slowly seeping away.

Ortyg Larghos was jubilant.

"Stick him, Rapas!" he was yelling.

I fended a thrust on my main-gauche, essayed a pass, took the other rapier rather too low and so had to give and bend to let the blade hiss past my side. I brought my wrist around for the next pass and a steel-tipped clothyard shaft sprouted clear through the Rapa's long roosterish neck. His companion had no time to make a sound as a second arrow feathered itself through his own scrawny neck.

Without turning around I shouted and I leaped for the men surrounding the Emperor.

I shouted just one word: *"Seg!"*

And then followed as marvelous an exhibition of shooting as any man can ever have performed and any man can have had the privilege of witnessing. For as I fought those remaining third-party men in their green and purple, slicing them, spitting them, so Seg shot out anyone who sought to close with me. His arrows sped silently above my shoulders and feathered themselves into the breasts of the men facing me. They could not stand against this whispering death, and they turned, and ran, and they were all dead men, for now the shorter arrows from my clansmen's bows fell among them.

Ortyg Larghos, Kov of Zamra, staggered across the stones of the square to fall at his Emperor's feet. His chest and back sprouted the steel heads and the bright feathers of many arrows.

"You pulled my hair, Dray Prescot."

"Aye," I said viciously. "And I'll pull it again if you rush upon naked steel like that again!"

He lowered his strong square face upon me. "I am the Emperor," he said, but he was not boasting, he was not trying to overawe me. Come to that, he had crawled out of the thicket of dinosaur bones to face my victorious men, and so he could never really boast of being emperor in quite the same way again. He was trying to explain something that saddened him. "I am never allowed to enjoy myself," he said. "Never. It is always inexpedient, bad politics, unsafe."

This was the man who had intemperately ordered my head cut off. I was to marry his daughter, and so that must have made some change in his attitude. I could understand him a little now, and, anyway, some emperors feel that ordering heads cut off is all a part of their function.

I turned away from him, not smiling, letting him see I was not impressed, to greet my men.

Seg had collected arrows from the battlefield as any frugal bowman does, and he and my wild clansmen marched up with all the swing and panache of the immortal fight at The Dragon's Bones still clinging to them. Inch swung his long Saxon ax with an air. Korf Aighos swung his Great Sword of War of the Blue Mountains and I caught some of the pride he and his Blue Mountain Boys felt in thus resurrecting their ancient weapon. Varden stared about with a city-bred eye.

Hap Loder and Vomanus were talking together, and I wondered what deviltry they were cooking up. Vomanus was handling Hap's broadsword, and I hazarded a guess Vomanus was telling my Zorcander of the longswords of the inner sea, the Eye of the World.

Delia said: "If you do that again, Dray Prescot, I may be a widow before I'm married!"

I held her right arm with my left, and turned her, and so, together, side by side, we walked through the main entrance-way of the Emperor's palace in Vondium, capital of Vallia.

"I may do anything for you, Delia," I said. "Anything."

On that beautiful and terrible world of Kregen under Antares there exist a number of forms of contract by which a man and a woman may agree to marry. When the bokkertu for our betrothal and marriage was being drawn up, Delia and I, without really having to discuss the matter, instinctively chose that form by which the two, the man and the woman, are bound the closest together. There were three separate ceremonies. The first two, the religious and the secular, were essentially private in character. I will say little of these, apart from the undeniable fact that I was profoundly moved. They took place a Kregan week — what I translate out as a sennight, for all that it is six days — after our arrival back in the capital. We were, after the two ceremonies, man and wife.

The third ceremony, the public festival and procession about the capital city, pleased me little.

"Oh, Dray, you great grizzly graint! I am supremely fortunate that the people of Vallia love me. And they will love you, too! So they want to see us happy, they want to see us drive in procession to all the temples and the holy places and the various districts of the city. You'll—"

"I'll become used to it all, I suppose. But being a Prince Majister is something I didn't count on."

"Oh, you'll learn."

After the attempted coup had been put down there was a considerable amount of clearing up to be done. Kov Furtway had stirred up as part of his plan one county or province to attack its neighbor. I was not settled in my mind until I had had a flier message from Tharu ti Valkanium that my Stromnate of Valka was safe. Led by my old freedom fighters they had successfully held off the treacherous attack mounted from the neighboring island to the west, Can-thirda, by its inhabitants, the porcupine-like Qua'voils. Tharu said they'd had to invade after they'd smashed the first attacks, and march to the north to help the colony of Relts there, who had remained loyal to the Emperor. I told the Emperor that Can-thirda should be settled properly, and, to my amazement, he simply said: "Then settle it, Dray, and have done with it."

Later, Delia said: "You silly woflo!" Which is, as we might say on Earth: "You silly goose."

"How so?"

"Why — that is how the great lords manipulate my father. He just assumed since you are now a most powerful and puissant lord in Vallia — the Prince Majister no less! — that you wished to add Can-thirda to your holdings. He has given the island to you."

"Can he do that? I mean, just like that?"

"Why not? He is the Emperor."

"Um," I said, and went off to sort out one or two items that had annoyed me.

Seg Segutorio, than whom no man ever had a finer comrade on two worlds, had been made a Hikdar of the Crimson Bowmen of Loh. This infuriated me.

I said: "Look, Emperor: who was it stuck loyally by you in the ruins in The Dragon's Bones? Who fought for you? Who feathered those rasts of Kov Zamra's men when they were about to do you a mischief? Seg Segutorio, that's who."

He was slowly coming back to his usual pomp and mystique of being the Emperor, and I knew I must strike quickly before he took once again the full reins into his hands. With the dispatch of his enemies, or their flight abroad, he was now in a stronger position than he had ever been. If he wanted to repudiate all the bargains he had struck with me, he might seek to do so, and slay me, as he had once ordered. From Seg and Inch I knew I could count on absolutely dedicated loyalty. Hap Loder and my clansmen and Gloag with the men of Strombor would have to return home soon, although they were staying on for the great public ceremonies marking my wedding. I was safe for a time. I did not forget the way King Nemo of Tomboram in Pandahem had served me.

I never did trust kings and emperors, and I was not about to begin now, for all that this emperor was the father of Delia of Delphond.

"What is it you want of me, Dray?"

"Me? It's Seg Segutorio I am talking of! Of your personal bodyguard, the Crimson Bowmen of Loh, half betrayed you, with their Chuktar in the lead. The other half fought to the end and a remnant now serve you—"

"I have sent to Loh for more Bowmen mercenaries."

"Very well and fine. And who is to lead them?"

"I have asked for a certain Chuktar Wong-si-tuogan. I am told he is a most excellent officer."

"Fine, just fine." We were seated in a private chamber of the palace, and the Emperor sipped a purple wine of Wenhartdrin, a small island off the south coast. The Emperor offered me a glass. It was exceedingly good, and I guessed he drank it as much for its quality as through any nationalistic pride. The wines of Jholaix are very hard to excel. "If you believe you are doing the right thing, then so be it. But I would have thought that Seg Segutorio, as a master Bowman, could not be bettered as Chuktar of your Crimson Bowmen of Loh."

The Emperor sipped. On the morrow Delia and I would drive about the city in a gaily decorated zorca chariot, and the bands would play and the flags fly and the twin suns would shed their opaline radiance upon us, and all would be merriment and laughter and joy. This night sitting closeted with the Emperor, I had the conviction I must saddle a few zhantils before it was too late.

"Rank your Deldars," said the Emperor, referring to an opening move in Jikaida which can be translated out something like our "put your cards on the table," although with the suggestion that this is an opening bet of a protracted bargaining session.

I duly ranked my Deldars.

"You should forthwith make Seg your personal bodyguard Chuktar. He is intensely loyal, to you and to Delia. You should reward him and Inch — and I suggest you bestow on them the titles and estates of the men who so foully betrayed you. You can have suitable presents made up for others of the men who saved your throne — aye! — and saved your life, too."

"And for yourself?"

"I need nothing beyond Delia. It seems I've acquired Can-thirda... I shall rename it, for that name has baleful associations to my people of Valka, and it will serve as a useful sister state to Valka."

"Nothing else?"

"We are talking of other people—"

"Your friends."

He sipped more wine, and looked at me. He had mellowed. I'll give the old devil that. He was the most powerful man in this part of Kregen, make no mistake about that. I had a hold on him only through his daughter. For all that I had done for him personally he would discount, put it down to what any person ought to do, must do, to preserve the life of the Emperor. But — he had fleshed out a little, he had lost that abstracted look, as though waiting for the dagger thrust in his back. I had made him far more secure than he had ever been.

"Aye. My friends."

"So they will become powerful. And loyal to you. But I—"

"Do you think I could possibly countenance — let alone take a part in — any plan or plot that would harm you? You are Delia's father. Although," I said, and, Zair forgive me, took a pleasure in the saying, "your wife, Delia's mother, must have been a wonderful person. No, Majister, from me you are safer than if you wore armor even a gros-varter could not penetrate."

I think, looking back, that he half believed me.

Being a prudent man, he would never wholly trust another person. I am prudent, or I think I am, yet I have committed the folly of trusting other people wholly. As you have heard — and if these cassettes last out will hear more — sometimes I have paid for that folly of trust, paid for it in agony and blood and slavery. But I did trust Seg, and Inch, and Gloag, and Varden, and Hap Loder, and having removed valuables from his reach, I trusted Korf Aighos. Trusting these men meant I trusted the men under their command. I had no doubts of Valka.

And, too, now that I knew Vomanus was Delia's half-brother, I could trust Vomanus again, too.

"I believe you, Dray." He had already made up his mind what he would do. "I shall make Seg Segutorio Chuktar of the Crimson Bowmen of Loh. In addition, the estates of Kov Furtway have been confiscated. I shall give them to Seg and create him Kov of Falinur."

"That is indeed munificent—" I began. He held up a hand.

"Furthermore, since the long man Inch roused the Blue Mountains on our behalf, and the Black Mountains are now vacant, by reason of Nath Larghos' treason, I shall give them to Inch and create him Trylon of the Black Mountains."

Now I had to think about this. There are many ranks in the nobility of Vallia which are not at all complicated once one grasps the essential pecking order. A Kov approximates out to a duke, as I have said, and a Strom to a count. Between these there come a number of ranks — some I know I have already mentioned. A Vad, a Trylon. By creating Seg and Inch of unequal ranks, I felt unease.

I said: "I think Kov of the Black Mountains sounds a richer note."

He chuckled and poured wine.

"You will find titles are grabbed after and fought for, Dray. They mean nothing. It is land that counts. Land! Canals, corn, cattle, wine, timber, minerals. Make Inch Kov, if it pleases you."

"It will please Seg." That was true.

Seg and Inch had become firm friends. I own I felt a thump of relief at that.

The Emperor drank and swallowed and wiped his lips. He cocked his head at me. "As for you, Dray Prescot. My poor daughter has caught a tartar in you." He said "clansman," but his meaning was as I have translated it out. "You mentioned Valka and Can-thirda. That fool Kov Larghos of Zamra set himself up as Pallan of Vondium. He is dead. Zamra is yours, and the title of Kov, if you want it, Prince Majister."

The old devil could be sarcastic, too, when he liked.

I thanked him. I did not stutter in surprise this time. I had an eye to the future.

He said: "With all the titles you have collected, Dray Prescot, I think we will need an extra-special sheet of vellum to write them all down on the marriage contract."

Face-to-face, I said: "All I want is to be the husband of Delia."

Then I retired for the night. Tomorrow was the great day.

Two

Marriage

The great day dawned.

On this day Delia and I would be truly wed.

As I watched Zim and Genodras rise into the Kregan sky over Vondium I found it hard to understand my own feelings. Long and long had I fought and struggled for this day. I had traveled many dwaburs over this world of Kregen. I had fought men, and half-men, half-beasts, and monsters. I had been slave. I had owned vast lands and many men had looked to me as their leader. Much I had seen and done and all of it, really, aimed at this outcome.

There is much I could say of that day.

Some parts of it I remember with the absolute clarity of vision that cherishes every moment; other parts are cast in a vaguer shadow. Here on this Earth the people of China wear white in mourning, whereas my own country chooses to regard white as the color of purity and bridal happiness, of virginity. The Vallians hew to the latter custom, which I think gives brides the opportunity to glow and radiate a special kind of happiness of their wedding day.

When I saw Delia clad in her white gown, with white shoes, a white veil, and — with the happy superstitions that mean everything and nothing on these days — tiny specks of color here and there — a flower posy, a scarlet-edged hem, a yellow curlicue to her wrists — I could only stand like a great buffoon and stare.

They had decked me out in some fantastic rig — all gold lace, brilliants, feathers, silks, and satins — and when I saw myself in a mirror I was shatteringly reminded of that rig I had worn in the opal palace of Zenicce, when the Princess Natema had unavailingly attempted her wiles. I ripped the lot off. Memory of Natema, who was now happily married to Prince Varden, my good comrade, brought back unbidden memories of other great ladies I had known in my career on Kregen. The Princess Susheeng, Sosie na Arkasson, Queen Lilah, Tilda the Beautiful, Viridia the Render, even Katrin Rashumin, who would, as Kovneva of Rahartdrin, be among the brilliant throng at the wedding. I thought of Mayfwy, widow of my oar comrade Zorg of Felteraz, and I sighed, for I dearly wished for Mayfwy and Delia to be friends. I must say that Varden had sent a flier to Zenicce and brought back Princess Natema.

I had greeted her kindly, if feeling a trifle of the strangeness of the situation. She was just as beautiful, and, I knew, just as willful. She was a little more voluptuous, a little more superb in her carriage, for she had had two children. But she and Varden had made a match, and they were happy, at which I was much cheered.

So I ripped off the gaudy clothes that turned me into a popinjay. I wrapped a long length of brilliant scarlet silk about me, and donned the plain buff tunic of a Koter of Vallia, with the wide shoulders and the nipped-in waist and the flared skirt. Long black boots I wore, and a broad-brimmed hat. In the hat I wore the red and white colors of Valka. My sleeves were white silk of Pandahem, for despite the intense rivalry between the islands, Vallia is not foolish enough to refuse to buy best Pandahem silk.

From Valka had come all my notables and those friends at whose side I had fought clearing the island of the aragorn and the slave-masters. They brought with them the superb sword from Aphrasöe that had been Alex Hunter's. This I buckled on to my belt with a thrill I could not deny. With this marvelous Savanti sword I could go up against rapier, longsword, broadsword, shortsword, with absolute confidence. Even then, in that moment, I admit, like the greedy weapons man I am, I longed for a great Krozair longsword to swing at my side.

But that, like Nath and Zolta, my two oar comrades and ruffianly rascals, could not be.

What they would say — what Mayfwy would say — away there in the Eye of the World when they heard that I had married and they not there to dance at my wedding, I shriveled to think.

There would be much calling on Mother Zinzu the Blessed, that I could be perfectly sure of.

When, in casual conversation, I had mentioned to the Emperor, turning what I said into a light remark, careful not to inflame, that a flier might perhaps be sent to Tomboram, he replied in such furious terms as to dispel the notion. His fury was not directed toward me, for I have cunning of a low kind in this area of elementary conversation-tactics, but against all the nations of the island of Pandahem. I mentioned this to Inch and Seg, for I had in mind asking Tilda the Beautiful and her son, Pando, the Kov of Bormark, to my wedding and, also, if she could be found in time, Viridia the Render. The general opinion was that the thing could not be done.

Only that week news had come in of a vicious raid by ships from Pandahem upon a Vallian overseas colony port. I could imagine the hatreds of the spot; they might be of a different kind, they could not be more intense than those festering in the capital. This saddened me. But I refused to be sad on my wedding day, and so with a last draft of best Jholaix, went down to the waiting zorca chariot.

Delia looked stunningly marvelous — I refuse to attempt any description. We sat in the chariot and Old Starkey the coachman clicked to the eight zorcas, and they leaned into the harness, the tall wheels with their thin spokes spun, reflecting blindingly the opaz brilliance of the twin Suns of Scorpio, and we were off on our wedding procession.

The Crimson Bowmen of Loh with Seg as their new Chuktar rode escort. And — an innovation, a thing I dearly wanted and had spoken hard and short to the Emperor to gain — an honor guard of Valkan Archers rode with us also. I had

13

spoken to Seg about this thing, and we both knew what we knew about bows, but he had agreed, for my sake.

In the procession rode all the nobles of the land high in the Emperor's favor.

There, too, rode Hap Loder and my clansmen. Inch as the new Kov of the Black Mountains rode, talking animatedly with Korf Aighos, and, again, I wondered what the rascally Blue Mountain Boy was hatching.

Between the Korf and Nath the Thief from Zenicce there was little to choose.

I said to Delia, leaning close: "We must keep a sharp eye on the wedding presents, my love. Nath, I am sure, has a lesten-hide bag under his tunic."

Those wedding presents meant a great deal, for it had been through manipulation of them as symbols that Delia had managed to remain so long unwed. Now I had scoured Valka for the best and finest presents the hand and brain of my people could devise. I had brushed aside poor Kov Vektor's presents. The Blue Mountain Boys had them in good keeping, but I scorned to use a beaten rival's gifts. Truly, I had been amazed at the wealth and beauty that had poured from Valka. Ancient treasures had been unearthed from where they had been hidden against the aragorn. Such treasures! Such beauty! And all given freely and with love to Delia.

So we rode in stately procession through the boulevards and avenues of Vondium. The Koters and the Koteras turned out in their thousands to wave and cheer and shout their good wishes. Vondium is not as large nor does it hold as many people as Zenicce, whose population must be a million souls, but I guessed very few people remained indoors on this day of days.

Delia's fingers lay in mine and every now and then she would squeeze my hand. She waved and acknowledged the cheering. Flower petals showered down on us from balconies from which gay shawls and banners and silks streamed. The noise dizzied us with the incessant volleys of good wishes.

Delia said: "I have spoken to Seg, and Inch, and they will free all the slaves in their provinces. It will be hard—"

"Aye, my love, it will be hard. But already my men have been working on Canthirda. And now Zamra, too, will be cleansed of the evil."

"Oh, yes!"

"Then," I said, with a mischievousness somewhat out of place, perhaps, given the subject and the day, "we will have many more free Koters and Koteras to cheer for us!"

"And aren't they cheering!"

Delia drew back that shimmer of veil from her face. The veil, I knew, had been the gift of her grandmother, laid by in a scented cedar-wood chest against the day when it would frame the glorious face of my beloved. Her eyes regarded her people of Vallia with a warm affection, and her cheeks flushed with a rosy tint that, however naive it may make me sound, captivated me again. And her hair! That glorious chestnut hair with those outrageous tints of auburn, her hair glowed and shone against the whiteness of the veil.

"You are happy, my Delia?"

"Yes, my Dray, yes. Oh, yes!"

We performed the necessary functions at the sacred places and we did not miss a single fantamyrrh. The people lined the streets and boulevards as we passed at a slow zorca pace. I saw flowers, and ribbons, flags and banners, many silks and shawls depending from the open balconies. Petals showered upon us in a scented rain. The Suns of Scorpio shone magnificently upon us. Truly, then, as we drove to the acclamations of the multitudes, I had grown into a real Kregan!

At my special request — which Delia, with a regal lift of her chin, had instantly translated into a command — we drove past the Great Northern Cut and past *The Rose of Valka*. There had been wild moments in this inn, and the raftered ceilings had witnessed many a scene of joyful carouse. Even with the crisp and concise stanza form adopted for that song, *The Fetching of Drak na Valka*, it takes a deucedly long time to sing it in its entirety, and usually we sang a shortened version. The old friends of Valka were there, hanging out of the windows, cheering and shouting and waving, and then someone — it was Young Bargom for an ob! — started up the song, and they were singing it out as we drove past. I knew they'd go on singing and drinking all day and all night, for that is the Valkan way.

As was proper we were to finish our promenade of the city by narrow boat.

The water glittered cleanly as we stepped from the zorca carriage and went aboard a narrow boat so bedecked with flowers and colors, with flags and banners, I wondered where we were to sit. The bargemasters had everything organized, and soon Delia and I found ourselves sitting on golden cushions high on a platform in the bows, sumptuously decorated, with a side table bearing tasty snacks, miscils, various wines, gregarians, squishes, and, of course, heaping silver and golden dishes of palines.

No happy function of Kregen is complete without as many palines as may be managed.

The water chuckled past the bows. I knew that water. Sweet is the canalwater of Vallia — sweet and deadly. I felt a comfort to know that through the immersion in the pool of baptism in that far-off River Zelph of Aphrasöe, my Delia was, as I was, assured of a thousand years of life as well as being protected from the fearful effects of the canalwater.

And now it was the turn of the canalfolk to cheer and shout and wave. The Vens and the Venas turned out on their freshly painted narrow boats, lining the banks of the cut as we passed. We had a specially picked body of haulers to draw us, for I had — rudely, viciously, intemperately — refused the Emperor's offer of a gang of his slave haulers. We did not see a single slave that glorious day, and although we knew the poor devils were hidden away in their barracks and bagnios, we could take comfort from our determination to end the evil, once and forever.

All day we traveled about Vondium, and as the twin suns sank we saw the monstrous pile of the imperial palace rearing against the last suns-glow and knew we were going home.

"I am so happy, my love, happy and not at all tired," said Delia, and then yawned so hugely her slender white hand looked more slender and moth-white in the dusk than ever.

"Yawning, my Delia, on your wedding day?"

She laughed and I laughed, and we watched as the narrow boat was drawn through the rising portcullis of the palace's water-port. We stepped down from the high platform and the Crimson Bowmen of Loh surrounded us and the Archers of Valka were there, too, and the Pallans, and the nobles and the high Koters, and we went up the marble stairs into the palace.

It had been a perfect day.

A girl's wedding day ought to be, should be — must be — a perfect day.

I was taken off by Seg and Inch and Hap, by Varden and Gloag, by Korf Aighos and Vomanus. We spent some time drinking amicably, but in low key, for none of us subscribed to the barbaric code that demands a groom become stupidly in-toxicated on his wedding night. Grooms who do that have scarce love for their new brides.

The room was low-ceilinged and comfortable, with softly upholstered chairs and sturm-wood tables, with Walfarg-weave rugs upon the floor, and with an endless supply of the best of Jholaix and all the other superlative wines of Kregen. Even so, as the Prince Majister, I could order up Kregan tea, than which there is no better drink in two worlds.

Off in a corner I was able to have a few words with Vomanus.

"So you're my brother-in-law now, Vomanus."

He cocked an eye at me, lifting his glass, and drinking.

"Half-brother-in-law, Dray."

"Aye. I doubted you, when the racters told me you sought the hand of Delia." I am a man who never apologizes and never begs forgiveness — at least, almost never. Now I said: "Do you forgive me for doubting you, Vomanus?"

He laughed in his careless way and tossed back the wine. He was a rapscallion, careless, lighthearted, but a good comrade.

"There is nothing to forgive. I know how I would feel toward a man who tried to take a girl like Delia from me."

"You are engaged — no, that is not the word — you have a girl of your own?"

"A girl, Dray? Of course not." He yelled for more wine. "I have girls, Dray — hundreds of them!"

Hap Loder came across, bringing more tea for me, and a handful of palines on a golden dish. We talked of the clans and of the new chunkrah herds he had been building up. He was now the power in the Clans of Felschraung and Longuelm, but he had given obi to me and I was his lord and so he would remain faithful to me forever. I knew that he was my friend, and that was more important than mere loyalty.

Tharu of Valkanium and Tom ti Vulheim were there, and I was joyed to see they had brought Erithor of Valkanium. I shouted across: "Erithor! Will you honor us with a song?"

"Right willingly, Strom Drak," he began, bringing his harp forward, and then halting, and, striking a chord, said: "Right willingly, Prince Majister."

"Strom Drak," I said. "Well, it is Strom Dray, now, in Valka for me. But the great song will never change."

16

Others broke in, begging Erithor to sing, for he was a bard renowned throughout all of Vallia. I recalled the song Erithor had been making, after we had cleansed Valka, and the girls of Esser Rarioch, the high fortress overlooking Valkanium, had unavailingly badgered and teased him into revealing its words and melodies. He might sing that song now. If he did, this would be another historical mark to go down beside the other great songs he had made that would live forever.

He saw me looking at him, and lifting his head, he said: "No, Prince Majister. I will sing the marriage song of Prince Dray and Princess Delia only when both are there to hear it together."

Someone — I do not know who it was to this day — roared out: "Then you won't sing it this night, Erithor!"

They all shouted at this, and Erithor struck a chord, and broke into *Naghan the Wily,* which tells how Naghan, a rich and ugly silversmith of Vandayha, was trapped into marriage by the saucy Hefi, daughter of the local bosk herder.

Everyone roared. Kregans have a warped sense of humor, it seems to me, at times.

How wonderful it was to be here, in this comfortable room, drinking and singing with my friends! I am a man who does not make friends easily. I can always rouse men to follow me, to do as I order, and joy in the doing of it… but friendship. That, to me, is a rare and precious thing I seek without even acknowledging I seek it, except in moments of weakness like this.

Seg's Thelda would be busily clucking about Delia now, and knowing Thelda, I knew she would be full of her own importance as a married woman with a fine young son — called Dray — and with all the good will in the world exasperating by her own importance and knowledge of the marriage state.

It was time I rescued Delia.

I stood up.

Everyone fell silent.

Erithor had been singing on — the time passes incredibly quickly when a skald of such power sings — and now he finished up an episode from *The Canticles of the Rose City* wherein the half-man, half-god Drak sought for his divine mistress through perils that made the listeners grip the edges of their chairs. The thrumming strings fell silent.

I cleared my throat.

"I thank you all, my friends. I cannot say more."

I believe they understood.

They escorted me up the marble stairs where the torchlight threw orange and ruby colors across the walls and the tapestries and the silks, where the shadows all fled from us.

Delia was waiting.

Thelda bobbed her head and Seg put his arm around her and everyone carried out the prescribed gestures and spoke the words that would ensure long and happy life to Delia and me. Then, already laughing and singing and feeling thirsty again, they all trooped downstairs and left Delia and me alone.

The bedchamber was hung with costly tapestries and tall candles burned unwaveringly. Refreshments had been tastefully laid out on a side table. Delia sat up in the bed with that outrageous hair combed out by Thelda gleaming upon her shoulders. I confess I was gawping at her.

"Oh, Dray! You look as though you've eaten too much bosk and taylyne soup!"

"Delia—" I whispered. "I—"

I took an unsteady step forward. I felt my sword swinging at my side, that wonderful Savanti sword, and I reached down to take it out and throw it upon the table, out of the way — and so, with the sword in my hand, I saw the tapestries at the side of the bed rustle. There was no wind in the bedchamber.

They must have waited until they heard everyone else depart, and only Delia's voice — and then my voice. That had been the signal.

Six of them there were.

Six men clad all in black with black face-masks and hoods, and wielding daggers.

They leaped for the bed in so silent and feral a charge from their concealed passage behind the arras that almost they slew my Delia before I could reach them.

With a cry so bestial, so vile, so vicious, so horrible they flinched back from me, I hurled myself full upon them.

Their six daggers could not meet that brand.

The Savanti sword is a terrible weapon of destruction.

Had they been wearing plate armor and wielding Krozair longswords I do not think they would have stood before me.

So furious, so ugly, so absolutely destructive was my attack that I had slashed down the first two, driven the sword through the guts of the third, and turned to strike at the fourth before they could swivel their advance to face — instead of the beautiful girl in the bed — me.

"Dray!" said Delia.

She did not scream.

In a lithe smother of naked flashing legs and yards and yards of white lace she was out of the bed, snatching up a fallen dagger, hurling herself upon the sixth man. He stood, horrified. I chopped the fourth, caught the fifth through an eye — the mask could not hope to halt the marvelous alloy-steel of the Savanti blade — and swung about to see Delia stepping back from her man.

The six would-be assassins lay sprawled on the priceless Walfarg-weave rugs.

"Oh, Dray!" said Delia, dropping the bloody dagger and running to me, her arms outstretched. "They might have slain you!"

"Not with you to protect me, my Delia," I said, and I laughed, and caught her up close to me, breast to breast, and so gazed down upon her glorious face upturned to my ugly old figurehead. "Sink me! I feel sorry for the poor fools!"

Later I carried the six out to the door and dumping them in the passage roared for the guard and half a dozen Crimson Bowmen appeared. The Hikdar wanted to rouse the palace, but I said: "Not so, good Fenrak." He was a loyal Bowman who had fought with us at The Dragon's Bones and had been promoted, to his joy. "This is my wedding night!"

He shook his head.

"I will see to this offal, my Prince. And in the morning, then…" He started his men into action. He was a rough tough Bowman of Loh, and thus dear to me. "I wish you all joy, my Prince, and eternal happiness to the Princess Majestrix."

"Thank you, Fenrak. There is wine for you and your men — drink well tonight, my friend."

As they carted the black-clad assassins off, I went back to Delia and closed the door on the outside world.

I must admit, knowing what I do of Kregen, that this was a typical ending to a wedding day. It had roused the blood, though, set a sparkle into Delia's eyes, a rose in her cheeks. How she had fought for me, like a zhantil for her cubs!

In the morning — and I a married man! — we made inquiries. The story was simple and pathetic. The would-be assassins, being dead, could not tell us what we wanted to know, but one of them was recognized by Vomanus as being a retainer of the Kov of Falinur, who had fled. This had been his last throw. This is what I believed at the time. Then, the truth did not matter; later I was to wish I had prosecuted more earnest inquiries, for what Vomanus told us was correct. What he could not then know was that this assassin had left the employ of Naghan Furtway, Kov of Falinur.

When we talked of this, and used the name, Thelda pushed up very wroth, her face flushed. "I am the Kovneva of Falinur! And my husband Seg is the Kov! Do not speak of the Kov of Falinur as a traitor!"

Delia soothed her down. Being a Kovneva was greatly to Thelda's liking, although Seg had laughed and said that being a Kov would not drive his shafts any the straighter when he was hunting in his hills of Erthyrdrin.

Naghan Furtway had been stripped of his titles and estates. Henceforth I knew we must think of him as Furtway, and he would seek to injure us in some way. And this was the man, together with his nephew Jenbar, whom I had rescued from the icy Mountains of the North at the behest of the Star Lords!

I will not go into details of my life after that in Vondium, the capital city of Vallia. That life was remarkable in its activity, for I had much to do, and in its uneventfulness. I took the palace architect, one Largan the Rule, and we went ferreting about in the secret passages. I have mentioned the usual custom in great palaces of having secondary passageways between the walls. These I inspected, and found many fresh alleyways of which even Largan the Rule had no knowledge, and so had those that would be weak spots bricked up.

It seems I had the knack of poking my beaked nose into all the places I was able to investigate and find some way of improving what went on. High on my list of priorities was organizing the canals better, in such a way that arguments over rights-of-way need not take place at crossings. Until a great program of canal building could be undertaken to create overways and underways on the cuts, I instituted a country wardens service, which provided for families of men and women to live near the crossings and superintend the traffic.

As was to be expected I spent a great deal of time at the dockyards and slipways making myself thoroughly familiar with the great race-built galleons of

Vallia. I looked into their artillery, the catapults, the varters, and the gros-varters which Vallia herself had developed.

As for the Vallian Air Service, a body of fliers I had always held in the highest respect, we discovered that Naghan Furtway had contrived through his contacts to disperse the Air Service during the time of his abortive coup. I met again Chuktar Farris, the Lord of Vomansoir, who aboard *Lorenztone* had plucked Delia and me from midair where we flew astride Umgar Stro's giant coal-black impiter. I thought I detected about his exquisite politeness an edged air of pleasure, as though his love for Delia found equal pleasure that she had at last married the great ruffianly barbarian she had chosen — against all common sense.

"We searched for you, Prince Majister, and found instead the Kov of Falinur and his Kovneva."

I saw Delia smile at this, and had to chuckle myself.

How high and mighty we all were with our titles these days, and then we had been a draggle-tailed bunch running and hiding across the Hostile Territories!

I asked after Tele Karkis, the young Hikdar of the Air Service, and Farris frowned and said: "He left the Air Service. He — disappointed us in that. I have not seen or heard of him for a long time."

Naghan Vanki, he of the sarcastic tongue and the silver and black outfit — an approximation to Racter colors, those — was still active, although away in Evir in the north at the time.

My sojourn in Vallia had already given me a feeling that blue was the color of Pandahem and therefore of an enemy. I was able to instantly quell this irrational feeling my own way by thinking of Tilda of the Many Veils, and her son young Pando — a right little limb of Satan if ever there was one. But, still, it was strange to see the Vallian Air Service men clad in their smart dark blue, with the short orange capes. The blue was so dark as almost to be black, and I guessed had been given that blue tinge to take away the odd dusty shabby look unrelieved black gives.

Delia and I flew a considerable amount of the time on our journeys to the Blue Mountains and to Delphond. Court officials worried over this, for the airboats were always giving trouble and were not to be relied upon. We visited Inch in the Black Mountains, and soon found he had palled up with the Blue Mountain Boys, and he and Korf Aighos, who ran the place from that eerie and cloud-capped mountain city of High Zorcady, were hatching plans that would further unite in friendship the whole mountain area. We flew all over Vallia. We went up to Falinur where Seg had betaken himself, with Thelda, to take charge. Seg had chosen an ord-Kiktar to run the Crimson Bowmen of Loh in his stead when he was away on his estates. This man, a veteran, intensely loyal, was called Dag Dagutorio — I believe I have not mentioned the system in Erthyrdrin over names and what the *torio* means, but that must wait for now — and I saw the Emperor felt more at ease when Dag was around and Seg was away up in Falinur. That must have been the motive of the munificent gift of a Kovnate to Seg.

An ord-Jiktar meant Dag had risen eight stages in the rank structure as a Jiktar. Two more and then he might become a Chuktar. I doubted if the Emperor would employ two Chuktars to command his Crimson Bowmen; and I surmised that Seg would be not too unhappy to let the job go to Dag.

Certainly, I had insisted that a Chuktar be appointed to command the new Vallian Imperial Honor Guard of Valkan Archers. The Emperor had smiled at this, and said: "Then, since you love Valka so much, son-in-law, and since you insist on creating the Valkan Archers as a bodyguard, you may pay the Chuktar his wages. For me, I can only pay a Jiktar."

I fumed, but I paid.

Anyway, what was mere money? Valka, Can-thirda, and Zamra brought in immense amounts. And Delia's Delphond and the Blue Mountains brought in more. We could have employed an army of Chuktars.

One man of the court surrounding the Emperor I should mention at this time: the Wizard of Loh, whom men called Deb-so-Parang. I spoke with him a number of times, and told him of Lu-si-Yuong, the Wizard of Loh to Queen Lilah of Hiclantung. Deb-so-Parang nodded, and stroked his beard — like all Wizards of Loh he was strong on the artifices of his craft, but I could not underestimate their powers — and said that he was not acquainted with him personally, although since the fall of the Empire of Loh the Wizards, by the seven arcades, had spread all over Kregen. He was a pleasant old buffer and, a mark against him, he had not forewarned the Emperor of the plot against his life and his throne.

I had, of course, questioned the Todalpheme in Vondium, who monitored the tides, about Aphrasöe. All they could say was for me to ask the Emperor. This I did and he said, simply enough, that when Delia had been crippled from her fall from a zorca he had heard the Todalpheme of Hamal — where the Vallians bought their airboats — knew of a mysterious place where cures might be affected, miracle cures. So now I knew.

I think you will not be surprised when I say that I did not, as I most certainly would have done a few seasons ago, immediately call for a flier and take off for Hamal. I had become so much more settled than I ever had been before. I did not recognize myself as the same man who had swung a great Krozair longsword and set off across the Hostile Territories on foot to reach my Delia, the man who had vowed that nothing and no one would stand in his way. It had always been Delia first and then the quest for the Savanti of Aphrasöe, those mortal but superhuman men who had thrown me out of paradise.

But, for me, Vallia and Valka and my Delia were paradise. Paradise enough.

So I stored the information away and went busily about my business. We honeymooned on Valka, my marvelous island with its wealth and its beauty, and we sang songs in the high hall of Esser Rarioch and we had a tremendous time. We traveled to Strombor. My emotions when once again I beheld the enclave city of Zenicce and strode the opal palace and thought of all the things that had happened there — they defy description. And Gloag, who had become grand chamberlain and the strong right hand to Great-Aunt Shusha — who still lived — could not do enough for us. We rode out onto the Great Plains of Segesthes and I caroused once more with my clansmen, and they roared out the great Jikai for Delia and me. Oh, yes, I lived very high off the vosk in those rousing days!

So much, I had. So great a wealth of everything that when I said to Delia I wanted to go to Zamra and sort out some problems arising out of the freeing of the slaves, and she said, "I think, dear heart, I will wait another week before I know," my heart leaped and I consigned everything else to the Ice Floes of Sicce. There are stories on Kregen as well as on Earth wherein a man does not know his wife is expecting a baby until she tells him. It is a poor husband who is not at once aware of the possibility of a child by reason of nature's interruption, and proof positive is what is awaited. The proof came.

"You will wish to be with your own people, Delia. Thelda will be useful, although I fear a sore trial to you. And there is Aunt Katri. We leave for Vondium at once."

Aunt Katri was the Emperor's sister, childless now, her offspring having perished one way and another, and she was a kind and warmhearted soul. And, in Vondium, there would be the greatest doctors of the land with their acupuncture needles at the ready. I would call in Nath the Needle, for I had a high regard for that particular doctor. So, in the fullness of time, Delia bore twins. A boy and a girl. The boy was to be Drak. The girl was to be Lela. She was named for Delia's mother.

I walked about like a loon. Any onker had a brain twice as big as mine in those days, and nothing in two worlds held more foolish pride. How could an ugly lump like me produce two such marvelous children? Delia, of course, with her superlative beauty, was solely responsible for the babies' gloriousness. The twinned principle is strong on Kregen, by reason of the twin suns in the sky. Very early on, on Kregen, twins were regarded as lucky and means were devised of keeping both children alive and well, whereas here on Earth twins were regarded as bad luck, and very often would be killed off — or one of them. Twins! A boy and a girl! By Zair, but I was a lucky fellow!

A summit of happiness had been reached.

Further problems arose in Zamra, and Delia was nursing well and everything was fine and wonderful in the palace of Vondium, and at last she said to me: "You great onker, Drak! I know the slave problem on Zamra is worrying you. You'll have to go there. I shall be perfectly all right, here in my father's palace."

"Tell Thelda to get Seg down here, and I shall send for Inch. Then I will go to Zamra."

So it was done, and I bid them Remberee and took off.

I called at Valka first, and then flew north. We touched down on a small island for the night and I wandered about the camp, restless, fretful, feeling the hilt of the Savanti sword swinging at my hip. I was a great man, now. A Prince Majister, married to the most beautiful and glorious girl in two worlds. I owned vast tracts of land. Money by the sackful was mine. And I was the father of two perfect children.

Pride, pride!

The blue glow grew swiftly, treacherously — and I all unprepared. I stared in a horror made all the more horrible by my complete unpreparedness. I felt the blue radiance calling me and the gigantic outlines of the Scorpion beckoned and enfolded me and then I was lying on harsh and stinking dirt, stark naked, with the smell and groan of slaves all about me, and a harsh boot kicking me in the ribs, and a voice snarling:

"Get up, rast! Get up, you stinking cramph!"

Three

The Scorpion sets a task to my hands

I was naked.

I was unarmed.

I was a slave in a slave bagnio.

My only hope was that I was still on Kregen.

You may judge of the shock of this transition when I tell you I did not instantly grab that cruel kicking boot and topple the fellow down and twist his neck.

I lay there, choking with the horror of it, shaking, feeling waves of nausea rush and flutter over me as though, once again, I sped down the great glacier of the Mountains of the North. But this transition into another part of Kregen struck home with shrewder intensity. I had waited while Delia had been delivered of our children, and I had wanted to suffer along with her, uselessly, of course, for the techniques of acupuncture ensured the birth should be painless. She had smiled up at me and reached out her arms to me, and I leaned down and kissed her dear face, and together we joyed in an experience that she alone had to bear, and I alone had to wait in useless suffering. The boot smashed into my ribs again.

"Get up, you stinking yetch!"

Perhaps I had been feeling that this was my punishment for being so high and mighty, for letting Delia bear our children — although, Zair knew, I had done everything a mere man can do on these occasions — perhaps the pride that comes before a fall had humbled me. But that second series of savage kicks made me take stock of my new situation.

I had been a slave before. I had been dumped down unarmed and naked before on Kregen. I knew the Star Lords had picked me out once again to perform some task for them, and if this task bore any resemblance to those that had gone before I must sort myself out quickly.

The boot felt warm and slick in my hands.

I pulled.

The slave-master fell.

I took his throat in my hands and choked him a bit, and leaned over him and snarled into his ear: "Kick me again, rast, and your neck will snap." Then I threw him from me.

I stood up.

Around me the groan and moan of naked slaves ceased.

They stood cramped up in a small chamber hewn from soft rock, crumbling, with the ceiling threatening to fall at any moment. Condensation on the walls and drops of niter glittered in the radiance of the twin suns pouring in the barred opening to the cave.

The slave-master scrabbled up.

He tried to lash me with the whip.

I caught the lash and pulled and took the slave-master again by the throat and lifted him up.

"I told you, kleesh—" I began.

A little Fristle female, all furry and curved, with her tail lashing in frenzy, caught my arm.

"Do not kill him, dom! They will be cruel to us all if he is found dead."

Well, I had no love for Fristles, those cat-faced half-men I had known before. But I remembered Sheemiff of the warrens of Magdag, and so I did not break the slave-master's neck. I choked him a little and then threw him against the wall. He fell and lay limply.

A big barky Brokelsh shouldered up, angry.

"Now we are in trouble!" All the slaves were naked. There were about a dozen of them. The Brokelsh started off for a black hole in the back wall. "I'm off."

The other slaves ran after him, including the little Fristle woman, who chittered in her fear as she ran.

I went over to the barred opening. The bars were solid logs of lenk. Outside I could see a clearing with papishin-leaved huts, a backing of jungle unfamiliar to me, and guards patrolling with ready weapons. There were some unusual circumstances about the slave compound, something I couldn't then put my finger on. I shook the lenk logs in fruitless anger, raging against the fate that dragged me from Vallia and Delia and hurled me contemptuously somewhere else on Kregen, summarily bidden to do the dictates of the Star Lords.

A sound at the back of the cave brought me around, snarling. Being weapon-less I lifted my hands in the discipline of unarmed combat of the Krozairs of Zy. Any man without a weapon on Kregen is at a disadvantage, but the Krozairs of Zy as part of their mystic devotions practice their own brand of hand-fighting, and very deadly it is, to be sure.

"Come away, dom," said the girl who faced me.

She was young, filthy, dirty with long and tangled black hair. Her face showed the gaunt look of the half-starved, but her body was firm and supple, and she looked fierce and wild.

"Why do the guards come here alone?" I pointed to the unconscious slave-master.

She shrugged her dirt-caked shoulders.

"He wanted pleasure, and would clear all but one out of here for that, into the other cells and passages."

I did not need to be told that this girl was the one the slave-master sought.

She nodded. "I am Tulema. But come away, quickly—" She pointed into the clearing. A couple of guards were walking toward the barred opening. They could not see into the cell, or so I fancied, but very quickly they would, and then there would be trouble. I nodded and followed Tulema.

24

There must be absolutely no pining after Delia. I must not think of Vallia, or of Valka, until I was safely out of this mess. I had to do the bidding of the Star Lords, and then get myself back home as quickly as may be.

Then I cursed.

It was crystal clear why the Star Lords had brought me here.

I had to rescue a slave from these pens.

There had been at least a dozen in this cell when I arrived. Now they had hurried out. I followed after Tulema, ducking my head beneath the rocky overhang, and found myself in a corridor that led to a maze of passageways and so on to a wider cave in which hundreds of slaves sat and squatted or paced about.

Which one was I expected to rescue?

The Fristle woman, the Brokelsh, and now Tulema — from these three I must find out who had been in that cell when the slave-master was knocked unconscious. I must not let them out of my sight.

I did notice, looking about the vast prison-cave, that there were a large number of halflings here. In general, on Kregen, there are to be found usually far more human beings than halflings, and the halflings, too, are not just one race but many. Here, the balance was quite otherwise.

A sudden commotion went up and then all the slaves were racing down toward a large opening cut in the cave. Tulema looked at me, shouted, "Feeding time!" and was off.

Perforce, I ran after her.

High in the rocky ceiling wide crystal facets showed the gleam of fire. I knew that crystal. It comes from Loh — exactly where is a closely guarded secret — and on it a fire may be kindled and it will not crack or distort. It is much used for holding heat and light above ceilings… I was to find that this crystal did *not* come from Loh, and thereby was cheap enough to light slave quarters — but I run ahead of my story.

That crystal is known as fireglass.

So it was that plenty of light in the cave allowed me to keep the supple form of Tulema in sight. Through the opening the cave passage debouched into a series of openings, each one walled off from its neighbor. Each cell was strongly barred off from the clearing, also. The slaves ran past these cells and on into another spacious cave where food had been left spread out over the floor.

The scene that followed, given the circumstances, should not have sickened me. The slaves fell on the food with cries and fought and struggled over the choicest portions. Coarse stuff, it was, plentiful, belly-filling. A kind of maize grows on Kregen, dilse, that can be mixed with milk and water and pounded, salted, and served up in a variety of ways. It is cheap where it grows freely, for it needs little cultivation. Great tureens of dilse stood about, the carrying poles all carefully removed from the handles of the tureens. It steamed. Also there was a little Kregan bread — those long fluffy rolls, although this stuff was stale and hard — sacks of onions, a few rounds of cheese, and what was clearly a single vosk cut into portions and cooked. By the time Tulema and I reached the feeding cave all the vosk was claimed, the bread was vanishing, the onions were rolling about with frantic figures in pursuit of them, but there was plenty of dilse for those unable to secure the better food, those too weak and feeble to fight for it.

Now I understood why Tulema's face showed a thinness her body did not reveal. That is the blight of dilse.

A large and somewhat ferocious Rapa was striding past me. He held a thick rasher of vosk, a piece of bread, and no less than four onions. He knocked an Och away, who attempted with one of his four arms to steal the vosk rasher. The Och tumbled against the wall, screeching. Tulema shrank back.

I said to the Rapa: "I would be obliged if you would share that vosk rasher, and a piece of bread, and half the onions with this girl, here."

The Rapas are notorious in their treatment of women. Once my Delia had been threatened with the horrible fate of being tossed naked into the Rapa court. The Rapa leered.

"You may go to the Ice Floes of Sicce," he said, and went to push past.

Well — maybe I was some kind of Prince Majister — but here and now I was slave in a slave pen. I knew slave manners. I hit the Rapa in the guts and took the vosk, the bread, and two of the onions. The other two rolled over the floor and were instantly pounced on by an old Fristle woman.

The Rapa tried to straighten up, hissing, his beaked face vicious, his crest swelling. But I hit him again, with my free hand, and turned to Tulema.

"Eat."

"But — you—"

"I am not hungry."

That was true. Only moments ago I had risen from the campfire, replete with the finest delicacies Valka could offer.

She fell on the food ravenously.

If you were not strong and determined and ruthless here you would not die of starvation, for you could eat dilse, but you would slowly decline. Maybe, I thought even then, there was purpose in this. I had some inkling of slave-masters' ways.

We walked away and I waited for Tulema to finish eating.

Then I said: "Tulema. Listen closely. I want to know the names and conditions of all the people who were with us in the cell when—" I hesitated. I could hardly say to her, "When I arrived," for that would demand explanations I would not give, and if given, would not be believed. I finished: "When the slave-master was knocked down."

The food inside her warmed her. She did not giggle — slaves only laugh and sing when something special happens, like the master falling down and breaking his neck — but she let me know she thought my remark highly apposite.

"I think I can remember. But why?"

Instinctively I had to quell my instant rush of bad language, my browbeating intolerance of any who would question an order. I said: "Does anyone escape from here, Tulema?"

"We believe so — we hope so — but I am frightened to go—"

That did make some kind of sense, but it was a tortuous thread. Tulema told me something of herself, and thereby something also of where we were. She came from a seaside town called Fellow, and she sounded sad when she told me of her home in Herrelldrin. She had every right to be sad. We were on the island of Faol, and she shivered as she told me. The island lay off the coast of Havilfar.

Havilfar!

So far on Kregen I had trod the land of the continents of Segesthes and of Turismond. I had touched at Erthyrdrin, in the continent of Loh. But the continent of Havilfar was all new and unexplored by me, virgin territory. I fancied I was in for some wild adventures and some seething action in the future, and, as you shall hear, I was not wrong.

After the meal a sudden shrilling of a stentor's horn made everyone jump and then rush madly for the exits. I stumbled along after Tulema, trying to keep her in sight in the frenzied rushing to and fro of slaves. Screams and cries rang out, people shouted for friends, and I saw the way the slaves kept darting frightened glances back, into the dimmer recesses of the caves.

We all pushed up against the lenk-wood bars.

I blinked against the glare of the twin suns and looked out. I knew we were in the southern hemisphere of Kregen now, and therefore the suns would cross the sky to the northward, but just where we were off Havilfar in relation to the equator I could not say. I guessed we were nearer that imaginary line than I had been in Vallia, nearer, even, than I had been in Pandahem. For the northern sweep of Havilfar rises out of the southern ocean east of southern Loh, below the rain forests of Chem. I fancied Inch's Ng'groga would not be too far away, down to the southwest.

In the clearing cut from the jungle I saw guards strutting, banging their whips against gaitered legs, swaggering in their tunics of forest green. Among them a number of well-dressed men and women moved as though on a shopping expedition.

I say as though on a shopping expedition, but then I thought that was what they were doing — shopping for slaves. In that I was wrong.

A group advanced to the cage where we stood and Tulema shrank back. Other slaves with us pushed forward boldly. Tulema held my arm. Without any sense of rancor I guessed she saw in me a meal ticket and did not wish to lose me. My sentiments were not to lose her, for she could tell me of the people in the cell when I arrived.

In the mob of slaves pressing up against the bars one man stood out. He was dark-haired, and his hair was cropped. He looked lithe and bronzed and fit. He had about him an alertness, an air of competence, and I saw the way he stood, loosely and limberly. The people with him pressed against the lenk-wood bars.

"A very fine bunch at the moment, Notor,"[1] a guard was saying to one of the customers. The guard I categorized in a moment: hard, arrogant, whip-wielding, a true slave-master, toadying now to the highborn of the land.

The man he had addressed as "Notor" also merited little attention, being fleshy, bulkily built, with a dark beard and moustaches. His eyes were like those of a leem. He wore a fine tunic of some fancy pale lavender silk, and boots, and at his side swung a sword. He carried a kerchief drenched in perfume. The party

27

with him, other nobles and their ladies, were likewise attired in silks and satins against the heat. They were a chattering, laughing, carefree group of people — and my heart hardened against them, for all I had been as happy and carefree in what, although it was but a bur or so ago, now seemed another world.

"Yes, Nalgre," said the lord. "I think so. What do you advise for this season? A dozen? Would that be enough for us?" He sniggered. "We are passable shots, Nalgre."

"The finest shots, Notor Renka," quoth Nalgre the slave-master. "I believe, with all due deference, you could easily accommodate a full score."

Tulema tugged me back again.

"Do not press against the bars so, Dray!" I had told her my name, Dray Prescot, without so much as a Koter for title. I had had my fill of titles for the moment.

I shook her hand off, for I wanted to learn as much as might be of the situation in which I had been placed, a problem to solve and someone to save — someone, I had no idea who.

At that instant, when I was about to press forward and so join the mob, slightly separated from the others, clustered around the lithe dark-haired man, I saw beyond the bars a man I knew. He walked with the notables and laughed and glanced over the slaves, and waved a scented handkerchief airily.

The man was Berran, Vadvar of Rifuji, a noble of Vallia who had been a secret member of the third party, and who had led his men to the aid of Naghan Furtway to fight at The Dragon's Bones. I had thought him dead. Now he was here. I wondered how many others of the leaders of the abortive coup had fled to Havilfar.

Feeling it was prudent not to be recognized I stepped back away from the bars. I must have stepped smartly, for Tulema let out a squeal, and I realized I had trodden on her toes. I do not apologize, so I said: "Who is that man with the dark hair and handsome face? A slave who looks unlike a slave?"

She recovered quickly. From the corner of my eye I could see the Notor Renka and his party, and with them Berran, moving away with the slave-master, so that danger had passed.

"He is a guide. They are brave men — I wish—" She swallowed. Her face wore a drawn look of misery. "I am frightened to go with them. I can offer nothing — but everyone says they can save us."

Four

Manhunters of Faol

A few quick questions established just what was going on here on the island of Faol.

Slaves were taken from the cell and, now that I understood, I was not surprised to see the willingness with which they went. They tried to hide that eagerness, they tried to dissimulate, but for all that they fairly skipped out of the cell. They were not happy merely because they were being let out of a cell. Their joy ran in deeper channels.

The man Tulema had called a guide went with them, and I could see him trying to hush his companions, and for a space they would slouch along like dejected slaves, only to go pushing on toward the slave barracks at the far end of the clearing. Guards surrounded them, harsh, vicious men in the leaf-green tunics, with whips and swords and spears.

The notables who had done their shopping had gone.

They were not here on Faol buying slaves.

They were on holiday.

They might even — and I hoped Zair might have mercy on them for so abusing a great word — they might say they were on a Jikai.

For these slaves would be hunted.

They were quarry.

On the morrow, given clothes and a knife apiece, they would be let loose in the jungles of Faol, and then the nobles and their ladies, dressed up in fancy hunting clothes, would take after them. Oh, it would be great sport. They'd hunt the slaves right across the island, making great sport of it all, shouting "Hai, Jikai!" like as not.

I felt sick.

That human men and women could so debase themselves frightened me. No wonder the men of Aphrasöe so passionately wished to cleanse the planet Kregen, to give it honor and dignity, to remove forever the stain of slavery.

One tiny spark of hope there was, one ray of hope in all this morass of horror and ugliness.

That hope made the slaves walk out so eagerly on what would be a dreadful chase through the jungles, hunted and slain for sport.

For the guards had no way of knowing that the young men the slaves called guides would lead the hunted creatures to safety.

Tulema told me.

"The guides are very brave men, Dray! They can find their way through the jungles, and they can lead the people out to safety! And then, they come back here, through the tunnels in the rock, at the back of the caves, they return to lead out more slaves to freedom!"

"They are brave, Tulema," I said.

"Oh, yes! They take who they can, but they are promised rewards for their help, and I cannot reward anyone, for my parents are dead and I was a dancer in a dopa den, and I am afraid…"

A thought occurred to me.

"Why does not everyone escape out through the tunnels in the caves?"

She shook her head. "The ways are terrible and fraught with danger. The shafts are steep. The stone crumbles. Men can slide down, no one can climb up."

Well, I could be sure that slaves had tried to get out that way, and had failed. Slaves do many things to escape. The fear of death will not stop them, only failure of a scheme will hold them back from escape.

An old crone wandered across the cell, sweeping with a rustly broom of twigs,

29

cleaning up. Everyone moved out of her way. She was not a human being, and here I saw for the first time a member of the race of Miglish, the Miglas, who inhabit a large and important island off Havilfar.

"Get out of the way, you onker!" said one of the slaves, pushing the crone. She spat back at him and waved her broom, her long tangled hair about her face.

"May Migshaanu the All-Glorious turn your bones to jelly and your teeth black in your mouth and may she strike you with the pestilence and your eyes dribble down your cheeks, you cowardly nulsh!"

The Miglish crone waved her broom, whose stiff twigs were no more wildly tangled than her dark hair. The slave fell back, but still he mocked, and, indeed, the Migla looked a strange and unwholesome sight. She wore a gray slave breech-clout and a gray sacking garment. Her words tumbled out in a torrent. Tulema pulled me back, saying, "She is an evil old witch, Dray!"

The Migla swiped her broom at the dusty floor and tottered across to the lenk-wood bars where a guard in the leaf-green opened the narrow, barred door for her. She went out, still complaining, her thin bent back hard and angular beneath the sackcloth. She was evidently a tame slave and employed to clean up. Truth to tell, cleaning up was always necessary in these slave pens of Faol.

The slave who had pushed her spat on the floor.

He was a fine upstanding young man, with a Umber body on which the muscles showed long and supple, clear evidence that he could fight his way to the choicest parts of vosk, the fattest and juiciest onions, the best knuckle of bread. Tulema glanced at him, and away. He stared boldly at her, and walked over, moving with an arrogant lilt to him, a cock of the chin.

"I have not seen you before, shishi," he said, and he smiled with the wide meaning smile of a young man who imagines he knows all there is to know of the world and its wicked ways.

Shishi is a word I do not much care for. It carries certain connotations when spoken in that way by a man to a girl, and is far from respectful. It had been used by various men to Delia when we were in captivity and most of the men who had so spoken to her were dead. I started to say something, in my usual intemperate way, but Tulema put a quick hand on my arm and spoke loudly over my words.

"There are many slaves here, dom. It is no wonder you have not seen me." And then, with meaning, she added: "Why have you not gone with a guide to freedom? You are a strong man—"

"Yes, I am strong."

And, there and then, to my amazement, he started in on a series of callisthenic exercises, bulging his muscles, striking poses, making his body an exhibition of muscular strength.

I did not laugh, for, as you know, I do not laugh often. Although, looking back, I see I seemed to do nothing else but laugh during that wonderful time in Vondium when Delia and I were first married.

"This man is a Khamorro of the land of Herrell," Tulema whispered to me, her eyes wide and fearful. "They know a very terrible means of breaking men's bones. Do not, Dray, I beg you, even think of fighting him."

"Do not be frightened of him," I said.

"You do not understand! I do not know what kham he may have reached, but if you touch him he will kill you."

About to make some noncommittally brave and no doubt foolish reply, I stopped my wagging tongue. A girl had walked into our cell and approached the bars, and stood staring out in hopeless longing upon the mingled opaline rays of the twin suns. There can be no shame about nakedness among slaves, for between us we did not own so much as a pocket kerchief to cover ourselves, but this girl's stance, the way her arm reached up to clasp a lenken bar, the long line of her body, moved me. Her hair waved in a bright and genuine golden color about her shoulders, and her face, pallid and clear, revealed a beauty that seemed to light up the dank dark cave-cell.

I fancied I remembered the glorious golden hair shining as she ran from the cell on my arrival, when I had thrown the whip-wielding slave-master.

The Khamorro, after taking my measure, as he must have supposed, and seeing that hesitation on my part, thereafter ignored me and fell into conversation with Tulema. I looked at them both and, for the sake of an honor that has often been a sore trial to me, as you know, vowed that if he troubled her I would break his neck for him, despite his secret knowledge.

If I simply walked up to the golden-haired girl and began to talk to her, she might think my intentions were the same as the Khamorro's toward Tulema. I was saved a solution to that dilemma by the entry of another girl, beautiful and lithe, but with a yellow hair that in its dustiness and lack of shine could in nowise compare with the golden glory of the first girl, who stood now so sadly at the lenken bars.

"A princess!" said this second girl, in a high and mocking voice. "The proud Lilah says she is a princess! Is not this a great joke?"

Slaves can relish a joke, if it suits their somber moods, as well as anyone else. And, too, most of these slaves knew that with the help of the guides they would win free of the chase and so escape with their lives and liberty. So they were in nowise as downcast a mood as are slaves who see before them only another day's toil as hard and agonizing as today's, and after that another, and another, and the only surcease in death.

The beautiful girl with the golden hair did not turn around. She spoke in a low musical voice that gave full expression to the beauty of language universal Kregish undeniably possesses.

"I am a princess, Tosie, in all truth. But what good that will do me I cannot say."

"You cunning liar!" This Tosie was furious, now, her head thrown back, her hands on hips, her whole stance indicative of intense personal anger and frustration. "You promise the guides much money and great rewards if they will guide you out, pretending to be a princess. Well, then!" Tosie's face took on a triumphant look as she screamed: "If you are the Princess Lilah, then I am the Queen Tosie! You should bow and scrape to me! I'll promise the guides anything to take me away from this awful place!"

Tosie was no queen, that appeared certain. But if this Lilah was a princess, then she was the one the Star Lords wished me to rescue. What their ends might be I did not know, but the rescue of this glorious Princess Lilah was a task to which they had set my hands. I would not fail them; I must not, for until I had completed their mission I would not be allowed to return to Vallia and my Delia, my Delia of Delphond.

"It is because I am Princess of Hyrklana that I may not do as you intend, Tosie. I can only offer rewards to the guides when I return home to my father's palace."

"And I shall offer rewards, too! Money! Lands! Zorcas! Totrixes! Women — and money again! Whatever you offer I will double. If you think you will escape and leave me here to be hunted, alone and without a guide, you think wrongly!"

A blast on the stentors' horns cut into the argument. The sound was different from the call that had driven everyone in such great panic out of the feeding hall and into the cells to crowd up against the lenken bars. The slaves began that surging movement, shouting and pushing, and all rushed off toward the feeding cave. By this time I fancied a juicy chunk of vosk would not come amiss, so I started off, too.

I looked back.

Tosie, who called herself a queen and was probably a dancing girl in a dopa den like Tulema, had gone. Tulema herself was just running out, assisted by the Khamorro. I would find her again, if necessary, but now, with the knowledge that it was the Princess Lilah I must rescue, I could let Tulema go.

Lilah turned listlessly from the bars.

"Come, Princess," I said. "If you would eat we must hurry to the feeding cave."

She looked at me.

Her eyes were blue, and though I could guess they would normally be bright and clear and frank, now they were clouded with suspicion.

Before she could say what so clearly lay in her mind, I said swiftly, "There will be a struggle for the food, Princess. We must hurry."

She stood there, drooping and defenseless, and the thought occurred to me that if ever my Delia found herself in this position again — which Zair forbid! — there would be a man ready to protect her without thought of reward.

"You — call me *princess*—"

"I see you are. Now, come."

She went with me through the barred cells and passageways and so into the feeding cave. We were too late. Most of the other slaves had already taken what they could snatch and the remainder were clustered about the dilse tureens.

My instincts were to knock down the nearest person eating a hunk of vosk and chewing on onions and snatch the food away. Perhaps I was growing weak and feeble, but I did not. I said, "We must eat dilse today, Princess. At the next feeding time you must run very swiftly."

She made a small dismissive gesture with her hand. I noticed her fingers, very long and slender, and I tried to imagine them plunging into the heaped food on the floor and bunching into tiny fists to strike away those who would snatch the food first. She would not starve, but she would grow lean of face and listless on dilse.

We were fed at regular intervals, I guessed every five burs or so — something like three and a half hours — and the reason for this lavish expenditure of food was quite clear. Whoever owned this island of Faol, where slaves were run and hunted as quarry, had to please his customers; and these came from many islands and lands even from beyond Havilfar, so the slaves must be well fed and active to furnish good sport.

I would relish a short interview with this fellow.

At the next feeding call, when the stentor horns boomed and clamored through the passageways and cells cut in the rocks, I grabbed Lilah's hand and fairly dragged her along. Many slaves clustered about the entrance to the feeding hall, of course, just before they guessed the call would come, and these rushed in first. I plowed my way through them and halfway to the mess of food let Lilah go and lunged on.

How had my pride been humbled!

Here I was, a naked slave grubbing and fighting for food scattered on a filthy floor, when only a day ago I had eaten all the delicacies my heart could desire — and then I shut all self-pity from my mind. I hardened — and I am only too prone to being a soft man in many things, as you know.

Lilah accepted the food. She might have thought to stand on her dignity, but when she saw the dripping hunk of vosk I snatched up, and felt the firm lusciousness of the onions, smelled the cheese — it was a dreadful smell, in truth, but it was food — she could not hold back. She ate with a strange pathetic mixture of ravenous hunger and a finicky set of table manners. I just wolfed the stuff down.

And then, again, that clamoring of stentor horns broke out afresh and with wild cries all the slaves ran out of the feeding cave to press themselves against the lenken bars.

But I had not quite finished the chunk of hard bread, for in my lazy, wealthy way back in Vallia I had grown used to the finest food, and so was slow with this lenklike loaf.

Lilah said, "Dray — we must run! It is the call for the jiklos! Hurry!"

She might know what in hell a jiklo was; I did not, and I wanted to finish this confounded chunk of iron-hard bread. Lilah was terrified. She did not catch my arm, as Tulema would have done, to drag me away. She started for the exit, and turned, her golden hair swirling, and cried, "Hurry, Dray! Hurry!"

Chewing on the bread I walked after her.

Truly, pride is a foolish item in a man's baggage!

I heard the jiklos, then.

I heard an eerie, spine-chilling, frightful, and obscene hissing and howling, a scrabbling of claws, the rush of bodies. Lilah screamed and ran. I turned to look back.

A glimpse, I had, a glimpse back through a freshly opened entrance to the cave. Ruby light spilled out from the space beyond.

Through that bloody radiance dreadful forms ran on all fours over the filthy floor. I saw matted hair crested into upswept combs, and trailing out to the rear. I saw flashing eyes. Teeth glinted like rows of daggers. Hands and feet pounded the dust and filth of the floor. Red tongues lolled. The jiklos howled at sight of me

33

— and then Lilah was there, pulling me on. We stumbled back through the entrance to the feeding cave and iron bars clashed down, almost crushing us.

The leading jiklo threw himself against those bars, slavering. His eyes regarded me with the utmost malevolence.

I looked at him.

And I saw what he was.

I felt the sick nausea welling up.

So I first made the acquaintance of the Manhounds of Antares.

Five

Manhounds

"But they're *men!*"

I have seen many and many a sight that might drive any normal man insane. I have never considered myself a normal man, and for that hubris I have suffered. But I do believe that the Manhounds of Antares made as strong an impression of decadence and evil and horror upon me as anything I have seen on Earth or on Kregen.

They were men.

But they ran on all fours. Their faces were human faces. But they had fierce sharply serrated teeth, they had pricked ears, pointed and mobile, they had squashed pug noses that could wrinkle up and sniff and follow a scent that might baffle bloodhounds. They had the bodies of men. But their hands padded against the ground, and their rear legs were shorter and thicker than those of a man who walks upright. Their nails were sharp hard claws, glinting evilly. Their hair was brushed and combed upward into a cock-fighting crest, and streamed out in a loose mane, like that of a horse, from the stiff crest.

They wore brave red jackets, cut like a dog's jacket. They wore gray breechclouts. Around their necks were strapped leather collars, studded with metals.

They were hunting dogs.

But they were men.

The Manhounds of Antares, the jiklos of Faol.

Pressed up against the lenken bars Lilah still held my arm. She had not shrunk from touching me, from pulling me away. Just beyond her I could see Tulema and the Khamorro. Now I understood a little why Tulema, for all the promises of the guides, hung back from escaping, was so terrified of the manhunt.

"Yes, Dray Prescot," said Princess Lilah of Hyrklana. "They are men."

Men. They were not halflings, even, men-beasts for beast-men with a weird mutation of head or body to mark them out from true men — and who, on Kregen, is to say who is a true man and who is not? Gloag was a man for all his bristle-hide and bullet-head. Inch, too, was a man. But these — things? These Manhounds of Scorpio? Were they truly men?

The answer could not be denied.

Some agency had so guided their development, over the seasons, as to transform them from ordinary men into jiklos. I could with revulsion imagine some of the training. They must have been strapped into iron cages from birth, made to walk always on all fours, taught to run and hunt, and by evolving senses regained man's lost capacities of smell and hearing. They might be unable to stand upright at all, now.

And the final blasphemy, at least in my eyes, was to dress them in red coats, to sully the image I held of my own old scarlet, the scarlet of Strombor!

Shadows moved in the jungle clearing beyond the bars. The slaves huddled, waiting to be picked as quarry. Tulema hung back and the Khamorro, arguing with her, at last slapped her across the face and pushed her back. He moved toward the bars with arrogance, and other slaves shrank back from him.

Lilah said, "Here they come now..."

Into the cleared area before the barred rows of cages, rather like a shopping arcade, stepped Nalgre, the slave-master, with his guards, and his customers. I ignored all that, started to push my way toward the Khamorro. Tulema was sobbing, now. She had lost this Khamorro and she must have assumed she had already lost me, absorbed as I had been with Lilah. Tulema could not know that it was by the Star Lords' command that I must rescue Lilah.

"No, Dray Prescot," said Lilah. I recognized the tone. She was a princess, I felt no doubt. "You will be killed."

Again she put her hand on my arm. I could feel the softness of it, and yet the firmness, too, as she gripped me.

What might have happened then, Zair knows, for a Fristle nearby, whose fur was much bedraggled, said quickly, "Here is Nath the Guide."

The guide pushed through to the bars, and I left off trying to reach the Khamorro. This guide was much like the first one I had seen — lithe, well built, fleet of limb, as I judged, with a handsome head and a mass of dark hair. Nath the Guide...

Well, there are many Naths on Kregen.

Around him perhaps a dozen people clustered. They were eager. They had been able to arrange deals with the guide to be taken out. And all the time Lilah's hand gripped my arm.

Nalgre the slave-master cracked his whip. The customers with him jumped, and then laughed, and pointed out to one another choice specimens of slaves within the cages. It was all a part of the show Nalgre put on.

These nobles and wealthy men and women who hunted human beings for sport were little different from the bunch I had seen before. A quick check showed me that Berran was not with them. The Notor who, by his appearance and gestures, considered himself the most important personage there was a heavily built man, with brown hair, a face pudgy from too many inspections of the bottoms of glasses, too many vosk-pies, and smothered in a mass of jewels and silks and feathers.

He was pointing now and Nalgre was nodding.

Nath the Guide whispered: "It will be all right. He will choose us. Now remember! Act as slaves, for the sake of Hito the Hunter!"

This Notor fancied himself as a great Jikai, it was clear, for the guards swung open the lenken-barred gate and began to herd out more than a dozen of the slaves. One fragile Xaffer was rejected, and I guessed the poor devil had been subsisting on dilse and nothing else for too long. In the heat and dust of the compound, with the smells of sweat and fear all about us, we were prodded out. Lilah clung to me. I caught a glimpse of Tulema hanging back, her face agonized, tear-streaked, and then the lenken bars smashed shut against the slaves who remained unselected.

"We're in for it now, Lilah," I said. "We'll soon be free."

"I pray it be so, Dray Prescot."

With guards around us, their spears everywhere ready to prod mercilessly, we were taken through the clearing to the slave barracks. Here we would be prepared for the next day's hunt.

You will already have realized that the Dray Prescot who walked so docilely with the slaves, prodded by spears, was a very different person from the Dray Prescot who had so witlessly and violently resisted any slave attempt upon him — as when, for instance, I was captured and flung down before the Princess Natema, and had thrown Galna at her, for good measure. I was trying to calculate out if escaping now, this instant, would serve our ends better than waiting. Once I had taken this lovely girl Princess Lilah of Hyrklana back home, I would then strike at once for Vallia. I did not wish to make a leem's-nest of it.

I have been hunted as quarry for sport since this occasion on Faol — notably by the debased Ry-ufraisors, who sacrifice to the green sun, calling Genodras by the name of Ry-ufraison. That was many seasons later, of course — many years ago, now, too — and I wander in my tale. It is worth noting that here on Faol I found the people referring to the red and green suns, the Suns of Scorpio, not as Zim and Genodras but as Far and Havil.

While I had no doubts that I could survive in the jungle, and this without boasting, which is a fool's trade, I had doubts about Lilah. Nath the Guide told us we would be given clothes, and boots, and a knife apiece. Also food. Almost decided in my mind to consign these trinkets to the Ice Floes of Sicce and make a break for it right away, I witnessed an event that changed my mind.

The arrogant Khamorro would have nothing of waiting. He had chosen his time, and now, by Morro the Muscle, he would break a few backbones and escape into the jungles. His name was Lart. I had had trouble with a Lart very early on during my second visit to Kregen, and so I watched with great care.

Lart the Khamorro flexed his muscles in the slave barracks. Other men walked small when a Khamorro passed. We were given fresh food, although the promised clothes were denied us, and the food was good — thick vosk and taylyne soup, beef roasted to a prime, fresh roandals, the bread of Kregen in long loaves and done in the bols fashion as well, and, lastly, palines.

We were packed off to the first floor of the building, leaving the hard-packed earth below empty. By leaning out over the sturm-wood balustrade we could see the guards patrolling down there. One test of the walls showed they would resist bare hands. The only way out was down the stairs, past the guards, and through the doors.

Lart the Khamorro flexed his muscles and started down the stairs.

Three guards stood up, alert, and their spears twitched down into line.

"Get back, cramph!"

Lart laughed. He jeered at them.

"If we kill you, rast, the cost of your worthless hide will be deductible." One of the guards, with a thin black goatee, swung his spear so that the point glittered in the light falling through the windows at his back. "But I would willingly pay that to degut you!"

Lart laughed again and then he moved and that guard lay on the ground with a broken neck.

The other two cursed and swiveled their spears. Lart the Khamorro swerved very lithely and ducked and another guard was caught and, for an instant, held in a terrible grip. He catapulted over Lart's back and when he hit the ground his little round helmet rolled away from what was left of his skull.

The third guard shouted, high and filled with terror.

"Hai! Guards! A madman is loose!"

"The fools!" whispered Lilah, at my side. "Don't they know he is a Khamorro?"

"Evidently not, Lilah." I watched, fascinated. I saw how Lart worked, the smooth play of his muscles, the cunning tricks of body-contact, all the skills I had absorbed under the pitiless tuition of the Krozairs of Zy were here being put into action, under my nose, and me skulking on a stair!

But I knew what I was doing.

The main doors were fast bolted by a massive beam of lenk.

Lart rushed for them and began to lift the beam. The third guard, still yelling, made the mistake of trying to thrust his spear into Lart's back. The muscles rippled on that sinewy back. Lart slid the spear — and that was neatly done, by Zair! — and cut the guard under the chin with the edge of his palm. The guard choked and writhed and died. The trick was an old one but reliable if you were quick enough to hit the target.

Again Lart began to lift the lenken beam that took two men to place. He got one end up and was about to slide it down when with a rush and a volley of oaths three more guards raced into the dirt-floored chamber. Up on the stairs we all yelled in warning.

If Lilah expected me to run down to help Lart, she was mistaken. Anyway, I had the hunch that if I did so a haze of blue radiance would engulf me, and a giant scorpion would enfold me in its pincers and I would be flung — where? Back to Earth, probably. Then I would have to languish how many years before the Star Lords once more thought to employ me about their mysterious business on Kregen?

For the sake of Delia, not for Lilah, I remained where I was.

Anyway, even as Lart, in a sudden and destructive flurry of blows, chops, stabs of finger and knuckle, body-swerves and cunning lifts and back-breaking holds, disposed of the three guards, what I knew must happen came to pass with the furious advent of a Deldar. He came in through the side door, waving his sword, and with him came three crossbow-men.

"You stupid, dopa-sodden cramphs!" The Deldar was bellowing. "Have you no sense in your onker-thick skulls?"

I perfectly agreed with him.

"Feather me this rast!" screamed the Deldar. The three crossbows leveled.

Even then, even then Lart the Khamorro with his marvelous skills in unarmed combat almost got them. He dodged the first bolt, almost missed the second, taking it high in his left shoulder. But this slowed him a fraction, jerking him off balance, and he took the last quarrel clear through his belly.

He coughed and doubled up.

Still, he moved on, lifting his hands. And now, because he was mortally wounded, he moved slowly enough for that cunning hand-pattern to be clearly visible. I recalled the burs of training spent with the Krozairs on the island of Zy in the Eye of the World. My body responded to the remembered thump and smash of fist, and hand-edge, and knuckle, the way Zinki could always throw me until I learned the secret ways of counterbalance, and weight-shift, the poise, the blows, the whole mystic art of body-fighting I had learned as I had learned how to wield a Krozair longsword. Well, give me a sword anytime, but without a metal weapon — or a wooden one, to come to that — a man may do terrible damage with his bare hands.

But Lart had been slowed too much.

The guard Deldar could bring his sword down in a vicious blow and so finish Lart the Khamorro.

Lilah gasped and turned away.

I admit, I felt queasy about leaving a fellow human being to fight alone, like that. But — and however brutal and selfish this sounds, I do not care — what was Lart to me beside my mission for the Star Lords that must not fail, my concern for Lilah — my love for Delia, my Delia of the Blue Mountains?

"The stupid rancid-brained onkers!" the Deldar was shouting. He kicked Lart's dead body. "They didn't know to keep away from a Khamorro. You!" He swung violently on his three crossbowmen. "Never get within reach of a Khamorro! Never! It is certain death." He fumed on, and as the bodies were cleared away he shouted up at us, gawping from the balustrade. "Get back up there and rest! Aye, rest! Tomorrow you run and will need all your strength. And if any cramph among you wants to break out of the door — he'll taste my steel!"

There was one furious Deldar. No doubt, Lart would be deductible.

There were palliasses and thin blankets, and before we went to sleep, Lilah said, "Lart fought well, Dray. He was very skilled, a high kham, I have no doubt. And he was very brave."

"Aye, Lilah," I said, turning over and pulling the blanket up. "Very brave and very stupid."

Six

How Nath the Guide aided us

The morning broke fresh and glorious with the twin Suns of Scorpio bursting up over the jungle levels and casting down their streaming mingled jade and ruby light. The air smelled clean and invigorating, and however dank it might become in the jungle, as we ate a huge breakfast, I own we slaves felt happier than any of us had any right to be.

Lilah had told me that she had been on a visit of state with an uncle to a neighboring country of Havilfar when her airboat had been attacked and captured. She called the fliers vollers, and when I mentioned that they always seemed to be breaking down, she turned a puzzled frown my way, and said, "Not reliable, Dray? You do an injustice to the voller builders! Why, our vollers can outfly the fastest saddle-birds in all Havilfar!"

I let the matter go, but I did not forget it.

She was not completely sure how she had come to be brought to Faol. She knew the island, of course, off northern Havilfar; and she had heard casual tales of great hunts to be had there. She had no idea that this Jikai was the hunting of people, and she had met the jiklos with utter horror.

Like all the continents and the nine islands of Kregen — with the exception of Vallia — Havilfar is divided up into different countries. I set myself to learn their geography and histories, as well as Lilah could inform me, and when it is necessary for you to know any part of these, then that is when I shall introduce it.

In the circle of vaol-paol all things may come to pass.

Nath the Guide winked at us as we shuffled outside and into the cleared area before the slave barracks. Waiting for us and backed by a strong guard contingent stood Nalgre and his customers. Today the great hunters were dressed in leathers, with tall boots, wide hats, and a massive armory hung about them. The chief weapon of the hunt would be the crossbow. As always, I studied the weapons of those who were my foemen and who sought to slay me.

The fashion in swords here was for the short straight blade, perhaps not quite as robust a brand as the shortswords of my clansmen, but a useful and all-purpose cut-and-thrust weapon that would do its work efficiently and without fuss. The crossbows were beautiful artifacts, the wood a close-grained hurm — a close relative of the ubiquitous sturm-wood — and the butts and stocks shone in the mingled rays of the suns. The bows themselves were of tempered steel. Most of these crossbows were spanned by cranequins, one or two by goat's-foot lever. I did not see a single windlass. The bolts were notched in leather. In addition these infamous hunters had loaded themselves with various bloodthirsty weapons. It infuriated me to see, for instance, a plump and laughing woman, her hair looped up in a net of priceless pearls, leaning on her crossbow and talking to her companion, who kept digging the point of his vosk-spear into the ground. They all looked a little self-conscious in their hunting leathers and they handled their weapons rather as tourists handle implements with which they are not totally familiar.

All this spending of money and time and effort — to hunt a raggle-tail bunch of half-naked slaves through the jungles!

Half-naked: we were issued with gray slave breechclouts which we put on, out there, on the ground, in sight of everyone. Lilah acted as though the hunters did not exist.

I waited for the clothes and the knives, but Nath the Guide whispered fiercely and at his words I forbore to inquire, sensing a part of the secret the guides kept against the man-hunters of Faol.

In this little group of slaves — sixteen of us — only Lilah and I and two others, a man and woman, were humans. All the rest were halflings. I couldn't equate Nath as a slave. Despite the air of docility and fear he assumed there was about him the unmistakable sense of the free man, the man who fought against odds, and expected to win.

This fine morning Nalgre had his little pet with him.

He clicked his fingers and a jiklo ran across the clearing toward him, tongue lolling, eyes bright, frisking about him. I watched, sickened. This jiklo was a woman. She panted about her master on all fours, pricking her ears, emitting little gobbles of pleasure at his notice of her, and at the dribble of ground vosk he let fall, which she lapped up greedily. She wore a red bolero jacket, and a gray breechclout, and she ran on all fours, and she was a manhound of Antares, and she was a woman.

The studs and plaques on her leather collar were all of gold. Her brown hair frizzed up into that angry matted crest, and blonde streamers of hair fell back in a tail from the central mass. Her naked rump frisked about Nalgre, and had a tail sprouted there, I suppose, one might have accepted the picture more.

Lilah's supple figure quivered at sight of the jiklo, then she controlled herself. The halflings were whispering to one another, and a couple of Fristles unashamedly clasped each other in their furry arms.

I had no doubt why Nalgre played with his pet before us. "Look," he was saying. "This is a manhound. These are the creatures who will chase you and hunt you and pull you down."

The jiklo trotted over to us. The halflings went rigid with fear. I looked down as the red bolero swung past. The thing emitted little gasps and wheezes, and the pug nose wrinkled up. The thing was smelling us! She was taking our scent!

"Get away, you filthy kleesh!" snarled the human man, a husky youngster called Naghan, who came, so he said, from Hamal itself. He told us this with pride. The girl with him screamed as the jiklo's tongue, all lolling and wet and red, rasped down her naked calf. Naghan kicked out and then he, too, screamed and writhed as a guard lashed his back with a cunning whipblow called the rattler.

"Stay in line there, you rasts!" shouted Nalgre.

He turned and spoke quietly to his customers the hunters, and then they glanced swiftly and at an angle beneath their hands at the suns, to tell the time, and then all turned and walked off out of the clearing, back to their comfortable Jikai villas to await the time to be off.

The time for the slaves to leave was now.

With the whips cracking about our heads, and words of advice from Nalgre, we set off. His advice amounted to: "Run and run, cramphs. If you do not afford good sport and are taken without a good chase, you will be more sorry than you may imagine!" He snickered as he said this, and fondled the female jiklo, who crooned in pleasure at the touch of her master's hand.

We set off due east.

The jungle closed above our heads and strange noises rose from the depths of the greenery. The brilliant light of the twin suns muted to a long lazy green-gold radiance, and here and there mingled shafts of ruby and jade struck down through interstices in the leafy cover. The trail was hard-packed for the first dwabur. Five miles was a fair distance to travel, and when we came out to a little clearing the slaves were happy to flop down, panting, to rest.

Nath the Guide crossed to a heap of lichened stones and lifted one to the side. I looked over his shoulder.

In the hollow between the stones lay clothing, food — and knives! Also there were clumsy-looking shoes. The halflings pounced on the shoes first. Well, that made sense. I have been accustomed all my life to going barefoot, and I had walked across the Hostile Territories, and the Owlarh Waste without footwear. The journey across the Klackadrin, too, was not without a lively memory or two, and then I had been barefoot.

I said I did not want a pair of shoes.

At this Nath the Guide protested, saying I would slow the others up. They were putting on the clothes, simple gray tunics and floppy hats, and Lilah, too, implored me to don a pair of shoes. In the end I did so, to quiet her noise.

We ate and rested and then set off again.

"When will they catch up with us, Nath?"

"Not until the suns have passed the zenith." He chuckled. "And if we press on boldly they may never catch up with us at all. There are secret ways."

He kept us going east. The jungle looked like many another jungle through which I have traveled, with trees and growths familiar to Earth as well as Kregen. Lilah was holding up well. If we could keep going and get well ahead, we might clear right out for good.

Toward early evening we left the edge of the jungle, which had thinned considerably, and came to an immense ravine cut through the earth athwart our path. A light rope bridge hung above the abyss. We crossed, not without a deal of swaying about and a few screams, and after we had reached the other side Naghan from Hamal said: "Let us destroy the bridge."

That seemed a sensible idea.

"No," said Nath the Guide. "If the bridge is gone the Jikai will surely know which way we have gone."

41

Well, that seemed sensible, too.

In the end, bowing to Nath's superior knowledge of the problems of the man-hunters, we left the bridge intact.

For a space I walked along with Nath, while Lilah walked with Naghan and his girl, Sosie. The guide intrigued me. I questioned him, casually, about his life.

"We are of Faol, too," he said. "I live in a village on the southern shore, and the young men are dedicated to helping the slaves. The manhunters are very terrible masters."

I congratulated him, thinking of the dangers he and his comrades faced. "I think," he said to me, glancing sideways as we walked, "you have been on many great Jikais yourself."

"Aye," I said, thinking of the great days when my clansmen had hunted across the Great Plains of Segesthes. "But I have never hunted humans for sport."

"Humans?" He looked at me oddly. "But only Naghan and Sosie, Lilah, and yourself are humans."

The Fristle man was at that moment helping the Fristle woman along, putting his furry arm about her waist and half carrying her. I was about to make what I considered a fitting reply when Nath broke away from me, looking up, shouting a warning.

"Vollers! Quick! Into the bushes — and remain still, for the sake of Hito the Hunter!"

From the shelter of the bushes we looked up as a flier passed overhead, traveling slowly due east. Well, that answered one question I had intended to put to Nath — how the manhunters would know in which direction we had gone. He had been right about the bridge.

When the voller had gone we stood up, breathing our relief, and set off again. The country was opening out now. From the edge of the jungle beyond the ravine at our back the sky filled with the quick darting shapes of flying foxes, hereabouts called inklevols, black against the dying suns-glow.

Nath the Guide pointed ahead across the open land, dotted here and there with clumps of trees, gently rolling and gradually undulating away to a distant horizon.

"Tomorrow we cross the plain and then—"

"Then we are free!" exclaimed a Brokelsh, rubbing his black bristle body-hair in his excitement.

We made our little camp in a hollow, surrounded by trees, in the bend of a small river. Nath showed the usual skills of the hunter in preparing a smokeless fire and of shielding the flame-glare by a palisade of twisted rushes. The knives he had provided were poor things, it was true, but they did enable us to cut wood and leaves and so fabricate a softer bed than the ground. We ate and drank water from the stream, and Nath had been able to provide a little wine for us. Truth to tell, freedom was the wine we all craved.

We sat for a short space, talking, Nath and I. I had said to Naghan earlier: "Sosie and Lilah will sleep side by side, and you and I will sleep outside them." And he had replied: "It is a good plan."

Now I said to Nath: "And is manhunting the chief occupation of the high ones of Faol?"

"Yes. It is their ruling passion. Nobles come from all over Havilfar, and the lands beyond, to go on a Faol Jikai."

He sounded proud of that, which was strange, but he added: "They bring in money, which helps my people, and we arrange for the escape of the slaves."

"The hunters did not reach us, as you suggested they might."

"No. Tomorrow will be a day of careful marching."

I was itching to ask about Lilah who, as a princess, would in the societies I had previously known on Kregen be far more valuable as a subject for ransom than as a subject for a hunt. I put the point to Nath the Guide, who yawned, and said carelessly: "Oh, there are many girls who claim to be princesses and queens, and, mayhap, some of them are. But then — if a customer knew he was hunting a princess, and with all that would follow at the end of the hunt, think how much more the pleasure!"

"I see," I said.

It did make sense, of a kind that sickened me anew. I rolled over and pushed up against Lilah where she lay asleep, one arm outflung across Sosie, and so let my eyelids close.

Tomorrow we would cross the plain and reach safety and then I could deliver the Princess Lilah of Hyrklana to her friends and take off for Vallia. As sleep overcame me, I wondered vaguely if I might not prosecute two of my obsessions on Kregen as I was so near Havilfar. For on Havilfar lived the scarlet-robed To-dalpheme who had taken Delia to Aphrasöe and who might therefore tell me where that marvelous Swinging City was situated on the face of Kregen. And the other obsession was to discover more of the fliers, the vollers, and their manufacture.

So I slept and with the first rays of Far and Havil striking low over the plain I awoke, sat up and rubbed my eyes, and reached for the cheap knife and stood up — and Nath the Guide was gone.

Seven

Princess Lilah of Hyrklana rides a fluttrell

In a babblement and confusion the slaves ran about looking for Nath the Guide. They shouted along the stream and broke through thickets, and looked behind clumps of rocks. I studied where the guide had slept. His gear still lay where he had left it — blanket, shoes, knife, a leaf with a few palines — and as he had slept a little apart from us, whatever had taken him in the night had rested content with the one meal.

Lilah shivered. "Poor Nath!"

"Leem, by Hanitcha the Harrower!" Naghan said fiercely.

"We are on our own now." The squat-bodied Brokelsh rubbed his black body hairs as he spoke. "We had best move now!"

"We will eat first," I said. "And then we will march."

I did not anticipate an argument, and broke bread and gave some to Sosie and Lilah. We shared out what we had. In truth, it was little enough, and I fancied I must hunt our meat before the suns sank beyond the western horizon. "Also," I said, "we will set watches through the night."

I took up the knife left by Nath. It was of the same cheap manufacture as our own, but it was steel, for which I was thankful. His shoes, too, would be useful. Like ours they were cheap, crudely made from a single piece of cattle hide, pierced for thongs all around and then drawn up on a slip-string, like moccasins. There hung about them an odd little odor, as though they had not been perfectly cured.

We set off, striking due east by the suns, walking smartly.

After a time, thinking to put a little heart into the slaves, for they were mightily downcast by the savage and inexplicable disappearance of Nath the Guide, I struck up a song. I took the first one that jumped into my head. It was *Morgash and Sinkle,* all about a man and a maid and the laughable plight of their marriage, and was known all over Kregen. These Havilfarese knew the song, and some of them joined in with me, and so, singing, we marched on across the undulating ground.

I kept that old warrior's eye of mine well open.

This night, I vowed, we would not sprawl out and sleep like a bunch of school-children on an outing; we would march on by stages under the light of Kregen's moons. She of the Veils and the Twins would be up early, and the maiden with the many Smiles would follow later, to make the land almost as bright as an Earth day.

Despite the horror I knew slavered at our heels, the march would have been pleasant had I been in certain company. Had Seg Segutorio been with me, or Inch of Ng'groga, or Gloag, Hap Loder, Varden, or Vomanus. Delia — well, I was not foolish enough to wish my Delia here in this situation. But she would have responded with her marvelous spirit and enjoyment of life, her brave smile and her untiring love. This Princess Lilah was a fine girl, but I could understand the air of strain, her distrait appearance of barely suppressed terror. I wondered how that other Lilah, that Queen Lilah of Hiclantung, the notorious Queen of Pain, was faring now.

And so, marching across that gardenlike plain, I fell to maundering in my thoughts about Nath and Zolta — and Zorg, my oar comrade, who was now dead. I missed my two rascals, Nath and Zolta. I remembered many a fine carouse and singing session we had indulged ourselves in, back in Sanurkazz. There was Pur Zenkiren, too, Grand Archbold elect of the Krozairs of Zy. One day the great summons would come and I must return to the Eye of the World so that all the forces of the Zairians of the southern shore might go up against the Grodnim of the hostile northern shore of the inner sea.

That day would come.

If Nath and Zolta were with me now — there'd be some wild goings-on, by Zim-Zair!

44

Twice during that long march we saw fliers crisscrossing above. We hid. I felt an invisible net was closing about us.

Some of the shoes we wore were thinner in the sole than others, and a Relt, one of those more gentle cousins of the ferocious Rapas, soon complained that his bare foot was hurting. We inspected the hole, and pursed our lips, and I gave him one of Nath the Guide's shoes. The other shoe went in similar fashion to Sosie. We slogged on. In my usual fashion — a cross laid on me I do not seem able to be free of — I had taken charge of this little fugitive band in the absence of the guide. They looked to me — Zair knows why people always look to me in moments of crisis — and so I had to respond with due propriety. I told them when to rest, and I caught one of the little six-legged rabbitlike animals of the plains called xikks and we cooked and ate the poor creature. Presently I roused them and we set off again, and now, ahead of us and spreading to encompass both north and south, a massive and darkly brooding forest spread its waiting wings.

Everyone looked ahead, pointing and chattering.

A harsh and demoniac croaking blattered down from above.

I looked up.

Up there, circling in wide planing hunting circles, rising and falling on the air, flew a giant scarlet and golden-feathered hunting bird. A magnificent raptor, the Gdoinye, the messenger and spy of the Star Lords, who had snatched me from Vallia and dumped me down in a stinking slave pen.

I shook my fist.

The raptor circled, its head cocked and no doubt one beady eye regarding us and relaying what it saw back to its masters, the Everoinye. I wondered, for a moment, if the blue radiance would engulf me — but the raptor emitted another raucous squawk and flew off. I did not see the white dove of the Savanti.

"What in the name of the Twins was that?" said Lilah.

"A bird," I said. "Had I a bow—"

"You would not shoot so wonderful a creature, surely?" said Sosie, shocked.

I knew what I knew, and so I did not reply.

I looked back.

Dark against the ground the dreadful shapes of jiklos pressed hard on our trail.

At once all was confusion and the slaves began a mad run for the forest. I kept close to Lilah. One of my shoes loosened, the slipstring slipping, and I kicked the thing off. I could run more fleetly in my bare feet than clogged down with these clumsy shoes, and so I loosened the other and kicked that off, too. We all ran.

We neared the trees, and I could see rocks and gullies in which the trees grew at crazy angles.

Lilah was panting and gasping, her golden hair blowing.

I picked her up and ran.

Naghan had picked up Sosie, too, as the Fristle man had picked up the Fristle woman. We were all hunted slaves, no longer simply men or halflings.

I flung a glance back.

The manhounds were terribly close. Beyond them rode zorca-mounted hunters, yelling, waving their weapons, having a fine old time. I ran.

We plunged into the first outlying trees and I picked a gully and ran up it, dodging tree branches, hurdling fallen trunks. Naghan, carrying Sosie, ran with me. We plunged on into the thicker trees, clambering over rocky patches, diving into underbrush, scratched and torn, plunging on and on.

Of course, my every instinct impelled me to dump Lilah down and, knives in fists, turn and battle these filthy manhounds, these high and mighty hunters. But I quelled that primeval instinct. My mission was to rescue Lilah, not to get myself killed in however enjoyable a way slaying manhounds and devilish hunters astride their zorcas.

Now we could hear the high excited keening of the jiklos. They were men! Men! Yet they were more fiercely predatory hunters than any bloodhound, any wersting, and to fall into their clutches would mean a hideous death.

We struggled and scrambled on, and came to a wall of rock.

"Put me down, Dray. We must climb."

"Get started, Lilah. When you are at the top, I will follow."

Sosie was already climbing, and Naghan following. Of the others I could see or hear nothing.

Lilah sprang at the rocks, began to haul herself up by ridge and crevice, her long golden hair very bright in the waning light of the twin suns.

I waited.

After what seemed a very long time I heard Lilah call, and about to wheel about and follow her, I caught the feral movement in the greenery opposite, the dagger-bright flash of jagged teeth.

A manhound sprang out from the trees, hurtled straight toward me.

And then — something for which I had not been prepared, the jiklo shouted to me, shouted words of a thick local language that, through the gene-manipulative pill of Maspero's in far Aphrasöe, I was able to understand.

The manhound spoke in a thick rasping whine, a hoarse and bloodthirsty howl.

"You are done for, you two-legged yetch!"

He bounded straight for me. The long mane streamed back from the central crest. His nails glittered. His eyes were bloodshot. And his teeth — could they ever have been the teeth of normal man? Sharp and jagged, serrated, as he opened his mouth to snarl at me those teeth looked like the teeth of risslaca honed to rip hot flesh and blood!

I poised, let fly one of my knives.

He tried to duck, but he was not quick enough.

The knife buried itself in one eye.

The jiklo let out an insane scream.

He was bounding into the air, rearing, his face a demoniac mask of hate and blood-lust. He pawed up at the knife hilt.

He twisted, he toppled, he fell.

There was no time to recover the knife.

Up those rocks I went like a grundal.

From the open space the fresh sounds of a second jiklo struck over the slobbering shrieking of the first. Lilah screamed something incoherent. If that had been my Delia up there she wouldn't have been screaming, telling me something I already knew; my Delia would have been hurling rocks down to protect the back of her man.

Without looking back I lashed out with my foot and felt my heel jar into something hairy and hard, and the howling changed key into a yowling. I scrambled up the last few yards of the rock face and swung about at the top, on all fours like a damned jiklo myself, and so peered over the lip.

The bounding demoniac shapes of more manhounds ferreted through the trees and sprang into the space before the rocks.

"Sink me!" I said. I stood up and grabbed Lilah's wrist. "The rock won't stop them. By the Black Chunkrah, woman, stop that blabbering and run!"

Oh, yes, I, Dray Prescot, ran.

We fled through the rock gullies with the overhanging trees making the way alternately dark and light, shot through with the last rays of the sinking suns, so that all the world turned an angry viridian blood color, most unsettling.

Farther on I caught up with Naghan and Sosie, who ran, gasping and panting, in a way distressing to me.

We paused for a quick breather and in that space of hard-drawn breaths we heard the click and patter of jiklo claws following us. Sosie screamed again, and Naghan clapped a hand across her face — but gently.

"If we split up we will stand a better chance," said Naghan, the young man who claimed with so much pride to come from Hamal.

"Agreed," I said. Then: "I wish you well, Naghan, and you, Sosie. May Zair go with you."

Of course they had no idea what or who Zair was, that was quite clear, but they understood, and commended me to the care of Opaz.

"Remberee!" we shouted, and then ran as fast as we might over the rocks and splinters up separate gullies.

After only a short time I hoisted Lilah to my shoulder and was able to progress at a faster rate. Only a short time after that we heard the most horrendous screams and shrieks, the snuffling howling of jiklos, the blood-crazed shrieking, and we knew that Naghan and Sosie would never return home to Hamal.

There was nothing I could do about that, and I thrust all thoughts of the despicable way I had been acting lately out of my mind. I had to free this Princess Lilah, otherwise the Star Lords would hurl me back to Earth.

This I knew.

She of the Veils rose into the sky and very quickly the Twins added their combined pink light so that we could press on without fear of falling into a crevasse or pitching over the precipice of a river bank. The trees thinned away and we had to decelerate our rapid onward march as the land trended downward. We skidded and rolled in a great sliding whoosh down a sheer scree-clad slope — highly dangerous, is scree, to one without experience — and at the bottom we found rocky inclines which led us out onto the hard banks of a river. Perforce, we had to turn south and follow the river, seeing its waters slide and gleam below us in the encompassing pink light. Occasional rocks and falls interrupted the river's flow, but I made Lilah walk on all night, with stops to rest now and then, and in the end carried her, fast asleep on my shoulder.

There was no question of my being tired.

By morning the river banks had sunk to a nice level meadow-like embankment. Through the early morning mists I could see the supple sheen and glide of the river, smooth and unmarred, and presently, after a little rise and a few gorse-like bushes, we came to the sea.

The sea.

Well, I wondered if that harsh interdiction of the Star Lords against my venturing out onto the sea still prevented me from doing what I had for so long missed.

As to that, ever since my cruel transition here to the manhounds' island of Faol I had not been acting as Dray Prescot would ordinarily act, and I had rationalized that out. I was most dissatisfied.

Lilah let out a cry of joy.

"Look, Dray! Across the strait! The White Rock of Gilmoy!"

I looked across the sea. Over there the dark bar of land penned in a strait which was, so I judged, in flood. Standing proudly forth, like a sentinel finger, was a tremendous pillar of rock on that opposite shore, white and blinding on its eastern edge where the light struck it, shadowed on the west.

"You know where we are, Lilah?"

"Yes! That white rock is famed throughout Havilfar. It stands on the northern shore of Gilmoy and I have flown over it many times. I had no idea Faol was close." She shivered at this.

"Then we must find a boat."

The notion struck my fancy. The Star Lords had forbidden me to journey by sea; they had also bidden me rescue Princess Lilah, and to do that I must take to a boat. Now let the Star Lords unravel that knot — I cared not a fig for them. We walked along the beach. I could see no boats at once, and in that I felt disappointment.

A house, set back against the line of gorse-covered hills backing the beach, showed a thread of smoke from its chimney. In a pen at the side two dozen or so flying beasts flapped their wings and shrilled. They were sitting on lenken bars into which their claws sank, and they were chained by iron. They looked to be not as large as the impiters, those coal-black flying animals of The Stratemsk, but larger than the corths. Their coloring varied, tending generally to a beige-white and a velvet-green, and their heads were marked by large vanes after the fashion of pteranodons. They looked to be nasty brutes, well enough. Lilah took an eager step forward.

"Fluttrells!" she exclaimed. "We are in luck, Dray. The wind-eaters will carry us swiftly over the strait to Gilmoy, and from thence home to Hyrklana!"

Before I could answer the door of the house burst open and a ragged mob of men wielding weapons sprang out. They did not stop or pause in their rush but came on with an intent I have fronted many times. The pen was to hand. There was only one thing I could do. I grabbed Lilah and fairly ran her across to the sturm-wood bars of the pen. I selected the nearest fluttrell, and gave it a great thumping flat-handed smack around its snouted face to tell it who was master — I had no shame in this brutalization, for death ran very close to our heels — and hoisted Lilah onto the bird's back.

"Can you fly one without stirrup, clerketer, rein?"

"I am perfectly at home in or on anything that flies in the air."

The feel of the flying beast between her legs had changed Lilah — either that, or she was scenting her homeland. She looked at me with a triumphant expression.

"Mount up, Dray! Let us be off!"

"Not so, Princess." Swiftly I released the locks of the chains holding the fluttrell. "You must fly for your home. If I take off with you these men will follow and we will surely be caught. You must go — I will hold them off until you are well clear."

"But, Dray! They will slay you!"

"I do not think so, Lilah."

I gave the fluttrell an almighty thwack and with a bad-tempered squawk it fluttered its wings and rose into the air. Lilah had to cling to its neck, ducking her head beneath the great balancing vane. She looked down on me. I snatched up a length of timber from the pen and with this cocked in my fists — and my fists spread in the old Krozair longsword way as I had done aboard Viridia the Render's flagship when I fought her Womoxes — I awaited the onslaught of the men from the house.

"You will be slain, Dray Prescot!" she called down.

"You are safe, Lilah! Now go!"

She kicked the sides of the magnificent flying animal. "I shall not forget you, Dray Prescot!" And then, faintly as she rose into the limpid morning sky: "Remberee, Dray Prescot!"

I admit it now — I can look back and see and understand my feelings then — I welcomed the coming fight. I had run and crawled and pulled my forelock long enough. These men might be justified in their instant attack upon us — although I doubted that — but they would rue the day they tangled with me.

No doubt the Star Lords thought that a good joke, too.

As I held that length of lumber prepared to show these yokels a little sword-practice, I felt, suddenly, treacherously, the shifting sensations and the blue radiance close about me, and I could no longer feel the wooden longsword — and I was slipping and sliding into the radiant blue void.

Eight

Prey of the Manhounds of Antares

The stink of slaves lay in my nostrils with that thick choking odor so familiar to me.

A voice said: "I can guide you out, Golan, by Hito the Hunter! But you must run—"

"I can run, Anko! And I will reward you, liberally, magnificently! I am a Pallan—"

"And me! And me!" other voices lifted, beseeching, begging, pleading to be led to freedom.

I opened my eyes.

I had failed the Star Lords.

The brazen notes of a stentor's horn filled the caves and passageways and like swirling weeds at the turn of the tide all the slaves raced madly off to the feeding hall. I stood up. By the Black Chunkrah! I'd go down to the feeding cave and take my food if I had to snatch it from all the Khamorros in Havilfar and all the guides in Faol!

So the Princess Lilah of Hyrklana with the golden hair and the beautiful form had not been the one I had been sent here to rescue.

There was but one thing I could do.

I must find the correct slave to be rescued and take him or her out to safety. Guide or no guide.

Down in the feeding cave I saw a lithe and limber young man with dark hair, very alert in carriage now he was alone with only slaves about him, talking earnestly with a bulky man who had once been plump. His face, much sunken in, still contained traces of the habitual power of command he had once wielded. This was Golan, and he had been a Pallan, and had been betrayed, and so sold into slavery and found himself dispatched to Faol, where slaves brought a high price.

Golan?

I lifted my chunk of vosk — a Rapa who had thought to dispute with me its possession lay on the floor unconscious — and shook it at the rocky ceiling. "You stupid Star Lords!" I said, but I did not speak aloud, for I did not wish to attract unwelcome attention to myself, and although insanity was common enough among slaves, it was still regarded with a leery suspicion. "Idiot Everoinye! How am I supposed to know whom to rescue out of this mad crowd?"

I received no answer, and expected none, and so sank my teeth into the vosk and stared sullenly at my fellow slaves.

My beard had grown and my hair, too, making me look even more wild and uncouth and slavelike. All the same, Tulema recognized me instantly.

"Dray! I thought — how did you—? Have you crawled back through the caves?"

"No, Tulema. I didn't go." Then, to allay her suspicions, I said: "Here, finish this vosk for me. I am heartily sick of this place, for I thought I was safely away, and then I was not."

Instead of saying, as one would, "Tell me about it," she seized the remaining chunk of vosk with my teethmarks sharp upon it and wolfed it down. No one, it was clear, had been looking out for Tulema.

Could my target be this girl, with her lithe body and dark hair, all matted with dirt, her savage ways, this girl who had been a dancer in a dopa den? I did not think so. It was, in truth and given the circumstances of my return, far more likely to be this Golan, who had been a Pallan. A Pallan, as you know, is a minister of state, a high official, and if he had been disgraced and sold as a slave, it might be my duty to return him and thus affect some great design in the political structure of Kregen. Lacking any other clues, I decided it must be Golan.

Of one thing I could be sure. If it was not Golan then I would be seized by the blue radiance and hurled back into the slave pens tunneled into the caves.

Then again — if it came to the worst, I might not be. I might be flung back to the Earth of my birth.

"Listen, Tulema. I mean to go again and this time I mean to break through to freedom. Will you come with me?"

"I dare not, Dray! You know why — the manhounds..."

"They are most fearsome beasts — no — fearsome men. But I will look out for you."

As you will instantly perceive, I was trying to copper-bottom my bet. If by chance Golan was not the target, and Tulema was, then I would be safe.

"You will, Dray! I think — I believe—"

Then this rough tough dancing girl from a dopa den turned away, and I saw her smooth shoulder with the dirt marks upon it quivering as she sobbed.

I felt pity for her — of course I did. But she was just one in exactly the same situation as all of us. I started to work at once. I took her shaking shoulder, and shook it, and her, so that she quivered, and I said: "This Golan, who was once a Pallan. Was he there when you and I first met?"

"Yes, he was." She sniffed and sniveled, and I brushed the tears from her eyes.

"There is no need for tears, Tulema. We will go out together from here, you and I, in safety."

She eyed me from under her long lashes where the teardrops trembled. "Lart the Khamorro. Did he?"

About to say, "He is dead," I paused. I lied. I said: "I do not know, Tulema. I told you, I was thrown back unwanted."

"Oh."

That evening after the meal I fixed up with Anko the Guide that he would include me in his party. He looked at me with approval.

"You look as though you can run."

"Oh, yes," I said. "I can run."

The tame slaves were let in and they swept out the refuse and muck. Most of them were sly, inventive, cunning creatures. The old Miglish woman whacked her broom about crossly, swearing at everyone in her vile way, threatening them with all manner of horrendous fates at the hands of Migshaanu the All-Glorious. Tulema squeaked and caught my arm and we moved into another cave.

I kept my eyes open for any other Khamorros. They would be useful on the hunt if only they would learn to rein and bridle their arrogance and contempt for other people.

The following sequence of events was much the same as before. Nalgre came with his whip and his customers and guards, and the bunch of slaves who clustered most urgently against the lenken bars were chosen. Anko the Guide gathered his little group about him — fourteen of us — and the barred gates were open.

I looked about for Tulema.

She was not visible.

Golan was about to be herded through. I seized him by the arm intending to haul him back and go find Tulema, for I did not wish to split my options, but a hefty guard seized Golan by the other arm and pulled.

Golan yelled.

"Let me go! Let me go, you hairy yetch!"

The guard hit me and I put my hand up and another guard hit me, and Golan was gone and two guards lay on the floor, unconscious, and then I was bundled out with the rest. At once I shoved my way into the middle of the crowd of slaves blinking in the sunshine. Tulema would have to take her chances, now, and I must not miss Golan. She had evidently allowed her fears to overwhelm her at the end. Anko the Guide looked at me in some surprise as I shuffled along with the slaves.

Nalgre and his guards were dragging out the two unconscious guards in their leaf-green tunics — their helmets had rolled and were instantly snatched back into the crowd of slaves, as is the slave way with all unattached objects — and were yelling and banging their whips and looking for whoever had done this heinous crime.

"You are not a Khamorro," said Anko the Guide.

"No. And look downcast, slave."

He gulped. "Yes. Yes, that is right."

We were taken to the slave barracks, where all went as before, except that there was no pathetic brave and foolish Lart the Khamorro to throw away his life so uselessly.

In the slave barracks this time there were two other parties of slaves ready for the great Jikai. We had some conversation, but I knew none of them, and now was more convinced than ever that Golan was my man.

Next morning Nalgre, with his admiring customers in attendance, went through his little routine with his pet jiklo. The female creature frisked about, lolling her red tongue, rubbing her flanks against his legs, sniffing us. Then we set out through the jungle. The other two parties went north and east. We struck south. As Anko said: "We do not wish to draw too many hunters down upon us, no, by Hito the Hunter. We cross the great plain, and then we will be safe across the river."

This Anko was much like Nath, and I hoped no untoward accident would befall him, also. He found his cache of clothes and food and shoes and knives, and cheerful at the prospect of liberty before us, we set off. The jungle was left far in the rear and we tramped across a wide plain where palies and that deer-like animal of such grace and beauty, the lople, ran and grazed in herds. We might run across leem here, too, and I kept my hand on the hilt of the cheap knife Anko had passed out from the cache.

The palies were the easiest to catch of the plains deer, and we caught, cooked, and ate one before settling down for the night. I own I felt the tiredness on me. I had suggested we march on by the light of She of the Veils, but Anko had laughed and said the high and mighty hunters did not relish hunting by night. He added, losing his smile: "They like to see their quarry."

Faol, as I was to learn, is mostly jungle in its northern half, nearer the equator, but a shift in the land height and the more southerly aspect give this part of the island a more open terrain. The plain over which we now trod curved around to merge with that over which I had marched previously, right across to the river. Now I felt an unease I put into words to Anko the Guide before sleep.

"We are exposed here, Anko. Would not the jungle have afforded us more cover?"

"There is some truth in what you say. But to the north the chances of complete escape are more limited."

Well, he ought to know. Once more I was struck by the bravery and self-sacrifice of the guides. Anko told me a little more of their philosophy, which was not based, as I had thought, on the twin-principle so common on Kregen, in which the Invisible Twins and Opaz figure so prominently. The guides came from a people of Faol who believed in absolute evil as a principle of life, unarguable and factual, and they were therefore dedicated in opposition to this force. He would not speak of the manhounds. I took this as a wise precaution, for the fears that had destroyed the courage of Tulema were rife among all the slaves. Only the presence of a guide gave them the courage to run. When a bunch of slaves were chosen to be hunted without having arranged for a guide to be among them their chances were nil. Luckily, so Anko said, the guides usually contrived to be with a party due to be hunted.

When I said to him, "And what do you guides seek in this work?" some of my old uncouth sailor ways slipped out. But he smiled.

"For every successful party guided to safety, we receive great honor in our own land, which is on the southern coast. Our young men regard this as a duty laid on them for the honor of their forefathers. Also, the more runs a young man makes, the prettier are the girls from whom he may choose his bride."

You couldn't argue with that.

Yes, he had heard that the Kov of Faol's name was Encar Capela, that his greatest pride was his packs of manhounds, but beyond that he knew nothing of him.

We slept.

In the morning, Anko the Guide was gone.

Zair forgive me if I had slept too long or too heavily.

There were tracks in the short grass of the plains, and blood spots, and signs of a struggle. I could not tell the others with me of Nath the Guide's disappearance, but here the tragedy was too obvious and too unnerving for them to take much in except for the need of instant flight.

It seemed clear to me, then, that the guides were being murdered. Someone had discovered the work they were doing. Probably Nalgre, with that confounded female jiklo of his, had been told by one of the tame slaves — and I instantly suspected that the old Miglish witch was the one. She nauseated me, I confess, with her twisted face like a gnome's, all bulbous hooked nose and rubbery thin lips, and bright agate eyes that saw so much, and her foully breathing mouth that told the secrets of the slaves and the guides.

53

Perhaps, just perhaps, I thought, if Golan was not the right target and I was thrown back into the slave pens I would take the old crone and shake the truth out of her.

The horror of it made me angry. The guides, fine upstanding young men, were risking everything to bring the slaves to safety, and the dark and devious ways of spies were bringing them to their deaths.

Golan wanted to run with the others. I managed to hang on to him and convince him he should eat something. Then, munching roast paly, we set off marching after the others.

We were on our own now. If we went due south we should reach the land of the guides, where we might look for shelter. I angled our march, striking a little to the west in the southerly direction, and soon we were able to see the other fugitives as dots, jerkily rising and falling over the small undulations of the plain away on our left front.

There was in me no desire to sing, and I kept a weather eye cocked aloft for Gdoinye or flier. A voller arrived first and the damned thorn-ivy bush into which I pitched Golan and myself was deucedly hard and prickly and sharp. We cursed as we crawled out. That was only the first. All morning as Far and Havil wheeled across the sky in their mingled lights, we had to dive and burrow our way into bush or crevice or rock shadow.

Golan had completely accepted me as his mentor, and, in truth, he was almost witless with fear. We pressed on and I made him keep up a good pace. From a thicket I cut a stout cudgel for him and a length that might serve as a wooden longsword. I swung it about. Wood it might be, it still felt good in my fists.

Maintaining a straight line of direction is often difficult, although to me, an old sailorman, navigation is an old habit and I knew we had not circled around when I heard the voices off to our left. I said to Golan, viciously: "Keep quiet!"

He did not say a word. His big, fallen-in face showed the horrors that rode him.

We crept forward carefully.

Through a screen of bushes I looked down and saw half a dozen of our fellow-fugitives running and stumbling, falling and picking themselves up, to run wildly on again. Then I saw the reason for that mindless fear.

Bounding in long loping leaps after the slaves raced the outriders of a pack of manhounds. I have seen the work of William Blake, here on Earth, and muchly admired it. And who is there who does not inwardly shiver at the terrifying images of "Tyger, tyger burning bright!"?

There is a picture by William Blake, a print, now, I believe, in the Tate Gallery in London, depicting Nebuchadnezzar. The king of Babylon was stricken, and became as an animal, and crawled away into exile. Blake's picture shows him crawling, with long beard, and hairs, as it were, growing into eagle's feathers. There is on his face a look of such inward horror, and pain, despair, and terrifying madness as would drive pity into the heart of any man.

There is about the picture much orange and brown and somber ocher. There is a static quality about it.

For all that the Manhounds of Antares are vicious and filled with a febrile energy, slavering, quick, and deadly, there is about them, too, something of that awful quality of uncomprehending doom.

So they ran and howled and the thick saliva slobbered from their mouths from which the red tongues lolled.

I saw the leader leap full upon the back of the last straggling fugitive.

The wretch emitted a despairing shriek and fell. He was a Rapa. And then a strange thing happened. The manhound did not kill him, for all their fangs can rip the reeking flesh from their living victims. He lifted the Rapa up in his arms, squatting back, and so waited.

His companions poured on in wild hue and cry.

A bunch of zorca riders galloped up — and the manhound released the Rapa, who shrieked and fled.

And now I saw the great Jikai.

The zorca hunters emitted wild whoops and spurred their mounts, and charged after the crazily running Rapa. He ran and ran, in a dead straight line, without the wit to dodge, although I do not think that would have done him the slightest good. The crossbows winked in the streaming mingled light of the Suns of Scorpio. The bolts loosed. The hunters were poor shots. Many missed. Three or four bolts struck the Rapa, all aquiver, and he stumbled, fell, and then tried to struggle on.

Their crossbows discharged, the zorca riders bore on. They hefted their spears and they cast and only one pierced the Rapa. This was clumsy butchery. The hunters unsheathed their swords, and now they reined in around the Rapa and I saw the blades rising and falling.

Golan was being sick.

"Keep quiet, calsany!" I said.

I took notice of the youth who had flung the only spear to strike. He had a rosy laughing face, very merry, and he was now red with exertion. But his face was no redder than the sword he waved wildly above his head and with a shrill yell plunged downward yet again.

"Well done, Ortyg! Well done!" his companions called.

Then — I went stiff with rage and passion.

For these miserable cramphs, these misbegotten of Grodno, shouted out the words, the great words, "Hai! Jikai!"

Almost, I rose up and flung myself upon them.

But Golan, who once had been a Pallan, was being sick in the grass, and the Star Lords had commanded me to rescue him.

I watched, trembling, hating the poltroon I had become, as the zorca riders spurred away. The flanks of the zorcas showed the blood-red weals. Spurs and zorcas are not a fit combination for a true rider!

A single manhound, sniffing after the rest, trailed up toward us.

Maybe he caught our scent on a vagrant breeze; maybe he was the rogue of the pack. But he came straight for us, head down, rump high, his hair blowing in a mane behind him, his crested topknot stiff and arrogant, his jagged teeth exposed.

Golan's sick spasm had passed. The other fugitives were almost out of sight beyond a grassy clump, the manhounds well up to them, and the great and puissant hunters spurring madly after. One turned, and shouted, and I guessed he was calling the manhound who doggedly climbed toward us. This man, in his leaf-green tunic and small round helmet, was a guard, probably the packmaster, in charge of the jiklos.

Then I had to concentrate on the manhound. He was a big fellow, very vicious, and had he possessed a tail it would have been lashing angrily. He had seen us now and he let out a slavering screech and charged for us.

For just an instant I saw the guard wheel his zorca, and then I leaped up, the wooden longsword cocked in that special Krozair grip. The manhound leaped. I saw his teeth, jagged and sharp, the saliva flecking from his thin lips, and his eyes all bloodshot and mad with hunting lust.

His clawed hands reached for my throat, and his teeth sought to rip out my jugular, for with the intelligence I knew these fearsome beasts still retained, he had recognized I was not a meek victim, but stood there with a club to meet him and bash out his brains.

In that he was mistaken.

This length of wood cut from a thicket was no clumsy bludgeon. It stood in lieu of a deadly Krozair longsword, second only to the great Savanti sword itself.

I took my grips, brought the wood around and back, and so, with a chopped "Hai," drove the splintered end full in the manhound's savage face. He tried to swerve, but he was too slow. He bundled over, screeching, splinters mantling his cheeks and one eye gone and then — and only then — did I bring the wooden longsword down in a blow that caved in his rib cage. Two more blows finished him.

The soft plop of zorca hooves on the grass brought me around.

The guard was a fool.

The first rule of a crossbowman is always: "Reload!"

He came at me with his sword.

He was angry, annoyed that a valuable jiklo had been slain, and he did not even have the same sense as that jiklo to recognize I was not an ordinary fugitive slave run as quarry.

He slashed violently down and I slid the blow and smashed him across the thigh — a favorite stroke, that, with the Krozair longsword — and had the weapon been edged steel he would have been less one leg. As it was he screamed in pain and I was able to reach up, inside the curve of the zorca's neck, and take him and so hold him and drag him down. When I stood up, grasping the zorca's reins, Golan staggered across.

"By Opaz! I have never seen the like."

"Mount up, Pallan, and let us ride. Otherwise you will not have the chance to see the like again."

And so, mounted up, forward and aft, and damned close together, too, on so short-coupled a mount as a zorca, we rode hard for the south.

Nine

The fears of Tulema, dancing girl from a dopa pen

The Pallan Golan was not the man the Star Lords wished me to rescue from the Manhunters of Faol.

Once more I found myself hurled disdainfully back to the slave pens cut from the rocks fronting the jungles, once more the stink of slaves filled my nostrils, and the stentors' brazen notes called us all to push and herd like vosks to the feeding cave. I had taken Golan safely through to a village where the headman, who knew nothing of the guides and so convinced me we had strayed from our course, promised to care for the Pallan. We had passed over a wide river by means of a raft I had fashioned, and we learned we were in another country on the southern shore. Clearly the villages and land from which the guides came lay farther to the east. The headman of the village knew little of what went on in what he called North Faol. The Trylon of South Faol had long ago refused to bend the knee to the Kov of Faol, and the headman kept himself aloof from what went on across the river.

After a good meal and a bit of a sing-song with the girls of the village dancing in the firelight — for I had foolishly thought my mission for the Star Lords accomplished — I was whipped up by the blue radiance and… well, here I was again, and all to do over.

If you think I was growing mightily annoyed by this time — you are right.

Although enough time had elapsed for my hair and beard and moustache to grow somewhat shaggy, still Tulema recognized me.

This time my original excuse would not satisfy her, and so before she could follow on her first quick exclamation of surprise, I said: "Yes, Tulema. I have come back. Like the guides, I feel it important to do so. Perhaps this time you will come out with me."

"Oh, Dray — the manhounds!"

"I am here, am I not? And I have been out — *there!*"

She was still as absolutely terrified as ever.

Something would have to be done about Tulema. I knew the person I was supposed to rescue was still in the caves. Unless, of course, he or she had been killed and the Star Lords were punishing me for failing. I would not contemplate that. Some of the original group in the pen when I had first arrived here had gone out; some were left. I could not explain to Tulema, but I managed to get her to identify them for me. I still could not bring myself to believe that Tulema herself was the right one. I had had experience then of the way in which the Star Lords worked. I did not know what their plans for Kregen were, but I had previously rescued people for them who I could see would be important in the scheme of things. Much as I respected the tough hardness of Tulema, and her pitiful fears of the jiklos, I could not envision her as a mover of politics, a maker of nations.

"There is Latimer," said Tulema. "He is frightened to go."

I grunted. "Suppose he is picked to go, anyway, without a guide? What then?"

"Don't say it, Dray!"

Latimer turned as I approached. We had just eaten, but there had come no stentor call to parade before the bars of our cages. He was a middle-aged man, say a hundred and fifty or so, still virile, with dark hair and a broken nose and eyes that did not quite meet mine when we talked. He showed by his rib cage — or rather by its absence against his skin — that he could fight well enough to secure good food. In conversation I learned he was a shipping merchant of Hamal. Only after a little cross-purpose talk was it borne in on me that he was a voller shipping man, and not a galleon owner, as I had imagined. At once I decided this must be the man I sought. Vollers were important. Latimer was a voller owner. Ergo, the Star Lords wanted him out in the world again so that some great scheme to do with the Havilfar fliers might come to fruition.

How snobbish all this sounds! How stupid, that I should seek out people I thought important by what they did! Tulema I intended to persuade to come with me; if she would not, I could not find it in my heart to force her. Only if this Latimer were not the one, would I force her.

We went out, we struck westward, I rescued Latimer — again the guide disappeared and again I vowed to try to get to the bottom of that mystery — and saw the voller magnate safe, and again I was tossed back in a radiance of blue fire into the slave pens.

Tulema said: "You have come back, Dray."

I was so desperate that I had to make an effort to be polite to her. She had to be the one. And she was frightened to go. Well, there was a cure for that.

More slaves had been brought in, a consignment from the mainland had evidently arrived, and the pens and caves were full again. To be safe, I said to Tulema: "Are there any slaves still here who were with us when—?"

She shook her head. "No, Dray. They are all gone."

"Except you."

"Yes. And you!"

"Oh. Me." At the stentors' call I smashed my way through the crowds of newcomers and took two heaping helpings of the best. I wanted Tulema fit and well for the break, and she had been eating dilse for a long time.

There seemed to me a need to keep a record. I ticked off all the people as Tulema recited their names. "And Tosie? She went out?"

"Yes. Right after that Lilah who put on such airs."

"I hope she is safe."

"Oh, she'll be safe. Anyone like her who pretends to be a queen will be safe, no matter what."

Yes, I thought, more cheerfully, yes, Tulema must be the one. There was a rough fire about her, practically obliterated in these conditions by her uncontrollable fears of the jiklos. She had heard too many stories of what the manhounds did to pretty girls.

The old Miglish crone began her eternal sweeping-up and Tulema shuddered and drew me away. I thought the dark thoughts I had thought when I'd seen the blood spots near Anko the Guide's blankets... but I was going out and Tulema was the one, so — did it matter?

Of course it mattered.

I took the Miglish woman by the shoulder and I could feel the narrowness of her, the bony hardness. She tried to twist away, leering up at me with her pouched eyes, her witch-face hideous, like a rubber mask melted in the fire. She revolted me, this halfling monstrosity.

"Do you betray the guides, Migla?"

She cackled, trying to hit me with her broom.

"I betray nothing! By Migshaanu the All-Glorious, may your eyes dribble out and your guts cave in—"

"Enough of that, crone!" I snarled. "Remember: if any guides are betrayed, you will be flayed and your skin hung up for all to see!"

Of course, I could not prove anything, and she would not be frightened into revealing her guilt. She might have nothing to do with the tragedy, but she was an old witch, and hideous, that was plain to see, as Tulema said, with a shiver.

I remembered what Nath the Guide had said about human beings, and I could see a point. There were no Chuliks among the slaves, as I have remarked; they are a very fearsome race of half-men, half-beasts. But something about this old Migla made all my Homo sapiens ancestry rise up in revulsion.

In that foul nose of hers black hairs sprouted. She always kept herself tightly covered up by her gray slave blanket and the breechclout was capacious and droopy enough to conceal her legs down to her knees. Her calves were always smothered in filth. Her hair remained a wild and tangled mass of knots and mud and caked filth. Truly, she was an abomination.

But, for all that, I could not prove she was the traitor.

Last time, when I had rescued Latimer to no avail, I had kept awake most of the night and still the guide had disappeared. I had not seen or heard it done. As usual, the guide had slept a little apart from the rest of us, to be on guard. This time, I vowed, I would afford him the protection he tried to give us.

The reason for this stealthy betrayal seemed obvious enough to me. Surely, by this time, even Nalgre, the slave-master, must have noticed how willing the slaves were to be run, to be sent out to a hideous death. This would please Nalgre and his master, the Kov of Faol. They would wish to maintain this satisfactory state of things, and continue the guides in their desperate undertakings. I wondered, not without a shiver of anger, what the guides' villages were making of the non-return of their fine young men. Truly, the ways of man and man are mysterious and barbarous beyond belief.

In addition, these thoughts also showed me that the old Migla witch, if she had been truly to blame, had no further need of betrayal. Once Nalgre caught wind of the conspiracy to free the slaves, then he would take up the savage and sorry business from there.

With all the numbers of fresh slaves within the barred caves cut into the rock I could not easily find a guide. Most of the slaves pushed and shoved, seeking better sleeping places, arguing, fighting, the girls looking for protectors, and everyone racing whooping like mad people when the stentors' horns blew for feeding time. Tulema had to be built up in strength before I could risk taking her out to be hunted. While there was a ready supply of slaves, Nalgre could not care how many managed not to be selected for a Jikai; so long as there were enough for his customers and they were kept happy, then Nalgre would not worry over the few slaves who were never picked.

I did see one incident that indicated how he solved the problem if it became too acute.

An old slave — it may have been the same Xaffer, or another, for they are a strange and remote race of halflings — was dragged out, screaming, and lashed to a wooden stake. He was flogged to death there. Tulema stared dry-eyed, hard and contemptuous, seeing in the fate of the Xaffer the possibility of her own ending.

"That is what happens to skulkers who are too old for the hunt," said Tulema. "If they are not employed as tame slaves to clean and cook like the old Miglish witch and her friends."

"That will happen to you, then, Tulema, if you can eat only dilse."

"Better, perhaps, ol' snake, than the manhounds."

I shook my head. "You are coming out as soon as you are fit and strong, Tulema. There is no argument. But the guides are few."

"They know when there are customers. Who can blame them if they do not wish to spend time they need not, in here, with us slaves?"

So there was time for Tulema to eat well and to shed that half-starved look on her face that came from dilse, and for her supple body to be genuinely lithe and firm again, on good food. A day came when the stentors" horns blared out in the call that summoned the manhounds, and drove us slaves to the lenken bars, to be selected for the great Jikai. I looked at Tulema. As always, she shrank back, but she was as fit and well as she might ever be in this dreadful place, and I could not wait any longer.

Out on the compound splashed with its jade and ruby light stood Nalgre, with his whip and his guards, talking in his important, belly-thrusting, strutting way with a group of customers. I recognized one man there; he was the heavily built Notor with the pudgy face from too many vosk-pies who had led the hunt when Lilah and I had escaped. Nalgre was speaking to him.

"Indeed, it is strange, Notor Trelth."

"And you have no explanation, Nalgre? A long way, we went, a very long way, and a scuffle in rocks and trees. I looked for a kill on the plains."

"Why not try the jungles this time, Notor Trelth?" Nalgre spoke with quickness, eagerness, anxious to please.

"Yes. I will give it thought," said this high-and-mighty Notor Trelth.

Tulema whispered: "There is a guide here, Dray—"

"Good." At once I looked about for the lithe young man with the dark hair who was risking his life for us. I saw him with a group and pushed my way across with Tulema. Whether the guide might be persuaded to take us or not, he would listen to me when I told him the disastrous news.

60

Ten

Of the two faces of Hito the Hunter

Of course the guide would not believe me. He scoffed. His name was Inachos and he was as young and athletic as the other guides. Also he was a little impatient.

There had been no time to tell him in the barred caves, for the guards had thrust through and taken out the slaves Notor Trelth selected, and in the resultant confusion Tulema and I had been pushed out with the rest. There were eighteen of us, this time, a large party, and only when we had settled down for the night in the slave barracks had I been afforded the opportunity of talking privately with Inachos.

"What you are saying is lunacy. By Hito the Hunter! No guide would be taken unawares."

"So I had thought. But it has happened, three times to my certain knowledge."

"And you have told no one else?"

"To alarm the slaves would not have been wise. Their fate rests in the hands of the guides. You must take the news back to your villages and warn them."

He looked at me, his head on one side, looking very alert and handsome. "I cannot believe what you say. But a warning must be taken, just in case."

"I shall stay awake all night," I said.

"If it pleases you."

A cocky youngster, I thought to myself, one who believes no secret party of assassins can creep upon him in the pink moonlight.

Inachos the Guide must act his part as a cowed slave the next morning as we went through those ghastly preliminaries Nalgre the slave-master carried out with such relish. With Tulema near me, generally held by my left hand, I kept very close to Inachos. If he refused to take me seriously, I knew that tonight his eyes would be opened.

Nalgre approached us and Inachos stiffened up, but the slave-master flicked his whip lightly over me — I bore it! I, Dray Prescot, bore it! — and then turned away as Notor Trelth called. Inachos relaxed, breathing hard through pinched nostrils, looking frustrated. I felt sorry for him.

Very soon thereafter we were trotting away. Inachos said we could strike north through the jungle and find the coast easily where we might pick up a vessel from the island of Outer Faol whose people, simple fishermen, he called them, would call for the sake of the alligators in the mud-swamps. Faol was not really close enough to the equator or well-watered enough to possess a really dense rain forest. The jungle was capable of being traversed by many trails, although, of course, not being a pleasant place. I thought of what had previously been said about the northern jungle offering no real safety, but Inachos knew his business, and fisherfolk and a boat so close to hand sounded more tempting than another long slog over the plains.

Just over half a dwabur along the trail through the dim green and russet twilight of the forest, Inachos halted us to produce his cache of clothing, food, and knives. I put the shoes on, with a grimace, and took the cheap knife with the thought that around me there was literally a forest of wooden longswords.

The longswords existed literally within the tree branches, as the greatest statues of two worlds already existed within the stones from which they were carved.

From my previous experience I did not believe the hunters would tackle us before the next day. That night Inachos found a comfortable dell by a small and somewhat marshy stream and we set up camp. He handed us the wine and my fellow slaves upended the leather bottles with great gusto. Tulema was exhausted. She sat with her back against the bole of a tree, licking the last of the paline juice from her fingers. I took a wine bottle over and she drank greedily. Inachos called:

"Have some wine yourself, Dray Prescot. You will have need of it."

"I like wine," I said casually. "But I prefer tea."

"Drink," he said.

Tulema had left a few dregs swilling in the leather bag, but to please Inachos, for he had risked much stowing the wine away in the cache, I lifted the leather and drank what there was and went on drinking thereafter, miming. Inachos chuckled.

"Tomorrow we will be through the jungle. We will find a boat. And tonight, nothing will disturb our rest."

We took precautions against the nocturnal denizens of the jungle. There are but a few snakes on Kregen, and these poor and miserable of spirit — with the exception of a breed of horrors of which I will speak later — but there were other perils and we twined vines about ourselves on the branches of trees, and rammed hard and thorny spikes in the wood to make a palisade. Already the slaves were yawning. Tulema was fast asleep. I fancied a conversation with Inachos, but he grunted and took himself off to a branch lower than those on which we slaves perched, saying that we must rise early.

A Gon moaned uneasily in his sleep. His chalk-white hair glowed an eerie color in the light of the Maiden with the Many Smiles striking pallidly through the leaves. Even in the warrens of Magdag the Gons had been able to shave that white hair of which they are so ashamed. I kept my weather eye open for Inachos, who lay, a darker blot, against his tree lower down.

My eyes closed.

How long I sat there, wedged against a branch springing from the main trunk I do not know. I remember I recollected there was some powerful and compelling reason why I must keep awake this night. I had slept well on those other nights when we slaves had been run as quarry for sport, and the last time, with the voller merchant, Latimer, I had kept awake most of the night, or so I believed. I opened my eyes, blearily, gummily. I looked down.

Inachos no longer sat in his tree perch.

Instantly I was wide awake.

I picked out his form, creeping down the tree, going carefully, and as he went dropping dark drops down onto the wood from a wooden vial he had unstoppered, a wooden vial I had taken to be a stick. He was going carefully so as to make the dark drops splatter effectively, and so as not to lose his hand- and foothold; he was not, I judged, going carefully so as not to awaken the slaves.

Quietly — and when I wish to be quiet it takes a very sharp ear indeed to hear me — I unlashed the vines and crept down the tree after him. He jumped very lithely to the packed leaf-droppings of the forest floor and ran swiftly along the trail ahead. Quietly, I followed.

After a few moments we reached a clearing, and on the brink I paused. Inachos stood in the center of the clearing, bathed in the radiant pink light of the Maiden with the Many Smiles, with She of the Veils adding her own luster to the scene. He reached up his arms.

Silently, a flier ghosted down into the clearing.

No further evidence was needed.

The man in the flier had no need to lean out and shout cheerfully to Inachos: "Ho, there, Inachos. By Hito the Hunter! I shall sink much wine this night."

And Inachos the Guide had no need to reply: "And I, also! This work makes a man thirsty! The yetches stink so!"

No, there was no need for them to say these words to convince me, to make me see what a credulous fool I had been.

Everything fell into place.

With a shout full of bestial hatred I charged into the clearing, bounded across the open space, struck Inachos senseless with a smashing blow to the nape of his neck, and reached in my hands and hauled his companion all tumbling onto the jungle floor.

Even then, I swear, I did not mean both of them to die, for I wished to question them. But Inachos must have had a weak skull, or my blow must have been too hasty and impetuous. As for the flier pilot who had come to pick the guide up — when I turned him over I saw the hilt of his knife thrusting up from his chest. As he tumbled out of the flier the knife had sliced whicker-sharp between his ribs. I wrenched it out with a foul Makki-Grodno oath.

What a credulous idiot I had been!

The guides were not being murdered by assassins sent by Nalgre. Oh, no! Nalgre hired the guides. They came into the caves and told the slaves they would take them out to safety, and the poor deluded fools went out, gaily, expectantly, filled with hope. They thought they were being taken to safety, and then, every first night, the guide would disappear and the slaves were on their own. They would be ripe fodder for the great Jikai! How much more cunning this system was to get the slaves out and running. Without hope, they might run, but they would not give sport.

The quarry were given a reason to run by the guides. They thought that with a whole day's start they stood a chance. And, too, I saw another sound reason for this dastardly plot. The different parties of slaves could be channeled into different parts of the island. Then different hunts would not become entangled and Nalgre would not have to face irate customers whose quarry had been snapped up by neighboring hunters.

And — that doughy-faced Notor Trelth had agreed to hunt through the jungle and the guide, Inachos, had directed us northward so as to keep within the confines of the jungle!

The more I considered the foul scheme the more I saw its elegance and simplicity — and its horror.

Maybe there were no real rear entrances to the caves.

Certainly, the manhounds had entrances there, to herd the slaves out for selection. All the time I thus reviewed the diabolical schemes of the Kov of Faol and his slave-master, Nalgre, I paced back and forth in the moonlight.

Then I went back to the tree where my companions slept and tried to rouse them.

Every last one was fast asleep in a drugged stupor.

That provided the last evidence. The wine so thoughtfully provided by the guides, which they did not drink through care for their charges, was drugged. The guides simply got up and walked away and were picked up by flier.

If I bashed a length of timber against the tree in my anger, I feel that needs no explanation.

In the end I had to unlash all the slaves, every one, and Tulema first, and carry them, snoring, over to the airboat. The flier would just take all the eighteen of us, although we were jammed in — no novelty to slaves accustomed to being jammed in hard together in barred prisons.

Delia had given me instructions in the management of airboats. I took the flier up quickly, savagely, sped low over the jungle in the streaming light from the moons of Kregen.

The flight had to be undertaken right away; it would have been madness to have waited until the morning. Come the morning, though — and here I believe my lips ricked back over my teeth in a most ungentlemanly fashion — the great hunters on their manhunt would find no quarry for the manhounds to drag down, for them to loose at with their gleaming beautiful crossbows, for them to chop down with sword and spear.

When, at last, Zim and Genodras — or, as here in Havilfar, Far and Havil — dawned over the jungle levels I brought the airboat down into a cleft in the trees. Below, a river ran, a broad sluggish ocher-colored river, with mud-banks and the scaled and agile forms of water-risslaca active about their own form of hunting. At least, much as I was wary of risslaca and with horrific memories of the Phokaym, they, at least, hunted for food.

I took the airboat low along the dun water and at last found what I sought, a place where the banks had eroded and fallen and the jungle had voraciously grown over the tumbled earth and so created a roofed space beneath. Management of the voller was a tricky business, but I got her neatly inserted under the overarching leaves. She was a craft built along somewhat different lines from those I had been accustomed to in Vallia and Zenicce, being altogether sturdier of construction, with lenken planking and bronze supports, although still of that swift and beautiful leaf-shape.

The Gon rolled over, snorting, and pushed into Lenki, a Brokelsh whose black bristles were the thickest I had seen on one of his kind, and Lenki snorted in his turn, and turned over, and struck a Fristle, and so, with much groaning and blowing and yawning, the whole pack of slaves woke up.

Leaving them to sort themselves out I swung down beneath the trees to the water's edge.

Certainly there is much beauty in the greenery of Kregen. A profusion of gorgeous flowers was opening to the first rays of the twin suns, and I stood on the ledge of soggy earth watching as moon-blooms opened wide their second, outer, ring of petals, and as scarlet and indigo and yellow and orange flowers of a myriad convoluted shapes prepared themselves for the day. A swim, which I would sorely have welcomed, filthy as I was, was not to be recommended. Many risslaca had woken up and were prowling. I scooped a handful of the water and splashed my face and body and heard a harsh and malevolent croaking in the air above my head.

I looked up.

The Gdoinye hung there, his pinions beating against the dawn breeze down the river, his head cocked. In the streaming mingled light of the suns he looked glorious, shining, refulgent. I shook my fist at him.

"You are an idiot, Dray Prescot!"

"You told me that before, on a beach in Valka!"

"An onker of onkers, Dray Prescot, a get-onker!"

"So I know!" I shouted back as the accipiter swung there, squawking hoarsely at me. Without a thought I knew those in the airboat could not be a witness to this astounding confrontation.

"You will be allowed a little more time to play your games. We trust they amuse you. There is yet time."

"Time for what? I play no games with you. Why do you force me against my wishes—"

But, with a hoarse cry, the raptor interrupted.

"We do what we do for reasons beyond your understanding, Dray Prescot. When you grow up, you may then grow a brain to comprehend the simple facts of life on this planet. Now you are as a suckling baby, as your antics here in Faol have shown."

"Antics!" I roared. "Antics! I've been trying to do what I thought was right — and no damned help from you! How do I know who—"

"When you reach Yaman you may discover answers you will never find in Aphrasöe."

"I didn't ask to be brought to Kregen! But now that I'm here I have found my own destiny! If you want my help you'll have to—"

But the Gdoinye had heard enough of my puling roaring, for he winged up and away, a golden and scarlet messenger of glory, from a bunch of Star Lords I'd as lief squeeze between my fingers and let drip through in a red mush. He soared up, shining in the mingled light of the twin suns.

His last harsh cry streamed down with that opaline light.

"You are a fool, Dray Prescot!"

Then he was a mere black dot against the suns-glow.

I cursed.

Oh, I cursed!

But, of course, there was nothing for me to do but go back and do as the Star Lords ordered and get Tulema out to a place of safety. After that… and then I knew that after that, before I could investigate the scarlet-roped Todalpheme, before I could spend pleasant days discovering more about the vollers, before, even, I could return to Vallia and Delia, I would have to return to the barred slave pens of Faol and warn the slaves. I would have to defeat the Kov of Faol and Nalgre and put paid to this foul and despicable game they played with their two-faced treacherous guides.

When I turned back to the cleft in the river bank with its camouflage of trees the slaves were out of the airboat and clamoring their wonder like a pack of jackdaws. Of them all, apart from Tulema and myself, only one was a human being, the rest being halflings of one sort and another. This young man, who had fed himself well in the caves, kept much to himself and spoke little. He said his name was Nath, but I did not believe him. He had red hair, and so might be a Lohvian. When a Brokelsh had pressed him, this Nath had said he came from Thothangir, and, again, I did not believe him.

This Nath na Thothangir walked toward me swinging one of the guide's swords. I eyed him meanly.

"Where are we, Dray Prescot? How did we come here?"

I gathered the rest of the slaves about and told them what had happened. They were, as was to be expected, exceedingly enraged, and a Relt, ordinarily one of the kindest of peoples, began threatening to have the guides tossed into a neighbor's pit back home. The neighbor, he informed us, was a Rapa of some wealth and power. We all agreed. The guides deserved such a terrible fate, for their duplicity and heartlessness as much as for their cruelty.

After that, with a flier at their disposal, the slaves began a volatile and acrimonious wrangling as to our destination.

I said to Tulema: "Where in all of Kregen do you wish to go, Tulema? Where is your home?"

She laughed, and the tears stood in her eyes.

"I have no home since I was abducted from Herrell, and I have no wish to return there. Where you go, Dray Prescot, there will I go, also!"

Eleven

"Where you go, Dray Prescot, there will I go also!"

This was a right leem's-nest.

I stood gawping at Tulema who had once been of Herrell.

She said it again, stamping her foot.

"Where you go, Dray Prescot, there will I go, also!"

She meant it; that was perfectly plain.

She could not go with me; that, too, was perfectly plain.

What had the Gdoinye meant, that I was playing games here in Faol, that my antics amused them? If I was to rescue Tulema for the Star Lords' devious purposes, did that mean I had to take her back to Vallia?

What, then, would Delia say?

As to that, I had no doubts. No other woman in two worlds means anything beside Delia. But I still had a duty to perform, and Tulema, because of that — and because she was young and frightened and alone — must be cared for.

Deciding that the most prudent course was to say nothing more of our destination to her — and seeing that that, too, was the cowardly way and thereby, as may surprise you, feeling a gust of amusement rather than of anger — I set about sorting out the halflings. They had to be told what I intended to do. If left to themselves they would have begun fighting bitterly over the different places they insisted on reaching immediately.

The only justification I can offer for my decision was that these halflings, escaped slaves, did not have the Star Lords breathing down their necks.

Those that had necks, that was.

Sammly, from distant Quennohch, for instance, only with extreme kindness could be said to have a neck, his head, as it did, sprouting from between his two upper limbs. But he was a good-hearted fellow, and said he wouldn't mind being set down somewhere convenient in Havilfar. He could work his passage home aboard any of the regular voller lines. His left center limb scratched at his carapace as he spoke.

"Does anyone," I said over the hubbub, and quieting them by the rasp in my voice, "know the way to Hyrklana?"

"I do," said the youth who said he was Nath na Thothangir.

"Then that is where we shall fly." I silenced the immediate babble of protest. "If anyone wishes to alight earlier, they will of course be allowed to do so."

By Zim-Zair, I said to myself, with another uncharacteristic chuckle, I was running a coach service!

Tulema grabbed hold of me and started in slapping. I fended her off, astonished.

"What, Tulema? What the blue blazes is the matter with you?"

"The matter, indeed! I know! You lust after that yellow-haired Lilah, that calls herself a princess!"

"By the Black Chunkrah! What other friends do we have in Havilfar if you won't damn well go home?"

Also, although I did not tell her so, I wanted to make sure Lilah had indeed reached safety.

None of them seemed to consider my warning about the guides; they refused to face up to the fact that those people they had seen leave the slave pens in such high hopes were all dead. Tulema simply assumed that Lilah was free. I devoutly hoped that was so, remembering those vicious men and the pen of fluttrells waiting to be mounted and sent in whooping pursuit of the golden-haired princess.

Without arguing further I went up to the flier and we ate what little food there was and drank from the river and then I shouted: "I am leaving now. All aboard who's coming aboard." That was enough to make them pack themselves in as best they might. They settled down with a considerable amount of flutter and argument as I inched the voller out over the river, turned her, and sent her streaking skyward.

The direction we needed to travel was southeast, according to this Nath na Thothangir, who sat up at the controls with me. We had to strike due east for some way before risking turning south. We had no wish to fly directly over the slave pens, for we knew other fliers would rise to challenge us.

"Hyrklana is on the east coast of Havilfar. It is a large and powerful kingdom." Nath spoke with a bitterness in his voice I had no explanation for, and I had no inclination to find the reasons. Then, with a fleeting sideways look at me, he said: "That dopa-den dancing girl. She mentioned a name—"

About to snub him for speaking in such a way about Tulema, for I did not miss the scorn in his voice, I paused for two reasons. One was that I was surprised he should reach the same conclusions about Tulema as myself; the other that, after a pause, as it were, to gather his breath, he went on: "She mentioned the name of the Princess Lilah."

"And if she did?"

"You know her? That is why you wish to travel to Hyrklana?"

"Perhaps."

I did not believe in giving away information.

"You will be sorry if you venture into Hyrklana uninvited. As in Hamal, the arenas there are ever hungry for fresh fodder."

"As to that, we shall see what we shall see."

And with that pompous reply this redheaded young man who claimed he was Nath na Thothangir had to rest content.

We crossed a stretch of sea and left Faol to our rear, at which, I confess, I felt much relief. New land spread out before us, and this youth Nath told me it was Hennardrin. We turned and flew south, along the coastline. Presently, with much of the day gone, and a smooth eight-point turn to starboard we flew over the White Rock of Gilmoy. So, if Lilah had not been caught this was the way she would have flown.

We went on and Nath began to fidget as our southerly course swung us inland. Below unrolled a massive forest, with clearings here and there in which towns had been built. No one so far wished to get off this aerial excursion. We were all hungry and thirsty by now, and so I said we would descend and hunt for our supper.

One of the halflings pushed his way through the jumbled passengers at my back and, puffing a little, smoothed down the yellow fur around his eyes and mouth and polished up the laypom-colored fur beneath his chin.

"If you will continue for another four or five dwaburs, on this course," he said in his smooth honeylike voice, "you will come to a fine city built by a great orange river. That is Ordsmot. There, I believe, you will find all the food and wine you may require. You see," he finished, and I detected a huge relief and happiness in him, "I am Dorval Aymlo of Ordsmot"

Over the chorus of voices declaring that this was splendid news, I considered. This Dorval Aymlo was a member of the halfling race sometimes called Lamniarese — the Lamnias — of whom at that time I knew little. You must understand that, in accordance with my original plan, although surrounded by many different kinds of half-men I introduce them to you only when they come upon the stage of my story. I believed this Aymlo of Ordsmot to speak the truth. *Ord*, as you know, is the Kregish for "eight," and a *smot* is a large town, large enough, at times, to be considered as a city. I guessed why it had been given the name of "Eight-town" — it would be divided up into eight sections, each occupied by a different race.

"Done," I said. "And many thanks to you, Horter Aymlo."

Horter is, of course, the Havilfar equivalent to the Vallian Koter, or Mister.

The airboat sped onward in the gathering darkness with only two of the lesser moons hurtling close by above.

We had traveled a considerable distance since leaving Faol — thanks be! — and I fancied this voller was a far speedier craft than any I had flown in before. Also, I had the hunch that the confounded thing would not break down as frequently as those the Havilfarese sold to Vallia and Zenicce and their other overseas customers.

Tulema was looking ahead and she saw the great bend of the river, shining faintly in the growing light of the Maiden with the Many Smiles rising away to our left, and she cried out in delight. A mass of twinkling lights in an immense circle, crisscrossed by the four main boulevards in a huge wagon-wheel demarcating the eight precincts, showed us without mistake where lay Ordsmot upon the orange river. I sent the airboat slanting down to an enclave near the river at Aymlo's directions. The lights spread out around us. The dark masses of trees rushed past and I slowed our descent. Buildings flashed past beneath.

"There!" said Dorval Aymlo, pointing over my shoulder. "Where that tower rises, beside those warehouses and the beautiful godown!"

By his words and his tone of voice I knew he was pointing to his home.

We landed in a courtyard with buildings on three sides and the river on the fourth. Doors opened and lights flared. The Maiden with the Many Smiles was hidden for a space by buildings and trees, and it was unusually dark upon Kregen where we were in Aymlo's home in Ordsmot.

He cried out in a great voice: "It is me! Dorval Aymlo! I am home, my children! *I am home!*"

I know how I felt, and I am sure that everyone aboard felt just the same. How we longed to be able to shout the same words, filled with joy and happiness!

I climbed out and Aymlo, who would have alighted next, was pushed aside by Tulema. She hated to let me out of her sight. I stood on the hard-packed earth of the courtyard and I smelled the wonderful sweet scent of the night flowers, and I saw the people from the house running toward us, bearing torches that flared their glowing hair upon the night.

"It is me, Dorval Aymlo!" the Lamnia called again.

He started to run forward.

The youth Nath, who said he was from Thothangir, stood at my side. In his hand the guide sword gleamed from the torchlight. I had kept the other sword. Nath swore.

"The old fool! Cannot he see they bear weapons?"

Truly, in the torchlight the flicker of spears showed bright in the forefront of those men toward whom Dorval Aymlo ran with his arms up, crying aloud in his joy.

And a voice lifted, a harsh, brutal voice.

"Aye! We know you are Dorval Aymlo! This house and this business are yours no longer! Know that I am Rafer Aymlo, your nephew, and these are my men, and this house and this business is mine! And know, also, old fool, that you and all those with you are dead, dead, dead!"

Twelve

How Dorval Aymlo the merchant of Ordsmot came

home

Even as Dorval Aymlo shouted in a high and shocked scream of utter disbelief and despair, I jumped forward, the sword low. This was no business of mine. But the old Lamnia had been so happy — he had been so overjoyed and he was a kindly old soul — and now, this!

So I jumped forward, like a headstrong fool, and Nath of Thothangir leaped at my side, his red hair black in the torchlight.

Aymlo screeched and stumbled and fell — and that for a surety saved his life, for the spear thrust passed above his prostrate body. In a twinkling I had thrust in my turn, and recovered from the lunge, and taken the next spear and so, twisting, hacked down the furry face of the Lamnia attacking me.

Nath fought with a series of clever but overly vigorous cut and thrusts. I smashed into the other Lamnias, for I knew that they would in truth kill us all if they were not stopped, and that would not please the Star Lords. Among the Lamnias were Rapas and humans and these fought, on the whole, with more skill and viciousness than the Lamniarese, which was only natural. Very quickly I found three Rapas at my side wielding fallen spears, and these were released slaves, my fellows. We fought and for a space the compound resounded to the shrill of battling men, the slide and scrape of steel, the shrieks of the wounded, and the bubbling groans of the dying.

The very savagery of the ex-slaves' rush, the sudden reversal of their own weapons, the blood spouting from gaping wounds, unnerved our opponents. One of our Brokelsh was down, with a spear in his guts, but that was the extent of our casualties. Our opponents fled. Dorval Aymlo stood up, holding his hands in the air in horror. The Maiden with the Many Smiles floated serenely above the rooftops with their notched outlines and upflung gable ends, and her pink radiance streamed out upon that scene of destruction.

"By Opaz the All-Merciful!" exclaimed Aymlo, scarcely able to speak. "What devil's work is this?"

A Rapa laughed nastily, wiping his spear on the clothing of a dead Rapa he had slain. "It is very simple, old fool. This bastard nephew of yours stole your house and your goods and he would have slain you to keep them!"

"Well," said Dorval Aymlo, in a voice of pain, "the deed has brought him nothing but sorrow. For, see, here lies the body of Rafee Aymlo, all dead and bloody."

And, indeed there lay the nephew, with the laypom-colored fur beneath his chin dabbled with blood and bisected by a great swiping gash. I knew that was not my handiwork. The redheaded youth who said he was Nath of Thothangir was more than a little of a hacker with a sword.

We all went into the great house, on the alert, and found a frenzied attempt on the part of female Lamnias to pack up the stolen wealth of Dorval Aymlo and to depart. We stopped them, Aymlo wanted nothing of revenge. We discovered his wife and six children, still alive, penned in a filthy basement, and we released them to hysterical scenes of sobbing and laughter, to which we slaves left them and so found ourselves food and drink. The business as merchant carried on by Dorval Aymlo was extensive and he was a relatively wealthy halfling. His nephew had trapped him and sold him into slavery, and he had wound up on Faol, sport for the great Jikai. Now he was home, and he could not do enough for us.

The next day we had to consider what to do. From Ordsmot many of the released slaves could find their way home to various parts of Havilfar, and Aymlo was only too happy to give them, freely and without interest or thought of return, sufficient gold to get them comfortably home, broad gold deldys, the Havilfar coin corresponding to the Vallian talen.

Aymlo's next-door neighbor, and others, crowded in to congratulate him, for he was a kindly man and well thought of. Among those whom the news brought hurrying to Aymlo's house was a man. He was, in the Kregan way, tall and well built, with a handsome open face with a fine pair of black moustaches, and it would be difficult to say how old he was between, say twenty and a hundred-and-twenty — as is the Kregan way.

His name was Tom Dorand ti Ordsmot, and he took an instant shine to Tulema. This Dorand did a considerable business with Aymlo, and all the time, between congratulating the old Lamnia on his remarkable escape and bargaining over new deals, his bold eyes kept straying toward Tulema. She knew, at once. She did all the things that, I suppose, most women have done since the very first Delia of Kregen captivated the very first Drak of Kregen, many thousands of years ago, as the old legends have it, when Kregen itself first emerged from the sea-cloud to receive the light of Zim and Genodras and be blessed by the dance of the seven moons.

She was talking to me, most animatedly, and she kept tossing her hair back and laughing, and arching her back the better to reach for a glass of wine, or a miscil, or stretch for the platter of palines on the sturm-wood table. We had all been through the baths of nine, and were sweet and clean, and, truly, Tulema looked very desirable, with the lamplight shining on her hair and sparkling in her eyes. I often think that the light from a samphron-oil lamp is particularly kind to a woman.

I felt a great relief, and took myself off, and let Dame Nature, who operates as successfully on Kregen as she does on this Earth, get to work.

Come to that, I took the trouble — which was no real trouble and was, in any case, a duty of friendship — to find out what I could of this Tom Dorand. He was a solid upstanding citizen of Ordsmot, respected in all the eight precincts. He carried on a lighter business, ferrying goods up and down the orange river from Ordsmot, the entrepôt hereabouts. Between them, he and Aymlo had a good thing going with regular contracts.

With all the halflings rescued from the manhunters taken care of, with Tulema almost certainly off my hands, there remained only Nath.

"I care not where I go, Dray Prescot. Do not worry your head about me, although I give you thanks for my life."

"As to that," I said, "so be it."

Later Tulema spoke to me. She was very serious. Her dark eyes regarded me solemnly.

"You may think it strange, Dray. But I have not been a dancing girl in a dopa pen for nothing. I know men. I know your heart is somewhere I can never reach."

It may have been flowery — Kregans love a fine phrase — but it was true.

"I hope you will be happy, Tulema. Tom is a fine man."

She flushed at that. "Oh, so you noticed!"

I didn't chuckle, but my lips ricked up a trifle.

"I did not wish to hurt you," she went on. "But I am hard enough in this world to know a chance when one comes my way. You do not love me — and—" here she flared up, and spoke with a great show of bravura contempt— "and I do not love you! I shall marry Tom. I think, though, I shall choose a lesser contract, just to be safe. I shall be happy. He owns many lighters, and will soon go into the voller business. And Dorval Aymlo is rich and is our friend."

"May Opaz bless you, Tulema."

It seemed to me, then, that I had fulfilled the wishes of the Star Lords. I tried to imagine how a lighter owner, and a man who might go into the voller business, might have some effect on Kregen that had drawn him to the attention of the Star Lords. I knew they did nothing without good cause. They had wanted Tulema rescued — and she now was engaged to marry Tom Dorand ti Ordsmot and no doubt they would have children, possibly twins, and it would be these children in whose interest the Star Lords operated. I guessed the Star Lords worked with an eye cocked very far into the future.

My task appeared, as I say, to be finished. Truly, I was a simple onker in those far-off days!

Prevailed on to remain as a guest with Dorval Aymlo, and then specifically invited to the coming nuptials, I agreed to wait twelve days, two Kregen weeks. Then — Vallia!

Halfway through the first week, dressed up in a fine dark red tunic, with white trousers, and a turban of white silk upon my head — very fashionable gear in Ordsmot, then, the turban — I wandered about the town. One could walk quite freely in any of the eight precincts, only taking a little care not to be too far from the area of one's own race by nightfall — and then only if none of the greater moons were in the sky — for skirmishes and clashes between the races were relatively rare. There was no Chulik sector, and I saw none of those fierce yellow-skinned tusked halflings in Ordsmot at that time.

Coming in one evening I was halted by Aymlo, who was in a high old state of excitement. He was dressed up in the most profuse and lavish clothes, with jewels smothering his turban, and a golden belt, and curled slippers of foofray satin. The house blazed with many lights and the expenditure of samphron oil must have been prodigious.

"Dray!" he said, clutching me by the arm, his yellow fur glowing. "Dray — the Vad of Tungar visits me!"

I congratulated him.

Tungar, I knew, was a large and prosperous province of the country whose boundaries ran ward and ward with those of Ordsmot. Ordsmot, of course, was a free city, with her own elected council and Kodifex, chosen by rote, a term at a time, from each of the eight precincts.

"He has large ideas, Dray! He owns much land, dwabur after dwabur, and wishes to develop. If my old business head will aid me now, he and I will strike a pretty bargain or two!"

"May Opaz shine on you, Dorval, my friend."

"And but for you, Dray Prescot, I should be bait for the Manhounds of Antares!"

"Don't think of such things, Dorval. They are of the past."

A commotion began outside, with the sound of zorca hooves, the tinkle of bells, and the soft silver sound of trumpets. These were not the famous silver trumpets of Loh, but they made a brave welcoming sound. Aymlo darted outside to greet his guest by the light of flaring torches.

I strolled after.

The conviction grew on me that I should not push myself forward here. This was business — and, Zair knew, I had done enough of business during my time as Strom of Valka, and later as Prince Majister of Vallia, when I had worked hard with the Companies of Friends — and my instincts were that Aymlo would want to prosecute his plans to his own fashioning. So I wandered out to stand in the shadows of the entranceway as the Vad of Tungar alighted from his zorca.

He made an impressive sight.

Clad all in crimson silk, with a lavish display of gold and jewels about his person, the straight sword of Havilfar they call a thraxter swinging at his side on a silken baldric heavily embellished with jewels and gold thread, he ran up the steps, hand outstretched, calling: "Lahal, Dorval! Lahal! Your happy return brings joy to my heart."

It was Aymlo's business, but this man was a Vad, a rank below that of a Kov, though a high rank, nonetheless. I felt an itch of apprehension, and then every other thought was banished from my head as I saw Tulema move forward into the torchlight. Tom Dorand moved, a vague shadow, at her back. Tulema looked radiant. She wore a sheer gown all of white silk, with crimson embroidery at throat and hem, cunningly slit so that her long legs showed in a gleam of warm flesh. The baths of nine and much scented oils and costly perfumes had transformed Tulema, the one-time dancing girl from a dopa den. Now she was the great lady.

I saw her face. She stared at the Vad of Tungar as risslaca stare at a loloo's egg.

And — he halted in his impetuous greeting of Aymlo, and stared up at Tulema there in the torchlight, and his business was done for him.

So they stared at each other, and I looked at them, and a hateful croaking voice sounded in my ears, coming from no earthbound denizen of Kregen.

"Truly, Dray Prescot, you are a prince of onkers!"

And the blue radiance took me, and swirled me up, and twisted me, and so departed... I felt stinking rock beneath my naked body and the stench of slaves in my nostrils and I knew I had been thrust brutally back once again into the barred slave pens of the Manhunters of Faol.

Thirteen

Concerning the purposes of the Star Lords

I didn't believe it.

I couldn't believe it. I didn't want to believe it.

How could I, again, have brought out the wrong person from under the slavering fangs of the Manhounds of Antares?

It was all a cruel jest of the Star Lords, to punish me for being a prince of onkers.

Surely, after taking Tulema safely out, and spending so much time in her company, after she was safe, in Ordsmot, she had to be the right one! I lay there in the stink and gloom of the barred caves and I confess I came as near as I ever allow myself to despair.

Then I roused myself.

There had to be an explanation, and I was too stupid to see what must so clearly be dangling in front of my nose.

Princess Lilah. The Pallan Golan. Latimer the voller magnate. And Tulema the dancing girl.

Well, none of these four was the one I had been sent here to seek.

Then an awful thought struck me.

Tulema had said, distinctly, that she was the last of those who had been with me in the cave when I arrived.

There was no one left for me to rescue — apart, that was, from a milling mass of a hundred or more filthy, unwashed, clamoring slaves.

74

So that must be the answer. I was to release them all.

I pondered on this carefully, for as I have indicated, the rash freeing of slaves, no matter how desirable that may be, is not wisely undertaken without much forethought. If these miserable creatures were released they would rush screaming into the jungle, and the Manhounds of Antares would lope after them, red tongues lolling in human imitation of hunting dogs, and devour them all. They would perish in the jungle. They would die on the plains. How many, if any at all, would reach safety?

I had vowed with my Delia to end the abomination of slavery on Kregen, thinking that a part of what the Savanti wished. But how would that vow help me now?

"By Hito the Hunter!" said a voice in my ear, a startled voice. "I thought you were dead for sure!"

I looked up from the floor and there was Nath the Guide, bending over me, wearing a mightily puzzled frown. Of course he could recognize me, for I had gone through the baths of the nine, and had my hair and beard trimmed, and so looked something like the Dray Prescot who had first arrived here. And, also, something else I should have observed much earlier then struck me. These so-called guides who claimed to guide people out to safety would hardly swear by the name of a mighty hunter. No, I should have seen that earlier.

"And I thought you dead, also, Nath."

I refrained from immediately leaping up and dealing with him as he had left us to be dealt with by the great Jikai. It was through no help of his that Princess Li-lah and I had escaped. "You disappeared, and we feared a leem had taken you."

He cobbled a story together swiftly, and, truth to tell, he was more concerned with his lies than he was to find fault with my story of running and walking until strange beast-men had taken me and so, eventually, sold me back here.

Nath talked on, very volubly, about his concern for the slaves and how he sorrowed that he had been snatched away by wild beasts, and fought them, and so won free. In truth, there in the barred caves cut into the rocks, we had a high old time swapping lies, and this brought me back to something of a better humor.

"I would like to go out again, Nath, and this time escape clear away."

"Of course! A party is due tomorrow. You must be with us." Then, meaningfully, he added: "There are three Khamorros among us, and they are very fierce men."

"So be it."

There was no doubt in my mind why I needed to go out with a hunted party of fugitives. I would take their treacherous flier from them, as I had done before. I had to take care not to betray any knowledge of what had transpired here after my Jikai with Nath, and nothing of the disappearance of Inachos the Guide passed my lips. But I guessed Nath and his fellows, and Nalgre, may Makki-Grodno rot his liver, were mightily perplexed.

If I make keeping my fingers off Nath the Guide's throat sound easy — believe me, it was not.

Wild plans scurried through my head, and I slept fitfully, awaking with the others to rush at the stentors' call to the feeding cave. In the morning we would be taken out and prepared in the slave barracks. Fantastic and unworkable schemes flitted into and out of my imagination, as a flick-flick shoots its tendrils out to gobble flies.

Many of the slaves had been beaten into submission and could not respond to the meal call, and the usual Kregan custom of six or even eight square meals a day did not always impel them to answer the stentors' summons. I noticed a little Och with a chin fuzz and skinny arms and legs who, so Nath told me, was due to go out with us in the morning. Then this Och, a man named Glypta, pulled back as an ancient, yelling female Och rushed into the chamber beating her broom wildly behind her. Screeching like one of those devil-bats from the hell-caves of Karsk, the old Miglish crone rattled into the chamber, thwacking her broom at the Och woman, raising a great dust and commotion, catching the Och woman cunningly around the head, then switching to trip her legs and so tumble her sprawling into our filth.

"Keep off! Keep off, Mog!"

"I'll see Migshaanu the Ever-Vengeful tears out your liver and your tripes and strips your skin off!" The Migla was stuttering in fury, thwacking with her broom, a very witch in truth, from her mass of tangled hair to her bare and filthy feet. "You don't trick Mog and regret the day you dropped into this world!" And *thwack!* went the broom and the little Och shrieked and tried to spring up and run, and *thwack!* down came Mog's broom again in a gigantic rustling and swishing of twigs.

Bedlam broke out with scuffling and dust flying. Then the Och managed to scuttle out. Mog leaned on her broom and the liquid sheen of her eyes as she leered after the Och sent a shiver up my spine, as I remembered Tulema's avowed declaration that this Miglish crone was in very truth a witch.

"She'll think on!" said this Mog the Migla, in a shrill cackling tone of satisfaction. "Ar!"

There was no Tulema to pull me away.

I stared at Mog.

And the thought dawned. The thought I felt a deep reluctance to face. The thought that must be a true thought. "Now, may Zair take my ib for a harp-string!" I said, but to myself. And so I continued to stare at this old harpy, this filthy harridan with the rat-tail hair, crooked nose, and nutcracker jaws, and I thought that I had taken four people out of here and all of them wrong and this — this monstrosity of a halfling witch — had to be the right one.

She had been here when I arrived. Tulema had said so. And she was still here.

Mog the Witch!

Incredible!

What could the Star Lords be about, to want this object restored to the outside world of Havilfar?

However much I did not wish to believe what I had so belatedly discovered, I had to believe. And if I freed all the slaves and did not set Mog at liberty, I had the nastiest of suspicions that I would be hurled back here yet once more.

I set myself to talk with the witch, and she beat at me with her broom, and spat, drawing her filthy old blanket up around her shoulders as though I assaulted her, and bade me clear off or, by Migshaanu the Mighty-Slayer, I'd be sorry!

"But, Mog," I said, "I can get you out of here."

She cackled at that.

"Get me out!" she mocked. "Onker! Nulsh! And you'd take me out for the manhounds to gnaw on!"

"Not so, Mog."

"Yes, yes, you great ninny!"

"But, Mog—" I said, breathing hard and gripping both my fists together lest they do harm I would feel sorry for after. "The guides!" I repeated what the deluded slaves believed. "The guides will take us through to safety."

She leered at me, mocking, spitting, drool running down that promontory of a chin, the black hairs in her nose quivering. "Onker! Idiot! Nulsh! The guides are—" She swung a bright beady eye to where Nath was deep in conversation with a fair-haired girl, and she cackled like any loloo laying a square egg, and drew a corner of her gray blanket up over her face. "May Migshaanu the All-Glorious turn your belly to porridge and your back to paste!" And she scuttled from the chamber. I lost her in the gloom of the maze of passageways.

There was only one way to settle her hash for her.

I tried to get some sleep and vowed that if there was a bigger fool than me on Kregen he belonged to the Star Lords.

I had been blowharding a lot just recently. Mind you, I felt fully justified, but it was enough unlike me to make me take stock. Old Mog called me a nulsh and I knew that was as foul a term of abuse as most on Kregen. The rast, which is a six-legged rodent infesting dunghills, is often contemptuously referred to as a disgusting creature, and the term of abuse is likewise powerfully disgusted; but a rast is only one of the creatures set down on Kregen like us all and must act out its duties in its own nature. This old Migla crone was only acting as her nature impelled her. Surely, the circumstances in which she found herself were enough to make anyone scream, and the fact she had become a tame slave to sweep and cook meant only that she had a slightly less precarious grip on life than the rest.

Anyway, she was coming out with me the next morning and that was all there was to that.

I awoke to Nath's ungentle toe in my ribs and I yawned and sat up with much play of knuckling my eyes and stretching. Although the air was foul, I came alert and ready for action the instant I awoke, the result of long years at sea being called in the dark of the middle watch to face crises of all imaginable horrors... but I had the idea of putting Nath off guard.

All went as before. Again, and to my distaste, the Notor leading the brave band of hunters was this Trelth. His doughy face gleamed under the morning suns.

The band of runners lined up for Nalgre's inspection. As was customary we all cringed back — even I, for I had no wish to start something that, in finishing, might end up disadvantageously for the Star Lords — and, as you may guess, I was not thinking of them when I wished no foul-ups to occur.

77

The thin old Och, Glypta, did not cringe.

He simply stood, upright, a distant lost look on his face, and I knew I watched a man who had already given himself up for lost and who put no stock by Nath the Guide's encouraging words.

"Why do you not bow to me, Och?" demanded Nalgre. He was interested. He was accustomed to the instant servility of slaves. His whip twitched in his thick fingers.

"I have reached the bottom, the end. There is nothing more you can do to me. I have no more fear, for I am finished."

Nalgre laughed.

"Aye! I have heard political prisoners speak like that, Och. They imagine — oh, they imagine many things, the degradation, the hollowness, the utter irrationality of imprisonment. They believe that in negation they overcome." He laughed, and the sound chilled the blood. "I tell you, Och, you have no conception of the hell that can be yours if I wish." He flicked his whip and the female manhound gamboled out. "I have no need, even, to cause you suffering from my manhounds you do not as yet comprehend. The whip, ol' snake, will quickly teach you that you have not reached the end of suffering. I can make you fear again, Och — as many political prisoners have found before."

I knew he spoke the sober truth.

I was thankful to see that Glypta, too, through the miasma of his suffering, had been jerked back from that self-congratulatory abyss of suffering so many politicals, believing themselves beyond fear, indulge in. He cringed and Nalgre laughed.

What the slave-master might have done next for his amusement remained thankfully unknown, for Notor Trelth with a thick impatient rasp to his voice said: "Have done with the rast, Nalgre. If a slave will not bow the neck, have his head cut off and thus make him bow for good and all."

A woman with Trelth, with pearls in her hair and a plump and well-fed figure she had somehow crammed into tight hunting leathers, so that she bulged, tinkled a laugh. "Let him run for our sport, Ranal! I shall joy to tickle him!" And the fat fool had the effrontery to finger the thraxter at her side.

Ranal Trelth chuckled. "He shall be all yours, Lavia, yours for yourself, my precious."

I did not miss the tip of her scarlet tongue as it licked her rich lips, shining in the radiance of the twin Suns of Scorpio.

As we trudged off to the slave barracks, I heard the slavemaster Nalgre have the last word.

"Ah, but, Notor Trelth, if you take off the head of an impudent slave, he does not suffer!"

There would be no chance whatsoever of convincing my fellow slaves that Nath the Guide, the one man to whom they looked for deliverance, was a traitor. I did not stand in the same danger vis-à-vis him as I had done with Inachos, for I had told Nath nothing, as I had blabbed to Inachos. I had to wait my time, and then strike, and trust in my own skill and strength to bring me through. Of one thing I was absolutely, irrevocably sure. I could expect no help from the Star Lords beyond an insulting jibe from their spy and messenger.

Up in the first floor above the hard-packed earth of the slave barracks we found two other parties waiting to go out, and a third joined us later on, when Nalgre had attended to them. There were sixteen in our party, of whom nine were halflings. The three Khamorros did not appear to me, at first glance, to be friendly to one another, and there were two human girls, the fair-haired one and one with very short dark hair, who by that token had been slave for a very short time. The girls were frightened of the Khamorros, and everyone else was, too. Nath himself trod warily, and I remembered the brave futile fight of Lart on that very dirt below us.

Glypta the Och, with the return of fear, also needed the return of reassurance, and Nath spent some time with him. I welcomed that. I took myself off to the darkest corner and ate my food alone and attended to what it was necessary to do without crossing any of the others. The Khamorros kept up an argument, but I made no attempt to follow its ramifications. There were two of them against the third. I did gather that they were khams of different training disciplines, different syples, but that the point of dissension was not, as might have been expected, the relative superiority of their own syple.

A certain amount of luck was with me, for when the suns went down I knew I would have two burs at the outside when only a couple of the lesser moons were in the sky. I waited with what patience I could muster.

When all was dark I carefully felt my way down the wooden ladder. Below, the guards were thrown into black relief by the glare of torches becketed into the walls alongside the door with its lenken beam. Lart had had difficulty in lifting that beam.

Like a wild leem of the plains, I crept up behind the first guard, silenced him, snaked across to the second, and served him likewise. I looked about for more, guessing they would be well on the alert for fear of the deadly men so well versed in the art of unarmed combat.

There was time for me to slip into the leaf-green tunic of a guard whose shoulders were almost the equal of my own, and to don his helmet. I extinguished one of the torches and cursed, a good Hito-the-Hunter oath.

The Deldar walked in from the guardroom, cursing in his turn. They all carried crossbows, ready spanned. Him, I tapped on the nape of the neck and dragged into the shadows. Two more I served in the same way so that there were six unconscious guards, sprawled on the hard dirt of the slave barracks. Then I lifted up the lenken beam and went out.

Getting into the barred caves was easy. No guard challenged me, for I was dressed as a guard and therefore above suspicion. And, too, no one had escaped from the caves of the Manhunters of Faol for many many seasons.

Inside the barred opening I ripped off the leaf-green uniform. Guards came in here in search of pleasure, and some, at least, never returned. I padded on towards the feeding area. Mog the Migla lay asleep on her filthy pallet in her den, surrounded by discarded bones and cracked and rimed platters — and her great bristly broom stood against the wall. I lapped a length of her foul blanket about her mouth and seized her and lifted her upon my shoulder and so, without a cry or a struggle, carried her swiftly outside.

A guard lowered the point of his spear as I stepped through the unlocked gate. Its bars were barely visible in the faint filtered light of the tiny hurtling moons.

"Now, by Foul Fernal himself! What is this?"

Had he talked less and used his spear more, he might have discovered what this Foul Fernal, whatever demon he might be, would now never tell him, for I stepped inside his spear and with my one free hand gripped him and cross-buttocked him with such force that his spine snapped. But he did have time to scream, whereat I let out a low Makki-Grodno oath.

I took his sword and spear and left him where he fell. I gathered up the leaf-green uniform and helmet, and carrying all in an awkward bundle, raced into the darkness.

Some distance along the trail the fugitives took to leave the compound I found a nice comfortable spot partway up a tree bole, and with movements very rapid and barely seen in the gloom, lashed Mog safely to the trunk. Her tattered blanket provided gag and bindings. Her eyes glared at me and I saw no terror in them, only a mindless and shaking sense of outrage and feral hatred. I slammed in a palisade of thorns that, although skimpy, would serve, and then dashed back. If you ask why I did not at once flee with Mog through the night jungle, you have not yet rightly understood me.

I knew the fliers were kept nowhere near the caves. Where they were kept I did not know. The Jikai villas were some way off and would be guarded. If I aroused the compound now there scarcely would be a hunt the next day. I had left the barred cage door open. The dead guard lay sprawled just outside. That would cause commotion enough.

Back in the slave barracks I flung the uniform back on the guard, kicked the Deldar, who was moaning, and scampered up the stairs. Up there all was quiet. I crept to my corner and lay down. A shadow moved. A man eased gently up to me.

A voice said: "You tried to escape, dom. You came back. Why?"

I recognized the voice of the third Khamorro, a light, pleasant voice, to come from such a deadly kind of man.

"If you wish to know," I said, "go down and see."

He chuckled. "I am going to escape tomorrow. I would not wish anyone to spoil that for me. I hope you have not done so."

"Go to sleep."

I was perfectly ready in case he leaped on me. But he did not. I heard him ease himself back to his pallet. His voice trickled through the darkness. "You are a strange man. Tomorrow, we will see."

With the morning there would be the final nonsense with Nalgre, and his female manhound, and then we would set off through the jungle. I hoped this Khamorro would welcome what he then discovered.

All followed exactly as before.

80

The only difference that a dead guard had made, and an open cage door, was a strong body of guards marching into the slave caves and beating about, aimlessly, and then marching out having found nothing and accomplished nothing. The slaves ready for the run today were counted, and then counted again. The Deldar, who had awoken first, must have said nothing of the inexplicable sleep he and his men had indulged in. But, as none of the slaves had escaped, there was no harm done. If anyone noticed the absence of old Mog, they would scarcely credit that she had slain a guard and taken off into the jungle, witch or no witch.

The Khamorro who had spoken to me, whose name was Turko, gave me a meaningful glance. I ignored him. Strange, how to look back on that day I can so clearly recall how I wished this Turko the Khamorro to hell and gone! Strange, indeed, is the way of fate.

With which not particularly original reflection we all began our march into the jungle, hunted men and women and halflings, sport for the great Jikai.

Nath the Guide led off very smartly, acting his part as the guide and mentor of this little band of fugitives. He had decided we should strike north, and his words were the selfsame words that Inachos had used. They learned their duplicity by parts, these treacherous guides!

When we came to where I had left Mog I sprinted ahead, and with the dead guard's thraxter cut her down.

She came all asprawl into my arms and I caught her odor and I gagged.

"You nulsh! Migshaanu the All-Glorious will fry your brains and frizzle your eyeballs and rip out your tongue and—"

I said: "If you do not still that wagging tongue of yours, Mog, I will probably rip it out, instead of Migshaanu." I was bending forward, glaring at her, mightily wroth. She looked up with those bright agate eyes, and saw my face, and she stopped talking. I have noticed that effect I have on people. It is not something I am proud of. But it is, nevertheless, mightily useful at times!

Nath shouldered up, flustered, shouting: "What is this! What is she doing here? Mog — Dray Prescot — what—?"

One of the Khamorros, the largest of the three and a thumping ugly great fellow, bellowed out in anger:

"The old crone cannot march! She cannot come with us — you must leave her, cramph."

"I will carry her, if need be."

For I had felt a surprising strength in that thin figure when she had tumbled out of the tree upon me.

"We shall not wait—"

Turko walked up with a lithe swing, his dark hair tumbled about his face, his features bronzed and clear, and, as I noticed for the first time, a look about him at once reckless and contained. With all this his build, all muscle and sliding roped power, advertised his enormous physical development, and, if that were not enough, he was damned handsome too, into the bargain.

"Leave it, Chimche," he said. "This nul Dray Prescot will carry the crone, as he says, or be left behind."

The bulky form of Chimche started to quiver and Nath said quickly: "We had best press on. There are shoes and food and wine ahead — and knives."

I had to keep my fingers still. I knew that wine.

So we hurried on along the trail, with Chimche turning often to give me a glare. But I had given him no further cause of offense, and I was carefully watching Mog. Having seen how matters stood, and at her first immediate rush back down the trail being firmly stopped by me, she screeched and waved her arms but trudged along. Every now and then I had to give her a push. I watched her, as I say, very carefully; the impression had formed that she play-acted rather more than she cared folk to perceive. And her walk, once the shuffling scuttle she habitually adopted in the caves proved troublesome swinging along the trail, changed imperceptibly into a much firmer and longer tread. She would not be the first woman to make herself look old and hideous in captivity.

Still, she was a halfling and, by Zair, she was hideous in reality!

When we reached the cache of food and clothing Mog was more than happy to rest. We donned the gray tattered tunics and took the knives and put on the shoes, and all this petty finery was designed to make us feel we had outwitted the manhunters, to give us hope, to make us run!

Mog wouldn't wear the shoes Nath offered.

Toward the end of the march I had to carry her, slung over a shoulder, and every now and then a filthy dangling leg would give me a sly kick, just to remind me.

When we made our camp up a tree, erecting a palisade of thorns, and Nath prepared his lower aerie, I knew the time approached. Nath hefted up the wine bottles, their leather bulging. I was looking at Mog. She was tied in place. I knew she had the willpower and the courage to march back through the jungle. Now, as Nath offered her the wine, she cowered back, trembling.

"No, no, Nath. I do not want the wine."

Chimche bellowed at this, his dark florid face flushed.

"Then give it here, you crone!"

"Why will you not drink the wine?" persisted Nath. He upended the spout over Mog's mouth, trying to force her, letting the wine drop through in that frugal way Kregans have.

"No!" She was terrified now. "No, the wine is drugged! We will all sleep and the monsters of the forests will eat us!"

Turko laughed at this, but Nath backhanded Mog across her rubbery lips. "Drugged!" he shouted, in a fury. "You lie, old crone! You lie!" And he hit her again.

I took Nath the Guide's arm and bent it back.

"She does not lie, Nath. The wine is drugged so that you may creep off in the night, and leave us prey to the man-hounds."

He stared at me, his arm bent back, and a sickly smile distorted that frank and manly face. We all saw. We all saw the guilt that glazed on that face.

"By the Muscle!" bellowed Chimche, shoving forward. "It is true!"

The other Khamorro, Janich, elbowed up, pushing me out of the way, reaching for Nath the Guide.

"The wine is drugged and the guides are false!" screeched Mog. Her agate eyes glared up in the terror of the moment.

Janich's hefty push and Nath's convulsive effort broke my hold on his arm and he scuttled back up the tree branch. He stared down on us, and saw the murder in our eyes, and he screamed at us.

"It is true! It is true! The wine is drugged and you creeping yetches will be dead tomorrow when the Manhounds of Faol tear your limbs apart and splash your blood into the jungle."

Shouts and calls broke out as the slaves tried to get up the tree at Nath. He lifted his knife. I think, then, he knew he was doomed, for the Khamorros are frightful fighters, and he with all his forest experience knew he would not elude them among the trees. But he would make the effort. You could feel sorry for him, as you might feel sorry for a risslaca — about to kill and eat a dainty lople — being suddenly caught in a snare and feathered with barbed arrows.

"You are all doomed!" Nath the Guide screeched it down at us. "And the witch shall die first!"

The whole reason I was here, in this hideous situation, was to rescue Mog the Migla and take her to safety. And now, with the speed of a striking leem, Nath hurled his knife at the old Miglish crone.

The knife flew, a darting sliver of steel in the forest gloom, full at Mog's unprotected throat.

Fourteen

Turko the Khamorro

Straight for that stringy defenseless throat the knife flashed. The movement of the knife struck everything else into a paralysis, a stasis wherein Nath's throwing arm remained outflung, Mog recoiled against the bonds, Turko and the other Khamorros stood caught in the passions of the moment, the halflings below stilled in their clamor.

The sword I had taken from the guard rasped as it cleared the scabbard.

That old Krozair trick of striking away flying arrows with the superb Krozair longsword must serve me now — and before I had time to finish the thought, everything happening so fast events blurred, the thraxter flicked out and the knife struck the blade with a high ringing pinging and spun away into the gloom of the forest.

Nath the Guide galvanized into motion, screaming, clawing back up the tree.

From below a Rapa — one I had noted as of that fierce, predatory, arrogant kind that meant he had once been a mercenary — threw his own knife. It flew true. Nath the Guide stood, arms spread, transfixed, his face twisted with the defiant-fear — and he fell. Nath the Guide, son of treachery, fell full-length down the tree and so into the greenery to smash face-first into the mud and detritus of the jungle floor.

"Let his foul Hito the Hunter aid him now!" quoth the Rapa, and went down very agilely to retrieve his knife.

This Rapa was one Rapechak, and I remember that he must have been less offensive to smell than most, or I was growing accustomed to the typical Rapa stink. Those Rapas who had fought with me in Dorval Aymlo's courtyard, too, I recalled, had been in nowise as offensive as other Rapas I had known.

"Now what do we do?" demanded the big Khamorro, Chimche.

Mog remained petrified and dumb. The halflings were raising a great hullabaloo. Janich was yelling at them to cease their noise or, by the Muscle, he'd break their bones to powder.

Turko said: "This nul Dray Prescot knew the guide was false. So did the old witch. What is fitting that we should do with them, khamsters?"

"Did you know, witch?" shouted Chimche, thrusting his nose at Mog. She cowered back, blinking.

"Only stories!" Her shrill voice poured words out in a torrent. "May Migshaanu the Ever-Radiant stand as my witness! Rumors — we heard stories — the wine was a sleep potion — the shoes were baited — the tame slaves were frightened. Enil was found dead in his den, and Yolan went for water and never returned." She shook as she screamed. "We dare not speak! The guides murdered us! By Magoshno and Sidraarga, I swear it!"

Janich went to strike her, so wrought up was he; but Turko took his arm, saying: "Leave the old nul, Janich. She is harmless and in fear for her life."

"Aye." Janich looked down at Turko's hand on his arm. "She should be. And so should you be, nul-syple!"

Turko took his hand away.

He removed that hand from Janich's arm neither too quickly nor yet too slowly. I admired that coolness. I could guess what had transmogrified the situation. The syples were the different kinds of Khamorro training and belief, and a nul, clearly, was anyone not a Khamorro. So that for Janich to call Turko a nul-syple was a great insult. Yet Turko did not instantly retaliate. He had put his hand on a man who was not a syple-brother. The answer must be given.

I said: "If you wish to yammer and quarrel here all night, you may do so. As for me, I am going to take a flier off these Makki-Grodno guides."

I still held the thraxter naked in my fist. I reached across to Mog, and with my left hand wrenched her bindings free, lifted her up, and slung her over my shoulder. She screamed and then tried to bite me, whereat I thwacked her narrow bottom with the flat of the blade. The thraxter is a medium-long straight sword, with a blade heavier and wider than a rapier, a vertical blade, and it smacked with a satisfactory smack. Mog yelped.

Down the tree I went, slipping and sliding most of the way. At the bottom the Rapa, Rapechak, straightened up with his knife freshly cleaned on Nath's breechclout. "You mentioned a flier."

"Aye. This way. And keep silent."

So I set off with the halfling Mog draped over my shoulder and a rout of halflings following me through the forest. I found the clearing and thumped Mog down and said: "Stay there, old witch. If you try to run I'll draw your guts out for a knitted vest."

Without knowledge of any signal the flier up there might be awaiting I could only wait patiently for him to descend. Inachos had stood out and waved; I could not do that. The Twins were up, the two second moons of Kregen eternally revolving one about the other, casting down a pinkish sheen of light in which details stood out clearly. A rustle on the back trail heralded the three Khamorros.

"You, Turko," I said. "If you stand in the clearing and wave up, and then scamper back here, and look lively about it, we might see the flier this Zair-forsaken night."

Again Turko favored me with that long, almost quizzical look. I turned away and went to stand by Mog.

Turko walked into the clearing, looked up, waved his arms, and then walked back. As a performance it would not have done for Drury Lane, but it worked.

The flier ghosted down, shimmering in the pink moonlight, drifting gently to the clearing's mass of rotting vegetation, fallen trees, and creeping shoots. A guide looked out and shouted something about Hito the Hunter and the stupid yetches of slaves to be run in the morning and needing a drink... and Rapechak the Rapa's knife buried itself in his neck so that he pitched over the lenken side of the flier, choking and writhing in convulsions, before Chimche reached him and twisted his head in a single savage crunching action.

I was working with fearsome allies, now, but they did not have the unwanted responsibility of Mog the Migla on their hands.

Janich said with great satisfaction, "I can fly a voller."

I said, "We will have to squeeze everyone in most carefully. There is not too much room—"

But Chimche and Janich both stared at me, as though I were mad, and then they laughed, and Chimche said: "You? A stinking nul? We do not take you aboard our voller."

And Janich chuckled and added: "But we will take the two shishis. They will make brave sport!"

The two girls, the fair and the dark, screamed at this and cowered back from the forefront of the group of halflings. Truth to tell, I had taken no notice of the girls, for I had had Mog to concern myself with. Now Turko said in a quiet, even, leaden voice: "And me?"

"You?" Janich threw back his head and laughed aloud. "You nul-syple! You will be left with these others, for the yetches of manhounds to gobble up! I am only sorry I cannot be here to see it."

I moved forward. The sword glimmered pinkly in my hand.

"I do not think you will take off and leave us, Janich. The airboat belongs to us all. We are all slaves together."

If I had expected an argument from a Khamorro I was a fool.

All I had heard about these fearsome men flashed through my mind. Tulema came from the same land, from Herrelldrin. She knew. "Terrible in their cunning, Dray! They practice devilish arts that let them crush a man's bones, that make the strongest man as a straw in summer in their hands! They do not fear the sword or the spear, for they know arts to outwit swordsmen. Come away, Dray, from a Khamorro, if you value your life!" And, I had seen Lart the Khamorro die and so I knew that all Tulema said was true — at least, the results of her observation if not the causes of the Khamorros' skills.

Janich rushed across the tangled floor of the jungle clearing.

He came at me with the intention of taking me in a grip that would snap my neck. I was familiar with the trick from long training and discipline with the Krozairs of Zy, of whom these Khamorros would never have heard.

I sidestepped and at the same time slid into an instinctive avoidance routine. Also, I slashed the thraxter down Janich's side. He slipped most of the blow and elbowed away the flat of the sword. He roared in enjoyment.

"See, Chimche! The stupid nul believes himself a man with a sword!"

"I seldom slay unarmed men, Janich."

At this Turko called out: "A Khamorro is never unarmed, Dray Prescot."

If it was a warning it could not help; if it indicated Turko would not interfere, it was useful. I did not know how deeply ran the animosities between syple and syple in Herrelldrin.

Janich circled, like a leem. In the clear pinkish light of the Twins I could see the shadowy interplay of his muscles. Beautifully built are the men of the Khamorro! He circled me and he was not in the least afraid of the sword, and I saw with great sorrow that this could only end one way — I would be forced to slay this Janich the Khamorro.

As we circled I saw Turko standing immediately to the rear of Rapechak. The Rapa's arm was twisted up and there was no knife stuck down his breechclout.

Then I had to concentrate on Janich. I admit my sorrow at what followed, for all that Janich had proved himself a mean-spirited man, but, as Turko had said, he was not unarmed.

He taunted me.

"I shall break your arm off, Prescot, and drive your own fingernails into your eyes! I shall twist your head so you may view your shoulder blades! A Khamorro cannot be mastered."

Why I said what I did, I do not know for sure; perhaps I was sick of the whole stupid affair already. We should be flying to safety in the voller instead of brawling!

"Unarmed combat, Janich, is very wonderful and brave. But people who develop it are slaves and without liberty, men kept down by a superior people who have weapons, real weapons, of their own. A man fights with his hands, or a stick, if he is subservient and not allowed a steel weapon."

By this time Janich was really annoyed and yet he did not lose his temper. He came in, weaving and ducking, very quickly, to take me in another grip I recognized. I eluded him and again I found that reluctance in my sword arm to plunge the blade home.

"You are done for, Dray Prescot," shouted Turko.

Well, it is all a long time ago, now, and Turko's voice spurred me in a way I did not then understand.

Janich kept on taunting me, and I replied once more.

"A man with a sword is not to be bested, Janich, even by so marvelous a hand-fighter as you. I would not slay you—"

He let loose a torrent of invective, foul words and many of them incomprehensible to me then, although I grew well-enough acquainted with them in later days. I could see he was puzzled and annoyed that he had not slipped my blade and taken me and gripped me and so broken my neck or my back. He bored in again, and he used a trick the Krozairs of Zy would never practice on one another — although only too happy to employ against an overload of Magdag — and he nearly got me so that I had to furiously twist aside and let his iron-hard toes go whistling past. My body did what it has been trained to do, released at last from compunction of my reason, and the blade slashed down. Janich the Khamorro staggered back with a ruined face and blood everywhere, ghastly in that streaming pink radiance. Then Turko yelled and I went flying as Chimche smashed into me from the side.

Somehow I clung onto the thraxter and shoved up and saw Chimche and Turko locked, and Turko flipped into the air to land with a smash. Chimche glanced at Janich, who was dead, and at me, and he roared mightily.

"Stinking nul of a sworder! You will die now!"

He rushed. I staggered up, for a fallen branch had not rotted enough and a jagged splinter of wood had sorely bruised me and taken my wind. I circled the blade, sliced at his wrist, drew blood, and made him stagger back, roaring.

"You have not learned, Chimche," I got out. "A sword will settle for you, you cramph." And I started after him.

Turko leaned up on an elbow, gasping, his face drawn with pain. I circled the thraxter again and then, and I suppose for the first time, Chimche got a clear look at my face.

He turned, bolted for the voller, clambered in, and the next instant the flier rose above the treetops, fleeing into the pink moonlight flooding down over Kregen.

I admit, then, I shouted a few uncomplimentary things after Chimche the Khamorro, comprehensively anatomizing his ancestry and his lineage and his personal habits and his eventual fate and where I would like to see him. Oh, yes, I was annoyed!

I had handled the whole affair like a green onker straight out of nursery school!

Where, I said to myself, is the Dray Prescot of the Clansmen of Felschraung, of the bravo-fighters of Zenicce, of the Krozairs of Zy, not to mention that puffed-up Drak of Valka? Had the Star Lords and their bedeviling demands completely addled my brain?

I swung back to Turko and helped him get up, for he had been thrown heavily and had been struck a shrewd blow.

"And don't prate to me, Turko, about not laying hands on a Khamorro. You have seen how I deal with Khamorros. And now, by Makki-Grodno's diseased left armpit, we have to deal with the manhounds and those perfumed idiots who think they are on a great Jikai. We're all in this together, now."

Turko stared at me, his eyes half-closed, rubbing his bruised side.

"We march with the moons!" I shouted to the beast-men. "We take the trail away from the slave pens. And, first—" And here, at the mouth of the trail we must take, I cut a long stake and pointed it and thrust it at an angle into the ground, camouflaging it with leaves. "May a manhound degut himself on that, to the glory of Opaz!"

Then, with Mog the Migla witch slung over my shoulder and my other arm around Turko supporting him and helping him along and followed by a jabbering crowd of halflings and two pretty girls, I, Dray Prescot, set off to outrun the Man-hounds of Antares.

Fifteen

Of mantraps and medicine

Along the jungle trail we left a fine old collection of traps.

There was no time I would spare to dig pits, but whenever we came across a natural hole that a few murs of labor might turn into a mantrap we happily spent that time, barbing the bottom with spikes, laying thin branches and many leaves across the top and sprinkling about the stinking detritus of the rain forest to camouflage the trap.

We constructed deadfalls, of a variety of patterns to make their discernment less easy. Rapechak entered into this work with great gusto. Turko had been badly knocked by the fall and although I had prodded his ribs, to his silent suffering, and found nothing broken, I was not happy that he did not have a broken bone in that magnificent body of his somewhere. I would not listen when he wanted to help with the trap making, and snarled at him to lie down and rest. "If you must show how brave and noble a Khamorro you are, Turko, keep your eyes on Mog. I don't want her to run off."

She had moaned and shrieked, but now she was silent, except to say, now and then: "No one escapes the manhounds, Dray Prescot, you nulsh. We are all dead."

Whereat I shouted across: "Keep the old witch quiet, Turko, or, by thunder, I'll gag her in her own foul breechclout!"

We left many pointed and cunningly positioned stakes along the trail. I hoped a manhound, loping after us, sniffing the scent from our baited shoes, would leap full onto the sharp point of the stake and so wriggle with the dark blood dropping down until he died.

I'd far rather see, I own, one of the hunters in that position, but I knew them.

They used the manhounds to track and corral the quarry; then they stepped in with their beautiful and expensive crossbows, their swords and their spears.

Once, Mog shrieked at me, "You ninny, Dray Prescot! The shoes the guides give us are baited. The manhounds can pick up the scent a dwabur off! Why do you not kick off the shoes?"

"Quiet, you old crone!"

Rapechak took his shoes off and was about to hurl them into the jungle when I stopped him. His fierce beaked face swung down to look at me, and his eyes glared, ready for an instant quarrel. I had suffered much from Rapas in the past. But I was prepared to explain to this Rapechak.

"Later. Later we will dispose of the shoes. Not now."

He would have argued, but I swung away, shouting about a tree trunk the halflings were trying to angle as a deadfall, and threatening to crush their own stupid brains out in the process. Rapechak put his shoes back on.

We could march for some distance yet. There was plenty of light from the Twins and later from She of the Veils; the enemy would be fatigued. Already, as seemed to be their custom, a Fristle man carried a Fristle woman. I didn't want to have to help the two human girls, for I had Mog to worry about and, to a different degree, Turko. He was in great pain, but not a murmur of complaint passed his lips. And, to me a strange fact, he still looked handsome. Suffering sometimes ennobles and makes one look radiant; not often.

When I calculated that we would exhaust our strength without adequate return by pressing on, I told everyone to take off their shoes. We found a great tree and climbed into its lower branches and there with the rammed-in thorns formed our palisade and made camp. We ate the rest of the food, and water was found in a nearby stream. I looked at this bedraggled band.

"Rapechak," I said. And, to a Brokelsh, "You, too, Gynor. Are you done yet, or are you for a little sport?"

They didn't understand. When I explained, both Rapa and Brokelsh gave expressions of pleasure in their respective halfling ways.

We three, then, struck off along the trail where it turned along by a river. We had prepared stakes which we used to make of that trail a death trap, unless one went cautiously, and inspected every fold of leaf. Presently, after a bur or so, we came to a gorge into which the stream fell. We threw the shoes down, having rubbed them well along the brink.

"May all the manhounds go to the Ice Floes of Sicce!" said Gynor, the Brokelsh. He was strong and his black body-bristles sprouted fiercely.

We went back to the camp and Turko looked up and said, "Mog is still here, Dray Prescot," to which I replied, "Good," and so we all rested. We set watches, for that was prudent, here in the rain forests of Northern Faol.

In the morning, by first light, a mingling of opaline radiance, we set off again along the small trail leading off from the other side of the tree. Here we set no traps but pressed on as far and as fast as we might. Those of the slaves whose feet were in the worst condition had rags wrapped about them, and we all struggled and slipped through terrible country, half-naked, gleaming with sweat, for it was very hot, panting and plunging on. We looked very much like fugitives then.

At a resting place, when it was time to move on, for I would not stop to catch food and eat, Turko looked up as I lifted him.

"Leave me, Dray Prescot. I cannot go farther. I am done for."

I ignored him and got him on my back.

Mog cackled as Rapechak, who understood I meant what I said, prodded her on.

"He is a fool, that Khamorro!" The old witch spat out the words. "Migshaanu the Pitiless witnessed it! He attacked the great kham Chimche when Chimche would have broken you like a reed, Prescot! And now look at him, his guts caved in."

I said to Turko: "I believe you attacked Chimche, Turko, and for this I thank you. Now do not prattle like a baby onker. I will not leave you for the manhounds."

"So be it, Dray Prescot."

I could not tell him that great kham or not, Chimche would have been a dead man if he had fought me, without Turko's assistance which, truth to tell, had thrown me off balance. A fighting-man, used to the melee, as it is known among my fighting clansmen, keeps the eyes in the back of his head well open all the time. As witness poor Alex Hunter, back there on a beach in Valka. And that seemed a long time ago, by Zair!

That day we hurried on rapidly, and turn and turn about the stronger helped the weaker. I noticed the two girls, who claimed to be rich merchant's daughters, kept close to me. Beyond learning that their names were Saenda — the fair one — and Quaesa — the dark one — and that they came from different parts of Havilfar and already were putting on airs, one claiming superiority over the other, only to have some other remarkable fact brought to life in opposition, I took no notice of them except to see they kept up with the party.

My plans had gone disastrously wrong, all because of those fool Khamorros, although Turko was a Khamorro and was proving a tough and reliable companion.

Although, as you will instantly see, I have forged ahead in this story; for at this time Turko was badly injured, in great pain, and a liability on our onward progress. Once he saw that I did not mean to abandon him he remained quiet and did not suggest I leave him again. Mog, however, mentioned the idea more than once, having discovered how much more pleasant travel was across my shoulder than struggling and stumbling through the gloomy aisles of the forest.

And perhaps, if you guess I did this to spite the Star Lords — you would not be wrong.

We were attacked by a species of risslaca, all squamous and hissing and tongue-flicking and claw-clicking; but I was able to slide the thraxter into an eye, and then into the thing's scale-white belly, and so dispatch it. Turko stared up at the fight from where I had dumped him beside the almost-invisible trail. When it was all over, he grunted as I lifted him, whereat I said: "I would not cause you pain, Turko. For the sake of Opaz, man, tell me!"

All he would say was: "It is better than lying on the ground and rotting and being eaten by ants or snapped up by a risslaca such as you have just slain."

Oh, yes, he was tough, was Turko!

After a time, he said, "You have handled a sword before."

"Yes."

"The trick with the knife, when Nath sought to slay the old witch. That was clever."

Truth to tell, I had looked back at that old Krozair trick and knew it to be not at all bad. I had not been using the great Krozair longsword which, with its two-handed grip, is suitable for the quick subtle twitchings and flickings necessary, and I had been aiming for a flashing sliver of a knife and not a clothyard shaft. Yes, that had been something of a little Jikai. I said, "A knack, Turko. Now, rest as best you may."

Presently Rapechak, prodding Mog, pressed up to my side.

"I will carry Turko the Khamorro, if he will allow, Dray Prescot, if you will take charge of this — this—" Rapechak rubbed his thin shanks and glared at Mog. "She is a devil from the Ice Floes of Sicce, by Rhapaporgolam the Reaver of Souls!"[2]

I did not chuckle, although I believe my lips ricked up.

"And what do you say, Turko?"

He faced a struggle, then, did Turko the Khamorro. Only later when I learned more about the Khamorros and the awful power their belief in their khamster sanctity has over them could I realize that for a Rapa to touch a Khamorro was far worse than, for instance, the touch from an Untouchable of old India.

Not understanding all this at the time, I said, "Rapechak has shins that are black and blue from the old witch. I shall not allow her so to maltreat me. Let Rapechak carry you for a space, Turko, my friend."

Turko yielded. He said something under his breath, and I caught the trailing words: "...Morro the Muscle's recompense and atonement."

We pressed on, for by this time the Manhounds of Antares lolloped on our back trail, and the traps would only hold them up for as long as they were stupid enough not to do the obvious. When I caught a glimpse through a gap in the overhead cover of a skein of fluttrells winging past, and ordered instant stillness until the magnificent flying beasts and their armed riders had passed, I suspected that they must be a part of the manhunters' search.

"Fluttrells and vollers," cackled Mog. "They will catch us, you nulsh, Dray Prescot, and rip our throats out and feather us with barbs for their sport."

"Maybe," I said, making it a casual statement. "But they will be sorry they found us, that I promise you."

So, with many rests that grew more frequent and of longer duration, we pressed on. I caught one of the little jungle palies, similar to the plains species but with zebra-striped hindquarters, and we all ate. By the time Far and Havil sank and the Twins appeared and we made camp we were pretty well done for. A complete night's rest was imperative.

At this camp I took the opportunity of making a bow. Oh, it was a poor thing, vine-strung, and of a pitiful throw; but with the fire-hardened points of the arrows, quickly fletched with feathers from a bird brought down by a flung stone, I fancied it would give us just that little edge of time. We might have to buy the time we needed dearly.

"Weapons," said Turko. He lifted his hands, and turned them about in the screened fire-glow in its crook of tree-trunk, for the trees hereabouts were powerful and large of bole. "I have been taught all my life that a man's hands — and his feet and head — are more potent than artificial weapons."

"Sometimes, Turko. What I told Janich is true. I know you boast you can dodge and deflect arrows; and certainly you may outwit a swordsman if he is not reasonably good with his blade, but—"

"Aye, Dray Prescot. *But.*"

"Now sleep, friend Turko. Tomorrow we will show these Opaz-forsaken cramphs of manhunters the error of their ways."

"Tomorrow?"

"They will find us tomorrow."

There was no answer to that, and with watches set, we slept.

Turko had a bad night. He awoke with a groan he could not still and I fetched water and bathed his forehead, which felt feverish, and gave him a little to sip, for I feared internal injuries. Mog woke up and swore at me. By this time she must have realized there was some special interest in her for me, and she would have been thinking very carefully on what her future would be. She could have no knowledge of the Star Lords, or so I believed. That I looked out for her was clear — the other halflings looked out for themselves, and the two girls, Saenda and Quaesa, had already shown signs of anger at my concern over old Mog — and so she must be racking her evil old brains for the explanation. That she could never find one that would make sense was obvious. I had no idea why the Star Lords should bedevil me with the old witch.

Now she swore at me, vilely. "Get your rest, you great nulsh, Dray Prescot! Why waste your strength on the Khamorro? He will die tomorrow. I can see that, for I have great powers in healing, and he is done for."

Turko looked at me and I saw his lips rick down. The hand holding the roughly fashioned leaf-cup shook. That was from weakness and pain, I guessed, never from fear.

With Turko looking at me I went down to old Mog.

I took her by the neck and I glared into her eyes.

"You say Turko will die tomorrow? You are sure?"

I let her breathe and she gobbled: "I know!"

"You have skill in medicine?"

She started off to boast of her secrets and her mysteries, and of how Migshaanu the Great Healer would aid her — and then she stopped, aghast, glaring at me, a hand to her mouth. She saw, at last, what the situation was.

I nodded. I have given orders in my life that I dreaded to give. One demand must be measured against another, and there is no certainty when it comes to command. Hesitation is a sin the fates punish by destruction.

"You will be able to gather plants from the forest, herbs, leaves, fungi — you will be able to fashion needles from the thorns — you will cure my friend Turko. If you do not, Mog the Migla, I shall certainly leave you for the manhounds."

She tried, shrewd enough to have read much of my intentions, for, after all, they were very patent.

"You took me from the slave pens, Dray Prescot. You saved me for some great purpose of your own — or your masters. You will not kill me or leave me to the monsters."

"Cure Turko, or you will be turned off into the jungle."

By this time for her to return to the caves was beyond her strength, wiry and whipcordlike though it might be. She gibbered and mewed, but I remained adamant. Just why I did this I can see quite clearly, now, was to make the Star Lords pay. Oh, poor old Mog was the instrument to suffer — although she had had an easy ride compared with the others — but the Star Lords would, I hoped, suffer a little along with her.

With many imprecations and mutterings Mog gathered what she would need and soon was concocting potions. She stuck thorns into Turko, and watching her, I saw the sureness with which her gnarled fingers worked, and knew she had the skill of Doctor Nath the Needle, back in Vallia. She felt him all over and pronounced nothing irremediably broken, and gave him the draft to drink. He lost his pain the moment the last needle had been inserted, so powerfully beneficent is the art and science of acupuncture upon Kregen. Presently he slept and Mog crept back to her place, pronouncing him as well as could be expected, that she had done all she could, and now it all lay in the merciful hands of Migshaanu the Great Healer.

A gram of Earthly comfort I took was that Turko had not bled from his nose or mouth or ears.

He had tried to save me, charging Chimche, who must be of a higher kham and thus almost certain to defeat Turko. He had sustained these injuries trying to help me. I could do nothing less than use every effort I could to save his life.

From the time when I had flown over the jungle escaping with Tulema and Dorval Aymlo and the others, I could only estimate the distances to be traversed to the coast. Once there I had no doubt we would steal a boat well enough. Had Turko not been injured we might have made it, and he realized this and said nothing, and looked at me speculatively.

We were, in truth, a sorry-looking bunch. When we creaked our way down out of our tree in the morning, and shivered, and stretched, and looked about on the dim vastness of the jungle, pressing us in to a narrow circle of hostile greenery all about, I realized we could not go on. The two girls' feet were lacerated and torn despite the muffling clumsy rags they wore. Some of the halflings were in a worse case, although many were holding up reasonably well; but with that stupid prickly pride, I had, without any conscious volition on my part, decided we would all get out together. By this time I was heartily sick of the jungle. I know we spent a weary time in the green fastness, and I contrasted it with others of my marches upon the hostile, terrifying, beautiful face of Kregen, but it was a chore laid on me and it was something I had to do.

I said, with that harsh intolerant rasp in my voice, "Stay here. I will return."

Most of them simply sank down, thankful not to have once more to plunge into that steaming hell. I left them and walked carefully along what was left of the trail. All about me, almost unheard, rustled the vicious life of the forest. Soon I came to a clearing — not large — but I fancied it would do. To bring everyone there and safely sheltered up trees, with palisades, took a frightening long time. But, at last, we were ready.

Turko opened his eyes and stared at me and I could have sworn amusement curved his pallid lips as I spoke to cheer him.

"Now, friend Turko! Let the manhounds come! We'll make 'em sorry they sniffed us out!"

"Yes, Dray Prescot. I really think you will."

Sixteen

The fight for the voller

Almost immediately half a dozen fluttrells bearing armed warriors passed in a skein over the clearing. I remained still. I hungered for a voller.

As the morning wore on and Far and Havil crawled across the sky and the temperature rose and we sweated and steamed, more fluttrells pirouetted above us until I began to think we would have to decoy them down, enough for all fourteen of us, for we had lost three and gained one. In the end I saw what must be the truth of the matter and cursed; but having deliberately walked all this way through jungle in order to decoy a suitably proud hunting party, the loss of a few more burs hardly counted. When the next skein of fluttrells was sighted I stepped out into the clearing and waved.

"Have a care, Dray Prescot," called Turko. "Remember, they will have real steel weapons, also."

His light voice sounded stronger, which cheered me, and I did not miss that underlying mockery. Truly, he counted me a nul, never a true khamster, and this was inevitable and right.

The fluttrells slanted down. There were five of them, and they looked bright and brave against the glow of the suns.

This was just another of those occasions on Kregen when I faced odds. I hoped the fluttrells would wing away after an inspection to report to the manhunters that they had discovered our whereabouts. The mighty hunters on the great Jikai were almost certainly sitting with their feet up, sipping the best wines of Havilfar — or possibly, if they could afford it, a fine Jholaix — and waiting until a sighting report had been brought back by their aerial scouts.

My hope was vain.

The first four fluttrells continued their descent; the fifth winged up in a flash of velvety green over the beige-white, his streamlined head-vane turning. He disappeared over the jungle roof before his comrades alighted. The men astride the fluttrells, although new to me then, were of a type, if not a nation, with which I was perfectly familiar. I had seen their like strutting the boulevards and enclaves of Zenicce, lording it over the slaves in the warrens of Magdag, supervising the

Emperor's haulers along the canals of Vallia. Hard, tough, professional, man-managers and slave-masters they were, like the aragorn I had bested in Valka. They jumped down with cheerful cries, one to another. They unstrapped their clerketers, and their weapons clicked up into position, the crossbows spanned, the moment their feet hit the tangled ground of the clearing.

They wore flying leathers, and braided cloaks cunningly fashioned from the velvet-green feathers of the fluttrells themselves. Their feathered flying caps fitted closely to their mahogany-brown faces, and streamed a clotted and flaring mass of multicolored ribbons, very brave to see in the slipstream of their passage across the sky. They advanced without any caution whatsoever.

My bow felt the ill-made thing it was in my fist. I could have no hesitation here. The Star Lords' commands impelled me.

The first arrow took the first flyer in the throat. The second arrow, a fraction too late, struck the second flyer in the face as he ducked to the side. I had read his ducking and his direction but the clumsy arrow loosed not as accurately as a clothyard shaft fletched with the brilliant blue feathers of the king korf of Erthyrdrin would have done. By the time the third arrow was on its way crossbow bolts were thunking about me.

They had difficulty seeing me against the gloom of the jungle and the third arrow pitched into the third flyer's throat above the leather flying tunic. The fourth flyer looked dazedly at his companions, at what must have seemed to him to be a deadly wall of jungle sprouting arrows — and he turned and ran for his fluttrell.

Much as I dislike shooting men in the back this was a thing very necessary to be done.

When it was all over Mog crackled out: "A great Jikai, Dray Prescot! You shoot well from ambush. Hai, Jikai!"

Which displeased me most savagely, so that I cursed the old witch in the name of the putrescent right eyeball of Makki-Grodno.

"They are flutsmen, Dray Prescot," Rapechak called. He walked across, carefully cut out the arrow from the nearest body, turned it over with his foot, and bending lithely, took up the man's thraxter. "I have served with them, in the long ago. They are good soldiers, although avaricious and without mercy. Because they ride their fluttrells through the windy wastes of the sky they consider themselves far better than the ordinary footman. They are disliked. But they earn their pay." He waved the thraxter about a little, and I saw the feelings strong upon him as he once more grasped a weapon in his Rapa fist.

The flutsmen, so I gathered, were not in any sense a race or a nation. Rather, they recruited from strong, fierce, vicious young men of similar natures to themselves, forming a kind of freemasonry of the skies, owing allegiance to no one unless paid and paid well. True mercenaries, they were, giving their first thought to their own band, then to the flutsmen, and, after that, to their current paymaster. Men from all over Havilfar, aye, and from over the seas, served in their winged ranks.

Gynor the Brokelsh approached. He looked determined. "There are four fluttrells, Dray Prescot. Will you four apims take them and fly away and leave us halflings?"

Apim, as you know, is the slang and somewhat contemptuous term used by halflings for ordinary human beings — for, of course, to any halfling *he* is ordinary and the apims are strange.

"You have put an idea into my head, Gynor, for, by Vox, I hadn't thought of it." He eyed me again. "You may speak truth. You are a strange man, Dray Prescot. If not that, then, what?"

"We must capture a voller—" I began, but with a rush of long naked legs and a hysterical series of screams, the two girls were upon me, panting, breathing in gulps, their hair all over their faces — very distracting and pretty, no doubt, but quite out of place in the serious work to hand.

"You must take us, Dray!" they both wailed. "Fly with us to safety in Havilfar!"

I pushed them aside, and they clung to me, sobbing, pleading to be taken away instantly from this horrible jungle.

"I want to get out of this Opaz-forsaken jungle more than you do!" I blared at them, outraged. "Now for the sweet sake of Blessed Mother Zinzu — shut up!"

They had no idea who Mother Zinzu the Blessed was — of course, the patron saint of the drinking classes of Sanurkazz — but everyone swore by their own gods, and so everyone was used to outlandish names in the way of oaths. They recoiled from my face.

"Look!" I said, pointing to a couple of Lamnias and the Fristle couple, all of whom were far gone. I marched over. "You, Doriclish," I said to the Lamnia, who was making an effort to smooth his laypom-yellow fur down. "Can you ride a fluttrell?"

"I have not done so since my youth, when the sport was a passion—"

"Then you can. And you? And you?" to the others.

It turned out that when it came to it, most everyone in Havilfar was quite at home in the air, whether aboard a voller or astride a fluttrell or other flying saddle bird or animal, and so I could shovel out another load of responsibility. "Very well. You may take the four fluttrells and make a flight for it."

If I had expected argument from the other halflings, I did not receive it. Only Saenda and Quaesa reacted, and they had to be told, pretty sharply, to behave themselves.

"Your feet are well enough," I said. "And there will be a voller before long."

"I shan't forget this, Dray Prescot!" shouted Saenda.

"You'll be sorry, Dray Prescot!" screeched Quaesa.

I saw the four halflings safely strapped into their clerketers, the straps buckled up tightly, and then with a final word of caution, sent the four great birds into the air. They flew over the jungle, going strongly, until they were out of sight. I thought they had a very good chance, for no other fluttrell patrols came by until, sometime later, the voller arrived. No doubt the mighty hunters had stopped for a final drink before setting off.

Between us we now disposed of four crossbows and five thraxters. I was disappointed there were no aerial spears, like the toonons used by the Ullars, but Rapechak snorted and said the flutsmen were kitted out for light patrol, not for battle. Then, he said, they were flying armories. Some people have talked and even written of aerial combat with shortswords from the backs of flying birds; it is doubtful if they have ever tried it. But, as is the way of Kregen no less than that of Earth, there are to be found people who believe nonsense of this sort. I looked at the crossbows. They were beautifully made instruments of death. Not as shiny or as flamboyant as the hunters' bows, they were weapons of professionals. I felt very satisfied with them. I changed the guard's thraxter for one of the flutsmen's swords; the one I chose was nicely balanced, firm in the grip, with a blade very reminiscent of the cutlass blade of my youth, although not quite as broad and strengthened with a single groove. The grip, of red-dyed fish-skin, and the guard, reasonably elaborate, of a kind of open half-basket pattern, pleased me well enough. Oh, the sword was no great Krozair longsword or that superb Savanti weapon, but I would use it to good purpose in the service of the Star Lords, for my sins.

The flutsmen employed a novel form of goat's-foot lever to span their crossbows, and although I knew it was perfectly possible to span an arbalest with cranequin or windlass when flying by use of adapted equipment and if one was skilled, I appreciated this goat's-foot lever of the flutsmen.

Gynor said he could handle a crossbow. Rapechak, of course, was an old mercenary. Two other halflings came forward saying they wished for nothing better than to sink a bolt into the guts of the manhunters. So we waited, rather like leems, I confess, as the voller came in.

Instead of an eager hunting party of untrained and amateurish nobles jumping down from the voller to slaughter, there leaped with vicious howls four couples of manhounds.

The change in our fortunes rattled in so subtly, so quickly, so disastrously.

"Do not miss, my friends!" I called in a voice I made firm, driving, intolerant. I do not think that was necessary, now, looking back, but *then* I felt the precipice edge of disaster at my feet.

The jiklos picked up our scent at once and with fearsome howls bounded toward us. They looked their hideous selves. If any nobility exists in beasts, as I believe it does, then these men-beasts had lost all. Jagged teeth glinting in the suns-light streaming into the clearing, leaping fallen trees and tangled undergrowth, blood-crazy, they bounded for us.

Four crossbow bolts sped true, driven by brains and eyes trained in hatred and loathing. My bow loosed, and loosed again. That was six down and the seventh took a shaft along his flank and was on me.

My thraxter rasped as it drew from the scabbard and I went over backward with the manhound all bloody and messy upon me, screeching, his teeth clicking together in rage and pain, seeking my throat. The sword was deeply buried in him somewhere low, and my left hand gripped his neck and forced those clashing jaws away. Blood and spittle fouled me. His mad blood-crazed eyes glared on me, and his thin lips worked, his tongue lolled out, and then to my infinite relief the light of intelligence faded in those crazed eyes and he slumped. I stood up carefully, throwing the carcass away so that my right hand could drag the thraxter free.

Men were yelling over by the voller.

Gynor and Rapechak and the other two halflings with swords left off plunging their blades into the mangled body of the eighth manhound. This one had been a female, and, sickened, I turned away to stare with hatred at the hunters.

They had heard the shrieks and the muffled howlings, and, too, they had seen some of their manhounds fall, stricken in mid-leap.

"Span your bows!" I spoke as I used to speak in the smoke and thunder of the broadsides, when the old wooden walls drifted down to bloody battle, and I must see my battery of thirty-two-pounders kept on firing until only myself, perhaps, was left to sponge, load, ram, and pull the lock string.

The people from the voller were uncertain. One called in a loud, hectoring voice: "Gumchee! Tulishi!" That would be the female manhound, I guessed. "Colicoli! Hapang!" They could call until the Ice Floes of Sicce went up in steam but they'd get no answer from those four couples of manhounds.

Rapechak said, "We are ready, Dray Prescot. May your Opaz go with you."

Turko shouted. He spoke loudly, angry, raging, shoving up from his bed of leaves. His face lost its look of pain and took on the semblance of superior anger more habitual to it.

"And is no one of you stinking half-men going with Dray?"

Of the nine halflings who had started with the party, only five were left now, and four were ready to do damage with the crossbows. The last, a little Xaffer, would be of no help in a fight.

Mog started to cackle something and the two girls were sobbing, clutching each other. I shouted back: "I will have to go alone. Now, *cover me!*"

Even then Turko tried to get up, to stand and to rush out with me, but his legs buckled and gave way and he fell. Then I waited for no more but started a mad dash for the voller.

I say mad dash, for I was mad, clean through, and I dashed, for the mighty hunters of the great Jikai had their crossbows ready.

I lived only because they were such lousy shots.

The only one from whom I expected real danger would be their guide, a man similar to the one I had snatched from his zorca on the plain with the Pallan Golan. Rapechak knew this, also. By the time I reached the voller three of the hunters lay with bolts skewering them. I had dodged and weaved in the last few yards. Up there and peering over the voller's side the guide looked down. His face showed contempt and rage and only a tinge of fear — and I fancied that was for his dead clients. He lifted himself to get a good shot at me — and the last crossbow quarrel, loosed by Rapechak the Rapa, penetrated his face and knocked him back.

The hunters drew their thraxters to face me. There were five of them and I must draw a veil, as they say, over what followed. I did not kill them all. Three of them were unarmed and then my halflings had reached me, and before there was anything further I could do, there were no hunters left alive. Truth to tell, apart from not really being able to blame the fugitives for their ready justice, I could only have left the hunters there in the jungle. That would have been a more prolonged end, if they were not picked up in time.

This time I said to Rapechak: "Keep an eye on the voller, good Rapechak. We are all comrades, now, in adversity, and this flier is our means of escape."

He took my meaning clearly enough.

Before I went back for Turko and Mog I respanned the bow, the most handsome of them all, I took from the dead hunter who lay so messily among the rotting detritus of the clearing.

With Mog, Turko, the two girls, and the Xaffer I returned to the airboat. We went some time stripping the dead and cleaning their clothes and putting them on. I could not find a tunic to fit and so had to content myself with fashioning a breechclout out of the only scarlet length of material there, and of slinging a short scarlet cape over my left shoulder. Then we all climbed in and, with a feeling of some relief, I sent the voller up into the clean blue sky of Kregen, where the twin Suns of Scorpio blazed down with a light so much more genial than before.

Seventeen

Of Havilfar, volleem — and stuxes

"You are a get-onker, Dray Prescot! You're a fool, you nulsh! I wouldn't go back to Yaman for all the ivory in Chem!"

So spoke Mog, the Migla witch, as we flew out over the sea from the manhunters' island of Faol.

This voller was a larger and more handsome craft than that in which I had escaped before, and in the comfortable cabin aft Turko could lie on a settee and drink the wine we found aboard and make sarcastic remarks about Mog. The girls had recovered, and chattered about what stories they would tell at all the marvelous parties to which they would be invited on the strength of their marvelous adventures.

When they heard Mog shriek at me that she would never set foot in her city of Yaman again, the girls looked up.

"We are agreed, Dray Prescot," said Saenda, somewhat sharply. "Quaesa and I are going to Dap-Tentyrasmot, my own city, where she will be received with all ceremony. Then the halflings may return to their homes, if they wish."

The effrontery of the girl was amazing only because she had recovered so rapidly from being slave; and was sad because these halflings were her comrades of captivity.

I said, "We go to Mog's city, Saenda."

Quaesa said, with a fluting sideways glance from her dark eyes, "If you wish, Dray Prescot, we shall fly to my homeland of Methydria, the land of Havil-Faril, where my father owns many kools of rich grazing and where you will be most welcome."

By Havil-Faril she meant beloved of Havil, that is, beloved of the green sun.

That was not, in those days, calculated to make me, a Krozair of Zy, amenable to her suggestion.

"Yaman," I said. "Let there be no more argument."

Of course, I was being selfish. I recognized that. I could have taken all these people home and then gone to Yaman. But I was tired of Mog the witch, and I wanted to get to my home, which was in Valka, or Vallia, depending on where Delia might be, and the quickest way to do that was to dump Mog where the Everoinye wished her. We could drop off a number of the halflings on our way, as we had planned to do before. Turko said, flatly, that he could not return to Herrelldrin. I did not press him. This might be because he had broken some of his syple vows with the slaves, or he might be a wanted man there. A more likely explanation, however, lay in the argument I had had when I had pointed out that a people learned unarmed combat when they were subject to another, and could not afford or were not allowed real weapons. Tulema had not wished to return home, either. I would find out soon enough; now I had to find out what the hell was up with Mog.

"My people have been enslaved, you nulsh," she said.

I spoke quietly. "I do not believe I am a nulsh, Mog. I do not call you rast or cramph — or not very often. I own I am an onker — a get-onker, as you will. But watch your tongue or I'll see what your Migshaanu the Odoriferous can do about it."

Turko laughed. He was much better, and that was a relief.

Mog took a deep breath. She still wore her stinking slave breechclout hanging down, and she smelled. I promised myself to give her a damned good wash at the first opportunity. Now she explained, remarkably lucidly, all things considered, and with a refreshing absence of insults, just what was wrong with her city of Yaman in the land of Migla.

Her story interested me only to the extent that I was always eager to learn about Kregen, my adopted planet. There was much I knew already, but I have not as yet related it for it does not fit in with my narrative. I hope I am managing to keep unentangled all the various skeins of fate and destiny that both manipulated me and which I, in my own way, attempted to manipulate, to the confounding of the Star Lords.

The Miglas had been a quiet, contemplative, peaceful race, much given to religion. Mog said she was the high priestess of the Miglish religion, using many strange expressions I will tell you of when necessary. But they had been overthrown and subjugated by a fierce and warlike race who invaded from the island of Canopdrin in the Shrouded Sea in Havilfar where terrifying earthquakes had destroyed cities and flooded fertile valleys and laid the land waste.

"They were few, the bloody Canops, but they were clever. They destroyed my religion. They took me and chained me and defamed me before the eyes of my people. They slaughtered all the royal family. But it was our religion, our love of Migshaanu the All-Glorious through which they enslaved us." She looked shrunken and miserable, and my feelings toward Mog the witch were forced to undergo a change. "My people believed their lies. They worshiped their false images. They made sacrifices, where we of Migla have not sacrificed for a thousand seasons — more! They made of Migshaanu a mockery. And if I return, Dray Prescot, they will surely slay me before all the people of Yaman."

So, I said to myself, what of the Star Lords' orders now?

"Not sacrifice, Mog?" I said. "But you are continually threatening me with what this Migshaanu will do to me."

She stared up, her bright agate eyes hard on me, her witch's face slobbered with tears, her hooked nose running. She looked a horrible object, but she also looked pathetic, and I suppose, for the first time, I really thought of Mog the witch as a person.

"Migshaanu the All-Glorious is peaceful and calm and gentle, and her love shines upon all, twin rays from the suns, in glory and beauty! It is the foul nulshes of Canops who do the things I threaten! I merely put them in my mouth as from my Migshaanu the Ever-Virtuous to — to—"

She had no need to go on.

"I have heard that no religion can be crushed utterly. There will be people who would welcome you back, the high priestess?"

"Yes. There are a few. Scattered, weak, feeble, hiding their adherence to the true beliefs under a mask, bowing to the bloody Canops in the full incline with despair in their hearts."

"Well, it is settled. I will take you to your friends."

All the fight seemed to have been knocked out of her. She just squatted down in the aft cabin, and presently she started rocking back and forth and crooning. Saenda shouted at her crossly to keep quiet, but the old crone hardly heard and went on rocking and crooning. I heard her say, between a clear change of musical pattern in the crooning dirge: "Oh, Mag, Mag! Where are you now?" And then she went on with her crooning and her rocking, and Saenda cursed her and came up to sit by me at the controls.

The girl started in at once, chatting gaily about how wonderful it was that we were free, and flying to Havilfar, and she tried her arts and wiles, but I took little notice. Old Mog worried me. I'd said that, by Zim-Zair, I'd rescue her and take her back, and that was what I was doing. She hadn't wanted to come. I'd put that down to fear, and, as was afterward proved, her suspicions of the treacherous guides. But the truth lay deeper. As a high priestess she had been defamed and sold into slavery, for she had said that the Canops, with all their vicious pride, had quailed from having her killed. Now, if she returned, they would not hesitate to do what they should have done in the first place.

The impression grew on me as we flew over the first scatterings of tiny islets fringing this part of the coast of Havilfar that this Mog the high priestess of the Miglas had many more surprises in store for me. Certainly the little Xaffer, when he discovered just who Mog was, reacted in a way that left me in no doubt that the powers of the priesthood of Migla had reached his ears.

Calling Rapechak, I asked him if he would care to fly the voller for a space. I phrased it like that, carefully, and in the doing of that apparently simple thing surprised myself. I realized I had been relying on Rapechak rather too much as a loyal lieutenant; he was a Rapa, fierce, predatory, one of a race of beast-men who had given me much grief in my time. He twisted his beaked face in that grimacing way Rapas have and said, "I recall when we flew down on Harop Mending's castle, Dray Prescot. I flew a voller then that had been half shot away by a varter and with a shaft through my shoulder."

"You are still a mighty warrior, Rapechak, for all that you were a slave with the manhunters. You were on the losing side in a battle, I take it?"

"Surely. It is over and done with, now. I think I might venture to look at my home, a Rapa island to the south and west of Havilfar. I have not seen it for nigh on sixty years."

If I noticed then that he did not give me the name of his home I made no comment. His business would be Rapa business and I wasn't interested in halflings — with the exception of Gloag, always, of course. We flew on with Rapechak at the controls and I went aft to talk seriously to the Khamorro, Turko.

I found him being fed a potion by Mog, mixed with wine. She had given over her crooning, and she glanced up at me the moment I ducked my head to enter the cabin, her old hooked nose and chin fairly snapping at me, like a crab's claws.

"I've decided to go to Yaman, to find my friends, and to keep out of trouble, Dray Prescot. By Migshaanu, if you insist on taking me home, I'll go, although I won't thank you."

I brightened. This was more like the Mog I knew.

"Very good, Mog. That is settled." She rose and left Turko, with a final quick wipe of a clean cloth to his lips, in a gesture that, I realized, moved me. Turko leaned back on the settee, his overly handsome face eased of pain, staring at me with rather too much mocking knowing in his eyes. "Now, Turko, we must decide what to do with you."

"What would amuse me, Dray Prescot, is to take you to Herrelldrin and there see how you fared against a Khamorro or two — without edged weapons in your hand."

Oho! I thought to myself. So that is what itches the good Turko. He might get his wish yet, if the Star Lords willed it, but I doubted it, although, of course, not being in any way privy to their devious schemes.

"Perhaps we may meet a khamster or two—" I began. He pushed up, frowning, and yet relaxing, as it were, all in a movement. I knew what had goaded him. Khamster was the name used by Khamorros of themselves between themselves. I started over, amazed at my softness. "Perhaps you Khamorros travel Havilfar. We might yet amuse you."

"As to that, we are not allowed — that is, yes, we do travel, as guards and servants. I was indentured to the King of Sava. The caravan was attacked and with a crossbow bolt aimed at my guts I was taken to Faol. Iron chains may not easily be broken, even with syple disciplines."

"I know," I said, remembering.

The shape of Havilfar is interesting, looking something like a rounded rectangle that has been badly bitten and hacked about. Gouging into the southeastern corner is the Gulf of Wracks, which leads to the great inland sea called the

Shrouded Sea. To the northeast of this sea lie many kingdoms and princedoms and Kovnates. To the west lie wilder lands, although the coastline contains many ancient kingdoms, for philosophers say that it was here, along the coasts surrounding the Shrouded Sea, that men first settled Havilfar. The whole northeastern corner of the continent consists of the puissant land of Hamal. Hyrklana, a large island, although not counted as one of the nine islands of Kregen, juts wedgelike from the eastern central coast in temperate and pleasant climate. Far to the west and just below a great beak-nosed promontory that extends southward of Loh lies Herrelldrin, with Pellow tucked into a great bay.

"If not Herrelldrin, Turko, then where?"

"You fly to Mog's Migla, do you not? That will do."

He amazed me.

Migla, situated at the western point of the Shrouded Sea, consisted of three large promontories running out northeastward and a tract of country inland. The Shrouded Sea is thus named for volcanic activity, which must be fairly frequent, as much as for the mystery it posed to the first inhabitants of Havilfar.

I ought to mention that the northern coastline of Havilfar extends upward past the latitude of southern Loh, almost reaching the equator. Ordsmot and the Orange River lie north of Ng'groga in Loh. And Loh, as you know, has the shape of a Paleolithic hand-ax, with the point northward — and that point is Erthyrdrin.

"Then we shall go to Migla by the Shrouded Sea and I will leave you with Mog and her friends."

"If Morro the Muscle so wills, Dray Prescot."

He had shouted so passionately at the halflings when I had been about to attack the voller, and then he had called me Dray.

The two girls called me Dray all the time, of course, and I wondered when I'd shout at them to address me as Horter Prescot. My name is Prescot. I try to allow friends only to call me Dray, although friendship is a rare and precious thing to me. Maybe that is part of the reason. To digress; there was once a man — an apim — called Rester who familiarly called me Dray while insulting me and what I was doing in his sneering insufferable way, and when he staggered up with a smashed nose crying and vomiting, I could find little pity in me, for he had considered himself so superior and knowing and all the time he had been acting, as I well knew from other sources, out of spite, cliquishness, and a petty denial of human dignity to a fellow human.

When he had been carried off I broke into laughter. I, Dray Prescot, laughed. But I was not laughing at the pitiful rast Rester. I was laughing at myself, at my folly, at my arrogant puffed-up and foolish pride.

We flew due south after a space to avoid Faol, and the voller sped through the air levels with her firm steady movement so unlike the pitching and rolling of a ship at sea. Turko explained what had itched the redheaded youth who called himself Nath of Thothangir when we flew inland on that previous flight. Somewhere among the forests of central northwest Havilfar lay a region over which vollers would not fly for fear of what — they knew not. But it was an area to be avoided. We drove on southerly down the coast, and we would swing southeast when we were opposite Ng'groga, although Turko identified the place by reference to Havilfar, and so strike across the narrow neck of the continent here to reach Migla.

To the west of Hamal and extending north and south ran a range of mountains that, so I gathered, might rival The Stratemsk. There was much to learn of Havilfar, the fourth and last continent of this grouping on Kregen.

We had a long distance to travel and, accustomed as I was to employing the free winds to blow my vessels along, or the oar when occasion was right, I could afford to think with some scorn of the clumsy steamships appearing on Earth's oceans and their dependence on limited supplies of coal. The vollers, by reason of that mechanism of the two silver boxes, needed no refueling and would fly as long as was necessary. For food and wine we would have to descend sometime, and I counted us fortunate that the mighty hunters after their fashion had a goodly quantity of golden deldys among their clothing. These coins were of various mintings, from a variety of Havilfarese countries, but as a rule the golden unit of coinage in Havilfar is the deldy.

Gold and silver, with bronze also, seem always to be the noble metals for coinage; men and halflings alike hewed to the style. I have come across other systems of monetary exchange on Kregen and these all will be told in their time.

There occurred one fright that made us realize we were not on some holiday jaunt with picnic baskets and thoughts of pleasure.

Emerging from a low-lying cloud bank the voller soared on into the sunshine and I saw a cloud of what at first I took to be birds winging up from a broad-leaved and brilliant forest below. By this time Turko was able to walk about without discomfort, although still fragile, and it was he who shouted the alarm.

"Volleem! Volleem!"

He needed to say no more. Shrieks arose from the girls and curses from the men. The leems, those feral beasts of Kregen, eight-legged, furred, feline, and vicious, with wedge-shaped heads armed with fangs that can strike through lenk, are to be found all over the planet in a variety of forms and all suitably camouflaged. There are sea-leem, snow-leem, marsh-leem, desert, and mountain-leem. These specimens were volleem.

They flew on wide membranous wings extending from their second and third pairs of legs, very conveniently, and like the flying foxes they could really fly. Their colors were not the velvety green I might have expected, seeing that their camouflage might seek to ape the fluttrell; they were all a startling crimson as to back, toning to a brick-red underbelly. The wings shone in the light, the elongated fingerlike claws black webs against the gleam.

"Inside the cabin!" yelled Turko, and bundling the old Xaffer before him, he pushed us into safety.

Turko might know these parts and be aware of the vicious nature of the volleem, but skulking in a cabin was not my style. I know I am headstrong and foolish, but also I feared lest the volleem damage the airboat.

"Their fangs will rip us to pieces," I said.

"We are on a rising course," said Turko. "They will not follow us far from their forest treetops."

He was proved right.

Even then, as I looked at this superbly muscled Khamorro, I wondered why I had listened to him instead of doing what I had felt right, of rushing out, sword in hand, to battle the volleem. One reason for his action was clear: unarmed combat against a leem usually results in a verdict of suicide.

Because of this the Xaffer and the other two halflings decided they would get off at the next stop. I had to quell my reaction, thinking that, once again, I was doing nothing more than running a coach or an omnibus line. Gynor the Brokelsh said he would alight, also, so we divided up the remaining deldys fairly, not without some rancorous comment from Saenda and Quaesa, and we bid Remberee to our departing comrades.

Rapechak looked thoughtful when the voller swung to the southeast, over the land toward the Shrouded Sea.

"My home is down there, Dray Prescot, not over far from Turko's Herrell. It is cold, but I think of it often."

"I will be pleased to visit, Rapechak," I said. "After Mog is unhung from around our necks."

"Perhaps." He said that the southernmost part of the continent was called Thothangir. I thought of the redheaded Nath, and was more than ever sure that he had never come from Thothangir.

So we sped on southeastward across the neck of Havilfar and after a lapse of time, for the voller was swift, we saw the clouds rising ahead and then the intermittent gleam of water. The temperate regions were very welcome after the heat and sweat of Faol. Mog roused herself and gave her instructions. I was reminded of that arrival with Tulema at Dorval Aymlo's home. Well, this time we would land among friends.

"You must go in at the darkest portion of the night, you great onker. The bloody Canops have patrols and soldiers and guards and mercenaries and spies everywhere."

"We will do that, Mog, and we will keep a watch."

Yaman was situated a little inland up from the broad sluggish river that ran down to the second of the large bays separating the three promontories. We waited until Far and Havil had sunk and only She of the Veils rode the sky, for this night she would be joined later by the Maiden with the Many Smiles and by the Twins and then it would be almost as light as a misty day in the Northern parts of Earth, although the shifting pinkish radiance from the moons always created that eerie hushed feeling of mystery inseparable from shadowed moonlight.

Mog insisted we hide the voller in a grove of trees on the outskirts. She said the trees were sacred to Sidraarga. Then, hitching our clothing and weapons about us, we set off for the home of one Planath the Wine, who owned a tavern that one might take a newly wedded bride to, as Mog put it with a cackle. Coming home had brightened and invigorated her. If we ran across a Canop patrol I felt she would not be the one to run screaming in fear.

Once again I trod the streets of a strange city in a continent of Kregen new to me. The houses reared to either hand, strange shapes against the starshot darkness, with She of the Veils riding low in the clouds, and very few lighted windows there were to see, and only a few hurrying pedestrians who avoided us with as much fervor as we avoided them. An air of mystery, of an eerie horror no one would mention aloud, hung over the city of Yaman.

As we hurried along in so strange a fashion I could feel the excitement rising and rising in me. Only a few short steps to go and then Mog the Migla witch would be in the hands of her friends, and I would be free! By this time I felt convinced Mog must be the one whom the Star Lords had sent me to Faol to rescue. I had felt this about Tulema, and been proved a fool. That could not happen again, by Vox, no!

But, all the time, I kept expecting at any moment to see that hated blue radiance and the enormous insubstantial shape of a scorpion dropping upon me from the pink-lit shadows.

The cobbled streets of Yaman passed by, and the darkened fronts of houses and shops, the ghostly emptiness of squares and plazas. I saw the moon-sheen upon the sluggish waters of the River Magan and the black blots of islands riding like stranded whales, the fretting of river boats against stone quays and wharves. In my ears the night sounds of a city ghosted in thinly. We pressed on and Mog led us down past the narrow entrances to alleyways, past wide flights of steps leading to the quays, down and through even narrower alleyways, and across slimed steps where, below, barges sucked in the mud.

At last we reached the tavern of Planath the Wine.

This was, I thought, a strange place to find a remnant of an outlawed and proscribed religion.

A gnarled tree hung over the crazy roof of the tavern. All the windows leered at us, dark ovals pallidly reflecting a pink sheen of moonlight. Around to the rear padded Mog, with many a cunning glance about, and so she rapped upon the door, a complicated series of rhythms, like a drum-dance.

The door was snatched open and a hoarse breathy voice whispered: "Get in! Get in, in the name of Migshaanu the Virtuous, before we are all taken!"

In we all bundled, with Mog cursing away at barking her skinny shins against the jamb, and so came into a dark, breathing space where I knew people stood about waiting for the door to close so they might turn up the lamp.

And now, to give you who listen to this tape an understanding of what then happened, there in the back room of *The Loyal Canoptic* as a concealed taper re-lit the samphron-oil lamp, it is necessary to tell you a number of things all at the same time.

The first thing I noticed, something I had been wondering about ever since my interest in Mog had been so brutally forced on me, was the physical appearance of these halfling Miglas.

They were not apim.

The people gathered here, about a score, sitting on benches along the walls so that the central floor area of polished lenk remained clear, all possessed two arms and two legs, and one head with features. But those features could never be mistaken for human features — always bearing in mind what I have said about that prickly word, "human." The old women looked a little like Mog, although nowhere so bent or vicious or cunning. The old men looked like nothing so much as those thick-legged, thick-armed, stumpy-bodied, and idiot-headed plastic toys the children on Earth nowadays play with. Gnomes, if you like, thick-heads, bodies as squat as boilers, dummies, grinners, with ears that swung like batwing doors, they all stared at Mog with looks of reverence and shock and holy awe — and vast surprise.

The younger men and girls, although far more prepossessing in the manner of bodily proportions, all wore that idiot grin, that flap-eared dog-hanging look of bumbling good humor that masks a cranial cavity filled with vacuum.

They all wore ankle-length smocks with scooped-out necks and no sleeves. The color was a uniform rusty crimson, as though the dye used, probably from a local berry or earth, had not taken properly in the coarsely weaved stuff. Their hair was dark and vivid and cropped, even the girls'. I stood behind Saenda and Quaesa as the lamp flared up and Mog stepped forward. Turko moved at my side, and Rapechak moved out from the other side.

Insane shrieks burst from the Miglas. The women clawed the children to them, the girls flying to crowd around the old folk at the far end of the room. The noise burst inside my head with the unexpected force of a magazine explosion. The Migla men rummaged frantically behind the benches.

They swung around to face us, pushing past Mog, who yelled at them.

"Do you not know who I am? I am Mog, your high priestess!" She used a number of those special words and phrases that meant a great deal in the religion.

The men — eight of them — stood resolutely before us, their womenfolk and children screaming behind them.

The eight looked highly comical, their flap-eared faces slobbering with fury and fear. They held the spears they had snatched up from behind the benches in grips that — I guessed Rapechak would have seen and Turko never failed to miss — were amateur in the extreme.

"Do you not hear, migladorn? These are my friends. They are the friends of the high priestess of Migshaanu!"

The heftiest man, with a fuzz of side-whiskers, spat out: "You are the Mighty Mog! But these cannot be your friends! They have tricked you! Two are apim warriors, one is a Rapa warrior, and two are shishis! They must all die!"

From the lighting of the lamp to the utterance of that word — "die!" — scarce a handful of heartbeats had passed.

The eight spear points leveled. Then, with sudden and astonishing speed, a ferociously lethal and completely unexpected reaction, the front three Migla men hurled their spears.

And — there was nothing amateurish about that spear throwing. With terrifying accuracy the deadly shafts flew toward us.

107

Eighteen

Saenda and Quaesa exert themselves

Three spears flashed toward us.

We were: one, a Rapa mercenary; two, a Khamorro; and, three, an Earthman who had made Kregen his home.

We reacted in three different ways.

With a fluid litheness of movement so fast no untrained eye could follow him, Turko slid the spear and it thunked solidly into the lenken door.

With the least amount of physical effort, Rapechak let his body lean to the side, and as a precaution, thrust up his forearm, so that the spear hissed past, to thunk into the door alongside the other.

I, Dray Prescot, had to show off — and yet, in truth, my way had been proved in the past and was to prove in the future by far the superior — and I had not needed the Krozairs of Zy to teach me this. I took the spear out of the air, my hand closing around the shaft with that familiar solid-soft chunking of wood against flesh, and so I reversed it and hefted it and said, "I will let you have your spear back, if you wish."

Over the women's screaming Mog lifted her voice and, there in that bedlam in the back room of *The Loyal Canoptic,* I heard for the first time the high priestess.

"Put down your spears! I am Mog the Mighty, high priestess of Migshaanu! Put down your stuxes or risk my certain wrath! These apim and this Rapa have aided me and brought me here."

Then old Mog the witch glared at me as she ducked her head as the spears went down. And I knew! Oh, I knew! She was saying to me: "Well, Dray Prescot. You brought me here, why I know not, so now what to do, hey, onker?" And, also: "And you put your spear down, too, idiot, or they'll cast for sure and spit you like a paly!"

I lowered the spear.

A moment of natural tension was heightened as both Rapechak and Turko turned and jerked the spears from the lenk. Even then, I had time to say, just so that they could hear: "What, friend Turko? A spear?"

To which Turko the Khamorro replied: "I thought you might need another if your first missed."

I chuckled. Oh, yes, that seemed a worthwhile moment to chuckle.

After that, with Mog the witch acting very much as Mog the Mighty — by Makki-Grodno's worm-eaten liver! Old Mog, called Mog the Mighty! Incredible and laughable and hugely enjoyable! — after that, as I say, we all sat down to eat and drink and for Mog to tell her news and to catch up on what had been happening in Yaman in the land of Migla in her absence.

Somehow or other Saenda had seated herself on one side and Quaesa on the other, and they were both holding my arms and snuggling up against me, pouting their lips and trying to claim all my attention, and I couldn't be too hard on them. By Vox! But they'd had a scare!

Even then, Saenda said to Quaesa, "Did you hear what that awful one with the ridiculous side-whiskers said?"

"That's Planath the Wine—"

"He called me a shishi! I'll give it to him when I get a chance. Nobody calls me a shishi and gets away with it."

"Nor me!"

"What will you give him, Saenda?" I hoped I was stirring things up.

"Humph!" she said, with her nose in the air, and so disposed of my question.

I didn't care. Mog was home with her people. These Migla were gathered in secret to celebrate a rite of Migshaanu and so the news of the high priestess' return would that more quickly spread over the city. I had done my work. Now I would go home.

Yes, I had decided. There would be time in the future to find out about the airboats and to question the scarlet-roped Todalpheme on the whereabouts of Aphrasöe. Do not think I had dismissed the importance of either of these projects, but I hungered to see Delia again, and to hold little Drak and little Lela in my arms, and tell Delia of my undying love.

Momentarily, I shuddered at the prospect of that blue radiance dropping about me with the great presentation of a scorpion, but I thought I knew, now, that I had done the Star Lords' bidding. The two girls prattled on, one in each ear. Although only half listening to them, being far more interested in what Mog and Planath were saying of conditions in Migla, I could not fail to become aware that the girls' intentions were becoming far more serious by the mur. Each wished me to take her to her own home, the idea that one should go to the other's as an honored guest having, apparently, been abandoned. They waxed warm.

"My father's totrixes are renowned over all southeast Havilfar."

"My father's merchant house has agencies far beyond southeast Havilfar."

"The Migshaanu-cursed Canops took Mackili, only last week, and impaled him over by the ruins of the temple."

"The ruins are infested by rasts."

"Methydrin is a wonderful country, with riches to spare!"

"In Dap-Tentyra we could be so happy. It is more of a city these days than a smot."

"We starve if we do not work and work is only given to those who worship Lem, the silver leem."

"And, dear Dray, you would not find me unappreciative."

"And, my Dray, I would be kind to you."

"It is death, slow and horrible and certain, to be found on the streets with a weapon."

I leaned forward, to ask a question about the spears, which had been restowed beneath the benches. These spears were ash-shafted, with heads wide yet short, exceedingly sharp, and fairly heavy in the hand so that a cast from them would spit a target with most ferocious thoroughness. So I leaned forward and the soft breathy whispers in my ears sharpened.

"Dray! You're not listening!"

"Dray! You haven't heard a word I've said!"

"On the contrary, appreciation and kindness are fine. But they are not for me. I am not going your way."

Their soft bodies, pressed so suggestively close to me, stiffened, and moved away, and bright color mantled their cheeks. Their competition remained as fervent as ever; for neither would give an inch and almost immediately I felt them approach to engage yet again in this allurement for their own ends.

Standing up, I left them whispering sweet nothings to each other across six inches of empty air, and went across to Planath the Wine. He cocked his eyes up at me, somewhat apprehensively, I thought, so I sat down and did what I could about making my face less the unholy figure-head lump exposed to wind and weather it is.

"Tell me, Horter Planath. These spears of yours. You may not carry them openly on the streets?"

Turko butted in, mockingly. "They would be difficult, by the Muscle, to carry concealed."

I ignored him.

"That is so, Horter Prescot. The casting spear, the stux, is our weapon — for we are a peaceful people and know little of swords and bows — and hitherto we have kept ourselves to ourselves. We hunt the vosk with the stux, for they roam in their millions among the back hills and forests."

"A goodly weapon. And the Canops?"

Mog worked herself up into a denunciation, to which all the Miglas listened with profound attention. When she had finished, Planath the Wine said with grave politeness, "They are fierce and vicious and horrendous. They crushed us with ease. But we would have fought, despite that we would certainly have lost, but for—" Here he paused, in some distress, until Mog jumped up, swinging her arms, and finished for him.

"Aye! But for the degradation of your religion and the profanation of Migshaanu's shrine and the defamation of your high priestess! Aye, they were reasons enough."

They all began talking then, as Mog sat on the floor and drew up a crimson covering they had given her. I thought of the stux, the usual name for the heavy throwing spear of Havilfar and of how they would have fronted these deadly Canops and all hurled, with their deadly aim, and then the arrows would have whistled in and the sword-wielding mercenaries would have cut and thrust them to pieces. Maybe they were better off, now; at least, they lived.

With only a little more conversation, in which the name of Mag was mentioned — I did not pick up the reference and so pushed it away to be dealt with later — the Miglas rose and took their leave. They did not take their spears, however, and these remained secreted in the cavities beneath the benches. Even so, the adherents of Migshaanu took their lives in their hands as they made their way home under the lights of the moons.

We were quartered in a garret room under the crazy roof, and, as we had during the nights of our escape, we all slept more or less together. Mog, alone of us, was conducted elsewhere. Tomorrow, I told myself, before going to sleep, tomorrow I would start for home.

In the night both Quaesa — first, and very prettily — and Saenda — second and most urgently — came to my pallet. I turned them both out, and I did not scruple to kick Saenda's remarkable rear to help her on her way to her own pallet. In the morning neither girl referred to the night's pantomime, but I knew they were storing everything up against me.

Discovering that the busy and highly populated country over on the eastern shores of the Shrouded Sea contained the homes of both girls, I could afford to forget them. That part of Havilfar, extending from the river border of Hamal in the north, the coast opposite Hyrklana in the east, and open ocean in the southeast, to the river running from the southern end of the mountain chain into the top of the Shrouded Sea on the west, had been settled for thousands of years. Kingdoms and princedoms and Kovnates riddled it with boundaries and capitals and petty rivalries. All the girls had to do was hire a passage aboard a voller or a ship and cross the Shrouded Sea and they would be home.

Planath the Wine looked at my scarlet breechclout and my scarlet cape and clicked his teeth. He was not a human being of Homo sapiens stock, but he was a man.

"Crimson is the color of Migshaanu the Blessed. We wear it only on high occasions, for it is proscribed." Truly, this morning he wore a brown smock with wine stains upon it. "I think, Horter Prescot, if you will pardon, that the Canops will resent that brave scarlet."

I pondered. As you know, previously I would have made some uncouth remark, involving a diseased portion of Makki-Grodno's anatomy, and said that, by Zim-Zair, scarlet was the color of Strombor, my color, and the color of Zair. No monkey-faced Canops would tell me to strip it off. But I pondered, as I said, and thought of Delia and the twins, and so changed into a dull and offensive brown sack Planath called a robe.

But I kept the breechclout even as I unstrapped the sword.

Rapechak surprised me — but only for a moment.

"I am a mercenary. I could take service with these Canops. If they paid enough."

"You could, Rapechak." I eyed him.

"I do not think I am old enough to return home. Anyway, it is too cold down there. I have grown used to warmth."

"Very sensible."

"And I have not made my fortune — so far."

"It distresses me to hear it."

Turko stood by, listening, that mocking half-smile on his damned handsome face. Rapechak cocked his beaked head at the Khamorro.

"Turko has nowhere to go." He rubbed that beak of a face of his, that Rapa face of which so many have been beakless and no longer faces when I got through with them. "You have not as yet said where you are going, Dray Prescot."

"That is true. I have not said."

111

There hung a silence in the back room of *The Loyal Canoptic*.

Both girls started in presently claiming that I was taking them home, and may Opaz rot the idea of going anywhere else.

"There are deldys enough to pay your passages," I said. "And you may have all mine, except a handful for food and wine. I am not going your way."

"Well, then! Which way do you go?"

"That is my affair. Come. I will see you to the voller offices — or the shipping agents, if you prefer."

Backward though Migla might be, and relatively poor if compared with many of the nations of Havilfar, nevertheless I knew there would be passenger services operating.

Migla was a case of a mild and overly religious country being taken over and subjugated by a smaller but infinitely more ferocious group of people. The other nations around the Shrouded Sea would not help; probably they had all been relieved when after the earthquakes that destroyed their island home the Canops had gone to Migla.

From all that I heard of them, these Canops were a very nasty bunch indeed.

The halfling Miglas went in deadly fear of them, the beast-men convulsed by terror at the thought of acting in any way that would bring down the sadistic and destructive retribution of the Canops. The tiny handful who still met to worship Migshaanu did so with terror in their hearts and, as I was the first to say, with high courage and selfless devotion to their own ways and religion. I am not an overly religious man, as you know, but I know what I know, Zair knows!

Into the back room of the tavern from the stairway entrance walked a halfling woman clad all in crimson, with heavy gold lace and embroidery, with jeweled rings upon her fingers, and a massive golden, silver, and ruby crown upon her head. Her face shone. Her lips were rubbery-thin the Migla way, and her hooked beak nose and toe-cap chin jutted arrogantly. She carried a great staff of plated gold in one hand — the likeness of the head of that staff I shall not say, at this time — and jewels flashed and coruscated from every part of her crimson and golden person.

Hovering with a mixture of awe and pride Planath the Wine and his wife, Ploy, followed this gorgeous halfling creature into the room.

Saenda and Quaesa ceased their silly babbling. Turko flexed his muscles, and was still. Rapechak twisted his great beak of a face, and hissed beneath his breath, and was silent.

"All hail!" called Planath, a little huskily. He wore his crimson robe, but now across it had been slung a glittering gold cloth baldric, and in his hand he carried a small silver replica of the staff of power in the Migla woman's hand. "All hail!" Planath said again, and his voice grew and the quaver vanished. "All hail the high priestess of Migshaanu the Glorious!"

No one said a thing. I didn't care much, one way or another, for all my selfish thoughts were set on Delia and Valka, but I felt that those gathered there looked to me. For the sake of Mother Zinzu the Blessed I cannot say why, but, not then wishing to spoil the effect, I lifted up my voice and said loudly: "All hail the Mighty Mog!"

Which, I thought, was a suitably ironic comment, when all was said and done. The old witch caught my meaning at once.

"You may mock me, Dray Prescot! But I am what I am. One day, Migshaanu willing, I shall return to a rebuilt temple and once more the people of Yaman shall worship their true god."

You couldn't say fairer than that.

"I devoutly hope it will be so, Mog," I said.

With that, as though she had achieved what she had set out to do, Mog swept her stiffly brocaded garments about and swept out — in the sense that a loose scrap of straw caught in her skirts swept away with her. I did not smile. Truth to tell, I already knew there was more to Mog the witch than appeared. The Star Lords did not fool with worthless people.

"Well!" said Saenda. "Such airs! Anyone would think she was a queen."

I admit to a relief that Planath had gone, also.

I said, "With regard to Mog, Saenda — and you, too, Quaesa — you will oblige me by keeping a civil tongue in your head. Otherwise I shall not hesitate to show my displeasure."

"If you were in my father's hacienda!" began Quaesa, very hotly, her dark eyes regarding me with fury.

"If my father ever found out about you, Dray Prescot!" began Saenda, interrupting. The girls started another of their arguments. For a moment they forgot me in their quarrel, which suited me fine. Neither of the little idiots had much idea of how they had become slaves. They might live in different countries, but the way of their taking sounded suspiciously alike to me. They had gone to a party and had thereafter remembered nothing until they were en route for Faol. I thought that the Kov of Faol paid hired kidnappers to procure pretty girls and handsome men for him to run as quarry for his customers. There was still, in my mind, the idea that I might pay a call on this Kov of Faol one day.

On our way through the suns-lit streets of Yaman with the Miglas hurrying about their work and not looking too happy about it, I pondered on what had so far befallen me in Havilfar. I knew that nothing I did for the Star Lords was without a reason. Ergo, if I had rescued four people the Star Lords did not require they would hardly have let me rescue them and return them to safety. Of them all, Lilah, the first, had been in the most peril at the end, and I was in two minds to go and visit Hyrklana, to make sure. The Star Lords guided me; what I did today might be of use twenty seasons into the future. That this was true you shall hear, and the wonderfully cunning way of it too, into the bargain.

Miglas ahead of us on the street began running.

These houses were strange spiky houses, tall and narrow, with crazily pitched roofs and toppling tall chimneys and roosts jutting up at geometrically alarming angles. Many of the roosts gave resting places to fluttrells and other saddle birds. The idea of this, with my experience of the Hostile Territories, affronted me. But then I saw that here in Havilfar everyone was accustomed to saddle birds and flying animals; therefore they were merely a part of the armaments of each country, and thus deployable in war as any other force. Given that Havilfar was in many

113

respects further advanced than Segesthes or Turismond, they were not faced with the implacable barbarian winged horde.

"What is happening?" demanded Saenda, in her imperious, petulant voice.

"Protect me, Dray!" screamed Quaesa, clutching my arm. The little onker clutched my sword arm. Granted I had no sword — but: "If you trap my sword arm, Quaesa, I shall not be able to help myself, let alone you."

"Oh! You're impossible!"

With Miglas running every which way around us I hauled the girls into the shelter of an awning-draped store where a few amphorae stood in sardine-rows against the wall and an old Migla who looked like a washed-out edition of Mog shrieked and fled indoors and slammed her shutters. We had seen a few apims, human beings of Homo sapiens stock, walking about and we had attracted little attention, even Rapechak. We had seen a couple of Ochs, a Brokelsh, and a few Xaffers chewing their eternal cham; we had seen no Chuliks. So it wasn't us that caused this commotion.

Down the center of the street came a body of men. They marched in step. They wore armor, scaled and gleaming in the light of the suns. They carried thraxters belted to their waists, and crossbows all slanted at one angle across their bodies. Their sandals had been solidly soled, and the clicking crack of iron studs on the cobbles sounded loudly, harsh and dominating. Their helmets were tall, crested with the peacock-bright feathers of the whistling faerling — which is the Kregan peacock — and they looked hard, confident, and extraordinarily professional.

At their head marched four men with brazen trumpets, but they had no need to sound these. Following the trumpeters strode the standard bearer. He was gorgeously attired. The standard consisted of a tall glittering pole, wrapped around with silver wires, a multicolored banner flaring, and atop that and arranged most ferociously, the silver representation of a leaping leem.

Strange, I thought at once, that men should take the leem as their symbol!

Then I saw the men's faces as they marched with machine-like step in their quadruple ranks. Harsh, domineering, intolerant, yes, all these things. But I have seen many men's faces with those characteristics and, as you know, I admit to my shame that my face bears those betraying marks. There was about this something more, something yet more horrific. The halfling Miglas were running now and scurrying out of sight. The old Migla put her head out of a crack in the shutter and called to us: "Bow your heads! Bow your heads or you will be sorry!" and, smack, down came the shutter fully.

Rapechak, the old mercenary, understood at once.

I suppose I did, in a weird way I would not tolerate or believe. Turko came from an enslaved people and so he, too, bowed his head as the silver leem, the symbol of Lem, went by.

The officer — he was a Hikdar — strutting at the head of the main body, with his armor splashed with silver and golden medallions, turned his head. He saw the girls, and under the visor of the helmet, thrust upward and hooked, his dark eyes betrayed all the thoughts I could understand so well.

Turko reached out with both hands and, with his supple khamster skills, bent the heads of the girls down. He couldn't reach me, and, anyway, even then I doubted if he'd try.

The Hikdar looked down his nose at me and yelled.

"Nulsh! Bow to the Glorious Lem."

I did not bow.

Me, Dray Prescot! Bow to a stinking leem! Even if it was only a silver toy called Lem.

The Hikdar rapped out a command and every right foot bashed down perfectly alongside a left and the column halted.

The Hikdar strode over. He swaggered. He drew his thraxter as he came and there was on his dark face that look of enjoyment that has always baffled me.

"You bow, nulsh, before it is too late."

I said, "You are Canops?"

He reared back as though I had struck him.

"Filthy nul! Of course we are Canops! I am Hikdar Markman ti Coyton of the Third Regiment of Canoptic Foot. And you are a dead nulsh!"

The horror of it almost made me slow. The horrendous, the vile, the vicious, the despicable Canops — were human men like me! I felt the sick revulsion strong upon me. I saw the thraxter jerk back for a lethal thrust.

I said, "So you are Canops! I do not like you, Hikdar Markman, and I detest your race of kleeshes."

And I kicked the Canoptic Hikdar in the guts.

Nineteen

I visit Turko and Rapechak in Mungul Sidrath

I say I kicked him in the guts. I had not forgotten he wore armor, and so my kick went in lower and at an angle and it did the business I intended well enough.

Before he had time to spew all over me, although he was turning green in the face already, I yanked him forward, took away his thraxter, clouted him over the nose with the hilt, and said to Turko, Rapechak, and the girls: *"Run!"*

To our rear lay a maze of alleyways and hovels and I fancied the smartly disciplined men of the Third Regiment of Foot would not welcome breaking ranks and chasing about in there. I knew, also, that in the next few seconds the crossbow bolts would come tearing into our bodies. Turko did not hesitate, and neither did Rapechak. They grabbed a girl each — Saenda fell to Rapechak and she squealed — and they vanished into the mouth of the alleyway where the crazy houses hung their upper stories over the cobblestones.

As you may well imagine, I was furiously angry.

Angry with myself.

What an utter onker! Here I'd been, all nicely set to take off for Valka, and this stupid imbroglio had burst about my ears. I had been too stupid for simple cussing.

Mind you, the shock of discovering that these detestable Canops were apims, men like myself, had been severe.

I recognized their breed, all right. They were not the mercenaries to which I had grown accustomed in the other parts of Kregen I had up to then visited. These were men of a national army. Their discipline would be superb. They had a far more sheerly professional look about them than had had the rather unhappy army of Hiclantung. These men were trained killers, and they fought and killed and, no doubt, died not for cold cash but for hot love of country.

Theyvwould present a problem far graver than I had anticipated.

The Deldar leaped out from the leading rank and began yelling and the lines of crossbows twitched up. If I hung about any longer it would be pincushion time. The mouth of the alleyway struck cold across my shoulders. I dodged against the near wall and ran — oh, yes, I ran! — and the bolts went *chink, chink, chinka-room,* against the far wall. Maybe these soldiers would have been trained to penetrate alleyways, to leap up and down steps covered by fire from their files. This Kasbah-like maze might hold no terrors for them. I ran. I had been running a lot lately, and that, I assume, was the reason I hadn't bowed to the silver leem. I just do not like running, although it can be, as I had demonstrated on the jungle trail back in Faol with underhand and cunningly vicious traps, an absorbingly interesting pastime.

There was no sign of the others and I guessed they had pelted hell-for-leather as far and as fast as they could.

Following them, as I thought, I rounded corners, leaped offensive drainage ditches, hared through archways, and roared down the flights of narrow steps, flight after flight I saw no one, but, of course, many eyes watched me as I ran, and, no doubt, as well as marveling consigned me to Sicce as the greatest onker ever spawned.

By the time I reached the last alleyway and debouched onto the wide steps leading down to the quays, I knew I'd missed Turko, Rapechak, and the girls. For the first time in a very long time, I was on my own. That could not, however much I welcomed it, be allowed to continue. Through my stupid action the others had been put in danger of their lives. I had, if for no other reason than my stupid stiff-necked pride — which I detest — to ensure that they were safe.

A disguise would seem appropriate.

I was not a Migla and I would need a rubber mask even to approach the look of one. I was a human and must therefore disguise myself as another sort of human. I found the man I wanted in a low-ceilinged taproom with the smell of mud and stale wine everywhere, and the acrid tang coming off the flat and sluggish waters of the River Magan.

He was a wherryman — I knew about those — and he willingly parted with the dark-blue jersey of his trade, together with the flat leather cap that went with it, for a silver coin that bore the likeness of a man-king of some country somewhere in Havilfar. His eyes opened wide at sight of the thraxter, which I had carried beneath the old brown robe.

"Those Opaz-forsaken Canops see you with that, man, you're dead."

"They might be dead first, though. You get along with them?"

"Huh!" He had sized me up — as he thought — and without questioning my motives, was ready to talk. "I had a nice little line going here before they came. Worse'n eight-armed devils from Rhasabad, they are! Can't abide 'em. It's all regulations, regulations, regulations now. I'm thinking of moving on. No family; sell me wherry. There's plenty of openings across the other side." He meant on the other shore of the Shrouded Sea, and I learned a little more. "I got along real fine with the Miglas. Now — why they can't abide the sight of me. Remind 'em of the Canops! Me — who took their kids on outings when it was Migshaanu's special days!"

Sympathizing with him seemed in order, and we had a jar together. The wine was a thin stuff, palely red and nothing like the rich color of a rose, and was shipped in from a country over the Shrouded Sea that must be making a fortune from fourth and fifth pressings.

He told me there had been a brisk trade in the old days before the Canops came. The Miglas exported vosk-hide, which they knew how to cure to a suppleness of surprising strength and beauty by a secret process, and colored earths. But most of that had stopped now and the Canops were trying to develop a quite different economy. "Bloody fools!" said the wherryman, who was called Danel, and looked about him in sudden remembering fear.

Bidding Danel Remberee I took myself off with the thraxter rolled in the old brown robe to *The Loyal Canoptic*. I had not missed the irony of that name for a tavern where gathered a remnant of those loyal to Migshaanu. My traveling companions had not arrived back. Planath told me, with a quiver, that the city buzzed with the news. A Hikdar of the Canoptic Army had been struck. He had been kicked! Patrols were everywhere seeking the madman responsible. I upended a blackjack of a wine little better than that I'd drunk in the taproom with Danel, and waited, and fretted, and the suns passed across the heavens. In the end I had to admit that Turko and Rapechak and Saenda and Quaesa were not returning to *The Loyal Canoptic*.

When She of the Veils sank into the back hills of Migla and the sky was filled with the shifting light of the Twins, Planath brought me the news I quailed to hear, had known I must hear, and which distressed me greatly.

"They were taken, Horter Prescot. Taken by a patrol and now they languish in the dungeons of Mungul Sidrath."

I sat there, on the settle, the blackjack in my hand, and I could have broken into curses that would have frizzled this comical worried ugly little halfling's ears off.

Mungul Sidrath, I was told, was well-nigh impossible to break into. The citadel stood on a solid bed of rock jutting into the River Magan and it dominated the city. In the old days the royal family had lived there with their hired mercenary guards, and they had smiled on the city of Yaman and on the daily worship to Migshaanu, and the suns had shone. Now the city commandant lived there, controlling the city by terror. He had many regiments under his hand as well as mercenary troops, very wild and vicious, quite unlike the old king's mercenaries, who had served him all their lives and grown fat and happy with their job, which consisted, in the main, of providing honor guards and rows of guardsmen with resplendent uniforms and golden-headed stuxes. Well, I had to break into Mungul Sidrath.

There was no need for me to do this foolhardy thing.

The Star Lords had commanded me to bring out Mog, and I had done so, and she was safe. After that, I was free to return home. There would be no blue radiance and no scorpion this time. I felt sure of that, now; now when it was too late. Of course I could fetch the airboat from the sacred grove of Sidraarga and fly north-northwest and so come to Valka.

I could.

There was nothing to stop me.

Turko and Rapechak and the girls were hanging in chains in the dungeons of the Canops in Mungul Sidrath, but they were no concern of mine. My concerns were all with Delia and little Drak and little Lela, and Vallia and Valka, with Strombor and my clansmen. What was this local petty matter to me?

It was no good cursing. All the Voxes and Zairs and Makki-Grodno oaths would not change one iota of this mess.

I stood up.

"I have to go to Mungul Sidrath, Horter Planath. Would you give me food and drink?" I took out the golden deldys.

Planath bristled. He thrust the money away.

"Ploy!" he shouted. "Hurry, woman, and prepare food. Horter Prescot is hungry!"

After I had eaten and drunk I wiped my lips and laid down the cloth and looked at these Miglas. Old Mog had silently walked in. Now she said, "You are a fool, Dray Prescot." Her voice had lost all its stridency. "A get-onker. But you are a man, and, I now know, beloved of Migshaanu. She will go with you on this desperate venture."

"That is good—" I was about to say just her name, Mog. But I paused, and then said: "I shall be glad of the help of Migshaanu the Glorious, Mighty Mog."

Her hard agate eyes appraised me and her nutcracker jaws clamped, then she relaxed. I think, even then, she realized I had given over mocking her — for a space, at least.

Wearing the wherryman's old blue jersey with its rips and stains and with the flat leather cap pulled down over my forehead I went up against the citadel of Yaman. I went without weapons in my hands. I kept to the shadows and as I went I bent over and shambled. And so I came to the outer stone wall of the fortress where it reared, pink in the moonlight, rising against the stars of Kregen.

The place was old, for there is much that is ancient in Havilfar, and although well-built in olden time was much crumbled and fallen away in parts. An arm of the Magan encircled the fortress like a moat and the bridges were guarded by smart and well-drilled infantrymen of the Army of Canopdrin.

As I skulked in the shadows from the towers, where the Twins threw down their roseate-pink light, I saw something I had never seen before on all of Kregen.

I stared, for a moment letting the urgency of my mission slide, staring at the soldiers who guarded this massive pile. These foot soldiers wore armor, like the men of the Third Regiment of Foot I had earlier seen. They wore bronze helmets with tall plumes, weird under the streaming moonslight, and their greaves gleamed in that light. They carried the stux, and at their waists were belted thraxters. They did not carry crossbows. I stared at what made them, as far as I was concerned, unique in all of Kregen — if you did not count my old slave phalanx from the warrens of Magdag, and they must now be scattered and slain or slaving once more on the monolithic buildings of the overlords. Not even the Ochs counted here.

For these soldiers carried shields.

The shields were oval, like the windows in *The Loyal Canoptic,* of a goodly size, much decorated and embossed, with a broad silvery rim. The men handled the shields as though they knew what shields were for. In Segesthes, in Turismond, I had never come across the shield as an article of warlike equipment, the men of those continents regarding the shield as the coward's weapon, behind which he might cower.

That I knew different — and, perhaps, gloated a little in my so-called superior knowledge — meant now that I had just been my usual foolish self.

I went around the angle of a bastion — for the towers were square-angled and not rounded — and prowled on, brought back to my senses by the hurtling passage of a lesser moon across the heavens. I found the man I sought leaning on his stux and opening a packet made from soft leaves to get at the wad of cham inside. I hit him cleanly on the back of the neck, below the neck-guard, and he pitched to the stones.

Dragging him back into the shadows of a wall and stripping him took little time. I had been careful, the man I wanted not being the first sentry I had seen, and his equipment fitted — but only just.

Dressed and accoutered as a soldier of the Army of Canopdrin I stepped out, leaving the man bound and gagged, and marched boldly for the bridge.

While it is true to say that the necessary demands of discipline and organization make one army very much like another, and the better an army is the nearer it approaches to an unattainable ideal, there must of necessity be many differences between army and army, details that are unique to any fighting force. I felt confident I could bluff to a great extent; after that, I would just have to take my chances, for there was precious little chance of finding another way into the fortress as quickly as this.

Common sense had dictated that I find a bridge as far from the one the sentry's comrades would be guarding as I could. On my shield, below the embossed image of the leaping leem, there had been painted in white the stylized representation of a fluttrell, with the figures for six and five. By their relative sizes I judged this would be the sixth regiment and the fifth subdivision of that regiment, called what I did not know as yet, for Planath had no knowledge of military organization. The men guarding the bridge I chose, besides having a different color arrangement of the streamers over their shoulder armor, carried on their shields the silver leem and, below it, a blue-painted zorca with the figures for eight and two.

I marched in boldly and, as I had seen the men do on the bridge, brought the stux up and across in a salute. Without breaking step I strode on. An ob-Deldar looked across and called: "It's your guts, is it, soldier?"

An ob-Deldar is the lowest one can get — as any ranker will say — and so I answered hoarsely: "Too true, Deldar. They pain something awful."

The ob-Deldar laughed with great malice and so I passed on into the dark shadows of Mungul Sidrath.

Observation that had helped me thus far could no longer give me a guide on the behavior patterns of the men of this army.

Down in the dungeons, Planath the Wine had said, shaking his head. Therefore, I must go down, and to descend I had to find a stairway of some kind. I had ideas on the proper situation of stairways in fortresses, and I found that whoever in the ancient times had designed Mungul Sidrath had come a long way along the path of fortress construction. The stairway was exceedingly narrow, and spiraled the wrong way — that is, it had been designed so that a man going down, as I was, had the advantage of the curve. This could only mean the designer had recognized the possibility of entrance below and had decided on the main-gate level as his central stand-area. He had ruled out any idea of defenders running below against a successful entrance by attackers through the gate. Going up into the towers the curve would be against a man.

The stones were surprisingly dry, considering the Magan flowed nearby, and only occasional runnels of water trickled across the stones. Where they did so they stained darkly and lichens grew. The air grew unpleasant but breathable.

At the bottom the stair curled in on itself, so that a man might stand and loose against men running up the passageway. The ceiling here was low and I took off the tall helmet. Farther along the way widened and two guards, their stuxes leaning against the wall, were crouched over tossing dice. They looked up suddenly as I approached, saw I was a mere ranker, and pulled back to get out of the way. Farther along there might be a single sentry; so leaving these two to a mercy they had no idea had touched them, I went on.

They had not spoken. The language used by the ob-Deldar had varied only minutely from the universal Kregish, and I guessed it was Canoptish, the local language of Canopdrin. The sound of rushing water ahead and a marked cooling and freshening of the air made me lengthen my stride.

In a man-made cavern carved from an original bubble in the rock, water poured through from a black cleft high in one wall, dropped in a great weltering and rushing of foam and spume, sped sheeningly through a wide conduit, and passed in another broad shining curve of water down and out of sight beyond an arched opening in the opposite wall. The passageway opened onto nothingness and the path was carried on a narrow wooden bridge across the pelting water. Steps led to a neat contraption after the fashion of a waterwheel by which water could be lifted from the stream and raised, level by level, until it was carried out of sight into the mouth of a shaft. Buckets hung from the shaft mouth. Here guards cracked their whips and slaves of all kinds turned the great waterwheels, level by level, and lifted the fluid up and into the fortress so that, no doubt, the great men of the Canops might drink and wash and waste the water that had cost so much effort.

The noise blattered unceasingly. Water splashed and hissed. Whips cracked. Men screamed and guards yelled obscene orders to work faster, faster, and smash went the whips, and around and around hauled the slaves, all filthy and naked and hairy, and in fountains of silvery leaping spillings the water lifted high. The name on Kregen for water fitted that scene.

Passing on, with a salute for the Deldar in command, I came into an area of gloom, for the torches guttered low and there were no fireglass panels above, as there had been in the cavern of the waterwheels.

The sight of these hairy naked devils writhing and struggling and hauling, the spouts of water slopping everywhere, the insufferable noises, affected me profoundly. Truly, there was a foretaste of the Ice Floes of Sicce here!

"In the name of Lem! Who are you?"

From a side passage barred by an iron door, now open, a Hikdar stepped out. He carried a shield like my own, except that the fluttrell and the numerals six and five were raised from the surface and colored silver. He glared at me with his hard, mahogany-tough face filled with a surprise that swiftly changed to suspicion and then to certainty as he spoke.

"I know every man of the eighty in the Fifth Pastang! You are not one of my men — there is no desertion from — by the Great and Bone-Crushing Lem himself! You are Dray Prescot!"

And his thraxter whipped out and his shield came around with a thump and he charged straight for me.

Even as I responded in kind I had to fight the nausea of knowing that these devils of Canops had forced information from my friends; this Hikdar could never otherwise have known my name. He came in very expertly, shouting the while to summon more men. He had to be dealt with quickly. Using a shield like this, with a sword, came strangely at first, but I had not forgotten what I had taught my old vosk-helmets of the warrens. Thraxters clashed against shields, and I bashed him low, against the swell of the lorica over his belly, and then slipped a nasty little thrust in that finished him. The thraxters were suited for this work, being not too long yet long enough to make swordplay of some value, coupled with a shield used as an offensive weapon. The sound of iron nails on the stone blattered echoing along between the walls.

There was just the one way to go and that was the way I took. Around me now barred openings revealed cells. Hairy bewhiskered faces pressed up against the bars and a dolorous chorus of catcalls and shrieks echoed through the dimly lighted way. Many prisoners, there were, and yet they were all probably segregated, there on punishment detail, military prisoners serving sentences. Those I sought would be lower, in the dungeons. A crossbow bolt hissed past and a voice lifted, ringing between the stone walls.

"Do not kill him, nulsh! He is to be taken and questioned."

That, I feel sure, had little bearing on the bolt that bounced off my head. It is doubtful if even the tall bronze helmet would have done much. I felt the blow, saw a blinding stream of sparks flaring across my eyes, and then I fell into darkness.

Unconsciousness could not have lasted long. The blow had been a glancing one and when I opened my eyes I could feel the wet stickiness of blood down my face. Hands were placing a rough bandage around my head, tucking the ends in, most painfully. I tried to kick the offender, but he avoided the blow, and a voice said: "The nul is conscious."

They used the word nul as the Khamorros did, did these Canops, to mean a person who was not one of themselves.

They had stripped off the armor and the white tunic beneath and the short white kiltlike garment that was all they considered a shield-carrying man would need there in the way of defense. I was clad only in the old scarlet breech-clout. They dragged me along by my hair, whereat I turned, sluggishly I know, and tried to bite the wrists of the hands that dragged me, and was beaten back for my pains.

The broad-flagged stone chamber into which they dragged me was clearly a guardroom. There were seven Canop soldiers and a Hikdar. Also there was a Khamorro. I knew this lithely muscled man must be a khamster from every lineament of him. That he wore a green breechclout meant nothing. Around his head a broad risslaca-leather strap had been cinctured tightly and from it dangled an assortment of objects that, at the time, meant nothing to me. He was obsequious to the soldiers, and ready to do their bidding, and I guessed he stood in their employment as Turko had suggested the Khamorros would be employed — not as slaves but as special and highly prized body servants.

The Hikdar had already sent word of my capture up through the underground ways to the nobles above, and they would soon want me dragged before them, if they did not save the trouble and come down here themselves to witness my punishment. I guessed Hikdar Markman ti Coyton would be in their forefront. I just hoped his guts still hurt.

Unlike the guards of Prince Glycas of Magdag, these Canops had not heard of me. They tied me up with thongs and bundled me into a corner to await the chaining and the questioning when the city commandant and his retinue arrived. So there was time.

The thongs came free with a series of wrist movements and a final bursting surge. I stood up. The soldiers turned, gaping, and I knew they might all die but that the Khamorro, without a weapon in his fist, must be the man I must consider most. So after I kicked the first guard and broke the neck of the second, the thraxter I snatched up and flung took the Khamorro between the ribs. The second thraxter I scooped up did not last much longer, breaking as it wrenched free of the fourth guard. The Hikdar was raving, swirling his sword, urging his men on to attack me and at the same time yelling for them to span a bow and shoot me in the legs. By the time he had sorted out his priorities he had run out of men. The seven of them and the Khamorro lay where they had dropped.

But this Hikdar of Canopdrin was not without courage and he came at me with his thraxter held most neatly — but he fought without a shield, for there had been no time for him to snatch one up from the arms racks along the wall. This

122

was a tremendous disadvantage for him, and he went down, still trying to fight. Now I would have to hurry. No time, therefore, then, to feel sorry for these Canops — vile reavers though they were.

I took two crossbows and two thraxters, the finest I could find. I did not stop for shields or armor but padded out and very quickly ran across a guard party marching back off guard duty. The three soldiers went down with ruthless speed. The dwa-Deldar I showed the point of a thraxter and then jammed it into his throat just enough to draw blood.

"Where are the prisoners, kleesh? The Khamorro, the Rapa, and the two apim girls?"

He told me. I hit him over the head, for that had been our unspoken compact, and ran off down the tunnelway indicated. The dungeon was barred by an iron grille. The guard there was most happy to open it for me. Beyond that lay another grille and this guard — large, surly, and evidently in a foul temper for rating this duty, wanted to contest it with me. I cut him up — I had to — and passed on. Inside the dungeon only my four companions waited to greet me.

They had been stripped stark naked and hung against the wall in chains.

The two girls glared at me with mad eyes, not believing this half-naked apparition with the scarlet breechclout and the red blood splashed all over him could be me, the Dray Prescot they had been trying to cozen.

Rapechak said, "You are welcome, Dray Prescot."

I placed the crossbows and the quivers of bolts down and turned my face up to look at Turko. He looked in bad shape, clearly he had not fully recovered from that experience in the jungle of Faol. He looked at me and then his eyes flicked in a sharp gaze over my head.

"Lahal, Dray Prescot," he said. "Yes, you are most welcome. But you will have need of your weapons, I think."

I turned swiftly.

Ten paces from me stood two Khamorros. Both were large, superbly muscled, fit and tough, and both stood with hands on hips regarding me as they might a plate of palines.

Around their heads both wore wide bands of soft risslaca-leather and again a mixed assortment of objects hung down.

"They are only Khamorros, Turko," I said, prodding. I wanted to get his spirit back.

"The reed-syples," said Turko, in a strangled voice. "The headbands," he added, for my benefit. "These are great khams, both. Without your weapons, Dray Prescot, you are a doomed man."

Perhaps there was no mocking taunt in his voice. Perhaps I read into his words what my own guilty conscience put there. I do not know, but I acted as the most callow and vainglorious onker of a boaster could act.

"Great khams, Turko? I do not believe I need mere steel weapons to deal with them."

And I pitched the two swords onto the stone floor, where they rang like tocsin bells, and swung to face the two Khamorros, my hands empty.

Twenty

The Hai Hikai creates a shield

"You great nurdling fool!"

Turko's anguished cry racked up from the foundations of his being. Now he gave himself up for lost.

Rapechak the Rapa shouted: "Now by Rhapaporgolam the Reaver of Souls! You are a dead man, Dray Prescot!"

Saenda screamed almost incoherently: "You horrible onker, Dray! I'll never forgive you for this!"

And Quaesa simply burst into a long howling shriek.

The two Khamorros stared as though they could not believe their eyes. One of them, the slightly smaller of the two, even went through a quick routine of flexing his muscles and rippling his strength at me. He looked up at the naked bodies of the girls and, again letting that stupid bravado overwhelm me, I clapped my hands.

"Excellent, nulsh," I said. "A great performance. I hope you do as well when your head rolls into the north corner and your body rolls into the south."

Oh, yes. It shames me now when I look back at that long-gone day, and seeing the whole scene as though brightly lit upon a stage, recognize my own youthful headstrong passions and my own stupidity! I was a bit of a maniac in my younger days, and here I'd been boasting to myself that I had been conquering that hasty arrogance of mine, that harsh intolerance, that desperate desire to kick and smash anyone and anything that smacked of authority and sadism and attempts to put me down. I had bowed the knee and kowtowed and done the full-incline — and here it had all ended with as foolhardy an act of onkerishness as any two worlds witnessed.

For these were great khams. They had reached enormously elevated heights in the hierarchy of the Khamorros, their khams sky-high. They were of a different syple from Turko — had they been of his own syple they might have rescued him — and they were as contemptuous of him as of me.

They thought to make of it a sport, and, not without a certain charming politeness, debated one with the other who should have first crack at me. Remembering the sage counsel of old Zinki during those painful sessions of combat on the island of Zy in the Eye of the World, I was content to let them come to me.

The shorter, the one who had gone through the quick exercise drill, stepped forward. He had yielded because he was that much fractionally the lesser of the two, as he admitted. "I am Boro, and I am a great kham." He went on then to describe himself and his renown, his attainments and his exploits. At each word poor Turko moaned, and I heard him say: "By the Muscle! You have picked the wrong men to demonstrate to me, Dray! They are masters! Great khams!"

When this Boro had finished he stood waiting.

So, to humor him, and because if I did not end this farce soon guards with real weapons would burst in, I said, "I am Dray Prescot, Krozair of Zy."

If he didn't understand, as I didn't understand all his titles and accomplishments, that was his loss.

Then, very swift and deadly, he was upon me.

I did what I had planned to do... almost...

He was quick, and he was strong and he was very, very good. I felt his blows. I could feel it when he hit me. I slid his rush, for, of course, it was no blind-chunkrah rush, and he laid a hand on my arm and I had to do a quick double-twist and near break his fingers before he would let go. He stepped back and a great pleased smile lit his face.

"So you know the arts, Dray Prescot! I shall enjoy this!"

This time I managed to deflect his attack, and for a short space we twisted, body to body, doing all the things I had no desire to do. Everything he did I matched, but I was in defense all the time except for a single opportunity and that ended with Boro going up in the air and landing on his shoulder blades. He roared as I jumped on him, and rolled away, so that I missed and gouged the stone floor instead. Like a leem he was on his feet, and now his face was dark and congested with anger, which proved that his kham was a trifle shaky.

"I shall tear your limbs off and—" he started.

"Save it, Boro the Boaster! There's no time!"

We set to again, and again he used all his skill and avoided the grips and blows that would have flattened a lesser man. I could feel my anger at his strong obstinacy boiling up and I had to keep it down. I'd gone into this childish exhibition and now I had to pay the reckoning.

He circled, came in from the side, and I bent and took him and he took me. We rolled on the floor and he tried to break my arm, as he had threatened, and I cross-checked him so that he cried out, shocked at the sudden pain, and managed to break and leap clear. My parting blow hissed past his ear.

His comrade, the bigger Khamorro, said, "It seems, Boro, that he bests you." At which Boro roared his anger. "I am Morgo. I am a greater kham than Boro. You will not escape so easily from me."

I circled them both, warily, for they were both after me now. I shouted up to Turko, high: "Are all these Khamorros such braggart boasters and such spineless fighters?"

Turko said something, I know not what, and Boro and Morgo charged. I backed swiftly and in a succession of flurries of dodges and weavings, of arm blocks and of kicks, I won free. This could not be allowed to go on. The next time I would have to do something drastic. Old Zinki had laughed, one time, telling us of what Pur Zenkiren had done to a couple of Magdaggian overlords. I had a great affection for the austere Pur Zenkiren, who was Archbold-Elect. If I could pay him the compliment of imitating him, I would do so.

Boro and Morgo split me between them and came in from both sides. I backed again, circling, and my foot hit against a sword where I had tossed it down so contemptuously.

"Pick up your sword, Dray! For the sake of the Muscle, man! Use the weapon you understand! They have only been playing with you!"

If that was true, of course, life would become exceedingly complicated and remarkably interesting in the next mur.

Deliberately, I kicked the sword aside.

Turko moaned.

The two Khamorros flexed their muscles. The sweat stood out on their skins like liquid gold. Working as a team they rushed me again and in a flurry of chops and grips that failed and hooks that barely missed, Boro wrenched away the bandage around my head so that blood flowed down over my face and left eye. I blinked and cursed.

"By the Black Chunkrah! You fight foul!"

They did not answer; they were both panting, their magnificent chests heaving and glistening with sweat.

This time, I saw, they meant to finish it. Boro came in a little ahead of Morgo, and he designed, I saw instantly, to feint an attack and then roll under me so that I would fall into the arms of Morgo. When Boro rushed I sidestepped. He came with me and our forearms smashed together and I stepped back.

For an instant he had an opportunity, for the distance I had gone seemed to him to be overlarge, giving him the chance of taking two skipping steps and putting in the jagger. This is that blow delivered by the feet with the body wholly off the ground. He chose the double jagger, with both feet. He did it superbly well, and for any ordinary wrestler it would have been the end, for those iron-hard soles of his would have crushed into the chest and knocked all the wind out and smashed the fellow over, to be gripped and thrust facedown into the dirt, finished, if his ribs weren't all cracked to Kingdom Come.

Turko's scream ripped into the stink of the dungeon.

Morgo's bellow of "Hai Hikai!" passed unheeded.

Everything happened in a fluidity of motion beautiful to behold, making me wish I'd been there when Pur Zenkiren did this to those overlords of Magdag. I took Boro's ankles in both fists and I leaned back, as a hammer-thrower leans in the circle, and spun. He carried all that forward momentum into a sideways rotation, with my body leaning back, muscles ridged, acting as the hub. Around me he spun, parallel to the ground. I lifted a little higher as his head flew around and aimed him, and, as though wielding a great Krozair long-sword, I laid his head smack alongside Morgo's head.

I let go.

Both Khamorros collapsed. Blood and brains gushed from their nostrils and their ears.

"By the Muscle!" I heard Turko whisper.

Quaesa wouldn't stop screaming. Saenda had done things she afterward would never remember. Rapechak said, "I believe the correct term is Hai Hikai, Dray Prescot! Hai Hikai!"

He was right. The unarmed combat masters, like the Khamorros, like old Zinki, do not use the swordsman's great Hai Jikai — instead, they say: "Hai Hikai."

Turko the Khamorro looked at me. His face held a frozen look of horror. Then he spoke, in a husky whisper.

"Hai Hikai, Dray Prescot! Hai Hikai!"

Freeing the four prisoners was simple enough, for the keys had been in the keeping of Morgo the Khamorro, who was now no doubt practicing his art somewhere under the alert eye of Morro the Muscle himself. They were stiff and sore and the two girls collapsed, moaning, for Quaesa had stopped screaming the instant she felt my hands on her, unlocking the chains. Turko picked up the blood-soaked bandage and rewound it around my head. He looked at it, his dark eyes filled with a pain he did not believe.

"As a reed-syple, Dray Prescot, that bloody bandage is extraordinarily fitting."

As you know I make it a rule never to apologize; I would have apologized to Turko, then, for acting in such a stupid way, when Rapechak, picking up a crossbow and quiver of bolts, said with an evil chuckle: "I think we may fight our way out now, Dray Prescot."

I handed him one of the swords. I made up my mind. I said, "Turko, you called me Dray, back there. I would — like — it if you and Rapechak dropped the Prescot."

This was no trifle.

We said no more, but I know Rapechak, the Rapa, at least, was pleased. At the iron grilles we took clothes from the guards and sketchily gave the girls a breech-clout each and a few rags for the men. Turko stopped. He looked down at the guard's thraxter, still in his fist. The shield lay to one side. Turko's face was completely expressionless.

I watched him. He bent and picked up the sword. He held it for a space, the guard's open hand like some mute testament below. Then he tossed the sword down. I started to turn away and then halted. Turko picked up the shield. He hefted it, looked at the straps inside, turned it around, slid it up his left arm, swung it about. Then, turning to face me, holding the shield up, he said, "I am ready to follow you, Dray."

"Good, Turko. We march now to freedom."

But we both knew we meant much more than merely escaping from this fortress-prison of Mungul Sidrath.

With both crossbows spanned and ready, with Turko at my back with his shield, and the girls following on, we padded on away from the dungeon and on toward the cavern of the waters.

Halfway across the bridge I halted. In the noise and confusion of water spouting, great wheels creaking, and slaves screaming as whips whistled down, we could not fail to attract attention. But the danger lay ahead. On the far side of the bridge a body of men appeared and instantly they were revealed as the nobles and officers come down to question their prisoners, and, perhaps, to have a little sport with them.

In the forefront, as I had cynically expected, stood Hikdar Markman ti Coyton.

He screamed and pointed and dragged out his sword, his words unheard in the din of rushing water, creaking wood, and other screams so much more brutally dragged forth.

At Markman's side stood a man who blazed with the stiff regalia of pride and authority. This Canop had to be the commandant of Yaman. For good measure I put the first shaft into him. I saw his mouth open as he fell, but did not hear his dying scream. Rapechak let fly and slew a Chuktar directly to Markman's rear. Markman turned and tried to push back through the officers. Being officers and having come on a sporting occasion they had no bowmen handy, but very quickly bowmen could be deployed and then we'd be skewered, there on the open bridge with the roaring water beneath.

I put my face close to Turko's ear.

"Over with you, Turko! And breathe deeply!"

I said the same to Rapechak.

They both wanted to argue and Rapechak, bending his great beaked face close to mine, barely avoided the quarrel that sizzled past to thunk into the wooden railing in a showering of yellow chips. They were arguing about the girls. There was no time to reload. Turko moved forward, and in a twinkling crossbow bolts stood in his shield like angry bristles. He screened us. I was not sure of the Rapa's capabilities as a swimmer, and Turko was in no real condition to look after anyone but himself.

I pushed them both over and grabbed the girls about their waists and leaped. Half a dozen crossbow bolts ripped the wood of the bridge as we hurtled down. We hit the water in a fountain that vanished almost instantly in that smooth, heavy flow and the current swept us frighteningly fast down and into the arched opening leading onto darkness.

Sword and crossbow had gone and I now had armfuls only of wet and terrified girls. I lunged up, my head above the surface, and dragged them up. There was no sign of the others. "Breathe!" I yelled, and then took a frantic quick breath, as deeply as I could in the time left, and then we were over and falling in the midst of the cascade, with only darkness, and water, and noise all about us.

Accounted a superb swimmer and able to dive for long periods I may be, but that gulp of air had not been enough. I felt the pains in my chest, the flecks of fire before my eyes that were wide open and staring blindly into the roaring darkness. On and on we were tumbled, turning and twisting like chips in a drainage ditch. I felt then that for a surety I was done for. This was the end. This was where they tossed the broken and bleeding corpses of the dead slaves after they had worked until they died, this was where they disposed of the prisoners they had questioned beyond the limits of tolerance. Down and down we went and on and on and then I knew I had finished and there was nothing else to do but end this agonizing pain and open my mouth.

But, being Dray Prescot, a stupid onker, I kept my mouth shut and I fought the pain and we swirled along like refuse. I felt a sudden rising shock as lights stung my dazzled eyes, and cool night air laved my face and we were afloat on the surface of the River Magan.

Turko waved an arm and yelled. I did not see Rapechak.

We swam into the bank and on the oozing mud a severe session of arm-pumping and kissing brought the girls around. They were shattered by their experiences and unable fully to comprehend that we had escaped. I felt that we would have little time. Finding a boat was easy enough and I selected a craft typical of river work, with sharply flared bows and a broad beam, shallow-drafted and with a sail and awning. At the oars — at the oars! How eerie and strange a feeling that was to be sure! — we pulled around in circles, calling as loudly as we dared for Rapechak. But we did not find the Rapa. I would not think of that. At last, and with regret, I set the bows downriver and pulled steadily away in the dying light of the Maiden with the Many Smiles.

By dawn we were well down the river. We had a few scraps of clothing, no weapons, and no money. But we had our lives.

"I can sail this boat well enough," I said. Hell! If I, Dray Prescot, couldn't sail a boat the end of two worlds was in sight! I felt relieved, light-headed, and yet let down. This was the end of this adventure, for there was food and wine in the boat and fishing lines and bait, with a breaker of water, and so all this evidence pointed to a fishing party this day. We might be pursued. If the boat had belonged to a Migla, I did not think the halfling would report its loss to the Canoptic authorities.

Turko said, "The girls ought to know this country, Dray. If we can sail out of the country of Migla we can find friends. If what Saenda says is true... and what Quaesa boasts of is so."

The girls shivered in the dawn as the mists rose from the sluggish river and a little breeze got up. We could set some canvas very shortly, for the wind blew fair.

"My father—" began Saenda. She swallowed. "If we could reach Cnarveyl, on the coast to the north, or Tyriadrin, the country to the south, we would find agencies of my father's. Or we might try one of the islands — but they are infested with renders."

"Take your pick," I said with a cheerful note in my voice. "The wind is fair for either."

Quaesa spoke up then. Both girls had drunk a little wine and pulled their fingers through their hair — a sovereign remedy, that, for miserable feelings — and they fell to arguing which country would be the better, having a mind to their father's vast interests and agencies. Turko looked at me and raised his eyebrows, and smiled.

Turko, who had taken half a dozen crossbow bolts into and through the shield, arguing with me there on the bridge, before I pushed him over. I would not think of Rapechak. He must have swum clear and been taken in a different direction by the sluggish current. He had to.

Well, whether it was to Cnarveyl to the north or Tyriadrin to the south, we would equip ourselves with clothes and money and the girls would go home aboard one of their father's ships or vollers, and I — I would go home, too, to Valka. And Turko would go with me. He wanted that, I knew. And, now, I wanted him with me. He did not know what a Krozair of Zy was, but he had seen what their unarmed combat techniques could do, and he was prepared to grant me all the khams he cared to.

The banks lightened under the suns and I considered. They were well wooded, with many muddy creeks, and again I cocked my eyes at Zim and Genodras just glowing through the mists, turning them into a chiaroscuro of emerald and ruby, and I considered, and then turned the boat toward the opposite bank.

"We lie up for the day," I said. No one thought to argue with me or question the decision.

That day, hidden beneath overhanging missals, we saw the boats passing down the river, long lean craft propelled by a single bank of oars, twenty to a bank, and I could guess the Miglas were rowing there, under the lash of the Canops.

From time to time fluttrell patrols passed overhead, swinging in their ordered skeins across the pale sky. Vollers, too, searched for us. They could not see us through the screen of leaves, the oared boats did not push far enough in up the creek, and the land patrols riding totrixes or zorcas could not approach the banks here by reason of the mudflats, which were very treacherous. So we waited the day out, eating and drinking frugally, and the girls calmed down completely and fell to arguing over me, and trying their wiles on me, whereat Turko harrumphed and took himself off.

Just before I was ready to push off I, too, went up the bank. I stared up at the sky and thought that very soon I would see my Delia again, my Delia of the Blue Mountains, my Delia of Delphond! And, too, I would hold in my arms those two tiny morsels of humanity we had called Drak and Lela. Oh, yes, I yearned to return home. I had done what the Star Lords commanded. No blue radiance had dropped about me. No hideous Scorpion had lowered on me to transit me back to the Earth of my birth four hundred light-years away, the planet that, I admitted with joy, I could no longer call home.

In the last of the light, in that streaming mingled radiance of the Suns of Scorpio, I turned to go down to the boat and push out into midstream and so ghost down to the mouth and sail away from this miserable land of Migla.

I turned, one foot was in the air — and a beat of wings above my head, a flash of scarlet and gold, and a hated voice screeched down on me from above.

I looked up.

The Gdoinye circled there, low, terrible of form, glorious and shining and altogether hateful.

"A fool, Dray Prescot! Nothing less!"

"Go away!" I shouted up. My passion broke out then in foul words. I shook my fist, for I had no other weapons of steel now, and yet I had proved that a man's hands are more terrible than the sword.

"You think you obey the Star Lords? You who do not understand a tenth, no, a millionth part of their purpose? You are an onker, Dray Prescot! Why did you bring the Mighty Mog here to her home in Migla which is cursed by the Canops?"

When I heard him refer to the Migla witch, old Mog, as Mog the Mighty, I knew. I knew! The agony of it struck in shrewdly and almost I fell to my knees and begged the Gdoinye to let me be. But I knew the penalty of refusal. I knew I must do what the Star Lords commanded, or I would be banished to Earth four hundred light-years away, and might languish there for years as my twins, my Drak and my Lela, grew up into wonderful children, and my Delia pined for me as I hungered for her.

"What is it the Star Lords command, bird of ill omen?"

"That is better, Dray Prescot! You should know you have not completed your task. Not until the land of Migla is cleansed of the Canops and Migshaanu is returned to her rightful place — for a time only! — will your work be done."

"I am almost naked, I have no weapons, no money, two girls depend on me, the whole country is up in arms against me. You are hard taskmasters—"

"You have been naked before, Dray Prescot, and weaponless. You will do this thing."

With a loud and harshly triumphant squawk, a cry of triumphant rage, the raptor winged away into the fading suns-glow. Zim and Genodras, which hereabouts I should call with all hatred Far and Havil, sank in a smoldering angry blaze of jade and ruby, firing bloodily into a savage crimson glow dropping down over the horizon. Darkness closed over the land of Migla upon the continent of Havilfar on Kregen.

Stunned at the enormity of the sentence passed upon me I went down to the boat.

In the darkness, before any of the seven moons of Kregen rose, I pushed off and in silence took the looms of the oars into my hands.

What I must do I must do.

Oh, my little Drak, my little Lela!

And — my Delia, my Delia of Delphond — when would I see her again and hold her dear form in my arms?

Arena of Antares

A Note on Dray Prescot

Dray Prescot is a man above medium height, with straight brown hair and brown eyes that are level and dominating. His shoulders are immensely wide and there is about him an abrasive honesty and a fearless courage. He moves like a great hunting cat, quiet and deadly. Born in 1775 and educated in the inhumanly harsh conditions of the late eighteenth century English navy, he presents a picture of himself that, the more we learn of him, grows no less enigmatic.

Through the machinations of the Savanti nal Aphrasöe, mortal but superhuman men dedicated to the aid of humanity, and of the Star Lords, he has been taken to Kregen under the Suns of Scorpio many times. On that savage and beautiful, marvelous and terrible world he rose to become Zorcander of the clansmen of Segesthes, and Lord of Strombor in Zenicce, and a member of the mystic and martial Order of Krozairs of Zy.

Against all odds Prescot won his highest desire and in that immortal battle at The Dragon's Bones claimed his Delia, Delia of Delphond, Delia of the Blue Mountains, as his own. And Delia claimed him in the face of her father, the dread Emperor of Vallia. Amid the rolling thunder of the acclamations of "Hai Jikai!" Prescot became Prince Majister of Vallia, and wed his Delia, the Princess Majestrix.

Through the agency of the blue radiance sent by the Star Lords, Prescot is plunged headlong into fresh adventures outwitting the Manhounds of Antares. After rescuing Mog, a high priestess, and Turko the Khamorro, and Saenda and Quaesa, Prescot brings them safely out of danger — when the giant bird of prey of the Star Lords appears once again to him...

One

The Star Lords command

"What is it the Star Lords command, bird of ill omen?"

"That is better, Dray Prescot! You should know you have not completed your task. Not until the land of Migla is cleansed of the Canops and Migshaanu is returned to her rightful place — for a time only! — will your work be done."

"I am almost naked, I have no weapons, no money, two girls depend on me, the whole country is up in arms against me. You are hard taskmasters—"

"You have been naked before, Dray Prescot, and weaponless. You will do this thing."

With a loud and harsh squawk, a cry of triumphant rage, the raptor winged away into the fading suns-glow. Zim and Genodras, which hereabouts I should call with all hatred Far and Havil, sank in a smoldering angry blaze of jade and ruby, dropping down over the horizon. Darkness closed over the land of Migla upon the continent of Havilfar on Kregen.

Stunned at the enormity of the sentence passed upon me I went down to the boat.

In the darkness, before any of the seven moons of Kregen rose, I pushed off and in silence took the looms of the oars into my hands.

What I must do I must do.

Oh, my little Drak, my little Lela!

And my Delia, my Delia of Delphond — when would I see her again and hold her dear form in my arms?

The two girls, Saenda and Quaesa, ceased their silly chattering at sight of my face, and they shivered. Turko looked at me, hesitated, and did not speak, for which I was grateful. Turko had stood upon the bridge there in the great cavern of rushing waters beneath the citadel of Mungul Sidrath and had taken the crossbow bolts on that new shield of his. He was to become a good companion. His superb muscular development and the cunning khamster skills of unarmed combat were to stand me in good stead. But, just then, by remaining silent he did me the best service he could.

His ropy muscles moved with the ease and suppleness that all the bunched and massive bashing power of a warrior's hardened muscles might never match. He understood at once that we were not to escape easily down the River Magan away from this eerie town of Yaman in the land of Migla.

Out across the water, lights moved in the starshot darkness. The armored men of the Canopdrin army continued to search for us. I pulled down gently, letting the ebb take us. Occasionally a hail floated across the water. The girls shivered in the bottom of the boat. If we were caught their fate would be horrible, worse than it would have been before I rescued them.

135

They were no longer my concern.

Those aloof beings, the Star Lords, had commanded me to erase the blight of the Canops from this land, and from the very first I had seen the enormous difficulties of that. I had no desire at all to involve myself in fresh fighting and scheming and planning; all I wanted to do was return home to Vallia or Valka, depending on where Delia and the children might be staying, and clasp them in my arms once more.

But if I refused to help the Miglas turn the Canops out, I would be seized up by the ghastly blue lambency of the scorpion-image and hurled back four hundred light-years to the planet of my birth.

That must not be allowed to happen.

Therefore I must begin at once to scheme and plan to aid old Mog the Witch, the old crone who was now the Mighty Mog, to regain her rightful place as high priestess to the all-powerful Migshaanu. Migla was dominated by religion. Mind you, if this Migshaanu was really all-powerful, then she would never have allowed her high priestess to be defamed, her temple razed, and her religion brought into contempt. If Mog or any of her friends and adherents thought of that, I guessed, they pushed the obvious consequences of the thought aside with the kinds of arguments that have sustained proscribed religions through the ages.

Lights glimmered upon the water and the two girls crouched down, frightened and shivering, and Turko looked at me. All about us in the moonless darkness lurked danger. No hand would be raised to save us. Darkness and danger and the creeping sense of impending doom cast a shadow upon the boat, a shadow that had not existed only moments before, when I had gone up to the bank for the last time before pushing off.

Our whole situation had changed.

Now I must go boldly ahead into fresh dangers and new adventures, and never reckon the cost until the bidding of the Star Lords had been done.

All that had passed meant nothing.

This was a new beginning, a fresh assault upon the destiny that had brought me to this fantastic planet of Kregen beneath the Suns of Scorpio.

Lights moved upon the waters.

Our little boat drifted with only a faint gurgle and splash, a shadow among shadows.

"They draw close, Dray," said Turko, his voice a whisper in the gloom.

"Aye."

Plans and schemes tumbled through my head like a cloud of those infernal midges of the marshes men call kitches, cursing and swiping, and no plan was a good plan.

One of the three lesser moons of Kregen rose and hurtled low over the horizon.

That speck of light racing between the star clusters served only further to enhance my mood of restlessness, of unease, of a mindless shifting of forces I could not control or even come to terms with, and so hated and detested. Water splashed nearby and a voice cursed, the deep rolling cadences of a man who swore by Lem, the silver leem.

We peered in that scant and erratic illumination and made out the dark loom of a boat, ghosting along, low in the water. I could feel the hard lenk of the boat's gunwales beneath my hands, and I gripped tightly, feeling the frustration choking me. I have told you many times that on Kregen a man must possess a weapon and be skilled in its use if he wishes to survive, and this is no less true for the marvelous skills of the Khamorros, the khamsters famed for unarmed combat, like Turko. I had not revealed all my mind to Turko on the subject of unarmed combat against edged and pointed weapons, and would not do so unless Zair commanded in a moment of intense danger, and so I fretted that I did not grasp a sword or a spear or a bow as that creeping dark boat ghosted over the water as we drifted down.

Those men over there, those Canops, hard tough fighting-men from the devastated island of Canopdrin in the Shrouded Sea who had invaded Migla and made the land their own and subverted the peoples' allegiances, they would not scruple to kill unarmed men. And I knew they possessed the skill to slay even a great Khamorro like Turko.

Our boat drifted, and I, Dray Prescot, peered over the gunwale at that other craft, and I cursed, and I was very conscious of my shame.

"She of the Veils will be up soon," said Turko. He spoke low on two counts, as I well knew. One, so that the armed Canops should not hear, and two, so that Saenda and Quaesa should not hear, either, and begin a frightened squeaking.

"There are more of these Opaz-forsaken cramphs about than I had bargained for, Turko."

"They slink like leem."

"A leem may be slain with a sword."

"Morro the Muscle faced and breasted and slew a leem, Dray. It is not left for mortal men."

"Maybe not."

He cocked an eye at me sharply. Some of his old quizzical appraisal of my prowess showed through. He must clearly have wondered if I spoke thoughtlessly, or boasted emptily, or — but he could not know of the existence of Sanurkazz and the Eye of the World even as he had been unaware of the unarmed combat disciplines of the Krozairs of Zy.[3]

For a space we drifted silently and the Canops' boat angled away from us, with an occasional faint splash. The torchlights dimmed. This would not do. I was acting as though I intended to take the two girls to safety, either to the land of Cnarveyl to the north or to the land of Tyriadrin to the south. I had to see them safe. That was a task I had laid on myself, for all their bitchiness and squabbling and their lofloo-like hitchings and squirmings. They were just two silly girls, whom I had happened to rescue from slavery and the Manhounds of Antares, and they could not weigh in the scales against what the Star Lords had commanded me to do.

A faint pinkish wash of light sifted above the eastern horizon, away across the mudflats and rushes fringing the River Magan. The river runs generally in a northeasterly direction into the Shrouded Sea; but in its sluggish windings a reach opened up due east, and She of the Veils rose and cast her streaming pink light full along the length of water.

I was looking up, watching the pinkly glowing orb as it rose, and I saw a black and angular silhouette for a moment flitter before the moon, dark and sharp and ominous, and as suddenly flicker away and vanish.

Turko sucked in his breath.

The two girls had not seen, and so were silent.

'Tell me, Turko.'

"By Morro the Muscle! A volrok, Dray. A yetch of a volrok."

Many and various are the beast-men and men-beasts of Kregen. Away in The Stratemsk and the Hostile Territories I had encountered monstrous flying animals and reptiles, and here in Havilfar there were many beasts of the air. I kept a wary eye open aloft, and took up into my hands the boat hook. It was a poor thing, with a clumsy bronze point and hook; but it was all we had.

The thing had seen us, that was sure, and it must have correctly surmised we were a small party. In a rush of wings and a harsh clacking cry, it was upon us.

Now Turko had called the volrok a yetch, which is a Havilfarese term of abuse generally used for a human being, and this should have warned me. I was not facing a flying beast.

I faced a flying man.

The volrok had intelligence, and quick wits, and a supple sinewy strength for all that he was lightly built. He was no impiter, no corth, no fluttrell; he was a man, a halfling. His wings beat against the starlight and I caught the gleam of a weapon. She of the Veils threw down a fuzzy pinkish radiance, and in that glow I saw his eyes, glaring at me, as he circled and dived.

"Watch his feet, Dray!"

I grunted and leaned away from that first vicious onslaught. Wings buffeted air and I smashed the boat hook up and caught the descending blow of a long spearlike weapon, something after the fashion of the Ullars' toonon, and so deflected the blow. The encounter had given me a closer look at the volrok.

He circled, screeching, and his wings folded, and he dived again. He had evolved from an eight-limbed stock, for his back bore real wings, wide and narrow, sharply angled, wings that enabled him really to fly. His arms held the toonon. His third pair of limbs consisted of legs — real honest-to-goodness legs — with attachments that made of them ghastly weapons of destruction and not honest or good at all. His remaining pair of limbs had fused in a fan to form a tail.

Turko brandished an oar above his head.

The volrok dived, and swerved, and the bronze head of the boat hook clashed against the toonon and then I saw the truth of those legs. On each heel had been bound a long and wickedly curved blade, like twin scimitars, and as the volrok screeched and rose so the blades whickered down toward my head. I ducked. I felt a grazing blow across my scalp.

Turko prodded with his oar.

Saenda and Quaesa were screaming. There was no time to do anything about them.

The volrok swerved there in the level air, turned, and I saw his narrow head peering down to regard us more closely. He wore a tight leather tunic, much decorated with feathers, and a belt from which hung a sword in a scabbard whose lockets held it so that it kept out of his way when flying. His legs scissored and the deadly wink of those scimitar blades made me dash the blood from my eyes and take a fresh grip on the boat hook.

The cut I had sustained in Mungul Sidrath had opened again and the bandage could no longer hold back the blood.

Turko was swearing on about the Muscle and swords and spears and devilish flying man-monsters.

The volrok folded his wings and plummeted.

This time I had to ignore his toonon. The spear had to be slipped, as Turko and I knew how, and I had to get those scimitar blades of his in good sight in that treacherous illumination.

I switched grips on the boat hook.

Instead of holding the sturm-wood shaft with my left hand forward, like a spearman, I held it right hand forward, like a swordsman.

A wooden longsword had been used before. This time it was of unhandy length, of ridiculous length; but it had a bronze point and a bronze hook. The volrok dropped down and I had time to realize the scimitar blades had been strapped to his heels to give a straight-line strength and control from his legs; had they been strapped to his feet or toes he would not have been able to deliver the same power. He would not have been able so easily to drag the blades free and lift off after a strike, either. As it was, he couldn't stand up easily for the blades curved to form a continuation of his legs.

The dark form swept in toward us. The glitter of the spear meant nothing. He would jerk his legs forward in the last moment of his dive, impaling me, or slicing my head open, and then fly on, trailing his legs, and so wrench the scimitars free.

With a yell to Turko, "Get down, Turko!" I ducked and let the toonon go past. It cracked the lenk gunwale of the boat and skidded on. Then I swung. The boat hook circled and smashed with awful force against the volrok's thighs. Both his legs broke. The blades abruptly dangled.

He shrieked.

In that tiny moment I was able to drive on and up, hard, and the bronze point tore up into his body.

Turko's oar battered his wings.

The volrok screamed. His wings churned the air as he sought to drag himself away. The boat hook had caught him. I leaned back, savagely dragging him down. The oar smashed down now on his head. With a convulsive effort, which tore his insides in a shower of blood, the volrok broke free from the bronze hook. He rose unsteadily, shrieking, and his wings beat feebly, and wavering and lurching, he flew away in the moonlit shadows. I was not content to let him go, and cursed.

"We could have used his toonon, and those vicious blades."

"He was a fighter—"

"Oh, aye, he was a fighter."

"Vicious, the volroks." Turko turned back and looked down into the boat. "Stop yelling! He's gone."

The girls yelped into snuffled wailings.

"Do they hunt in pairs, Turko, or singly?" I ignored Saenda and Quaesa. This was something a fighting-man had to know. "Or — in packs?"

"It depends entirely on which town or province they come from. I do not claim to recognize all their markings. But, they are men, they have intelligence—"

"I see."

I scanned the night sky with the warming glow of She of the Veils spreading out upon the dark waters. Our noise had attracted attention. Lights moved across the water, waving, clotting into a bunch, growing in size, nearing.

"They've spotted us, by the Muscle!"

"Aye!"

I dropped onto the thwart, chucked the boat hook along the bottom boards and was rewarded by a shriek from one of the girls, and unshipped the oars. Now my training as an oar-slave aboard the swifters of the inner sea and the swordships prowling up along the Hoboling Islands would come into full use — not to mention my early years as a seaman of Earth's late eighteenth century wooden navy.

The blades bit deeply. Water surged. I put my back into it, uncaring of the blood that clotted on my forehead and stung coldly in the night breeze. I pulled for the north bank. It was the nearer of the two. Coming up fast from astern the long low shape of a galley, a liburna, hauled into just a prow upflung against the stars and what appeared a single oar, rising and falling, each side, starboard and larboard.

I pulled.

But those whipped Miglas slaving aboard the liburna pulled too, and the galley foamed along in our wake, closing.

"Where away ahead, Turko?"

He jumped for the bows, past my back. In a moment he called: "To the left — that is your right, Dray—"

"Aye."

The little fishing boat, a mere dinghy in reality, surged ahead. If any more volroks attacked now we were done for. We would be done for, too, if I did not reach the shore with time for us to leap out and escape into those alleys of darkness between the mudbanks and the mudflats. I pulled. We had passed a quiet day, and rested, and my strength was restored. I would not tire yet; but there was little chance of a single man in a clumsy boat like this outrunning a galley crewed by oarsmen at forty oars, at the least.

"By the Muscle! Volroks! Scores of the yetches!"

I did not waste effort looking up. I pulled. The water splashed and hissed and at each stroke the boat leaped. The liburna following cleft the water with a fine pink-tinged white comb in her teeth. She gained. I pulled. The boat leaped as Turko, waving his oar, for there were two pairs aboard, leaped and slashed wildly above his head.

A wing buffeted me, over the head and for a moment a dark haze dropped over my eyes; but I fought it. I had to. This was no way for Dray Prescot, Krozair of Zy, Lord of Strombor — and much else besides — to die.

The girls were simply huddled together and screaming in mindless fear. The galley smashed her way after us. And the volroks descended in clouds from the pink-tinged darkness about us.

"This is the end!" shouted Turko, bashing with his oar. "We're done for!"

Two

Obquam of Tajkent keeps order

Neither the Star Lords nor the Savanti had made any attempts to save me when I stood in mortal peril of my life in obeying their aloof commands. I could look for no help from them.

There seemed no hope.

If the Star Lords moved the volroks, I did not know then and I do not know now.

But the cloud of winged men swirled up, their wings an evil rustle in the darkness, the pink sheen from their weapons rising and swinging, their eyes glittering, and then, in a single close-bunched mass, they swooped upon the galley pursuing us.

In an instant all was commotion and pandemonium aboard.

I did not cease from pulling.

"By the Muscle…" breathed Turko, in awe.

Any ideas I might have entertained of remaining in the boat and of slipping past along the river were banished as more galleys appeared, pulling up with the kind of individual precision obtained by a smart whip-deldar and drum-deldar, and a skipper who knew his business. A brisk little action was being fought back there. The volroks, of whom I was to learn a great deal later on in Havilfar, had flown in from their aerie towns far to the north and west. They had a plan. Although I could only guess what their schemes might be, I did know they would aid me in my own.

The conceit appealed to me.

One of the galleys had hauled around the main area of conflict. I knew they could still see us, as we could see them, a dark blob against the pink sheen along the water. The galley ignored the fight off to her side and settled down to a strong steady pull. We would reach the bank first, I judged; but it would be a touch-and-go affair.

Now it was just a question of a long strong pull across the ebb toward the bank. Rushes and reeds grew there tall enough to shield us for a space, enough to give us time to cross the mudflats and so escape into the shadows. Behind us, and full in my view, the clustered galleys were putting up a doughty fight against the swarming clouds of volroks.

Arrows skimmed upward, their tips chips of glittering light in the pink glow; crossbow bolts also, I guessed, would be loosed among the flying men. Many I saw fall. One of the galleys swayed drunkenly out of line, her oars all at sixes and sevens, and reeled into a second. Her upperworks, which were, in truth, low enough to the water, were dark with the frantic agitated forms of volroks, like flies upon jam.

Now the Twins edged into the sky, and the two second moons of Kregen, continually orbiting each other, shed sufficient light in their nearly full phase to pick out details with that pink and typically Kregan semblance of fuzzy ruby clarity. Neither the galleys nor the volroks were winning, I judged. The galley pursuing us must be constrained under the most severe orders to recapture us to leave the fight. I pulled and went on pulling as I watched that furiously waged fight, clamoring and shrieking into the night. We had traveled in our flier from the west coast of Havilfar clear across the narrow waist to the northwestern tip of the Shrouded Sea. We had soared over a mountain range. In those peaked valleys, I guessed, lay the towns and aeries of these volroks, these flying men of Havilfar.

The boat's keel felt the first kiss of mud. The boat shuddered; but with a few long, powerful strokes I forced her on until the keel grated unpleasantly on gravel and coarse mud.

I grabbed Saenda. Turko grabbed Quaesa. Also, with a semblance of a grimace that might be called a smile, I seized the boat hook. It was our only weapon.

Over the side we plunged, thigh-deep, and at once the water roiled and clouded with disturbed mud. We staggered on.

Wasting breath, but considering the waste justified to cheer my comrades, I said: "This shallowness of the bank side will hold the galley farther out. We have a better chance."

Saenda, her fair hair streaming over my shoulder, her arms and legs wrapped about me in a clinging grip, shouted: "You'll be sorry for all this, Dray Prescot! By the Lady Emli of Ras! What you've done to me since we—"

I chose at that moment to stumble over an old tree stump half buried in mud and water, and recovered reasonably quickly; but Saenda went under and took a mouthful of that mud and water, and her sharp complaints changed to a choking gargling, in which I caught her attempts at further swearing and promises of the dire things that would happen to me when I took her home to Dap-Tentyrasmot. If ever there was a time for chuckling this night, I suppose that was the time; but I did not chuckle. I simply blundered on up the bank, slipping and sliding in mud, hearing the mud slop and suck at my legs, hoping that I would not fall into a patch of quicksand or that the mud leeches would not get a good grip on my naked legs. For I wore only that old scarlet breechclout. Saenda, for her part, wore a dead Canop guard's breechclout and a piece of cloth hung around her shoulders, and the leeches would relish the fine blood they would discover beneath that fair skin.

Quaesa, with her darker skin and jet hair, would also provide luscious bloodsucking territory. So it was that I was most thankful to blunder out on top of the bank and slip and slide down the other side where the rushes grew wild and in great profusion and leave the sluggish and highly unpleasant River Magan behind.

"They stuck, Dray, just as you said," said Turko as he followed on. His breath came as evenly and his chest moved as smoothly as though he had not plunged into muddy water and carried a girl up a slippery bank at top speed.

"But they'll wade ashore, as we did. Let us *move!*"

That old devilish crack whiplashed in my voice, and the girls jumped, and Turko chuckled, and so we put the girls down and we ran as best we could through the reed beds.

The harsh and mystical training through which I had gone with the Krozairs of Zy — a period that would never really end, for the Krozair usually makes time to return and refresh not so much his physique but his mental attitudes to life and the secret disciplines — enabled me to push on quickly enough and to assist Saenda. The Khamorros, too, taught physical and mental disciplines that enabled Turko to forge on with Quaesa. This was lung-bursting, thew-tearing, heart-hammering effort. Some people when referring to what I have called unarmed combat talk about bloodless combat. There is such a thing, of course, and it is what, really, the Khamorros do in practice — most of the time. But the unarmed combat man is seeking to down his man, and blood will flow then just as though he had sliced him with a sword as hand-chopped his ear so the blood gushes from his nostrils and mouth. There is nothing bloodless about the kind of unarmed combat Turko the Khamorro and I, Dray Prescot, Krozair of Zy, shared.

So we were able to outdistance the pursuit. Soon we ran across a road, muddy and full of potholes, but, nonetheless, a road, and here we saw the beings waiting for us to emerge from the reed beds.

Turko stopped with a low hiss of indrawn breath.

The two girls began to squeal — and two hard and horny hands clamped across their soft mouths. Turko knew as well as I the importance of first-footing with strangers, especially strangers encountered on a lonely road at night with the pinkly golden light of Kregen's moons glinting back from the muddy ruts and potholes and throwing details into a hazy blur.

Often and often has the understanding been brought home to me that this kind of situation is what life on Kregen is all about: This continual headlong advance into danger; this confrontation with the unknown. These beings might turn out to be friends, attracted by the commotion on the river and waiting to see what manner of men or beasts emerged from the reed beds. They might choose to be hostile, and so demand all Turko's skills and a measure of hefty thwacks from my boat hook. They would act according to their natures, and, of a surety, Turko and I would act according to ours.

"Llahal!" I called, using the nonfamiliar form of the universal Kregish greeting.

"Llahal," responded the leader, a being who stepped a little in advance of the others.

There were ten of them, and I saw the gleam of weapons; but I fancied that if

Turko and I were quick we might see them off. Certainly I would not tamely submit. I had been trying, as you can bear witness, to quell that hasty and violent streak of mine that will not tolerate oppression in any form. I had been trying, you might say, to talk first and then strike, rather than the vice versa method to which I had been accustomed.

"We come in peace," I said.

I know this does not sound like the Dray Prescot you may think you have understood, listening to these tapes spinning through the recorder; and I know I told a blatant lie if we were not received in peace; but I meant it. I had more important concerns than a brawl on a muddy path in the light of the moons. The being advanced cautiously. He looked not unlike a volrok, having long narrow wings, neatly folded, but there was about him a difference that marked him out. Those differences could best be described, perhaps, by saying that if a volrok was equated with a Latin of our Earth, this being would be equated with a man of Nordic stock. But the same eight-limbed original body-form was there, with the upper limbs extended into wide narrow wings, the two arms forward — and holding weapons! — the two legs and feet on which there were no scimitar blades, and the rear pair of limbs fused into a tail fan.

"We, too, seek peace. You have been fighting the volroks?"

Turko laughed and started to say "By the Muscle! We've fought the—" when I kicked him in the shins. He said, instead, "—The whole wide world in our time. Do you, then, fight the volroks?"

Another flying man pushed up from the pack. In that light it was difficult to tell them apart. But there is one curious fact that I own to with a certain silly pride, and that is with every successive season I spent on Kregen I was able to pick out more clearly and with greater certainty one halfling from another. Men of one race on Earth will say that all men of another race look alike to them; this is natural if regrettable. Rapechak, for instance, the Rapa mercenary with whom we had fought in Mungul Sidrath and whom we had lost when we escaped into the River Magan, had looked like Rapechak to me, and not like any other Rapa.

This second flying man said: "They are apim. I say we do not trust them."

"And I say," said the leader, in a fashion I admired, "that I will stick you if you do not keep quiet, Quarda."

"We are apim," I said. "But we are not Canops."

The leader laughed. It was a good belly-laugh, rich and round and boiling up from a well-filled stomach.

"We know that, dom. Had you been Canops you would have stepped upon the road as dead men."

"That's comforting to know."

He thought I meant it was comforting to know we had not been killed. What he did not know was that I scented allies here in the straggle to come against the iron men from Canopdrin.

One of the other flying men in the pack shouted: "The Miglas will be here soon. There was enough noise and torches on the river — let us kill them and be gone."

The leader did not turn.

He said, "Quincher — hit that onker Quilly for me."

There came the sound of a blow and a yelp from the dark mass of flying men. The leader nodded, as though satisfied. I rather liked his style.

"You tell me who you are, dom," he said. "And then we will decide to kill you — or not."

I am not given to idle boasts. "Tell me who you are."

He spoke in a very reasonable tone. "You are unarmed. We have weapons, of bronze and of steel. Surely, you must see it is in your own interests to tell us first. After, I will be happy to tell you, and, by the Golden Feathers of Father Qua, it would sadden me to slay a man without weapons in his hands."

I glanced at Turko. He did not betray his thoughts, but they were clear enough.

"What you say is indeed reasonable, dom. This is Turko, a Great Kham, and these are two foolish girls, Saenda and Quaesa, who live on the opposite shore of the Shrouded Sea."

"And you?"

The dark eyes regarded me with a closer intent.

"My name is Dray Prescot."

A buzz of conversation from the flying men, which told me they had not heard of me or of Turko, was followed by the leader bellowing for order. He took a few steps forward, his tail high and arrogant in that pink moonlight.

"I am Obquam of Tajkent. I seek for a certain cramph of a volrok called Rakker — Largan Rakker of the Triple Peaks. Know you of this vile reaver and his whereabouts?"

"No, Horter Obquam," I said at once. There was no sense in beating about the bush here. "We were attacked by the whole pack of volroks and escaped only because they attacked the Canops in the galleys. This Rakker — he has done you an injury?"

"Aye! And more, may the black talons of Deevi Quruk rip out his entrails and strip his wings so that he falls into the Ice Floes of Sicce!"

For the moment I had learned all I needed to know. Local detail could be filled in later. At any moment the commotion which had attracted so much unwelcome attention would bring a patrol of Canops to the scene. There was light enough still to see the wheeling flock of volroks above the galleys, although they were hidden from direct view. I fancied there were fewer flying men over there. I put it to this Obquam of Tajkent.

"If the one you seek flies with that pack there, why do you not wing over and discover the truth for yourself?"

He drew himself up, not so much with hauteur as with offended pride. I had suggested blatantly enough that Turko shook his hands and arms, loosening up, readying for the fight he thought must be imminent.

"Look there, apim!" Obquam pointed.

Out over the river the volroks were in turmoil. Their thin screeching reached us blown on the wind. Now among them appeared the larger and bulkier shapes of men astride flying beasts and birds, flutsmen astride fluttrells, as I thought then. The gleam of weapons turned to a bright glittering. I saw volroks falling,

145

and fluttrells, too, with their riders pitching off to dangle by their clerketers all the way into the water.

The aerial battle raged and drifted away from us.

"The Canops from the galleys will be ashore now," I said. "If you seek this Rakker you had best follow, Horter Obquam."

He gestured. "I am a Strom, Horter Prescot. You really should address me as Strom of Tajkent."

"If it pleases you. But as for me and my friends, we are for Yaman, and the streets will not be friendly at this time of night, so we will take our leave now."

I could feel Turko's brisk brightening at my words.

The girls, whose mouths were now free of our hands, let out gasps of surprise and annoyance and, as was inevitable, fear.

"I am not going back there, Dray Prescot!" yelped Saenda.

"Not for all the ivory in Chem!" snapped Quaesa.

"Then you are perfectly willing to stay with this Strom and his flying men?"

Their outrage was both pitiful and painful. If this Strom Obquam of Tajkent tried to stop me I was fully prepared to deal with him and his flying band. As for the girls, I knew I would have to devise a scheme to get them back to their homes on the other side of the Shrouded Sea, and a good scheme at that. But Turko surprised me. I did not then understand why he wanted to go back to Yaman, the city of eerie buildings where Migshaanu had been contemptuously ousted as the Great Goddess by the Canops. He had no particular love for Mog, the old witch who had so surprisingly become Mog the Mighty, the high priestess, for all that she had doctored him and healed him of his hurts back there in the jungles of Faol.

So it was that I turned to walk off, and said rather sharply: "You understand what it is we are about, Turko? We are making a fresh beginning. We are going to Yaman in the full knowledge that we might never leave, that we might hang by our heels from the ramparts of Mungul Sidrath?"

"I know. I doubt it will happen, Dray."

I grunted, for I could find no words to express what I felt just then.

The flying man — I suspected these were people who would not welcome being called volroks — called Quarda, who had already spoken out of turn, stepped before me. He held a weapon very like a toonon. The short and broad-bladed sword had been mounted on a shaft of a bamboo-like wood, with cross quillons also daggered. He held it as a man who knew his business.

"You do not walk away so lightly, apim Prescot."

I did not reply. I looked with a hard stare at the Strom.

He spread his hands, a gesture of resignation. "In this, Horter Prescot, a matter of honor, I may not intervene. It is between you and Horter Quarda, now."

The distance from my left kneecap to Quarda's groin was almost exactly what one might have wished in the exercise yard. My knee smacked it with a crunchy *whop!* and Quarda stood for a moment, absolutely still, his mouth open. Then he dropped the toonon. His eyes began to bulge. They bulged quite slowly, and shone, a most curious sight. Slowly, he began to fold in the middle. I stood watching him, quite still, not speaking. Quarda put his hands to his middle, moving with a slow underwater finning movement, and bending forward and over, more and more, and his eyes bulged and bulged, and the cords in his neck stood out like a frigate's sheets in a gale.

He rolled right over into a ball, and fell on his side, and his legs kicked for a moment. He had not vomited yet, and that showed he must have been in good control. But he could not yell, and what with the yell inside him that couldn't get out, and the stream that wanted to spurt out as well, he lay in a coil and twitched.

I turned to the Strom of Tajkent.

"Remberee, Strom," I said, quite cheerfully. "Maybe we will have the pleasure of meeting another day."

His eyes on me remained unfathomable.

"Remberee, Dray Prescot."

Taking Saenda firmly by the upper arm, as Turko took Quaesa, I marched off.

Marched off along that dismal road toward the city of Yaman where waited horrors and battles and stratagems, were the other three, and I could not find it in my heart to pity them. As, of course, I could never find pity for myself.

Three

A wall beneath Mungul Sidrath comes to life

"Mag," said Mog, the high priestess. "Nothing can be done until Mag is found. The religion cannot be truly useful to us — to my shame — until Mag is freed."

"Unless," said Planath the Wine, "he be dead."

Old Mog surged up at this in her stiff and gorgeous robes, all crimson and smothered with gold lace and embroidery, the massive golden crown with its rubies toppling dangerously. She banged the great gold-plated staff upon the floor. She looked impressive and dominating and yet, remembering her as the mewling slave I had seen in the jungles of Faol, I felt the irony and pathos here. Her old face with the witch's beak of a nose and the boot-cap chin scowled most ferociously, and her agate eyes gleamed most furiously upon us in the back room of *The Loyal Canoptic.*

She might be an old halfling woman who had been defamed by the invading and conquering Canops, her temple razed and in ruins, her king and queen slain, this important Mag a prisoner or dead — but she cowed the assembled Miglas here. The tavern had seen many of these secret gatherings, but on this night the back room bulged with Miglas, more than ever before, collected together from all over the city of Yaman.

And yet they were a pitifully small number to pit against the might of the iron men from Canopdrin with their superlative drill and discipline, their bows and swords, their armored cavalry of the air. But I had had the task of creating a revolution thrust upon me by the Star Lords, so, therefore, a revolution there was going to be, by Zair!

"So we rescue Mag," I said, over the hubbub.

There was a great shaking of Migla heads, those ludicrous rubbery, flap-eared, pop-eyed faces like children's playthings all swaying in unison. Everyone wore a crimson robe; the men held their stuxes, the throwing spears of Havilfar. But, as I well knew, the brave crimson robes and the deadly accurate stuxes would all be safely hidden away before these Miglas would dare creep out under the radiance of the moons to slink home by back alleys and slippery stairs.

Turko sat back, his bright eyes on me, and, as always, I felt his quizzical glance and knew he weighed me up. A great Khamorro, Turko, a master of his syple, cunning in unarmed combat. He would follow me, for he had said so. But into what harebrained adventures was I proposing to lead him now?

The general consensus was that Mag must be rescued before any move against the Canops could be made. Even then, I wearily suspected, these Miglas were not the stuff from which could be forged a fighting force fit to stand against the disciplined ranks of the men from Canopdrin. I had seen a little of this occupying army, and I recognized their expertise.

But, first things first.

After we had rescued Mag, we could then weigh the situation afresh.

"He is of a surety imprisoned in Mungul Sidrath," said Planath the Wine. He looked troubled.

None of them had appeared surprised that I had returned with Turko, Saenda, and Quaesa. They knew I had rescued them from the citadel of Mungul Sidrath. They did not even show surprise at my announcement that I would help them in their fight against the Canops. Either they were too far gone in apathy, or they did not really believe, or they regarded this as merely a further happy result of the return of Mog the Mighty, their high priestess.

"Then it is to Mungul Sidrath I must go."

Turko lifted his head. But he did not speak.

I said: "How am I to recognize Mag?"

At this old Mog the Witch cackled. She bent her forefinger and pointed it at her nutcracker face.

"You have seen me, Dray Prescot. Therefore you have seen a likeness of my brother."

We were drinking beer, a thin and rather bitter stuff I did not much care for, although the Miglas lapped it up smartly enough. Now a man stood up, splayed on broad feet, his ears flapping, beaming the idiotic Miglish smile. He lifted his blackjack, beer slopping down the dark cracked leather.

"A toast! A toast to Dray Prescot who will go in the safekeeping of Migshenda of the Stux."

"Aye," rumbled from the assembled Miglas, and they stood and lifted their goblets and glasses and blackjacks, and drank.

It was a pretty gesture. But that was all it was, a gesture.

As the Miglas resumed their seats one man remained standing. He lifted his pewter mug to me.

"I will go with you, Dray Prescot."

I looked at him.

Apart from the facts that he was a young man, that he looked fit and healthy, that he held his chin high, there was nothing to distinguish him from all the others.

"You will be killed for sure, Med Neemusbane!"

"Oh, no, Med!" A girl leaped to him, clasped her arms about him. He stood there, and for all the ridiculous appearance of the typical Migla morphology, an aura of dignity and determination made him not ridiculous at all.

Planath the Wine said, again, "You will be killed for sure, Med Neemusbane. But if you must go, we will pray for you."

"Aye," said the others. "At the temple, among the ruins, we will pray for you."

"Oh, Med!" moaned the girl, clasping him.

I had no desire to push this youngster into a danger he probably did not understand. I knew from his name that he had already won fame. A large proportion of the economy of Migla revolved around wild-vosk hunting in the back hills. From the vosk came rich and succulent joints, and supple voskskin, and this Med Neemusbane must be a hunter of great repute.

He said, "I shall go."

Turko said, "A neemu is a most vicious and beautiful beast, a machine of destruction. Even a leem will not willingly encounter two full-grown neemus."

"So be it," I said. I had a plan for this headstrong youngster. "And the thanks of us all, Med Neemusbane."

Although as you know I had figured in a rebellion before, when I had led my old vosk-skulls against the overlords of Magdag, I had been cruelly wrenched away from that final victorious battle by the Star Lords. The rebellion had had no time to flower into a revolution. The time when, as the great song, *The Fetching of Drak na Valka*, says, I had cleansed my island of Valka of the slave-masters and the aragorn did not really count as an organized rebellion. That had been a people aroused in a just anger against rapacious oppressors who raided and reaved. Here, in Migla, the Canops had taken over every aspect of the country and had settled in as the masters. I had no real experience of revolution as I knew it must be handled here. But, as in my avowed way, I would learn.

The problem of returning Saenda and Quaesa worried me; but Planath the Wine assured me he could arrange travel for the two female apims, one to Dap-Tentyrasmot, the other to Methydria, without too much trouble, provided they did as they were told. They had become accustomed to doing as they were told during their period as slaves, when they were being readied to run as quarry for the Manhunters of Faol. Just lately, after our escape, they had tended to revert to their usual hectoring and faultfinding ways. I spoke to them and I deliberately put that old vicious cutting rasp into my voice.

They quailed as I spoke.

"You both claim to be high-born ladies. You have prated on about the kools of rich grazing land and all the merchant agencies your fathers own. This may be so. But if you wish to cross the Shrouded Sea and return to your homes, you will do exactly as Planath the Wine tells you. He is a man to be trusted. If you give any trouble at all, I'll clip your ears, by Vox, and send you back for sport in the fangs of the Manhounds of Faol!"

"Oh, Dray!" wailed Saenda.

And, "Oh, Dray!" wailed Quaesa.

A vivid image flashed into my mind.

I saw myself in a muldavy with her dipping lug of the Eye of the World, and I heard myself cutting the Lady Pulvia na Upalion down to size. I hate and detest berating women. It is a cowardly pastime. But, here, these two silly gigglers demanded no less than a real honest-to-Zair tongue-lashing. I spared them. I recognized my softness and weakness; but they had suffered, by Zair, and I thought they would understand and respect the risks Planath and the Miglas were taking for them.

"You will need many golden deldys, Planath. These I will secure tomorrow."

"Hush, Dray Prescot! We will be happy to furnish all the lady apims may require. Also—" Here Planath the Wine rubbed his chin and squinted up at me. "Also, if you knock any more Canop guardsmen on the head and steal their money the whole city of Yaman will suffer."

"Sink me!" I burst out. "I wouldn't want that — but, equally, I would not wish to sponge on your charity."

After a long and pleasant wrangle, during which a great deal more of the beer was drunk, we agreed that Planath and his friends should outfit the girls and buy them passages aboard the most convenient ship or voller traveling to the eastern shore of the Shrouded Sea. There would have to be matters of disguise, and secrecy; all that I left to the Miglas. It was no part of the plans of the Star Lords, I thought, to become embroiled with these two silly gigglers.

The frowning pile of Mungul Sidrath waited.

In order to rescue Turko and Saenda and Quaesa I had dressed myself up as a Canoptic soldier and marched in boldly. The commandant had been slain; I guessed the new commandant would have tightened up security so that it would be fatuous to suppose we could break in that way again, and, of course, Med could never disguise himself as a Canop, I thought. During the rest of the meeting there was talk of ways and means. I suppose because he looked more and more agitated as the night wore on I took stock of an ugly old Migla called Malkar, who kept rubbing a bald spot on his head, and pulling his flap-ears, and burying his hooked nose in his blackjack, and coming up spluttering to wipe the thin froth away. He had been the old boy charged with the duty of cleaning the drains in the temple. Now the temple of Migshaanu lay in tumbled ruins.

At last Malkar got his courage up, as I thought, although in that I did him an injustice. He took a huge draft of beer, spluttered, choked, and then bellowed so abruptly that everyone fell silent.

"May the divine Migshaanu forgive me, for she will understand why I speak! I know the drains and the sewers, for that is my work, and I joy in serving Migshaanu the thrice-bathed. But — I know more! There is a—" He paused here, screwing himself up to the point. He was, in his eyes, betraying a secret which he should never have known. "I know! Often and often have I seen the king and queen, may Migshaanu enfold her golden wings about them, come to the temple from their palace by the secret way—"

"Ah!" said Turko, leaning forward.

"Yes! There is a way, a tunnel, dark and dangerous, and guarded in a most horrible way I do not know. The king and the queen knew. But they are dead, slain by the Canops, by the foul and rast-loving King Capnon whom the yetches call King Capnon the Great."

"Show us the entrance, good Malkar!" said Med Neemusbane. He spoke with a quick eagerness that warmed me. If there were other brave young men like him among the Migladorn, the chances of a successful revolution were greater than I had surmised.

So it was arranged. Turko and I said Remberee to the two girls, Saenda and Quaesa, and they were suitably tearful at parting. They were not the shishis they had been called. They were simply two young girls who had fallen on evil times and had tried to retain their sanity by clinging to their own old ways. I was in no real position to pass judgment on those ways, for all that I knew they involved slave management, and, as is notorious, women are infinitely more cruel to slaves than are men.

We slunk through the night streets of Yaman, with the eerie old houses, tall and narrow, crooked against the stars, hemming us in. The ruins of the temple glimmered in the hazy pink light of She of the Veils. The Canops had thrown down the columns and the walls and the roof had fallen. Malkar led us past a black hole that stank of sewage. We penetrated down past stone blocks with weird hieroglyphs incised on their hewn surfaces; but we had not lit our torches and so the secret and magical inscriptions were only fitfully revealed in the pink moonlight. When a stone overhang brought us into deep shadow, Malkar whispered and his voice rustled and echoed among the tumbled stones.

"You may light the torches now, Horter Prescot."

Flint and steel clicked and scraped, the tinder caught, and a torch flared. I held it aloft. Before us lay a narrow flight of stairs, hewn from the rock, leading down into inky darkness. Weird and ungainly forms of animals and birds crawled in the light across the walls. The atmosphere of decay and of doom hung about this shattered temple, dedicated to gods of a halfling race.

With a screech and a great rustle of membranous wings a Kregan bat fluttered madly in the light. The woflovol chittered and flew in crazy zigzaggings, seeking the darkness. I put my foot on the first step. Turko closed up. Med, also, began the descent.

Malkar hung back.

"It is down there, Horter Prescot. A great bronze-bolted door. And, after that, Migshaanu the All-Glorious alone knows!"

"I thank you, Horter Malkar. Now get you gone in safety."

"Remberee," he called; but his voice dwindled and faded, for he was already scuttling back and away from this place where, if I allowed myself the fancy, eldritch horrors awaited us.

We three pressed on, descending that narrow stair in the flare of our torches.

I wore my old scarlet breechclout, for the weather was mild. I carried the thraxter and the crossbow and a quiver of bolts we had earlier relieved of those who had no title in the higher warrior-justice to them. If this sounds a high-handed judgment I stand condemned. I knew what I knew of overfed, pampered, and decadent people who hunted other people with crossbow and spear.

This land of Migla stood on approximately the same parallel south as the parallel north running through the Black Mountains of Vallia. I wondered how Inch was faring. But the dark hole yawned beneath my feet and the steps, greasy and treacherous, trended downward inexorably to that massive bronze-bolted lenken door. I suppressed the instinct to hammer on that portal of ill-omen with the thraxter and I kept the sword in its sheath.

Turko, as was his custom, was unarmed. That is to say, he did not carry weapons of steel, edged and pointed. While he had his hands and his feet and his head, he remained a most formidable fighter, a Khamorro and therefore a man to be feared. Med carried eight stuxes in an interesting gadget. From a flat disc of wood eight near-circular notches had been cut around the edge. Each notch had a small spring of carved horn which, when a stux shaft was pressed into the notch, held the stux in place. A simple jerk would flex the spring and release the weapon. There were two discs, and the heads of the spears were so arranged that they staggered downward to give clearance to each fat wedge-shaped blade. A carrying strap could be attached to this stuxcal, when necessary, so that it might be slung over the shoulder and be ready for instant use. Also, Med carried a large hunting knife similar to a scramasax.

The shadows clustered thickly and fled reluctantly before the flare of our torches.

Each individual bronze bolt head of the lenken door gleamed at us like a single malicious eye.

"There," said Turko, and, stepping forward, seized the sliding bolt. I saw the way his muscles slid and bunched, roping like great cables as he drew back the bolt. It had not been used for some time, and verdigris made that drawing difficult. A stale and musty odor puffed out, fetid with unnameable miasmas. Med coughed. Turko grunted. I stepped in, holding my torch high.

"Malkar prated of a great and horrible danger, Dray. Best tread warily."

And, as he spoke, Turko moved up and attempted to take the lead.

I simply increased my stride, plunging headlong into the tunnel beneath the ruins. Sink me! I was still young and foolish enough to think it not pride but a proper sense of martial valor that I should go first. Turko muttered something about a Muscle-bound onker, but he fell in to my rear. Our torches threw ghastly shadows fleeting before us, contorted phantasms from jagged edges of rock. I kept up my brisk advance, for I was not willing for Turko, all unarmed as he was, to take the lead.

We were all breathing lightly, tensed up, cautious, and yet anxious to be through this melancholy tunnel with its aroma of death and decay.

Little echoes from disturbed stones beneath our feet chittered ahead, reverberating tinnily, disquietingly. I stopped.

"Let us move quietly, my friends," I said. "As though we hunted leem."

The way grew warmer. The fetid breath on the air near choked us. Presently the sound of rushing water trembled nearer, until we came out to a cavern where steaming water, boiling and bubbling, spouted from a cleft in the rock and ran, hot and angry, in a channel cut alongside the path. The channel continued into the tunnel, and steam rose about us, slicking upon our skins, so that we gleamed and sweated as though passing through the baths of nine.

Through the steam I tried to espy what lay ahead. I could hear nothing above the boiling rush of waters. Our torches twirled their flaming hair, dampened and fading, so that the shadows closed in. Was that a movement there, up ahead along the tunnel wall? I slowed down and moved forward warily. Yes... that *was* a movement. Something waited for us at a bend in the tunnel, something I could not make out, something lethal and horrible and waiting to pull us down.

Now I put each foot down soundlessly. The torchlight wavered along the slimy walls. White-yellow vegetation grew here, and at the very corner of the bend a gap in the rock ceiling revealed a chink, and a thin streamer of pink light falling through. We were near the surface, then. I advanced.

Med's voice, whispering, reached me.

"Dray — there, by the wall! By Migshenda! A syatra!"

The wall writhed. Many thick and fleshy tentacles sprouted from a central trunk, corpse-white, spine-barbed, rippling and writhing and seeking us. I saw the barbed leaves of the trap opening, ready to snap on its victim. Each Venus's-flytrap would gobble a grown man. The steam rose bewilderingly. The tendrils swayed and writhed like beseeching arms, like the serpent-hair of the Gorgons. But this syatra was no Medusa; rather, it must be one of Medusa's sisters, Eurale or Sthenno. It lashed its tendrils about and its spined trap yawned, barring our way along one side of the tunnel.

I edged forward on the other, the sword in my fist, the crossbow slung over my back.

The tunnel widened a little. The horror opposite lashed its tendrils at me. I ignored them. Until they reached me I would refrain from smiting.

A few bones crunched underfoot.

I pressed on, the steam swirling confusingly in my face, the swishing, thrashing sounds of the blind tendrils seeking those who passed whistling by my ears. Turko closed up. Med followed.

The shadows gyrated madly. Crimson torchlight bounced from the corpse-white trunk and tendrils. The leaves of the trap, like doors hinged flat, quivered. I felt a light sliding glance on my arm and halted instantly.

But — Turko!

The wall at our side had opened. In some way the tunnel was wider still and a second syatra growing from the wall, its roots seeking the hot water, flailed its tendrils above us. We were directly between the two. Their tendrils locked and closed about us. Turko yelled. Two tendrils wrapped around his body were pulling him two different ways, toward the two opposite traps. In scant seconds Turko would be torn in half.

Four

The Miglas demand revolutionary vosk-stuxing

Instinctive reaction lifted my sword arm. I was ready to slash through the tendril nearest to me. Then I, Dray Prescot, paused. Sheer blind bloodthirsty passion had almost condemned my new comrade Turko to death. Instinct to action here was useless. If I slashed through this near tentacle, then the other would have nothing holding it and so could spring back with all its hideous power and snap Turko into the barbed coffin of the trap.

Turko's magnificent body strained. His enormous strength concentrated in resisting the twin pulls. His body was being torn in half, but his training, his discipline, and his muscles fought every inch of the way.

One tendril cut would be followed instantly by the springing of Turko into the trap. The coffin-leaves would close and the spines bite, like a vegetable Iron Maiden, and perhaps a thin trickle of Turko's blood might seep past those clenched vegetable lips.

Instinct had been quelled, and thought had taken over; but to tell you all this has taken ten times longer than the facts of action. In almost the same moment the tendrils lapped Turko and he yelled, I had seized his body in my left arm, throwing the torch to Med and trusting to his quick-wittedness to catch it, had reached across and slashed the tentacle and almost had my feet pulled from under me, so savage and powerful was that force pulling from the opposite syatra. There was time — but only just, only just! — for me to follow that swiping swing with a second and sever the far tendril.

Turko was on his feet in an instant.

"By the Muscle! Burn the monsters!"

He thrust his torch at the nearest syatra and the thing went crazy. Tendrils lashed and writhed, the torch went spinning, to plunge to a fizzing extinction in the boiling water. Med yelled. He was slashing with a stux, not the most handy of weapons for the business, managing for the moment to keep clear of the Gorgon's hair. My thraxter was circling and hacking and hewing all the time, leaving a growing heap of dismembered tendril tips scattered on the floor about us.

This whole scene was awry. How could the old king and queen of Migla have come walking through here in secret to their devotions in the temple? In the ceiling, erratically lit by the two remaining torches — Med had flung mine back — I could vaguely make out a straight line crack, some six inches or so wide. Now if…

I whirled the torch in that crazy steamy atmosphere. The king and queen would have brought samphron-oil lamps. I saw the long lenken lever protruding from the wall well past the syatras and a look back showed its counterpart. We had missed it in going past, an easily done thing in that treacherous light.

With a wild yell I whirled the torch at the near syatra, slashed more of those tendrils away, hacking and slashing, jumped for the lever. A tendril lapped my thigh as I reached the lenk. I ignored it. I felt the vegetable strength of the thing, horrific, dragging me back. With a single last heave I laid my hand on the lever and dragged it down. It resisted and I used all my strength, and with a clashing of gears and a great groaning, the lever fell.

"Look out, Dray!" Turko yelled savagely.

I whirled.

A single stroke from the thraxter severed the tendril around my thigh; but the stroke was unnecessary. From those two six-inch wide slots in the ceiling, one on each side of the tunnel and parallel to it, vast slabs of slate descended smoothly, their massive weight in some way counterpoised behind the walls. As they slid downward so the tendrils wriggled backward, bunching, coiling, avoiding the descending edge of slate. The last corpse-white wriggling tentacle slipped back beneath the slate and the two edges struck the ground with a hollow and reverberating clank.

The running water which gave sustenance to the syatras also must power the counterweight mechanism.

Turko peered over his shoulder, frowning. He never did like having his body ripped up — well, no one does, of course. But for a Khamorro the sanctity of his own body is very close to his heart.

"By Migshenda the Stux!" breathed Med. "We were nearly cast adrift on the Ice Floes of Sicce then!"

"Aye," said Turko. He breathed deeply and flexed his biceps gingerly, testing. Everything seemed to be in order, which put my mind at rest. "By the Muscle! They were strong kobblurs."

Trust Turko for a comment on the aspect that affected him!

We advanced, relighting the torch after some trouble, and found no less than four more levers and slate barricades which, descending with a rumbling roar, walled off the voracious syatras. Although I had not previously encountered this famous plant of Kregen, I had heard of it. It liked hot damp climates in general, and I understood Chem was choked out with the things. No doubt the builders of the temple and Mungul Sidrath had thought it a capital scheme to employ them when they had a ready supply of hot water. The cracks in the roof were not casual cracks at all but carefully constructed ventilation tubes, and no doubt their upper ends would be concealed in innocent-seeming masonry of an innocent-seeming building.

During the day the twin Suns of Scorpio would shine down here for a space sufficient to sustain the syatras.

We padded on and were thankful to leave that tunnel of dark and dank and danger to our rear. We came up into a shaft around the inside of which a narrow spiral stair led upward to — to more darkness and danger, for a surety.

We had, of course, no idea where Mag, twin brother of Mog, would be imprisoned. We did not even know if he was still alive.

Many and many a time have I crept into a fortress, a naked brand in my fist,

155

bent on one nefarious scheme or another. This time I was out to rescue an old Migla and take him back so that the religion of which his twin sister was high priestess might regain its former glory and puissance. Then, if we were lucky, we could turn the Canops out of Migla. We padded through the lower levels of Mungul Sidrath and we were not gentle with those whom we met. We did not run across that dolorous cavern of the waterwheels, where slaves heaved and struggled to hoist water up to the high towers, so that the nobles and lords and ladies of the occupying Canoptic army and court might bathe and wash and refresh themselves. I took the time to don a Canoptic soldier's uniform, the white kiltlike lower garment, the greaves, the lorica, the helmet, and I took up his shield. As he had done before, Turko ignored the weapons, but he took up a shield and slid it up his left arm. I remembered what Turko had done with his shield on that fragile bridge above the rushing waters of the cavern, and I own I felt greatly more happy about life with Turko at my back with his shield.

And, of course, as you must guess, Turko soon became called Turko the Shield.

Presently a Jiktar, sweating, frightened clean through, the point of my sword drawing a bead of blood from his throat, was only too happy to tell me what we needed to know. I knocked him senseless, for that was his due, and we prowled on along the dungeon-lined corridor he indicated. Men and women crowded to the bars. Hairy and whiskery faces peered out, arms beseeched us through the iron bars, a wailing chorus of utter despair which senses that utter despair may be ending screamed at us as we passed.

"When we return, Med," I said, hard and unpleasantly.

"As you will it, Horter Prescot."

I did not blow up at his formality, taking it as a reproof.

'Take your formality to Makki-Grodno, Med! I have been Dray to you — there is no need for 'Horter.' We will release them when we return, for otherwise they will raise the citadel about our ears."

He glanced at me, and away, and gripped his stuxcal. For a Migla he had a spirit I admired. He must have had, for since when did I, Dray Prescot, the Lord of Strombor, condescend to explain my every order?

These were political prisoners, which in Migla meant religious prisoners.

A Deldar, arrogant in his brilliant uniform, strutted down toward us as we reached the end of the corridor where an iron-barred gate concealed the final cell. Med hurled his stux. The squat wedge-shaped blade smashed into the Deldar's lorica, punched on to lodge fatally in his heart. Gouting blood from his mouth — for the wide blade must have severed all his veins and arteries there about his lungs — he toppled without a scream.

"Stupid calsany," commented Turko.

The final cell yielded up Mag.

Mog had spoken truthfully. The oldster after the fashion of very old people was hard to differentiate as to sex. He looked just like Mog. The same beaky nose, the same rat-trap jaws, the same toe-cap chin. He blinked as the torches glittered across his eyes.

This was where Med Neemusbane proved the value of his coming with us. He

156

was able with quick words and the right and correct references to the religion of Migshaanu to convince old Mag that we were friends, come to take him to freedom. The Canops no doubt had plans for him, for they could not be absolutely sure they had crushed the religion, and old Mag, with suitable encouragement of a kind I would not seek to dwell on, would have been a pawn to reimpose their will. We helped him back along that dismal corridor of incarceration, and we opened all the barred doors on our way, swearing vilely at the inmates to be silent. Like released slaves from a swifter, they could not contain their joy, and they ran about, some picking up weapons, others kicking prostrate Canops, others falling to their knees in thankful prayers.

"Mag!" I shouted. "Tell this rabble to follow us. And, by the diseased left armpit of Makki-Grodno, if they don't stop that caterwauling they'll have the whole Canoptic army at our throats."

Mag tried to calm them, but I saw he never would, and as my duty was to him I hustled him away. Turko and I hefted him between us, and he whistled through the air, his feet six inches off the ground and flailing.

We had to put him down half a dozen times to deal with isolated parties of Canops come to investigate the uproar. We noticed that none came upon us from the rear, and from this we took heart. The released prisoners were fighting, then.

Some came with us. Men hardy enough to want to get out with Mag and begin the struggle from the outside, when they were prepared, and not to idly throw away their lives in here.

At one point one of the Miglas, who looked just as stupidly flap-eared and rubbery as any of the others, but who had a rolling muscular look about him, hesitated as we were accosted by a detachment of Canop soldiers. A Migla next to this one, whose name was Hamp, screeched as a crossbow bolt thunked into his belly.

Hamp held a stux he had picked up from a dead Canop.

"Imagine they are vosk, Hamp," I said. I spoke quietly, without drama, reasonably, as though discussing an abstruse point of their own religion with him. "Hurl with Migshenda's skill."

The idea struck him as novel. "Vosk!" he shouted. I loosed and hit a Deldar in the mouth. Hamp bunched up, poised, and threw. His stux battered away the shield of a Canop soldier and slashed out the side of the fellow's face.

"It is done!" Hamp shouted. His curious Migla face looked dazed. "Canops are vosk, to be stuxed!"

Looking back, I saw that was the crux of the problem. The Miglas *had* sought to fight off the Canoptic invasion, but I had put down their complete failure against what were so few men as being due to the superb organization and military discipline of the Canops. But the reasons ran deeper than that.

Here on our own old Earth the East has a tradition that only certain races or tribes are warlike. Others are never reckoned as being of martial spirit, as being of any use as soldiers. Certain developments in the last few years have undermined this belief. In Europe we are a warlike lot, it seems, for the West does not have the same tradition. So the Miglas were a religious nation, and warfare something with which they were unfamiliar. For the Canops, the army represented the ideal. The Canops, with a few regiments and a tiny air arm, had subdued the whole country of the Miglas. Now they sought to maintain their conquest.

With more Miglas like Med Neemusbane and Hamp, I judged, the task I had considered almost insuperable might have a solution that was one I could accept. We reached the open air and climbed back through the tunneled stair and so came out into the ruins. The Maiden with the Many Smiles shone down on us. We made our surreptitious way back to the tavern leaning so crazily on the bank of the River Magan. *The Loyal Canoptic* buzzed with activity that night. I worried over that. The two girls were gone, having been sent on the first stage of their journey home. *The Loyal Canoptic* was a sarcastic name for Planath the Wine's tavern. Before the time of tragedy it had been called *The Loyal of Sidraarga*. Now I fretted that Canop patrols, or any of the mercenaries they employed, would hear the sounds of merrymaking and investigate.

If they did so, of course, every man of the patrol would be dead. But that would only stir up fresh trouble.

The tangled skein of politics in Havilfar, and the delicate balances of power, I found fascinating. The Canops had been able to carry out their conquest of Migla, their own island of Canopdrin in the Shrouded Sea being made uninhabitable by the volcanic activity there, because no one wished to fight them on this issue. The Canops were no more powerful now than they had been. This was not an empire-building conquest. On the other hand, there were many countries around the Shrouded Sea which would welcome the downfall of the iron men from Canopdrin. Their army discipline and organization, I discovered, was not peculiar to them, or remarkably exceptional. The Canoptic army was a fair representative war machine of most countries of Havilfar.

Against that war machine we must pit only religious-minded halflings with vosk-hunting experience. In the normal course of events we could not hope to win; but I held ever in my mind what had been accomplished with the slaves and workers of the warrens of Magdag, and I did not lose hope. I had no right to lose hope, for that would have displeased the Star Lords, and my overriding duty was to stay on Kregen — no matter how.

A camp was established in the back hills of Migla and here collected disaffected halflings prepared to fight. They came in, in small numbers; but as the message was spread by word of mouth throughout the land that both Mog and her brother Mag were returned the stream of recruits thickened. The full rites of Migshaanu were celebrated every sixth day, as was proper on Kregen, and due observances were restored every day also.

I was kept very busy.

A small cadre of dedicated Miglas gathered about Turko and me. Hamp, as one of the better potential officers, and Med also, could be trusted to carry out orders faithfully. I spelled out various of the difficulties to them as we watched Miglas straggling to stay in line and advance shoulder to shoulder over the slope of a hill.

"We face a number of problems," I told them. "One is the absolute absence of hand-to-hand fighting experience here. Not only are you deficient in the art, you do not even have the weapons."

"I have this," said Med, ripping out his big knifelike scramasax. "My veknis has slit many a vosk throat — aye! And a neemu's also, into the bargain."

They solemnly nodded their heads, these ugly little Miglas.

"Aye, Med Neemusbane, you speak the truth."

Whereat Med lowered his head, and looked away, ashamed of thus boasting of his prowess and calling attention to the deed for which he was both famed and named.

"And," I said cuttingly, "what of your little veknis against a real sword? Answer me that!"

I was harsh about his scramasax, for that Saxon weapon is a knife built like a sword, and is very ugly and deadly, although of beautiful shape. But a thraxter, the cut-and-thrust sword of Havilfar, would deal with the veknis with ease.

They shuffled their feet and the Miglas in the line advancing up the hill weaved about like those tendrils sprouting from that horrific syatra in the tunnels beneath Mungul Sidrath. I looked up. At least, the Suns of Scorpio still shone.

"We need shields, and bows, and we need the skills to use them."

Here there were no masses of slave workers skilled in all manner of arts and crafts, as there had been in the warrens of Magdag, as ready to produce a bow or a shield as to produce a statue or a decoration for the megaliths of the overlords.

Mog waved her arms. She insisted on attending every planning meeting, and this was her right, I suppose.

"We must collect all the money we can. All the deldys my people will give — aye, and more. Then we can hire mercenaries. I am told Rapas are very good, for I do not think we could afford to hire Chuliks. There is your answer."

They could do this, of course.

"You can do this," I said. "But who holds the treasury of Migla now? Who controls the state chest in Mungul Sidrath? Can you outbid the Canops in hiring soldiers? For every Rapa you hired they would hire two Chuliks. And, I tell you, for I know these things, no mercenary likes to be hired to fight for a side so obviously doomed to lose."

That, I realized at once, had not only been a tactless thing to say, it had been also offensive.

I went on bluntly and offensively: "Until you learn to fight for yourselves, you will not regain your own country."

"We will fight!" yelled Med Neemusbane. He jumped up, waving his stux. "We will fight!"

"Then learn, you wild neemu! Learn!"

Turko said, in the hush that followed, "If we fight and begin to win, will not the Canops then hire more mercenaries?"

"If they do that, good Turko, they admit defeat. Then, I would be happy to see contingents of Rapas and Brokelsh and Fristles landing in Yaman. For then we would be winning!"

One important fact I must make clear at this point is that I felt myself cut off here in halfling Migla. I was a Homo sapiens, as was Turko; apim. We were the only apim among all these halflings, people whom I would have dubbed, when I first moved among the races of Kregen, as beast-men. I knew a little better by this time. But the oppression of being stuck away here in this backwater of Havilfar, when all I really wanted to do lay across the Southern Ocean, filled me with a haziness as to my proper course for the immediate future. Building up an army seemed to me the only sensible course to follow. The army grew slowly, and shields were produced, and I hammered out a system of tactical combat that I felt would serve its purpose on the day of battle.

We had the advantage of numbers. But, had I been a Canop Chuktar commanding my brigade of regiments, I would have chuckled and in the old uncouth and savage way have said: "All the more targets for my fellows."

As far as the numbers opposed to us were concerned, I was amused to notice how the oddly intricate mensuration of Kregen hampered estimates. Kregen measures in units of six and also in units of ten. In the ancient and misty past we here on this Earth used to measure in units of six; but the decimal system ousted that, and a last rearguard action was fought when shillings vanished and twelve pennies were no longer a unit. There were eighty men in a Canoptic pastang. Six pastangs formed a regiment. With ancillaries like the standard-bearers and the trumpeters and grooms and orderlies and cooks and others of the un-glamorous duty-men necessary in every army, there would be, I judged, something like five hundred and fifty men in a regiment. The commandant in Yaman held no less than twelve regiments, of crossbowmen and of footmen. With extras here, also — say between seven and eight thousand men. He had an air wing also, of which I knew nothing; tough aerial cavalry mounted on mirvols and not on fluttrells as I had previously thought. There was a ground cavalry force, riding totrixes and zorcas, and I had been told that here in Havilfar the half-vove also was used.

In addition there would be the Canop Air Service, flying vollers, those airboats which were at the time manufactured solely in certain of the countries of Havilfar.

All in all we faced a formidable fighting machine.

They hadn't understood my reference to being glad to see contingents of mercenaries, and I had to explain that I meant that these would be mercenaries we hired, for then they would be happy to come to join the winning side for booty and glory.

I had for the moment discounted various Canoptic regiments stationed outside the capital city, for I meant to make the decisive struggle in and around Yaman itself. By the time those regiments scattered throughout Migla arrived they would march into a debacle and could easily be dispersed and captured.

The air of impatience among the Miglas grew with every new bunch of arrivals. They were excellent spear-throwers. I told them what I wanted, what, indeed, I could see as their only chance.

"Shield-bearers will protect your flanks and your front and the stux-men must hurl as they have never hurled before. By sheer weight of flying stuxes you must beat down the Canop shields and slay their bowmen. Then, once you can charge into close quarters, you must use your veknises to strike savagely upward and in, past the edges of the devils' armor. That is your only chance." I stared at the group of Miglas I had chosen as officers, not finding it at all strange that they and Mog had allowed me to take overall command. "I shall show you how to create a new kind of stux that will strip a man of his shield. It will be hard and bloody work. But with a continuous supply of stuxes" — and, Zair forgive me, I did not add, 'and a continuous supply of men' — "you should beat down their strength and their will and so slay them as you slay a wounded vosk."

That, too, was not a clever image, for a wounded vosk is atrociously dangerous, the time when vosks lose their usual placid stolidity and become fighting mad. But, then, the image was correct, after all, for the iron men of Canopdrin were far more dangerous than any vosk, wounded and raging.

And as well I must not lose sight of the fact that Med and his fellows hunted wild vosk out here in the back hills. The domesticated vosk is the stupid sluggish animal of story and legend, and I recalled how we had used them and their appetites in the Black Marble Quarries of Zenicce. The wild vosk, as I discovered, was another kettle of fish altogether. They were wild. Their horns would impale a man and his totrix together given half a chance. The Miglas prized them, though their meat was stringier and tougher than that of the domesticated vosk, because their skins were infinitely more supple and strong, and the export of voskskin had been of great economic value to Migla. The Canops were altering that, as I knew; but for us, here and now training up an army in the back hills, the wild vosks had served to create men — Migla men — with unerring eye and aim, and muscles that could drive a stux with deadly accuracy.

More and more Miglas joined the growing army and shortly a vociferous claque began to demand we march instantly to Yaman and smash the Canops in fair fight.

However much I tried to explain the truth, the hotheads would not listen. They were the victims of an old illusion. Once a man joins his regiment and puts in a little training his whole life changes, he knows he is fitter and tougher than he has ever been, and possessed of fighting skills he had not dreamed existed. He sees his comrades all in line and charges valiantly with them against straw-filled dummies. He believes he is then a soldier. He imagines he is ready to fight.

They would not listen.

Mog and Mag, ugly old twins, whipped up the passion for immediate action. The crimson of Migshaanu appeared everywhere.

I did what I could to depress this premature enthusiasm; but everyone, including Turko, looked at me askance, and could not wait to march.

As promised the new spears were made under my instructions and issued. All I had done was to tell the smiths to convert a stux into a pilum. This was simply done, and in the crudest of fashions, by inserting a rivet halfway along the shaft which, when the spear bit into a shield, would bend and snap and so allow the pilum to droop. The trailing shaft on the ground would impede the soldier and drag down his shield. He would not be able to drag it free for the barbs, and he would be unable to cut it away with his thraxter for the metal splines running down the forward portion of the shaft. When the pila flew shields would be cast away — or so I hoped.

The men were divided up into regiments, and shield-men, stux-men and pilum-men formed into units for the tactical plan.

We had a small totrix-mounted cavalry force, mostly of young Miglas who had been shaken from the placid lethargy of their elders by their resentment of the Canoptic invasion. The totrix, a near relative of the sectrix and the nactrix, is a somewhat heavier beast than either of those and will carry an armored man more easily. They had nothing of the fleetness and nimbleness of zorcas, and nothing of the smashing power of voves, but we had ourselves a cavalry screening force.

Of course, it was not easy. I had to be everywhere and superintend everything, and I own I was tired in a way strange to me, enervated and depressed and struggling vainly to whip my enthusiasm up to the giddy heights of all those around me.

We possessed no aerial cavalry whatsoever.

Hamp was a transformed man.

"They are vosks, Dray Prescot! You said so yourself!"

"Yes — but, Hamp, we are not ready—"

"Look!" Hamp waved his hand at the men who now ran forward steadily in long even ranks, hurling their pila, the air filled with the flying shafts. The stux-men threw, hard and accurately. Then the whole mass drew their veknises and charged, whooping and skirling and roaring. They made a brave sight.

"Not ready," I repeated. My face was ugly.

"You cannot be afraid, Dray Prescot," cackled old Mog. "I saw you at work, in the jungles of that Migshaanu-forsaken Faol. You perhaps fear for the lives of my young men?"

"I do."

"We are happy to give our lives for Migshaanu the All-Glorious!" yelled Med Neemusbane, waving his knife.

"Aye, you are happy. But I am not. Suicide is no way to find Zair and to sit at his right hand in the glory of Zim."

"Heathen gods, Dray, heathen gods!"

I had to bite down my angry retort. I was, as you would say in this day and age, losing my cool.

Despite what many men — aye, and many women! — have said, I, Dray Prescot, Krozair of Zy and Lord of Strombor, am a human being. I am only human. I was tired in a way that irked me. If I let the decision slip away, if I did not fight them more forcefully, I own the fault is mine. Worry and concern pressed in on me, and I gave way. Their enthusiasm and confidence were treacherous pressures. I should not have allowed it. But, to my shame, I did.

"Very well! Give me two more sennights. Just two. Then, by Vox! Then we will march on these men of Canopdrin!"

I was a fool.

162

The Miglas would not wait twelve more days.

Hamp was the ringleader; chosen by me as a commander, he took full control, actively encouraged by the twins Mog and Mag. Med Neemusbane was his enthusiastic lieutenant. The Migla army, a creation wholly new to them, and a thing not seen in Migla for many and many a season, marched out.

They marched singing.

They carried their shields over their backs. Their stuxcals were filled. Their pila were ready. Their veknises were sharp. They sang as they marched and the long winding columns of crimson, with the great staff of Migshaanu borne at their head, rolled down from the back hills and took the road to Yaman.

Turko and I sat our totrixes on a little eminence and watched them go.

"Fools!" I whispered.

"They are brave, Dray. They will fight well, for you have taught them."

"I have sent them to their deaths…"

"They chose to go."

"Aye. And I cannot let them go without me." I shook out the reins.

Turko lifted his great shield, specially built and strengthened, behind my back. The Suns of Scorpio streamed their mingled red and emerald light about us as we trotted down from the hills, our twin shadows moving with us. All this was happening because of the direct orders of the Star Lords. I did not much care for the Everoinye then. We trotted down from the hills and so rode with the Migla army for the city of Yaman and for disaster.

Five

Turko the Shield and I sup after the first battle

That disaster did not strike exactly as I had imagined it must.

The raw army of recruits of Migla fought well.

I fought with them. The memories I retain of that battle are scattered and fragmentary, of the charges and the falling spears, the glitter of armor and weapons, the clouds of crossbow bolts, the solid chunking smash of masses of men in close combat. The fliers astride their mirvols rained down their bolts from above, and the Miglas lifted their shields, and the crossbowmen afoot loosed into them.

But the pila dragged down many a shield, and the stuxes flew. The Miglas fought magnificently. They outnumbered the army of Canopdrin. They did not consider their own losses. They charged again and again, their veknises gleaming crimson with blood, and again and again they were hurled back. Yet still they charged. The supplies of stuxes I had arranged to be brought up by wagons were late arriving, and when they did at last reach the field, which lay in wide meadows about a dwabur west of Yaman, there were pitifully few hands to grasp them.

I had four totrixes slain under me. When there were no more riding animals to be had I charged afoot at the head of the Miglas. I found the thraxter to be a useful weapon, used with a shield, and I also discovered — as I had always known — how inordinately powerful a shield wall could be if it remained intact.

The Miglas broke two shield walls.

They toppled two Canoptic brigades into rout.

But the supreme efforts spent their strength and the remaining two brigades were able to drive in, charging in their turn now under showers of bolts, and tumble the Miglas back into destruction.

Trapped in a close-pressing melee Turko and I were tumbled back with the rest. Yes, I do not recall many of the details of that battle, which, from a windmill nearby owned by a Migla called Mackee, was henceforth known as the Battle of Mackee; but one scarlet memory stands out and runs like a thread through the whole conflict.

How strange it was, I thought, not to have to worry over my back!

For, where I went, there went Turko the Shield.

With those lightning-fast reflexes of the Khamorro he picked up the flight of a bolt and interposed the shield between it and my back or side. He hovered over me, an aegis through which no single bolt, no single arrow, no single stux could penetrate.

And — more than once a Migla, inflamed by the homicidal fury of combat, seeing in Turko and me two hated apims, would hurl at us. Turko's muscles roped and twined as he held the great shield up, its surface bristling with shafts. Whenever he could he took the opportunity of ripping them away. He had the Khamorro strength to rip a barbed bolt out where a normal soldier would have no chance of doing the same.

A pilum smacked into the shield. I remember that. I remember seeing Turko hoisting the shield up, seeing bolts glancing from it, seeing the way he held it despite the dragging effect of the pilum. For a space we were clear of the press. Dust and blood and the shrieking screams of wounded and dying men created that insane horror of a battlefield all about us.

Turko bent and ripped the pilum away—

And then I remember looking up at the night sky and seeing the Twins eternally revolving one about the other sailing across the sky, cloud wrack driven across their faces giving them the illusion of movement. Turko at my side lay senseless, blood clotting his hair. He wore a red band around his head now, as a reed syple, and I knew why.

All about us the horrid moaning of hundreds of wounded men, Migla and apim, rose into the cool night wind.

Occasionally shrill shrieks burst out, to sputter and die away. Canops were out with lanterns searching among the dead. I discovered the blood dried along my head. All the famous bells of Beng-Kishi rang in that old head of mine; but my skull is a thick one, and I had bathed in the pool of baptism in the River Zelph in far Aphrasöe, and so I was able to hunch up and get Turko on my back and stagger away from that awful and tragic field.

There was nothing to be done here, the disaster was on so great a scale, that all there was left for us was to save our own skins. Then, I vowed, then we would come back and do properly what we had so signally failed to do this day on the field of Mackee.

A voice hailed.

"Over here, dom."

Armed Canops, with samphron-oil lamps and flaring torches. If I ran they would split Turko and me with accurate bolts. I took Turko across to the fire. Many Canops lay on blankets around the fire, and I saw Canop women tending them. The smoke drifted in the cool wind.

"Let's have a look at you, soldier."

This Canop, this one with the lined haggard face, the haunted eyes, must be a doctor. In mere seconds he had stuck his acupuncture needles into Turko and so could banish my comrade's pain while he tended the gash on his head. My own wound needed merely cleaning and poulticing and bandaging.

"A nasty crack that one, soldier." The doctor handed me to a Canop woman, a mere slip of a girl with dark hair and eyes I knew would be merry in other circumstances. Her long slim fingers bandaged my head. We were apim; therefore we were Canops. We were not Miglas, we were not the enemy.

The situation was not without its piquancy.

Turko breathed easier now. We had both been wearing armor taken from Canops, and we would pass.

We were put down carefully on blankets in a ring around the fire, and broth — good vosk and onion soup — and a rolled leaf filled with palines were handed to each of us. We drank and ate with relish. Later there was wine, rough army issue wine, but refreshing and invigorating at the time.

"Those old cham-faces," said a soldier next to me, who had a bandage covering most of his stomach. "They stuck me in the belly. But I feel sorry for 'em."

"Sorry for 'em?" I was genuinely surprised.

"Well, look at the crazy onkers, charging us like that." The soldier moved and suddenly, unpleasantly, he groaned and I saw his face go set into drawn haggard lines.

"Nurse!" I called, and the girl hurried over. She knelt, her yellow tunic and skirt, not unlike the kilts worn by the men, glimmering warm in the firelight. There were many fires over the battlefield, each with its ring of wounded. She looked cross.

"Have you been drinking, soldier?"

He winked at her.

"You silly onker! You've been cut up in the belly — no more wine until the doctor orders. Understand?"

She had given one of the needles sticking in him a twirl and his pain receded. He looked properly subdued. "Orders is orders, nurse. But I'm fair parched."

"Suck palines, soldier."

When she had gone in answer to a muffled scream from across the ring of wounded men, I returned to the source of my puzzlement. "Those Miglas. They were out to kill—"

"Well, wouldn't you be? If your land had been taken from you?"

The disorientation of all this could not be explained merely by his mistaking me for a soldier and a comrade. The soldier next along lifted on an elbow. He had a broken leg which had been expertly set and splinted. He spoke over the man with the stomach wound.

"How much do we get out of it, then, I ask you? We do the fighting — aye, and I'm proud to fight for Canopdrin. But I'd like a little more booty."

These men I had already summed up as soldiers fighting for their country, not mercenaries, and therefore urged on not by cold greed but hot patriotism. They talked on, quietly, and I came to understand the viewpoint of the Canoptic soldier much better. A rough lot, like soldiers almost anywhere, they enlisted for enormously long periods and expected hard fighting, for they had had a long-standing feud with a neighbor island of the Shrouded Sea. When Canopdrin had been made uninhabitable they had welcomed the decision of the king and his pallans to make a new home in Migla. But, as was usually the way, the high-born reaped most of the benefits.

The man with the belly wound, whose name was Naghan the Throat — he was always thirsty — rambled and muttered and I feared that he would be gripped by a fever and so taken off. He suddenly tried to sit up, his eyes wide and brilliant, and he cried: "I fought, by Opaz! I fought!"

Then the man with the broken leg, one Jedgul the Finger — I was too delicate to inquire why he had acquired the name — sat up sharply and dragged himself toward Naghan's blanket and took Naghan and thrust him down, his hand splayed over the face.

"Quiet, you onker!" He spoke breathily, quickly, and then, in a louder voice: "By the Glorious Lem, you will live!"

The picture came clear to me in those few words. Lem, the silver leem, was the supernatural being worshiped by the Canops, and his statue was everywhere, for a soldier most noticeably in the form of a silver leaping leem atop the standard. This leem cult had broken the religion of Migshaanu. But Naghan the Throat had cursed in his delirium by Opaz, the great twin deity, invisible and omnipotent, that represented the major religious beliefs of the peoples of Pandahem and of Vallia and of many other civilized places besides. So, I reasoned, Lem, the debased silver leem, had ousted the followers of Opaz before he had started in on Migshaanu. Now I have made no attempt to outline the beliefs or practices of the religion of the Invisible Twins, of Opaz. I have told you of the long chanting processions streaming in torchlight through the cities and all chanting "Oolie Opaz, Oolie Opaz, Oolie Opaz." The stresses come on the first syllables of the words. It is always "Oolie Opaz!" over and over again.

But — there is a very great deal more to it than a mere chanting procession.

Jedgul the Finger looked at me over the prostrate form of Naghan and I saw his eyes glittering in the firelight.

"Naghan the Throat is a good comrade of mine, dom. You are a soldier. You would not betray him?"

"Never," I said.

Jedgul slumped back, as though relieved.

"It's all the fault of the officers," he said, his voice low, grumbling. This is so common a complaint in every army I would have taken no notice of it; but Jedgul added, "They think themselves so high and mighty. A common ranker may never enter their shrines to Lem. Everything of the best is always theirs. I bet you your officers are doing what ours are now, drinking themselves silly and pestering shishis... You didn't say what your regiment was."

I had seen his shield, with the embossed image of the leaping leem at the top, below that a black neemu, painted on, with the figures eleven and one. He was of the first pastang of the eleventh regiment of foot. At the beginning of the battle I had made it my business to make a note of all the regiments arrayed against us, and now was able to choose one on the opposite wing from the eleventh. Also, in choosing this particular regiment I could exhibit a little hard-won knowledge.

"Third," I said casually. And added, "Hikdar Markman will be occupying two shishis, if I know him."

Jedgul chuckled.

"Aye, Nath," he said, for I had told them I was called Nath. "And King Capnon can sleep safe in his bed this night."

"Better get some sleep yourself. Here comes the nurse."

"Aye," he said, yawning. "Paline Chahmsix is a sweet kid. Her old man ought to be proud of her."

"Six" is one of the common suffixes denoting daughter, as "ban" often denotes son. The nurse, Paline Chahmsix, came up, tut-tutting, and bid Jedgul and I sleep as soundly as Naghan. "Lem keep you," she said, which is a way of saying good night.

Jedgul answered with a snore.

I turned over and closed my eyes. When the light tread of her little feet had gone I rolled across to Turko and shook him awake. The sounds around us were dying. The wounded were finding peace in sleep. Tomorrow would see the collection and burial of the dead, with their memories dedicated to the greater glory of Lem, the silver leem.

"We have to leave now, Turko. And don't make a sound."

He was awake quickly enough. He touched his bandaged head and checked the needle. "What—?"

"A doctor attended you, and a charming little girl not really old enough to be out here at night with all these desperate soldiers. We've been lucky, Turko. Now let's get out of here without a fuss. I wouldn't want anything to happen to little Paline Chahmsix."

His glance contained all that old quizzical appraisal; but he rose, and together we silently crept away from the glow of the fire out into the moon-drenched shadows of Kregen.

Late on the following day we caught up with what was left of the army of Migla and with these sorry remnants we returned to the camps in the back hills. We had lost a sorrowful lot of men. Hamp and Med had both been wounded; but they were unrepentant when I started to tell them a few home truths.

"We were not ready, as you said, Dray. But we have learned. We know now we can beat them next time."

"There will be no next time," I said. I was savage and cutting and angry and contemptuous — of myself. For, I, too, had seen my own crass stupidity. "There will not be a next time until I give the word."

Mog waved her arms about at this, and quieted Mag, who had been about to try to say something, and she yelled: "I am the high priestess! We must strike, and strike again!"

"Agreed. But we do it my way. The common soldiers of Canopdrin are just ordinary men. They are driven into fighting by their masters, who crack the whips over them, and who dazzle their eyes with statues of Lem, the silver leem."

As I spoke these words Mog and Mag and the others shuddered and put up their hands, warding off the evil of that foul name.

"Opaz," I said fiercely, proddingly. "Aye, Opaz is known among them and some still love the Invisible Twins. They would welcome you of Migshaanu if a way could be found."

"They would cut us down with swords if we tried," said Med.

"Agreed. You cannot face them in battle, not for a long time. You must accept this as a truth. But there is a way, and I shall take that way, and bring you help. You must wait here, recruit more men, train them up as I have shown you. When the time is ripe Turko here, or one bearing a message from me, Dray Prescot, will come to you. Then, my friends, strike at Yaman!"

They jabbered on at that; but all I would say — for fear I should fail — was that they must prepare themselves for the day. When that day came, they would be told.

And, even as I cursed myself for my own stupidity, I cringed a little at the thought of what the Star Lords would do. For I had not disobeyed the Everoinye. I had done what the Star Lords commanded, through their spy and messenger the golden and scarlet raptor, the Gdoinye. But — for the first time on Kregen — I had failed the Star Lords.

I had not failed them in Magdag but had been too successful.

I had not disobeyed.

I had failed.

What would they do to one who proved a broken reed?

The thoughts of Delia, and our twins, drove mad phantasms through my mind. What if, through my failure, I was banished from Kregen forever? If the Star Lords had no further use for me? The thought was impossible; I could not face it. I must recoup this situation, bash on, trample down any and everything that stood in my path. Oh, I did not relish my avowed intent, there in that ring of hills in backward Migla. But — better the Ice Floes of Sicce than being hurled back to the Earth of my birth and never more see my Delia, my Delia of Delphond!

Never before had I failed in what the Star Lords had set me to accomplish. This was no time to start.

Turko would come with me.

I bid Remberee to Mog and Med Neemusbane and Hamp, and set off for Yaman. We traveled secretly and by night, and I wore my old scarlet breechclout and carried weapons, and Turko wore the scarlet band about his forehead that was his new reed syple, and a shield strapped on his left arm. And so we came under the moons of Kregen into the ruins of the temple within the grove of trees sacred to Sidraarga.

Shadows dappled the stone where lichens already stained and obscured the sacred symbols. The moons rode the sky above and the pink moonlight flooded down. I moved into the shadows beneath the trees, and my brand gleamed naked in my fist.

The flier was still there.

This was the voller that had brought us out of Faol and away from the slavering if human jaws of the manhounds.

Turko said, "I have never inquired why you had to bring old Mog home, Dray, being content to follow you. And, now, I am filled with joy that I may lift a shield at your back. But—"

"And much do I value that, Zair knows!" I climbed up into the airboat. "In me, Turko the Shield, you behold a great and misbegotten fool! An onker of onkers, a get onker."

"If you say so, Dray, I would be the last to correct you on so weighty a point."

He was laughing at me again, this muscular Khamorro!

I checked over the flier and saw she was intact and ready to go. I would not give Turko the satisfaction of rising to his sarcasm; for all that we owed each other much, I still had that prickly feeling that he weighed me and sized me up at all times. I had proved to him through the disciplines of the Krozairs of Zy, of which he had never heard, that I was as good as any Great Kham produced by the Khamorros, and I had earned his shocked "Hai Hikai!" But, still, he wanted to know more of me. You could not fault him for that, I did realize, somewhat ill temperedly; for I own I am a great shambling bear of a fellow when it comes to human relations and I know what I want to do and say and, Makki-Grodno as a witness, I say and do the exact opposite. I have overcome that defect a great deal in later years; but it is a burden many of us bear.

With a finicky delicacy on the controls I edged the voller out from under the trees. Mog had truly said no one would venture into the sacred grove. We cleared the last boughs and I looked up ready to haul the lever into the ascent position, when I saw the black shape of the Gdoinye hard-etched against the glowing pink and golden face of the Maiden with the Many Smiles.

For an instant the accipiter hung; then it vanished.

No mistake was possible; that had not been some nocturnal, completely ordinary bird of prey. The Everoinye watched over me, watched me in my failure!

"Where away, then, Dray?"

"Do you know where lies Valka?"

"No." Then he added, "I've never heard of it, I think."

This did not surprise me. Kregen is a world where rapid transport by flier rubs shoulders with quoffa carts, where men in one continent cannot be expected to know very much of another continent, and that in the other hemisphere. And yet one expects travelers, businessmen with overseas agencies, military personnel, and, above all, the men of the air services, to be aware of vast numbers of names and places scattered across the islands and continents in this part of Kregen.

"Valka lies a trifle west of due north." At this time on Kregen the magnetic variation was approximately naught degrees naught minutes and ten seconds west — which was very handy for calculation — and a due north course would serve admirably. "It must be something like two thousand or more dwaburs which, in this excellent voller, are a mere nothing."

I said no more.

Around me in the flier a blue nimbus spread. I was aware of outside sounds slipping away, of Turko's light voice fading. The blue radiance grew and began to coalesce around me into the gigantic form of a scorpion.

This was idiocy.

This was sheer lunacy.

Were the Star Lords then so abysmal a pack of cretins?

The blue radiance closed around me.

"You idiots, you onkers of calsanys of Star Lords!" I roared. "How will taking me back to Earth help you now? I am going to Valka and to Vallia to raise an army to fight the Canops and to free Migla! As you commanded! Are you so stupidly dense as not to see that?"

The blueness wavered, not thickening; but not thinning, either. I sweated. Would these lofty Star Lords heed my impassioned call? Or were they truly less than perfect and blind to my purposes? I had fooled them before — or, rather, not so much fooled them as twisted their motives to my own ends. "I have to raise an army somewhere, and the Migla money will not serve against the Canops' control of the treasury!"

Familiar falling sensations swung me and I felt the faintness overcoming me. They were not listening! They were contemptuously hurling me back to Earth! This was unlike that other time I had struggled against the Everoinye, there in the courtyard of the Akhram as the Star Lords and the Savanti had through the agencies of the raptor and the dove sought to determine if I should stay on Kregen and to which side of the Eye of the World I should venture. I had gone eventually to the green north, to the land of the Grodnim. Who was to say what my fate would have been had I gone to the red south, to the land of the Zairians?

So, again, I struggled. I roared and raged and cursed and pleaded. The blue glow about me wavered uncertainly.

"If you banish me back to Earth now, you Opaz-forsaken cramphs, you will never free Migla! By the Black Chunkrah! Let me go to Valka and raise my own men. Then we will see how the army of Canopdrin fights!"

The scorpion leered down on me, at once surrounding me in the blue radiance and also hovering over me, that arrogant tail upflung as the constellation of Scorpio flings its tail across the night sky of Earth. I felt the beginnings of a fading, of a lessening of power and of a lightening of that lambent blueness. The glow blinded me. All I could see, suddenly and with a shocking clarity that told me the vision came from within my mind, the face of Delia blotted out everything else in the world of Kregen. But I did not utter her name aloud. Even then, onker that I am, I kept my wits about me. Instead, cunning with the cunning of the desperate, I screamed: "Let me go to Valka and there raise an army to fight for you, you — you Star Lords." The thought had occurred that cursing them might not help, either.

The blue radiance rippled, as a pool ripples from a flung stone, trembled, and — instantaneously — was gone.

Turko was looking at me quite normally and saying, "I agree this is an excellent voller. We can make about fifteen db[4] and with stops to pick up supplies should be there in three and a half or four days."

As far as he was concerned nothing had transpired. He did not know I had fought as hard a battle over my fate, dangled between two worlds four hundred light-years apart, as ever I had done — but not, Zair rot the Star Lords, as I was to do, as you will no doubt hear in due time.

Whatever their mysterious purposes were they clearly wanted me to reinstate the religion of Migshaanu — and her twin brother Migshenda the Stux, who was in something of a decline even compared with Migshaanu — pretty badly, enough to allow me to call them a bunch of onkers and calsanys and many another vile word I could put my tongue to. The voller drove up past that grove of trees sacred to Sidraarga and sped out over the face of the land spread beneath the moons of Kregen.

I was on my way home — home to Valka and to Delia.

Six

A stowaway and I part on the field of the Crimson Missals

Delia held me fast and would not let me go.

She clung to me, not sobbing, holding me tight, her arms wrapped about me, her dear form pressed against mine so that I could feel the beating of her heart.

And I held Delia, my Delia of Delphond, my Delia of the Blue Mountains — and, now, to our eternal glory, Delia, the mother of the twins, Drak and Lela.

We could have stood thus, breast to breast, locked in a thankfulness and a joy that was a mutual rapture, until the Ice Floes of Sicce went up in steam.

But, eventually, outside forces broke in as the Emperor strode testily into that inner chamber in the high fortress of Esser Rarioch overlooking my Valkan capital of Valkanium. The room was low-ceiled, and tastefully furnished with sturm-wood and tapestries, with rugs of Walfarg weave and silks of Pandahem strewn upon the low couches, and in the corners vast jars of Pandahem ware with many colorful and scented flowers springing in a blaze of beauty. On the windowsill sat a flick-flick in its pot; but it was likely to go hungry here, where the very cleanliness and beauty of the place must repel flies.

"Well, son-in-law, so you deign to return home to your deserted wife!"

Reluctantly, I released Delia. She wore a sheer gown of silk — not Pandahem silk but silk from Loh — of a pale glimmering laypom color, and her brown hair with that outrageous auburn tint shone in the mingled streaming radiance from Zim and Genodras shining splendidly in the sky of Kregen. I had taken time to wash myself after that mad dash across the skies in the voller with Turko. I would not voluntarily present myself before my princess in any other condition than of utmost cleanliness; but there had been no time to take the baths of nine. I wore my old scarlet breechclout, still, and a Havilfarese thraxter swung at my waist.

How Delia had shrieked when I appeared in the door, thrusting impatiently past guards and attendants and footmen. We kept no slaves, Delia and I, on any of our estates. She had shrieked once, and then thrown herself into my arms and held me — and now her father, the puissant Emperor, was here and demanding explanations I could not give him.

"Well, Dray Prescot," said Delia. "Am I your deserted wife?"

"Alas, my heart, to my shame, you have been." How much could I let the Emperor know? Delia already knew of my absences so inexplicable to her, absences which she met with the sturdy resources of a loving heart. She must be told the truth, and I knew that even if she could not understand — as, by Vox, neither did I understand myself — she would not call me a madman and run for the guards.

"I have been away on business near to us all," I said. And then I plunged. "I have brought back a voller — an airboat — that I do not think will break down or fail us."

"That I cannot believe."

"Indeed you would not, and I do not blame you for that. But I have been in Havilfar—"

"Havilfar!" They both said the word, astounded.

"Aye. There are secrets to be learned there it much behooves Vallia to learn."

"That is true, Dray, by Vox!" The Emperor scowled as he spoke. Every Vallian resented the dependence on the manufacturers of Havilfar for the supply of airboats that continually failed.

"How are you here, Emperor?"

"That daughter of mine — she insisted we bring every resource into looking for you. You vanished on your way from Valka to Zamra. We have combed every stew, every alley, every barracoon — although, Delia and you, between you, are closing the bagnios so fast you'll bankrupt us all."

"We will not talk of that, my father, at this time."

"As you will, daughter, as you will. Come, where is wine? I would like to drink a toast to this wild leem of yours, who swings a sword and pulls my hair."

This was the man who had yelled a harsh command to his men to cut off my head — instantly. Well, times changed.

The twins were thriving wonderfully. Delia was blooming. Seg Segutorio and Thelda, his wife, the Kov and Kovneva of Falinur, were here also, aiding in the search for me. Inch, too, the Kov of the Black Mountains, with all his seven foot of height, was here. How we chuckled at these titles, for had we not all, at different times, been foot-weary nomads wandering with only our swords and our wits between us and destruction?

Also I saw my elders and council of Valka, and assured myself that everything ran smoothly. As I told Tharu ti Valkanium: "I warned you, Tharu, that I might be taken away on business. I am happy the island prospers so under your wise direction."

To which he replied: "I have the help of the elders and of fine young men like Tom ti Vulheim, Prince. We shall not fail you."

That evening in Esser Rarioch we caroused and sang in the Valkan way. The songs burst upward to the rafters, all songs we knew and loved. And, to my intense surprise, I found my Valkans singing that notorious song, "The Bowmen of Loh." Since I had introduced an honor guard of Valkan Archers to the imperial court, and since Seg had proved by deeds as well as words that he was a true friend to Dray Prescot, Prince Majister of Vallia and Strom of Valka, the Valkans accepted the Lohvian bowmen as equals. Seg and I exchanged wry smiles at this; but we kept our thoughts to ourselves.

"Crossbows it is in Havilfar, mostly, Seg."

"We can put ten arrows into the air while they wind up their monstrous contraptions."

"We will have need to. We cannot take all the men I would wish for."

I had conceived that the Emperor would prove a problem, and had not been altogether pleased he was here on my island of Valka when I would have thought him safely back in his capital of Vondium in Vallia. But since the abortive revolution had been put down, as I have told you, he was a much freer man. Now he surprised me by wholeheartedly flinging himself into preparations for the venture to Havilfar. He would be the mainspring that would enable me to collect airboats and men and to transport them to Migla. If he questioned why we must go to Migla and aid a halfling race against the Canops, who were apims like ourselves, he did not mention it. He did say, however, that the Miglas did not manufacture airboats, did they, Dray?

And I said they did not, but that they would be useful allies to us for the future.

He had a long eye, had the Emperor of Vallia. He nodded and set about collecting men and weapons and fliers.

If this was a confidence trick I was pulling on the empire of Vallia, it was on a gargantuan scale, and I was gleeful at my thoughts.

Vomanus, who was my half-brother-in-law, was away in Port Tavetus at this time, on the eastern coast of Turismond, no doubt drinking and wenching in his reckless way, and so was unavailable to come with us. Korf Aighos was in the Blue Mountains. But with Seg and Inch I wanted no other companions. Except for Nath and Zolta, my two oar comrades, those two rascals I had not seen for long and long.

In all this preparation Turko wandered like a man in a dream, dazed, and every time he saw me he would say, "Prince Majister," and shake his head. Then he would flex his muscles and so I would know he was all right. He would get on with my comrades, with Seg and Inch, for all that they were Kovs these days.

The day dawned when our preparations were ready. In the end his Pallans persuaded the Emperor it would be folly for him to go with us, and grumbling and reminding us of how he had fought the last bloody remnants of the third party led by Ortyg Larghos outside his own palace, he gave way. I felt relief.

Seg was bringing three thousand of his Crimson Bowmen of Loh. Tom ti Vulheim was bringing a thousand Valkan Archers. There were five thousand of my old Valkan fighters, men I had trained myself in the arts of war and with whom I had thrashed the aragorn and the slave-masters and so cleansed my island of Valka. Many of them still addressed me as Strom Drak. I did not mind. It was a name of honor.

We did not take a single mercenary. I had no desire to lead Chuliks or Rapas or Fristles up against the apims of Canopdrin. I had received a new insight into them, on the battlefield of Mackee, around the fires, among the wounded. They were men. We must deal with their noble masters, and then, I devoutly hoped, we could come to terms.

By the Emperor's express commands we collected an impressive fleet of fliers. They might fail us on the way. We had to accept that. The Vallian Air Service, trim in their blue uniforms and orange cloaks, would do all they could to bring us through. Chuktar Farris, the Lord of Vomansoir, would lead. I was pleased, for although we had met and got on well, our paths had not crossed as often as I would have wished.

We even had a few commercial airboats, and I was amused to see a couple of ice boats there, gray and ugly — but fliers, able to take a platoon of men into Havilfar.

So it was that under the light of the Suns of Scorpio we took off, a great aerial armada of better than a hundred and fifty fliers, slanting up against the rays of the suns, heading due south.

I had bidden farewell to the twins, Drak and Lela, and wondered what they made of this ugly-faced old graint of a fellow, who claimed to be their father. I could not find Delia. This was odd. I raged about the high fortress of Esser Rarioch, shouting, and maids and servants and guards ran hunting, but she was not to be found. My flier, which should have been up there leading the host alongside that of Chuktar Farris, waited on the flight platform overhanging the sea.

Then I slapped my gauntlet down on my thigh.

I should have known my Delia!

Seg and Inch had left, each leading his own contingent, and Inch had brought eight hundred bonny fighters from his Black Mountains, for we had not called on Korf Aighos for any of his Blue Mountain Boys. We were remiss in that, as Delia had prophesied, and the Korf followed us, in what fliers he could scrape up, swearing and cursing and his fingers itching for plunder.

So I vaulted up into the flier, and nodded to young Hikdar Vangar ti Valkanium, who had been a Deldar when I had been in most desperate straits in Vondium, and who now commanded my airboat. He saluted and started to yell his ritual orders to cast off, for he had seen how I had observed the fantamyrrh as I came aboard.

In the aft cabin, and hidden beneath a great pile of silks, I saw a rounded bottom in tight buff leathers only half concealed. I did not slap. The itch was there, but I did not.

I hauled her out.

She came, laughing, joyful, her gorgeous face glowing with fun and pleasure, that marvelous hair tumbled about her, her glorious brown eyes filled with the light of love.

I stood back and looked at her, and I put an expression on my face that would have cowed a leem and she laughed — she laughed! — and shook me and kissed me and so I was done for.

She wore buff leathers, and a brave scarlet sash around her waist, so narrow, so slender, so beautiful. Her form was something to take a man's breath away. She wore buff boots of supple lesten hide, reaching to the knee. At her side swung a rapier, and opposite the Jiktar she wore the Hikdar, the main-gauche. Her face glowed upon me.

"You did not think, darling Dray, that you could escape me again?"

"I had thought to leave you mewed up, in Esser Rarioch, to care for the sewing and the darning, the pot-washing and the clothes-scrubbing and the floor-cleaning. They seem fitting occupations — and the twins?"

This was a serious note.

"They are safe and cared for as no other children in all the world, my heart. Aunt Katri is there, and Doctor Nath the Needle, and there are so many nurses and handmaidens the children will never remain unwatched. And, Dray, they are so young! And, too, there is my father..."

"All right, you female schemer. But remember, as soon as we have freed the Miglas from the Canops — it is home for us!"

"Amen to that, my heart."

So we pressed on through the air levels. Due south we drove, keeping mainly over the open ocean and retracing the course taken by Turko and myself. We passed the Koroles, the group of islands extending tongue-like from the eastern seaboard of Pandahem. We kept a lookout, for the Pandaheem do not buy airboats from Havilfar, but they had a few examples, all the same, and we wished for no trouble from the ancient foes of Vallia. I wondered how Tilda the Beautiful fared, and her son Pando, the Kov of Bormark, an imp of Satan if ever there was one. And Viridia the Render — was she still pirating away over there up the Hoboling Islands?

Over the northern coast of Havilfar we passed, crossing Hennardrin but too far east to see the White Rock of Gilmoy. Now we crossed the vast plains and the enormous areas of cultivation, until we sped above the wild lands. We avoided that area where no flier would go — but not by much — and we saw only a few spots in the sky to indicate we might be observed. We understood the risks we ran. More than one flier had to descend because of these infernal faults of the airboats supplied to us by the manufacturers in Hamal. We pressed on, and those left behind carried out repairs and so took up the chase again. Straight to the northwestern shore of the Shrouded Sea we flew, independent of air currents or winds, and so swung away to the west and gave Yaman a very wide berth, to land within the circle of the back hills of Migla.

The Miglas greeted us in stupefaction.

Hamp and Med Neemusbane gaped, their ears flapping, their eyes goggling. Only Mog retained her composure. She cackled and her old nutcracker face snapped at me.

"I always knew you were no ordinary man, Dray Prescot. You conjure an army out of thin air—"

"An army I should have brought at the start. Then you would not mourn so many of your dead."

"Migshaanu the All-Glorious counts the cost. We who serve her do not. Go out to war, Dray Prescot, and the light of Migshenda the Stux shine upon you."

Which was all very nice and magniloquent; but the idea still rankled that I had allowed these cheerful flap-eared, rubber-toy Miglas to march off singing to a war which was quite outside their experience. I knew those gathered here would be by far a fitter and more efficient army than that first one; but the cost came high, too high for me, I fear, and thereby I betray just how soft I had become.

That evening as the final plans were made and the Miglas caught a little awed insight into the way my fighting-men of Valka and those other fighters from Vallia behaved, Delia and I stood looking up at the last of the suns' glow.

The giant golden and scarlet form of the Gdoinye swept over us. I pretended to ignore it. The Star Lords were observing me and making sure they received their pound of flesh.

"That bird, Dray. I have seen it before."

"Possibly. It is of no consequence—"

She put her arms on my shoulders and forced me to look into her face. How sweet she was, clean and fresh and smelling so delectably of all the fabulous perfumes of paradise!

"Do not put me off, Dray. We both know the strange things that have happened to us — we have only to think back—"

"There is little I can tell you, dearest heart. I am constrained by forces I do not understand. I love only you. I love only you, and yet I love the twins, and I love this beautiful and cruel world of Kregen. I would not choose to leave all this—"

"How could you leave Kregen — unless you were dead? Oh, Dray! I did not mean to speak like this, on the eve of a battle."

I kissed her, a long, long kiss, and so silenced her.

When we drew back, I said, "Remember always, my Delia of Delphond, my Delia of the Blue Mountains. I love only you. Whatever I may do, that is why I live and breathe, that is why I am anything at all. If what I do seems strange, think only that I love only you."

I could not go on. I would have to tell her something, but I quailed from opening my weird story to the one person in two worlds from whom nothing should be hid. I would tell my Delia, one day...

The sound of laughter and loud voices heralded the arrival of Turko, Seg, and Inch. Turko had been telling them of the Canops, and of the Battle of Mackee, and of how the army of Canopdrin used the shield. I, also, had told my men of the uses of the shield. But, as I have earlier told you, the men of Segesthes and Turismond, as of Vallia and Pandahem, rate the shield as a cowardly weapon, something to hide behind. I knew they would find out differently in the morning, and I prayed the discovery would not come too high in blood.

The plans were laid. If the Canops scouted us with their aerial cavalry, we would deal with them. Seg had the skills for that. We had both watched an army cut to pieces from the air, when the impiters of Umgar Stro destroyed the army of Hiclantung in the Hostile Territories. Now, we had bowmen who would do more damage than a hundred stux-men.

Of shafts the Emperor had scoured his empire and we had brought so many arrows that I had devoted all the draft animals and all the totrixes we could spare to bring them onto the field. Our fliers were equipped with efficient varters, varters and gros-varters made in Vallia. They would not fail us.

The Miglas with their shields were apportioned to the various formations from Valka. I bore down all opposition. I told them, in a very high and mighty fashion, that I was the Prince Majister of Vallia. I was also Strom of Valka. My men *would be* shielded by the Migla shield-bearers.

"If I see a man wantonly exposing himself to the Canops' crossbows, Seg, and you too, Inch, I will be most severe." And to Tom ti Vulheim, in command of the Archers of Valka, I said the same things. "We use our superior rate of discharge, and we swamp them with shafts. When we get to close quarters they will be shot to pieces. Then your rapiers, daggers, and glaives will have to stand against thraxter and shield." I didn't like that bit of it at all. But I showed my officers a few passes that would serve, and the Jiktars passed these on to the Hikdars, who in their turn instructed the Deldars. The Deldars with their brazen lungs bawled it out to the men, and I fancied that at least some of the instructions would penetrate those blockheaded if valiant warriors of mine. One day I would forge an army that was an army, here on Kregen...

The day dawned brightly. She of the Veils had risen late and her pale orb gleamed bright pink against the blue, fading as the suns climbed, but remaining. I pointed this out to the men as an omen of good fortune. The ranks formed up after breakfast was eaten. My cavalry scouts informed me that the Canops, who I was sure had not spotted the fleet of fliers, had scouted the camp and that the main force, confident of an even greater victory than the last, had marched out. They would be breaking camp at about the same time as we were, and would be marching west as we marched east. I frowned. The suns would be in the eyes of my men.

Orders were given to the Vallian Air Service to prevent any aerial scouts from observing our movements. We saw one or two skirmishes in the hazy distance, dots swarming and sweeping about our fliers. The Canoptic vollers put in an appearance and were quickly seen off.

I said to Seg, "Take over the command, Seg. Keep them moving, but slowly. I do not want to engage with the suns in our eyes."

"Aye, Dray."

Hikdar Vangar had my airboat ready. She was the voller we had taken from Faol and flown to Valka and back. We rose into the air and swept toward the army of Canopdrin. From up here I was impressed by the dressing and alignment of the

Canops. The silver gleam from their standards, where Lem, the silver leem, was flaunted, splintered into my eyes. Their whole mass advanced with a steady tread, perfectly confident. They were disciplined, professional fighting-men. My Bowmen of Loh were professionals too, but of the rest of my army all were rough and ready warriors, some drilled and trained by me, but ever ready to let warrior passions inflame them. Oh, we were not a wild undisciplined body of men claiming to be an army, as my savage clansmen were. We were a drilled army. But Vallia has been famed for her navy. She has always hired mercenaries for her fighting. This was, as I knew, the first time since beyond any memory, when Vallians themselves had stepped onto a foreign field in such numbers to do battle.

When I had seen what I needed we slanted back to the army.

I sent a messenger to Seg, telling him to trend his men away to the north. Along there a valley lay athwart the path of both armies. When I saw Seg reach the crest on the western side and halt I knew we had, for the moment at least, achieved a considerable advantage.

By the time the Canopdrin army formed up on the opposite crest the suns had risen enough to satisfy me, and, because we were in the southern hemisphere of Kregen, the suns would circle the heavens to the northward, behind us. I felt a little more pleased, then. A cavalry scout came in to report he felt sure the Canop king was with his army. He could not be sure, but…

If King Capnon, whom his nobles called the Great, was really with his army we might finish the thing in three hours of hard fighting.

Now the suns were high enough so that they formed no hazard to us at all. I lifted my sword. As you must guess I was carrying that Savanti sword I had taken from the dying hand of Alex Hunter. I wore Vallian buff, with a great scarlet sash, and sufficient armor to protect my vitals. Turko was there, at my back, a great shield upraised. Seg and Inch had both given me looks when Turko, un-speaking, unsmiling, had thus positioned himself. I had said, "Turko the Shield follows me," and they had nodded, pleased, I liked to think, that they had someone else to keep me out of harm's way.

The sword slashed down.

The whole army advanced.

The Canops must have been puzzled. For instance, where had all these vollers sprung from? They did not recognize the markings. And now, an army of men — apims — marched toward them. But they were soldiers. They obeyed orders. And, led by King Capnon, their masters urged them on. With a great brazen roar from their trumpets, and with the silver leems high, they charged.

At once Seg halted. The Bowmen of Loh lifted their weapons.

Well, it is all a long time ago now, and so I shall not go into every gory detail of that battle. It took place along that valley, called the Valley of the Crimson Missals. Crimson missals are very rare, for the trees usually carry white and pink blossoms, and the valley was thusly famous and well known throughout Migla. So the Battle of the Crimson Missals began with the Crimson Bowmen of Loh, shielded by the crimson-clad Migla shield-men, shooting in a long series of controlled discharges that tore huge rents in the ranks of the Canops.

Powerful and deadly is the longbow of Loh. Those steel bodkin-tipped cloth-yard shafts, expertly fletched and flighted, skewered through the Canops like — well, to liken that sound and that sight to anything is to lessen it. The Lohvian longbowmen tore the heart out of the Canops.

Here was where Seg was able to show beyond dispute the superiority of the longbow over not only the Canoptic crossbow but the Valkan compound reflex bow. My Valkans raged, and led by Tom ti Vulheim, they raced forward, brushing aside the Migla shield-men, getting themselves into range so that they too could join in that sleeting storm of shafts.

The Canops, although dreadfully stricken, did not lose their formation or their dressing. They closed up and charged, shields high, straight for our bowmen.

Many and many a Canop went down. I had to harden my heart, and I suffered. I remembered what Mog had told me of the devilish practices of these iron men of Canopdrin. Now their iron was of no avail against those withering shafts pouring down on them from the sky. A few soldiers reached our ranks so that our rapier-and-dagger men could get to hand grips. The lines swayed and roiled, and then it was all over.

The crossbowmen had been shot down, their splendid weapons tumbled into the green grass. The crimson missals glowed in the light of the suns above them, and clumps of Canops formed in the shelter of the trees. They formed a shield wall and the branches deflected the arrows from them. The Miglas were yelling and prancing. So many men were involved that complete views of the scene were impossible without taking to the air.

I had a mind to let the remnants of the Canops alone, to survive. I remembered Naghan the Throat and Jedgul the Finger. They might be safe in the hospital in Yaman. But there were other men like them in that army trapped among the trees. Also, there were officers like Hikdar Markman ti Coyton. The face of Kregen would smile more cleanly if they were removed.

The decision was not too difficult, for there was a precedent.

"Tell Seg — tell the Kov of Falinur — to leave off now."

The message was taken by one of the small corps of aides I had quickly organized from young men anxious to play a part. His totrix bounded away. The Miglas were inflamed. This was their first heady taste of victory. The field presented a dreadful spectacle and I wanted to get in touch with the Canoptic hospital organization and arrange a truce so that the wounded might be speedily treated. We had brought doctors and medical equipment with us, but the Miglas were ill prepared. And the Miglas were inflamed. I caught a glimpse of crazy old Mog, wearing all her regalia, her golden staff lifted high, racing across the field astride a totrix, yelling blue bloody murder, thirsting for the blood of every Canop alive there.

Another aide was dispatched to bring her back.

I had done what the Star Lords commanded, but in my own mind this was only a beginning. Now must begin the harder task of reestablishing Migshaanu and of integrating the Canops with the Miglas. Failing that, I would find them a country they might make their home without bloodshed or dispossession of the people native to that land.

It seemed clear to me that the task must begin with the banishment of their king, if he still lived, and of the reversal of roles between common soldier and noble — judging by the examples I had met.

An attack made by armored Canops astride mirvols was beaten off with an ease that made me think back with some savage self-contempt to the way the mirvollers had ripped up that first raw Migla army. I thought I caught a glimpse of the scarlet and golden raptor, among the whirling bodies of the mirvols; but the glimpse was too quick for certainty. It would be like the Star Lords to keep this close an eye on what went on.

Delia rode out to me, her totrix an old nag and well worn down; but she had refused anything better, saying the best animals were needed by the fighters. Her presence thrilled me as always. She rode with a free fine grace. She hauled up, dust kicking from the totrix hooves, and she was not laughing.

Rather, she said, "This is a terrible business."

"Aye. But it is over now. Now we begin to put everything back in place."

"Those poor men — the arrows are so cruel."

"Some deserved it, some did not. Seg is ordering a cessation. We will get help for the wounded."

We dismounted, for her totrix threatened to keel over any minute and I wished to talk seriously to her. We went a little apart from the others, from my dwindled group of aides, from Mog and Mag, from the trumpeters and the standard-bearer. Oh, yes, Delia had not forgotten to bring a brand-new and impeccably stitched flag with her. My own old flag — the yellow cross on the scarlet field, the flag that fighting-men called "Old Superb" — had floated over our victory.

Turko the Shield gazed after us, but he had sense enough not to intrude.

"We have won a victory, Delia, my heart. But you must wonder why it had to be, why I became involved with this backward country in Havilfar which is generally more advanced than other places—"

"Really, Dray!"

"I know what you think. But Vallia cannot produce fliers."

"No. But Father says this is a first step in the right direction."

"So it is. But I would like to tell you why, my Delia."

She looked up at me, perfectly aware of the seriousness of the moment, her soft lips half parted, her brown eyes brilliant upon me, waiting for me to speak. A little movement scuttled in the dusty grass at her booted feet.

And now I must relate a thing that seemed impossible to me at the time, and still strikes as strange and weird as anything I encountered on two worlds.

For Delia looked down sharply, and without screaming or starting, said, "Oh, Dray! A scorpion!" I looked.

The reddish brown scorpion scuttled past Delia's boots. It halted before me and that damned arrogant tail lifted. I did not move. Delia, with a single glance at my face, remained silent.

And then — Dear God! — the scorpion spoke to me.

180

I thought I was hallucinating again, as I had done in that first dreadful attempt to cross the Klackadrin when the Phokaym had captured me. I put a hand to my head, staring at the scorpion.

"Dray Prescot," said the scorpion in a reedy and shrill voice not unlike a buzz saw ripping through winter logs. I did not think anyone else might hear that baleful voice.

"Dray Prescot. Perhaps you are not so great a fool as we thought." The Gdoinye had spoken to me. A bird had spoken to me. Was a scorpion any the more strange in this weird and wonderful, beautiful and horrible world of Kregen? "You have done what you were commanded to do. We acknowledge your deeds. Now you have our leave to depart from here, to Hyrklana—"

I shouted in my old savage, intemperate way. "I am not going to Hyrklana!"

Just how it was done I did not know, could not know. But, on the instant, black clouds roiled across the sky. Huge raindrops began to fall, gouting the dust into fountains, spreading and joining and coalescing into rivulets trickling down into the Valley of the Crimson Missals. In a twinkling the darkness of the clouds shut off every other person from my sight. Thunder boomed.

"Delia!" I shouted. "Delia!" I screamed it out, spinning around, lost and shut away and condemned. *"Delia!"*

"Dray!"

I heard her answering call, but faint, faint. "Dray! Where are you, dearest heart?"

"Delia! Here — I am coming to you!"

I blundered in the direction of her voice.

"Dray! It is dark and I cannot see — Oh, Dray!"

The shape of a terrified totrix reared above me in the gloom, his hooves wicked.

I ducked and heard a faint and dwindling cry: "Dray—"

And then the blue radiance swamped down about me and that greater representation of a scorpion caught me up in its ghastly blue embrace and I was falling and spinning and tumbling away into a long blue tunnel of nightmare.

Seven

Of the descent of a slate slab and a scarlet breechclout

Yells of panicking men and shrieks of terrified women burst all about me as I sat up, cursing, and looked upon a bedlam. Trust the damned Star Lords to pitchfork me headlong into frantic action. I knew why I was here — wherever here might be. Someone was in danger. Someone was in deadly peril and the Star Lords wanted them rescued — so, send for Joe Muggins, Dray Prescot. He'll land flat on his back, stark naked, unarmed, and he'll sort out the problem, never you fear.

181

Oh, yes, I cursed the Everoinye to the Ice Floes of Sicce and gone as I climbed to my feet and started to sort out what the hell now the Star Lords had chucked me into.

I stood in a cavern carved from virgin rock, the marks of chisels sharp and distinct upon the walls and roof giving no indication of the age of the place. It was clean and only a little dust puffed as the crazed mob of people ran and struggled madly from the square-cut opening through which streamed the mingled streaming rays of the Suns of Scorpio.

I could hear brazen lungs yelling orders out there, and the harsh blocky silhouettes of halflings in armor packed the entrance. Men and women ran screaming past me and plunged headlong into a farther opening, smaller, in the back wall. About twenty people were left to struggle through, away from the armored halflings raging to get at them. These people wore decent blue robes and dresses, had sandaled feet, combed hair, clean faces and arms. Most of the women wore bangles and bracelets of cheap imitation jewelry: Krasny ware, but pretty in their way. Now every face was a mask of horror. There were a few children there also, running fleetly between the legs of their elders, skipping for the far opening and safety.

Then I saw the smooth slab of slate descending. It dropped smoothly and slowly down over the exit and when it touched the floor it would wall off the way of escape from the halflings and give safety to those who had passed through.

But there were still these last twenty to pass through. And the descending slab would shut them out of safety, shut them back in this cavern with the swords and spears of the halflings, who, I now saw, were Rhaclaws, most savage and unpleasant. So I, Dray Prescot, pawn of the Star Lords, must rescue them.

"By Zair!" I said feelingly. At my side on the floor — and next to an overturned sturm-wood bench and a gilt cup still rolling and spilling its dark wine across the rock, a positive indication of how suddenly and how recently all this panic had begun — lay a length of scarlet humespack. I grabbed it on my way toward that descending slab of slate, wound it roughly about my loins. People tended to get in the way as I ran, trying to thrust their way through the narrowing opening.

"Out of the way, onkers!" I roared, and barged on. I got my fingers under the hard edge of slate and then my shoulders. I braced my legs apart. I could feel the weight coming on. It grew and grew and pressed me down so that I felt my feet would puncture the rock of the floor.

Men and women flung frightened glances my way, but they did not stop, and scurried past me, to left and right, as I stood there like poor old Atlas, chained by the weight of Kregen.

I could feel my muscles cracking. I bent a little — I had to — and the massive slate slab inched down. Now there were barely ten people left, and I heard a woman — a short but plumply rounded woman with a tumbled wealth of dark hair falling across her face and the shoulders of her blue gown — calling to her son and daughter, as I judged.

"Hurry, Wincie, hurry, Marker! This great paktun is holding the door! It will not crush you!"

The children squealed and the little girl, Wincie, all disarrayed black hair and long naked legs and flickering petticoats, dived between my legs. Those legs of mine corded under the strain. Sweat ran down my body, and my muscles bulged, my chest arched and resisting, backbone taut. I knew I could not hold much longer, for the weight of the slab was immense. But now there were only five people left, and then three and then one.

This one halted, ducking his head to pass by my left shoulder. The edge of the slab pressed cruelly into the flesh, denting it to the bone. My fingers were bone-white as I gripped die slate, heaving against the dead weight.

"I would not believe it possible, my friend," he said. He was a well-set young man, with quick direct eyes flecked with green. His blue robe had been tucked up into a lesten-hide belt from which swung a small, curved, overly ornamented dagger. His brown hair clustered in curls. "You must let go or you will be caught, too."

A stux pranged off the slate above our heads and I said, "By Vox! Get inside, onker, and run!"

His handsome face flushed and he stepped past me.

Another stux barely missed my side.

I had to now let go this monstrous thing bearing down on me, and somehow summon the strength and agility to dodge backward and so let it rumble all the way down and bar off those blockheaded Rhaclaws. I was breathing in jerks and gasps, and specks and shards of fire splashed across my eyes. Sweat stung and near blinded me. Another stux nicked my calf and I cursed and tried to move my hands away and found they would not obey my will.

I could not move my body!

So great had been the pressure bearing down on me my body had locked in defiant resistance. Now I could not move. The gigantic slab of slate trapped me as a silversmith traps a bangle in the jaws of his vise.

Yet if I did not drag myself free those Opaz-forsaken rasts of Rhaclaws would be able to pass under the slab and so enter the escape tunnel. Then all my efforts would have been in vain. The halflings would be upon the terrified fugitives, hacking and cutting and capturing. I fought with my own body, there in a rocky cavern, trapped between a massive descending slab of slate and the rocky floor beneath my feet.

I felt a nudge in the small of my back.

A voice said: "I am Mahmud nal Yrmcelt, oaf, as you must very well know. And I do not take kindly to being dubbed onker." His finger jabbed me in the back again. "But I will condone it now, for you are a remarkable man. Now, oaf, let me take a part of the slab—"

I managed to speak. I truly felt if I had not interrupted he would have gone prattling on until the Rhaclaws were upon us. They were advancing more cautiously now, and I guessed their eyes had not fully adjusted to the interior of the cavern from the brightness of the suns without.

"No." I hacked the words from a corded throat. "No. I cannot move — so you must push me."

183

"My oafish friend! You will fall into the rasts!"

"There is no other way — you cannot pull me — *push!*"

A woman screamed shrilly and most distressingly from somewhere in the greater darkness at his back. He did not hesitate more. "May Opaz the Mighty and All-Beneficent have you in his keeping, and may the Invisible Twins smile upon you—" And he put his booted foot against my back and thrust.

At the same time I summoned up every last shred of willpower I possessed and forced my body to obey. I got my hands free and moved my feet and then Mahmud nal Yrmcelt's thrust kicked me clear. The slab smashed down with a great and horrible thunking, so that slate chips flew from the bottom edge.

Hands caught me as I sprawled forward. My body felt as though it had been knotted and starched and then unwound, aching inch by aching inch. I shuddered and drew huge gasping breaths. I tried to twist my arm away. Slick with sweat as it was it should have sprung away easily. But the locked grip of the Rhaclaw held fast. My limbs trembled. I felt a trilling vibration all through my poor abused old body and I knew I wasn't going to clamber to my feet and bash a few skulls for some time yet.

Mind you, I promised myself as I was swiftly carried out into the sunshine, some skull-bashing seemed an inevitable prospect.

Once more my duty — imposed and arbitrary — to the Star Lords had flung me headlong into danger and perils of a kind I could not then conceive, but which were to become hatefully familiar in the succeeding days.

Assuming two things — one: that my transit here from the battlefield of the Valley of the Crimson Missals had followed immediately in time, and I was not caught in another of those weird and damnable time loops of the Star Lords (and, as you will hear, that was a mistaken assumption); and, two: the weather had not changed drastically — I fancied I was not very many dwaburs nearer the equator. The suns gave me that impression. Of course, as Kregen swings about the Suns of Scorpio they will appear to change in size, and their size changes are visibly greater than that of old Sol from Earth. The air had a warmer feel, and there were unfamiliar scents from the trees and flowering bushes surrounding the entrance to the cavern.

Twin shadows fell from my horizontal body as I was hauled out.

I was dumped into the back of a quoffa cart. Above me reared a craggy cliff face, its fissures dappled with the glowing colors of rock plants and the green of shrubs. A fringe of thorn-ivy grew in a level line I did not think natural about a hundred feet up that cliff. I had the hope that the terrified people would escape from secret exits tunneled into the rock.

The quoffa were whipped into action. I frowned. Of all the animals of Kregen the quoffa least need chastisement. With their huge, patient old faces and their perambulating hearth-rug bodies, they are docile and obedient and completely lovable and dependable. The carts creaked and moved forward. There were seven carts and each was stuffed with half-naked men and women and halflings, all bound with thongs, and most groaning and crying and sobbing and lamenting.

No need to inquire what was going on, or who we were.

I was partially wrong in that instinctive assessment, as you shall hear. But the difference was, if Zair will forgive me, a difference I was to welcome.

The fact that I was also bound made little impression, for my muscles seemed still locked in the stasis caused by holding up that damned great weight. The thongs were of a kind and thickness — they were not lesten-hide — I would have snapped by a single muscular surge.

We bumped along and I took in the new sights and impressions around me as a matter of course. That length of scarlet cloth I had picked up in the cavern worried me. It hung around my hips now, and I was as respectably dressed as many of the slaves. Always — so far — the Star Lords and the Savanti had brought me to Kregen stark naked. The Star Lords dumped me down into diabolical situations naked and unarmed and with only my wits and strength and cunning to get me through. I had understood that I would think less of them as they of me had they provided me clothes and weapons, a helmet, and a spear, say, a sword and shield. But this time a damned scorpion had chittered words at me, and called me by my name, and in this new emergency I had found a length of scarlet humespack. Was that coincidence? Or had the Star Lords decided to give me a little more assistance than they had ever done before?

We bumped along between the trees and so came out onto a reasonably good road, dusty but firm. On either hand stretched vast fields ablaze with flowers. Soon this purely decorative agriculture gave way to crops thriving under the suns. I saw marspear and sweet corn — which I detest — and crop plants of kinds unfamiliar to me then. Because I could see out only backward, like the man who always sits with his back to the engine, I had no idea of where we were being carried. The fields opened and I saw good quality fat cattle grazing, with men riding zorcas among them. We passed occasional hamlets with small cottages made from honest brick with thatched roofs, and a village well. The procession wound on and I felt hungry and thirsty; but we stopped only once to be given sips of water from huge orange gourds, and a mouthful of palines each. The palines were thrust into our open mouths by skinny, gaunt lackadaisical girls with stringy hair, who ministered to the Rhaclaws. Then we creaked and groaned on our way.

This was a rich land. That was very clear.

We passed a gang of slaves digging ditches, and I marked the Fristles who stood guard, as well as Ochs who wielded the whips.

Suddenly there came a bustling commotion and the old quoffas were lashed to the side of the road, the wheels of the carts slipping into the drainage ditch. I heard the crash and stamp of metal-studded sandals.

A column of infantry passed. I thought, at first, they were Canops. But no pagan silver image of Lem, the leaping leem, crowned their standards. These soldiers with their tall helmets, tufted with feathers from the whistling faerling, with their scaled and plated armor, greaves, shields, stuxes, thraxters, and crossbows, marched following a golden image of a zhantil.

If I thought of Pando, boy Kov of Bormark, then, who can blame me?

185

Of almost all the wonderful wild animals of Kregen, I might have chosen a zhantil for my standard.

We were hauled out of the ditch and went on, and a bur or so later, again were driven off the road by the passage of a brilliant body of zorcamen. They were resplendent in armor and gems, silks and embroideries, their lances all slanting at the same angle, their helmets ashine under the suns. They trotted past most gallantly. I wouldn't have minded ripping each one from his ornate saddle and breaking his back across my knees. But I, Dray Prescot, still felt the effects of that damned great slate slab. By the time we passed under an archway and I heard the muted roar of a great city all about me, the stiffness was wearing off. The suns hung low to the sky and the horizon sheeted in emerald and crimson, opaz colors filled with a dying radiance. Then towers and ramparts and roofs jagged against that sky glory and the shadows dropped down.

The carts pulled into a flagged courtyard and the Rhaclaws yelled commands. Torches flared. Stone walls, frowning and somber, rose about us. We were hauled out and pushed and prodded into line. Although the stiffness had quite worn off now, and I had bulged my muscles and found to my satisfaction that my battered old body responded once more to my will, I fell down and lay on the stone flags. I was kicked. I continued to lie there. I was looking for the man in command.

Then I saw him. A Jiktar, he strutted out, rather paunchy as to waist and puffy as to feature, but a fighting-man for all that. His armor glinted redly in the torchlight.

"Won't get up, Notor," reported the Deldar in command of the slave detail.

"If he's damaged goods he is of no use to us." The Jiktar's words carried a nasal whine. He glared down on me.

This, I felt, must be the time. I had suffered a very great deal. I had been kicked and prodded and mauled, and I was bound with thongs and I was destined for slavery. Well, someone would be sorry for all that before I was finished.

I broke the bonds with a single convulsive jerk.

I stood up.

The Rhaclaws began to yell at once.

The Jiktar took a step back, and then I took his pudgy throat between my fists. I did not kill him. I threw him at the nearest bunch of Rhaclaws. They are a stocky lot, the Rhaclaws, with two arms and two legs, and heads that are so large and dome shaped that, lacking a neck, their chops seem to rest on their shoulders and, as Zair is my witness, are almost as wide as those shoulders. I say they do not have necks; this is not perfectly true. They do have a small disclike neck that enables their massive domed heads to swivel. Now their two legs apiece did not stop them from toppling over in a muddle as the Jiktar struck them. "Seize him!" someone was yelling, as there is always someone willing to shout those easy words rather than to dive in.

I picked up a Rhaclaw who was driving in with his stux low at me, and whirled him about my head. I yelled, then, like a fool: "Hai, Hikai!"

The huge domed head of the Rhaclaw cut a swath through his fellows. I forged on. Things were becoming interesting. One or two of the slaves were beginning to jump up and down, and at least three of them had freed themselves from their bonds. We might make a tasty little party of this yet.

The gate lay open. No one had thought to close it on a rabble of cowed slaves. The Rhaclaw-club in my fists cleared a path. I aimed for the gate. Torchlight spattered the scene with drops of ruby radiance. Shadows writhed at the gate and I saw a Hikdar — he was apim — hurling his stux.

A quick roll of the wrists interposed my human club and the Rhaclaw made no sound, for he was already unconscious, as the stux penetrated his chest.

I bashed my way on, and dodged two more flung stuxes, and then a Rhaclaw came at me with a thraxter. He was smashed to the side. His great domed head struck the gate, burst, and blood and brains splashed out, vivid in the torch glare.

I felt sorry for him. But then, he should never have hired out as a mercenary had he not envisaged some such bloody ending.

"Run with me, comrades!" I roared at the slaves. Some responded. I saw a burly fellow with a shock of villainous black hair slashing about him with a thraxter. He handled the weapon as he would handle a cutting knife in the cane fields. Others ran to follow me.

Swinging back to the gate I started through, and this time I draped the senseless Rhaclaw over my back and so heard the individual sick chunk of three stuxes as they smashed into him, poor chap, instead of my naked back.

I was through the gateway.

The torchlight dimmed, but the Maiden with the Many Smiles floated serenely above, a little cloud drifting across her smiling pink face.

Fresh torches blazed before my face. A group of men. riding half-voves halted and the glitter from their accouterments near blinded me. I shook my hair back and glared up at them.

Their leader stared down, remote, in complete command, with a haughtiness I recognized and loathed.

"Hai, Jikai!" I roared, and swung the dead Rhaclaw and let fly at this supercilious rast astride his half-vove. He ducked. The Rhaclaw flew past.

The half-vove rider spoke in an icy tone of voice.

'Take him alive!"

The half-voves closed in.

Well, they were tougher opponents, but I could handle them.

From nowhere a net descended about me, enveloping me. I had no knife, no sword. I fought the strands, the smothering folds tangling and obstructing. Men dropped from the high saddles of the half-voves and closed in. Their thraxters gleamed most wickedly in the confused lights of the torches and of the Maiden with the Many Smiles.

I took two strands of the net into my fists and wrenched, and wrenched two more, and so tore a hole in the net.

I thrust up through the net, kicking it from me.

The first man was upon me.

I slid his sword, chopped him across the neck, took his sword away, and parried the immediately following onslaught from three of his fellows.

They sought to strike me with the flat and so knock me senseless.

I used the edge, for I cared nothing of them.

They wore armor and billowing cloaks, very romantic in the streaming moonlight. I was near naked, clad only in an old scarlet breechclout I had had no time to fasten properly.

That I, Dray Prescot, Krozair of Zy, Lord of Strombor — and much else besides — should be laid low by a breechclout!

And — my own old scarlet breechclout, at that.

I sprang and leaped and fought and beat them back and so took stock of a fine half-vove and readied myself to leap upon his broad back and so urge him away with those special clansmen's words that only we and the voves may understand.

I leaped all right — but I was heading downward instead of upward.

The scarlet breechclout had finally untwisted and fallen about my legs. Tripped, I pitched headlong.

In the next moment something extraordinarily hard and heavy sledged alongside my head and there was no time for a single chime from the bells of Beng-Kishi.

Eight

In the Jikhorkdun

Nath the Arm glowered on the recruits as we stood on silver sand in the wooden-walled ring, blinking in the suns-light, shuffling our feet. We were coys, for anything that is young and green and untested on Kregen is often dubbed a coy, with a sly laugh, and we screwed up our eyes and stared up at Nath the Arm as he looked down on us from his pedestal.

"Unequal combat is the secret," he roared at us. "That is what pulls the crowds. You'll be unequal, and if you live, maybe you'll be unequal the other way." Nath the Arm chortled, his massive black beard oiled and threaded with gold, his wide-winged ruby-colored jerkin of supple voskskin brilliant with gems, his kilt a splash of vivid saffron. He wore silver greaves. His black hair, graying at the temples, was savagely cut back around his ears.

The villainous fellow with the black hair who had thrashed about with the sword, back where I had chastised the Rhaclaws, swallowed and grimaced at me. "Unequal?"

"Silence, rasts!" Nath the Arm thumped a meaty fist onto the wooden rail before him. His face, leathery, whiskered, and lined, crisscrossed with old scars, loomed above us, the huge blue-black beard glittering with gold. "You talk when I tell you. You do *anything* when I tell you."

As though we had been faced with a victorious render crew we had been given the alternatives. We could become slaves and work on the farms or in industry or the mines. We might become fodder for the Jikhorkdun. We might, if we thought ourselves apt enough with a weapon, become kaidurs, beginning, of course, as coys. Or, we could be slaughtered, there and then, out of hand.

Some, who with a shake of the head said they knew of these things, had chosen to go as slaves.

Those of us here, in the small sanded practice ring hot and sticky beneath the Suns of Scorpio, had chosen to become coys and so perhaps, one day, if we lived, to become kaidurs.

Escape, we had been told, was impossible, and then, with many a sly wink and nod, Nath the Arm pointed out to us the wonderful advantages enjoyed by a great kaidur: the gold he received as purses, the girls who sighed and lusted for him, the wine he might quaff, the soft living between bouts in the Jikhorkdun where the maddened crowd showered him with plaudits.

The arena, Nath the Arm told us, was the life for a man.

Well, I had heard a little of the arenas of Hamal and of Hyrklana, and we were in the capital city of Hyrklana, Huringa, just as the scorpion had promised me.

Listening as Nath the Arm threatened and promised I had already agreed with myself that at the first opportunity I would test if escape was impossible or not. I needed to get back to Migla and discover what was going on there, after the great Battle of the Crimson Missals, and assure myself that Delia was safe. I shuddered more than a little, as you may well judge, at the thought that any of my comrades might discover how I had tripped over my own scarlet breechclout. How Seg and Inch would roar! How Hap Loder and Prince Varden would chuckle! How Turko would lift a quizzical eyebrow! How, in short, all my good comrades would think it a great jest that I, Dray Prescot, had been brought low by a breechclout.

Questions as to dates produced the same bewildering and conflicting replies as one would find over all of Kregen. Men called their days by names they fancied themselves, and sennights likewise. With seven moons floating in the sky the month — surprisingly moon-cycle mensuration was known and practiced — hardly counted. As for seasons, men dated the beginning of a seasonal cycle from many and various occurrences. Usually it would be from the founding of a city, as in the case of Rome on Earth, or a great game cycle, as of the Greeks and their Olympiads, or the birth of a great philosopher, or the travel of a seer from the place of his birth to the place of his ministry, very familiar to us on Earth. Hyrklana dated her seasons from the foundation of the Lily City Klana — the old capital away down in the south of the island, long since tumbled into ruin. By that reckoning this was the year 2076. A relatively new nation, on Kregen, then, the people of Hyrklana.

I wondered if I would meet Princess Lilah. That, I owned as I sweated through the drills prescribed by Nath the Arm, would be pleasurable. I was human enough to admit that a great deal of the pleasure would come from what I hoped would be her immediate adoption of me as friend and her instant removal of my ugly old carcass from the arena. But I knew, too, that the deeper part of that pleasure would be in the knowledge she had escaped successfully astride that fluttrell from the Manhounds of Faol.

189

We were afforded an early opportunity to see what occurred in the Jikhorkdun of this city of Huringa.

The suns shot their brilliant rays across the raked silver sand. Blood spots were covered with fresh sprinkled sand, raked and leveled. Deeply into the ground, in a great natural hollow, had been set the arena. Around it and sloping up the sides of the honeycombed hill rose tier after tier of seats and private boxes. Above these towered the walls, lofting high, carrying the terraced seating away up to dizzying heights. I have mentioned that the telescope is known on Kregen, and a spectator up there would have need of one when the combats were staged down in the arena. When the peculiar Kregan form of vol-combat was produced, then everyone had his or her own chance to see everything that might occur.

The coys clustered at iron bars covering the exit from an apprentice kaidurs tunnel.

I could see the opposite loft of the amphitheater. The spectacle presented a dizzying perspective of towering multicolored masses, of thousands of faces, mere white or tan or black dots, thousands of people, both halfling and apim, cheering and screaming and gesticulating, hurling down flowers or fruit rinds, old cheeses, rotten gregarians, hurling down golden deldys and silver sinvers and copper obs.

The roar, the noise, the sheer caterwauling bedlam of it all broke about our heads like a rashoon bursting in primitive violence.

"By Opaz!" breathed Naghan the Gnat, at my side. A little fellow, all gristle and bone, he stared out in great apprehension.

"No wild beast will wish you to fill his belly, Naghan the Gnat!" bellowed Lart the Stink. He was aptly named and we gave him a wide berth. We had fallen into a rough comradeship, these coys in this training bunch, about twenty of us. We lived and ate and talked together. We trained in the wooden-walled ring, one of many set in the complex of buildings and courtyards to the rear of the amphitheater. Now we were watching what we would be doing in a sennight or less.

Men strutted out there, their armor blinding in the light of Far and Havil, the twin Suns of Scorpio, named thus here in Havilfar. We saw the quick twinkle of swords, the bright gush of blood. We saw and understood what Nath the Arm meant about unequal combat, for swordsman was not pitted against swordsman; rather, the Hyrklanish relished a swordsman against a stux-man, or a rapier-and-dagger man against a shield-and-buckler man, a retiarius against a slinger. We saw the way the fights went. We sweated out all one long afternoon there, clutching those iron bars, hearing the horrid yells of the crowd and the despairing screams of the dying. As a final fillip a bunch of slaves who had not been selected for anything useful in the land were herded out, and wild neemus, black and sleek and deadly, devoured them with a great crunching of bones and a spilling of blood.

There were many things that went on in the Jikhorkdun of Huringa I will not mention to you, for we are supposed to be civilized people, and such things are abhorrent to us.

Yet was not the land of Hyrklana civilized? Did they not manufacture air-boats? And was not that beautiful girl, the Princess Lilah of Hyrklana, one of the inhabitants of this island? Truly, civilization means many different things in the different worlds of space.

Naghan the Gnat said, "They will not get me out there!"

The Hyrklanish who organized the games for the arena employed Rhaclaws and other beast-men to control the kaidurs. They told Naghan the Gnat what would happen to him if he did not venture out upon the silver sand with us. He shivered; but he took his stux in hand and crept out with us when it was our turn, the day appointed for us to show if we could live through the unequal combat and so begin the long path of combat and victory that might lead to perhaps just one of us becoming a kaidur.

The amphitheater had been built in a classically oval shape. The lofting terraces had been divided vertically into four sections, each section, rather naturally, with one of the four full colors: blue, green, yellow, red. It fell to our lot to walk out onto the sand wearing red breechclouts, a red favor tied about our left arms, and a small leather helmet with tall red feathers. As you may imagine, I was not displeased that chance had brought me to fight once again under the red.

We each had two stuxes.

From the blue corner trotted half-men wearing half-armor, with blue favors and feathers, and carrying thraxters and shields. I frowned. This was unequal combat with a vengeance!

And yet there were twenty of us and only fifteen of the blues.

The beast roar from the crowded benches had to be ignored, to be rubbed away from the consciousness. We advanced over the silver sand and the suns burned down and the smell of beasts and the smell of human blood and sweat dizzied us. The blues formed a neat line and walked slowly towards us. We had been told what we must do. If we won, very well. But, as Nath the Arm had said, one thick hand searching his gold-threaded beard: "Whatever happens, you reds! Die well! Die like men! In dying show that you might have become kaidur!"

Each color had its own complex of training rings behind the amphitheater. I could not fail to understand Nath the Arm's passionate desire for the reds to do well. This utter obsession with the Jikhorkdun besotted almost everyone in the city. Huge bets were wagered. Enormous sums of money, and land, zorcas, and vollers too, changed hands every day.

Through that crazed blood-lusting thunder of voices we heard Nath the Arm's fierce last words.

"Fight well, reds! Fight for the ruby drang!"

The thought that for almost no extra reason at all Nath the Arm would leap out after us and join us in the fight was not an idle one. Nothing in Hyrklanan Huringa could arouse the passions as the chances and thrills and excitement of the Jikhorkdun.

The reds fought for the ruby drang.

The blues fought for the sapphire graint.

I knew that the yellows fought for the diamond zhantil.

The greens fought for the emerald neemu.

People were still crowding into the amphitheater, running down the steeply sloping stairs and edging along the terraces. This was still early in the day and the coys were put on as a mere appetizer, to keep the crowds amused before the main bouts. All the important combats would take place just before and during and after noon, so that the twin suns shining down would cast as few shadows as possible from the uplifting walls. After that, the spectacles tended more to the mammoth and bloodletting-in-droves style, with the skill and professional daring of the kaidurs over for the day. Usually — not always, as I was to find.

The blues advanced in their neat line. I judged they were apprentice kaidurs, just out of the coy stage. They were not apims. They were Blegs. If you have seen a representation of the face of a Persian leaf bat you may have some faint idea of the appearance of the faces of the Blegs. They do not possess the large and typical bat ears; their coloring is brilliant green and yellow and purple, with bright fur and skin patches; their lower jaws hang and the thin membrane there droops, to reveal a row of small, thin, and intensely sharp teeth. They have arms and shoulders very apimlike; their bodies are not unlike a man's; but they have four legs from which the trunk springs almost vertically, rather like a tower rising from a four-legged support. Over their backs lies an atrophied carapace and it is thought they once had the power of flight.

The Blegs are considered, on a planet famed for its prolific life, as among the most hideous of quasi-humans.

Like almost any species on Kregen, the Blegs may be found in any of the continents and islands; but they are more usually to be found on Havilfar. Given that wide spread of the temperate regions north and south of the equator that makes so much of Kregen comfortably habitable to intelligent beings, one would expect to find a wide spreading of life-forms, flora and fauna, particularly as through the use of fliers, seeds and spores and people may move relatively freely from landmass to landmass.

The beast roar of the crowd, the reek of thousands of people crammed together, the heat of the suns, the crisp sliding feel of sand beneath my feet — I can feel them all as though they happened this morning. Yet I felt no animosity toward these hideous Blegs. They were halflings, beast-men, and yet I was being forced into fighting them for the debased amusement of these decadent spectators massed around me in the amphitheater.

Naghan the Gnat kept close to me. His thin, wiry frame looked more scrawny than ever beside the massive muscle of Lart the Stink and of Cleitar Adria. These advanced boldly toward the Blegs.

If what I am about to tell you appalls you, makes you sick, gives you a strong sense that I, Dray Prescot, am a very beast in truth, I cannot blame you. We had been given wine before we stepped into the arena, a rough red wine much like vinegar, poured carefully by Fristle women from leather bags into our leather cups. We had drunk deeply, for the day was hot and we faced dangers we would rather not face.

Cunning are the ways of the managers of the Jikhorkduns!

Not only were the four colors pitted one against the other, in two, three, and four way combats, but the races and species were pitted one against another, so that it was rare except in special wagered combats to find apim against apim, Och against Och, Fristle against Fristle, Bleg against Bleg. The Jikhorkdun demanded a man fight against other men who aroused in him the deepest and most basic fears and furies of blood.

Among the ranks of the reds were Blegs, and they might on the following day be set against apims — men like me — wearing the blue.

But all that might be lived with. I was prepared to fight if that meant I might stay alive.

The subtle cunning of the Jikhorkdun managers — and, yet, not so subtle, not so cunning; rather, inevitable — saw to it that the wine was drugged with the crushed distillations of the sermine flower. Already I could feel a rage growing within me. I did not know then the wine was drugged. I did not discover this for some time. But I must mention it now, to try to explain why I did what I did.

Yes, I even felt a glow of prowess, as though I had performed a great Jikai! Deep was my shame, I acknowledge, for I had lived and others had died.

"Come, brothers," growled Cleitar Adria. His tanned skin showed a light dusting of golden hair; his braided hair had been caught up beneath his leather cap. He had told me he had been quoffa handler, until he had mentioned, when drunk, that the queen should be put down, and the king too. From that speech until his appearance in the arena his progress had been swift and inevitable. He had not been slave. Now he shouted and lifted his javelin. "Let us destroy these Blegs, and have done!"

And I, Dray Prescot, shouted, "With all my heart!" and so hurled the first stux. The cast was shrewd. It slid between the shield and the armor of a Bleg and transfixed him, whereat he shrieked and writhed and fell.

With four legs, a Bleg was a difficult foeman to knock over.

With a series of bloodthirsty shouts, the two lines met.

We should have had little chance. The Blegs were apprentice kaidurs, growing skilled in the ways of the arena. They had passed through their coy stage. I kept the second stux, unwilling to deprive myself of a weapon at this pass, and so dueled with a Bleg who kept spitting obscene words at me through his funnelmouth. His thraxter smashed against the cheap purtle wood of the stux-shaft, and that wood, poor stuff from the pine forests far to the south of Havilfar, splintered and cracked across. I seized the splintered end containing the steel stux-head and swung viciously and saw Naghan the Gnat, on all fours, thrusting his stux upward at the Bleg. He stuck the point in one of the fellow's legs. The Bleg yelped and swung his sword violently down at Naghan. I leaped. I put the stux into the Bleg's face with my right hand and with the left took his right wrist into my fist. I bent. He crashed over with me on top of him, and then I had the thraxter and was on my feet.

"The Invisible Twins!" screeched Naghan the Gnat.

Lart the Stink was down, his blue and yellow intestines greasily strewing over the silver sand in the glare of the suns.

A quick look about showed me that Nath the Arm had done his work well. Of our twenty, ten still remained on their feet, and six of the Blegs were down and one more went over, his four legs flailing, as a stux from Cleitar Adria took him full in that hideous vampire face.

Now the killing should in theory begin, for we had hurled all our javelins, and there were eight Blegs left to dispatch us.

"Gather up stuxes!" I roared at Naghan the Gnat. "And stay out of the way!"

A Bleg bore down on me and there was no time to snatch up a fallen shield. I leaped. I took the shield-rim in my left hand and parried off the sword blow and so dragged the shield down and thrust long and hard. This time I glared around malevolently, and I know my face held that old devil's look of maleficent murder, as I stooped to pick up the shield. The next Bleg tried a clever series of overhand and underhand passes and I simply smashed my shield against his, upset him on his four straddling legs, and passed the thraxter through his eye.

A quick glance showed me four more of our reds down and Cleitar Adria taking a stux from Naghan and hurling it with tremendous force and accurate aim. I went after the rest of the Blegs, who fought well — oh, yes, they fought well, for had they, poor devils, not also been given the drugged sermine flower wine?

When I learned the secret of that anger-stimulating wine I understood why there was kool after kool of beautiful flowers growing in Hyrklana. And I had thought that meant the people were civilized, beauty-loving! We grew flowers in Delphond, gorgeous blooms, and they delighted our senses. I did not think a happy Vallian of Delphond would care for the uses to which the Jikhorkdun put the sermine flower.

"Behind you, Drak!" roared Cleitar.

Already aware of the Bleg heaving up from the sand at my back as I turned, I yet shouted an acknowledgment to Cleitar.

"By Opaz! A persistent fellow, Cleitar."

We stood upon that blood-soaked silver sand. The suns poured down their radiance upon that scene of horror. Stretched upon the arena floor lay the bodies of fifteen Blegs and seventeen apims. Only Cleitar Adria, Naghan the Gnat, and myself survived. With the fading of the effects of the drugged wine, Naghan vomited all over the sand.

"Brace yourself, oh Gnat!" said Cleitar. There was about his blond face a look that did not puzzle me. He had fought and he had won, and he was feeling marvelous. I suspected that the quoffa handler might have found his true vocation as kaidur.

The amphitheater was filling with spectators. We saluted the royal box, empty as yet, and marched back to face the wrath of Nath the Arm. Slaves ran to sprinkle and rake. The beast-howl of the crowd muted as we entered the iron-bound tunnels and so made our way back to our quarters. Nath the Arm looked at us.

"Three!" he said, shaking his head in wonderment. "I had thought the whole twenty of you marked for the Ice Floes."

"Maybe you trained us well, Nath," I said.

He looked at me, and his dark eyes swelled in their sockets — then he chuckled. "By Kaidun! You three may yet become kaidurs! A miracle, a veritable miracle, as the glass eye and brass sword of Beng Thrax is my witness!"

Cleitar Adria chuckled, flexing his muscles, the blood wet and slick upon his body, clogging the blond hairs. He was a man who would never need drugs to fight as kaidur; he had tasted the power, and he had found his vocation.

Naghan the Gnat winked and said, "Nath the Arm! Where are all the shishis sighing for our favors you promised us?"

"Cramph!" roared Nath, mightily outraged. "You are coys! When you are kaidurs! And then, oh puissant Gnat, who will care for your scrawny body, hey?"

"You'd be surprised," said Naghan the Gnat.

Nine

I fight for the ruby drang

Tilly peeled a grape most carefully with her long, slender golden fingers and popped the juicy squishy morsel into my open mouth. I lay on my back, supported by heaped silken cushions, clad in a light lounging robe of sensil whose touch is softer than the ordinary silk, a massive golden bracelet upon my left wrist, a trophy flung down by an admirer the day before. Around me the high-ceilinged marble chamber with its tall windows letting in the glorious rays of Far and Havil was crammed with trophies, feathers, weapons, gold and silver, flowers and laurels, the whole gorgeous and barbaric loot of a successful kaidur. A chest of jewels open at the foot of the couch spilled pearl necklaces, diamond rings, brooches and torques of a hundred varieties of gems.

Much of this lavish wealth, of course, had been won by wagers. A table whose legs were formed into zorca hooves supported a lavish display of wines. Needless to detail them all. Each was a superlative vintage. There was even a flagon of Jholaix. What that had cost I did not know, for commerce on Kregen follows common sense routes and parameters, and an importer will fetch his wine from only so far off, and an exporter will scarce wish to venture farther than he need to sell his wares.

"Enough of grapes, Tilly," I said. "Palines!"

She giggled. Tilly was a Fristle girl. I detested Fristles as a general rule, and yet — remembering Sheemiff — I had to admit I cared for their women. A cat-people, the Fristles, yet quite un-catlike in their social habits. Tilly had a golden body fur covering a shape that would drive most men's mouths dry. Remembering my Delia — a shallow and silly remark, that, for I would never be able to forget her, my Delia, my Delia of Delphond — I could still admit that Tilly was a most beautiful female. Her face with its wide slanted eyes, its full moist mouth, and — even — her delightful little whiskers, so unlike the Latin woman's heavy moustache, all delighted me.

She began to toss palines into my mouth and I to suck them down. I had respected her. I was a successful and, so far, exciting new kaidur. I was not yet a great kaidur. Everyone said that would come.

I did not agree.

Escape for the slaves, the workers, the coys, apprentices, and kaidurs was impossible. All the working exits to the warren of workrooms, rings, and barracks adjoining the massive amphitheater were closely guarded. And there was no way of climbing up into the lowest ring of seats and escaping through the many exits used by the public of Huringa. Only the greatest of great kaidurs were allowed freely to stroll in the city. They had the scales weighed in their advantage and they had everything to gain by staying, and nothing to win by escaping. I did not think I would stay around long enough to become a great kaidur.

So I could loll in my grand sensil robe and eat squishes and palines and grapes and chatter pleasantly with Tilly; for on this night I would escape from Huringa, and from the land of Hyrklana, and return to Migla. If Delia had left I would then fly to Valka. I own for a concern. It had begun to ram through the diabolical interference of the Star Lords on that field of the Valley of the Crimson Missals. A force of Canops had remained unbeaten. If the rain prevented my longbowmen from shooting… But, I felt, Seg would master that problem.

Nath the Arm strutted in then, his gorgeous robes worn when off duty lighting up that already dazzling chamber. He looked cheerful.

"I have had three more offers, Drak the Sword. And one from that pimply idiot, the Kov of Manchifwell."

"You will accept, of course."

I had to let Nath the Arm believe everything went as usual. These special wagers were a profitable source of his income. Other famous kaidurs were already beginning to measure their prowess against the strides made by Drak the Sword. Nath had promised, with tears in his eyes, that he would make me the greatest kaidur in all of Hyrklana, aye, in all of Hamal, too!

The reds prospered, to the greater glory of the ruby drang. Naghan the Gnat still lived, and was now, at my request, not used as a kaidur in the arena but served as our armorer. His sinewy strength was more adapted to the cunning blows required in the fashioning of armor than in the different skills of parting warriors from essential portions of their anatomy. Cleitar Adria, too, still lived, and was winning a renown for himself. There were a number of kaidurs in the barracks controlled by Nath who were still regarded as greater than I; this had no power to disturb me. I merely fought that I might stay alive. Well, in that, as you who have listened to my story may guess, I am less than honest. A fight is a fight. I have given you something of my philosophy of swordsmanship already, and I admit to a fascinated interest in the chance that each fresh day, each new challenge, would bring me at last face to face with a greater swordsman than I am.[5]

"There are also fifty coys all green and dripping."

I sighed. We needed recruits, for the reds were fighting many unequal combats on the silver sand of the arena. But I disliked the way we obtained our coys. Anyone who displeased the queen or any of her nobles was liable to be swept up to serve as fodder for the Jikhorkdun. Those people with whom I had been captured had been leaving a meeting called to discuss ways and means of bringing the queen down. She was, everyone agreed, a bitch. Her husband, the king, was a weakling, a mere cipher. She was, also, this haughty Queen Fahia, the twin sister of that Princess Lilah I had rescued from the Manhounds of Faol.

Many a time had I seen the queen sitting enthroned in her ornate box, covered by the regal awnings, decorated with flowers and vines and many banners, sitting there, chin on fist, gazing down as men and beasts, and beast-men and men-beasts, hacked at each other and gouted blood and died — for her pleasure.

Not once had I seen Princess Lilah. During every spare moment in the arena I had looked along the boxes and tiers of seats reserved for the aristocracy, searching for her beautiful face and golden hair among all the other faces there. I had made discreet inquiries, but no one seemed to know. More and more I was coming to the dismal conclusion that she had not made her escape astride the fluttrell, or had been taken by another slave gang of Havilfar, or, perhaps, had not even survived that mad escape attempt.

"As to the coys, Nath," I said. "Cannot you shield them from the demands of the arena? With a little more training—"

He shook his head. "Alas, Drak the Sword. I would like to, Kaidun knows! But it is impossible. We reds must put on our part of the show. Already, and despite the work you among our great kaidurs are doing, the yellows claim they honor the diamond zhantil the highest among the four quarters."

"The yellows have been doing well." I flicked Tilly's long golden tail away from where she had been slyly tickling my side. "That riot last sennight — have the terraces been repaired? And what is the latest count of broken heads?" I was always asking for news from the outside world. To Nath the Arm, the world was here in the Jikhorkdun, and, possibly, he would allow some interest to what went on in Huringa. Apart from that, the whole wide world of Kregen might not exist as far as he was concerned.

"Tilly!" I shouted. "Take your golden tickler away and pour wine for Nath the Arm — or, you fifi, you will be whipped."

She slid from the couch with a soft shirring of her silken gown, her long golden-furred legs very wanton. She mocked me, her slanted eyes wide, her lips pouting. "You would never whip me, Drak my master. You are too softhearted."

"Beware lest I chain you up at night with an iron chain."

She brought the wine for Nath, and she pouted her lips at me. "If you chained me, Drak the Sword, it would be with a silver chain."

Tilly, like me, was a slave, although I was a kaidur and therefore the object of considerable envy.

How many and devious ways there are in the world, to be sure, for a man to earn a living!

Cleitar Adria came in as Tilly was pouring again and at once he lifted a goblet and she poured for him, carefully. It was not unknown for Cleitar Adria, kaidur, to strike even a little furry fifi if she spilled his wine. Still, I was pleased to see him, for he brought news.

He occupied a chamber constructed in the marble fashion of splendor of the Jikhorkdun builders of Hyrklana, although perhaps not as grandiose as mine. We were prisoners, but we lived in highly gilded cages. Far below us groaned the great mass of coys and apprentices and common kaidurs, pent into their barracks and cells. We, at least, could see the suns in their glory and revel in the sweet air away from the fetid breath of the arena warrens.

"I fight twice today, Drak the Sword." He quaffed his wine, his golden hair done up in braids, finely twisted by one of his slave wenches, his color high, his eyes fierce. He wore a corselet of gilded iron, and silver greaves, and carried a thraxter. He would have a lad — not necessarily an apim boy — to carry his massive helmet for him. The helmet would be of iron, heavily chased and carved, gilded, and with a face mask with breaths and sights let cunningly into the metal. On everything about him — as about me and the rest of us here — the red color was flaunted in feather and sash and favor.

"My felicitations, Cleitar. I wish you success twice over."

He was not so far drunk with his own image of himself as to forget to thank me. Then he stared at me directly. I knew he had been jealous — to put no baser construction on it — of the bestowal of the tag "Sword" to the name Drak I was using. He wanted to ask something, and his own newfound kaidur pride rebelled. At last he drank again, wiped his lips, and said, "The first is with Anko, an ord-kaidur of the greens, a Rapa. I do not trouble myself over the outcome."

I nodded. "You are kaidur, Cleitar. One who has two more accolades to obtain before that will scarcely evade your sword."

"Aye. But the second is a graint."

Oho! I said to myself. Here is the rub. I said to Nath, "Has Cleitar fought a graint before?" And then, quickly so as to negate any imputations of hostility, I added, "He fights so often and so well it is difficult to keep track of his victories."

"No, Drak the Sword."

As you well know, I have fought graints. I have also fought them with swords that did not kill. But that was a fading dream to me, in those days as a kaidur, and the paradise of the Swinging City of Aphrasöe had never seemed so far distant.

After some more drinking and talking I managed to give Cleitar the benefit of my experience, and hoped he would take it. I had made no good companions as a kaidur. The tragedy of that course was all too apparent. A good friend in the morning might be merely a mangled corpse, dragged by the cruel iron hooks from the blood-smeared silver sand, by the time the twin suns sank in their opaz glory.

I scratched my beard. I had let my hair and beard grow unchecked and I was now a most hairy specimen, like a shaggy graint in truth. This was done for a set purpose.

Cleitar left, and Nath, also, and I called young Oby to help with my armor. Oby was short for Obfaril — first beloved — and he was an engaging imp, an apim boy, with tousled fair hair, a wide cheeky smile, and fingers as dexterous in the manner of stealing palines as of buckling up armor. He was slave and was, of course, mad keen to become a kaidur.

I, too, was fighting twice this day. A kaidur's life was not all lolling on silken cushions being fed palines by delectable Fristle fifis and quaffing wine and counting golden deldys and adding up the winnings. Today I faced a notable kaidur of the greens, a Rapa like the green Cleitar was to face; but a kaidur. That is, he had passed all the destructive tests of the arena from coy and now, with a string of victories behind him (a defeat was almost impossible for sometimes the defeated were allowed to live), was looking for the supreme accolade of being dubbed great kaidur. He, like myself, would be a trifle pampered by his manager. The backers with the money, nobles in consortia, business people, great merchants, and landed gentry, would wager more and more heavily upon him. He would be sought out for combats from his peers; he would not be chanced too often in the melee. He would, in short, be a prize kaidur. Like Cleitar. Like the other kaidurs and great kaidurs of the Jikhorkdun. We fought the combats in theory as unequals, as the blood-lust and the blood-curiosity demanded; but we were arena professionals, and we met and matched our skills rather than the mere differences of weapons.

If Cleitar was killed this day, then his ord-kaidur Rapa opponent would be one step nearer to being full kaidur.

I had little fear for Cleitar. He was of the manner of man to whom the arena had come as the real purpose of his life.

Between Tilly and Oby I was accoutered in a clean white linen shirt, a padded vest, a corselet of gilden iron, shoulder wings — scarcely pauldrons — golden greaves, and I buckled up two crossed lesten-hide belts over the scarlet breechclout. Often Nath the Arm would glare at that scarlet breechclout, and say: "But, Drak the Sword! By Kaidun, but the color is overly scarlet for the ruby drang!"

And I would say: "It has brought the ruby drang fair pickings, oh Nath the Arm! Would you offend, perhaps, the ruby heart of Beng Thrax?"

"By the glass eye and brass sword of Beng Thrax! Do you then mock me, Drak the Sword?"

"May Kaidun forfend!"

We went down to our assembly place where the coys shuffled away with many a long look, at once apprehensive, fearful, envious, at the kaidurs. Cleitar greeted me. So did Rafee the Render, a giant of a kaidur who had been a pirate before being captured and offered the usual alternatives. He was a huge ruffian and a great hand with his ax. With the other kaidurs of the red who were fighting this day we took our places on ponsho-fleece covered benches behind the iron bars where we might sit and quaff wine and swap stories and stare out upon the silver sand. One by one the combats took place. Cleitar disposed of his Rapa, as I disposed of mine. At this time there might be as many as fifty separate combats going on in the arena, and wherever the public might sit, strictly in the color-quarters they would support from the day of their birth to the day of their death, they would have a fine close-up view of the fighting.

The suns crawled up the sky. The wine we drank, that raw rough red stuff the kaidurs called Beng Thrax's spit, served to slake our thirsts. It was practically non-alcoholic. But — it contained the hidden drug distilled from the sermine flower.

The day wore on and the most important of the combats especially staged as wagers went on increasing. We lost a great kaidur, one Fakal the Sword, who slipped in a patch of sand-strewn blood and so recovered to stare at a thraxter as it plunged over the rim of his corselet into his neck. We yelled and rattled our swords across the iron bars and made the shrieks and ululations from the paid mourners, starkly dramatic in their black robes, separated in their special boxes, seem like thin chittering whistling.

"Ornol the Chank!" yelled Nath. "We have him marked, by Kaidun!"

Ornol the Chank was a great kaidur of the yellow, and we saw poor old Fakal the Sword's head offered up as a tribute to the diamond zhantil. Out of deference to custom we must remain mute while the observances were being made. But we all looked at Fakal's dripping head, and we all wanted to get onto the silver sand and cross thraxters with Ornol the Chank.

I checked in horror.

This night I had planned an escape. What then, by Zair, was I doing vowing to revenge our injured red honor by dealing with Ornol the Chank in the future? I had no future I wanted here in the Jikhorkdun. Rather, having established what position I had, I would reject it all as trivial for the realities of my life which were, as you know, Delia and — well, the rest might go hang. Delia, and little Drak and Lela were all I wanted.

So — why shout and rave and shake my sword at the triumphant yellow benches?

There was no denying the excitement of it all, the thrills and terror, the narrow escapes, the great shouts of triumph or of raging despair that roared up at victory or disaster. I was one of the reds. We fought for the ruby drang. Out across that sun-soaked arena of silver sand lives were staked. The huge sums of money and jewels and property were all behind the scenes. Here, in the blood and the agony, the swift clash of combat, here was where it all happened.

Oh, yes, I was caught up in it all. I was a kaidur, and conscious of that, proud even, and I fought for the reds and as much as I joyed in my own victories I gloried in the victories of my fellow reds. I even think that a great kaidur, when at last he was beaten and so fell with his opponent's bloody weapon drinking his life blood, felt greater sorrow that his color had gone down in defeat than that he was losing his own life.

Eerie and powerful are the ways men may be twisted by systems and customs and the hot passions of blood.

The proud and remote land of Hyrklana gathered men from many other lands and nations and races to fight in the Jikhorkdun. The demands of the arena were insatiable. Of poor people to be used merely as fodder, to whip up the blood appetites, few might be found outside the criminal classes and the political opponents, and those betrayed by hidden enemies. But the land of Havilfar is wide, and there are very many different countries upon its surface, even if the wild lands in the central northwest are relatively barren. Slave dealers thrived. It had taken a mighty empire to support the arenas of our Earth's ancient Rome. But that empire, large as it was, could not compare with the resources open to the swift vollers of Havilfar.

Fighting in the arena were men from Pandahem, from Murn-Chem, from Ng'groga — their seven-foot height and incredible thinness could not be mistaken — men from Walfarg and Undurkor and Xuntal. Men like my good comrade Gloag from Mehzta who was not apim. There were the wild black-haired, blue-eyed men from the valleys and mountains of Erthyrdrin. There were men from Vallia, too. And, I believe, from Zenicce.

On a day before my plans for escape were complete, I had been engaged in the melee and the reds had been steadily wearing down our yellow opponents. The diamond zhantil remained in the ascendant over the red drang; but we were doing what we might to redress that balance. The four huge colored images on their movable staffs situated at one end of the gigantic oval of the amphitheater showed by their relative heights the state of the colors. If the reds emerged victorious we would lift the red drang another notch higher and bring the yellow zhantil a notch lower.

So, on this day, as we fought and I dispatched my man — for this was a skilled melee, where like fought like, and we were matched — I swung about to smash away a thraxter aimed at my back and so slew that one, also. Cleitar Adria was just stepping back from his man.

The yellow lay gasping on the sand, his face agonized. His oiled curly black hair in tight ringlets gleamed in the steaming light of Far and Havil as his helmet rolled away. Cleitar bent to finish him, as was proper, given that this was a fight-to-the-finish melee.

I saw the man lying there turn his eyes up. His face lost its writhing reflection of the agony he felt. He watched as Cleitar's sword lifted high against the suns. And then he spoke, quick, simple words, breathy and blood-filled. Words I heard in a kind of stupefied daze.

"I join you, my brothers, Krozairs of Zamu! I join you to sit on the right hand of Zair in the glory of Zim!"

Shattered, I sprang forward.

"No, Cleitar!"

I was too late. The sword slashed down. A Krozair brother had indeed gone to join his comrades in Zair. Aye, his comrades as a Krozair of Zamu — but, also, my comrades as a Krozair of Zy!

Cleitar bent to wipe his thraxter, there in the arena of Huringa in Hyrklana, so many many dwaburs from the Eye of the World and from Sanurkazz.

"What is it, Drak the Sword! What ails you? Are you hit?"

"It is nothing, Cleitar Adria."

But it was something.

I could not find another man from the inner sea fighting in the Jikhorkdun of Huringa in Hyrklana. I would ask, when I saw a man who looked as though he knew what a swifter was, who knew the difference between Zair and Grodno. But I never did find one, then.

So, now, on this day I was to escape, I watched as Cleitar Adria went out to fight his graint. He won. He managed to kill the great and noble beast. When he came back he was ripped and scratched and one arm hung useless. He stared at me, and licked his lips. His beard had been torn and bloody flesh showed.

"I did as you counseled, Drak. I took him, limb by limb." Cleitar looked all in. "I think — I think you counseled well."

201

I had to say it, for all that the words nearly stuck in my mouth. "You did well, Cleitar. Hai Jikai!"

I had never used those great words in the arena before. I considered the place and occasion base and unworthy. But Cleitar had fought well. He deserved the "Hai Jikai." "Jikai" is for warriors, I thought, hardly for kaidurs.

Nath the Arm had overheard. He glanced at me curiously.

"Now, by Kaidun, Drak the Sword! I had often wondered, but now I am sure. You have been a paktun — perhaps a Hyr-paktun."

A Paktun, as I have said, is a great warrior of fortune, a mercenary leader, or one who has achieved some feat of great renown. It has become a little debased in usage, and is often applied to any noteworthy freelancer. But, to be a paktun is to be a leader of a free company, or a mercenary so famous as to be hired at the highest fee obtainable. Many Chuliks were paktuns — and many were Hyr-paktuns, also; "Hyr" being a word for great.

"And if I have, Nath the Arm, does not that augur well for the ruby drang?"

He glowered at me and pulled his gold-threaded beard. He knew how I liked to mock him, and he could only take it, for we had become as friendly as men in our respective positions might. As to my references to the ruby drang, he could never make up his mind if I meant what I said, or merely mocked the more.

My own second fight followed, and it was a bloodthirsty affair which I prefer to forget. But I did what I had to do — had to do, for a kaidur who would not fight was a kaidur with a garrote around his throat and a stone lashed to his legs and a billet in the fast-flowing River of Leaping Fishes which pours around the northern side of Huringa.

After that I had no wish to sit further on the ponsho fleeces of the benches in the red quarter. Out on the arena stakes were being raised. Presently females of various races would be brought out, all naked, and lashed to those stakes. Their male counterparts would be let out, naked also, and armed with that very broad, very short two-edged sword the Havilfarese call djangir. Then, when all was ready and the crowds were leaning forward in expectation, the wild bosks would be driven out, mad with hunger and rage. The bosk is pig-like, and very good eating, and highly prized, a delicacy of Valka, as you know. The wild bosk has two horns upon its head, each at least two feet long, straight and sharp and deadly. It can lower its head and charge and skewer through good leather.

The men must defend their womenfolk, for the managers of the Jikhorkdun are most clever in this, and select married couples, or son and mother, or father and daughter, or lovers. The short djangir is scarcely the weapon with which to meet the wicked twenty-four-inch twin horns of the wild bosk.

But the spectacle affords amusement to the paying public of Huringa…

Ten

A voller flight over Huringa

Soft and gentle and very skilled were the fingers of Tilly, the girl Fristle, as she clipped and combed my hair and beard and moustache. I like a short, pointed, damn-you-to-hell beard, and moustaches that, whether I will it or no, thrust upward arrogantly. Tilly sang a little song as she snipped. It was "The Lay of Faerly the Ponsho Farmer's Daughter." Young girl Fristles with their soft fur and their sweet cat-faces and their exciting figures are notorious for their knowledge of the arts of love. Perhaps I am unfair in using the word notorious. It would be kinder to say famous. Of course, this meant nothing to me, for only Delia could ever stir me; but it was undeniably pleasurable to have Tilly thus minister to my wants. She would wash and rub me with oil and ease the stiffness out of my limbs and clip my hair and comb it and sniff at me and say, cheekily, "You are a veritable apim graint, Drak the Sword."

To which I was honor-bound to reply, "Tomorrow I shall buy a silver chain."

To which she, in her turn, would toss her pretty head and flick her tail around to tickle my ribs, while she went on snipping and combing and singing about the lay of Faerly, the Fristle ponsho farmer's daughter.

All this was meaningless. By tomorrow, far from buying a silver chain, or even threatening to, as I did almost every day, I would be aboard a stolen voller and winging my way northward to Valka — or southwestward to Migla, for I still felt great unease about that diabolical rain shower.

I have said I prefer a short pointed beard. I had deliberately allowed my face fungus to grow inordinately. Oh, it had not sprouted into the great blaze of jet threaded with gold that Nath the Arm sported. But now, when Tilly finished her clipping, she sat back, curling her tail up, and said: "By the furry tail of the Frivolous Freemiff! You look so different, Drak my master."

She knew I didn't like her calling me her master.

We were slaves together. I frowned. She opened those wide slanting eyes of hers, so catlike, so sensual, and flicked her golden tail.

"I am no different, you impudent fifi. I am still Drak the Sword, a great hairy graint of an apim."

"Aye! That you are!"

So, that being settled, I packed her off to her bed in an adjoining room, where she was perfectly safe not only from me but from any amorous kaidur who might wander the corridors of this high barracks. Somewhere below in a courtyard a poor devil was being flogged. I could hear the meaty thwack of each blow and the shrieks that gradually quieted to a moaning and then to a more horrible silence, punctuated only by that devilish sound of a man's bare back being lashed raw.

The contrast between my condition up here, with all its luxury, and that poor devil below sobered my high spirits for the night's enterprise. Young Oby came in, cheerfully whistling a scandalous song. He wanted my authorization for him to collect our allowance of samphron oil for the lamps. I gave it to him, sealing it with the crude signet stamp allowed me in the form of a thraxter crossed with a djangir. I had not chosen that signature.

"Who is that below, Oby?"

"Why, master, the onker Ortyg the Sly. He was caught stealing wine — purple Hamish wine, too."

Well, stealing rum was a crime for which I had seen floggings enough in the navy of my youth. I dismissed Oby.

Then I set about dressing myself for the night's adventures.

A nobleman or a Horter — that is, a gentleman — of Havilfar might well walk the streets of his city wearing a sword. He would not ordinarily carry a shield. They favored the curved dagger here, and with its ornate sheath and grip the one I slung to my belt was a flashy toy. But the thraxter was a warrior's weapon, bloodied this day in the arena. I put on my favored scarlet breechclout — a new one specially procured and washed and ironed by Tilly. Over this the white linen shirt and then a yellow jerkin, its shoulders and back a blaze of embroidery. The weather was too hot for trousers. I chose calf-high boots of a supple leather that would breathe, for I did not wish to wear sandals in the game I was playing.

A pouch contained a considerable sum in deldys and sinvers, and this I buckled to my waist. With due precaution I also wrapped a few extremely valuable gems into the scarlet breechclout. Around me in my marble chamber with its silks and feathers and furs lay a fortune I had won. All this must be left. It meant nothing. I wore a hat, one of the Havilfarese closely fitting leather caps, and could wish for one of the wide-brimmed Vallian hats with their jaunty feathers.

I knew nothing of the city of Huringa — save that its people liked to pay money to enter the Jikhorkdun and to wager if a man would live or die — and Oxkalin the Blind Spirit must guide me when I set foot outside the amphitheater. You may be sure I observed the fantamyrrh when I left that chamber, as I thought for the last time.

A stuxcal stood by the door, fully filled with its eight javelins. I had to leave it. A gentleman does not walk the streets of his city carrying stuxes, now does he? In a civilized city like Huringa? I thought not, judging by what I knew of Vondium and Sanurkazz and Zenicce.

Tilly and Oby were left. They had prepared me a good meal, and I had eaten well — roast vosk, taylynes, a pie of squishes and gregarians, rather too sweet, rich yellow butter and fluffy Kregan loaves, and — a triumph! — cup after cup of that fragrant superb Kregan tea. In my wallet I had stuffed a package of palines, and I carried two strips of dried beef, veritable biltong, which would sustain me for a long period.

Once past the corridors and passageways immediately adjacent to my chamber I was able to pass without notice. From my cap a great cascading mass of red feathers drooped and a red favor glowed on my left shoulder. These I planned to discard the moment I was out on the street and unobserved.

The success of my plan hinged on the evening entertainments of the Horters of Huringa. They would take their carriages, their sleeths, or their zorcas and ride up to the Jikhorkdun, unable, it seemed, to keep away from the blood-reeking place, to inspect the latest hyr-kaidur, or a newly imported wild beast, or to watch practices. Some of these Horters, I knew, fancied their luck and would don a kaidur's gear and venture into a practice ring. They would use rebated weapons — that went without saying. There must be many other entertainments for a pleasant evening in the city, I reasoned: taverns and dancing halls, dopa dens, even theaters. But the pull of the arena was stronger.

Down in a practice pit I saw a group of gentlemen watching a kaidur fence one of their number. The kaidur gave them their money's worth, letting himself be bested. The Horters laughed and joked, garish in fine clothes, flicking their thraxters about, sniffing from pomanders, chewing palines. Oh, yes, they were a brilliant parasitical lot. I joined them. I, Drak the Sword, kaidur, had the temerity to insinuate my way into a group of nobles and Horters from the city.

Had Nath the Arm appeared he might well have recognized me. I doubted that even Cleitar Adria would do so. I was confident that Naghan the Gnat would recognize me at once; he was a sharp little one.

So I had chosen a practice ring well away from the usual ones patronized by the coys and apprentices and kaidurs of Nath the Arm's barracks. I was jostled by a young Horter, who did not apologize but merely twitched his elegant shoulders away. I let him remain on his feet and with his senses intact. As in almost any group, a natural leader led this one, a young man in the bright flush of youth whom the others called Strom Noran. He joked and laughed with them and yet quite clearly remained aware of his position.

"By Clem, Dorval!" he shouted to one of his friends, older and leaner and, I judged, looking for any opportunity to make money. "I'll wager a thousand Deldys you could do no better!"

"I would refuse to take your money, Strom Noran," replied this Dorval. "Callimark might be a kaidur himself!"

Callimark, the youngster who fancied he had beaten the kaidur in the practice ring, lifted a flushed face. Sweat stood on his forehead. "By Clem, Dorval! Don't get out of it like that! Come down here and fight me!"

"Yes, Dorval," said Strom Noran. "And a thousand on it."

"Now, by Flem, you do push me, Strom Noran."

"And by Flem I want to see it, Dorval!"

I stepped back. Their silly pride, their stupid wager, meant nothing. A great and horrid suspicion overwhelmed me. These brilliant, carefree, rich young men swore casually by Clem and by Flem — gods or spirits or saints of whom I had never heard, although with so many cluttering the pantheon of Kregen that was not surprising. But I had not missed the hesitation as they swore. If the first consonant of any of the gods' names was omitted, one was left with *Lem*!

Then I knew the evil cult of Lem the silver leem had penetrated in secret into this city of Huringa in Hyrklana.

As I was to find, the people of Hyrklana are a fiery-tempered lot, hasty with the sword, bloodthirsty as their love of the arena testified to me even then. Yet there were very good and pressing reasons for much of this fierceness, this predatory urge to supremacy and violence. All along the southeastern coastlines of Havilfar the populations lived in a constant apprehension of the raids from those strange beings from the southern oceans. I had already met and fought one of their ships. But I had had little direct contact and knew nothing about them, except that as reavers they were viler than anything I had known on Kregen — the overlords of Magdag could not bear comparison — and as reavers ought to be put down. So Hyrklana, from her exposed and precarious position jutting out into the southern ocean from the eastern flank of Havilfar, received her fair share and more of these devastating raids. A viciousness of reprisal, a hardness of character, a streak of reckless daring ran through all of Hyrklana — aye! and many another country of Kregen, too. They clung to the belief that one day, someday, a final reckoning would have to be made with these reavers. They had so many differing and usually obscene names I have not bothered to give a single one; but one name they had given to them that chilled me by its implications was — Leem-Lovers.

From Quennohch in the south to Hennardrin in the north, the whole eastern flank of Havilfar knew and detested these reavers from the southern oceans. They came, this way around the planet, from the easterly southern ocean. Usually they limited their farthest advances to the sea areas around South Pandahem and the one we had fought must have been a loner. Not so very long ago they had captured and set up a base in the Astar group of islands approximately midway between Pandahem and Xuntal. Then a great Jikai had been called and they had been hurled out, reeking with their own blood, as men from this grouping of islands and continents dealt with them.

"By Gaji's bowels, Strom Noran! Very well, then, and the thousand deldys will buy me a new zorca chariot!"

The lean dark Dorval had been goaded enough. As he threw off his ornate cloak and jerkin to stand in his tunic and kilt, Strom Noran laughed delightedly. The young man Callimark looked up, still panting from his previous bout, and he laughed also.

"Welcome to our circle, Dorval! It will be a pleasure to cross blades with you."

Time was ticking along and the suns were now almost gone and the idlers and rufflers were drifting back from the Jikhorkdun at last to their other evening pleasures. I stood shoulder to shoulder with the Horter they had called Aldy and watched the mock combat. The youngbloods of Huringa catcalled and whooped and whistled as Callimark and Dorval set to. The kaidur who had allowed this youngster Callimark to beat him had done so with skill, so that it appeared Callimark was something of a sworder. Now the saturnine Dorval cut him to pieces — or would have done so had the blades been sharp and not rebated.

At last Callimark threw his thraxter down, his face angry and near tears, puffed with chagrin.

"You have the devil's own tricks, Dorval, by Glem!"

Dorval turned his thin dark face up to the Strom.

"A thousand deldys, I think the sum was, Strom Noran."

With a curse concerned with the obscene Gaji, Strom Noran lifted his hand. "I will settle with Havil in the morning." By this he meant he would settle when the green sun rose above the horizon.

The raffish Horter next to me, Aldy, chuckled and half to himself said: "By Gaji's slimy intestines! The Strom must pay, the devil take him!"

Then he shot me a swift suspicious look, and I could guess he was cursing himself for so openly allowing his feelings to be known by a stranger. During the planning stages of my escape I had made it my business to inquire for a remote and almost unknown and certainly unfrequented part of Hyrklana. An oldster whose job it was to muck out after the totrixes told me he had come from a land far to the south called Hakkinostoling. This was a mouthful so that few people bothered to recall it, and the land being ravaged, its people were almost unknown. I had asked old Wenerl about his home, plying him with wine, and with rheumy eyes he had obliged with a description of a place anyone would wish to leave. So it was that when this youngblood Aldy glowered at me, suspiciously, I was able to speak with a fine free assumption of bumpkin ignorance.

"I am Varko ti Hakkinostoling," I said, "and am but lately arrived in Huringa. Everything is strange to me, as you may well imagine, and I feel very lost."

"Get a bellyful of wine and you will find friends," Aldy counseled, and then yelled and dodged as Callimark came flying up out of the ring. Callimark landed neatly enough on the wooden edging; but then his foot caught and he pitched forward. I caught him under the armpits and stood him up. He was not at all pleased. He started to bluster, and Dorval, with his saturnine look, vaulted up after him, saying: "A fair fight, Callimark. You witness I did not wish it."

"Well, Dorval, by Gaji's bowels, you could have lost it then!"

Dorval chuckled and drew on his jerkin and cloak. "What! And lose a thousand deldys to a man who scarce notices them?"

So, arguing and expostulating, the crowd swaggered from the practice pit of the Jikhorkdun. Aldy mentioned my name to Callimark and Dorval, saying: "This is Varko ti Hakki-somewhere-or-other. He's drinking with us tonight."

They were a trifle rough and ready in a high-spirited way in their manners, not thinking much of the formal Horter, or of the Tyr or Kyr some of them ranked. Larking and shouting they made their way out of the Jikhorkdun past the watchful Rhaclaw sentries, out onto the broad patio fronting the amphitheater, and I, Varko, went with them.

Snug in the center of the group and talking to Aldy, I passed through the iron sentinel ring set around the Jikhorkdun. My red favors mingled with the flaunted red colors of the others. Maybe I would not have to dispose of them swiftly, after all. We swaggered down the long shallow flight of steps fully a hundred and fifty yards wide, thronged with people leaving the amphitheater. My escape had been comically simple. I think that somewhere, unknown to me at the time, above the clouds, perhaps, Homeric laughter was being roared out at my expense.

I could stare about me, enthralled, for was I not a bumpkin oaf from the backwoods? The outside of the amphitheater could never match the interior for grandeur, for a great deal of the seating was sunk in the ground; but the place reared up, alright, tall and imposing, with facade after facade of architecture rising on arches and colonnades. I looked where we were going. A wide boulevard led off southward. Three other boulevards led off to the other three cardinal points, but I discovered that no area of the city was given over wholly to one color; people lived cheek by jowl as to their color loyalties in the arena, and a baker of the red might shout jolly obscenities to a fishmonger of the green, while a haberdasher of the yellow tried to sell his goods to a housewife of the blues. All would wear their favors as a matter of course, and gnash their teeth when their quarter was down, and crow their triumph when in the ascendant. The reds, as second in the table, were able to swagger with a fine panache over the blues and greens, and yell shrill mocking promises of quick retribution to the yellows.

The main thing that took my attention about the four main boulevards of Huringa was the lighting. Down each side of the roadway a long string of lights flared. I found out about these lights — and marveled anew. They were illuminated by gas, by a natural gas source in nearby hills, which had been tapped and piped into the city and used in flaring gas jets. The sight was wonderful and impressive to me. This merely served to confirm my feelings that Havilfar was further advanced than the other continents of this grouping of four.

We soon passed down the steps and so came to the waiting carriages, and the zorcas and totrixes and sleeths. These amazing gas jets flared brightly and lit up the scene in garish colors, the red of the favors around us, the brilliant harnesses, the gems and gold and silver, the waving feathers, the eye-catching brightness of fresh colors everywhere. The waiting zorcas stamped their hooves, the sleeths scraped their claws, slaves in their gaudy liveries opening carriage doors and soothing impatient animals and folding up steps and whipping up their totrixes or zorcas, everything melded into a bright scene of splendour — but I could not see the stars or the moons of Kregen above me in the night sky.

This was my chance to slip away. Strom Noran shouted some witty sally and cursed his slave hostler to hold the Havil-forsaken sleeth still. He mounted, drawing up a very tight rein. The reptile reared on its two powerful hind legs, its claws biting into the ground, its silly forepaws flailing the air. Its small wicked head flicked a forked tongue and hissed demonically. Strom Noran stuck in his spurs and yelled and the sleeth went bounding off in that ungainly two-legged waddle they have, which can cover the ground at a fair turn of speed, for all that. The sleeth is an uncomfortable mount, and one I do not much care for, nothing being preferable to the zorca or vove. But these racing reptiles were all the rage in Havilfar, and the youngbloods risked their foolish necks in buying and riding the fiercest of them. To me, riding a dinosaur-like sleeth carried too many overtones of the Phokaym.

Now I was fairly out of the amphitheater and among the fashionable sporting crowd of Huringa and I noticed at once that almost no one was without a color favor. I chanced my arm and slipped between a gesticulating bunch of greens, hotly debating the very fight I had myself had this day, when the Rapa kaidur of the greens had fallen to my sword. They concealed me from Callimark and Aldy and the others. The last I saw was Dorval, very contemptuously mounting up on his zorca, and yelling at Callimark that he'd take him on his sleeth to the end of the boulevard, by Gaji's slit ears, for two hundred.

To which Callimark, foolish fellow, yelled: "You're on, Dorval! And I'll lick you—"

Sleeth and zorca sped off. I knew which one my money would be on. I let them go and cut away from the greens, who had come to no agreement why their great kaidur had failed against that kaidur of the reds, Drak the Sword, and so managed to slink off into an unlighted alleyway.

I confess I knew little if anything of Huringa, and I learned precious little more that night.

Once out of the glare of the gas jets I could look up and ease my eyes and see once again the glory of the stars and She of the Veils riding clouds high above. Colored lights festooned the sky up there, moving in long smooth arcs from horizon to horizon, dropping down and rising up. These were the riding lights of vollers. I watched where a group came to ground and set off walking. I went with care. My thraxter was loose in its sheath; and although I saw plenty of people coining and going about their business, and passed from torch-lit areas to other places of pitch-blackness, I was not molested.

The flierdrome lay before me, blazing with lights, and the expenditure of oil must have been prodigious. Most of the lamps used a cheap mineral oil called rock oil, and not the more expensive, infinitely purer, and more beautiful samphron oil. I selected the voller I wanted. A four-place craft with a low rail, without a cabin and with fast lines, it would, I fancied, take me swiftly to Migla — or Valka.

I vaulted the low drome rail, raced for the flier, leaped in and thrust the ascent lever hard over. The flier zoomed up in a graceful arc, and from the ground and dwindling in the rush of my passage, I heard the shouts and angry calls of the slave attendants. Their woes were not mine and although I felt sorry for them, for they might well be punished, this was just another of the burdens of Kregen I must bear — for a time.

The night sky enfolded me. I set the course at west-southwest and cracked up to full speed. Huringa sped past below.

I was free!

And then — and then the black clouds boiled solidly before me and a mighty wind rushed upon my craft, spinning it end for end and the noise blasted into my ears, and I was falling... falling... falling into blackness...

Eleven

The neemus of Queen Fahia of Hyrklana

Sparks and stars and planets and meteors shot and crackled about me. The airboat fell from the sky as though smashed in the paw of a gigantic leem. Whirled headlong the voller sliced through treetops and foliage whipped about my ears. No control was possible. That black maelstrom stirred the sky into a caldron. Other vollers there were being hurled pell-mell. I saw two smash together and the small frantic figures of jerking passengers fall through the storm to the ground.

No need to ask by whose malign power this gale had been sent!

Once again, as had happened before, I was being warned off by the Star Lords. They did not wish me to travel to Migla and they were giving me no chance to find out if I might travel to Valka, away to the north across the equator. This was no ordinary storm. The blackness, the massive billowing of the clouds, angry, lightning-shot, and violence of the wind and rain, all were supernormal. I clung to the gyrating voller and I cursed the Star Lords. Oh, yes, I cursed them blue!

Another voller narrowly avoided crushing mine, for this craft that yawed away was a monster and I could see the deck covered with iron cages. Weight is of no consequence to a voller. In those cages, illuminated eerily by the flickering shards of lightning, wild beasts leaped and yowled and screeched. This was a flier bringing prize specimens for the arena.

Both vollers hit the ground at the same time. Mine went somersaulting over a low brick wall, smashing a thatched roof, ripping through a loloo yard, came shudderingly to rest against a low thorn-ivy hedge. I scrambled out. I had no wish once again to go breeches first through a thorn-ivy hedge.

The cages had burst on impact. Screams and yells, horrid in the uncertain light, created a bedlam. The aftercabin of the flier, a two-deck construction, had splintered to destruction, and costly silks and satins, mashcera and damask, floated and strewed the shattered house. Men and women were running in crazy circles. I saw Rhaclaws carrying torches and whips trying to round up some of the beasts — I saw a strigicaw tear the head off one and spit it out before racing for a second.

In that incredible scene of confusion with maddened wild beasts, of a ferocity known only to Kregen, terrifying humans, halflings, and apims alike, I stood for a moment. I knew I must help but knew, also, I was likely to get killed in affording that help.

Any hesitation was instantly banished as from the shattered wreckage of the cabin's upper deck the slim and half-naked form of a girl leaped and ran, screaming. Her hair blazed flame in the torchlight, by which I assumed she might hail from Loh. Now the thatch of the house was alight and in that curdling orange radiance I saw the low feline shape of a neemu racing after the slender white form of the girl.

The neemu had been injured, for it ran favoring its off front foot. Four legs have the neemus, round and smooth their heads, with squat triangular ears, and wide slit eyes of a lambent smoky-gold. All black are neemus, sleek and deadly, their fur highly prized, their ways amoral and feral. Their red jaws and sharp white teeth love nothing better than closing upon rosy living flesh. Vaguely puma-like, the neemu, vicious and treacherous and utterly deadly.

No thought was necessary.

I leaped forward, drawing my sword.

The girl cast me one terrified, appealing look, and collapsed, her foot twisting under her.

I stepped forward and the neemu did not hesitate.

It leaped.

That long sinuous black body packed with muscle sprang and in that rounded smooth head the lambent golden eyes glittered at me with deadly intent.

I slid the first lashing claw and because the beast was injured in its right paw was able to lean to my left and bring the thraxter around and down in a short and savagely chopping stroke at the neemu's neck. It screeched as it went past. It landed short of the girl, who cowered back, one hand to her mouth, her eyes enormous. Without giving the neemu a chance to recover — for that blow, mighty as it had been and bringing a gout of blood from the gash in the beast's neck, had not killed it — I jumped in again. This time the sword cut and thrust as it was built to do and the neemu shrank back, hissing and screeching, its glossy black fur dappled with blood, and so rolled over, slumped, and died. It did not die easily. Seven lives, neemus have, so goes the old superstition. I gave it seven thrusts, and then seven more, just to make sure.

The girl could not rise. She lay there, her gauzy scraps of clothing only partially covering her glowing body. She tried to speak, and I heard the whispered words "Hai Jikai!"

And then rough and ungentle hands seized me, and a giant Rapa cunningly cast chains about my limbs, and his fellows, Rhaclaws, Rapas, Fristles, and apims, manacled and fettered me.

"What are you about, you yetches!" I roared.

But they struck me across the face and then gagged me, so that I could not yell the curses that boiled and spluttered in my head. What nonsense was this, that I should thus be chained?

The answer to that bore down on me with all the old sense of injustice that festers in many parts of Kregen, as, indeed to our shame, it does on this Earth in the here and now. I was taken swiftly aboard another flier, for the storm inspired by the Star Lords had died as swiftly as it had begun, and with the passengers from the beast-carrying voller was carried with the utmost dispatch to the frowning fortress of Hakal, which dominates the city of Huringa in Hyrklana.

In certain essentials one fortress is much like another, although in Valka I have made certain changes that make of the Valkan castles the finest and most impregnable in all of Kregen, or so I fondly believe. Almost all Kregan castles are comfortable, of course, for comfort and Kregan nobility are tolerably well acquainted. I was taken wrapped in my chains and bundled down into a cell, where sundry Rhaclaws picked me, a Rapa bit me (the Rapa beaks are notorious), and a Fristle flicked me across the face with his tail. Had my mouth not been gagged he, at least, would have regretted his conduct.

I kicked a number of them where it would materially impair their mating instincts; but in the end I was beaten down and chained up. They used a great deal of solid iron chain on me so that, finally, I was helpless.

After some time — time meant nothing among the nobility when dealing with their inferiors — I was hauled out and beaten again just to remind me. Then I was dragged helplessly up stone stairs and so through many back stairs and corridors into a low-ceiled room hung with many bright tapestries and furnished luxuriously with the wealth of empire, and flung down before Queen Fahia of Hyrklana.

I was hungry.

My chains chafed and my muscles were cramped and twisted. I had a headache and I was in the foulest of foul bad tempers.

The queen sat in a simple curule-styled chair, a zhantil pelt strewn carelessly upon it. A Fristle girl hovered with ready goblets of wine, another with tidbits on golden platters. A giant Brokelsh, dressed up in ridiculous finery, waved a feathered fan above her head, for it was full day and the suns pouring in through the open windows gave heat as well as light to the chamber. I took a quick squint — for my eyes were adjusted to the darkness of prison cells and not the glory of Zim and Genodras — to see whether or not the scarlet and golden Gdoinye or the white dove of the Savanti might not be looking in and having a damned good chuckle at my predicament.

"So this is the rast."

The queen's voice might once have been musical and low, but years of undisputed authority had coarsened it. She looked very much like her twin sister, the Princess Lilah; but there hung that coarseness about her, that reddening of artery and vein, that thickening of the flesh of her neck and chin, that cluster of lines between her eyebrows no amount of careful exercise and cosmetics could clear. Her hair had been plaited and dressed into a magnificent golden pile upon her head, ablaze with gems. She wore a long green gown and over that a bodice that seemed to be made from a blaze of jewels. Her feet were clad in satin slippers. She took a goblet of wine from the fifi and sipped reflectively, gazing at me over the rim. She was a beautiful woman, who was slowly losing the battle against too rich food and too much wine and too little exercise. She was aware of her beauty, and, probably, not completely able to grasp that she was losing that glory.

If I do not mention the lines of habitual cruelty that had sunk into her skin around her mouth and pinched her nose, I do so only out of pity for her. Zair knows, she had need of pity!

Now, when I was thrown at her feet, chained and gagged and helpless, she was at the height of her powers. She completely dominated all of Hyrklana, having pushed the kingdom's bounds out to every part of the island, and in the continual nagging misunderstandings with Hamal, the giant neighbor country in the northeast of Havilfar, having quite a few notable successes. Surrounded as she was by subservient pallans and courtiers, her merest whim was unbreakable law. She might live in a dream world, but where that world impinged on the greater world without, the dream world of the Queen of Hyrklana would always prevail.

Princess Lilah had said to me that she longed to return to her father's palace in Hyrklana. I was to learn that the old king still lived, in retirement, having abdicated in favor of his daughter Fahia. He had opposed this obsession with the Jikhorkdun, and Princess Lilah, also, had wanted no part of the arena scene. I remembered her horror at the idea of the Manhounds of Faol hunting people. The King's retirement had been engineered by his daughter Fahia. Fahia's husband, Rogan, the present king, was a mere cipher, a nonentity.

At the queen's side, reclining in a low couch wide enough for six, lay four beautiful girls. They were diaphanously clad and smothered with feathers and gems. One of them was the flame-haired girl I had rescued from the wounded neemu.

She looked at me now so piteously that I cursed my gag and bonds afresh, for I judged she blamed herself for my position, and I would have comforted her.

The gaunt figure of a pallan now moved forward. He wore a long robe of blue, girt with the symbols of his authority, and a face much like his must have promised hellfire to many an unbeliever before the fire consumed him utterly.

This was Pallan Ord Mahmud nal Yrmcelt. He was so addressed by the Deldar of the guard. My ears pricked.

The queen stared down at me as she sipped her wine. Then, in a gesture she might imagine to be regal but which was, in all truth, merely pretty, she flung the dregs in my face.

"Yetch! You destroyed my neemu!"

The flame-haired girl gasped.

It was quite unnecessary for the queen to spell out my crime. From the moment I had entered this luxurious chamber I had understood. For tied by silver chains, one on each side of that curule chair, the feral black forms of two neemus were pulling toward me. They yawned to reveal their blood-red mouths and their sharp white fangs. She liked to tickle them now and then with a golden tickler a Fristle fifi had charge of, and when the queen commanded the girl would hand the golden feather-tipped rod across and the queen would stroke and tickle her pets and they would purr like enormous black cats. I knew how deadly they were. But these possessed themselves, partially trained, I had no doubt, willing to be fussed and petted by a human woman in return for a warm spot to sleep and much milk and meat.

The neemus regarded me with their baleful golden slit eyes, and yawned, and the queen tickled them and they purred.

"Take his gag off!"

The gag was roughly removed. I worked my aching jaws, but I did not speak. I stared up evilly at this gorgeous golden woman with her jewels and her feathers and her sleek black neemus and her slaves. I stared at that whole barbaric picture and I thought that perhaps I did not have long to live.

"You have not been put to the question yet, yetch, for you have been gagged, and so have had no opportunity to lie. I shall ask you questions. You would do well to tell the truth."

I waited. Now I had to think. The Dray Prescot of only a few seasons ago would have rolled in his chains toward this woman and caught her leg and so dragged her down and hoped her head might be chewed off by one of her pet neemus. The Dray Prescot who would have done that had been almighty lucky to have survived. The Dray Prescot who had come so far on Kregen had learned — a little, not much, as you shall hear.

"What is your name, cramph?"

This was the obvious question. To tell them I was a kaidur in their arena would mean I was markedly inferior, nothing better than a pampered slave, and so marked for destruction. To claim a spurious ancestry and say I was Varko of Hakkinostoling would be merely foolish. But, if I was a lord, a Kov — even a prince — I might stand some chance.

I said, "I am Dray Prescot, Pr—" and was immediately interrupted.

"You slaughtered one of my neemus, a prize, a hyr-neemu I had paid for and had sent from a far distance. Your crime is a heinous one."

I knew she was playing with me, as her neemus might play with a woflo; but the test was yet to come.

So far I had concentrated all my attention on her and her immediate surroundings. There were others in the chamber, of course, high dignitaries and nobles, pallans of the realm. I ignored them. Dare I bring in the flame-haired girl? My eyes flickered toward her, and her pale face whitened more.

The queen fairly snarled at me.

"You look at my handmaiden Shirli! Perhaps you two have a criminal liaison? Perhaps you plot together against me?"

I shook my head, and those damned famous bells of Beng-Kishi clanged resonantly inside my skull. "Not so, Majestrix, not so. I have never seen the girl before the neemu would have killed her—"

"And if I believe you, does that give you the right to slaughter my glorious neemu so wantonly?"

"But the beast was about to devour the girl!"

"You yetch! Is that any reason to slay it? Of what value is a shishi compared with a glorious neemu, so black, so velvety, so smooth? You shall be slaughtered yourself, in a way that shall make you regret your criminal act! Oh, yes!"

I rolled over and struggled to stand up. I felt the indignity of my position. As I thus wriggled I saw a young man standing with the nobles and dignitaries, and he stared at me with so horrified a light in his eyes, so petrified a look of terror on his face, that he stood as one hypnotized.

I recognized him.

He was Mahmud nal Yrmcelt, the brilliant young man who had given me the kick that had freed me from the intolerable burden of the slate slab when first I had been pitched into this land of Hyrklana. And, more — his father was a chief pallan to the queen! And, more! He had been plotting treasons against his queen.

No wonder as he saw my eyes on him he trembled and that look of utter horror transfixed his handsome face!

I let my gaze travel across his face, pass him, and so stare at the others in that brilliant audience as I struggled to my feet. The guard Deldar moved in, his thraxter point pressing up against my side. I took a breath.

"I have committed no crime in any man's justice. I did not wish to slay the neemu; but the life of a girl is more precious in the sight of Opaz than even the life of so wonderful a wild beast as a neemu."

A frozen silence ensued.

The queen took more wine, and a slave wiped her forehead with a tissue-thin scrap of sensil. At last she spoke.

"Havil is the only true god."

She said this woodenly. I knew instantly that she did not believe this, that the worship of Havil was mere state policy, that she, herself, looked to other and probably darker deities for her inspiration.

"Yes," I said quickly, before they could get in. "Yes, Havil will relish the life of a girl over that of a neemu."

'Take him away—" the queen started to say, and I knew my blundering tongue had condemned me.

Mahmud nal Yrmcelt moved forward. Suddenly he was lively, light on his feet, smiling and smirking, bowing before the queen. "May I address the divine glory of your person, oh great queen?"

She looked down and she smiled, she smiled at this Mahmud nal Yrmcelt, did the puissant Queen of Hyrklana.

The moment was fraught with a great peril for us both.

"You may speak, Orlan, for you have always some jest, some merry jape to play. Proceed."

This Orlan Mahmud was sweating, and smiling and bowing, and was shaken clear down to his fashionable sandals.

"May it not prove a merry jest if this man faces his death in the arena, oh gracious queen?"

She put her hand to her chin. She pondered. Everyone waited on her words, for this was a weighty decision. Then she smiled on Orlan Mahmud nal Yrmcelt.

"You speak well, Orlan, and thus prove yourself a worthy son of a great father, who is my chief pallan. Truly, this yetch shall face his death in the arena!"

"Your Majestrix is too kind," babbled Orlan Mahmud. He bowed and backed away.

The queen shot him a sudden hard look.

If she wondered why this made her kind to him, she chose not to pursue the matter at the moment. I had read this Orlan Mahmud correctly. He had made his bargain with me.

"Don't tell the queen," he was in effect saying. "You are a doomed man; but this way you may save your life. There is at least a chance for a man who can lift a slate slab…"

"And if he wins the contest, oh puissant lady?"

Queen Fahia chuckled and reached for a handful of palines on the golden dish handed to her by a Fristle fifi.

"I do not think that likely. He slew a neemu, very dear to me. Therefore by the green light of Havil it is only just he meet a test of greater import in the arena."

A long susurrating sigh rose from the audience.

They guessed.

So did I, too; but I wanted to hear this evil woman say it with those ripe cherry-red lips of hers.

"Dray Prescot, you said your name was. Well, Dray Prescot, you will be taken to the Jikhorkdun and stripped naked and given a sword and turned out to face a wild leem."

Twelve

Token for a queen from a dead Krozair

All the familiar sights and sounds and stinks of the arena rose about me again.

This was a special occasion, a gala arranged by the queen for her own special pleasure. The stands and terraces bulged with spectators, for all they had been let in free this day, and wine had been distributed, also, so that the canaille might cheer and yell for the queen. All the nobles' and dignitaries' boxes had been carefully decorated, and now they were filled, for not a soul there would offend Queen Fahia. She controlled not only the army, who were loyal to her out of consideration for the pay they received, and not only the Hyrklanian Air Service, for the same reasons, but also a large and formidable force of hired mercenaries, paid for out of treasury funds, but answerable to her alone. Rebellions did not last long in Hyrklana.

After my hair and beard clipping done by Tilly, my frisky little Fristle fifi, I had been easily recognizable to Orlan Mahmud nal Yrmcelt. I was not, by the same token, as easily recognized by anyone who knew me as Drak the Sword, kaidur of the Jikhorkdun. The irony of my situation was not lost on me. Because there were remnants of red favors on my clothes when I had been chained and flung before the queen, and because she was a somewhat vindictive little person, she saw to it that I was equipped for the Jikhorkdun by any other color than red. It happened she chose the green color — and I guessed that was no chance, for sacred to the greens was the emerald neemu.

A gruff old hyr-kaidur with a potbelly and graying hair and with his green favor stained with grease about his shoulder looked me over, behind the bars of the green coys' entrance. He pulled his thick lower lip. He was apim, a man like me, and a comfortable sort, called Morok, and because he was a green, only a day ago I would have cheerfully killed him.

"Well, my lad," he said, pulling his lip. "You're in a right old leem's nest, and no mistake." And then he roared until the tears squeezed past his eyelids at his own jest.

Mind you — it made me feel like a good belly laugh, too.

This leem's nest was likely to be the last bed I lay upon, either here on Kregen or upon the Earth of my birth, four hundred light-years away.

When he had recovered himself a trifle, he spluttered out: "Can you use a thraxter, lad?"

"Aye."

He took me by the arm, looking swiftly about at the coys who had been shouted off from us, here up at the bars with the shine of the silver sand waiting beyond. "Hush, lad! We've had orders to give you a weapon you might perchance not savvy the use of. You slew the black neemu with a thraxter?"

"Aye."

He furtively looked around again, and wiped the back of his hand across his mouth. He was a green — but I had to pull myself out of this Jikhorkdun nonsense. He was a man, and he didn't much care for what he was being forced to do, sending a man up against a wild leem.

"Forget you said that, lad. I'll see you get a thraxter." Then he hawked and spat at a scuttling liki, and drowned it in the sand, its eight legs feebly writhing in a lake of spittle. "The leem will serve you like that, lad. Thraxter or stux or spear or anything."

"Perhaps."

"You're a cool one, by Kaidun! I'll say that." He looked at me and so did not see the tall gaunt form of the Pallan Mahmud walking from the milling coys toward us. "You'll get a thraxter, my lad, or my name ain't Morok the Mangier."

Pallan Mahmud spoke in that detached icy voice: "Your name may well be Morok the Mangled, kaidur, if you disobey the queen's express orders." He gestured behind him as Morok shrank back, his potbelly quivering, his face stricken. "The queen has given commands that this yetch, since he fancies the sword so much, is to be given a strange sword. One the like of which is unfamiliar to us. She believes the thraxter will give him too much advantage, and what the queen believes is so, kaidur!"

"Indeed, yes, Notor Pallan, indeed yes!"

Two Rapas came forward at the pallan's bidding. I was looking at Morok the Mangier and thinking how strange are the ways of men. Had he known I had fought as kaidur for the reds he would have cursed me, and here he had almost run headlong into punishment on my behalf. So I took no notice of the Rapas.

"We had a slave who swore by outlandish gods and blasphemed Havil the Green," said Mahmud. He, like the queen, no doubt gave only lip service to the state religion. "He wished to fight for the reds, and so, naturally, he was given to the greens. He brought his own outlandish and uncouth weapon with him; but we took it from him as a curiosity, and the queen hung it in her trophy hall." Pallan Mahmud sniggered. "No man can really swing the sword, so monstrous is it. But, Dray Prescot, by the queen's express command you are to go up against the wild leem bearing this steel monstrosity."

So saying Mahmud gestured again to the two Rapas. Between them they carried the monstrous object forward, bowed, and presented it to Mahmud. He stepped back, pettishly waving them away. "Give it to this loudmouthed Morok the Mangled! Yetches, must I tell you everything!"

Mahmud flicked a lace handkerchief — a group of coys out there had just been butchered and the smell was warmish — and the kaidur Morok the Mangier, of the green, stepped forward to take this queen's gift of a sword from the two Rapas. He whistled his astonishment.

"Now, by Kaidun! You are doomed with this useless rubbish, Dray Prescot! It is a show sword, heavy and slow..."

I stared.

I, Dray Prescot, stared at the weapon this kaidur held all uncomprehendingly. What did he know of its magical secrets?

A man had once died out there in the arena, at my feet, and had gasped a last word of greeting to his Krozair brothers of Zamu. And another man had come from the Eye of the World, and he had brought with him that which Morok now held, and these kleeshes had not allowed him to use it in the arena. Had he done so he would have become the greatest of hyr-kaidurs.

I had fancied the evil queen had designed to send me up against a leem with a rapier; that would have been a jest much to her liking.

But she had surpassed herself.

They would not let me take the weapon yet, for fear I ran berserk before I was thrust out with the iron rakes into the arena. I glared hungrily upon that sword. I knew what manner of sword that was. It had come here, to the Jikhorkdun of Huringa, in the land of Hyrklana, in far Havilfar, all the way from the Eye of the World.

Could I believe that the Savanti — even, perhaps, the Star Lords — had intervened on my behalf?

That was the reading I thought then to put on this miracle.

Neither the Grodnims of the north shore nor the Zairians of the south shore of the inner sea go much afaring in the outer oceans as mercenaries. But a Krozair had once done so, for reasons I knew were not important, and had fought his way around the wide curve of the world, and so, at last, found himself taken up by the foul slave-masters seeking fodder for the Jikhorkdun. I saluted his memory.

There was only one other possible sword I could have preferred for the work in hand, and that was the Savanti sword.

But I was content with the beautiful blade that Morok the Mangier so contemptuously condemned, and tucked under his arm with a curse for the retreating backs of the Pallan Mahmud and his Rapa slaves.

I kept trying to look more clearly at the scabbard, for both scabbard and hilt, as well as blade, are marked.

This happening, I felt convinced, marked a new and important phase in my relations with those unseen forces that controlled my life.

Brazen trumpets blasted the hot air above our heads. A huge roar welled up from the packed seats. The time had come. I was naked. I held out my hand to Morok.

He looked sorrowful. "You're a dead man with this, Dray Prescot." He hefted the sword. "By Kaidun! What manner of imbecile made it so long? So hefty! And the length of the handle — the pommel flies about like a gregarian on a string."

Again the trumpets blasted their brazen notes into the heated air. The twin suns — and now if ever was the time to call them Zim and Genodras — flooded their mingled streaming light down in an opaz glory. The silver sand glittered. The roar continued, thousands of throats yelling for the spectacle to begin.

Morok the Mangier held out the sword to me.

"May the glass eye and the brass sword of Beng Thrax go with you, Dray Prescot. Aye, and his emerald lungs blow danger away from your path!"

A group of Rhaclaw kaidur-handlers came up, prodding, and so the time had at last come. I said, "My thanks, Morok. May Opaz guide you."

He concealed his shock. He held the scabbarded sword in both hands. "Havil the Green—" he began unconvincingly.

The Rhaclaws shouted, and the uproar from the crowd outside increased so that the very air shivered. I said to Morok, "I will not need the scabbard."

And so I, Dray Prescot, Krozair of Zy, once more took into my two fists a great Krozair longsword.

With this as weapon I would fight three leems. Or so I felt then, so elated, so buoyant, so cocksure — alas, all youthful follies — but... but... once more to grasp a great Krozair longsword!

Memories ghosted up — to be instantly suppressed — of the clean onward rush of a swifter, of the shock of ramming and the wild elation of boarding, of the glorious red of Sanurkazz smiting down the hated green of Magdag. And, in my fists — gripped in that cunning Krozair grip — a great longsword!

I marched out into the arena and the howl that went up at the sight of me dwarfed anything before. The crowd had been inflamed. The queen had ordered this rogue slaughtered for their pleasure, and a man against a leem was a rare and wonderful sight. And, too, brother, the seats were free!

I had long experience as kaidur in knowing from which different pens the wild beasts would be let out. Not that I had fought a beast for some time, for kaidurs were reserved for more skillful combat one against another. So I walked slowly out, and I must have presented a lonely figure, a lone spectacle, a single man dwarfed to insignificance in that mighty amphitheater and the vast sanded arena below.

The animal roar from the crowd could be erased from my consciousness except as it might signal the leem's release behind my back. I could feel the sand under my feet — dear God! — I can feel it now! The warmth of the suns pressed on my back. I held the longsword in my left hand, under the pommel, loosely, the blade slanted up over my left shoulder. How the crowd enjoyed the sight of that monstrous blade! How incongruous it seemed to them. They were accustomed to the cut-and-thrust thraxter, with its medium-length straight blade. The Krozair longsword dwarfed the thraxter at every point. Truly, this longsword was no weapon for a man unskilled in its use. A kaidur might seek to use it, and no doubt would acquit himself well; but for a great Jikai one must indeed be a Krozair!

The hideous shrieks from the crowd reached incredible proportions — and then fell eerily silent, and so I knew the leem had been released. I turned slowly to face the pen, for the clever managers of the Jikhorkdun had waited until my back was turned to release the leem. Maybe they thought they were doing me a favor, and that it would be all over before I had a chance to turn. If that, then they risked Queen Fahia's regal displeasure.

There had been time, in that short interval, to look at the sword. It was a quality blade. Neatly incised, it bore a name — a name I will not reveal to you — followed by the letters KRZY. So I knew I had the best brand possible in my fists.

The chance I had accepted was that the queen might play a further jest on me and release a volleem, one of the flying monsters we had met on our journey to Migla, or some other of the specialized forms of leem. But the beast that slunk toward me over the silver sand, belly low, tail flicking, his clawed paws going up and down in a regular stalking rhythm, very menacingly, was the normal variety of leem I knew from my days with my clansmen guarding our herds of chunkrah on the great plains of Segesthes.

A leem is a feral beast, eight-legged, furry, feline and vicious, with a wedge-shaped head armed with fangs that can strike through oak. It is weasel-shaped but leopard-sized. Its paws can smash a man's head.

This one was a fine vicious specimen, with ocher-colored fur, and black paws, and a black tuft to his tail, which is unusual. He had been saved against a great occasion, and the crowd knew Queen Fahia would never release him against someone she did not want ripped into the tiniest of bloody scraps.

I do not believe myself to be an overly superstitious man. I know what I know about the dark forces that may — or may not — have their being beyond the walls of our senses. But when, with that damned leem stalking me across the sand, I saw a patch of blood not properly raked and saw the unevenness of the sand there, I paused. The slaves charged with sprinkling and raking and clearing away the corpses and the abandoned equipment had been in just as much a rush to finish as the crowd to begin. And the arena was a large arena. I kicked the rough sand. The first kick revealed the hilt of a thraxter, broken off. I frowned. This would be no place to make a stand when I would need all my agility. I kicked again. A scrap of red cloth showed.

Again — was it the Savanti — was it the Star Lords?

Who can say?

I bent and jerked the red cloth free. Someone of the reds had died here. I stuck the longsword point first into the sand and wrapped the breechclout about me, tucking the end between my legs and pulling it up and tucking that in, and this time I made a thorough job of it, thinking of my past ignominy.

The crowd started yelling again as I did this, and a few rotten gregarians came hurtling down. I took the longsword out of the sand and this time I held it in the Krozair grip. My right hand gripped firmly but most subtly close up to the guard, my left fist beneath the pommel. That way, with about two handspaces between my fists, the tremendous speed of leverage that makes the Krozair longsword so deadly was fully available. As to the power — I knew this leem would feel that.

The leem was hungry.

Well, that made two of us.

He opened his jaws in that wedge-shaped head, showing his fangs. There were shrieks from the terraces. That sight alone was enough to make a coy faint.

He paced slowly toward me, readying himself for the spring, no doubt already imagining himself settling down with me between his front paws to satisfy his appetite.

Leems are able to spring for enormous distances.

I moved away, making the crowd screech. I wished to clear that treacherous unraked area of sand. If the crowd did not wonder why I was not running like a crazed loon around the arena I put that down to the fraught feelings of everyone there. They all knew this was a confrontation.

I heard the odd single comment, spurting through the crowd's noise. The leem advanced. I set myself. The sword went up over my right shoulder. The crowd slowly fell silent. The suns shone, there was no wind down here in the arena. I was sweating a little, and the leem stalked forward. His head was low, his eyes upturned to me, and his jaws opened as his tail flicked from side to side. One after the other with menacing precision he put those eight great claw-armed pads down, the talons extended and gleaming brilliantly.

The leem sprang.

So fast it all was. So fast and deadly.

He soared into the air with his four front paws extended, his rear paws trailing, and his tail rigid. So fast… I went for a knee-bending roll one way and then came back the other and as he went past cut the great sword down. I put tremendous effort into that blow, an effort more of aim and precision than of mere muscular strength, knowing the Krozair longsword would do the work if it was handled correctly.

I am a Krozair of Zy, and in all humility I may say that, indeed, I do know how to handle a Krozair longsword.

The brand sheared through the leem's front foreleg. He went on and rolled in a great swashing of ocher fur, yowling, splattering blood from the stump; but wrenching himself around and standing on his remaining seven legs. Blood pumped thickly from the stump. I regarded him gravely. I decided not to pick up the severed leg and hurl it at him. He was a beast, and for all that we detested leems on the great plains of Segesthes that would have been an indignity to him, for a leem, like any other animal, man or beast, must follow his nature.

Also, the blood might have made my hands slippery.

He rushed again, and he sprang with as much sheer feral verve as before, having four back legs from which to make his spring. I removed the other front foreleg.

This time he came around more slowly. He was not weakened by loss of blood yet; that would take, in a leem, a little time. They are not easy to kill. When he charged me this time, I fancied, he would act differently, and not just because he had lost two legs.

He came in again. This time I leaped for him, got under him as he passed above me, and, ducking, I severed his rear hind leg. He went on, rolling, and this time he came back so fast, springing from his uninjured side, that a claw raked down my side and my blood dropped to mingle with his on that bloodstained silver sand.

But if he was taking the fight to me, I took it to him. He sat back, as a cat does, for an instant. Then he swiped at me with his second foreleg. I did not strike back but ran sideways, turned and feinted to hit him from that side. He pivoted and I went the other way — fast, fast! — and got six inches of steel between his ribs. That was not enough to reach his heart, of course, his main heart, and I had to skip back most circumspectly. I had missed my aim, but I did not curse. This was a game of life and death we played, this leem and I beneath the Suns of Scorpio in the arena of Huringa. He would not waste time spitting at me.

He did hunch his back, though, and I saw the way his stumps bled, and I knew the thing was really over; but before that he could squash my head with a single blow. I leaped again and swung and gashed a great slice across his shoulder. He tried to take me in his mouth and I drove the Krozair longsword at him, and again I missed and merely succeeded in slicing alongside his nose. The blade was sharp. Had it been blunt, as was the blade with which I fought the shorgortz, I believe I would not have been as quick as I was; I do not think the leem would have got me, for the blunted longsword is a great bone-smasher.

The crowd had been silent. Now they began cheering again. I banished the noise; but I did notice the shouts and calls came when I attacked the leem. So, being a show-off in some things, I made a great point of attacking the leem, of charging him, and of smiting and hacking. He lost another leg — and now he did not want to know anything at all more about this man-monster with the brightly shining metal tongue who so tormented him.

He backed off, hissing.

I do not like leems, as I told you, for their ways and damage they have done me. But I could feel it in my heart to feel sorrow for this great beast. He was done for, and I think he knew it. Blood fouled his ocher fur. His eyes did not glare with so much bestial ferocity. He hissed and he slunk away, his ears low, his tail dragging.

I had an idea.

The leem was hobbling — for him — on four legs, but he could still run. I herded him. I wove a net of steel about him and drove him back and back, chivying him from the side, making him go where I wanted. His muzzle was a mask of blood. He slunk back, hissing, and tried to leap aside, and I thrust into that flank and so forced him back. When he was where I wanted him to be, and he attacked again, I leaped and sliced the great sword and so took off his fifth leg. Now he would limp in very truth. He spat now, and hissed, and then he began to shriek. I circled him. He tried still to get at me.

When the moment came I sprang.

I landed with both feet on his shoulders — those beautifully articulated shoulders that swing two pairs of legs — and got my left arm around his head and

under his throat, and so passed the sword downward and through his heart —
both the main heart and then, unnecessarily, the subsidiary heart. I leaped clear,
and I leaped clear backward, deliberately. In death he writhed and slashed and
screamed and foamed and bled — but he died.

Anyone or any beast tends to die if a Krozair longsword passes through the
heart.

I cut off his tail. I held it at my right hand, by that tuft, and I sloped the bloody
longsword over my shoulder.

The place I had herded the leem to was exact. I looked up, and there, sitting regally in her royal box, directly over my head, Queen Fahia looked down, her
golden hair and white face unmistakable in that colorful brilliance surrounding
her.

Absolute silence.

"Here, queen!" I roared. "A token from a Krozair!"

And I hurled the bloody leem tail full in her face.

Thirteen

"Drak the Sword! Kaidur! Kaidur!"

Defiant, theatrical, ridiculous, that gesture.

As soon as I hurled the bloody leem tail I leaped nimbly away and to the side.
Eight stuxes and half a dozen crossbow bolts pierced into the sand where I had
been standing. If this was the way I, Dray Prescot, Krozair of Zy, was to die, then
I would make of it a great Jikai, and die well, by Zair!

I started for the tall wall festooned with silks and carpets and flowers supporting the royal box. I held that marvelous Krozair longsword before me,
double-handed, as I had been trained and as I knew how, and as I went forward
so I flicked and batted away flying stuxes and crossbow quarrels. The whole
crowd remained absolutely silent. That silence hung eerily over the enormous
amphitheater. Every eye, I knew, was fixed in a hypnotic gaze upon that macabre
scene, a half-naked man clad in a brave red breechclout, advancing with a monstrous brand in his fists, forging through a flying hail of death. I picked the way I
would climb up where no man believed a kaidur could climb. I seized on the flying stuxes and bolts and swatted them away with the wrist flickings that are the
joy of a Krozair.

Queen Fahia looked down and saw my face.

She flinched back.

I think she recognized that I would reach her.

She stood up.

Tall and regal, her pile of golden hair ablaze with gems, she lifted her white
arms upward, and spoke harsh words that instantly halted the flickering streams
of bolts and stuxes.

She lowered her arms and placed her hands on her breast, crossed, and she looked into my eyes and I stopped and waited for her to speak.

"You say your name is Dray Prescot. You cry upon unfamiliar spirits. What token is it that smears blood upon a queen's face." And, indeed, her pale face showed daubs of leem blood, spots splattered across her gown and hair. She stared at me with wide and brilliant eyes, willing me, I knew, to submit to her beauty and authority.

I threw my head back, challenging. "What queen is it that sends a man to his death in the paws of a leem?"

"You merited that death."

"You merit a death no different."

Some hot-tempered young mercenary of her guard could not contain himself longer at this and he let loose. I flicked the bolt away and stared evilly at this Queen Fahia.

But she was a queen, long used to absolute authority.

"You are very clever with that monstrous steel brand. What if I order two of my guardsmen to loose together?"

"Order them."

I think she had now reached a conclusion I had already come to — and the crowd, in the way of crowds who sense these things, already guessed. She did not wish to have me killed until she had satisfied her feminine curiosity and slaked her pique. But the challenge I had issued was direct. She nodded curtly to her guard Chuktar. He was a Chulik. I had seen very few Chuliks so far in Havilfar. I guessed he was a most expensive paktun, hired to train and command her private bodyguard.

Two crossbowmen lifted their weapons and, at the Chuktar's barked command, let fly.

At the moment of this word *"Loose!"* I took three neat little side steps. The bolts whistled through thin air.

Every throat in that vast amphitheater roared out — a great volume of raucous noise — for they were laughing!

Only Queen Fahia and those about her did not share the jest.

Fahia spoke again, swiftly, to the Chulik Chuktar. He nodded and sent a file of his men running down the concealed stairs that would enable them to pass onto the sand of the arena through doors solidly bolted only on the inside. I braced myself.

"You will not be harmed, Dray Prescot. I wish to talk with you, before I decide what is to become of you."

I knew that part of it. I considered what was best to do.

The dead leem lay bleeding in the sun. I walked across to it and looked down. The flies were already gathering and I swatted the sword about, aware that this was not a lowly task for that marvelous brand. The leem was wearing a silver collar. During the fight I had not thought about it, for the Krozair steel would shear through silver as though flesh and bone. Now I bent and unlocked the silver collar, lifted it up so that it glittered in the mingled rays of the suns.

224

The queen's guardsmen appeared from the hidden entrances onto the arena, other guards always alert and vigilant there.

And then — I suppose Naghan the Gnat started it, for he was a quick-witted rogue, and cunning, and yet a staunch armorer-kaidur — from the red benches a great storm of cheering rose. The kaidurs there, the apprentices, even the coys, were jumping up and down and yelling and shouting and, almost at once, the whole red corner of the amphitheater began to erupt in a bedlam of victory shouts.

"Drak the Sword! Kaidur! Kaidur! The red for the ruby drang! Drak the Sword!"

So they had at last recognized me. I felt a fitting further gesture might be in order, for I much disliked the queen's new silky approach. I walked slowly over to the red corner and I lifted the silver collar taken from the dead leem and I hurled it high. It spun and glittered in the sun as it fell among the trophies of the reds, proudly displayed in their sacred prianum under the red and gold awning. Absolute silence from blue and yellow and green. Rapture unbounded from red!

Then the two files of mercenary guards closed up and I went with them, out of the arena with its blood-soaked silver sand and down the long secret tunnels and up the secret stairs into the regal presence of Queen Fahia of Hyrklana.

They made me wait, all blood-splashed and sweaty as I was. Wishing to reinforce my advantage and to consolidate what little hope I might have, I had given up the sword. A Rapa had placed his curved dagger at my ear at the time. I could have fought the lot of them, and slain them, and so raced from the secret passageways. But life thereafter in the Jikhorkdun would have been impossible. And I did not forget the great storm that had first thrown me into contact with this catlike Queen Fahia and her black neemu pets.

More and more I was understanding that it was well-nigh impossible to anticipate the wishes of the Star Lords. They had been patient with the escape I had made with Princess Lilah, and they had — even then — been storing up that information against a later day. I wondered about the other people I had rescued on Kregen at different times and places, and wondered how they were destined to fit into the pattern of the future.

All the time I waited I guessed Fahia would be taking the baths of the nine, no doubt in ponsho-milk, relaxing and preparing for an interview she would be absolutely without doubt must go her way. She would be perfuming herself, and donning marvelous clothes of fabulous value, adorning herself with gems and feathers and silks and furs, her face painted and powdered and perfumed, her fingernails lacquered green, her eyes heavy with kohl, her lips rich and moistly red. And her hair — hair of that brilliant gold would be coiled and coiffed to display all its luster and brilliance, and sprinkled with gems so as to bring out with great artifice every last beauty.

When, at last, the Chulik Chuktar with a bodyguard came for me and I was ushered into her presence I felt cheated.

She knew her own power, did Queen Fahia. She sat in that curule chair with its zhantil-pelt coverings, and the barbaric furs and jewels and feathers and silks were all there, each adding its contribution to the gorgeous spectacle filled with light and color. She herself sat there in a classically simple red gown, slit to the thigh on both sides, girdled by a golden belt. Her golden hair, her face, retained still the splotches and stains of the dead leem's blood.

The black neemus yawned and opened their lambent golden eyes, and stretched, tinkling their silver chains. The slave shishis huddled in their transparent silks. There were no councilors or pallans present, but Orlan Mahmud was there, and a few other young men I did not recognize. Women also were there, and at least two Fristle women of exceptional beauty and power in their looks, not slaves but free halflings at the queen's court.

The Chulik positioned his crossbowmen in a single line to the right and left of the curule chair, facing me. I noticed the way the courtiers moved out of the area that could be turned into a sieve of death.

"You told me a lie, Drak the Sword." Those were her first words.

I did not reply.

Her color was still pale, still wan; she had had a nasty fright. I knew the way the crowd's fickle behavior would be read by the queen, how she must seek to placate them as she detested them, despite her power.

"You are a kaidur, and now, after the exploit today, a hyr-kaidur. Your name is Drak the Sword. What, then, this nonsense about a fanciful uncouth name like Dray Prescot?"

"A man may have a name before he gains a name in the Jikhorkdun."

Her eyes regarded me. "Aye, that is true. And my Jikordun divides the leems from the ponshos."

She said *Jikhorkdun* as *Jikordun*, as many people did, slurring the word for ease of pronunciation. Few kaidurs spoke it that way.

"Had I known you were a kaidur, Drak the Sword, perhaps I would not have been so swift in my just vengeance."

There was a very great deal to be read into that statement.

I decided to play the most obvious reading, the one most likely to reflect the state of the game. I said, "I believe I did not express my very real sorrow at the destruction of the neemu." I was deliberately refraining from calling her queen or majestrix or any other of the many terms for referring to royalty I spare you. "I feel I am able to make restitution."

"Ah!" she said, and she sat forward, and again her chin settled onto her upturned fist. Her eyes regarded me now with a look reminiscent of the look that leem had first given me. "Yes, Drak, I think you may!"

Again pushing what I fancied the Star Lords, in their usual obscurantist way, were urging me to, I said, "You have but to command."

"I know that!" Her chin went up, off her fist, and her eyes blazed at me. "My commands are obeyed. But before that, Drak, I would talk of your great victory, for the leem was a mighty and powerful beast, and notable for its kills."

So we spoke for a space, of this and that, and presently she motioned for me to come and sit on a stool brought forward by a flunky — a little Och in embroidered livery — and placed at her feet. I sat down and told her a pack of lies, about swinging the sword as one would an ax, and of how I rather fancied I would use it again, Havil willing, in the Jikhorkdun. She nodded and sucked in her breath, her bosom rising and falling, her eyes bright and leechlike upon me as she heard talk of other combats, some she had seen and some not. Her passionate interest in the arena was not faked. Statecraft, love, food, money — all were of secondary interest to her beside this consuming passion for the Jikhorkdun.

Knowing this, thinking I knew what the Star Lords were about, I forced down my desires to smash them all up and get out of here and aboard a voller and make for Valka — for I knew another great supernatural gale would brutally beat me back.

This game here must be played out first.

As a queen and a despot she had her pick of the kaidurs. Her chambermaids would bring them to her chambers at night, and she would use them as she saw fit, and so send them back to fight for her in the arena. I already knew that apart from the four color corners, there existed a small and select band of kaidurs devoted to the queen — Queen's Kaidurs — and on special occasions these would fight wagered combats of phenomenal value. Usually they won, and would dispose of the opponent fighting them, no matter what color he happened to be. Much later, long and long, I discovered just why the Queen's Kaidurs almost invariably won.

She did not make me an offer to become a Queen's Kaidur. She had said, though, "You are a hyr-kaidur now, Drak. And as a great kaidur you may wander the streets of Huringa. Would you seek to escape? I remember the flier..."

Here was where I took two korfs with one shaft, as Seg would say.

"No idea of escape enters my head. There was a girl — I have completely forgotten the shishi, now, since — since—" And, artfully and contemptuously, I hesitated, and looked at her, and looked away. "No, I would on no account seek to escape from Huringa which is ruled by Queen Fahia."

The performance sickened me. But if the Star Lords wished me to remain here, and I was to do so with my head still affixed between my shoulders, the pace must be forced a little. All that natural charisma I have told you of was working for me now, keeping me alive, as I know; I had to give nature some assistance, some better chance.

"I believe you, Drak the Sword."

This first interview — first in our altered circumstances — drew to its close. But she was a sharp lady, and a queen, and so as I was retiring, she said, her voice roughened and back to its habitual coarseness from the more mellow tones in which we had conversed: "And, Drak the Sword! You swore to make restitution for the slain neemu!"

"Aye. Point out the way—"

"Sufficient that you remember. Now go. I shall send for you again."

Amid much scraping and inclining — she insisted on the full incline in matters of state — we went out. I guessed I was expected to report back to the red barracks where no doubt Nath the Arm and Naghan the Gnat would greet me kindly enough, even if Cleitar Adria might glower with jealousy.

I found myself walking along the corridors with the marble wall-facings and Pandahem jars of flowers and Lohvian mirrors from Chalniorn in company with Orlan Mahmud nal Yrmcelt and his friend, a commanding-looking apim with a somewhat pudgy face and plump body, sumptuously dressed, who I gathered was Rorton Gyss, Trylon of Kritdrin. Orlan Mahmud had been overeager to push up to my side, nudging other people out of the way, for a hyr-kaidur is assured of constant attention from admirers and well-wishers. I knew what was troubling him.

"Simmer down, Orlan," said the Trylon of Kritdrin. "The hyr-kaidur is a man, by Havil! He knows the value of a closed mouth."

Orlan Mahmud shot me a glance. "My father," he said, all his liveliness gone. "I still fear him."

"That, my boy, is why I never married. I like women, Havil knows, but I prefer to cast my bread upon private waters." And Rorton Gyss chuckled. A genial, pleasant, thoroughly civilized Horter, this Rorton Gyss, and, as I was to find, with a mind of his own and a will of alloy-steel.

They took me down from that high fortress of Hakal, frowning over the city of Huringa, and by more open ways this time we crossed to the Jikhorkdun. Here we stopped by a tavern into which, by virtue of my new status, I was now allowed. Many taverns and inns had been built into and alongside the Jikhorkdun and its surrounding warrens but inevitably never enough for all the public. Only nobles and high Horters might venture into the amphitheater tavern. One seldom ever heard anyone addressed as plain Horter; it was all Kyr and Kov and Tyr and Rango and Strom. We sat at a plain sturm-wood table and an apim girl served us light yellow wine from Central Hyrklana — reasonable stuff, light and refreshing and ideal for the heat of the day. If a deal was to be proposed, Mahmud and Gyss were going about it in a civilized manner.

The deal was simple.

I kept my mouth shut about Orlan Mahmud's involvement with those people plotting the queen's downfall, or I had my throat slit by certain paktuns whose names needn't be mentioned among Horters.

"You would take my word?"

"Of course. You may be a kaidur, but we can tell you are also a Horter."

I sipped my wine and inwardly I laughed at them. Fools! I was no gentleman — I never had been, save by a king's commission to walk the quarterdeck of a King's Ship, and I never would be. But, for all that, if I gave them my word I would keep it. Also, and I did not discount this aspect, they knew that it would take more than one paktun of very great skill indeed to deal with me, and further, that the queen would be most wroth and would relentlessly pursue an inquiry.

"Perhaps," I said. "You do not ask yourself what I was doing there, at the time the great slate slab fell."

This had occurred to them. It was not a weapon they might use against me except after I had denounced them, as they knew.

"You, too, are against" — Orlan's gaze flicked around the tavern and back — "the queen?"

He whispered that, a conspirator to the life.

"It might very well be," I said. And added, "Or, it might not. For I think the queen will smile on me now."

"Aye!" Gyss drank his wine at a single gulp and called for more. "And we know where the queen's smile leads! A garrote, and a stone lashed to the legs, and a hole in the River of Leaping Fish."

Then someone recognized me and a crowd gathered and I had to rise and smile at them — most painful — and so make my escape in a shower of backclaps and handshakes and adulatory speeches. We walked quickly along the alleyways threading the warrens of the Jikhorkdun, and my state attracted so much attention that in the end I had to bid Orlan Mahmud and this Rorton Gyss farewell and run for the red barracks.

"We will see you tomorrow, Drak the Sword!" called Rorton Gyss. This Trylon of Kritdrin had impressed me. He seemed a man who knew his own mind, and went for the truth, no matter what or who stood in his way.

He was a supporter of the yellow; that was unfortunate, but as I have said, color supporters might mingle freely with only the occasional fight, for Mahmud was of the red. And, if Gyss was of the yellow it would mean he could bring a whole new dimension of support to the cause he espoused with Mahmud.

Nath the Arm greeted me with a great bellow.

"By Kaidun! Drak the Sword — you are a hyr-kaidur now! It was superbly done, Kaidur to the life! Just remember: easy come, easy go. There are many coys pushing up, and the glass eye and brass sword of Beng Thrax may smile on them also!"

Naghan the Gnat jumped up and down in his excitement, and all the red barracks waxed warm over the triumph. The silver collar of the leem was a great trophy. I thought of the leem's tail — and I did not smile.

I had not missed the shifty liquid eyes of the little fellow who had followed me, keeping as he thought out of sight, his plain brown tunic and kilt worn without color favor. A spy, he was, spying on me... following me through the Jikhorkdun to the red barracks of Nath the Arm. He could not follow me inside, and on that I cursed him and forgot him...

Fourteen

The life of a hyr-kaidur in the Jikhorkdun

My life in Huringa proceeded much as any other kaidur's at this time, for I was waiting for the signal to which I might respond. If the queen was to be overthrown, poor soul, for all her evil, then the plan must be good and absolutely watertight. She controlled everything personally, with pallans to convey her orders and, sometimes, to venture on advice. I palled up with Mahmud and Gyss, and was sent into the arena from time to time, usually to rapturous applause, and otherwise lounged around fretting over this damned interdict of the Star Lords, and drinking and having what fun was offered. Here I brushed up on my knowledge of Havilfar, as you shall hear when overt knowledge is essential. A parcel of Chulik slaves were brought in.

We all went down to the bagnios to see them.

Now Chuliks are not often kept as slaves. Their chief value lies in their fanatical obedience to orders and their absolute loyalty while they are being paid. They are superb fighters. I had met a Chulik render captain; that had been unusual.

Chuliks are an extremely fierce manlike race of people with oily yellow skin, the head shaved so as to leave a long pigtail, two three-inch-long tusks thrusting upwards from the corners of the cruel mouth, and round black eyes. On the Chulik islands stringing off the coast of southeastern Segesthes the training of the males from birth is designed to produce high-quality mercenary soldiers, and they generally command higher fees than other races. There are large colonies of Chuliks in other islands and continents, of course, as I had found in the Eye of the World and in the Hostile Territories, and these people, like the other races about them, know nothing of the outside world. Chuliks may share some of the normal attributes of mankind, like two legs and two arms and two eyes; but they have little of the attribute of humanity.

So it was that the idea of Chulik coys intrigued us all.

"Well, Drak, and how do you fancy their chances?"

"By Kaidun, Balass," I said. "They are a mean bunch."

Balass laughed. Balass liked laughing. He was a black-skinned man from Xuntal, with fierce predatory hawklike features, and brilliant eyes, and he was a fine fighter, a kaidur. I had found in him a chord of friendship that I was loath to touch, for fear he would be dragged across the silver sand smearing his lifeblood, hauled out by the cruel iron hooks. He was named Balass the Hawk. Balass, as you know, is an ebony wood, often used for purposes of correction and chastisement.

"A cage voller flew in today with many volleems," said Balass the Hawk. His bright eyes showed all the mischief and merriment the news meant.

"Oho!" I said. "Then it behooves us to see this, kaidur. Indeed, yes, Balass the Hawk, this must not be missed."

"Beng Thrax's silver kneecaps must support us all." Balass chuckled. We both knew what these Chulik coys would face, pitted against volleem.

Volleem, the flying form of the leem, is a nasty brute at the best of times, and we wondered what the Jikhorkdun managers would think up to make the spectacle more interesting.

You see — I have reported this conversation as I remember it — how bound up I was becoming with this whole evil business of the arena. And yet, it was not wholly evil. In straight combats between men of equal skills and armed in the same fashion, many virtues for a warlike nation must accrue, especially when that nation is faced with ferocious depredations by vermin like the Leem-Lovers from the southern oceans.

Each of the four colors received their quota of Chulik coys and the managers designed a different test in each case.

The greens were caged, a Chulik and a volleem together, and left to fight it out with spears.

The blues were herded in altogether, with a variety of weapons, into a vast cage erected in the center of the arena and all their quota of volleems released upon them at once.

The yellows, being in the ascendant, were kept in reserve.

The reds were given an assignment that brought howls from the red benches where the kaidurs lolled on their ponsho fleeces and shrieks from the red terraces soaring up in the amphitheater.

Each red coy had a strong steel chain attached to his left ankle, and the chain passed to a ring riveted around the front rear leg of a volleem. The thraxters the Chuliks were issued would not cut the steel chain, light as it was.

The resultant spectacle raised a pandemonium of noise and screams and yells. Silver sand puffed. Bright blood flew. The battering of the volleems' wings, the shrieks as men and beasts were torn and slashed, all blended into a bedlam of horror and revulsion — and yet men and women of many races sat in the terraces and enjoyed it as a spectacle!

And all the time the citizens of Huringa thus disported themselves their slaves labored to manufacture the produce and grow the food that kept the city and the state great.

I felt the Star Lords had set a purpose to my hands, and I itched to prosecute it with more zeal than the careful machinations of Rorton Gyss and Orlan Mahmud and their friends would allow.

The volleems massacred the Chulik coys. All their weapons-skill could not overcome the tremendous odds. Only one Chulik survived, badly lacerated and injured. He was a red coy, and when he was carried in, dripping blood, we all rose to him, Chulik though he was.

His name was Kumte Harg.

The volleems would be cared for, rested, fed, and then when they were back to full strength again, would be starved ready for the next bloody spectacle.

The only subject of conversation from then on was just who would be sent out to face them, and with what.

I fancied that Drak the Sword would find his fool self mixed up in that confrontation somehow.

For a successful kaidur whose ambitions lifted no higher than the plaudits of the crowd, the rewards of victories, the acclamation of his comrades and peers, this life I was now leading could scarcely be matched. I had continually to fight against its seductive sway. The real tests came in two forms: in the first that I would forget who and what I was and revel in the better aspects of the Jikhorkdun, overlooking or excusing the wilder and more bloody aspects; in the second that I would be sent out against an opponent better than I.

Ascent up the scale of success was relatively rapid. An unknown coy one day would be the apprentice of the next few sennights, and then with each successive accolade would climb the ladder until he made kaidur. Some men managed this very rapidly, others at a more sedate pace. For them all, the descent would be swift.

So it was that I rigidly kept myself apart from the other kaidurs, even Balass, to my sorrow, for he was a fine man, and trod the lonely path of the true hyr-kaidur.

During this period I was well aware that I was, as it were, serving an apprenticeship of a different sort and to two different masters — rather, to a clique of masters and to a mistress.

The would-be rebels contacted me from time to time, and always it was big talk of what they would do, and how, and never when. The queen sent for me, particularly after a great Kaidur, and we would talk. Always, these audiences I had with her were in the chamber, with her sitting regally on the curule chair. Her neemus and her shishis flanked her, fifis fluttered to and fro with wine and palines, and the giant Brokelsh waved the gorgeous feathered fan.

The cunning managers of the Jikhorkdun ensured my fights were carried out with weapons familiar to them. Each time I saw the queen my question was always the same.

"And when are you going to put that great sword back into my hands?"

She would give a little frown, and, out of custom, I would add: "Queen?"

She would laugh lightly, an evil little tinkle.

"When the time comes again for a great Kaidur, Drak."

So I would not press the matter.

She said, once, I remember: "It says in the *Hyr-Derengil-Notash* that all things are as they seem to all men." This famous book, the *Hyr-Derengil-Notash* (the title means, very roughly, the high palace of pleasure and wisdom), is often resorted to by philosophers. It had been compiled by a Wizard of Loh some two thousand five hundred seasons or so ago, and copies existed in various forms, each with its bibliography and separate notations, and you may be very sure the Kregan academics argued long and earnestly over their wine as to the analysis and interpretations to be placed on each separate word and phrase. She looked at me with those bright blue eyes of hers, so like her sister's, speculative upon my ugly face. "It says, Drak the Sword, that where there is evil there must be good. And where there is good there must be evil."

I nodded. "The interpretation is still debated, Queen."

"My interpretation satisfies me. Evil must of necessity exist. The *Hyr-Lif* says so explicitly."

One of her neemus yawned. His fangs were very bright and sharp. He closed his eyes, yawning.

"Yet does not the book say also something of the relative amounts of good and evil? Does it not say that an ounce of evil is enough for a ton of good?"

"It does, Drak my smooth-tongued kaidur. And, also, as you know well, the *Hyr-Lif* says that an ounce of good is enough for a ton of evil."

"The *Hyr-Derengil-Notash* means all things to all men. It is read as the heart commands."

She nodded, for the statement was so prosaic, so universal, no answer was needed. Kregans often refer to the heart as the seat of emotion and knowledge, although the doctors, so skilled with their acupuncture needles, are well aware that it is the brain that controls the body. She waved for wine and a neat little fifi with sleek black fur glided across, her silver vestments and diaphanous robes billowing, her ankle bells chiming softly. I still had not formed a final opinion on ankle bells.

The wine was good; light, for it was daylight, yet pungent and redolent of the sunny north.

I drank with pleasure. I should say that I still did not know the crude red wine the kaidurs quaffed before combat, Beng Thrax's spit, was drugged with the sermine flower.

Truly, as I sat there with the Queen of Hyrklana sipping fine wine, munching palines and miscils, waited on by scantily clad jewel-entwined slave girls of surpassing beauty, I was a part of the Jikhorkdun that many and many a coy would give his ears for. The life, for all its horrors and bestiality, could claim a man utterly.

Of course, many women were available to the kaidurs, for if a great lady could flaunt a hyr-kaidur as her latest conquest she would score a notable coup over her fashionable rivals. Huge sums were paid by some of these ladies of Huringa for the favors of a kaidur. I gave none. Pressures were brought to bear, and I hurled them back, concealing my contempt, pleading other excuses. The queen, I know, was apprised of this and approved. For she, Queen Fahia, assumed I was deeply enamored of her. I appreciated the dangers of this course, and was somewhat apprehensive in a distant way for what might follow. But I felt it imperative that my freedom of maneuver should not be impaired.

As an example I attended a secret meeting of the Horters and a few nobles in a house at the end of an unlighted back alley. It was all talk and speeches and wild declamations and, a thing that made me perk up a little, a counting of weapons and men available. They were small enough, to be sure. We left unmolested, and sang as we wended our way through the streets, Rapa and Fristle slaves lighting our way with flaring torches. The armed guards of the queen, prowling the streets on the lookout for any mischief they might knock on the head, let us go, for we were merely a gang of drunks. But for me, as a hyr-kaidur, these excursions were fraught with a peril quite foreign to the Horters.

At subsequent meetings I tried to insist on a more practical approach and in this Rorton Gyss backed me up.

"We need to think more forcefully," Gyss said. He spoke in his own downright way, direct and yet charming. "We must so organize the people who share our views that the government is attacked simultaneously on all sides. We must do this thing, for this evil queen is leaching the life-blood of the country away. I came over the road from Shander's End today, and the surface is not fit for troops to march, and the money for its upkeep was spent in Chem buying boloths for the arena. Is this the way to run a country?"

I tell you, you who listen to these tapes spinning through the recorder, I, Drak the Sword, kaidur, took more interest in that part of his speech wherein he mentioned that boloths had been purchased for the Jikhorkdun. I confess it. I sat up. The boloth can be best described by imagining four elephants affixed in such a way that there are eight tusks facing forward, eight legs a side down the body, and a tendrilous mass of whipping tails at the other end. Its hide is hard and gray like a rhinoceros along the back, a brilliant leaf-green along the sides, and yellow beneath. It is slow. But it can still gather enough speed from its sixteen legs to build pace sufficient for a few hundred yards to outrun a totrix. After that it must pause for some time to allow its three hearts to pump fresh oxygenated blood around that ponderous body.

As an afterthought — it has an underslung jaw that can gobble a strigicaw, all spitting and snarling, at a gulp.

When I got back, Nath the Arm was frantic. "The queen has sent for you, Drak, by Kaidun! You must go to her at once! By Havil the Green," he said, lapsing into unfamiliar theistic regions for him. "Hurry, lad, hurry! Or all our heads will roll!"

"I will wash and dress myself in fresh clothes," I said. "Nath, if any heads are removed they will all be mine."

As I prepared — for this summons from the queen came at an inconvenient time — I pondered what Orlan Mahmud had reported at the meeting. He claimed to have set ablaze two of the state manufactories for vollers. He said his men had burned not only fifty fliers, but the sheds and yards also. When I was ready I took up my thraxter and, with a last flick of her tail from Tilly, with Oby opening the door for me, I went up to see what Queen Fahia wanted of me.

Fifteen

Of Rorton Gyss, Balass the Hawk, and wine

This time Queen Fahia received me in a low-ceiled intimate chamber high in the Chemzite Tower of her fortress of Hakal.

She reclined on a low couch strewn with zhantil pelts and furs, silks and sensils, propped on one white elbow. She knew she looked incredibly seductive, for the tall and unflickering candlelight gleamed in mellow warmth from her skin and hair and that soft haze concealed the lines of arrogant power stamped on her face. She wore semi-transparent billowing trousers, and a translucent jacket artfully half open, and their silk blazed a brilliant scarlet into the scented bower.

I was ushered in, my thraxter taken from me, and fifis already giggling to themselves showed me to a low stool beside the couch. Nearby stood a hurmwood table loaded with golden goblets and glass bottles, the dust removed only from the labels, with many glass and porcelain dishes loaded with fruits and a golden dish upon which miscils lay ready to crumble into instant deliciousness upon the tongue.

"Drak the Sword! I have been waiting for you and fortunate you are that I had affairs of state to occupy me."

If this pantomime was to begin at all, I would start by laying down the ground rules myself. She was clearly bent upon complete conquest. I had evaded her, as I knew, before; this time the test had to be faced.

"Pour me wine, Drak." She gestured vaguely at the table, and so, determined to please myself, I chose a bottle whose shape and color I recognized. The date on the label referred to the Vallian calendar, and it was, I saw, a damn long time ago this wine had been prepared. I poured carefully, and handed her the glass. She looked over the rim at me.

"Vela's Tears, Drak?"

"Aye, Queen. It is a wine of Valka. You have heard of Valka?"

"Friends of the cramphs of Hamal." An old sore had been itched here. She was the queen, concerned for her country, for this moment her role as a seductive voluptuary momentarily forgotten. "The Emperor of Hamal supplies Vallia with vollers and the rasts of Vallia do not venture so far south as here to Hyrklana. Our vollers are as fine as those of Hamal. But the empire blocks our commerce."

As you may imagine, I drank this up with as much pleasure as I sipped that superb wine, Vela's Tears from my own Valka.

The strong red wine suited my fancy. Usually I frowned on this drinking of unmixed wine, for that is a fool's trade; but I fancied I needed the assistance the alcohol would give me in dealing with this wanton woman, for if she became a trifle fuddled I could then slip away and leave her to sleep it off. So I drank sparingly, and replenished her glass.

"Two of my manufactories were burned, Drak. Many fine vollers are ashes; but they may be rebuilt. But the yards and sheds are gone, and the tools — when I lay my hands on the yetches responsible I will deal with them!" She was panting, and the color flooded her cheeks. Candlelight flamed in her hair and glittered from her jewels. She held out a hand to me.

"I need a strong man, Drak. A man to make me forget my cares and worries." She was smiling now, her moist red mouth open and inviting. "A hyr-kaidur, Drak! One who knows what a sword is for."

Into that appealing hand I placed a fresh glass. This time the wine I had poured for her was a brilliant green concoction from eastern Loh, crushed from the fruit of the pimpim tree, thick and cloying on the tongue, overly sweet — and strong!

She continued to look at me as she drank. I merely touched the tip of my tongue to the pungent liquid.

"You speak of swords. When am I to receive that great sword—?"

She drank, and swallowed, and interrupted me. "You saw Hork the Dorvengur?"

"I did. He was brave, but a fool."

Hork the Dorvengur had been a hyr-kaidur of the green. He felt a personal slight that I had performed a great Kaidur with this strange sword and with a leem and had sought to do likewise. The leem had ripped him to shreds.

"If I give you the sword, it may be to face a foe far worse than a leem."

"There are many more dangerous foes than leems, although few as vicious, and, even, if your treasury can afford it, you might buy larger and stronger cats. There are risslacas. There are the boloths you have just bought, and the volleems which destroyed the Chulik coys. And there are many many more hideous horrors in this world of Kregen you might buy and send against me in the arena. But, I think—"

Again she interrupted. "You think that with that monstrous sword you would stand a chance?"

"Better than with a djangir, at all events."

She laughed. "I love to see the bosks running with their heads down, their long horns outstretched; it is a great Kaidur against the shortsword."

With some amusement I noticed that of all subjects we had got on to, the one consuming her passions was the one most calculated to make her forget why she had invited me up here. We talked Jikhorkdun for some time, and she drank steadily as I pressed her. Her knowledge of the arena was prodigious. She had the great feats of the past off by rote, dates and times and states of play, and all the records of the color champions for many seasons past. She knew so many names of hyr-kaidurs that she made me feel very small beer indeed — which was a most useful ploy, as I discovered.

By careful and callous manipulation of Jikhorkdun talk and of wine I jollied her along as the night wore on. She was in reality a cruel and evil woman; but she was also aging and losing her beauty, and a trifle drunk and maudlin, and, I judged, more lonely than any person should be condemned to be. After a time she slobbered after me; but I laughed — I did! — and gave her more wine, and started on about how she had never allowed neemus into the arena, and so diverted her attention to areas in which she felt far more passion.

"Never, Drak-ak the Sword! Neemus are a part of me! They are so sleek and slender and all the female secret things a man will never understand." A tear cut its way through the powder on her cheeks. Her flush was now wine-red, startling against the cosmetics.

I might never understand women's wiles and secrets, but this case was too plain. She was the twin sister of Princess Lilah. Lilah although cold and aloof had been slender and beautiful and young. This Queen Fahia, the same age, was growing fat, her face was lined, her bones and sinews, as I guessed, feeling creaking and old. Yes, evil as she was, one could find a pity in one's heart that was not put there through mere duty and form to any of the better creeds of Earth or of Kregen.

She hiccupped again, and knocked a goblet over, and laughed shrilly, and Oxkalin the Blind Spirit guided me as I said: "I fight tomorrow, Fahia. You are exceedingly lovely, but the husband your king… I must leave you." I deliberately did not phrase that in the usual way in requesting permission to leave. I stood up. I had guessed that for at least the opening sessions of the night's business she had had eyes spying on us. A golden bell stood on a lenken stand. If she struck that, once, probably, armed men would pour in. I wondered if she struck it twice the eyes would withdraw.

"You fight tomorrow, Drak the Sword? Then I will cancel the combat — cancel combat — fight tomorrow…"

With her mouth open and her eyes slowly closing, she sank back on the couch, breathing in rapid shallow breaths that slowed and drew out to a deeper rhythm. I lifted her naked feet up into a comfortable position on the couch. I looked about at the table with the wreckage of the night's drinking. I popped a handful of palines into my mouth and saw the second bottle of Vela's Tears, untouched. About to pick it up, I paused.

Those eyes...

I picked up the bottle. I held it in my left hand, even in that moment relishing the feel of something that had been born in my Valka, and I picked up in my right hand the small mahogany-handled gold-headed hammer and I struck the golden bell.

The chamber filled with armed men.

Their Hikdar stared about, at the sleeping queen, at the golden hammer in my hand, the golden bell still quivering. He commanded a detail of armed and armored men and halflings, and he stared at me like a loon.

I held up the bottle of wine.

"Have you a clean glass, Hikdar?" I said. "The queen and I have used up all that were here."

Queen Fahia gave a little snore just then, and mumbled her lips about, and dribbled a trifle.

The Hikdar's chest swelled. His eyes threatened to pop like overripe squishes. He could barely turn his neck in the iron collar of his corselet for its swelling.

"Deldar Ropan! A glass for the kaidur! And jump!"

Dear Zair! How I plagued those guardsmen!

That was the first time we had a cozy tête-à-tête, Queen Fahia and I.

She would give me no sensible answer about the Krozair longsword. Other kaidurs made the gallant attempt to use it in the arena and most were slain, although a fighter from the blues, surprisingly, bested his opponent, a strigicaw, and so scored a notable triumph for the sapphire graint. The queen insisted that the longsword be returned immediately after every bout. It hung among a splendid display of arms in her trophy chamber, magnificently decorated and appointed, in a great hall of the high fortress of Hakal.

Balass the Hawk was only too pleased to give me the benefit of his assistance and contacts when I made a certain request of him. Shortly thereafter, in exchange for a boskskin bag containing quite enough golden deldys, I received a small dark purple glass vial of a curious shape, heavily stoppered.

"One drop, Drak," said Balass, chuckling. "Guaranteed to knock over a dermiflon."

That blue-skinned, ten-legged, idiot-headed monster grew so fat and ungainly that it could barely waddle and only its sinuous and massively barbed and spiked tail saved it from extinction at the claws and fangs of strigicaw or chavonth. To say anything would knock over a dermiflon was guarantee enough.

So, armed with my secret purple vial with its drop-by-drop dermiflon guarantee, I could face those ultimate little drinking nights with Queen Fahia with greater equanimity. She did say, and more than once, that my company was very soothing to her in her great worries and problems, for she always slept well after I had visited her.

Poor soul!

But she could wield as much power as an absolute despot ever can over his or her subjects, and my head was still a-rattling between my shoulders.

I often wondered what the results for the island of Hyrklana would have been had the fifteen-minute interval that separated Fahia's and Lilah's entrances onto the stage of Kregen witnessed a reversal, so that Lilah had been the elder.

You will forgive me, I know, in my cynicism, if I suggested to myself that Queen Lilah would have been little different from what Queen Fahia in reality was. If the Star Lords truly had commanded me to a work here, I must also be aware that the realities of the situation, in political terms, could never obscure the greater human realities.

Only those people who have had to sign another person's death warrant can truly know the realities, the miseries, the agonies, of power.[6]

* * *

"...once and for all that evil queen! Drak — it must be you who slays her! You are the chosen one!"

"But, Orlan — to kill a woman, like that — I care nothing that she is a queen—"

"It is a deed done for all Hyrklana!"

"But I am not of Hyrklana."

At this Rorton Gyss lowered his wine glass and stared at me. Always charming and courteous, the Trylon of Kritdrin now spoke in a smooth sensible way that admitted of no argument.

"You may not be of Hyrklana originally, Drak the Sword. But you are a hyr-kaidur, of the Jikhorkdun in Huringa, and that does make you indisputably of Hyrklana. Whether you will it or not, my friend, it is so."

"Maybe. But there are armed guards she can summon instantly."

"We know. But, Drak" — Orlan looked with a sickly smile at me, at which I pondered how much he really cared for the queen — "you are a kaidur. When you caress her, and bend over her, your arms about her, kissing her. Then you may place your hands upon her neck, so, and twist, so, and she will go quietly, and you may lay her, so, upon the couch."

And Orlan Mahmud placed upon the table the two halves of the ripe fruit he had twisted apart.

We all looked at the two halves of that rich fruit as its juices seeped onto the sturm-wood. It was a shonage fruit, I remember, larger than a grapefruit, as red as a tomato, crammed with rich flesh and sweet juices. No one spoke.

The little secret meeting room hidden in the rear of a hovel in a dingy portion of Huringa had never seemed more remote, clandestine, and filled with dark menace. I could do to Queen Fahia what Orlan Mahmud had done to the shonage; and I could do it silently and shielding the deed with my body from the alert gaze of the watchers outside the queen's chamber. I could.

I doubted if I would.

I said to Orlan Mahmud nal Yrmcelt: "You know the queen's chamber in the Chemzite Tower. You have perhaps been there yourself?"

His young face flushed and that sickly smile returned to his features. "I have. Once."

Before I could push any further the Trylon of Kritdrin interposed, smiling, charming, forceful. He had seen how it stood with me, I think, for he was a shrewd man. "Let us leave this portion of the plan for now, comrades. We will return to it when we are sure the quarters will rise."

On that the treasonable business of the meeting could be concluded and we could get down to aspects more agreeable to me, the drinking and singing. If I give the impression that I drank a lot or was some kind of drunkard, this is not so. Water of most of Kregen is drinkable except where fouled by men, and the varieties of fruit juices are immense and wonderful. Also, I always prefer Kregan tea. The cover, that we were a drinking club, had to be maintained. So, singing, rolling along, our arms across one another's shoulders, we staggered happily back into the street and so wended our merry way toward the south boulevard which led to the Jikhorkdun. Before we reached it, in an alley where a torch threw lurid gleams across the stones of the walls, and with Orlan hanging on to me and roaring out about 'Tyr Korgan and the Mermaid,' Rorton Gyss leaned across and whispered fiercely in my ear.

"We are followed, Drak! A thin little rast in brown."

Trust Gyss to have his eyes and ears open in this wicked world.

I looked back. It was the same man. I had forgotten him; now I remembered. He wore a djangir, and he looked mean, and he hovered at a corner where the stones had been grooved by the centuries of wear from the iron-rimmed wheels of passing quoffa carts. Hyrklana is rich in iron.

He hung back there, waiting for us to pass beyond the torch before following. Orlan stopped singing, just where Tyr Korgan takes his third great breath of air and dives to inspect the Mermaid in wonder. He was not so far gone as to call on Opaz as he halted, all wine-flushed.

"What is it, in Havil's name?"

"Hush, Orlan!"

Some genuinely staggering, some shamming, the conspirators turned to look back. The spy realized he had been discovered. He took to his heels at once. With a wild whooping the whole bunch pelted after him.

Only Gyss and I remained standing beneath the torch.

"Onkers!" said Gyss.

I knew what he meant. "I doubt he is a queen's man, for she would have already struck." I told him of seeing this man on the day I had become a hyr-kaidur. He frowned. "It is inconvenient. We must tread cautiously, leave for the country for a time. The day of wrath is postponed." He added, without rhetoric or bombast, false to his nature as they would have been: "But it will come, Drak the Sword. The day of judgment will come."

So we left the conspirators, like would-be leems, to go chasing after the spy as leems chase a running ponsho. We calmly walked back and I said to this quiet, contained man, "I think so too, Rorton Gyss. Remberee, Trylon of Kritdrin."

"Remberee, Drak the Sword. Remberee."

That night Queen Fahia summoned me to her perfumed bower in the Chemzite Tower of the high fortress of Hakal frowning down from its rocks over the Jikhorkdun. Armed with the purple vial of curious shape, dressed finely, I went. As usual the guards took my thraxter. Strangely, secure in the protection of the purple vial, I welcomed these philosophical discussions touching the arena.

The queen would talk of the high excitement and the peril and the blood of the Jikhorkdun with a panting eagerness, her full moist lips shining, the lower lip locked by her teeth as she listened to tales of a great Kaidur. This absorption with the scintillating evil surface of the Jikhorkdun did not prevent her deep obsession with its inner philosophies, and we explored areas both of analysis and synthesis, of ideas and theories, that showed she understood far more than her voluptuous figure and jeweled body might give one to think, assuming she had no brain at all. She put great store by the *Hyr-Derengil-Notash,* that *Hyr-Lif.* Only the greatest books of Kregen are dignified by the description "Lif," and only the greatest of these may expect to be honored by the "Hyr." Her amorous advances would be reserved for a later time, when she had molded me, as she would think, into the kind of kaidur suitable to her high-flown fancies.

Once she was in a black temper. "I have had word out of the chief place of Hamal, that vile city of Ruathytu. They seek with their left hand to throttle realms to their south and with their right hand they prevent men from Zenicce and Vallia reaching us to buy our vollers. By Havil the Green — one day…"

Then she laughed, a little shrilly, wildly even. "The yetches of Hamal are like Djangs with four arms, for they clutch to the west over their mountains, and to the north across the sea."

I admit to a strange thump of the heart when she said that name — Djang.

So, on this night, with her prowling black neemus taken on their silver leashes by their attendants and with many kisses and cooings from her, Fahia received me. Interestingly, instead of the usual red she wore in honor of the ruby drang, she wore a shimmering white gown, and from the costliness of the silks and sensils I guessed it had been the work of many slave-girls' needles. Cunningly slit at thigh and belly, it clung to her, and slid and susurrated when she moved. Diamonds cascaded about her. Her hair of that brilliant corn-gold had been let down, and, without a single gem, swirled about her figure. In the rosy candlelight she did, indeed, I admit, look most alluring and desirable.

Her moist red lips parted in a smile.

This was the woman the conspirators wished me to murder. However much she deserved the fate, could I take that white neck, with its hint of pudgy fatness, into my fists and so twist and stare down upon her without compassion as she died?

Hardly.

Her Fristle fifis fussed about her, and a couple of new apim girls, glorious in their fresh beauty, brought in her toilet necessaries. One carried the golden bowl and a towel, the other a pitcher of scented water and a fluffy, soft, pampering towel. The queen retired behind a small screen of interwoven papishin leaves. The two apims, slaves, wearing clean white loincloths, would not look at me. They trembled with fear as they ministered to the queen.

Almost, then, I did as I had been requested.

The single drop from the purple vial of curious shape did its work, and I was able to drink moderately and watch as Queen Fahia slipped into a sound sleep. I made her comfortable and then went out. The Hikdar of the guard knew me by now. We exchanged a few words; but he remained resentful of that first prank I had played on him. I went back to the Jikhorkdun.

The next day I heard the report that a man had been found dead in a back alley of the city. His brown clothes had been cut to ribbons, and his body slashed in a score of places. So my fine drunken conspirator friends had caught their ponsho.

All the same, most of them found reasons to leave the city and go to their estates in the country of Hyrklana. For a space, then, the queen was to keep her life and my life at the Jikhorkdun would continue. Were the Star Lords, I wondered, really at work here? To test that I went out the very next night, stole a voller, and was battered and beaten back by a gale whose savagery sprang from supernormal forces.

I raged.

By Zair! I was trapped in this round of Kaidur, and I had begun to detest it urgently.

It has come to me as I tell you my story that you must conceive of me as a dour, brooding, humorless sort of apim, whose face hurts if he smiles, who does himself a serious mischief if he dares to laugh. I admit to a starkness of character, a feeling of doom that will not leave this side of the grave; but I do laugh, wildly and with great mirth, when a situation appeals to me in its incongruity, and I can smile most tenderly when my Delia is with me, and my twins, Drak and Lela, chuckle and laugh and grip my fingers with their tiny chubby hands. By Zair! But I talk now as I thought in those dark and scarlet days of the Jikhorkdun in Hyrklana. Babies grow up, as you shall hear, and their problems sometimes made my own seem mere pimples upon a boloth, trifles I scarce need mention beside the enormities of terror they were to face.

So I fought in the arena, and won — for defeat would end in death and the Kaidur would be over for me then — and I took a second purple vial from Balass the Hawk in exchange for a boskskin bag of golden deldys, and Naghan the Gnat was set to attend personally to my armor, at which I was much pleased, and Tilly plagued me with her long, supple golden tail, and Oby practiced swishing a thraxter about, and the long days passed. The twin Suns of Scorpio went on their eternal swinging paths about Kregen and the seven moons cast down their fuzzy pink light, and the air grew sweet with the scent of flowers, and the wealth in my marble chambers grew and swelled until in mere material terms I was a paladin of kaidurs. The queen, I knew, was kept happy by other kaidurs, and she had fallen into the habit of talking with me, seeing me when the circle of her life prevented other pursuits, and in these conversations I think we both realized our lives were restricted and circumscribed. Princess Lilah did not return to the kingdom. I never saw the king, Rogan. The hyr-kaidur Chorbaj the Stux was slain by Cleitar Adria. And on that night the queen summoned me. It was unusual for the pattern of living that had been established, and I was surprised. I dressed carefully and went to see her in the exotic chamber in the high fortress of Hakal.

"Chorbaj has got himself killed," she said, flinging herself down on her couch. She wore a brilliant green sarong-like garment, almost a shush-chiff, which was encrusted with gems, and yet her white body glowed through cunning interstices in the sensil. I remained alert, my hand gripping that purple vial of curious shape.

241

"It was a great fight, Queen," I said.

"Aye! A hyr-kaidur to the life. You reds crowed today, when the iron hooks dragged the bleeding corpse of Chorbaj the Stux from the arena."

"The greens were not pleased, I'll allow that."

"I had thought to send for Cleitar Adria, but he took a cut in his victory."

"I am here."

"Yes, Drak the Sword. You are here. And tonight we do not simply talk and you do not lull me to sleep with your fine stories, like Sosie and the Kov of Veruki-adrin!"

Sosie and the Kov of Verukiadrin is an incredibly similar story cycle to our Earthly *Thousand and One Nights,* and Sosie and Scheherazade are twin sisters separated by four hundred light-years.

"You were expecting Chorbaj the Stux," I said. "He was a great kaidur. The Jikhorkdun is the poorer for his loss."

"You, a red, can say that? A kaidur's life is short and violent, and he must take what pleasure and profit he can."

I did not reply.

She gestured for wine.

I went to the table, and as was my custom I poured her a mild wine to begin with, so that when I slipped into her glass the single drop that would knock over a dermiflon I could drown any trace by a wine stronger and more pungent. She rang her little silver bell for her attendants, and her fifis scuttled in, giggling, flicking their tails about, and a couple of apim girls came in, one with the great golden bowl covered with an embroidered damask, the other with the pitcher and the fluffy towel. Queen Fahia stood up and walked to the screen.

"Hurry, you useless yetches!" she snapped at the girls, and one of them gasped in terror, and ran with the pitcher of warmed and scented water. The other stood stock still, and Queen Fahia reached for her whip, with the silken bows and tassels and the exceedingly ugly and painful lashes.

"Must I slash you, cramph!"

I looked at this new girl, turning in curiosity, and so saw her, and dropped the wine glass and the purple vial and stared and stared…

Delia, my Delia, in a slave breechclout, stood there, her eyes enormous and fixed on me with a look of utter disbelief.

Sixteen

Delia shows me around the high fortress of Hakal

Nothing could have halted my instinctive reaction then. No thought of security or of peril, no other thought in all of Kregen obsessed me. I am a man obsessed with only one idea in the whole of my life. I am obsessed with my Mountains.

I simply rushed toward her and knocked the golden bowl spinning from her hands and so took her into my arms. I clasped her to me, and she clasped me, and we stood there, unable to speak, hardly breathing, locked together.

Delia! How she had come here I could only guess. I held her dear form in my arms and I felt the quick beat of her heart against me and the warmth and softness of her figure pressed against me, and all of Kregen might have gone hang.

Over and over again I have cursed myself for a blind selfish fool. An onker! A get onker, as the Star Lords dubbed me. Oh, how incredibly idiotic I can be, at times, I, Dray Prescot with all the fancy names and titles and honors! Oh, the most fitting title I can ever earn is idiot onker, fool of fools!

Rough hands seized me and dragged us apart even as the soft malicious chiming of Queen Fahia's golden bell rang in my ears. Armed men dragged us apart. I allowed myself to be pulled from my Delia for a heartbeat only.

Fahia was shrieking: "So this is the wench! This is the shishi! Rest assured, Drak the Sword, you will never see her again!"

I finished up my delayed business with the guard Deldar by kicking him where I once kicked Prince Cydones Esztercari. The fool had drawn his thraxter so that I was able to take it away and instantly parry a blow from a man who came in most brutally and so thrust him through the eye. They wore corselets after the fashion of Hyrklana; but they had left their shields in the guardroom for this kind of guard duty, for which they were sorry in due time.

In a frenzied flurry of action I chopped down two Rapas and two apims and went for the men grasping Delia. She struggled. She was no waxen effigy of a girl who would shrink and scream in a situation like this. I knew my Delia of old. Had we not, together, disposed of black-clad assassins on our wedding night?

Fahia was screaming on: "Seize him, you onkers! Chain him up with iron chains! Seize the rast! You fools, you cowards!" She was right to call them fools, for any man who lays a hand in animosity on Delia of Delphond is a fool, for he is a dead man. She was wrong to dub them cowards. They fought bravely. They tried to get at me and I simply leaped on them like a leem and slew them and their blood splattered horrendously into that perfumed, decadent chamber. The fifis had run screaming, their tails curled up past their shoulders in fear. The other apim girl stood, still carefully balancing her pitcher, and her mouth opened in one long scream of terror.

Delia broke free, I sliced her other guard, and she scooped his dagger. It was a Hyrklanan blade, ornate and heavily curved. It went in curving, as it was meant to do. Delia looked up at me and the glory of her face and figure, the brightness of her brown eyes and that gorgeous hair with its outrageous tints of auburn, spurred me as nothing else in two worlds can.

"Oh, *Dray...*"

"Out of here, Delia, my heart. This is fit country for leem, little else."

Fahia was raving.

"You will be cut down! You are condemned! I shall see to it you die a death so exquisite—"

I turned.

I was less than gallant.

"Cease your babble, fat woman! Know you not this is the Princess Majestrix of Vallia! That her father is the puissant Emperor of all Vallia? Beware lest an avenging army lays your land in waste and utterly razes your city of Huringa."

"You lie! You lie, by Lem, you lie! You are a kaidur and she is a slave shishi! You will die, by Lem, you will die!"

I left her there screaming and screeching and I felt sick at heart at her words. *By Lem!*

So the evil cult of Lem the Silver Leem had in truth penetrated into the highest ranks of Hyrklana, and I shuddered to think what doom must fall upon this land.

Outside in the corridor we ran through the ways I knew, and Delia ran fleetly at my side, for I had no need to drag her along with me, as I had dragged Princess Lilah, and Tulema the dancing girl from a dopa den, and those two silly girls, Saenda and Quaesa.

Guards tried to stop us, of course, mercenaries of various races. With the protection of Delia as my reason for living they had no chance. No blood lust obsessed me; as I have told you, fighting and killing are abhorrent to me except where they are inevitable, and Zair himself does not point a different path.

Fleetly we ran down the long curving marble staircase. Its walls were covered in carved representations of many of the marvelous legends and stories of Kregen, and we ran hurtling past hero and demon, god and devil, monstrous beast and beautiful woman, swirling pictures of love and combat, of sack and creation. A file of apim guards ran out below and I did not check but leaped the last fifteen stairs and so smashed among them and in the quick and bitter flashing of swords cut them down. A shriek rang out at the head of the staircase.

Delia and I looked up.

Queen Fahia had dragged herself to the marble balustrade and leaned there, panting, glaring down at us with mad eyes.

"You cannot escape from Huringa! Every hand will be against you!"

A Rhaclaw's immense head appeared beside her and he lifted a stux and hurled. I did not swat the stux away. I seized it out of the air, and reversed it, and so hurled it back.

"Any man who dares touch Delia, Princess Majestrix of Vallia, dies! Remember that!"

Fahia ducked and the stux took the Rhaclaw in his bloated head so that it burst and showered the queen with blood and brains. We left her to her shrieks and threats and ran on.

A terrified apim slave girl crouched away from us as we rounded the next corner. Ahead lay a long passage studded with many doors, and then we might go on to the outer ways and so the street, or down and through the secret passages to the Jikhorkdun.

The apim girl was slave to a pallan's wife, a noble lady who stared down her nose at us, at a savage-faced maniac with a bloody sword in his hand, and a stunningly beautiful girl clad only in the white slave breechclout of the queen's household. Ordinary slaves wore the slave gray.

"What tomfoolery is this?" the noble lady began. I had seen her fawning on the queen. "You will be severely punished."

She wore a fine deep-crimson robe, with a smart furred cape over that, with many jewels, and her sandals gleamed with gems. I took the robe in my left fist and twisted the noble lady about and so held her as Delia, with me at once, flicked her long slender fingers down the latchings. The robe fell free. The noble lady was screaming and struggling.

"Guards! Guards! Slay me these slaves, *instantly!*"

Her command would have been obeyed, instantly. Only two guards arrived on the scene, for the others hereabouts were dead, and these two joined muster with them shortly.

Delia donned the crimson robe. The noble lady wore a white sensil chemise.

"No time for the chemise, my heart—"

"The dress stinks!" said Delia. In truth, the noble lady's taste in perfume was overly strong for our nostrils.

Dressed decently in the crimson robe with the furred cape flung across her shoulders and with those jeweled slippers on her feet, my Delia could proudly face the city of Huringa.

We ran on.

No coldly calculating thoughts of victory or defeat entered my mind. I knew we had to get out of here. If we did not, it would be the arena for us. I had no need to be told what the stakes and the bosks would do. Queen Fahia would delight in putting us both to the supreme test. We sped past the hard and cold marble, and every now and then a mercenary guard sought to dispute our passage.

Delia gasped out words as we ran and I did not stop her, for she trusted in me and I was fascinated by what she had to say.

"Only four days ago, beloved, the battle. The Battle of the Crimson Missals! When you disappeared in the thunderstorm I heard you say you would not go to Hyrklana. And so — and so—"

"I will tell you, Delia, my heart." At this point I stopped talking and crossed thraxters with a Rhaclaw who bore a shield. He wanted to fight in the proper, ordinary, decent way of two men fighting each other. There was no time for that. I ran at him leaping in the air so that he lifted himself for my attack, and then I let myself drop to that polished marble floor and, feet first sliding on my bottom, I skidded toward him. My feet shot between his legs, I passed under the bottom rim of the shield. Flat on my back I whistled under the shield and so thrust upward with the thraxter most hurtfully, gutting him. After that we had a shield to lift on my own left arm.

"I did not wish to come to Hyrklana. But — but I did…"

"And I followed. Seg and Inch, we took our airboats and we came to Hyrklana. But, as usual, the airboat broke down and I was taken by Rhaclaws. This mad Queen Fahia saw me and bought me—"

"Aye. She has first choice of all the most beautiful young girls, by Vox!"

"And so I was instructed to become the chambermaid to the queen."

"That chambermaiding did not last long, thank Zair."

"I fancy the queen is mighty angry — look out, my heart!"

I had seen the crossbowman.

He leered at me over the bolt of his weapon and I saw his shoulder bunch to pull the trigger — poor practice, that, I remember thinking as I hurled the thraxter. He died with the steel through his mouth and spearing up into his brain. I put a foot on his head and hauled the thraxter free. Still with the shield shoved up on my left arm I stuck the thraxter, all bloody and smeared with brains as it was, into my mouth, puckering my lips in the old way to avoid cutting them, and snatched up the crossbow. I whirled. A Hikdar was running toward us waving his sword as though he acted in a play. The bolt took him through an eye. I threw the crossbow down and with Delia at my side sprinted on for the far doors. They were lenken and bound with gold. The uproar behind us boiled up. I could not go on swiftly enough and so out into the street. So it must be the dark and secret ways that led to the Jikhorkdun for us.

Staring down past the half-folded doors that led first of all into a narrow passageway and then a steep and slippery flight of stairs I heard a grunting gasp and a meaty chop and a mangled scream of agony behind me. I whirled. A Rapa staggered back with his beak hanging and dripping blood. Delia didn't bother to slice him again but pointed past my shoulder, so I turned back. Armed guards with weapons bright in the lamplight boiled up that stair and crowded out past the half-folded door. The Jikhorkdun was not for us. The massive gold-bound lenken door would not be opened without a fight, and even so wonderful a girl as Delia could not open it single-handed as I held off the guards. I cocked an evil eye upward.

A small arched stone entrance was barred by a sturm-wood door. I ran at it, and kicked it in so that the lock ripped away and the wood gleamed freshly splintered. Delia bundled in before me and I hung my shield over my back, and felt the glancing shock of bolts ricocheting from the bronze-bound wooden surface.

"Up, Delia, my heart!"

"Follow close, close…"

The door was a ruin and so valueless. The first one through was a Rapa and he went shrieking back into his comrades, beakless. The next was a Brokelsh, and he somersaulted back with half his face sheared away. The third was a Gon, and his cleanly shaved scalp abruptly gaped all bloody through the wreck of his helmet. The fourth did not appear. Instead a stux flashed through, and then another. These I caught and returned, and heard two shrieks.

Delia called from above.

"Doors, Dray — all bolted save one—" And then I heard a beginning scream from Delia of the Blue Mountains abruptly chopped off.

I went up those stairs like a devil.

A horrid screeching spitting, a diabolical hissing echoed down the stone staircase. Frantic, I roared up the stone treads and came out onto a landing with the bolted doors and one door open. In the doorway crouched the black form of a neemu, its wicked eyes smoldering gold, its sleek black fur electric in the-gloom, its mouth gaping, and the white fangs bared. On one knee the slender form of

Delia waited, the dagger held before her — and I saw the fresh blood on that dagger, the blood-matted fur on the neemu's throat, the claw marks ripped down the crimson robe, and the torn tufts of the furred cape. Delia had screamed — and had cut the scream off deliberately so as not to alarm me further as she faced a savage neemu with only a curved ornate dagger!

I hurdled Delia and, shield-first, crashed headlong into the great black cat and so, with four precise thrusts, finished it.

"Are you badly hurt, Delia — Delia...?"

"No — I surprised it — but it was — it was—"

"Through here."

I helped her rise. She gave me her smile, and then we were running into the long chamber beyond the open door with the ominous clashing of mailed men following us. Along the tessellated floor of the chamber we ran and then through a gallery lined with obscene idols of jade and alabaster and ivory, and so to a door, tall and narrow, hung about with emerald wreaths, hundreds of brilliant emeralds cunningly worked by a master artist into representations of triumphal wreaths. The door was of balass and it moved smoothly and silently as I pushed it open. We passed through into a great space of shadow and mystery. I closed the door behind us and lowered the counterpoised beam of lenk into its steel slots. A full-scale battering ram would be needed to smash down that high door.

We surveyed this place wherein we had fled, and saw that it was a shrine raised within the fortress of Hakal to the highest state spirit, the national god, of Hyrklana, for all that other cults and beliefs were undermining the strength of the old religion.

Samphron-oil lamps glowed a mellow gleam upon the shrine within that vast chamber, picking out the fantastic wealth of decoration, the abandon of riches, the exotic outpouring of art and skill. Central within the shrine and lofting higher than fifty feet rose the idol. The image was of a morphology serene and bland, with a bewildering wagonwheel of eight arms, each hand rigidly fixed in a ritualistic pose of power. The face might have been apim, with Chulik tusks, Womox horns, Rapa beak, Fristle whiskers. It combined many racial characteristics, and yet was of itself.

"Havil the Green!" whispered Delia.

"Had we the time, my love, I'd welcome the chance to prize a few of those emeralds free and tuck them into a lesten-hide bag." I laughed. "Korf Aighos should be here now!"

"Aye, Dray, if only he were!" She controlled herself, lifting her spirits. "And Seg and Inch and Turko the Shield!"

She went to move on and I placed my left hand, all bloody as it was, upon her shoulder.

"Do not move, my heart!"

She saw the four neemus, then, their heads low, their tails moving slowly from side to side, as they slunk out like four demoniac black shadows, creeping forward on their bellies.

Queen Fahia had released her pets to cleanse her palace of a man and a woman who had despised her before her people and thrown a stux at her, and defamed her.

I cocked an eye up at the statue.

With a sinewy thrust I lifted Delia so that she stood upon the idol's left foot. The leg had been encased in a greave of chased gold and emeralds, and at my urgent gesture Delia began to climb up the projections, as she would a ladder, so that soon she was some ten feet above my head. Then I slid the shield down before me and took a fresh grip upon the thraxter and faced the neemus.

They spat at me. Their lips writhed back and their fangs gleamed in the mellow samphron glow.

Delia did not speak.

A sullen booming began from the high balass door and the lenken bar in its steel sockets moved and groaned.

At that moment, with my Delia in so grave a peril, I think I can be forgiven if I say that had the four neemus been four leems they would have stood little chance. The first one sprang and I smashed the shield into its face and passed the thraxter through it, the sleek black fur clotting with blood, the claws grasping and scratching at the shield rim. On the instant I ducked and withdrew and slashed the sword in a flat arc that slit the second's throat as he sprang after his fellow. The third sprang, also, and landed on the shield; but I kept low so that his hind legs could not rake forward. The thraxter bit again. That left one. He circled, his tail lashing, his head turning from side to side, and he hissed and spat. And I charged him, and so took him, the shield smashing into his head and forequarters, and the thraxter sliding bloodily into his heart.

I stepped back.

Delia did not immediately climb down. I looked up at her and she lifted her right hand, and she said, "Hai Jikai!"

I laughed at her. "Rather, Delia, my girl, you should say as these folks here do — hyr-Kaidur!"

"Oh, they would, them and their debased arena."

She climbed down and I hugged her and then we prowled on toward the far end of that vast and shadowy chamber where the emerald idol of Havil the Green brooded through the centuries. The booming gong-notes from the balass door receded as we passed through the far opening. In this corridor I was completely at a loss. No one appeared. No guard, no courtier, no slave.

"The sacred precincts," Delia said, with her practical knowledge of palaces and fortresses and temples. "There must be a way out, if we can find it."

"We should be feeling like two trapped woflos," I said. "But I feel sorry for anyone who crosses our path. Lead on, my princess. After all, you are a princess — now let us see you put that elevated position to some practical use."

"You great shaggy graint! You, Dray Prescot..."

But I laughed and we went on, my thraxter and her dagger dripping bright blood, shining in a trail of red drops upon the priceless marble of the pavement.

We came at last to another vast chamber within the fortress of Hakal, which frowns down over Huringa, and now I stared about and whistled in admiration. We stood in Queen Fahia's trophy room. Almost all the collection gathered here referred to the Jikhorkdun, in weapons and armor and curious artifacts used in the arena. Delia was happy to throw down her curved dagger and take up an example of that long slender-bladed dagger in the use of which she is a master — or mistress, more accurately. I stopped. The hope had grown in my breast, but I would give it no credence, no room to burgeon — and now…

"Well, Dray, my shaggy Krozair, take it down and let us get on."

So I took down the great Krozair longsword.

This was the same weapon with which I had bested that silver-collared leem in the arena. My fingers felt the incised letters, feeling the power flowing from them, the miraculous magic of those simple letters KRZY pouring through me.

I threw down the thraxter, but I kept the shield and pushed it back on loosened straps so that it sat high on my left shoulder. I strapped on the scabbard, but I held the brand naked in my fist.

We pushed on.

Delia said, "I think there will be no exits in this direction, Dray. The balass door protected all this wing of the fortress. There will be secret ways only, and we do not have the time to find them."

"Very well," I said, like any tomfool hero from a shadow-play acted out to the glow of samphron-oil lamps in the pink-lit moonlight of Kregen. "We will go back and make our way through these cramphs—"

"There is always a window."

"And the stones will be worn, for the fortress is old, and our fingers and toes have enough skin on them to see us down. Perhaps you are a princess, after all."

"You are a prince, my hairy graint, or had you forgotten?"

"I've not had the same practice at it that you've had."

"Well, you will go jaunting off on various mysterious errands. Little Drak and Lela are likely to grow up orphans if you carry on like this."

All the time we spoke thus to each other we ran swiftly through the deserted corridors. We both heard the distant booming thud, like a gong that is beaten so savagely it breaks from its chains and crashes to the floor. We both knew that the guards of Queen Fahia would be upon us with feral swiftness.

Delia found the right corridor and chamber beyond. Her instinctive familiarity with palaces grown with her from childhood did stand her in good stead now — aye! and me.

We ran swiftly along the corridor toward this room and now we could hear the clank of iron-studded sandals following us, beating a menacing tattoo upon the marble floor.

We burst into the room.

A narrow window in the far wall showed a pinkish wash of moonlight. The Twins would be up, forever circling each other, and I took heart from that, as a sign from Zair.

I stuck my head through the window.

The pink moonlight picked up the scene and showed me the trap into which we had blundered.

"What is it, Dray? Let me see!"

Delia wriggled herself by me to look out.

The angle of wall beside us dropped sheer in an unbroken line for six hundred feet, sheer to the fanged rocks upon which the high fortress of Hakal had been built. Just beyond the rocks terraces dropped away, one below another, to the northern face of the Jikhorkdun, its massive pile dwarfed as to height by the Hakal, its oval shape easily discernible.

"May Opaz smile on us now!" breathed Delia.

All along that precipitous drop the moonlight picked out crevices and chinks, but I doubted if they would serve us all the way. Then in that moonlight I saw the wide band of marble about the wall, a band smooth and slippery and carefully repaired, so that angle of marble fitted against angle. We would need a stout stake to drive in as a piton and a rope to negotiate that, and in this bare storage chamber with broken chairs heaped against one wall, a few brooms and buckets of bronze and wood against another, and dust everywhere, ropes and pitons were not available.

I looked along the wall.

A shadow moved there, and a shape humped around and a wing flickered up to be tucked more comfortably back, and I knew that Zair had answered my plea.

"Into the next room, Delia, and swiftly, before the cramphs spot us."

We ran from that dusty storage chamber along the corridor and into the next room. It was empty of life, although fitted as a sleeping chamber for a guardsman or courier. Judging by the perch-pole outside the narrow window, it was more probably the latter. With her neemus prowling, Queen Fahia had withdrawn all her people from this part of the fortress, ordering them to steal away down the secret passageways. Now that her pet neemus were slain — and would I ever forget the picture of my Delia facing with so great a courage the coming spring of the savage black beast? — and her guardsmen had broken through the balass door, we could expect mercenary guards to come streaming in from every direction.

I looked out the window. Here in the heart of Huringa, capital city of Hyrklana, where saddle-birds were common, there was little need even for the minimal anti-flier precautions they took in Miglish Yaman. As for the flier-protection of cities of the Hostile Territories, here in Huringa such things were unknown and — given that an attack must cross the sea to reach the island at all, and then wing for dwaburs inland — unnecessary. A concession in the perch-poles was made so that they might in time of trouble be drawn inward. Feet clattered in the corridor outside and Delia swiftly closed the door.

I hauled in on the leather rope running from a brass ring in the wall. The flying beast out there stirred and flicked that wing again and gripped its claws into the perch and twitched around — and I cursed savagely.

The bird was a fluttclepper. It was a small high-speed racing bird, without the wide vane of the fluttrell, and it was capable of carrying only one rider. One rider. Used in races, or as speedy mounts for couriers, the fluttclepper is a most desirable flying steed; for Delia and me, then, it was practically useless.

Surely, I thought, surely Zair would not disown me now? As for the Star Lords and the Savanti, I had written them off in situations like this a long time ago. To save myself, to save Delia, I must depend on my own strength and my own wits.

The jagged-edge rocks into which the foundations of the fortress were sunk grinned up at me, their edges glittering in the pink moonlight. Beyond them the terraces trended downward, most containing walled gardens of flowers or herbs or greenery, some set out as practice courts for the ball games of Kregen, others with butts for crossbow practice. Beyond them the wide patio surrounding the Jikhorkdun spread invitingly. But to reach it we must fly.

Must fly.

I hauled the strap in.

Delia said, "I do not think that small bird will carry both of us, my heart."

Blows broke upon the door, and the iron bolt groaned. An ax-head appeared through the wood, which was a smooth-grained yellow vone from southern Havilfar's pine forests. It would not resist like sturm or lenk; it would go down into long yellow splinters and ruin in mere murs.

The fluttclepper was in a bad temper, for he had been awoken from a sleep and his master, as he thought, was most inconsiderate to drag him on his leading strap like this. He dug in his claws and resisted. I cursed the fool thing, and hauled. I saw long splinters split from the perch. Then I realized the fluttclepper was no fool; he was smart. He had recognized I was not his master, his usual rider.

The door groaned and chips flew.

I threw the shield to Delia and she caught it deftly and swung with it facing the disintegrating door. The stones on the windowsill had been set only a foot above the level of the floor for ease of egress and ingress. I moved through the window, gripping the stone edge, and put a foot on the perch-pole.

The wind, unnoticed inside the building, now whistled about me. There were four long paces to reach the fluttclepper. I took a breath. My short half-cape billowed and I unfastened and let it slip from my fingers. It flew up and out like a monstrous bat, caught in the air currents, eddying about, twining in on itself, and finally falling long and long to the rocks below.

When I took a look back through the window into the room, still holding on to the stone architrave, I saw the door buckling away from the frame. A hand reached in for the bolt. Without even being fully conscious of what I had been about, for all I wanted to do was get that damned fluttclepper under my hands and set Delia upon him, I saw the way Delia was half crouched behind the shield, facing the door, and the long straight slender glitter of the dagger in her hand.

"Hurry, my princess!" She turned to look up at me.

"You go on, Dray. The bird will carry you to safety—"

I never shout at my Delia — or not often. I said to her in a voice I thought was perfectly reasonable: "Get up here, woman, and do as you are told."

She stood up. Her eyes locked on mine, brown eyes staring into brown eyes. I could have drowned then. I took her wrist and hauled. She balanced easily on the sill. The door across the room burst open as the hand at last slid the bolt. I took the shield from Delia and skated it across. Its bronze-bound rim gashed into the throat of the leading Fristle, and he screamed and frothed blood and toppled back into his comrades.

The leather strap hummed tautly as I hauled. I took those four steps on that narrow perch across emptiness and got my fingers into the fluttclepper's neck and I squeezed. I put a foot back on the perch, and braced myself. Beneath me gaped an abyss floored with jagged rock fangs. The wind blew. I shouted. "Delia! *Now!*" She made of those steps across that dizzyingly narrow pole a superb dance of joy, a light skipping waltz that swept her effortlessly across and into my outstretched arm. My right fist twisted in the fluttclepper's white feathers. He tried to squawk and I kicked him, feeling my whole body sway.

"He will never carry us, Dray — but if we are to die, then I am glad we die together."

"Clack, clack, clack," I said. "Slide down and grasp his leg above the claws. And, my dearest heart — *hold on!*"

She slid down and gripped and, suddenly, looked up at me and I saw the anguish written on her beautiful face.

"Dray — oh, Dray, you will not send me away — alone!"

For answer I slid down by her side. My left arm encircled her slender waist, my right hand gripped fiercely into the legs of the fluttclepper. I yanked. The bird's claws scrabbled. He swayed. I jerked him again and the swing of our bodies overbalanced him so that he toppled screeching from the perch.

Angry faces appeared in the window and over the rush and batter of the wind I heard a high yell: "Crossbows!"

Much good that would do them in this wind and the hurtling pell-mell fall of the bird. He could not carry us both. That was true. But he had the instinctive reaction to, and fear of, falling and so he spread his white wings and beat frenziedly. We fell. But our fall was checked. The fluttclepper was acting as an animal parachute.

We plunged down and out and the edges of those fanged rocks whipped past us. We hissed down through the air. Now the terraces whirled away above. We were across the patio. We were nearing the ground, and the rustling shriek of the bird's wings tore the air about our heads.

We hit with a shock, but only enough to make us tumble head over heels across the edge of the patio and into a trellis of moon-blooms whose outer petals were greedily sucking up the moonlight from the Twins.

We scrambled up.

"You are all right, Dray?"

I looked at her. "As you are. We are out of that Opaz-forsaken place. Now we need a voller."

People on the patio and coming and going on the adjoining streets were rapidly left behind as we ran into the moon-drenched shadows. After a time we could walk as a normal couple, except for the chance I might be recognized. The great Krozair longsword I had unstrapped from my belt and carried bundled under my arm, a fold of cloth covering the hilt, where the fashionable cut of the sleeves permitted. For the rest of that magnificent scabbard, Zair must smile on its new owner.

The voller park we chose was not the same as that flier-drome from which, twice before, I had attempted to escape from Huringa. Again I went into a voller before the attendants were aware and sent the craft surging upward. Delia sat at my side as the wind slipped past our ears. Straight into the path of the Twins I sent the voller, and chance directed we would pass straight over the Jikhorkdun. That was cheeky, but safe, for I fancied Fahia would send her guards and her aerial cavalry searching the air lanes to the north. She might not believe my words on Delia and on Vallia, but she would act on them.

We had reached past the amphitheater and I was lifting the craft to attain a good height and maximum speed when what I could not believe, would not believe, occurred in all its horror.

Black clouds roiled in from nowhere. Lightning flashed from that abruptly jet-black sky. The wind velocity simply halted us in mid-flight and tumbled us back, like a dusty leaf, hurling us down with contemptuous colossal ease into the ground.

I remember yelling insanely, raving, almost incoherent with the scarlet, futile, frustrated rage burning within me.

"No! You who call yourselves the Star Lords! This is not possible! You cannot do this to me! Onkers — rasts, cramphs, yetches! Star Lords! Everoinye!"

The flier swung and swayed and in the supernatural gloom I gripped hard on to my Delia. If a hint of that hideous blue radiance swooped on me now...!

"Give me leave to depart, you Star Lords!" I bellowed. I was insane, then. I had won against fearful odds, and my Delia won with me, at my side, racing to freedom — and the stupid, vile, vicious, unspeakable kleeshes of Star Lords were driving me back, back to Huringa and the evil talons of Queen Fahia and the Jikhorkdun!

We crashed among the warrens clustering by the amphitheater.

My last conscious impressions were of the ground swooping up; of the warm and vibrant form of Delia clasped in my arms, and of her strong slender arms clasped about me; and of a crazed, upside-down vision of coys and apprentices and kaidurs running in the moonlight that, with a supernatural suddenness, burst through those roiling diabolical black clouds. Lightning struck down, a ferocious earth-shaking noise burst up all about me — everything coming together like a volcano in my head.

Even as I knew I was being knocked senseless, I would not let go my hold upon my Delia. And she would not let go her hold upon me.

Seventeen

The Arena

Queen Fahia sat in her curule chair, flanked by the sinister shadows of her pet neemus, and she taunted me. She enjoyed that. She had left to her only two neemus, and that pained her. But, she had me, she had Drak the Sword, hyr-kaidur, who had caused her that pain.

She would not be kind.

I had, of necessity, to crouch. They had loaded me with so many iron chains I could barely walk. But walking was not necessary, for they had stuffed me into a tiny square iron-barred cage where I had to crouch in a doubled-up position. The cage was carried by sixteen massively thewed Brokelsh. I twisted my head up to look at this Queen Fahia, for she interested me. They had not tortured me. I knew why that was.

"You have done much mischief, Drak the Sword. And I was foolish and weak enough to think you were my friend."

Delia was not here. She was all I was concerned about. All this talk about friendship with this fat little woman who sat upon the throne of Hyrklana would have made Delia smile. I felt convinced, through my own agony and misery, that because I had not been harmed, Delia would not be either. I thought I knew the way Queen Fahia's mind worked by then.

"My name is Dray Prescot. I warn you, Queen—"

"Silence, you rast! I am the queen! You are no more than a yetch of a kaidur who presumes." She threw her head back and laughed, an unprepossessing sight, to be sure. "What! You call yourself Dray Prescot, Krozair of Zy?"

"Aye. But you do not know what that is. I am Pur Dray. But, also—"

She flicked her fingers and the Pallan Mahmud passed her the scroll wherein was written my crimes. It was not paper, which would have interested me, thinking of far Aphrasöe, but a stiff parchment. She stabbed a jeweled finger down.

"You claim to be Pur Dray Prescot, Krozair of Zy, Zorcander, Lord of Strombor, Prince Majister of Vallia, Kov of Zamra and Can-thirda, Strom of Valka!" She lifted her head and stared at me with a jovial evil over the parchment scroll. "And you seriously expect me to believe this roll of rubbish? This tirade of tomfoolery? You yetch! Think of my neemus! Think of my guardsmen!"

"I have little need to think of them, for they are mostly dead. If only they all were."

She drew her breath. She stabbed the scroll again. "I know nothing of these impossible names — save Vallia and Valka. And Zamra. I once heard of a Kov of Zamra, for my stylors tell me his name appears in a secret document they brought from Hamal, where he visited. The Relts tell me his name is Ortyg Larghos."

I laughed.

"Ortyg Larghos was slain by many arrows, slain in foul treachery to his emperor."

"It is easy to claim a man is dead and take his name, when you are many dwaburs from his homeland."

I could see Fahia was enjoying this. She was working up to a great scene when I would scream and beg for mercy, and she could turn the screw tighter and tighter, until in the end I would admit all my sins. She licked her full red lips. Even then, I truly think, I pitied her.

So far no mention of Delia had crossed my lips. What I was absolutely certain was to happen would not be swayed, now, by what I said, and I wished to start the thing as soon as possible and so spare my Delia any further protracted agony.

We must have been scooped out of the wreckage of the voller after those damned Star Lords had brought all my proud plans of escape to nothing. I had awoken to find myself as I now was, loaded with iron chains and doubled up in an iron cage. I had been given food and drink. But I was in a foul state, for all the buckets of water had been hurled over me before I had been carried into the queen's presence. My clothes had been taken from me. I wondered where the Krozair longsword had gone, but forbore to ask. That would give one more item for them to crow about.

Presently the queen's taunts became cruder and cruder and there is no point in repeating them. She worked herself up into a veritable passion, her blue eyes flashing at me and her features twisting. She dribbled and slashed at her slave fifis who trembled and tried to wipe the spittle away with sensil cloths. She saw the way I looked at her, and I believe then she understood that if I could get my hands around her fat neck I would have had no compunction about squeezing her evil life out, for all that I pitied her, and had recoiled from that deed before, for events had moved on apace since then, by Vox!

"By the putrescent left eyeball of Makki-Grodno!" I roared at her. "You silly fat old woman! Get on with it, for the sake of that yetch Havil the Green. Or" — and I stared her full in the face as she flinched back — "may that hyr-kleesh Lem the Silver Leem devour your mangy body entire!"

She fairly exploded then.

Courtiers ran with whips to hit me, guards milled, a number of Horters fainted, and noble ladies leaned on their noble spouses' shoulders, shaking.

By the time the hullabaloo had subsided Queen Fahia had left her audience chamber, and her black neemus padded balefully after her, twisting their rounded heads, their wedge-ears low, their tails lolling. I laughed.

The preparations within the Jikhorkdun for this greatest of great Kaidurs were made with thoroughness. Barriers around the arena were heightened and strengthened, and solid marble walls were erected before the queen's box, and many crossbowmen were stationed there. Her Chulik Chuktar still retained his place; but I knew it had been a near squeak for him when I had so impudently slipped and deflected his bolts and stuxes, and so barbarically hurled the bloody leem's tail in her face. Thinking back, I would not have dubbed that a high Jikai. More likely a little Kaidur!

They brought my iron cage to a small newly created stone enclosure I did not recognize. All across one side of the stone-walled space stood a line of mercenaries, all with their crossbows lifted, loaded, and cocked, and aimed directly at me. There were fifty of them. At the Chulik Chuktar's command — for he had taken personal control of this wild leem of a prisoner — fifty bolts would flash toward me, narrowing in a fan and piercing my heart. There would not be a lot left of that heart by the time fifty steel-headed quarrels had bedded there.

Slaves wearing the gray slave breechclout unlocked the cage and the chains. The reasoning was, I suppose, that the slaves were expendable. As it was, the four of them shook so much their fingers made a sad hash of the locks, until I said: "Hai, brothers! I am not a slave-master. One day the light will reach this evil place of Huringa. One day slaves will be free."

They didn't believe me, of course. And, to my shame, it was a bravo's gesture, words out of an empty bladder of courage. They got the locks undone and then it was the old bloodstream twisting me about so that, for a time, I could not have faced a woflo, let alone a ponsho, and a quoffa might have had his way with me unmolested. When at last I could stand up, the guards with their crossbows aimed and their trigger-fingers white as death escorted me, all naked, through the far gateway.

Oh, yes, believe me, I can see that scene now, etched in acid on my retinas.

I stepped onto the silver sand of the arena. Everything was the same and everything was different. The terraces and boxes rose into the high blue sky. I was let out onto the sands of the arena exactly as the Suns of Scorpio reached the zenith. Shadows shrank small. Everyone would have a fine unobstructed view. The roar! The yells and shrieks in a bedlam of sound pulsed down from those thousands of throats. And I heard the tenor of much of that noise, the howls for "Drak the Sword! Hyr-kaidur!" Oh, yes, they loved to see the hot blood spurting, and if it gouted from a champion, from a favorite, there were always new accolades to be won by kaidurs forcing their way upward in the Jikhorkdun.

The silver sand gleamed under the suns. The smell of caged beasts wafted in a streaming fetid breath down here, down on the blood-soaked sands of the arena, where the action was. There was, as usual, no wind. I looked up as a skein of mirvols with watchful patrolling aerial cavalry passed, and guessed they would find an excuse to wing around and so hover near, taking their fill of the sport below. They swung away, and a smaller, slimmer flying figure appeared, slipping in over the roof of the western stand and so disappearing in a twinkling. I had caught no sight of a flier upon the flying animal's back.

The beast roar smothered reason. Men and women — apim and halfling — screamed and screeched and banged the benches and swung their rattles and beat their gourd-drums. The winesellers passed along the benches, and could not sell their wares fast enough to slake the throats that all this yelling turned into volcanoes of thirst. Young slave girls, apims, Fristles, Lamnias, sylvies, in particular, moved among the seated thousands carrying fresh paline bushes for sale. Their masters employed girls from those races which traditionally produced the most beautiful girls. I have not mentioned the sylvies before out of decency. But they were there, and doing a roaring trade with their palines and squishes and gregarians and all the exotic fruits of Kregen.

The royal box had never been more ornately decorated. It blazed with color and fire. Queen Fahia sat there, enthroned, and I could guess she would be sitting with her hand propped on her chin, absorbing all this pageantry of the Jikhorkdun with those blue eyes wide, her full lower lip caught between her teeth, mesmerized. If I say that I was to witness a similar spectacle that would surpass this Jikhorkdun of Huringa in Hyrklana, that is not to say that it was not a most impressive spectacle. Golden trumpets cut the air, shrieking their high notes above the din. A silence gradually fell, a silence of waiting, of lip-licking expectation.

I had been let out onto the sands, all naked as I was, from that special area near the queen's box from which her own Queen's Kaidurs — who owed no allegiance to any color — would march proudly forth to fight for her. They would halt and lift their arms in salute. There was nothing about the Queen's Kaidurs or their prospects in the arena to prompt them to cry anything about imminent dying and present saluting.

I walked out a little upon the sand. I had not been able — all the time I moved from that stone gateway onto the sand, all the time the corner of my eye had picked up that mysterious flier slipping over the roof of the amphitheater, all the time my senses had been drowned by the noise and smells — all that time, I had been quite unable to take my eyes from the stake positioned in the center of the arena.

I prayed she was unharmed.

Silver chains they had used to bind her. This was not because she was a princess, for Fahia did not believe that. The silver chains, I guessed, and felt the black rage in me, were a direct reference to the silver leem.

All naked she was suspended there.

Her glorious brown hair lay strewn about her shoulders and bosom. Her shape would set fire to any man. The silver chains draped her so that she could not move, and her arms were drawn up above her head and fastened with silver staples to the black balass of the stake.

She *was* a princess, and she looked more proud, more beautiful, more regal, than anyone there — *anyone!*

Soon, I knew, the horned bosks would be let out.

The thought of those long cruel bosk horns tearing into that slender form filled me with such horror, such rage, that I nearly allowed myself to go berserk and strive to climb that sheer unmarked marble wall to place my fists around the fat neck of that fat, evil woman.

I stood there, and I saluted her as her own Queen's Kaidurs might salute had they wished to die instantly.

There is on Kregen a gesture of such obscene connotation that I have made it a practice never to use, for I am squeamish in such matters.

Now I drew myself up and saluted the queen with this sign.

The sigh that rippled around the amphitheater might have been the sigh of the mourners around an open grave or gathered by the pyre.

257

I was naked and unarmed. I faced, as I expected, either a single bosk and his long horns, or two or three together. The Chulik Chuktar came to the edge of the arena and tossed me a djangir. The short sword, squat and fat and two-edged, landed in the sand at my feet. Being frugal in the matter of weapons, as you know, I bent and retrieved it. It was sharp. They wanted their sport, then, before I died. And with my death, the death also of Delia of Delphond, Delia of the Blue Mountains, fastened by silver chains to an ebony stake.

Once, she had said to me, "I wish to be known as Delia of Strombor."

But I had always thought of her as Delia of Delphond, Delia of the Blue Mountains. Now, perhaps in a few heartbeats, it would not matter.

Cunning are the ways of the managers of the Jikhorkdun of Huringa, which is the capital city of Hyrklana, in Havilfar. But, of them all, none so cunning or malefic as their queen, Queen Fahia, she of the blue eyes and golden hair and heart as black as the fur of her own neemus!

This time they did not wait until my back was turned to release the beast into the arena, as they had done when I fought the leem with the silver collar. This time they wished me to see at once the horror I faced.

One of the larger iron-barred gates swung up. Those bars were thick, and strong, and closely set. They had need to be.

I waited with the djangir in my fist, positioned halfway between the stake and the barred opening. I had not spoken to Delia. She had not spoken to me. We knew all there was to say to each other at a moment like this. I waited, then, poised and ready, for the first bosk to rush out, horns lowered.

A boloth emerged onto the silver sands of the arena.

A boloth!

Huge, impossible, sixteen legs, eight tusks, a massive monster of destruction, standing there with his bunch of whiplash tails swatting flies, staring, with his rapacious mouth half open so that its red darkness glistened and its rows of jagged teeth glinted in the Suns of Scorpio.

A boloth!

Impossible, inhuman, unstoppable.

And I — armed with a little shortsword!

There was only one thing to be done.

Without a shout, without a whoop, in a silent and feral rush I charged for the monster. I knew there was no hope; but then, my way is never to give up until they throw the grave-dirt upon me, and even then I'll likely as not claw up, cursing them all to the Ice Floes of Sicce.

The belly of the boloth, bright yellow, stood as high as my head. His green sides towered above that, and his gray rhinoceros-hide back lofted above. He just stood there, for they are slow beasts, savage when roused — and I was going to rouse him now!

I skipped aside as I neared him, away from the gravel-dredger mouth. The eight tusks formed a barrier of bristling ivory. I thought of the shorgortz and I thought of the Ullgishoa, and then I thought only of this boloth.

My spring carried me past his lowered head, so that I could get a grip on his flap-ears, like those of an African elephant, if four times the size; but, unlike an elephant, there was no deadly weakness behind those ears where a thrust might do his business for him. And, remember, he had three hearts!

Up I clawed and lifted the djangir high and so plunged it down into his right eye.

The mess that spurted had no power to sicken me. It proved that fifty percent of his vision had gone. He reacted with a frenzied bellowing scream, for the boloths have no trunk and therefore he could not trumpet out his pain. But he screamed and bellowed and that massive head shook and I went up in the air and head over heels and so came down flat on my back. Only that old training in the disciplines of unarmed combat enabled me to break the violence of that fall.

The boloth stared about, shaking his head, stamping his feet, lashing his tails about. He continued to bellow. For him, the world had gone dark on his right-hand side. But — disaster — the djangir had remained firmly embedded in that vast ruined eye! I cursed by all the foulest Makki-Grodno oaths I knew; I had to get that djangir back, for, puny as it was, it had already served nobly and must do so again, before that left eye saw the slim form of Delia wrapped in her silver chains.

The bellowing ceased and the boloth turned his head in a peculiar and meaningful way. I saw his nostrils quivering, for he had four of them, and their blackly red edges shivered as he sniffed. Abruptly the whole amphitheater fell silent. The boloth could hear me well enough as I slid on the sand; but he could smell! And, in that silence, I heard the voice of Delia, lifted to me.

"Dray! They have smeared me with scented ointment!"

And I cursed most horribly that devil-queen of Huringa.

I might put out the other eye of the boloth with my bare hands, as I would — I would! — but still the beast would take the scent from my beloved and so charge full upon her. One gulp, one single snap of those gigantic jaws, and all I cared about or loved on two worlds would be gone forever.

And so, as I stood there on the sand, knowing that this vast beast must soon sniff that treacherous scent smeared upon Delia's naked body, I saw that I must express to her a final caress of love. I turned my back to the beast that threatened the lives of Delia and myself and ran away from it. I ran straight toward the balass stake. The uproar from the amphitheater changed into a shocked upheaval of disbelief.

Delia hung in her chains, glorious, desirable, and altogether wonderful. Gently, I reached up and caressed her naked body. I stroked her shoulders and arms and waist and thighs, and every now and then I rubbed my hands over my own naked body. The touch of her stung me through with a whiplash electric bolt of exquisite agony.

"Oh, my Dray..."

"Remember what I have told you, my Delia. Remember the twins, Drak and Lela. But, remember, always, that I love only you of all women in two worlds."

Then I ran back toward the boloth.

He picked the scent smeared upon my body sniffing through those four nostrils and he charged. For that short mad dash a boloth runs faster than a totrix. At the last instant I skipped aside and he thundered past, his legs rising and falling in that smooth complicated rhythm. There was no chance to spring on his back. Next time, when he was slower...

The next time his charge carried him perilously near the central stake, and I had to race toward him, shouting and waving my arms, and all that battery of tusks nearly upended me. He had taken his breather with his three hearts pumping and he charged again. I leaped for his ear, got a grip, got my hand around the djangir hilt, but the pus and mucus slimed it so that I lost it and so fell, winded, to the sands of the arena.

This could not go on.

When I look back upon that brilliant scene, what I have to tell you now never fails to straighten my spine, to make me relish the love and honor between man and man, man and woman. The crowd sensed the boloth was approaching the final kill. He stood obstinately shaking his head in which the djangir remained embedded, too short to do more than darken his eye, and his whiplash tails flickered ready for the next charge. Then...

The roaring from the benches now drowned reason. An abrupt and astonished howling tore from all those thousands of throats there in the tiered Jikhorkdun.

I stared at the red corner.

Four figures ran out onto the silver sand of the arena.

I knew them all.

First ran Naghan the Gnat. In his hand he carried — oh, may Zair be praised over all of Kregen as I praised him in that moment! Naghan must have been there when we crashed in the voller. He ran on his spindly legs toward me and he carried high that great Krozair longsword all gleaming in the suns-light. The scabbard was belted to his waist, and he carried that magnificent Krozair brand all naked and ready.

Following him ran Tilly, my little golden-furred Fristle fifi, and with her ran Oby, that young rascal who dreamed of becoming a kaidur. This deserved the accolade!

And then, also, ran Balass the Hawk, clad in gilded iron of a kaidur's harness, with shield and thraxter and stuxcal, and his massive kaidur helmet was open so I could see his face. Why?

I could guess the scenes taking place at that moment in the queen's box. Foaming, she would be shrieking her orders — and — here came the results!

Crossbow bolts hissed into the sand around the flying figures of my friends. My friends! It was impossible. I cannot recall that scene without the most painful surge of emotions, a feeling that of all men I did not deserve such friendship.

Tilly ran one way and Oby ran the other, making a wide circuit of the arena. They carried jars, and a liquid, rich and darkly purple, spilled upon the sand as they ran.

Naghan the Gnat checked, poised, hurled. The longsword flew through the air. I took it out of the thin air by the hilt. That hilt was Zair-guided into the palm of my hand, and it smacked there with a rich and satisfying thwunk of flesh and hide-grip. I sprang for the boloth. The great beast swung its head and its nostrils quivered.

"Get out of it, Naghan the Gnat!" I yelled as I charged. He needed no second bidding. They had it all worked out. He took to his heels to run for cover and a crossbow bolt ricocheted up from the sand and sliced across that running heel and so laid him low. He lay, the wind knocked out of him.

I reared up to the boloth and dodged a vicious swipe of that battery of tusks and was able to slice off one of the nostrils. His lips were more darkly red when I had finished.

I sprang back and cast a quick glance behind. Balass the Hawk had flicked his faceplate down, and the sheer mask of metal with its breaths and sights covered his dark eager face.

No time, no time for thoughts. I swung to the beast and it was laying about itself, seeking that scent, seeking to puzzle out in that sluggish brain what was going on. For Tilly and Oby were spilling lavish quantities of that alluring scent upon the sand of the arena, in wide circles, decoying the olfactory senses of the beast, confusing it. I breathed hard for the safety of the two as they ran so fleetly, the little golden-furred Fristle girl and the reckless scamp of a boy, running as the crossbow bolts sprouted and gouted from the sand. Truly, one does not have to be Krozair to dodge a quarrel!

"Hai Jikai!" I roared it out ferociously, joyously, as I leaped in once more upon that super-mammoth beast. Screaming his anger and fury, his outer tusk grazed past my leg as I leaped and curled the balanced longsword in and so took out another nostril, and sprang back. Now I knew I would not fail, and to the Ice Floes of Sicce with what might come after!

This was a High Jikai! This made a hyr-Kaidur look the mean and base thing that is the heart and core of the Jikhorkdun as practiced then in Hyrklana. For the true Jikai lay with my friends, with Naghan and Tilly and Oby, with Balass.

The Krozair longsword sliced into the boloth and I leaped and sprang and so cut it to pieces, and the bewildering scents spread by Oby and Tilly worked most subtly and wonderfully upon the poor creature, for it merely pandered in its brute strength and hideousness to the evil hungers of the queen and her people. I saluted it as I took its other eye out. For now I thought the crossbow bolts would thicken about me into such a storm that a whole regiment of Krozair longswords could not keep them out.

I heard Delia yelling. She was not screaming. I was, at the time, leaping down from the boloth and hoping the poor beast would have sense enough to roll over, and not force me any further to hack it into pieces.

"Dray!" Delia shouted, her beautiful voice strong and firm and without a hint of panic. "Hurry, my heart! Hurry!"

I landed on the sand and whirled; the vast bulk of the boloth stood between me and the central balass stake. From below the queen's box files of her mercenaries were running out. The front ranks carried shields, high, and following them ran the crossbowmen. They had formed as though for battle, in ranks, and their shields formed that wall through which a wild and naked barbarian can seldom ever cut his way.

There was no sign at all of Tilly or Oby or Balass. The oncoming guardsmen, precise in their dress, aligned, thraxters and stuxes ready, the crossbowmen following on, bore down on me.

Again I heard Delia's voice: "Hurry, Dray, my darling!" I looked up. A voller from the Air Service of Hyrklana slanted down, and the faces of her crew showed over the side. With her flew a number of the queen's aerial cavalry astride their mirvols. I saw three mirvollers abruptly crumple up and fall in a wide spinning from the sky.

The mercenaries advanced. There was one quick way to get back to the central stake and there make the final stand, as Delia was calling me to do. I turned again for the boloth to jump up and claw my way over his back and leap down on the other side, for he was down on his knees now, his belly sagging, and there was no way under him. Then I noticed the guardsmen in their military formation, dressed for battle, were heading at a slant that would take them past the boloth and me. They were running with their military pace straight for the central stake, out of my sight, hidden beyond the boloth!

I yelled, then. I screamed at the cowardly assassins to fight me, and not bring all their armored might against a lone girl, naked and chained to a stake. The crowd noise was now so great that nothing else could be heard, even the sound of the armored men, the sound of my breathing, the hissing grunts from the boloth.

And then...!

And then I saw another wonder and, if anything, it was more wonderful than the first. But, no, that is not so. For the actions of Tilly and Oby and Naghan and Balass could have brought them nothing but death. And what I saw now came from men who wanted nothing to do with death — at least, with their own death.

For the neatly ordered ranks of the guards swayed, and writhed, and collapsed. Guards were falling in droves. And then I saw the sleeting rain of the steel-tipped clothyard shafts, and so I knew why Delia was calling to me to hurry.

I went up and over that poor old boloth like a steeplechaser at the first fence. I poised for just a second, looking down.

An airboat of a style unfamiliar to me hung a yard or so above the sand. But I knew the men who manned her! I saw their great Lohvian longbows bending in that smooth and precise rhythm, and the deluge of shafts that soared to pierce through with bodkin accuracy and penetration. I saw, also, the varters lining her sides angled upward, and loosing bolt after bolt toward the Hyrklanan Air Service vollers. And, the aerial cavalry astride their mirvols were not left out of that continuous pelting rain of destruction that sheeted from the airboat.

The voller was the largest I had seen up to that time. Her petal shape had been drawn out into a towering construction of terraced power, long and beamed, three-decked forward, four-decked aft. The varters spat and clanged and the bowmen loosed and she looked like a snarling demon of the skies. And — from every flagstaff floated the yellow cross on the scarlet field, that flag of mine warriors call Old Superb!

I roared out once, a mighty *"Hai! Jikai!"*

Then I was leaping down from the destroyed boloth and feeling that familiar genuine pity for a noble beast done to death to please the debased whims of people who should know better. His three hearts pumped more slowly now as his bright blood poured out upon the silver sands of the arena, and he gave a last long mournful hooting, very distressing. But what else could I have done, there in the Jikhorkdun beneath the Suns of Scorpio?

Delia waited for me aboard the voller. I knew Seg and Inch and Turko had had adventures. Seg waved an arm to me, in between shooting. Inch flailed his Saxon-pattern ax about, cursing, I could so easily guess, that he could not get into close action. Korf Aighos, too, was there, jumping up and down, brandishing that monstrous Sword of War of the Blue Mountain Boys. He would be longing for a fast looting trip to bring him final satisfaction. Away up forward Tom ti Vulheim controlled his band of Valkan Archers, putting shaft after shaft down in the dense defensive pattern. I could have strolled up to the voller. Then I saw Obquam of Tajkent, that flying Strom who disliked the volroks, and I understood he had been that slender flying figure I had seen, and also how Seg and Inch had found me.

Nothing could be heard save the beast roar from the crowd. Not even the shrieks of the wounded and dying as those cruel steel birds tore into them and their crossbows and shields spilled into the blood-drenched sands of the arena.

I wondered what Queen Fahia was thinking.

Halfway there I stopped. Naghan the Gnat lay on the sand, his heel wet with blood. He waved at me and his lips moved. I guessed what he was saying, for a crossbow quarrel at random chunked into the sand beside us.

"Sink me!" I said aloud, although no one could hear. "I'll not leave Naghan the Gnat!"

I scooped him up and a bolt hissed past and so I did not walk, out of concern for Naghan, but raced to the voller and bundled him up onto the deck, where eager hands grasped him. I took a grip of the side, a brass-bound lenk coaming near a varter platform, and the airboat shot into the sky. For a lurid instant I hung there, dangling by one hand, for the other grasped the Krozair longsword which I would as lief hold on to as to the voller carrying us to safety. Wind whipped past. With a wriggle and a squirm, and with Seg and Inch hauling at my wrists, I came aboard.

As I stood up a shadow flicked over me, and I swung around, and there was Turko the Shield, at my back, and a last despairing try sent a crossbow bolt clattering harmlessly from the massive shield Turko lifted over me.

The noise diminished as we rose.

A Hyrklanan Air Service voller shot past, ripped and torn, her crew strewn across her decks with the clothyard shafts feathered into them.

"By Zim-Zair, my friends!" I cried. "You are most welcome!"

Delia clasped me and Korf Aighos cast a swirling scarlet cloak about her glowing nakedness and I laughed and drew her close beneath that flame of friendly scarlet.

Seg Segutorio smiled very merrily upon us, his reckless blue eyes and dark hair very dear to me. "We would have been here sooner, with the good aid of Obquam, but our airboat broke down. We had to take this fine new flier from some onkers who wanted to imprison us and take us to Hamal."

Inch was standing on his head, looking very serious, and we laughed but respected him and his taboos, and gave him room.

"Tom ti Vulheim!" I roared up at that massive fore-deck. "Come down here and shake my hand!"

Korf Aighos produced golden goblets of refreshing wine.

"Seg and Inch, old comrades!" I cried. "Korf Aighos and Turko the Shield! Now we have an armorer with us in Naghan the Gnat. And a hyr-kaidur in Balass the Hawk. And, also—"

"And also, dear heart, a saucy Fristle fifi!"

"Aye! And also a rascal who will now aspire beyond the kaidur dreams of the Jikhorkdun. Oby, you imp of mischief! Let go—" But with a screech and a clang the varter with whose mechanism Oby had been tinkering loosed. Everyone gave a great cheer.

"A parting shot to a rast's nest!"

Oh, yes, as we lifted high and higher and sped far and fast from that reeking blood-fouled arena of silver sand in the Jikhorkdun of Huringa in Hyrklana, I saw before me a great and dazzling future. One day, one day, Zair willing, I would return and perhaps, if the people were willing, cleanse the Jikhorkdun.

Now the future opened out bright with that promise. For no ominous clouds boiled about our path and no supernatural winds contemptuously hurled us back as they had done when I had previously tried to escape from Huringa. I knew why the Star Lords had prevented my going before, for then I had been in the past relative to the freeing of Migla, and had I returned I might have met myself — so that I had been forced to wait in the Jikhorkdun until my two presents once again merged.

No such impediment had caused the Everoinye to prevent Delia and me leaving together, and now the Star Lords were allowing us to go where before they had smashed us back to be captured. A task I had had no idea I must perform had therefore been carried out in the interim, and, looking at Oby as he joked and laughed with my good comrades, I fancied I could guess something of the Star Lords' purposes. Oby, in running with our friends into the arena, had saved me twice over!

And, too, no insidious blue radiance crept out to toss me four hundred light-years back across the void to the planet of my birth. Once again, so I fondly thought in my joyful ignorance, once again I was free upon the face of Kregen.

In my arms I held my Delia, my Delia of Vallia, mother of our twins Drak and Lela, and the Suns of Scorpio streamed their mingled opaz light and the sky remained clear and serene above.

A Glossary of Places and Things
in the Saga of Dray Prescot:
The Havilfar Cycle

Editor's note: For the sake of completeness, this glossary is included here at the end of Arena of Antares *as Alan Burt Akers intended. However, it has also been included in a complete glossary of the Havilfar Cycle at the end of* The Havilfar Cycle II.

A

apim: Homo sapiens.

arena: See Jikhorkdun.

Astar: Group of islands midway between eastern Pandahem and Xuntal.

B

balass: A wood similar to ebony.

Barrath: An area of Hamal.

Beng-Kishi: These famous bells are said to ring in the skull of anyone hit on the head. This happens frequently on Kregen.

Bleg: A halfling with a face like that of a Persian leaf bat, without the large ears; fur and skin patches of green, yellow, and purple. The lower jaw hangs revealing row of thin sharp teeth. Two arms. Four legs arranged in a quadrilateral. Atrophied carapace on back.

boloth: A large animal from Chem with eight tusks, sixteen legs, a tendrilous mass of whiplash tails. The hide is hard and gray along the back, leaf-green along the sides, and yellow beneath. Normally slow, but fast in a short dash. Has an enormous underslung fanged mouth, keen sense of smell; with three hearts.

bur: The Kregan hour, approximately forty Terrestrial minutes.

C

Canopdrin: Island of the northwest Shrouded Sea, devastated by earthquakes.

Canops: Martial people of Canopdrin.

cham-faces: Nickname given to the Miglas. chavonth: Powerful six-legged hunting cat with fur of blue, gray, and black arranged in a hexagonal pattern. Treacherous.

Chemzite Tower: Dominating structure of the high fortress of Hakal.

Chuktar: Highest of the four main military ranks. There are many subdivisions varying with country of origin.

Cnarveyl: A country bordering Migla in the northwest of the Shrouded Sea.

coy: Slave or volunteer fighting to become a kaidur.

Crimson Missals, the Battle of: In which the Miglas with the assistance of
Dray Prescot and his comrades fought the Canops.

D

Dap-Tentyrasmot: Town to the east of the Shrouded Sea.

db: Abbreviation of dwaburs per bur.

Deldar: Lowest of the four main military ranks.

deldy: Gold coin of Havilfar.

dermiflon: Blue-skinned, ten-legged, idiot-headed animal, very fat and
ungainly, armed with sinuous, massively barbed, spiked tail. The
expression 'To knock over a dermiflon" is a cast-iron guarantee of
effectiveness.

diff: A man-beast, beast-man. A halfling.

dilse: A species of maize, can be mixed with milk and water and pounded and
served in a variety of ways. Grows freely needing little cultivation. Has
serious nutritional failings.

Djanduin: Country of the far west of Havilfar.

Djang: Inhabitant of Djanduin.

djangir: Very short, very broad sword.

Djanguraj: Capital city of Djanduin.

dom: Kregish equivalent of English "mate" or American "pal."

dopa: A fiendish drink guaranteed to make a man fighting drunk.

dwa: Two.

E

Everoinye: The Star Lords.

F

Faol: Island off the northwest of Havilfar, home of the Manhounds.

fifi: Saucy Fristle girl of exceptional liveliness and beauty.

fireglass: A crystal that does not distort or crack when used to hold fire for
illumination and heating purposes.

flutsmen: Mercenaries of the skies, fierce and vicious, of many species.

fluttclepper: A small racing saddle-bird.

fluttrell: A strong saddle-bird with large head-vane, coloring beige-white and
velvety-green, with powerful talons.

foofray satin: Expensive material often used to make slippers.

G

Gairnoivach: Capital city of Gorgrendrin.

Gdoinye: The giant scarlet and golden raptor, messenger and spy of the Star
Lords.

Gorgrendrin: Land of Southwest Havilfar. Its inhabitants are often called
Gorgrens.

green sun: Apart from Havil has many names: Genodras, Ry-ufraison, etc.

gros-varter: A larger and more powerful version of the ballista.
Gulf of Wracks: Gulf and channel in Southeast Havilfar leading to the
 Shrouded Sea.

H

Hakal: The high fortress dominating the city of Huringa.
Hakkinostoling: A remote province of Hyrklana.
Hamal: Empire in the northeast of Havilfar.
Hamish wine: A purple wine of Hyrklana.
ban: Common suffix denoting son.
Havilfar: A continent of Kregen south and east of Loh.
Havilthytus, River: One of the main rivers of Hamal.
Hennardrin: A land in the north of Havilfar.
Herrelldrin: A country in the southwest of Havilfar.
Hikai: The unarmed combat equivalent to Jikai.
Hikdar: Military rank immediately above Deldar.
Hirrume: Kingdom in Empire of Hamal.
Horter: A gentleman of Havilfar. Feminine is Hortera.
Huringa: Capital city of Hyrklana.
hurm: A hard close-grained wood, similar to sturm-wood.
hyr: Great, renowned, high.
Hyr-Derengil-Notash: "The high palace of pleasure and wisdom." A book of
 philosophy compiled by a Wizard of Loh two thousand five hundred
 seasons ago. Admits of many interpretations and analyses.
Hyrklana: An island realm off the east coast of Havilfar.
Hyr-Lif: A very important book.
hyrshiv: Twelve.

I

inklevol: flying fox.

J

jagger: In the syples of the Khamorros a kick with the feet delivered with both
 feet off the ground.
Jikai!: A word of complex meaning; used in different forms means: "Kill!"
 "Warrior," "A noble feat of arms," "Bravo" and many related concepts to do
 with honor and pride and warrior-status.
Jikhorkdun: The entire amphitheater, arena, and training and barracks areas.
 Sometimes slurred to "Jikordun."
jiklo: A Manhound of Faol.
jikshiv: Twenty-four.
Jiktar: Military rank immediately below Chuktar.

K

Kaidur: Renowned gladiatorial feat of combat.
kaidur: Gladiator.
Kham, Khamster: A Khamorro.

kham: Levels of achievement within the syples of the Khamorros.

Khamorro: A man of Herrelldrin expert in unarmed combat.

Kharoi Stones: Ruins of a city of the sunset people in west Havilfar.

kitches: Midges of the marshes.

kleesh: Violently unpleasant, repulsive, stinking. An insult.

kool: An area measurement of land.

Koroles: Small group of islands off east coast of South Pandahem.

Krzy: Abbreviation for the Krozairs of Zy, a mystic and martial order of the Eye of the World devoted to Zair.

L

laccapin: Ferocious flying reptile.

Lahal: Universal greeting for friend or acquaintance.

Lake of Dreaming Maidens, the: see the Wendwath.

Lamnia: Member of a race of halflings, gentle as a rule, with light-colored fur. Respected as honest and shrewd merchants.

Leaping Fishes, River of: Fast-flowing river to the north of Huringa.

Leem-Lovers: Insulting name for the reavers from the southern oceans.

leemsheads: Outlaws.

ley: Four.

lif: An important book.

liki: Small fly-catching spider.

Lily City Klana: Ancient capital of Hyrklana, now in ruins.

Llahal: Universal greeting for stranger.

lople: Deer-like animal of great grace and beauty.

Loyal Canoptic, The: An Inn in Yaman, renamed after the conquest.

Loyal of Sidraarga, The: Original name of *The Loyal Canoptic.*

M

Mackee, Battle of: First battle of the Miglas against the Canops in which Dray Prescot was unwillingly engaged.

Magan, River: Wide sluggish river on which is built the city of Yaman.

Manhounds: Apims of Faol trained to run on all fours and act as hunting dogs. Extraordinarily vicious and predatory.

marspear: A crop plant.

Methydria: Ranching land east of the Shrouded Sea, sometimes known as Havil-Faril, sometimes Methydrin.

Migladrin: Land to the northwest of the Shrouded Sea.

Miglas: Simple, thick-legged, thick-armed, gnomish-headed people, with stumpy bodies and flap ears, of the northwest Shrouded Sea. Also known as Migladorn.

mirvol: Flying saddle-animal of Havilfar.

moons: Kregen has seven moons. The largest, the Maiden with the Many Smiles, is almost twice the size of Earth's moon. The next two, the Twins, revolve around each other. The fourth is She of the Veils. The three smallest moons hurtle rapidly across the sky close to the surface of Kregen.

Mountains of Mirth, the: A mountain chain in the west of Havilfar.

Mungul Sidrath: The powerful citadel and palace of Yaman.

N

neemu: Black-furred, almost-leopard-sized animal with round head, squat ears, slit eyes of lambent gold, four legs. Their ways are amoral and feral, they are vicious, treacherous, and deadly.

Notor: Lord.

nul: Dismissive term for a person not of one's nation or creed or Order or Discipline.

nulsh: Term of abuse.

O

ob: One.

Ocean of Clouds: A name for the ocean east of Havilfar.

Ocean of Doubt, the: Ocean to the west of Havilfar south of Loh.

onker: Idiot. Term of abuse.

Orange River: A river of Havilfar running westward into the sea opposite Loh between Ng'groga and Nycresand.

ord: Eight.

Ordsmot: Town on the Orange River divided into eight species sections.

Outer Faol: Island to the north of Faol.

P

paktun: A mercenary leader; a notorious mercenary; a renowned soldier of fortune.

paline: Yellow cherry-like fruit with taste of old port.

Paline and Queng, The: An Inn in Djanduin.

paly: The easiest to catch of plains deer. The jungle paly has zebra-striped hindquarters.

Pastang: A military company, often consisting of eighty men, infantry, plus ancillaries, commanded by a Hikdar.

Pellow: City of Herrelldrin.

pimpim: Tree of eastern Loh. The crushed fruits yield a brilliant green wine, thick and cloying, sweet and strong.

prianum: A cheap pine wood from forests in the south of Havilfar.

Q

Quennohch: Island in the far southeast of Havilfar.

quoffa: Large draft animal, very mild and docile, powerful, shaggy, with a dogged head and a large patient face. Has six legs and looks like a perambulating hearthrug.

R

rast: Six-legged rodent infesting dunghills. Term of abuse.

red sun: Has many other names besides Far and Zim.

reed-syple: Headband with symbols worn by Khamorros to denote their syple discipline, their kham status and allegiances.

Remberee: Universal salutation on parting.

Rhaclaw: Manlike halfling with enormous domed head as wide as shoulders.

Rivensmot: Town of a small kingdom within the Empire of Hamal.

rofer: Very large multi-saddle-bird of Havilfar.

Ruathytu: Capital city of Empire of Hamal.

S

Sava: Kingdom in continent of Havilfar.

Savanti: Mortal but superhuman people of Aphrasöe.

sensil: An extremely soft and fine form of silk.

sermine: A flower from which is processed a drug inducing fighting fury.

Shander's End: Town connected by road to Huringa.

shebov: Seven.

shiv: Six.

shonage: A fruit of rich flesh and sweet juices, larger than a grapefruit and as red as a tomato.

Shrouded Sea: Large inland sea running from the Gulf of Wracks in the southeast in a northwesterly direction into the heart of Havilfar. Is plagued by volcanic activity; dotted with islands.

sinver: Silver coin of Hyrklana.

six: Common suffix denoting daughter.

sleeth: Saddle-dinosaur running on two legs used by the more sporting rider in races; an uncomfortable ride.

smot: Town.

so: Three.

stux: The Migla vosk-hunting throwing spear. Used as javelin by soldiers.

stuxcal: Device for carrying eight stuxes.

syatra: A corpse-white man-eating plant, with spine-barbed leaves and many thick fleshy tentacles sprouting from a central trunk. Venus's-flytrap-type growths larger than coffins grow around the trunk. Likes hot, damp gloomy climates. Chem is choked with them, according to Prescot.

syple: A training and mystic discipline of the Khamorros.

T

Tajkent: Mountain aerie of flying men of Havilfar opposed to volroks.

Thothangir: Region in farthest south of Havilfar.

thraxter: The straight-bladed cut-and-thrust sword of Havilfar.

totrix: Close cousin of the sectrix and nactrix. Six-legged saddle-animal, blunt headed, wicked eyed, pricked of ear.

Triple Peaks: A mountain aerie of the volroks.

Tungar: A vadvarate south of the Orange River.

Tyriadrin: A country bordering Migla to the south.

tyrvol: Large flying saddle-animal.

U

ulm: Unit of measurement, approximately 1,500 yards.

V

veknis: Scramasax-like hunting knife used by Miglas.
volclepper: Fast, small flying saddle-animal.
volleem: The flying form of leem.
voller: The Havilfarese name for fliers, airboats. volrok: One species of flying
  men.

W

week: On Kregen the week is usually six days, although it is seven days in
  Zenicce. Six-day week associated with Opaz.
Wendwath: Known as the Lake of Dreaming Maidens. With its associated sea
  inlets and fens cuts off the western promontory of Havilfar from
  Herrelldrin and the northwest.
wersting: A vicious black and white striped four-legged hunting dog.
whistling faerling: One of the kinds of Kregan peacock.
White Rock of Gilmoy: A tremendous pillar of white rock standing on the
  northwest coast of Havilfar opposite Faol
wo: Zero.
woflovol: Bat with large membranous wings. Wraiths, River of: River of
  Djanduin.

X

Xaffer: A race of diffs remote and strange; when slaves they are usually
  employed in domestic and light duties.

Y

Yaman: Capital city of Migladrin.
Yawfi Suth: Dangerous and difficult fen area of western Havilfar.
yetch: A term of abuse.

Fliers of Antares

A Note on Dray Prescot

Dray Prescot is a man above medium height, with straight brown hair and brown eyes that are level and dominating. His shoulders are immensely wide and there is about him an abrasive honesty and a fearless courage. He moves like a great hunting cat, quiet and deadly. Born in 1775 and educated in the inhumanly harsh conditions of the late eighteenth century navy, he presents a picture of himself that, the more we learn of him, grows no less enigmatic.

Through the machinations of the Savanti nal Aphrasöe — mortal but superhuman men dedicated to the aid of humanity — and of the Star Lords, he has been taken to Kregen under the Suns of Scorpio many times. On that savage and beautiful, marvelous and terrible world he rose to become Zorcander of the Clansmen of Segesthes, and Lord of Strombor in Zenicce, and a member of the mystic and martial Order of Krozairs of Zy.

Against all odds Prescot won his highest desire and in that immortal battle at The Dragon's Bones claimed his Delia, Delia of Delphond, Delia of the Blue Mountains, as his own. And Delia claimed him in the face of her father the dread Emperor of Vallia. Amid the rolling thunder of the acclamations of Hai Jikai! Prescot became Prince Majister of Vallia, and wed his Delia, the Princess Majestrix.

Through the agency of the blue radiance sent by the Star Lords, the Summons of the Scorpion, Prescot is plunged headlong into fresh adventures on Kregen. Outwitting the Manhounds of Antares, he rescues Mog, a high priestess, and defeats the Canops who have invaded her country. Forced to fight in the arena of the Jikhorkdun of Huringa he rises to be a hyr-kaidur and at a climactic moment is rescued with Delia by his comrades in a magnificent airboat. Now they are on their way to Migladrin across the Shrouded Sea...

Alan Burt Akers

One

I swim in the Shrouded Sea

"By Vox!" yelled Vangar ti Valkanium above the clamor of the gale. "This would be no time for this flier to break down."

From the forward starboard varter position I clung to a stanchion with my left hand and peered out and down. The sudden onset of the gale had cast a darkness over the bright day, and the twin Suns of Scorpio were dimmed. Through the drenching lash of rain and the erratic lightning-shot darkness I could see the lacerated surface of the Shrouded Sea. The wind slashed off the tops of the running waves, and the white roar below bellowed and flung wind-tossed spume flat and sheeting.

"This voller was built in Hamal, Vangar," I yelled back at him. He could barely hear me. "She won't break down like the rubbish they sell us in Vallia."

We were both drenched with rain. The decks ran with water which spouted out, foaming, through the scuppers. I had full confidence in the flier, for my men had taken her from a crew of foolish raiders from Hamal, so that they could come to my rescue in the arena of the city of Huringa in Hyrklana; it was now very clear to me that the shipwrights of Hamal applied double standards to their work.

"She flies well, my prince," shouted Vangar. He felt a particular concern for Delia and me, I well knew, for his appointment as captain of my flier brought him grave responsibilities as well as great joys.

The sea below raged and roared. We were lower than I liked, for we had tried to outrun the gale on our way back to Migladrin to finalize the new arrangements in religious and political matters of that country, and this confounded gale had seized us in its grip as we sped across the Shrouded Sea.

For a moment I lingered. The sea down there aroused strange emotions in me. The Star Lords had prohibited me from shipping in either swifter or swordship; but I admit that, despite the anger of that sea and the fierce and deadly power of wind and water, I stared a little hungrily at the element on which I had lived for so large a part of my life on the planet of my birth, four hundred light-years away.

"Get back to the helm-deldar, Vangar, and lift us. We will have to take our chances with the wind and storm higher up."

Vangar did not argue but went at once.

To this day I cannot in truth say how it happened. I know the black thought of treachery crossed my mind, for until the conspiracy against the Emperor of Vallia, who was my father-in-law, had been completely crushed, we walked in perilous paths. And his peril also menaced his daughter, who was my wife, the Princess Majestrix Delia, my Delia of Delphond, of the Blue Mountains.

The most probable explanation is that during that brave rescue of me from the arena when the flier was being shot at from all directions, a chunk of rock thrown by a varter had crunched into the stanchion, weakening it.

Now with my weight and the wind and the violent motions of the flier, the stanchion parted.

Instantly I was tumbled headlong into thin air, spinning head over heels, gasping as the wind and rain struck and sent me plunging into that fearsome sea.

I surfaced and dragged in a huge lungful of air; then the waves smashed me over and down and so I began a protracted period of intense struggle to survive. As you know, I am a strong swimmer, and may dive deeply and long, and believe me when I say I needed every ounce of skill and endurance. The flier vanished, whisked away as a clump of thistledown is brushed by the breeze.

I, Dray Prescot, of Earth and of Kregen, battled for my life with the sea — alone.

There are techniques for keeping afloat and I used all my knowledge to remain near the surface and not allow the vicious violence of the sea to weaken and overwhelm me. That I survived is clear in that I am speaking to you on these tapes; but it was a near thing. When I felt myself at last at the end of my strength and saw there low against a level break in the clouds the long line of rocks marking a shore, I knew I had to make a supreme effort. I am not a man who will give in easily. I had been learning caution, and tried to contain that intemperate recklessness that had many times brought me kicks and cuffs, and, may Zair forgive me, so many times failed. But against the insensate violence of the sea I would exert everything of me that is me, that makes me Dray Prescot, and no other in two worlds.

Gradually, with immense effort, I maneuvered myself toward the shore. For a moment or two I thought I would be flung end-over-end onto the black rocks that showed through the gouting spray like decayed teeth; but Zair aided me — for the damned Star Lords would not, and neither would the Savanti — and I felt myself picked up and flung between two jagged rocks and so hurled onto a tiered beach of coarse gray sand. I had to summon up all the reserves of strength I had left to prevent myself from just lying there, prey to the waves, and to force myself to crawl on hands and knees up above the high water mark. Then, between two crumbling rocks, I put my head onto that sand and passed out.

The next thing I recall is being turned over gently and feeling soft hands examining my ribs and arms and legs. I lay still.

A girl's voice, light and clear, said: "He has no broken bones, for which he may praise Mother Shoshash of the Seaweed Hair, when he awakes. Father Shoshash the Stormbrow has not been gentle with him. His ib is knocked fair out of him."

Another girl's voice, a little more giggly, answered. "Come away, Paesi. He looks monstrous ugly. And look at his shoulders!"

"Mmm," said Paesi, in a way I decidedly did not like.

Thinking it expedient to regain consciousness, I let out a few grunts, heaved myself around, and opened my eyes.

Two Lamnias stared down on me. They had run back a few paces, and now stood, poised for instant flight. I have told you that certain races are famed upon

Kregen for the beauty of their womenfolk, and the Lamnias, that gentle, shrewd, yellow-furred folk, are blessed with daughters who are as fair in the eyes of other races as any Fristle fifi, or apim girl, or aephar damsel of far Balintol.

The two girls, Paesi and her companion, wore simple short-sleeved white blouses and knee-length skirts of apple-green, and they carried woven wickerwork baskets over their arms. They stood regarding me uncertainly, a monstrous great hairy apim risen from the sea. Shades of Odysseus and Nausicaa! I was as salt grimed and unkempt, clad only in my old scarlet breechclout, as any shipwrecked mariner. But the two Lamnias stood, open-eyed, regarding me, and beneath the white blouses their bosoms rose and fell perhaps a little faster as I slowly stood up, and stretched, and gave thanks to Zair that I still lived.

Lamnias in youth possess that gorgeous laypom-colored dusting of fur upon their bodies that strokes as light as thistledown. Later in life the fur grows thicker and darker but seldom as thick as, for example, the fur of a Fristle. Now the two girls stared at me and the flush of blood beneath the skin showed clearly through that light yellow dusting of fur.

"I mean you no harm," I said, trying to make my bear-like voice as friendly as possible. But when I spoke they both jumped and took a step back.

After some time I managed to convince them that I was a human being — and by that I mean a human being, as they were; and not merely apim, which they could see — and we set off to walk to their village.

I had no means of knowing where Delia might be now. What I did know, unshakably, was that she would scour the sea until she found me. She knew of my mysterious disappearances, although not the cause of them, and this time the broken stanchion would show all too clearly what had happened. I fancied then, as I went with the two Lamnia girls up past the gorse-like bushes of the shoreline and through broad-leaved sough-wood trees, that very soon the flier would come ghosting in and my friends would yell and bellow for me and a rope ladder would come tumbling down and I would be rescued again.

If I mention, now, that the broken stanchion dumped me headlong into fresh adventures, I must add that the stanchion also contributed much to the destiny of the planet Kregen itself.

The people of the village greeted me kindly. They must have observed the way I was constantly looking up into the sky as Zim and Genodras sailed past scattered clouds, shedding that streaming mingled opaz light, and perhaps they put down those searching looks to guilt against Havil, or to some religious doctrine, or even — and this would be the nature of the Lamnias — to a stiff neck I was trying to ease.

My previous experiences of Lamnias, notably with Dorval Aymlo, the merchant of Ordsmot, had shown me that they were a gentle people, good merchants, shrewd at bargaining, not warriors. The village had a wooden stockade and was tucked neatly into the crook of a river with a bluff to defend it; but it was a poor place for all that, both in military might and in wealth. It was crowded with people all engaged in running about on tasks of the utmost importance to those performing them but incomprehensible to me at the time. I detected a note of competition in the air, and saw young girls dancing and singing in long lines, and young men running races and hurling blunted wooden javelins, throwing weapons quite unlike the formidable stuxes of Havilfar.

The Lammas seated on wooden stools at the entrance to the largest house, a two-story structure festooned with many varieties of flowers, I assumed to be the village council, and the headman, a shrewd and sad-looking fellow called Rorpal of Podia, greeted me with a punctiliousness I found touching.

"Llahal, stranger who has escaped from the house of Shoshash."

"Llahal, Rorpal of Podia."

Podia was the name of the village, and it was situated on one of the innumerable islands of the Shrouded Sea. On the other side of the river a steep, cone-shaped volcano emitted a lazy cloud of smoke. Perhaps the Lamnias thought I kept looking at He of the Yrium, the volcano, in my searching looks at the sky. *Yrium* is a word with profound meanings of force, meaning power, either power conveyed by office, or by strength of character, or given to a person in any way that unmistakably blesses — or curses — him with undisputed dominance over his fellows. To dub a natural phenomenon like a volcano as He of the Yrium was to convey in the most pungent way all the awful ferocity and power these people regarded as residing in the volcano. The Shrouded Sea is plagued with volcanic activity, as well as earth tremors and earthquakes.

"I am Dray Prescot," I said. Then, I added, "Krozair of Zy," because at times I am a boaster as well as an intemperate hothead, and I felt secure in the knowledge that they would not understand what I was telling them anyway.

"Llahal, Dray Prescot, Krozair of Zy. You are welcome to Podia. Will you tell us your story?"

I did not smile at this, for that would have been impolite; I simply sat on the wooden bench indicated and, with a glass of fruit juice and a plate of palines at my side, I told them a little. I mentioned the Canops, that fierce, martial race of people who had been driven out of their island home because of its near-destruction by earthquake, and of their settling in Migladrin, but before I had a chance to say that the Miglas, with the help of my friends, had taken back their own country, the Lamnias reacted.

To my surprise they were disappointed that the Canops had left the Shrouded Sea island of Canopdrin.

"They are honest traders," said Rorpal, rubbing the laypom-colored fur beneath his chin. "Now there is no one to stand against the aragorn of Sorah."

Well, as you know, I was acquainted with the evil ways of the aragorn. Slave raiders and slave-masters, the aragorn plunder their way to fortune over the agony and the blood of anyone unfortunate enough to be too weak to stand up against them. The valiant people of my island of Valka had driven out the aragorn of Vallia. I was in the midst of a political campaign to drive them out of Vallia altogether. And now, here in the continent of Havilfar, I found aragorn operating in the Shrouded Sea. This was not surprising. Slaves are required. Slaves are always needed. Slave-masters will always find a calling when there are weak people to be enslaved and strong and unscrupulous people to enslave them.

"You fear the aragorn of Sorah?"

"Aye, Horter Prescot. We fear them."

I sat back and considered. I had chanced here because a weakened stanchion of an airboat had pitched me into the sea. I might have drifted anywhere, or been drowned and forgotten. I had not been sent here by the Star Lords. No blue radiance had enfolded me, no gigantic representation of a scorpion had borne me away to a desperate mission for the Star Lords. No. No, I had no business here. If I occupied myself in every small corner of Havilfar — let alone Kregen — interfering with the ways of life that had gone on for centuries, there would be no end to it. This business was not my business.

All the same, I felt the thrill of blood through my arteries, and the word *aragorn* — remembering Valka and that great song, "The Fetching of Drak na Valka" — made my hands close as though they held a sword.

I now know I was wrong in shrugging off someone else's problems. But you must remember that I was young according to Kregan standards, to which I have become adjusted, and I was newly married with baby twins, Drak and Lela. I wanted to go home to Valka and take my Delia in my arms and forget all about Star Lords and slavery and the other pressing problems of Kregen. I was even considering leaving off my search for the Savanti, those mortal but superhuman men of the Swinging City of Aphrasöe.

It is not easy for a fighting-man to reconcile himself to the philosophy that teaches we are all responsible for each other, and that one person's loss is a loss to all.

So I changed the subject and said: "I see you hold a great festival, Horter Rorpal. Your young men and your young girls compete against each other."

Rorpal's sad face looked sadder than ever and he leaned forward, about to answer me.

An old Lamnia at his side put a hand on Rorpal's arm. This Lamnia's yellow fur showed silver tips, a clear indication of his great age, for I guessed he must be well past a hundred and seventy-five. He shook his head in warning.

Whatever Rorpal had been about to say, that hand on his arm and that shake of the head changed his mind.

"Yes, Horter Prescot." He took a paline and munched it thoughtfully.

I waited politely; but he said nothing more to enlighten me.

Although I wore my scarlet breechclout, cinctured up with a broad leather belt, and a sailor's knife lay scabbarded back of my right hip, I felt naked. On Kregen, that marvelous world that is so heartbreakingly beautiful and so horrendously cruel, a man must carry a weapon if he wishes to remain free in so very many areas of the globe. The unarmed combat disciplines of the Krozairs of Zy could keep me out of much trouble, but I hanker always for the feel of a sword in my fist.

The activities of the youngsters, which could be viewed with ease from this high verandah outside the headman's house, came to a climax with much shouting and hullabalooing, and at last a group of about fifty youths and maidens, their dusting of yellow fur bright in the declining rays of the twin suns, clustered

279

together, entwined with wreaths of flowers. Something of the sadness of Rorpal of Podia must have affected me, for these circlets of flowers could scarcely be wreaths. They must be the victors' crowns.

And yet the flowers, so brilliant, so beautiful, were linked together in long chains, so that the fifty were in very truth entwined about, bound, almost.

Masses of people moved away from the open space, laughing among themselves, and yet their laughter struck chill. I glanced at Rorpal.

He stood up. At his side a young man with as aggressive a cast of feature as any Lamnia might aspire to handed the headman his spear of office. Around the spear had been entwined flowers. Rorpal lifted the spear, and the gathering crowds below fell silent and shuffled into place before the verandah and the group of village elders, leaving the fifty bound in their flower chains some way off, isolated.

Rorpal was about to say something that might explain these proceedings. A woman ran urgently up and past the crowd's outskirts, pushed vigorously past the aggressive youth, who made no real attempt to halt her. She stopped in front of Rorpal. She looked agitated and yet determined, and her face, pleasant and mellow in the Lamnia way, set itself in lines of unfamiliar hardness.

"Rorpal! I call on you — Paesi — she it was — and it is decided that Polosi shall go!" She was stammering so much through her assumed hardness that she made no sense. At least, she made no sense to me. But Rorpal of Podia understood what she wanted.

He struck the butt of the spear on the wooden flooring three times. The silence became absolute, except for the evening breeze in the trees and a few dogs howling from the compound where they had been herded during the ceremonies. I noticed particularly, from my already vast experience, that no babies were crying.

"Very well, Mother Mala. Paesi it was, we all agree to that, it is attested."

"It is!"

Rorpal gestured in a way that might have embraced this woman, Mother Mala, the crowds, the fifty youths in their flowery chains, the elders on the verandah — or me — and he banged his spear down again, four times. Abruptly everyone burst into shouts and cheering. But, even then, that cheering struck a somber note, there on the dusty compound of the little village of Podia. I noticed that most of the cheering came from the young men and women mixed in the crowds before the verandah. The fifty bound in flowers remained silent, although everyone looked toward the elders on the verandah.

Then — one of those fifty burst into hysterical shouting. A young man broke the flower chain by a single movement of his hands and ran and ran and so was swept up into the arms of Mother Mala. I saw the girl Paesi, who had found me on the shore, also hugging and kissing both the boy and his mother.

Lamnias passed among the crowds carrying large gourd-shaped vessels of pottery that are sometimes called amphorae, although they are not strictly of that shape or form, for they have a stoppered spout, and their more proper name is holc. They were mounted on wicker carrying baskets upon the men's backs and it was remarkable with what nicety and skill the men could tilt the holc and direct a stream of wine into an outstretched cup without so much as spilling a drop. Fresh wine in fresh goblets was produced for the elders upon the verandah, and I took the goblet offered me. Rorpal of Podia banged his spear butt again, twice and a third time, and the silence fell.

Rorpal lifted his goblet.

Everyone raised their goblets or cups high into the air.

"Let us drink the parting toast!" called Rorpal. "The toast of daeslam! The farewell and the greeting! Daeslam!"

"Daeslam! Daeslam!"

We all drank.

Then, as is the way with Lamnias, everything was over and the people shuffled away. I put the goblet down and looked for the fifty — no, the forty-nine — and saw they were gone from their places.

Only the coiled chains of flowers lay there, abandoned, their petals wilting and losing their color.

One function of the meaning of daeslam, as I knew even then, rather like the vaol-paol, is the end and the beginning, and equally the beginning and the end. But whereas the circle of vaol-paol encompasses all things, daeslam contains a narrower vision connected almost always with a person's fate and destiny.

The Lamnias had summed me up shrewdly.

In the last of the light streaming and mingling from the emerald orb of Genodras, which is called Havil in Havilfar, and the ruby orb of Zim, which is called Far in Havilfar, I saw a small group of men walk from the stockade past the last of the houses and so come out onto the open space before the verandah and the elders and the headman.

I saw their faces, and instinctively my right hand crossed my waist, groping for the hilt of a sword that was not there.

Yes, the Lamnias understood men, even apims, even apims like myself.

The newcomers stood in the opaz radiance, their shadows long upon the packed dust where the feet of the Lamnias had so lately shuffled. I saw those damned faces. Thick black hair, greased and oiled and curled, hung about their evil faces. These beings were not apim. They were of a race of diffs I had not encountered before, and they were beast-men and men-beasts of so forbidding an aspect I truly thought that a Chulik might think twice before offending one of their number.

Low were their brows, low and wide, above flaring nostrils and gape-jawed mouths in which I saw snaggly teeth bared in grins of anticipation. Their eyes were wide spaced, brilliant, yet narrow and cold. These halflings wore armor, scale armor that was as commonplace as any I had seen. They wore close-fitting helmets which I then thought were brass, and only later discovered to be gold over iron. They carried weapons of the fighting-man of Havilfar — thraxter, stux, shield.

Apart from the impression of evil upon their faces, they would not have occasioned in me any further interest outside my usual fascination with the myriads of types and species upon Kregen, but for their tails. I saw at once that these tails were probably their most formidable armament. Long and whiplike, the tails were carried high and arrogantly, curved over the right shoulder. And every tail ended in a razor-sharp curved blade. The glinting light from the twin suns caught the serried blades, upflung on the flaunting tails, and glittered like a field of diamonds.

The faces of diffs are passing strange in the eyes of a man from this Earth. Some are beautiful, some are ugly, some misshapen in our estimation, others quite unremarkable. Yet how difficult it is to say with complete surety that a certain expression upon the face of a man who is not apim — is not a member of Homo sapiens — means exactly what you think it means. I took the gloating faces to portray evil at that moment, and although I was proved right — to my cost! — the assumption was made so rapidly, so much from instinct, that immediately I forced myself to relax and to believe that an alien's face cannot show what a man's face of this Earth would show and necessarily mean the same thing.

Below the scaled corselet each man wore a brilliant scarlet kilt. I stared. I suppose that, too, influenced me, like any onker. The diffs wore the old brave scarlet, the color that had in so many ways become associated so closely with me and mine upon Kregen.

They advanced with a steady step and I saw that they kept in step and to a wedgelike formation. The leader, broad and bulky, wore a multitude of feathers and silks, not on his helmet but about his person. He halted below the verandah and looked up. Once more I had to control myself, to make myself relax. Was I not learning the ways of quietness and peace upon Kregen under Antares?

"Is all ready, Rorpal?"

"All is ready, Notor."

"Then bring them out, you rast, or I'll sink my stux in your belly."

I straightened up at these words, for I understood a little of the thinking behind such uncalled-for insult and arrogance. As I straightened, I felt a hazy qualm or dizziness pass, as though my brain had moved within my skull, fractionally later than I had intended.

So then it was that I understood how easily the Lamnias had read me, how shrewdly they had taken stock of me, and what they had done. I understood now what had transpired here. There was no need for Rorpal of Podia to lean regretfully toward me as I stumbled, and clutched at the railing, and so, stupidly, collapsed to the wooden floor, and for him to say: "We express our deep regret, Horter Prescot. But we are driven by devils. We must send fifty of our youths and our maidens, and the aragorn will welcome you exceedingly in place of Polosi, the son of Mala and sister of Paesi, who found you and so had claim upon you."

Then Rorpal, who had the good of Podia at heart, called to the aragorn leader: "This apim is a great warrior, a Hyr-paktun. In him you will be well pleased."

Then the drug in the wine felled me utterly and Notor Zan engulfed me in blackness.

Two

Delia begins a story

It seemed to me that Delia was telling young Dray, the Strom of Balkash, a story. The Strom of Balkash was the son of Seg Segutorio, Kov of Falinur, and Thelda, the Kovneva. Delia sat curled up in a heaping pile of cushions whose glowing silks and embroideries could not compare in any way with the glory that was my Delia. The story was well loved in Vallia, and Delia, herself, enjoyed the retelling of it.

"Under a certain moon," she began, which is a way of saying *Once upon a time*, "a great and cruel Vad ruled a country and all the people groaned and were unhappy. Now it happened that in that country, at a place where a wooden bridge crossed a stream and silver fishes leaped into your hand, lived a poor man who had a beautiful daughter whose name was Ama of the Shining Hair. It chanced that the great and cruel Vad went a-hunting leem, which had been troubling the ponshos of the people in those parts."

Something tickled me in the ribs and I stirred and moved and then sank back on my cushions to listen to Delia. As for young Dray, who was Seg Segutorio's son, his little face was puckered up in absolute concentration and he was holding all his body tightly with expectation and glee at this marvelous story from this marvelous aunt.

"But one of the ponsho farmers was a young man who could talk to his ponsho-trag and who loved nothing better than to sport all day in the fields with his friend, as you would with your friends. Now this ponsho farmer's name was—"

The nudge in my side was less gentle, far from gentle. It was a positive kick. I rolled over, ready to find out who would thus dare to desecrate the enjoyment of the Prince Majister of Vallia's entranced absorption in a story told by the Princess Majestrix of Vallia, and a thudding kick bounced off my ribs, and a course and unlovely voice roared in my ear.

"Get up, you rast! Yetch! On your feet!"

I opened my eyes.

An aragorn drew his booted foot back ready to drive it into my ribs again. I rolled away, feeling a terrible pain in my gut, and tried to catch that wicked boot. I could not move my hands.

"Nulsh! On your feet!"

The kick landed. I got my feet under me. The pink-lit shadows of the Kregan night lay between the loom of trees, and I heard the susurration of the night wind. My hands were bound.

"You cramph," I said. "I wanted to hear that story."

My voice slurred horribly and I could feel the solid ground going up and down like the deck of a swordship in a gale off the Hoboling islands.

The aragorn brought his whiplike tail around and laid the flat of the curved blade against my head. That thick skull of mine rang as though all the bells in Beng-Kishi sounded off with maniacs at the clapper ropes.

"Get into line or I'll flay your hide off!"

He was genuinely annoyed. The pink moonlight from She of the Veils flowed over his gold-on-iron helmet, scaled armor, and brave scarlet kilt. I could see the vague shadows of Lamnias all about and I could hear the harsh orders to move, and so I understood that no great time had elapsed since Notor Zan had taken me entire. The aragorn were taking the young Lamnias selected for them, and, shrewd in their way, the Lamnias of Podia had saved one of themselves and thrown me in as a prize specimen of a slave.

Under the conjoined forces of the tail-blow on the head and the surgings of the solid earth beneath my feet and the rumblings of my gut, I staggered half a dozen paces beneath the trees. They had had the forethought to bind my wrists with thongs and had carried me out and dumped me among the forty-nine sacrifices.

The thongs were not lesten hide.

I broke them with a single savage surge, twisted, got the aragorn around the throat, and, ducking my head beneath his instinctive slash of the tail-blade, started to choke a little respect into him.

I had no desire to kill him. I was still ensnared in the repression of my savage and intemperate nature; but enough was enough. He garbled and choked trying to yell. Others of the slave-masters came running, and so I threw this specimen at them and turned to dash into the moon-shadowed trees. Oh, yes, I was perfectly resigned to leave them unharmed and to run away. I had some of the most important aspects of my life worked out now; as you would say today, I had my priorities almost right.

Delia would not welcome a dead husband lying rotting beneath the mud of some putrid island of the Shrouded Sea.

But these aragorn were cunning in the ways of man-management. Twining iron links whirred through the air and snagged my arms and legs, brought me down with a crash. Once the thongs had proved useless to hold me, they merely clamped chains upon me. I tested the iron. It would take long and long — if ever — for me to break the weakest link.

After that it was a question of being prodded along the track between the trees. The aragorn I had maltreated took some delight in prodding me with his stux. I clashed my chains at him, but he laughed evilly and avoided the swinging bight and struck me again.

"Leave off, you onker, Reterhan!" The leader strode up, and his anger made of his ugly face a devil's mask very like the face of the Devil of the Ice-Wind who guards the north shore of Gundarlo.

"He attacked me, Notor!"

"When he is sold — when we have golden deldys for him — you may take your own payment, then, Reterhan. Until then, by the Triple Tails of Targ the Un-touchable, you will care for the merchandise as you care for your tail!"

"I obey, Notor." Reterhan shrank back from his lord's anger.

We marched again through the forest, and I guessed we went to another village of the island where more people would be rounded up. I trudged on under the weight of the iron chains until gradually my senses returned and my gut stopped rumbling. I was now ready to pull a few tails.

"That was nobly done, Horter Prescot."

The young Lamnia looked like them all, yellow furred, meek in appearance, slightly built. I could barely envisage him hurling javelins so well as to out-throw some of the other Lamnia youths of Podia.

"These aragorn," I said. "They need to be cleansed."

"Aye, Horter Prescot. But we of Podia are not destined for that great work. We are too few and too weak."

The youngster said his name was Fanal and as we walked along he spoke to me softly, and I answered with a guiding grunt or question. I learned more, then, of the tangled politics of the Shrouded Sea, and of how these aragorn of Sorah wreaked their horrors upon the islands. They were of the race of diffs called Kataki, and they held their tails in especial esteem. I was not surprised at that. I saw the fashion of helmet they wore, close-fitting and smooth, without embellishment or ornament. They could whip their tails about over their shoulders and around their heads, lashing forward in lethal sweeps. They would make interesting antagonists. I wondered why I had not encountered any in the Jikhorkdun, the arena, of Huringa; but Fanal explained that the aragorn took good care that they themselves were not sold into slavery and thus avoided the fate of fighting in the arenas of Hyrklana or Hamal.

The Katakis gave most of the islands a bad time. The Canops, of whom I have told you, had forged themselves into a fighting nation of soldiers to resist them. My estimation of the Canops changed once more. And now I understand a little more of the fear-filled lifestyle of the Lamnias of Podia.

Forced to live as slave-fodder, they had worked out a modus vivendi with the Katakis of Sorah, and with their accustomed Lamnia shrewdness had agreed period by period to supply a stipulated number of slaves, both youths and maidens.

The games I had witnessed sorted out the strongest and fittest young men, and the most beautiful and graceful of the young maidens. But then — and I admit I ricked my lips up in what might have passed as the semblance of a grin — the Lamnias sent as slaves to the aragorn their failures, the least agile young men, the least graceful young women. All the winners, the best athletes, the most beautiful girls, were hidden away out of sight. This made so much sense that I marveled it had not occurred with more frequency, given that those willing to take the risks of fooling aragorn must be shrewd and smart and cunning bargainers.

"And what is to become of you, Fanal, once you are a slave?"

"I do not know." He looked apprehensive, as well he might. "I pray the eye of Lomno-Niarton may never close over me, so that I am spared the Jikhorkdun or the Heavenly Mines."

This Fanal had been a loser, one who had not been able to keep up with his fellows in the races, who had not hurled his javelin as far, had not jumped as agilely, with the consequence unfortunate for him that he had been packed off as slave. I did not envision him coming out well from his experiences as a coy in the arena; as an apprentice he would not, I judged, last long. His reference to the Heavenly Mines I then took to be an oblique way of talking about death. I was wrong in that, as you shall hear, dreadfully wrong, and the word *heavenly* embodied a great deal of that typical Kregan aptitude for mockery and deadly sarcasm.

The gale that had wrought my original destruction had blown itself out and She of the Veils rode free of cloud wrack. The trees swayed gently and the night breeze blew cool. Very soon we were ordered to halt and to wait while the Kataki aragorn went about their business.

"The village of Shinnar," Fanal told me bitterly. "Ochs live there, gentle enough and not overly bright in matters of trade. They supply fifty young people, as do we, every period."

Shortly thereafter we marched on, and the slaves were now a hundred in number. The next village yielded up twenty strong Rapas. I felt a mild surprise, for the Rapas are renowned for — apart from their smell, to which I was by now becoming accustomed — their ferocity and viciousness. But the Kataki aragorn stood no nonsense. I sensed that these Rapas did not come with quite the same willingness as the Lamnias and the Ochs. Maybe there was capital to be gained there...

One of Kregen's lesser moons swung low over the trees as we came out onto the shore where the waves glimmered pink in long, surging lines of foam and the wind blew free.

Again I stared with hungry longing upon the waters, for with a vessel under me and goodly spread of canvas I would be as free as the breeze. But now, quite apart from the Star Lords and the Savanti, the Kataki prevented me from taking ship and departing this sorry little island. Its name was Shanpo, and it was one of a multitude of islands in the Lesser Sharangil Archipelago. It seemed to be more obvious now why the Canops had not settled themselves on some other island grouping when their own land of Canopdrin had been so disastrously destroyed. The Katakis were a people either to avoid or to destroy.

"What happens now, Fanal?"

"We will be taken to Sorah — an evil place!" And he shivered — for the night breeze blew a trifle chill, I admit. "From there we will be sold to whoever will pay the Katakis' price."

There was the thwarted businessman's acumen in that.

The stars now showed through the tattered cloud wrack, brilliant constellations that had become familiar to me over the seasons of my life on Kregen. The Zhantil and Sword; the Leem and Shishi; Onglolo; the Headless Risslaca; many more, twinkling away up there with a fine disregard of me and my problems. Of them all, the Zhantil and Sword meant the most, for I was as sure as I could be — and still I am quite certain — that in this fabulous constellation glittered the star that is the sun of my planet of birth, our old Earth.

Perhaps old Sol is not visible at all from Kregen. But I prefer to believe it is, and that it twinkles there at the tip of the sword in the claws of the Zhantil's right paw.

The Shrouded Sea is named not out of mere fancy, and the horizon mist was enough to blot out a great part of the constellation of the Zhantil and Sword, for it is visible north and south, according to season. And so, looking up, I glimpsed the bulk of an airboat drifting among the stars, a tiny mobile constellation of its own.

Instantly every nerve in my body told me that aloft there, in that voller, flew Delia and my friends. They had to be there! I gazed up and the little grouping of lights swung lower. Others had seen the flier, and with harsh orders the Katakis beat us back to the treeline. I mused on this even as I ran in my chains. So the Katakis were wary enough of fliers to take these precautions!

My immediate reaction of resistance was speedily overcome as the chains were hauled up, I tripped and, helpless, fell off balance, to be dragged through the sand and shells and scrub and gorse into the trees.

With a curse I clawed my way up and stared into the sky.

The flier dropped lower, swinging toward us, so that the lines of her illuminated ports disappeared and only the fore lights showed. She dipped. The breeze had now sunk to a mere whisper in the leaves. I could hear the hoarse breathing of men and women all about me — men and women! — even if I was the only apim there.

"Absolute quiet!" The voice of the Notor cut into the silence, like a risslaca hiss.

At my side I felt Fanal go rigid with fear of the lash.

The flier swung down. I stood up. I shouted.

"Delia! Seg! Inch! Down here! There are foemen—"

That nurdling cramph Reterhan hit me then. He laid the flat of his tail-blade against my head and, although I broke most of its force with my arm, the thing smashed into my temple with force enough to admit the near presence of the Notor Zan and his blackness. I had been so intent on putting a quarterdeck bellow into my voice, as I would hail the fore-top of a squally night, that I had broken one of my own cardinal rules. It nearly broke my arm, too. I went over sideways and lay for a moment on the sandy grass, cursing my own folly.

By the time they dragged me to my feet and the procession of slaves started up again, the flier had gone.

Either she had not been the flier with Delia aboard, or my people had not heard me.

I was as sure as I could be about anything that had she been our flier, my people could not have heard me, for if they had they would have been here by now, with longbows flashing and swords chunking.

For the rest of that miserable night we lay confined in the next fishing village. Its inhabitants had been turned out for us. They were apim, but small and meek; their fishing boats were simple open affairs, the fishing grounds no more than a league offshore, and I felt — with no emotions I could feel ashamed of — that they would have difficulty in actually killing their catch. The Katakis took a few slaves from here, a few of the young girls; the rest were sent to spend the night as best they might on the beach. This, to me, exemplified the aragorn's contempt for them.

The crockery of the villagers was pressed into use and we were fed a thin fish gruel. As you know, I am not enamored of fish, but I forced myself to eat the revolting stuff, for like any sensible fighting-man I eat when I can against the certain privations in store in the future. There were no palines, which was an affront, but we got the word that there might be squishes in the morning — if we behaved ourselves.

The morning came with the twin Suns of Scorpio rising out of the Shrouded Sea wreathed in a flamboyant mantle of green, gold, and orange. We sat upon the packed dirt of the village square, yawning and knuckling our eyes. Everyone was thonged up, one to another; I wore the iron chains. More fish gruel was followed by a muttering clamor among the slaves.

"Where are the squishes? Where is some bread?" The new slaves were distinctly upset and, this early in their slave careers, annoyed. "We cannot live on this fish—"

The Katakis went about with their whips, right merrily, and soon no one was asking where the promised squishes were.

I confess I looked on my fellow prisoners with not a little superiority — foolish, I know, but understandable. They were just beginning the life of slaves. I had been a slave many and many a time, high and low, pampered and flogged, as stylor and as miner. They would find out. Slavery is an evil, and I grew every season more and more sure that the reason I had been brought to Kregen was to stamp out that evil. I was only partly right in that, as you shall hear if these tapes last out...

An aragorn ran into the square yelling and waving his arms. Instantly the square was filled with the sounds of blows and yells as the Katakis whipped and bludgeoned the slaves out of sight. A string of calsanys was prodded beneath the long verandah of the headman's house, and, being calsanys, they did what calsanys always do when upset.

It was now clear with the daylight that there were more Katakis than those who had brought us in, and there were more slaves. This miserable village had been taken over and was being used as an entrepôt for slaves, a barracoon on a grand scale. Katakis armed with crossbows ran across the square. Reterhan came rushing toward us, his tail high, its curved blade glinting in the suns. He carried a long strip of cloth.

In all the hustle and bustle I saw what was being done.

The village was being returned to its original innocent state. Not a Kataki in sight. Not a calsany that would look out of place. Not a weapon. All the fish-gruel bowls were collected and dumped into the nearest hut. Soon — in mere murs only — the village lay under the rising suns looking like just another poverty-stricken fishing village.

I looked up.

A flier cruised into sight.

I recognized her. I had seen her first in the arena of the Jikhorkdun in Huringa, when I had fought the boloth. Her decks were crowded with people. I would have known who those people were anywhere. And I would have known the flags that fluttered from her masts — every flag the scarlet field with the yellow cross. Old Superb! My flag! Oh, yes, my heart leaped when I saw that voller come flying so serenely over the fishing village.

Then Reterhan and a comrade wrapped the length of cloth about my mouth, ramming a chunk of wood between my lips so that my teeth grated, and knotted it tightly behind my head.

They did not wish to knock me out, for we would be marching soon. I thought that — fool that I was!

"Silence!" The Kataki Notor waved his tail-blade to impress on us the seriousness of the moment. "Absolute silence, all you rasts! I'll hang and jerk the first of you who cries out!"

I wondered if he would do that, for a slave with crippled arms is scarcely a salable commodity. But it impressed the cowed Lamnias, and Ochs, and Rapas.

Reterhan leered at me, his face filled with an evil I now recognized as being a true reflection of his evil mind.

"Lem rot you, apim! You may watch and suffer, but you cannot cry out!"

Now I understood exactly what ghastly scene was to be enacted here. Lines of Kataki crossbowmen leveled their weapons. They knelt under the cover of houses, in fishing-net sheds, behind walls. They would be invisible from the air. The voller ghosted down, her flags brilliant in the morning suns-glow, and descended to a landing in the village where the hard-packed dust made a descent inviting. Delia, Inch, Seg, and the others were looking for me, and they were searching here.

But when they touched down they would be deluged with a sudden, treacherous sleeting of crossbow bolts. Those who survived would be swept up as slaves. All my friends — so soon to be murdered or enslaved!

And I was bound and helpless in iron chains, gagged so that I could not cry out a warning!

Three

Of the pulling of a Kataki tail

The flier was in truth a magnificent vessel. She moved with a sure steady grace over the village huts, and her people were hanging overside and staring down, and some of them waving...

The iron chains about me bit into my flesh as my muscles bulged. Futile! I tried to gnaw through the wooden chunk in my mouth; but the wood was balass and I merely bit down with teeth-crunching agony. I writhed about in the violence of my movements and the iron chains clanked.

Reterhan looked most evilly upon me, and placed his foot on my neck, and pressed. Sparks darted and flashed before my eyes; but they were clear enough to see the flier turning, the scarlet and yellow flags dropping to their flagstaffs now as way came off. I stared. Then I dragged my gaze away.

The flier had to be warned.

Vangar ti Valkanium, as the flier Hikdar, was bringing her in smoothly and gently, a perfect landing approach. Those people up there would see below them merely a sleepy, poor and innocent fishing village, with precious few people about at this time of morning.

They would not expect serried lines of crossbowmen.

Here in the continent of Havilfar, south of the equator, we were far from our homes in Vallia and Valka. But Havilfar was accounted the most progressive, the most modern, of the four continents that made up this grouping upon the face of the planet. Around the shores of the Shrouded Sea men had settled here first, long ago, and in the tumbled ruins of long-forgotten empires, in the artificial features of the landscape, in the admixtures of blood within the different species and races, were to be seen clear evidence of that long history of civilization here.

Seg, that wild and reckless bowman of Erthyrdrin, was up there in the flier. He and I had fought our way through the Hostile Territories. He would never in ordinary circumstances be taken unawares in ambush. Likewise Inch, that seven-foot-tall ax-man from Ng'groga so obsessed with his taboos, and I had battled through adventures. He, too, was a seasoned campaigner.

And — and up there on the high quarterdeck stood Delia, my Delia of Delphond!

At any moment now the voller would touch down. And then the cruel steel-tipped bolts would flash in a raining cloud of destruction.

Reterhan's foot pressed with jovial power upon my neck.

Up in the flier was Korf Aighos, the leader of the rascally but loyal Blue Mountain Boys. Up there was Turko the Shield, that superbly muscled Khamorro of the magical murdering hands; but I felt his great shield would offer some protection, and I prayed Zair he would slap it across before Delia when the bolts whickered in. Tom ti Vulheim and his Valkan Archers were there, ready to be cut down before they could draw bow. Obquam of Tajkent, the flying Strom, would be there, and I longed for his slender powerful form to flash out on his narrow wings to scout this innocent-seeming deathtrap.

Also, up there in the voller, were those new friends who had saved me in the arena by their selfless devotion: Naghan the Gnat, armorer superb; Balass the Hawk, who had earned the distinction of becoming a hyr-kaidur, Tilly, my little golden-furred Fristle fifi; and Oby, that young rascal who had aspired to greatness in the arena, but had had his dreams shattered, to be replaced by a vision of a greater future — and who must, I suspected, figure in the shadowy schemes of the Star Lords.

All of them might in the next few murs be lying dead, pierced through and through with arbalest quarrels. Or they might be staggering up to be chained as was I and be carried off into slavery.

Oh, Delia, my Delia!

I rolled my eyes at the Lamnia youth, Fanal. He saw me looking at him. I could not cry out. But he could. He could warn the airboat. Across my face that old evil look of power and arrogance passed, and my eyes glared with a mad berserker brilliance, so that he flinched away. But he turned his head, and would not look at me, and he did not cry out a warning.

No one would shout voluntarily.

So I must do something horrible.

Reterhan's foot slid from my neck as I squirmed. I got my linked chains up and swung the small bight they had allowed me, and so snared that curved blade mounted at the end of his whiplike tail.

Metal splines ran down from the blade to give stiffening and protection to the end two feet of tail.

The chains snagged beneath the blade where it curved from its socket I rolled and lurched and staggered up and I pulled.

I pulled Reterhan's tail.

It was not a gentle pull. It was a savage, barbaric sinew-and-muscle-bursting jerk.

Reterhan yelled.

He could not stop himself.

The Kataki opened his mouth and yelled blue bloody murder.

His shout of agony bellowed across the open space.

I was not content.

Circling, I twisted the tail about me and jerked again with utmost vicious force. The Kataki leaped and toppled toward me, and I truly think had he not done so I would have wrenched his tail out all bloody by its roots.

His agonized screaming knifed through the air where the mingled streaming light of the Suns of Scorpio threw twin shadows of the flier across the packed dirt.

The chains so cunningly bighted around by ankles and knees would not allow me to walk, let alone run, and that stumbling circle was the only progress I could make. I fell to the dirt and tried to roll myself like a barrel of cheap dopa out into the cleared area. A warning! My brain blazed with the single desire to warn my comrades in the voller.

The rolling did not get me far, but it saved my life, for two crossbow bolts sizzled into the earth, gouting clods, where I had been.

Covered in sweat and caked dirt I dragged in a lungful of breath and glared at Reterhan, who was crouching up, his left hand clamped bone-white across his mouth, his right hand feeling his injured tail. He was in no position to hit me again for some time.

The flier halted its descent. It hovered a dozen feet above the open space.

The rows of heads that had been showing over the bulwarks had all vanished, and I heaved a great gasp of relief. Those men of mine up there were alerted! They would not know what was going on down here, but now they would not come down meekly to be massacred and enslaved.

I had expected a sheeting storm of crossbow bolts to rise toward the flier, and I was confident enough in her armoring to know it would take more than a hand-held arbalest to drive through. A good-sized varter would be needed, and the Katakis, as far as I knew, did not dispose of varters here.

But this Kataki Notor was a cunning lord. He also held his men under a strong controlling rein, for he had not given the order to shoot, and so no one loosed.

No one shot at me, either, so I guessed the Notor had a scheme afoot.

I saw him giving swift orders; then he divested himself of his war-gear. Off came the scaled tunic, the greaves, the close-fitting helmet. His thraxter and stuxes were grasped by an attendant. Two more worked rapidly on his tail and soon they unstrapped that wicked curved blade.

The Notor snatched up a net-needle and its spool of thread from a draping net by a wall. Clad only in his breechclout — that scarlet kilt! — he walked slowly, bent over and shuffling, into the central plaza. He shaded his eyes and looked up.

"You are most welcome, whoever you are!" he called up. "We are but a small village and poor. We have nothing for aragorn to plunder or for slave-masters to covet, for all our strong young men and beautiful girls are gone in the plague."

Reterhan was still totally absorbed in his concern for his tail, but his comrade stifled a little gust of merriment at his Notor's words.

I felt the chill of despair.

Vangar ti Valkanium leaned over the quarterdeck rail and bellowed.

"We wish you no harm, old man. The plague, you say?"

"The dropping sickness and the purple buboes. It is a visitation from Chezragon-Kranak for our sins, though we know not how we have offended the Great Ones."

I'll give this evil Kataki lord his due; he made a convincing liar.

"We will come and assist you, old man," yelled down Vangar. "We have medicines—"

I was on tenterhooks.

The Notor waved his tail, all innocent and naked as it was.

"I thank you, Notor, but we are few and the sickness passes."

Some further conception came to me then of the way these Kataki aragorn operated. The Notor could see the crowded decks and the glitter of weapons, he could see the varters ranked along the broadsides, all fully manned. He could not fail to understand that this flier and these men were a most formidable opposition. All surprise had been lost. A shower of crossbow bolts now would do little damage, and then the varters would loose and the return arrows would come in...

To give him his due, he preferred to go around terrorizing the villages and taking plunder and slaves without trouble. Much though the Katakis liked a fight, they would not fight if the odds were against them. There was no profit in tangling with this powerful adversary — or so I read his thoughts.

"You're sure you do not require assistance?"

That was Seg Segutorio, leaning over the rail, his black hair brilliant in the suns-glow.

"We do not, Notor."

An incredibly tall figure with waist-length yellow hair stood beside Seg. Inch lifted his battle-ax.

"You have food? Wine? Can we not help you, old man?"

"I thank you, Notor. But we have what little we need."

And then Delia stood on the quarterdeck. I could stare up and see her, there, above my head, leaning over the rail, radiant, glorious in her beauty, the true princess of an island empire, and yet, as I well knew, so softly firm and tender and filled with love for me and for our twins.

"Have you seen a man washed up from the sea?" She called down. "A man—" She paused then, and whether it was sob or laugh I did not know. "A strange man with brown hair and brown eyes, with shoulders that — with broad shoulders — a man of power, a man with an aura. Have you seen such a man — who would be very violent, I am afraid, if you or anyone tried to maltreat him."

"Is this man a Hyr-notor, my lady?"

"Oh, yes, and a great villain besides. He is my husband and I search the Shrouded Sea for him—"

"I have seen no man as you describe, my lady."

I was writhing in my chains and trying to break the iron links, trying to roll out into the open, trying — oh, trying to send my passionate thoughts winging from my mind into the mind of my beloved as she stood above me, looking down, her lovely face troubled and darkly shadowed by her grief — her grief for me!

Reterhan had assured himself his tail was still attached to him. He stood up in the shadow of the huts and the trees, and he strutted toward me, holding his tail in his left hand.

So close! So near at hand were my friends, just a tiny distance away! That just one of them might see me! I rolled and clashed my chains and Reterhan stood over me, his greave-clad legs wide-spread. He took out his thraxter. If I was to die now, then in what a fashion I was to go! This was no way that my Anglo-Saxon forebears would relish as dying well. I rolled onto my back and glared up murderously. The gag stifled me. I saw Reterhan lift the thraxter and I saw his wrist turn so as to bring the flat alongside my head.

The twin suns of Kregen and the seven moons all spurted up and were gobbled down into the blackness of Notor Zan.

The last thing I saw was the glorious and divine face of my Delia as she stared out, so woefully troubled, over the quarterdeck rail.

If I was to go down into the great darkness and find my way to the Ice Floes of Sicce, then I would take with me that last look of longing that contained all of love. So I fell into the blackness, and the darkness was irradiated for me by Delia, Delia of Delphond, Delia of the Blue Mountains.

Four

The ways of the aragorn

I, Dray Prescot, Krozair of Zy and Lord of Strombor — and much else besides — came back to consciousness sluggishly packed among my fellow slaves in an open flier. The stink and the groans and the shrieks were all familiar to me, not from this Earth but from Kregen, and I knew I must endure. I was still alive, which surprised me only a little, for slaves equate with money. We were worth many golden deldys and silver sinvers almost anywhere in Havilfar.

A dead Och lay at my side, his four little arms shriveled and wrapped around his wasted body.

The flier remained firm and solid in the sky with that peculiar way of a certain kind of voller which travels independently of the wind, and there was no pitching and rolling to add to our discomfort. The flier was of that kind I was to come to know well later, but which until then I had not encountered. She was long and wide in the beam, but shallow, being open and without a deck. A tiny cabin had been perched amidships to house the controls and crew. The slaves lay jammed like logs. They call these barge-like vollers *weyvers* in Havilfar, and sometimes they refer to them as Quoffas of the Sky. They are designed simply to cram as much cargo as possible into a flat space, without niceties of careful loading in tiers. The slaves were mere lumber.

Fanal lay miserably at my other side.

He would not meet my eye when I stirred.

He understood what I had asked of him, back there in the fishing village, and he had failed. I could not blame him. All men are not built in the same way, and Kregen, let alone the Earth of my birth, would be a strange place if all men were alike. And as for all women...!

Presently he said in a whisper, "I am glad you are not dead, Horter Prescot."

"What happened to the flier?"

"The Kataki Notor convinced them he was a harmless old fishing man, who needed no assistance with the plague. They flew away."

They flew away.

Well. It was a disappointment, but also it was a relief. I had, in the instant of awakening, been horrified that I would turn and see my people, my Delia, wrapped in chains and thongs and wedged in among the mass of slaves.

"The flier flew well?"

"I have not seen many vollers. She flew low away to the west, as though she were searching for this Hyr-notor — this man with the yrium — of which the lady apim spoke."

He looked at me then, a real Lamnia look, shrewd, sizing me up anew.

"You are the man they sought, Horter Prescot?"

"Yes, Horter Fanal. I am the man."

"I think perhaps if the aragorn realize this they will sell you for ransom."

"It would be paid," I said. I did not boast. I knew what I knew. To my shame, I knew that the coffers of Valka and Can-thirda, of Zamra and Delphond and the Blue Mountains, would pour forth gold and jewels and treasures if by those means my Delia could once more clasp me in her arms.

And if they were not enough, then Seg's Falinur and Inch's Black Mountains would bring more gold and jewels. And, if necessary, Delia would go to Strombor, my enclave in Zenicce, aye! and to the Clansmen of Felschraung and Longuelm to take of their treasures for my release.

These thoughts brought me no elation. I knew that the treasure of a country is not bought without sweat and blood and the labors of the working people who are the real originators of wealth. The comfort was that I could perhaps give of myself in after days so that my people, and my friends' people, could quickly recoup their losses and once more live comfortable lives, as I wished.

No mention of ransom was made then or thereafter, and maybe the aragorn of Sorah had no real belief in it, not recking of lands so far away across the equator as Vallia and Valka, of which they had barely heard.

Sorah itself was a large and prosperous island of the Shrouded Sea. Canopdrin lay not too far to the north. The weyver touched down inside the cleared central area of a vast barracoon, and we were herded out and given more revolting fish gruel. Then after washing in water lightly sprinkled with vinegar, our hair was cropped, and, stark naked, we were prodded into lenk-wood cages.

There was much shouting and cursing and belaboring with balass sticks. The Kataki also used their tails upon us most vilely, but in all this brutality they were careful not to mark or cut too severely the merchandise by which they made their evil living.

Rumors swept the barracoon as was to be expected.

A Rapa said positively that he would slit his throat with a sharpened flint before he would go to the Jikhorkdun of Hamal or Hyrklana. He refused to discuss the possibility of being sold into the Heavenly Mines or the pearl fisheries of Tancrophor.

The women were segregated; they would be sorted out into classes so that they might be sold to the best advantage. The men were also sorted, and here I parted with Fanal of Podia. He kept himself cheered by the thought that he might end up as a stylor or perhaps a steward upon an important estate.

The art of reading and writing had once before brought me an easier task among slaves;[7] but here in Havilfar the art was much more common. If I was sent to the Jikhorkdun of Hamal life might be interesting. There are many arenas in the Empire of Hamal, and there is more than one in the realm of Hyrklana. If I was sold as a coy to the Jikhorkdun of Huringa I scarcely relished what Queen Fahia would do. Had I not contemptuously tossed the bloody tail of the silver-collared leem in her face? Had I not shamed her in the arena before all her people, and, at the end, had I not slain the boloth and escaped? Queen Fahia and her neemus would be overjoyed to see me back in the Jikhorkdun.

So it was that as the rumors swept the packed barracoon I determined that I would not be sold back to the amphitheater in Huringa, the capital city of Hyrklana, to be fresh sport for that foolish, fat, and yet nasty little Queen Fahia.

Bunches of slaves were taken out from time to time to be oiled and cleaned up and paraded for prospective buyers.

Sorah is a large island and her slave pens are notorious. The aragorn do a good trade. They charge high prices for their merchandise and traders come from all over Havilfar.

A group of Shaslins was herded out one morning after fish gruel. They were just about the only people there who relished the foul stuff, for the Shaslins are a sea-people; they look not unlike what some wild mating of a human with a seal might produce, with their sleek streamlined heads, their sloping shoulders, and their arms and hands, legs and feet, beautifully adapted for swimming and diving. Their pelts gleamed in the sunlight, for the food was good for them. But they set up a tremendous racket, screaming and shrieking, and had to be dragged out to the waiting fliers of their buyers.

"They have been sold to Tancrophor and will dive until they die in the pearl fisheries."

The man who spoke to me, a Brokelsh, looked as annoyed as any slave has a right to be. His dark body bristles stiffened.

"But they are a fishing folk," I said, somewhat unwisely.

"Aye! The Shaslins can swim well. But the devils of Tancrophor drive them to their limits, and they cough blood and their heads split with the ringing of the bells of Beng-Kishi. I am glad I do not go to the pearl fisheries of Tancrophor."

This Brokelsh was sold with others to a Notor who owned many kools of land in Methydria. Other slaves were sold, and then it was my turn. I spent less than a day in the Sorah barracoon and I took no pride from the price I brought. I had taken one simple precaution during the ritual questioning of my abilities. I lied. I said I knew nothing of swords and battles and fighting, and whether or not the record-keeping Kataki believed me, I do not know. But he sold me to an agent from Hamal buying workers for the Heavenly Mines.

You have probably heard it said more than once that if you can keep your head when others all around you are losing theirs, then maybe you do not fully understand the situation.

There were two brothers, two apims, fine young men with strong shoulders and sinewy backs. When the understanding hit them that they were sold to the Heavenly Mines, they looked into each other's eyes and, with a previous arrangement clearly agreed between them, placed their hands on each other's throats. The two brothers stood there, facing each other, gazing one at the other in brotherly love, and choked each other to death. Guards bustled through with their balass sticks lashing and dragged the two apart. The finger-marks glared lividly upon their throats. One of the brothers was dead. The other was revived, and when he realized what had happened he sat in a ball, his hands over his head, crooning. He had become insane, and if I thought that would disqualify him from laboring in the mines of Hamal I was mistaken. This young man, Agilis, was taken out with the rest of us to the waiting fliers.

Many of us fought. The guards brought their balass sticks down viciously now, now that we were sold. I kept a wary lookout for Reterhan, but I did not see him — luckily for him.

"Treat them carefully, you onkers!" The agent from Hamal, a Rapa, screeched at the Kataki guards, and he tried to protect his merchandise without letting them beat him over the head. I joined in. After all, I knew the outcome of this; the slaves would be battered into submission and be dragged aboard the fliers. But I admit I wanted to get in a few whacks before that.

A surprised Kataki felt his tail pulled, and as he swung toward me, roaring, I took the balass stick away and clouted him over the head with it. Then I jumped into the melee.

Well, foolish as I was then, and stark stupid as I am now if I still recall some pleasure in laying about me at those evil Kataki faces, I feel only a little shame in saying that I enjoyed thwacking that long ebony stick down and stretching a few of the aragorn senseless.

We fought in a small enclosure at the side of the main barracoon, with a lenk-wood fence beyond. The gates were closed and the fliers from Hamal waited, hovering, to pick us up. The thought of escape flashed across my mind with con-siderable shock. At once I began to fight in earnest, bashing now with intent and working my way through to the nearest flier. But, as I have said, the Kataki are good man-managers, like so many of the aragorn and slave-masters I have met on Kregen.

At a raucous shout the fliers lifted out of reach, and reinforcements of Katakis pounded into the small enclave. They must have gone through this scene or similar scenes a hundred times. I guessed they did not bother to practice a de-ception on the slaves and tell them nothing of their destination because they wished to enjoy the sufferings and anticipatory horror of the slaves. I saw at last that any further joyous slashing and bashing would get nowhere and so I tripped a Kataki, kicked him in the belly, hurdled his screeching form, and dived into the safe shadows by the lenk fence.

When it was all over I walked out, unruffled.

I, Dray Prescot, had stood calmly and watched a fight going on and made no further effort to interfere — and that, mark you, a fight between slaves and ara-gorn! Truly, I was either growing old and stupid or old and wise. It is my experience that being a father is a wonderfully sobering device.

I most certainly did not bother to observe the fantamyrrh as I stepped aboard the Hamalian slave flier. I fancied I'd let the rasts take whatever sorrow their pan-theon of gods and devils might care to hand out.

The flier was a simple, practical, no-nonsense vessel with ample capacity be-low decks for slaves and with enough armament above decks to repel any expected normal attack by volroks or laccapins or volleem, or any combination of flying mount and rider. I understood that the free-flying brethren of the air, the flutsmen, might well be operating in the vicinity, for there had been unrest around the Shrouded Sea; the flutsmen, the mercenaries of the skies, had been called in by more than one worried ruler.

The slaves slumped down on the low tween-decks, a thoroughly subdued lot. Their terror remained, for they had heard lurid stories of the Heavenly Mines of Hamal, although when I asked more probing questions it soon turned out all the information anyone had was mere hearsay, mere rumor circulating and magni-fied. There was one very good reason why information of this monstrous kind should be by hearsay only; and this will become all too apparent as I speak to you. So the slaves lay moaning and groaning and nursing their bruises and bumped heads as we flew on north-northeast over the Shrouded Sea.

The flier carried a fair-sized crew of slavers, men of a number of different races. We were given water to drink, chunks of bread — which the first mouth-ful told me had been baked from dilse, that almost useless yet common cereal — and thin, stringy strips of vosk. Again there were no palines, although there was a small supply of overripe malsidges, those melon-sized, somewhat tart fruits that, at the very least, keep the scurvy off a man. We were thrown sections of the malsidges and we scrabbled for them as they flew among us, and I, at least, sank my teeth into the sharp pulpy flesh with its flushed green color, eating right down to the brown and wrinkled skin.

The journey from the island of Sorah to the Heavenly Mines of Hamal is about three hundred and fifty dwaburs. I calculated roughly that the speed of the voller could not be above ten db — that is, ten dwaburs per bur. So we could expect to reach our destination in something like twenty-four or so Terrestrial hours. I settled down to a patient negation of everything outside me, willing to start more trouble when we reached these notorious mines.

The only incident of any interest occurred after we had crossed the coast up toward Methydria and could see in the far distance on our larboard side the hazy snowglint of a giant range of mountains. Two rofers appeared above us, beating through the air with massive strokes of their enormous wings, their necks outstretched. The flying animals, sailing past, looked calm and majestic, and we could see that each carried seating for a family of Fristles, six or so, with the little ones perched high at junction of neck and body craning over to look at us.

Although the root syllable *flut* does not appear in its name, the rofer is a kind of bird. Not so the tyryvols which, with their riders brandishing welcoming tridents, surrounded us as we settled into a gigantic basin in the foothills. These tyryvols are large flying animals, with whip tails, wicked, intelligent eyes, and bodies clad in flexible scales that evolution has not yet changed into feathers; although their wings — given another few million years or so — will sprout true feathers, I shouldn't wonder. They come in different colorations, although the most favored color chosen by the aerial riders of Hamal is a lustrous mottle of black and ocher, with scarlet claws and bands of multicolored scales around their necks. They impressed me, these tyryvols, who had seen impiters and corths of the Hostile Territories, not to mention fluttrells and mirvols of Havilfar.

Their riders were short squat diffs with thin bandy legs. Their faces reminded me of the Ullars of Ullardrin of Northern Turismond, although there was none of that indigo dyed hair. There was, however, the same savagery about the square clamp of their mouths. At this time they habitually wore black and ocher scaled clothing made from the skins of the tyryvols, and they carried those damnably sharp tridents, and the thin flexible sword of the aerial fighter. These are the Gerawin of Gilarna the Barren in the Empire of Hamal. They proved to be immensely efficient guards and watchdogs over the Heavenly Mines for the Hamalese.

Around us stretched the barrens. The foothills trended up steadily toward the west and northwest. The task of escape from the mines on foot would be a daunting enterprise and one not to be considered without many days' food and water and, inevitably, a weapon of defense against the frightful dangers infesting all such spots.

The Hamalese are an efficient people. The dominant species happens to be apim; but the many species of diffs take a full part in government, industry, commerce, and all the other branches of activity that make up a thriving empire. Hamal was an ambitious and outwardly thrusting empire. They made airboats and sold them to Vallia and Zenicce and other favored customers, although they would not sell to Pandahem or Loh. That efficiency took us in, cleansed and fed us, and let us rest for a space. Then we were issued picks and shovels. An example was made of a Gon who wanted to shave his hair and so made trouble; the cold, calculating discipline administered to him chilled all the slaves' blood, and then that harsh impersonal discipline, that massive adherence to law and order, imposed its full weight on us. We marched down to the mines and went through the artificially illuminated passageways cut in the rock, and so came out to a vast and echoing space in the mountain. Here we set to work to hack the rock away and fill baskets with the broken stuff. The baskets were drawn on a track by calsanys, to the opening where crushers and refiners went to work, powered by the arms and backs of slaves.

That efficiency saw that every slave worked to the uttermost of his strength. Everything was regulated down to the last drop of water. Rock was cut, drawn out, crushed, refined, and parceled up into fliers to be sent somewhere in Hamal of which we had no knowledge then.

The whole process was inhuman.

The last ounce of effort was taken from every slave.

It was possible to survive, for I saw old men still laboring away, although the turnover was rapid, for the labor simply wore a man down until he saw no good reason to go on living. Absolute inhumanity reigned here. Work — slaving work — filled every day. Rest periods were calculated out with a nicety that allowed a man to recuperate just enough energy to return with his shift to work the next time around.

By comparison, the Black Marble Quarries of Zenicce, in which I'd spent some time, seemed to have been run by amateurs.

Order, law, discipline, rule. The lash, starvation, deprivation of water so that thirst tore a man's spirit and made of him a tool in the hands of the Hamalese, all these things conspired together to make of the Heavenly Mines a place that proved Agilis knew what he was doing when he strangled his brother and would have allowed his brother to strangle him in return...

So I entered another period of my varied life on Kregen that, even now, fills me with a most profound horror, a revulsion of spirit that brought me face to face with the man I thought I was, the man Dray Prescot, shorn of all titles and petty ranks and symbols. It was just me, Dray Prescot, pitted against inhuman will and discipline.

I knew only one thing.

I would not give in.

Five

The Heavenly Mines

Everything had a number.

Every pickax carried its number burned into the haft and punched into the ax. Every shovel carried its number burned and cut. Every drinking bowl. Every spoon. Every eating bowl. A number was branded on the hide of every calsany. Each tunnel, each chamber, each working face, every one possessed its own number.

We slept in rock shelters set against an old and abandoned cut's side. Each rock hut had a number painted above the open door, which was provided with no blanket or hide. We slept on packed earth and each little space had a number scribed in the earth. We each possessed a single thin blanket, and this miserable covering had its number also.

And, as was inevitable, every slave had his own number.

Dray Prescot scarcely existed any longer.

The slave, number 8281, stood in his stead.

The number was branded on my chest and on my back for all to see.

The Hamalese used the common Kregish numbering and in normal times that linear script form is most beautiful. Here they had adopted the square and blocky numerology, so that my chest and back shouted aloud to the indifferent world that I was 8281.

The weird distortion of reality that must take place in surroundings of this nature and under psychological pressures so matter-of-fact and ingrained caught me up, so that I became completely habituated to think of myself as 8281. Whereas I might have taken violently against the number, instead I embraced it. For the number was me. I was the number. Eight-two-eight-one was Dray Prescot. Eight-two-eight-one existed.

By thus rushing forward and embracing my numerical alter ego I was able to dissociate myself from the almost psychotic anger of some of my fellows, who would not answer to their numbers until beaten, who refused to think of themselves as a number because of the lessening of simple human dignity.

I knew a little about human dignity; but I wished to survive.

I had witnessed the punishment of the Gon who wanted his head to be shaved, as is the fashion of Gons, through what I consider to be a foolish matter of shame over their white hair. He was not thrashed unmercifully, for the Hamalese guards and overseers had nothing written down in their laws and rules about mercy. He was simply punished as the law ordained for refusing to do his quota of work. The summary court which sat on the matter dismissed his reasons as untenable.

He was beaten with the regulation number of strokes each day he refused to work. Everything was carried out with the punctilio and observance of the law that I had seen so many times aboard a King's Ship, when a hand was triced up to the gratings and given a red-checked shirt at the gangway. His crime placed him into most serious jeopardy, so that it was lawful to jikaider him, that is, flog criss-cross.

After he had been flogged jikaider for the regulation fifty lashes he would be cut down and then the medical men would see to him, as was required by law. His back would be doctored and the medic would pronounce him unfit to work for the period his back would take to heal. Then, when he refused to work again, he would be jikaidered again.

This went on until he died.

And when he died that long and flowing white hair of the typical Gon glittered silver and brave in the dying light of the suns.

He had been number 8279, and that was how I remembered him.

I lost count of the days, and that alarmed me. But the apathy of work and of numbers held me in a grip I could not break. Fresh fliers brought fresh slaves. A Bleg came into our hut with the numbers 8279 branded on his breast and back over the atrophied carapace, and I shook my head and called him that, although I did not forget the Gon.

The question of what was mined here teased me at the beginning; but gradually I grew indifferent. The mountains existed. We must chop them down and break them up and shovel them into the wicker baskets, they would be carried to the chaldrons, and the calsanys would draw them out to the crushers. The refiners, powered by a sickly green stream flowing over a bluff and falling into a scummy pool, rich in minerals, would do their work; then what was left over would be packed in wooden crates, lined with leather, and loaded aboard fliers. When the quota dropped, the law permitted an increase in working burs. A bur is forty Earth minutes long. It grew so that at the face a bur seemed to stretch to a Terrestrial hour. And still I had no idea what the refined rock was needed for, what the Hamalese, Zair rot 'em, did with it, why they forced this agony on fellow human beings.

The tailings stretched for dwaburs along the base of the foothills, ulm after ulm of them, spreading a powdery and ashlike detritus. What the refiners did, what sort of rock this was, what was taken from it — all these things I did not know and gradually came not to care about.

Early on I had said to a man, an apim, laboring alongside me, "What do they want the rock for, dom?"

"I do not know," he had said, bashing his pick so that chips flew. "I only wish I could choke the rasts with it."

"Amen to that," I said, striking with my pick.

No one knew.

Every day we labored. There were no rest days.

The knowledge that if I did not escape soon I might forget that escape existed drove me on. While loading the fliers one day — for the Hamalese rotated tasks according to their rules — a man was discovered secreted in one of the leather-lined wooden boxes. Where guards of other peoples perhaps would have had sport with him — for example, taking him aloft so that he thought he was escaping, and then pitching him overboard; or weighing the box and declaring it was short-weight and so pouring rock upon him until he was crushed — the guards at the Heavenly Mines acted strictly according to the law.

The Hamalians — or Hamalese, either term is quite correct — took him in chains to a summary court, where he was found guilty — for he was certainly that, having tried to escape — and sentenced to the prescribed punishment.

There are always sedentary jobs to be done in a mining complex like this, work that can be performed quite well by a man who cannot walk, by a man, say, who has no legs.

They found him that employment. The law had no wish for extra severity and would not take his life. Slaves of quality were hard to come by in great quantity, and would not be wasted, only refuse being sent as victims to the arenas. And only tough fighters would do as coys, apprentice kaidurs.

This man, number 5763, sat all day at his task, his stumps beautifully bandaged. He had shouted that he came from Hyrklana; but that did not help him.

If he tried to escape again, the law would be more severe on him; and, as was written down, at the third attempt would then demand his life.

He would be hanged in the most strict ritual procedure.

I witnessed only two hangings, one for a third-time escape attempt, incredible though that may be, and one for a slave who had struck an overseer.

This slave was a Chulik.

Had he killed the overseer the law admitted that the next of kin, or the dead man's superior officer failing a next of kin, might stipulate what punishment the murderer would suffer before death.

They were colorful in their thinking in those areas, were the bereaved in Hamal.

And there was no revenge, no bloodthirsty shrilling anger in all this. It was all written down in the laws of the land...

A new slave, number 2789 — for they filled up the old roster numbers with new slaves at the Heavenly Mines — said to me, "Eight-two-eight-one! I must escape! I'll go mad!"

I said to him, "Two-seven-eight-nine. To escape is so difficult it is scarcely worth the attempt. Better for you to go mad."

Only later, as I sat eating my chunk of bread — made from good corn, for the Hamalese wished to keep up our strength — and coarse pudding of vosk and onion, with a finger over the gregarian at the side of my bowl, was the truth of what I had said borne in on me.

I, Dray Prescot, unwilling to contemplate escape?

Number 8281 knew the truth. Dray Prescot was an empty boaster, a bladder of wind. Eight-two-eight-one knew the truth.

It took me a day to think of the subject again. We were opening up a new seam far down into the guts of the mountain. The rock we wanted held a gray metallic sheen which differentiated it from the yellower rock all around. Yet it held no mineral I could tell. We simply took all the gray rock, irrespective of minor dif-

302

ferences. This seam was narrow, and an overseer, a little Och holding with his four limbs a lamp, a wax notepad, a stylus, and a prodding stick, waddled up on his two lower legs to supervise. We were all crouched down, for the roof pressed close, and the oil lamp — it was not samphron-oil — smoked a little. I smelled the lamp; but, also, I smelled another nostril-tickling odor. In that confined space in the grotesque shadows of the lamp, the little Och prodding and writing, a Rapa guard with a spear bending almost double ready to spit the first one of us who did anything against the law — for the law would hold a guard within his rights if he killed protecting a Hamalian — I picked up the unmistakable scent of squishes.

Memories of Inch flashed into my mind, of his insatiable hunger for squish pie, and of the taboos he held in so great honor, and of that limb of Satan, Pando, taunting poor Inch with rich, ripe juicy squish pie.

The Och squeaked and backed away.

"All out!" He shouted so loudly some of the slaves jumped and a trickle of rock slid from the overhang. "All out at once! Guard, prod 'em along, you onker!"

We scuttled out.

We did not go back to that seam again.

Although I can recall that scene in all its clarity now, at the time with the same depressing grayness of days it passed from my mind; the little flicker of the idea of escape guttered like a candle in the opened stern-lantern of a swifter of the Eye of the World.

Number 2789 harked back to the idea of escape himself, and so forced me to contemplate reality. Was not 8281 also Dray Prescot? Was I not Pur Dray, Krozair of Zy? The Lord of Strombor? Prince Majister of Vallia? Kov of this and that, and Strom of Valka? Zorcander? Was I not? No title would help me now, but a Krozair brother is never beaten until he is ceremoniously slipped into the sea over the side of his swifter — if he can be buried decently by his brothers of the Order of Krozairs of Zy instead of dying in some stinking prison or under the longswords of those Grodnim cramphs of Magdag.

Despite all the horrendous difficulties, there had to be a way of escape.

The sheer efficiency of the Hamalese would make any attempt enormously difficult.

Probably escape was impossible. I wondered about it then, and I freely admit it, if it was possible for one man, even a Krozair of Zy, to escape from the Heavenly Mines of Hamal.

But, from somewhere, I found the determination to make that attempt. I did not care how foolhardy it might be. I knew, and I believe I understood at last, that merely staying alive was not enough. My Delia, my Delia of Delphond — who so far had not been called Delia of Strombor, as she had once wished — could not pine for me longer if I was dead than if I remained in these Opaz-forsaken mines.

So the decision was taken.

I would try to escape.

Number and order and law had worn me down. If you have listened to these tapes of my life upon Kregen you will know with what a hearty zest I detest and despise petty authority exercised in heartless and evil ways, without thought for those who are weak and unable to defend themselves.

Discipline is necessary in life — sometimes it is a necessary evil — but excessive discipline is a perversion.

Law dominated the men of Hamal.

I would turn their law against them.

Number 2789 would help. There were others, almost always newly arrived slaves who retained some shred of their old spirit. The Heavenly Mines in their soul-destroying regularity broke spirits as boys break twigs in sport.

I must have a plan ready to broach to the others, and then make it work. I worked out a scheme. Simplicity. Speed and simplicity. The seizure of a flier, for we would never walk out, offered our only chance, and the fliers were always well guarded. Strength. Well, we were strong from our unceasing and strenuous labors and the coarse but filling food.

The plans tumbled into my head and always the glorious face and figure of my Delia smiled at me, and her gorgeous brown hair with those outrageous tints of gold and auburn glinting filled me with uplifting determination. I collected a few loose scraps of jagged rock, for the law proscribed a slave possessing anything that might be used as a weapon when he came off shift, and all the picks and shovels with their numbers were checked into the stores.

In the hut I lay on the earth and drew my blanket about me. I turned over to think and I saw a reddish-brown scorpion scuttle out from a crack in the rock and stare at me, his tail high.

If you have listened to these tapes I believe you may have some faint inkling of my feelings then.

In that reedy scratchy voice I had heard before on the Battlefield of the Crimson Missals, the scorpion spoke to me.

"You get onker, Prescot!"

I knew no one else could hear that voice, or mine, in reply.

"I know."

"There is no escape from the Heavenly Mines of Hamal."

"You may be a messenger from the Star Lords, you and the Gdoinye; but I will escape."

The scorpion waved his tail mockingly. "The Star Lords know you, Dray Prescot; they know you are a fool, a get onker, an onker of onkers. They know many things. They know you are such a stupid onker you might succeed where noone else has succeeded before."

"Believe it, scorpion."

"The Star Lords have a use for you, Prescot. A use far from here in space and time."

Sheer terror hit me then, for if the Star Lords banished me back to Earth, as they could (as they could!), I might never be returned to Kregen beneath Antares. I started up, sweating, prepared to defy the Star Lords and all their superhuman power once again.

But the scorpion was growing, was glowing now with that damnable blue radiance, was bloating into a gigantic blue shape that filled the hut and burst the rock walls and so engulfed the night sky and all the stars and tumbled me headlong into that radiant blue confusion.

Six

The Star Lords blunder

Often and often had I cursed that I was merely a puppet, a mere hank of hair and blood and bone, dangling on the strings so callously pulled by the Savanti and the Star Lords. Well, that might be true, in its own way. But as you know I had been developing ways and means of circumventing the Star Lords. Oh, yes, they could still hurl me back four hundred light-years to the planet of my birth, perhaps never again to summon me to Kregen. They could forever sunder me from Delia, the only woman in two worlds that means anything to me — and I say that in due deference and love for all the other women who have been and are my friends. But this construction of artifices had more than once before kept me on Kregen. The Star Lords could be manipulated.

But this time the transition came with blinding suddenness. I yelled out, once again, in my own old intemperate bellow: "I will not return to Earth! *I will stay on Kregen!*"

I swear I heard a ghostly chuckle, and a voice that was in all probability in my head and not gusting from the blue radiance surrounding me, as I thought, say: "You get onker, Prescot! You would stay on Kregen even in the Heavenly Mines!"

"I would escape even where they say escape is impossible!"

"Maybe you would, Prescot, you wild leem. Maybe you would. But there is work under your hands, work for the Everoinye. And, Dray Prescot, you fail at your peril!"

I opened my eyes and the blue radiance fell away.

Above me blazed the twin Suns of Scorpio.

And — the red sun preceded the green across the sky!

Immediately I knew I was caught once more in a time loop cast by the Star Lords. Once again I had been thrown into the past. I could take great comfort from that, for my Delia was not waiting for me now in trembling apprehension, and whatever I had to do here — wherever here was — could be done and I might then rejoin my beloved and she would not have spent a single extra day in sorrow over my fate. Also, I knew, and the knowledge brought a shivery feeling of insecurity over me, that somewhere on the face of Kregen, I, Dray Prescot, was at this very minute fighting or drinking, slave or free, struggling on or living it up in luxury. At this very minute somewhere over the horizon a Dray Prescot that was me was walking and talking, fighting, and, perhaps, loving, and I own I found it all most weird, to be sure.

Then — why then the obvious thought occurred. If I was back to certain times past, there might be *two* Dray Prescots battling on the surface of Kregen! In Valka I had been thrown into a time loop.

I could be in the Hostile Territories right now, fighting on in our long journey with Seg, Thelda, and glorious Delia at my side; and at the same time I could be in Valka, fighting to free my island from the aragorn — and, at the same time, here I was, naked and weaponless as usual, ready to undertake some great new task.

I shivered a little at the power of the Star Lords.

I, Dray Prescot, who called them onkers and rasts and cramphs!

From my experiences in the Heavenly Mines I had emerged in reasonable condition, completely hairless, for the Hamalians with their rigid adherence to the rules shaved the slaves once a sennight, and without the brands on chest and back. I had to acknowledge that forethought to the Star Lords, although as I knew my dip in the Pool of Baptism in the River Zelph of Aphrasöe as well as giving me a thousand years of life and phenomenal powers of recuperation also enabled my skin to slough off brand marks. Sometimes, as when I had been a hauler for the Emperor's barges, that had not been too comfortable an attribute.

Unlike most of my previous transitions to various unfriendly locations of Kregen, this time I had not landed slap bang in the midst of danger, action, and headlong adventure.

Around the Heavenly Mines stretched the Barrens, a deadly waste of desert and near-desert. All food had had to be imported. I stood up slowly, taking stock of my situation. Around me now extended broad fields, heavy with corn, with brilliant flowers blooming in the hedgerows alongside narrow lanes. A house or two showed red-tiled gables, and smoke drifted lazily from tall twisted chimneys. A flock of birds — ordinary Earth-like birds — swooped and squawked about a clump of trees remarkably like elms. Had the two brilliant suns of Antares not blazed down from the sky above I might have thought myself back at home, in a rich and golden autumn with all the goodness of the harvest to be gathered in.

This situation, then, was like no other that had confronted me on arrival on Kregen.

I could see at once the dangers here, the difficulties. Perhaps, if the truth was told, more danger for me existed in this apparently peaceful scene than in the damned Heavenly Mines of Hamal.

Did I tread the soil of Havilfar? Had I been taken back to Vallia, or to Turismond? Segesthes, perhaps? Or, a continent I had touched only at the tip of Erthyrdrin, Loh? The thought crossed my mind that I might have been deposited in one of the remaining three continents; but I had no information of value on them, and no one of the people of this grouping knew much of them; they were foreign and strange beyond the understanding of ordinary men and women.

A mirvoller flew out from the trees and passed across the sky and, without having to think, I took cover in a hedge. The mirvol flew effortlessly, and I caught the wink of weapons from its rider. The flyer passed out of sight.

As far as I knew mirvols were found only in Havilfar. So I felt reasonably sure I was still in Havilfar. If this was a game the Star Lords were playing with me, I knew only too well it was a deadly game, and failure would result in death or a fate worse than death, if you will pardon the expression, in my return to Earth.

Perhaps, the treacherous whisper crossed my mind, perhaps I was still in the rock hut of the Heavenly Mines, and I had imagined I had seen and spoken with the scorpion, and all this was pure hallucination.

A quoffa cart rumbled along the road, and the apim sitting in the front with a straw in his mouth and a wide hat pulled low over his forehead looked real enough. Naked as I was, I must accost him. He wore a shirt and trousers, a fashion quite often seen on Kregen, and I would face some quizzing, I felt sure. But it had to be done.

The white dust of the road puffed under the six pads of the quoffa, and his huge, patient, wise old face cheered me as I stepped out. This was a crossroads. A tall tree stood in one corner of the cross, and a blackened *thing* hung from a branch, chained and gruesome. I perked up. Directly across the angle of the road stood an inn, whose white walls and red roof leaned lazily against the sunlight, the windows winking in the sun. A table and a bench stood outside. I fancied I might find information there, if I could not stand a drink and a piece of vosk pie.

The red roof of the inn was new, for the tiles were unpitted and still full of color, but the far end gable roof showed older tiles, darkened and cracked here and there.

This was a mystery, this whole occurrence, so unlike anything that had happened before. The peacefulness of the scene, the calmness of the surroundings, even the *thing* in the gibbet to indicate that law was upheld and troubles past, all drew together to make me believe that *something* strange was happening.

I stepped out and opened my mouth to shout to the apim in the quoffa cart — and a blue radiance swept about me and a violent wind seemed to whirl me head over heels. I was still standing upright and on the same spot, but my impressions whirled chaotically. I saw the quoffa cart spin around, the tree bend and sway, the fields ripple and run as though a great and silent wind scored them flat.

I struggled to draw breath in that glowing azure radiance.

I gasped.

The quoffa cart had gone. The tree had changed, for its foliage was now of early season, and not of autumn. And the inn! Its roof was now old all over, darkened cracked tiles where before had been new tiles. The fields had shrunk, for instead of ripe and golden grain they now showed the beginning shoots of new garden growths.

The Star Lords sent their blue radiance about me and I felt myself falling; I thought in my terror that I had failed to accomplish what I had been sent here to do. And I knew the Everoinye would punish failure with instant dismissal. I was on my way back to Earth!

"No!" I screamed out. This was not fair! This was to set a task without clue, without sign, without hope.

Then I could scream no more. For the solid ground returned once more under

307

my feet, the old inn, the new shoots in the fields, the burgeoning tree, all flashed again before my eyes.

But now there was a change, a drastic change.

The inn was on fire. Flames shot from the roof, cracking and tumbling the tiles away as beams fell. The windows glowed with the violence of the fire within. All about me rose that horrid screeching of men locked in mortal combat.

I had no time to thank Zair. For this — this horror, this screaming and screeching, this clang of iron weapons on armor, this noise of battle — this scene was my scene, may Zair forgive me. Now I knew I was where I must be in order to fulfill my destiny on the world four hundred light-years from the world of my birth.

Diffs were attacking the inn.

They pranced about it, shooting quarrels into the fire through the smashed windows, running and laughing and cutting down other diffs who struggled to break a way through that iron ring. Any thought that I might be hurling myself into the fight on the wrong side had to be dispelled. The Star Lords had tested me in that way before; I had been tested through my own stiff-necked pride, and had hitherto had the good fortune to pick the right side. Now I felt that the devils so wantonly attacking the inn must be my adversaries. Those within might have been a coven or a gathering of criminals, but I doubted it. As I had struck when I had taken Sosie na Arkasson from her tree of suffering, so I struck now.

I ran into the fray.

The diffs pranced and screeched, but I was able to trip one in half-armor and gaudy orange robes, to thump him as he went down, and so possess myself of a thraxter.

Is it a sin to confess, as I do, that the feeling of a sword-hilt once more in my fist uplifted me, gave me a thrilling sense of completeness? This proves without the shadow of a doubt that I am an incomplete man, a shadow man, a weakling, dependent on the shallow symbol of a sword for my moral and spiritual sustenance. Oh, yes, all that — but on Kregen a sword means life to its owner.

Or, as is the way of two worlds, death…

My prowess as a fighting-man gives me pleasure only when that skill may be used to ends which are in themselves worthy. The protection of the weak has seemed to me to be such a worthy end. But the judgment of worthiness remains with me, alone, and therefore in the eyes of everyone else must be suspect.

I saw these four-armed diffs attacking the blazing inn. I heard the shrieks and yells from within, and witnessed other four-armed diffs attempting to break out, and being shot down as they ran and stumbled; so it seemed right to me that I should assist those trapped in the inn.

All these thoughts of a schoolboy philosophy flashed through my mind in the moment that I scooped the thraxter, blocked a blow from a yelling halfling who tried to decapitate me, and thrust him through above his lorica. I turned swiftly, ducking my head so that a crossbow bolt flicked by above, and leaped for the clump who were attempting to smash down the door, almost enveloped in a blaze of sparks and flame. They had a tree trunk and they ran and swung with great and agile viciousness. These four-armed halflings were superb fighting-men.

The lenken door groaned back from bronze hinges. Then I was into the battering-ram group, laying about me, and catching them completely unawares. They dropped the log. They carried thraxters in their right upper hands; but their other three hands had been occupied with the log, and it seems to me now that small fact perhaps saved my life. They were fantastic fighters. I had to skip and jump, to parry and block more than I could hack and thrust. But they went down, first one and then two, and two more as I caught the knack.

Others came running, holding shields balanced high on their two left arms.

The streaming light of the twin Suns of Scorpio poured down on the scene and the blaze of the burning inn shed a ghastly wavering light into that sunshine. There would be no quick and easy escape into the shadows. As I fought I took stock of these four-armed diffs.

"He is only apim, by Zodjuin of the Rainbow!" A magnificent halfling yelled his anger that his men were being thus thwarted. He wore an iron-banded lorica that had been let out to its full extent, and a pair of gray trousers, with a broad, orange cummerbund wrapped around his waist, and a swirling orange and blue cloak fastened by jeweled golden brooches. He wore no helmet and his coppery hair gleamed in the light, cut into a helmet-shape itself, with a fillet of silver confining the curls across his forehead. He waved his thraxter with his upper right hand and hurled a stux with his lower right. He threw the stux with great skill and precision. I slipped it and cut down a diff who attempted to run me through. Things were becoming more interesting by the mur, by Zair!

A man I had chopped at and who had slid his thraxter across barely in time, so that instead of having his head laid open had been merely slashed down his face, yelled back hoarsely.

"He may only be apim, Kov Nath, but he fights like a devil of the Yawfi Suth!"

"Stick him, you yetches, and have done!" This Kov Nath whirled his sword at me, commanding, demanding. "We must break in and make sure Ortyg Fellin Coper is truly dead. His men will be here soon! Hurry, you rasts, hurry!"

A blazing mass tumbled from the roof then, falling from the porch, and we all skipped aside. Kov Nath yelled savage commands. His men closed in. There were something like twenty of them, and I knew this was no longer a pleasant muscle-exercising afternoon's romp. Twenty diffs with four arms each meant something more than eighty to two, for the combinations offered by the four-armed configuration are interesting and deadly. So I fought and leaped and jumped and kept the door.

Stuxes hissed past me, and those I did not snatch from the air and return from whence they came in best Krozair tradition thunked splinteringly into the lenken door. How much longer could this go on? My thraxter gleamed a foul and bitter red, now, with the blood of these diffs. They did not seem to reck the consequences of attack; they bore in vengefully, and only by the utmost exertions could I stop the final lethal thrust.

A crossbow bolt tore into my side. I ignored that. Kov Nath, raging, rushed forward. He had snatched up a shield and grasped it in his two larboard hands, while his two starboard fists wrapped around a sword that was, I swear, longer than those great Swords of War of the Blue Mountains in distant Vallia.

A window broke outward and a four-armed diff sprang out, wielding a sword, cursing, followed by two more. They charged into the attackers. All thee of them were smoldering, their cloaks and trousers smoking.

"Now by the blood of Holy Djan-kadjiryon!" yelled Kov Nath. "You will all die!" He charged.

Even in the shock of the engagement I thought he would do better to grip that unwieldy longsword in his two upper fists, or his two lower, so as to get the triangular leverage so important in two-handed play. But he was skilled and quick and vicious, and I skipped and parried and gonged my thraxter uselessly on his shield. He tended to keep the shield covering him and did not use it, as I taught my men, to thrust out and so use as an offensive weapon in its own right.

He, like them all, had taken no notice of my appearance. I had two arms only, and was therefore apim. My nakedness, my shaved head, my hairless body, appeared to them as merely a part of the custom of my people. We circled, and against my will I was forced from the door.

I leaped in with a fierce and savage lunge, ducked, felt that damned great sword go whistling over my head, and tried to stick him through the thigh. But the shield rim clanked across, and that rim was bound in iron, not brass.

"By Zodjuin of the Rainbow! You fight like a leem!"

I did not waste breath answering but got myself back to the splintered door and held him off yet again. I had to allow my fighting instincts full play. There had to be a way of beating him. While he leaped and sprang so agilely before me and I ducked and weaved in my turn his men would not chance a stux throw or the loosing of a bolt. This gave me heart.

The three men who, on fire, had charged into the fight were fully occupied. They were yelling and screeching strange oaths at one another, calling on outlandish gods and devils, and the way these four-armed diffs fought filled me with admiration. Whatever the rights and wrongs of the situation and wherever on Havilfar I might be, I had landed in a country of warriors, by Vox!

Kov Nath drew back a space, and I saw a face at the window at my side. At first I imagined a monstrous mouse-face looked at me. There were brilliant dark eyes, a trembling tender nose above wide white whiskers, and a small mouth which showed small even teeth in evident terror at the fire-filled scene outside. A scarlet velvet cap with a jaunty white feather stuck lopsidedly in it covered this diffs head. He squeaked.

"May all the Warrior Gods of Djanduin aid you now, apim!"

So now I knew where I was. And, as before, the very sound of that name, Djanduin, struck a responsive chord in me. I had experienced the same uncomprehending but thrilling spark of uplift when I had first heard the name Strombor and the name Valka. And now — Djanduin!

Perhaps all that has happened in the intervening years has given me a false hindsight; perhaps the names of Strombor and Valka and Djanduin and — but they must wait for now — ring and thunder in my head so much, enough to echo back over the years. All I know is that as the mouse-faced little diff yelled at me, the name Djanduin struck shrewdly. These four-armed diffs were Djangs. I had used their national weapon, the djangir, on a notable occasion in the arena of Huringa.

A crossbow bolt shattered into the window frame and the little diff jumped, squealing.

"Get your head down, onker!" I roared at him, and with the thraxter belted a stux out of the air. The keen iron point would have pierced him just where his whiskers joined beneath the quivering nose and above the trembling mouth.

"Mother Diocaster!" he yelped, and vanished.

The fire-fanned flames lay their burning hair across the inn and more of the roof fell in; but I was heartened to note that the splintered lenken door and the smashed window with the crossbow bolt embedded in the frame lay upwind. Here was a tiny portion of hope for the cause in which I fought. That I had no idea what that cause was all about added a spice I — thinking of the Star Lords — did not relish.

The far end of the inn was now doomed. I continued to fight, keeping a circle about the door, and with an evil cunning drawing Djangs in for combat so that they would screen me with their own bodies from their comrades' shooting.

Kov Nath, with his smooth helmet-head of coppery hair, tried again to get at me with that confounded great sword of his and I had to leap and then bend double to avoid the crunching back-handed swing. I circled him to his left, flickering the thraxter in and out like the tongue of a risslaca of the Ocher Limits, and then darting back and trying to cut him up in his right side. But those two damned right arms of his kept whacking the great sword about so that I had to take it on my blade and let a supple wrist twist slide it free. When, with the fighting-man's instinctive attack following defense, my blade merely scraped across his shield I grew hopping mad.

"Sink me!" I burst out. "You're a bonny fighter, Kov Nath!"

"Aye, apim," he said merrily, and came at me again. "And I'll split your head on my sword to prove it."

We clashed and banged and every now and then I had to jerk away and flick my thraxter up to swat a quarrel off or snatch at a flying stux. It seemed to me then that this could not go on much longer. I did not take a stux cleanly with my left hand and the broad iron blade scored up my forearm, at which I let out a curse.

"By the Black Chunkrah, Kov Nath! Let you and me settle this between ourselves, like true Horters."

He laughed.

"I am no Horter, apim. I am Nath Jagdur, the Kov of Hyr Khor!"

That betrayed him. For although I am not a gentleman, and do not pretend to be, having seen too much of their nasty ways, I do know that the Horters of Havilfar and the Koters of Vallia and all the other gentlemen of Kregen consider themselves Opaz-elect. Any noble considers himself a gentleman, by birth and

311

right, except in those cases or men who — like myself — fought and struggled to become Notors from lowly origins, and then they are nobles by right only. But, such is the custom of Kregen, birth means far less than achievement in the eyes of most peoples.

As we thus struggled before the lenken door of the blazing inn a Djang screeched and ran out from the streaming smoke.

"Kov Nath! They come! They come!"

Kov Nath went mad. His great sword whirled into a silvery-blue blur, for he had not tasted blood with it as yet. He bellowed his anger.

"By Zodjuin of the Stormclouds! I'll spit you yet, yetch!"

His face congested with blood. Apart from his four arms he looked exactly like an apim, and his face was darkly handsome, with bright merry eyes, a thin black moustache, and a chin that jutted with a dark bristle to show he had not shaved that morning. He bore down on me again even as his men yelled and began to decamp.

"Rast!" he yelled at me, and spittle flew. "I'll degut, debrain, dissect you, you two-armed weakling!"

"By Vox!" I ducked a swing and surged up to him and so took his throat into my left hand and dragged his handsome head forward. I glared into his congested face. "You'll know you've met me, Kov Jagdur the Boaster!" And I slashed the thraxter down. The blow would have finished any ordinary man. But this Kov Nath Jagdur was a Djang. He had four arms. The shield came around and caught me in the side, just beneath the ribs, and I grunted and let him go, and he brought the great sword around and down to finish me.

I rolled away and my thraxter came up just in time and slid that long wicked blade. The steel bit into the turf.

A crossbow bolt went *whirr-chunk* against the great blade. The double hilt was violently wrenched from Kov Nath's fists. The sword spun across the turf.

He roared and straightened up and another bolt hummed past his ear.

From the smoke more Djangs appeared, running and loosing crossbows, holding their shields high, their thraxters low. At their belts swung djangirs.

"Now by all the devils in a Herrelldrin hell!" bellowed Kov Nath.

He hesitated — he stood there, balanced, ready to lunge one way for his sword and the other in flight. A bolt pranged glancingly from his lorica, and that decided him; with a final blood-curdling curse he ran around the far end of the inn. Moments later the thud of animal hooves sounded and the band of rogues burst into view, racing with straining necks and heads low, riding fast away along the white dusty road.

I looked up into the point of a stux.

The Djang holding the stux looked as though he would like nothing better than to thrust down.

Just as I was about to teach him the error of his ways in thus treating a Krozair of Zy, four arms or no four damned arms, the little diff with the mouse-face came running out of the inn, squeaking. His whiskers were all a-twitch as he pushed the stux aside and dropped on a knee at my side.

"Apim! You still live! Now may Mother Diocaster be praised!"

I did not fail to notice the offhanded way this little fellow thrust the stux aside, nor the way the Djang soldiery stiffened up at sight of him. These were signs I recognized.

He was most solicitous.

"You are hurt, sir, you are hurt. You bleed!" He leaped up and tore into the gathered newcomers. "Deldar! Take this Horter into the unburned room and care for him. Bandages, water, needles, palines." He swung about. "Sinkie! Sinkie! I am coming, my love! It is all right now, the Opaz-forgotten leemsheads are gone! You may come out from under the table now."

I had to let myself be hoisted up to keep a smile off my face. Lord knew, I needed a smile then!

As we went into the unburned end of the inn I observed how the Djangs were going about dousing the flames, working with a swift eager efficiency that heartened me. Hauling water from the well in the rear courtyard, they had the fire under control very soon. Truth to tell there was little left of that end of the roof. The little fellow pranced at my side very solicitously.

"I have the honor to present myself to you, sir. I am Ortyg Fellin Coper, Pallan of the Highways."

He looked at me expectantly, his bright eyes alert, his whiskers quivering. He wore rich robes of a dark blue material liberally splattered with gems and silver lace. His scarlet velvet hat with its white feather looked now a sumptuous part of his costume. He wore no weapons, apart from a small silver secretarial knife in a silver sheath at his belt.

All naked and bloody as I was — although a cloak had been flung across me as I was half-carried in — I pondered what answer to make. This, I thought, must be the man the Star Lords had sent me here to rescue. I had done that, for if I had not stood before the door and prevented the leemsheads from getting at him before his bodyguard came up he would have been a dead man. If I was, as I sincerely believed, in my own past, then perhaps I was not Strom of Valka yet; certainly I was not the Prince Majister of Vallia.

"I am Dray Prescot, the Lord of Strombor, Pallan."

"Well, you are right well and heartily met, as Mother Diocaster is my witness!"

He introduced his wife, a charming little lady whose whiskers added, if anything, to her coy beauty. Her clothes, too, although simple were richly jeweled. I could not fail to notice the affection between these two, and, also, the affection and respect accorded them both by the tough warrior Djangs. O. Fellin Coper handled them with the casual unthinking courtesy of a man habituated to absolute authority tempered with concern for those that fate had put into his hands. Also in the unburned room were two other mouse-faced diffs like himself, lesser in rank and importance but still treated with grave gruff respect by the Djangs, and a Djang woman, very much pregnant and very near her time, as I judged.

She lay on a pallet, pale-faced, her long fair hair damp, her face streaked with sweat. She was still beautiful, despite the difficulty of the birth. Three Djang women were attending her but there was no doctor with acupuncture needles in attendance. This did not seem right to me and so I mentioned it to O. Fellin Coper. His gerbil-like head twisted.

"You are quite right, Notor Prescot. But when Mother Diocaster calls forth the babe at the appointed hour — why, then, the babe has to come whatever the circumstances."

A great bustle began as preparations were made for the Pallan to leave the inn. The pregnant Djang woman was not of his party. Her husband had been burned in the fighting and had died. For a moment I pondered, and then Ortyg Coper called to me from his decorated carriage which his men had brought up.

"I am returning to Djanguraj, Notor Prescot, and if the city was your destination before you fell among these leemsheads, I would be most honored — my wife and I would be most honored — if you would deign to take advantage of our carriage for the journey."

It was nicely said, and it explained why no one had commented on my nakedness. They assumed I had been set on and was fighting the leemsheads to get my clothes and money back. To dispose of another problem here and now, they also took me for a member of the Martial Monks of Djanduin, which would explain my hairlessness.

My wounds had been seen to, and I was busy as any old mercenary would be. The dead Djangs yielded clothes, weapons, and money. I rifled the dead men with as much compunction as I would sweep the table of breadcrumbs. A paktun is a paktun, when all is said and done.

So it was that when I walked toward Ortyg Coper's carriage at the far end of the yard I was suitably clad in a pair of gray trousers with an orange cummerbund and a white shirt. A lorica was collapsed and slung over my shoulder. In a pouch lay enough shivers and obs to last, and there were three golden deldys. No one, I thought, had seen that quick rifling of the dead. For weapons I took a thraxter, a pair of stuxes, a djangir and a shield, which I draped about myself. At the last moment I picked up Kov Nath's enormous sword, and so stepped into Ortyg Fellin Coper's elegant carriage for Djanguraj.

Seven

Pallan O. Fellin Coper of Djanduin

"We do not see many apims in Djanduin, Notor Prescot. Nor many other diffs, come to that." Ortyg Coper glanced at me obliquely as the carriage rolled along the road and left a wide swath of white dust in its wake. His bodyguard rode up front and well astern. I had noticed they rode totrixes, the awkward six-legged riding animal of Havilfar, and carried long slender lances upright in boots attached to their stirrup irons. "So," went on Coper, looking out of the window at the passing fields of corn and marspear and crops I did not recognize, "it seems you are the Lord of Strombor and so therefore cannot be a Martial Monk of Djanduin."

"I lay no claim to being a Martial Monk, Pallan Coper."

The dangers here were obvious. This man was a Pallan, a chief minister of state, and, as he had told me, one charged with the upkeep of the highways. He held a very real power. To judge by other parts of Kregen I knew he would think nothing of having me thrown into a dungeon if it suited him or his master the king, and the fact that I had saved him from the swords of Kov Nath's leemsheads would mean nothing. So I had to tread warily, for all that he seemed a pleasant enough little fellow.

He brushed his whiskers in a finicky fashion.

"Tell me of Strombor, Notor."

Had I been a man given to empty gestures I might have smiled then, for this was so clearly a cunning opening ploy in a conversation designed to trap me into giving away my secrets. No further mention of my nakedness — its fact lay there between us — but it was: "Tell me of Strombor."

I considered. If this past was far enough back he would not have heard of Strombor, for that enclave had been taken over by the Esztercaris in distant Zenicce. Had he heard of Zenicce? Had he heard of Segesthes?

"You know the continent of Segesthes, Pallan? The great enclave city of Zenicce?"

He inclined his head.

"Indeed. We have records in our libraries."

I said easily, "Strombor is an enclave in Zenicce," and then I went on matter-of-factly. "I, naturally, consider Strombor the most beautiful and the best, even if not the greatest; but we are a rich people and I am fortunate to be their prince."

His wife, Sinkie, fluttered up at this, but Coper gave me a sly sideways look and said: "You saved my life, Notor Prescot, and for this I am in your debt. I shall not forget. But there will be those in Djanguraj who will — ah — wonder what a noble prince of a great house of Zenicce is doing, wandering naked and hairless in Djanduin, so far from home."

Well, you couldn't say fairer than that.

"How are arguments that touch a man's honor settled in Djanduin, Pallan Coper?"

"With the sword."

"That will be quite suitable."

He chuckled then, this little mousy fellow, and stroked his whiskers in high good humor.

"You are apim, Notor Prescot! You have, like me, but two arms. How do you think to face a Djang champion, who has four arms?"

About to say, "I had thought you had witnessed that," I paused. To make that remark would be boorish, despite its other and intended meaning.

So I said something about fighting as Zair willed (he like most Kregans accepted strange gods, devils, and saints without turning a hair) and so we rolled on for a space in silence.

315

I found that to suggest I had been shipwrecked, an obvious stratagem, would not work, as the inn and crossroads were dwaburs from the sea. I told a part of the truth, and said I had tumbled off a voller. Like the Horter he was, he did not refer to it again.

In the southwest corner of Havilfar the sea surges in a cleft that, looking at the map, reminds me of the Bristol Channel, except, of course, that the scales are vastly greater, for Havilfar is a broad continent. The northern promontory sweeps out boldly south of Loh, with a ruggedly indented coastline and a wide and sheltering band of islands, some quite large, running off the northwestern shore. At the tip of the channel is sited the town of Pellow in Herrelldrin. Sometimes the smot[8] of Pellow is referred to as standing in a bay, but the bay shape begins farther out, below the Yawfi Suth. The Yawfi Suth is a frightful area of bog and fen, of marsh and quagmire, penned between a tonguelike intrusion of the sea to the north, and treacherous ground to the south, alongside the channel. Here, also, is the Wendwath, that vast, misty lake of magic and superstition, and, too, of a strange, haunting golden beauty when the twin suns slant through the mists upon the water. They call the Wendwath the Lake of Dreaming Maidens.

The promontory that extends westward south of the channel — that same Tarnish Channel — curves southward to the southernmost land of Havilfar: Thothangir. Off the jagged and wind-eroded cliffs there lies the Rapa island that had once been the home of Rapechak, the Rapa with whom Turko the Shield and I, with those two silly girls Quaesa and Saenda, had escaped from Mungul Sidrath. Rapechak had not surfaced in our sight above the waters of the River Magan. It hurt me still to recall that, but I did not believe he was truly dead.

But we were in the northern promontory, near its far western extremity, rolling along toward Djanguraj, the capital of Djanduin, which is situated at the head of a wide, island-protected bay notched into the southwestern corner, above the Tarnish Channel.

To the west, as far as man could know, stretched the Ocean of Doubt.

So I was in the southwest of Havilfar. Now I had to prove myself acceptable to the Djangs, and I had to see about organizing transport back home to Valka.

Then I froze.

I knew the Star Lords would never let me leave here until time had once more caught up with the present I had left at the Heavenly Mines. I had had experience of their ways before. A great storm would arise, supernatural lightning and thunder would bar my path, as rashoons had done on the Eye of the World, as gales and typhoons had penned me in Valka, as I had been prevented from leaving Huringa in Hyrklana.

It was no use cursing and crying and calling out against the injustice of it all. Where I was I must stay until the time was up, until once more the green sun preceded the red across the sky — and I knew where else on Kregen I would be when that happened! I took the only comfort I could from the fact that Delia would not share this enforced and lonely exile. To her, when I returned — for I *would return!* — it would seem I had but minutes before tumbled out of the voller.

This *would* be.

How I was to make the Star Lords keep their part of the bargain I did not know. I had only the haziest idea what their plans were, but I suspected they wished me to do something drastic about the omnipresent slavery of Kregen. Very well, while I sweated out my sentence in this prison of time I would amuse myself. I would take what satisfaction I could get from upsetting as many unpleasant people as I could. I would do the aragorns' business for them, if any came my way, or I would dot a few eyes for the flutsmen, or show the cramphs of Gorgrendrin the error of their ways.

By Zim-Zair!

I would!

But — how long? How long?

On the thought I cocked my head out of the carriage window and, shading my eyes as best I could, squinted up to get an idea of how far apart were Zim and Genodras. They looked a long way, a damned long way, apart. I remembered how in the warrens of Magdag and in the Emerald Eye Palace — which was the second best palace in all Magdag — I had waited and watched for the red sun to eclipse the green. When it had happened I had not been in either the warrens or the palace; and then — as you must guess — I felt that old life surge back. What were we all doing now, Zolta and Nath, my two oar-comrades, my two wonderful rogues of Sanurkazz?

If you think in those first few moments of understanding I grew overly maudlin, you are probably right. But I missed Nath and Zolta, oh, how I missed them! And Mayfwy, the widow of my oar-comrade Zorg. And Pur Zenkiren. The inner sea knew little of the outer oceans and cared less. Would that I were there now, if I could not be in Valka!

"You look troubled, Notor Prescot."

"I was thinking of old times, and that ill becomes a man, as I know to my cost."

Sinkie, the Pallan Coper's wife, gave a little cry.

"Oh, my dear Notor Prescot! Pray, do not alarm me so! You looked so stern and — and — oh!" And she buried her quivering little nose in her lace handkerchief that had come all the long way from Dap-Tentyrasmot across the Shrouded Sea.

We trundled on and the conversation came back to normal patterns. As is my usual custom I will tell you the details of this land of Djanduin — and fascinating they were, at least to me — as and when they are relevant to my story.

The Djangs with their four arms, powerful bodies, and great muscular agility were superb fighters, and they were conscious of their good fortune. Their land of Djanduin was walled off in the southwestern promontory of Havilfar by first the Yawfi Suth and the Wendwath and second by a dangerous and difficult range of mountains barring the path of an invader. But the Djangs had not won their independence lightly. Constantly over the seasons the Gorgrens mounted invasions. Gorgrendrin, the land of the Gorgrens, stretched inland from the head of the Tarnish Channel. The Gorgrens had carved themselves fresh living space and captured many slaves from the lands and free cities of the area. The smot of Pellow, in Herrelldrin, lay under their heel.

317

Turko the Shield, my Khamorro comrade, came from Herrelldrin, and now I understood fully, for he had always been reticent, that the Gorgrens had indeed enslaved Pellow. The Khamorros had developed their syple disciplines of unarmed combat because they were, in truth, not allowed weapons.

And the Gorgrens sought always to march into Djanduin and serve the Djangs as they had served the people of Herrelldrin.

Trouble, it seems, is endemic in any culture where peoples fret and struggle and seek to expand their frontiers.

The only problem with the Djangs was — and here Pallan O. Fellin Coper exercised exquisite tact as he sought to explain to me in a way that would not demean the Djangs in my eyes — that they were, in very truth, exceptionally fine soldiers, but they were seldom entrusted with high command. To be brutally frank about it, the Djangs were bonny fighters in the blood and press of the field, but were not overly bright when it came to the higher command. Tactics — yes, they were superb. Strategy — no. They were duffers.

"Up to Jiktar rank, and you will scarcely find a better soldier. But give a Djang a brigade and he sweats and groans and worries, and wants to go up to the front line to see how his men are getting on every bur instead of thinking and planning what they ought to do. There are Djang Chuktars; very few."

"And you, Pallan Coper?"

"Oh, I am a civilian administrator. I deal with the roads." At that moment the carriage gave an almighty jolt and pitched and swung on its simple leaf springs so that we were rattled about like a Bantinko dancer's peas in his gourd.

"Now may Djan rot the road!" burst out Coper and immediately turned in alarmed contrition to his wife, who let out a little shriek and waved her perfumed handkerchief.

When I discovered she was horrified at his outburst and not the shuddering of the carriage I felt my lips rick up. These two were likely to make me laugh before I realized!

When all was settled Coper explained that his own people handled all the affairs that demanded planning and higher administration for the Djangs. He called himself a Djang, too. He was an Obdjang, that is, a First Djang. He told me frankly that although his race of diffs were clearly not the same as the Djang diffs, no one had any memory of when their partnership had begun, and no records existed in their libraries. Always, so Coper said, the Djangs had fought and the Obdjangs had directed. Each respected the other. Each knew they could do nothing without the other.

"Except—" And here Coper looked as troubled as I had seen him so far. I chanced a guess.

"This Kov Nath Jagdur na Hyr Khor," I said. "The leader of the leemsheads. He would prefer to lead instead of being led."

Coper nodded rather forlornly and his whiskers drooped. "That is so, Notor Prescot. You are quick."

"You have to be quick to stay alive on Kregen."

"Those yetches of Gorgrens are quick, also. We have certain intelligence that they plan a new campaign — and that will play merry hell with my roads — and I am summoned to the palace. The king will need counsel. Chuktar Naghan Stolin Rumferling will be there, I am glad to say. He is a good friend and a great warrior. My part will be a civilian's, which pleases me, also."

"Yes, Ortyg." His wife spoke up. "Better for you to be a civilian and let the soldiers and the warriors fight. Chuktar Naghan is a very great warrior indeed."

"He knows the approaches the Gorgrens will probably take. You see, Notor Prescot, our frontier is protected by the Yawfi Suth and the Wendwath; but there are ways through and between these natural obstacles and an army must be so positioned as to cover all eventualities."

"You have to outguess your opponent," I said. "Yes, I know."

I had done a deal of campaigning with my fierce clansmen on the Great Plains of Segesthes. That time we had burned our foemen's wagons in the Pass of Trampled Leaves had been a great bluff and counter-bluff. They, too, had had an alternative set of routes, and Hap Loder and I had guessed right. Perhaps, the thought occurs, if we had not had the skill and generalship to pick the right answer, I would not be here now. My bones might be moldering away on the plains, my blood and flesh long since gone to feed the grasses grazed upon by the chunkrah.

Coper glanced at me and I saw the quick intelligence on his gerbil-like face.

"I know you are a great fighter, Notor Prescot, although I do not think you would have lasted much longer against the leemsheads — and I compliment you, sir, I compliment you — but may I take it you also have knowledge of the art of strategy? Of generalship? Of the maneuvering of armies?"

Somehow, whether from my need to be independent and free or from a resentment of being pushed, I said, "Oh, as to that, Pallan Coper, I have been a fighting-man for a long time. I am content to leave the higher command in the hands of those who believe they are masters at that game."

He sank back in his seat. He rubbed his whiskers and pulled his scarlet hat over one ear, and so we fell into a silence that, at least for me, came with unwelcome desolation. I had the uncomfortable feeling that there was more to O. Fellin Coper.

Over the rumble of the carriage wheels we did not hear the beat of wings, and an escort Djang thrust his head through the window as the carriage shuddered to a halt.

"Well, Deldar Pocor! What is it, what is it?"

"A messenger from Chuktar Stolin Rumferling, Pallan."

The door was opened and, fussing and complaining of delays, Coper and his wife alighted. The other carriage with its Obdjang attendants pulled up also and the escort sat their totrixes with the blind indifference of the soldier wanting to get back to barracks and the local inn. A fluttclepper curved through the air in a barrage of swift wing-beats to land beside the road. The rider, a young and athletic Djang wearing flying leathers of orange and gray, leaped off. A long flexible staff whipped aft of his saddle and flew a multicolored flag with many tails. This, I guessed, was a badge and the reason the guard Deldar had known the messenger came from Chuktar Rumferling.

Using a steel key strung on a golden chain around his neck, Coper unlocked the flat balass box the messenger proffered. He took out a narrow strip of paper and broke the seal with a practiced flick of his left thumb. He unfolded the paper and read. His whiskers quivered and then stood out, stiff and rigid.

He crumpled the paper in his small hand.

"Very good, merker. A verbal reply. 'Returning in all haste.' Now get airborne."

"My wings are yours to command," said the merker in the rote fashion of the messenger and leaped aboard his fluttclepper and took off immediately. Coper ushered us back into the carriage and squeaked up very hotly at Deldar Pocor.

"We must hurry, good Pocor! Great things are afoot in Djanguraj. I expect us to reach the city by sunset."

"By sunset, Pallan. Very good, Pallan."

Sinkie fluttered at her businesslike husband.

"Oh, Ortyg! Whatever can be the matter?"

Coper shot that shrewd look at me and then leaned forward and patted his wife's knee.

"This is terrible news, Sinkie, and you must be brave. I will tell you now, for Notor Prescot is not of Djanduin and is not concerned with our affairs, for all that he is a guest and will be made truly welcome in our house."

"Of course, Ortyg! Notor Prescot saved us from those horrible leemsheads and I am very fond of him. But, my dear, the news…?"

The news was, in truth, enough to shake any Pallan of the kingdom. "The king and queen have been assassinated. Chuktar Naghan has certain news of the Gorgrens' invasion. The two terrible events are linked. Now, Sinkie! You must be brave. We will win through, in the end, as we have always done before."

"Oh, the poor dear king! And the queen—" Sinkie burst into tears that shook her little body. She looked absolutely woebegone, with the tears dripping from the ends of her drooping whiskers.

Coper looked at me meaningfully.

"You are our honored guest, Notor Prescot. I can judge a man, even if he is apim, and I know you to be a Horter and a Notor. You will not divulge any of this until it is generally known?"

"You may rely on me, Pallan Coper. And, as you say, this is not my business. I have no wish to become involved." I had just been brought from the horror of the Heavenly Mines, and had fought damned hard, and I meant what I said. In my prison of time I intended to live it up and have a good time — nothing more.

Eight

In Djanguraj

I, Dray Prescot, of Earth and of Kregen, fell into low ways and low company.
I make no excuses.

The taverns I explored, the dopa dens, the theaters, the fighting arenas (Djanduin is mightily contemptuous of the Jikhorkduns of Hamal and Hyrklana and instead flocks to see real fighting by professionals that almost invariably results in no one dying at all), the dancing girls I gawped at, the zorca races and the sleeth races, the dicing, the gambling, the drinking! Money came in, for I have skills at certain of the hairier games of Kregen, and I never went hungry or thirsty — or, at least, not often.

Pallan Coper and his charming wife Sinkie had shown me tremendous hospitality and they had been horrified by my antics and pleaded with me to give up such a terrible life. But they would not hear a word spoken against me.

And the cause of all this wanton debauchery?

As I have told you, calendars and dates are highly individual idiosyncrasies on Kregen, and every people and every race and every country keep some kind of time in their own way, and to the Ice Floes of Sicce with everyone else's.

By the expenditure of a great deal of time and effort and by constant application at the observatory of the Todalpheme of Djanduin — a small and humble group compared with other Todalpheme I have known — I calculated out dates. The Todalpheme are those austere and dedicated men whose charge it is to work out the tides of Kregen, and give timely warning. So I worked on my figures and when I had finished I stared in appalled horror at the final figure, under which I scrawled a great slashing red line.

Ten years.

Ten Terrestrial years, it was going to take, for the present in which I now lived to catch up with the time I had left the Heavenly Mines.

I did not go mad; after all, this was a mere matter of waiting, and patience is a virtue, even for me, sinner that I am. And I would wait in as much comfort and pleasure as I could contrive. My only true comfort was that Delia would not know of my durance, and her sufferings could, if I ranked my Deldars correctly, be curtailed or obviated altogether.

So I plunged into the heady nightlife of Djanguraj and found most of the strong young men gone off to war, and their womenfolk moping after them, and war and talk of war filling everyone's horizons. This suited me ill.

Chuktar N. Stolin Rumferling had gone off to war.

Seeing him briefly before he flew off I was struck by the cunning way nature can produce entirely different end products from the same original material. Imagine a meek and mild little clerk, with contact lenses and a sinus drip, hunched over a computer in a glass-walled office in a great city of Earth, weak-chested, scrawny-armed, flabby where it would do the most harm, prim and precise — there, to slander him, you have a defamatory picture of O. Fellin Coper. Imagine a fullback, bulky, powerful, superbly muscled, charging head-down into a mess of footballers in his way, chunking them aside with massive energy — there you have a not unflattering picture of Chuktar N. Stolin Rumferling. They are both men. They both come from the same stock. But what a difference between them!

"This will be a bloody business, Notor Prescot." Rumferling spoke in a gruff way that told me he was perfectly capable of cowing the roistering, rough-and-tough barbaric Djangs he would command. "Those cramphs of Gorgrens must be taught a lesson, once and for all."

"They will return and return, Naghan," squeaked Coper. "We all know that, Djan rot 'em!"

There was no gentle Sinkie present to protest his language.

So the fighting-men went off to war and I frolicked about town, enjoying what I could of the fleshpots.

Ten years! Ten long damned years!

I witnessed the new king's coronation. It was a rushed affair, with a hushed and spartan wartime atmosphere. This king was a nonentity, the old king's nephew by marriage, and he would not, I fancied, last long in some places of Kregen I had been — Sanurkazz or Magdag, for example, or Vallia herself.

He did not last.

A palace revolution was the first upheaval and that placed another nephew on the throne. He was strong, but a fool. He was murdered after a season and the Chuktar of the palace crowned himself as king. He lasted until the next Chuktar of the palace bribed enough of the king's personal bodyguard and overthrew him. His body was dragged though a pool of fighting fish, something like piranha, and the new king was crowned.

All this time I caroused and drank and sang and watched the dancing girls — for they were dancing girls, unlike those fine free girls of my clansmen who danced for us beneath the moons of Kregen — and they were very skilled in the arts of the dance. Their four arms weaved arabesques of beauty, and their oiled bodies and gleaming masses of silver bangles and golden bells, of waving fans and swirling silks, charmed me even as they bored me.

I would have none of them.

Ten godforsaken years!

My Delia — I had to get the disaster that had overtaken me in proportion. My overriding duty lay to Delia, and through her to Vallia, and to my people of Valka because I was their Strom. Also I owed a duty to Strombor and my clansmen of the Great Plains. But Gloag in Strombor and Hap Loder with the clans did everything right, as I well knew, and my duty was fully and freely carried out by them. Delia — I had to think of other things. Like the teasing arguments we indulged in so often over the merits and demerits of the wonderful zorcas of her Blue Mountains' blue-grass grazing estates as against the fabulous zorcas of my clansmen.

So with some of my ill-gotten winnings I went to the zorcadrome to buy myself the best zorca I could.

The zorcas of Djanduin are fine animals. But then, it is difficult to find a zorca that is not a fine animal, for of all the animals of Kregen, I believe, it is the zorca who most nobly fulfills its ancestral breeding. This is not to gainsay the superb quality of the vove, that fearsome steed of the Great Plains. But voves — real voves — are found only there in the natural state, while zorcas are found in many areas of Kregen.

Passing the totrixdrome — as you know I have never been fond of the sectrix, the nactrix, or the totrix, or of any other of the *trix* family — and hurrying on with Khobo the So chattering away in my ear as he guided me through the throngs of people who seem forever to wander and push and shout through the markets of two worlds, we came out to a wide dusty space fenced in with lenken rails. A pair of zorcas were racing up toward us, having completed a circuit of the oval, and they were neck and neck. Even at speed like that a clansman can point a zorca, and the faults of both these were at once apparent. But a fat cortilinden merchant, sweating happily as he paid out golden deldys, bought them for his son, who looked as though a quick belt on the backside would suit him better than a zorca saddle. They were Lamnias, and so the merchant should have known better.

"Rubbish!" Khobo whispered in my ear. He was a jaunty rogue, a carousing companion I had rescued from a brawl and who had stuck to me since. "I know old Planath the Zorca. He will not cheat me."

I grimaced at the name of Planath's, for although it is common on Kregen for the occupation to decide the label — and very colorful that is, to be sure — there were places I knew where to be called anything at all to do with zorcas meant much effort and sweat, not a little blood, and general approbation from one's peers. As for that genial rascal Khobo, he was called *the So* for obvious reasons. He'd been in the army and as a young man had had his upper left arm lopped off. As *so* is Kregish for *three,* thus Khobo was *the So.*

As I casually inspected the zorcas on display — for some reason I have always disliked the use of the word horseflesh for horses and zorcaflesh for zorcas — I was vividly reminded of what my father used to tell me as he doctored up a lame horse, or patted a strong chestnut neck, his eyes filled with the love of horses. It was with a nostalgic thought or two that I came at last to a magnificent pair held by two Djang grooms of Planath the Zorca's establishment.

"Wonderful animals, Notor, wonderful!" Planath babbled on, but cunningly. "See their quarters, their fetlocks, see their teeth—" At this, like two rat-traps, the lads opened up the zorcas' mouths. "Both are guaranteed perfect! Never, I swear by Holy Djan Himself, have there been two such zorcas as these."

Khobo rolled spittle around his mouth and spat into the dust. He laid a finger on the soft nose of the larboard one.

I shook my head.

"This one, I think, Khobo."

At this everyone began to wrangle, thoroughly enjoying themselves in the dust and the summer suns-shine, having supple Djangi girls bring them beaker after beaker of that sherbet drink called parclear that tickles the nose and is a sovereign thirst-quencher. Khobo, I knew, had not spotted that tiny divergence in the shoulder blades of the zorca he chose so confidently. That one was a splendid snow-white and, indeed, was a magnificent animal. But the one I wanted, and would give no reason for so doing beyond a stubborn foolishness, was the one a clansman would have selected, for all that he was a dusty shabby gray color. But I liked the look of him, the bright light of intelligence in his eyes.

"So you rush upon disaster, good Notor! Well, I can say no more!" And Khobo the So threw up his three hands in despair. "Choose this Dust Pounder, Notor, and have done, then."

So, astride Dust Pounder, thrilling again to the feel of a blood zorca between my knees, I rode back to the tavern at which for the moment I stayed. This was *The Paline and Queng*, run by a fat and happy Obdjang who knew exactly where every last ob came from and went to, and who made the best vosk pie in all Djanguraj. I downed some of his better wine, a clear yellow vintage from east, beyond the Mountains of Mirth, and bade Khobo sup up, and roared out that now I would challenge all comers in the zorca races.

This, as you will see, was a highly cunning way for a Krozair of Zy to earn his daily bread. But as I have said, I felt bitter and betrayed and desolated, in those early days in Djanduin.

Well, I will not weary you with a recital of my daily doings, as those doings wearied me. Suffice it to say that I raced Dust Pounder, and we won handsome sums of golden deldys; and I made the acquaintance of my Lady Lara Kholin Domon, who herself raced zorcas and who, perhaps, felt annoyance that she had lost, and who yet concealed that annoyance because she fancied some affection for me. The Lady Lara — oh, yes, she was a girl with fire and spirit, who rode like the east wind over the Sunset Sea. Yet she had a humility that was totally amused each time some proud Djang buck proposed to her. Her middle name — Kholin — proclaimed to all Djanduin that she came of a most powerful and wealthy tan — or House or clan or tribe — of Djanguraj. The Fellins and the Stolins were not in the same class as the Kholins.

We raced our zorcas against each other, and old Dust Pounder carried me to victory, for I would not shame her by pulling on his rein and so allowing her a hollow victory.

Her wild coppery hair blazed under the suns as we rode, her lithe and lissome form, clad in gray leathers, bent urgently over the neck of her zorca, whispering in his ear, entreating, pleading, urging, commanding him to run faster, faster, faster! Fast enough, at any rate, to beat Dust Pounder. But Dust Pounder had an aversion to running with another zorca's hindquarters in his view.

Her four supple arms, rounded and aglow with beauty, could not aid her once she mounted a zorca. But when she wrestled with me, stripped, I found her a most slippery customer. We wrestled for our own private amusement — not as we raced, as professionals for gain — and I could not bring myself to use the disciplines of the Krozairs of Zy upon her and so hurl her flat upon her back, panting, and place my foot upon her neck. She did this to me, though, many times, laughing down on me, her eyes dancing with mischief, her vibrant form outlined above me, her coppery hair in disarray, superb.

"Now, Dray Prescot, who says four arms are not better than two!"

"I won't argue, Lara. But for the sweet sake of Djan Himself, take your foot off my windpipe so I can breathe!"

They knew of the Khamorros of Herrelldrin here, of course, being not all that far distant from Pellow, and their own Martial Monks were reputed masters of bloodless combat as well as more serious work with pointed and edged weapons. My hair was growing back and I was shaving, as I sometimes did, leaving my arrogant old brown moustache to thrust its way up from my lip. I wondered what Turko the Shield would make of my thus throwing a combat with a four-armed girl — and so cursed and groaned as again the realization of ten infernal years to serve in my prison of time brought me back to reality.

So the time passed in Djanguraj, capital of Djanduin.

Chuktar Rumferling had guessed right about the attack route of the Gorgrens. I knew there would be more of sagacity and experience than sheer guesswork in this decision as to which pass to throw most of his weight. The first of this fresh invasion from Gorgrendrin was hurled back. I stood silently in the crowded streets to watch the wounded come in. On that day the new king was fished from the river, its yellow mud disturbed by his finery and his jewels, and a new king installed himself.

The main strength of the army lay carefully positioned along the frontier under the cover of the Yawfi Suth and the Wendwath; those left at home in Djanguraj struggled to keep the country on its feet.

This period proved near-disastrous to the Djangs. Before the troubles there had been three kings who had ruled for over a hundred years each, and before that there had never been this weakening rapid succession. Djang and Obdjang had ascended the throne in the sacred court of the warrior gods at the center of the Palace of Illustrious Ornament. No continuity could be achieved, it seemed, and even the expedient of the Obdjangs and Djangs failed in allowing a diff of another species to ascend the throne. A Rapa, a Chulik, and a Bleg succeeded one another with the rapidity of utter ruin.

I saw Coper when the Bleg was cut down from the rafters of his own country house, and the Pallan of the Highways looked exhausted, shrunken. Sinkie was lying down.

"It is good to see you, Notor Prescot. These are evil days in Djanduin."

Rather too carelessly, I said, "The army will have to return to set a strong king upon the throne. You, my dear Pallan, or Chuktar Rumferling, or one of your friends who see eye to eye with you."

At this Sinkie sat bolt upright with a shriek.

"Notor Prescot! I consider you a good and valued friend! But to speak thus! Would you condemn my poor dear husband to a terrible fate — do you want his blood to stain the faerling throne?"

"Of course not, Lady Sinkie, as well you know. But there must be a man of courage and strength and sound common sense. The markets complain of the prices of food. Ships from countries overseas do not wish to trade because we cannot guarantee either their safety or payment. Why, I can only make a living by winning in the zorca races—"

"We have heard, Notor Prescot."

They were a straitlaced pair, these two, and yet I liked them much. We talked more and I believe it was then that Pallan Coper began to come around to the dreadful idea that perhaps Naghan Rumferling, or one of their circle, would have to chance his life as king. I was shown out by their personal servant, Dolar, a massive Djang of ferocious appearance and childlike mind, a man of enormous courage and strength and utmost loyalty. He had been the first of those Djangs who, on fire, had leaped from the burning inn to fight the leemsheads.

Back at *The Paline and Queng* I made a frugal supper of bread — not done in the bols fashion, I may say — butter a little too long out of the icebox, and a pon-sho chop that had seen better days. I had the money to buy better provender; the troubles had dried up markets and the country folk were frugally storing food against worse days to come. The whole countryside was in unrest, for the leemsheads now openly waylaid and slew any Obdjang they could find. If the Kov of Hyr Khor thought he would frighten Djangs like Chuktar Rumferling by these tactics, he was well out in his calculations. But Sinkie and Ortyg Coper were two worried Obdjangs.

At one time ships from Ng'groga used to call regularly at Djanguraj. The first time I had seen one of the tall, fair-haired Ng'grogans I had jumped forward with joy, expecting to find Inch; and then sober sense returned. Here in Djanguraj we were a mere three hundred or so dwaburs almost due south from Ng'groga. But the ships, simple single-decked brig-rigged craft, seldom reached in past the pharos of Port Djanguraj now.

The days of my enforced imprisonment limped past. And each day it seemed to me the state of the country worsened. If the army suffered a reverse now, Djan Himself knew what would happen. The Lady Lara Kholin Domon still wrestled me and one day, so occupied was I with my miserable thoughts, I forgot what I was doing, and caught two of her wrists. I twisted and pulled and sent her flying beautifully through the air to land with an almighty thump upon the mat. Three of her hands punched down to spring her back to her feet while the fourth rubbed her bottom, and then I was on her and tying her in knots and pressed my foot on her windpipe.

She glared up in a fury, and so, remembering, I let my foot slip and then she was on me like a leem and belted me down until I yelled quarter.

Even the zorca races were poorly attended, the lavish hippodrome, which they call *merezo* on Kregen, sparsely filled and the bets poor.

Lara had introduced me to her cousin, Felder Kholin Mindner, who was a Jiktar of the aerial forces and therefore as highly placed as a Djang had any right to expect in the military services. He had been wounded in an affray and was home convalescing. What he told me of the army convinced me that if the emergency at home was not speedily ended, then the army would simply march on the capital and compel some sense into the politicians. What that would do as regards the Gorgrendrin situation was not something any Djang would wish to contemplate.

There were few fliers in Djanduin, but the Djanduin Air Service, being manned by Djangs, was as smart and efficient as any other. Felder Kholin Minder was a Jiktar of the flyers,[9] riding a saddle-bird peculiar to Djanduin, called a flutduin, a powerful bird with wide yellow wings and a vicious, deadly black beak. We discussed the military situation; but he burst out with the usual realistic Djang observation: "May all the devils in a Herrelldrin hell take me if I understand strategy, Notor Prescot! How Chuktar Naghan does it I'll never know. But he peers down at his maps and he measures up with his ruler, and walks his dividers across, and then he thinks, and then, by Djan! we're all flying off helter-skelter and, as neat as you like, there are the Opaz-forsaken rasts of Gorgrens all lined up ready for us to belt into! I tell you, Notor Prescot, these Obdjangs are powerful clever fellows!"

"Both races of Djanduin get along well," I said. "I feel it a great shame that the country suffers so. If you Djangs accept the Obdjangs, as they accept you—"

"Absolutely right, Notor Prescot! We do and they do!"

"—then it seems that Kov Nath Jagdur is a mischievous man."

"I'd like to see him in the Ice Floes of Sicce!"

The use of the name Djang for either of the two peoples is quite correct; the little gerbil-faced fellows are often called Obdjangs. Very seldom are the four-armed warriors called Dwadjangs, which is a name to which they are entitled.

Eventually I came to find out why I had not come across a crossbow when I had rifled through the dead outside the inn on the occasion I had arrived in Djanduin. The Djangs use the curved compound reflex bow, a very similar weapon to those used by my clansmen and by my archers of Valka. The crossbow is a weapon they manufacture; not well, and they generally import examples for their crossbow regiments. So an arbalest is one of the first weapons a Djang soldier will snatch up on the scene of battle.

We went swimming in a scented indoor pool and Lara's parents joined us, laughing and splashing. I was invited to stay for supper, an invitation I accepted with alacrity, for although I had a sufficiency of money I had no influence, and the Kholins had both, and so could secure supplies.

We were halfway through an extremely fine meal, although Lara's father, Vad Larghos, would keep apologizing for the meanness of his table, and her mother, a woman still beautiful with her coppery hair bound with silver moon-bloom petals, kept throwing him reproachful glances as though the emergency and lack of the usual abundance of food were all his fault, when the majordomo announced a messenger.

"For the Notor Prescot, Lord of Strombor!" he boomed out.

Dolar stumbled in. His gray trousers, his dark blue cloak, the shirt visible beneath his lorica, were hideously splashed with blood. He looked exhausted. We all leaped up and I pressed a golden cup of wine into his hands. He drank like a leem.

"The Pallan!" he cried out, when he could get his breath. Then, remembering his manners, he said: "Lahal, Notor Prescot. The master and mistress! They send for you. Chuktar Naghan Rumferling is dead, assassinated, and they need all loyal help."

Nine

"You hairy graint, Dray Prescot!"

Wild alarums and excursions and mad dashes through the night sky of Kregen, well, they have been a pretty constant part of my life on that beautiful yet terrible world. The Maiden with the Many Smiles floated high above us as we saddled up, strapping the clerketers tightly over our flying silks and leathers, and sent the flutduins lunging into the air.

Chuktar Naghan Rumferling, who was now dead, had been visiting a base camp at Cafresmot, halfway to the Mountains of Mirth. Pallan Coper and his wife had visited him there; I wondered, as I stretched forward along the neck of the giant flying bird and battled through the rushing air, if that visit had to do with a kingly crown and throne.

Pink moonlight washed over the steadily beating wings of the flutduins, and their sharp black beaks jutted forth ready, it seemed, to impale any obstruction. We flew on, with a steady remorseless wing-beat to lull us into a false sense of security. Wounded though he was, although much recovered, Felder Mindner had insisted on coming with us. Lara, too, had borne down all opposition, and her father, the Vad, had thereupon announced that he valued Naghan Rumferling highly, and the Pallan Coper, also, and would come with us, Nundji take him if he didn't!

Dolar, the faithful servant to Coper, in his turn hadinsisted on rousing the other loyal friends he had been bidden to summon. Much of the blood spattering him, dried and caked as it was from his flight from the Mountains of Mirth, was not his own. He had merely said, "They would have prevented me leaving, Vad," when Vad Larghos questioned him.

Truly, the Djangs have thews of iron and a simplistic view of life!

So we knew there were others in the sky this night, outward bound for the base camp of the army of the east.

If the Gorgrens got wind of this night's doings, and decided to attack, who would there be capable of reading their plans and scheming to defeat them? So many of the Obdjangs had been slaughtered by this maniac, Kov Nath Jagdur, that the High Command was decidedly thin on the ground — or in the air.

Cafresmot stood a good long way from the fighting front, the Mountains of Mirth rise something like halfway between the Yawfi Suth and Djanguraj and have in the past proved the final insurmountable obstacle to armies invading from the east. That is why they are called what they are. How many and many a time, so I had been told with a chuckle, had proud and confident armies burst through one of the tortuous routes around the Yawfi Suth or the Wendwath and marched through Eastern Djanduin, full of hopes of easy conquest and glory now they had broken into the country. And then, they had seen rising before them the sharp and narrow peaks of a mountain range that extended north and south and curved in a bow that faced them. Not overly grand or full of hauteur, the Mountains of Mirth, standing no comparison whatsoever with The Stratemsk, and yet many and many a time they halted enemy invasions in relatively poor country, and turned them back. The shock had proved disastrous to many armies, not least the Gorgrens on the single long-ago occasion when they had managed to reach the mountains; and the men of Djanduin had roared their merriment.

Truly, they were the Mountains of Mirth!

From Djanguraj to the outermost western limits of the Yawfi Suth is about a hundred and seventy dwaburs. So this night we had to fly approximately fifty dwaburs, for the Mountains of Mirth stand roughly a hundred dwaburs from the capital, roughly seventy from the Yawfi Suth.

The firm steady beat of the flutduin I rode impressed me. I have ridden impiters, corths, fluttrells, mirvols, and many other of the marvelous saddle-flyers of Kregen, and it is difficult to choose the absolute best, for all have their good points as well as their weaknesses. We passed over the sleeping countryside and as She of the Veils rose before us and we blustered on against the rushing wind, the night filled with the pinkish moons-radiance. We followed the pink-glimmering reflections of the River of Wraiths. This river rises in the Mountains of Mirth and curving boldly southward flows westward through Djanduin and so to the Bay of Djanguraj where the Tarnish Channel meets the Ocean of Doubt. On that river stands Djanguraj, and also Cafresmot, our destination. Up and down, rising and falling with the long smooth wing-beats, we hurtled on through the level air and all about us fell the pink moons-light.

This part of Djanduin is rich in agriculture and husbandry, and we passed over the wide fields and the farms and the carefully tended grazing, and presently we saw beneath us the darker splotches of shadow against the pink glimmer, and so knew we had reached Cafresmot. The town is small but active, with a good cattle and ponsho market and with a thriving trade in corn and other staples. Felder Mindner, who knew the area well, had received directions from Dolar, and we swung a little north and swooped down toward a lightless ranch house set among missals. The night wind rustled the branches as Felder Mindner dropped his flutduin beyond the trees and we settled to the earth screened from the house by the missals.

Cautiously we crept along a track rutted by cart wheels and pocked by the hooves of calsanys. No one spoke. We were aware of the need of surprise, and I was quite content to let this Jiktar Mindner lead, for he seemed to know his business. Also, and the real reason, was that I recognized I was here only as a friend of Coper's. Dolar had been to other houses in Djanguraj and aroused friends of the Pallan. Chuktar Naghan, visiting here, had been met by Pallan Coper, but had been treacherously slain by disaffected members of an army unit stationed here, well back from the front. If Kov Nath had instigated this murder, and we had yet to prove that, he had struck a shrewd blow. It would have been useless for Dolar to have flown eastward to summon assistance from the army of the east, for, as he had told us, Coper suspected treason among them. If an army mutiny was to be added to the troubles of Djanduin I could see little hope for the country.

This troubled me as I crept forward through the pink radiance from the moons, my sword in my fist.

A Horter of Havilfar will carry his thraxter with him as a mere matter of dress; but I had taken nothing else in the way of weapons to what should have been a pleasant evening of swimming and feasting with the Demons, and so they had lent me a soldier's gear. The thraxter gleamed silvery pink. The shield I held high on my left shoulder. At my waist swung a djangir. Some of Vad Larghos' men carried crossbows, the others the compound reflex bow. We padded on like a wild hunting pack of drangs, scenting our quarry.

No lights, no sounds, came from the ranch house.

We passed the corrals on our left and heard the sleeping snorts of joats and the restless snuffling of totrixes. Mindner waited for us to come up and he spoke in a whisper to Vad Larghos and me.

"I fear we are too late, Vad. If the Pallan was not dead there would be sounds of fighting—"

"If you are right, Felder—" Vad Larghos took a shuddering breath. "If you are right, my boy, we must take our revenge upon these mad leem!"

As you know I am not a man much concerned with revenge. Justice — of a suitable kind — usually satisfies me. But I own I shared a little of the Vad's anger. Punishment must be seen to be inflicted, for the country was falling to pieces and good men were dead.

We crept on and reached the final packed-earth space before the row of tall windows fronting the house. I looked carefully in the streaming moonlight and could see no sign of movement.

The Vad waved his men to left and right and, their bows nocked, they spread out.

Lara stood close to me, breathing in quick excited gasps, her face pale in the moon-glow. I put my hand on her left upper arm, and pressed, and she turned quickly to me and would have spoken, but I took my hand and the thraxter away swiftly and touched the hilt to my lips. I was indicating silence upon her; I think, now, she understood that little gesture differently.

Those around me were aware of the tense and jumpy business this was. At any moment a storm of arrows and bolts might spurt from those dark windows and cut us down. Someone had to go up to the front door and find out the truth of the situation.

Why I did what I did, I think, is easy to explain. Such boredom, such bitterness, such hellish misery had been my portion ever since I had been parted from Delia that a kind of fey recklessness had overtaken me. As I marched up to the door with my shield high and thraxter low I knew — I *knew* — the ranch house would be deserted when I broke in.

I am not given to having my nerves racked by the various frightful experiences that befall me from time to time and which make life on Kregen so fascinating. If a bolt flicked toward me I would take it on my shield. I wanted to know what had become of Coper and Sinkie. I marched up to the door and kicked it in and smashed my way inside.

The darkness was partitioned by the long angular parallelograms of pink moonlight from the windows, paired from She of the Veils and the Maiden with the Many Smiles, softer and stronger, as one is the fourth and the other the first moon of Kregen. I padded in, vicious and ready for instant combat.

The house was empty.

Mindner followed me in and then the Vad and Lara and we searched, and gradually, with the lighting of torches and the shouting and running of feet, we made a nice little hullabaloo, as the Vad's men turned the house upside down.

"You take great chances, Notor Prescot," said Jiktar Mindner. He flexed his four arms meaningfully.

"Perhaps. Where will the rasts have taken the Pallan and the Lady Sinkie?"

"We must find them!" exclaimed Lara. "Poor Sinkie! Think what may be happening to her!"

"I fear they must all be dead, daughter," said her father, the Vad, somewhat gruffly.

"If they are, Vad," I said, in my old surly way, "I will not believe it until I see them lying before me — dead."

"Oh!" said Lara, and she put her sword down as though suddenly aware of what it was.

"Jiktar!" I said and I saw them all jerk up at my tone. I had spoken as I would have spoken to a Jiktar of the army of Vallia or Valka, or a wild clansman who had not jumped immediately when I asked a question.

"I think—" Mindner began, a little hazily.

"By Vox! Spit it out!"

"If, as Dolar said, this terrible thing was done by the local army unit, they might have gone back to their barracks."

"Are the Dwadjangs then so envious of the Obdjangs?" As he opened his mouth to make some sort of answer I chopped him off. "No matter. I know what I know of the Djangs. We fly at once to the barracks. Jiktar Mindner! You lead!"

"Yes, Notor Prescot."

And so once more we mounted our flyers and took the wide-winged wind-eaters into the night sky of Kregen.

As we hurtled through the rushing air I considered how strange it was that these big rough fighting-men, the Djangs, so desperately needed someone to tell them what to do in moments like this. In a battle or an affray Mindner would never have been at a loss. If I say that the Djangs fight in such wise as to turn even Chuliks a little more yellowly pale than usual, I do not exaggerate. But they need leaders!

They would have all gone flying off to the barracks, whooping, to plunge down into as bloody an affray as you could wish; I had had to tell Mindner to detail a man to stay at the deserted ranch house to warn the following flights.

Yet this was only a tactical move, nothing clever in it, and I suspected there were as many degrees of intuitive intelligence as well as learned skill among the Djangs as among any other diffs. A number of the young fighting-men of Djanduin would go off to become mercenaries; but the vast majority stayed at home to work the soil and serve as soldiers in their own army, constantly menaced by the Gorgrens. Therefore the formidable fighting shape of the four-armed Djang was seldom encountered in the empires and kingdoms and free cities of Kregen. Djanduin is a rich kingdom, and yet it holds itself aloof from the rest of Havilfar, secure behind its treacherous bogs of the Yawfi Suth, the mysterious waters of the Wendwath, and the serried peaks of the Mountains of Mirth.

There was action aplenty at the barracks.

We saw the lights flaring and heard the yelling and shouting, whoops of ferocious merriment, the discordant clanging and banging of gongs and punklinglings and drums, and the wailing of flutes, the brazen notes of razztorns and trumpets.

We touched down out of sight and Mindner looked over a screen of thorn-ivy bushes forming a kind of natural boma around the barrack area, and he looked as delighted, as fierce, as obsessively pleased, as any fighting-man has any right to be casting his avaricious gaze on his foemen.

"They are Dwadjangs of North Djanduin, very fine doughty warriors, and I have no doubt that the madman Nath Jagdur has besotted their minds with evil promises."

If it came to a fight between Djangs, as I knew, they'd fight, by Zair, they'd fight!

I wished to avoid bloodshed. Oh, I was bitter and savage enough in my self-misery not to care who got themselves killed; but I suppose the devil was working his dark and devious plans in me even then.

We could see Coper and Sinkie, with other Obdjangs and a few Dwadjangs who must have remained loyal to them, sitting in a corner of the compound, the light from the two moons bright upon them. They had been bound with thongs. They looked dejected and frightened, as they had every right to be. And yet I saw Coper leaning toward his wife, and the way her little body jerked upright, her whiskers quivering, and I could guess with what sweet and reasonable fire he was putting courage back into her. He was a fine man, Pallan O. Fellin Coper!

The noise came from a drunken band of soldiery who had broken out the musical instruments; each man with a piece that would make a noise was making a noise, and each man was playing a different tune from his neighbor. Other men sang and laughed and jumped, and continually they drank deeply of the liquor that poured from great barrels turned on their sides and wedged up on trestles. I sniffed. Dopa. Well, no wonder they were making this racket. Dopa is a fiendish drink guaranteed to make the coolest headed man fighting drunk in a second, if he takes it neat. The dopa dens usually water or soft-drink their dopa in the ratio of ten to one.

"Drunk!" said Vad Larghos, with great distaste.

"I think, Vad, that Kov Nath Jagdur has made them drunk, for otherwise it is doubtful, even though they are Northern Djangs, that they would do what they have done." Mindner looked a little sick, as he looked on this betrayal of the army in which he served.

"They may be too drunk to notice us," I said. I merely tested the wind as I spoke, for I was forming theories about the Djang fighting-man.

"The hulus!" said Mindner. "They're drunk enough to tangle with a leem. They'll see us."

There had to be a way around this. There were ten in the party of captives, and at least a hundred drunks cavorting about. Mindner had called them hulus. Well, here on Earth we apply insulting names, in amused despair, to idiots who are doing something wrong that we know, in normal circumstances, they would not do. It is all in the tone of voice, as when you call a man a bastard or a ratbag you can mean many different things. On Kregen one such term is hulu. And it summed up these onker-rasts perfectly, for they were more villainous at the moment than a simple stupid onker, and yet not quite as outrightly villainous as rasts.

I said to Mindner, "You will, on my signal, keep them occupied here. I am going to get them out with the flutduins." He started to huff up at this, but I was brutal with him. "Don't get yourself killed, Jiktar. And keep an eye open for the Lady Lara and her father. If you have to run away — aye! — run away from them, then run. Just give me a few murs in there, that is all."

He managed to get out, "I shall accompany you, Notor Pres—"

"Do not be a nurdling onker! You keep those hulus occupied in there, and, by the Black Chunkrah, they won't know a thing has hit 'em."

I gave him no time to argue. Back into that moon-spattered night I went, and the Lady Lara pattered along with me, and I turned my look on her, and I knew — Zair forgive me! — what my face looked like then. "Go back, Lara, and keep out of the way. If you do not, I shall tan you so that you won't sit a zorca for a sennight!"

"You hairy graint, Dray Prescot!"

And then I — Dray Prescot — chuckled. It was not in me to laugh, not then. "I have been called a hairy graint before, Lara, many and many a time — to my eternal joy!"

"Oh — you!" she said, and swung about and marched back to the distraction party outside the boma.

Managing the flutduins was not as difficult as I had expected, and they followed me into the air on leading lines, a smoothly rhythmical flight that slotted them into a pattern that economically took up the minimum space their wide yellow wings required. We passed over the boma and that was the signal Mindner awaited. As I went streaking over the packed earth I twisted to look at Mindner and his party. They were putting up a brave show, loosing arrows, yelling and shrieking, and they'd thought to twist up quick torches from clumps of grass which they tossed cunningly down just the other side of the boma. These served before they burned out to illuminate the boma and the drunken soldiery and, by contrast, to drown the pink light of the two moons and throw Coper and the captives into shadow.

The flutduins were birds that could not be easily hidden. I had no stupid ideas that I would not be seen. But the Vad's marksmen were aware of the importance of Coper. So many Obdjangs had been killed that the Pallan of the Highways was now a most exalted personage. Vad Larghos' men would shoot, and they would shoot to kill.

The flutduins landed and I was off the back of my bird and at Coper and Sinkie with a hunting knife. Their thongs sliced free.

"Oh! Notor Prescot!"

"Up, Ortyg!" I yelled, as Sinkie, calling on her husband Ortyg, fainted into his arms. "Grab Sinkie and get on a flutduin! *Move!*

Savage slashes that, I confess, drew blood, released the other captives and I herded them onto the remaining birds. The flutduins rose into the sky. A crossbow bolt sheared past my arm and vanished into the shadows. I whirled. Half a dozen drunken soldiers were staring at me, and shouting and gesticulating. One of them was trying to wind his arbalest, but the ratchet kept slipping and he kept falling over his own feet. Another drew his thraxter, waving wildly, and charged.

I knew what they would have done to Coper and Sinkie when Kov Nath Jagdur arrived, and so I could resign myself to cutting this hulu down. He fell without a screech. The flutduins were aloft now, their yellow wings powerful in the pink moons-shine. I jumped for my bird, the last remaining one, and took off without strapping myself up in the clerketer. I found the ready bow and I drew and loosed six deadly shafts before we rose past the boma, and six of those less drunk than their fellows, who were trying to shoot up, fell, screeching.

Out over the boma we whirled and a darkness descended as the crude torches flared and died. Then eyes adjusted and I was seeing my comrades rushing for the flutduins and mounting up. Each bird can carry three people, at push of pike, and we were not overloaded as we winged off into the Kregan night.

No surprise at all, none whatsoever, that the Lady Lara contrived to leap up before me and let me grasp her around the waist as the flutduin belabored the air. She leaned back and her coppery hair brushed my cheeks.

"I declare, Notor Prescot! Hai Jikai!"

We flew off, and, I think, perhaps that had been a good Jikai. Not a High Jikai. But, still, a Jikai to remember.

Ten

Khokkak the Meddler and the King of Djanduin

They say the devil finds work for idle hands.

Well, there are many devils of many different shades of deviltry on Kregen, as there are parts of that profoundly mysterious planet where devils are accounted of no value at all; and I suppose the devil who got into me was most likely to be Khokkak the Meddler.

I do not think it could have been Sly the Ambitious, or Gleen the Envious. No, on reflection, some few aspects of Hoko the Amusingly Malicious must have helped along the general deviltry of Khokkak the Meddler.

At any event, what with my own desperate boredom and savage misery, and the way the country was going, and the stupid succession of stupid kings, and what was happening to fine people like Coper and Sinkie, for something to do I decided I would become king of Djanduin.

This was a consciously mischievous decision.

As you will know, among my clansmen my success there had been entirely because I would not allow myself to be killed, when, in truth, I had no great reason to live, and through the accumulation of obi and a growing respect, culminating in the selection by the elders and the election of myself as leader, subsequently Zorcander. And in Zenicce no one had been more surprised than I had been myself when Great-Aunt Shusha — who was not my great-aunt — had bestowed on me the House of Strombor. And in Valka, I had fought, I and my men, for the island, and they had petitioned behind my back with the Emperor to make me their Strom. As for being Prince Majister of Vallia, that meant nothing. Delia, as the Princess Majestrix, had been the prize not only for me, but I as her prize.

So I had not gone out of my way to grasp for ranks and titles and honors. I had with some calculation accepted Can-thirda and Zamra, but they were political acquisitions, with an eye to the future.

Here, in Djanduin, with much inner amusement, I took a calm decision. I, Dray Prescot, would make myself King of Djanduin.

It would not be easy. That was all to the good. I had what was left of ten years to do it in, and the harder it was the more amusement I would have.

Oh, do not think I did not falter on occasion as the years wore on, when I saw fine young men, superb fighting Djangs, dying on some stupid battlefield, or in some affray that went awry; but I took the weakling's comfort in the knowledge that had I not struggled to put the country in order those fine young men would have died, anyway, and many more with them. When Nath Wonlin Sundermair was assassinated as he waited in my tent for me — while I was out repairing a varter that had been damaged by a chunk of rock thrown by the enemy artillery — do not think I was unmoved. N. Wonlin Sundermair had fought them and shouted for aid, and my guards had come running, too late. The assassins were caught. A military court sat, and adjudged, and they were hanged, all six of them, hanged and left to rot.

The fateful charisma that envelops me whether I will it or not worked for me in Djanduin. Many men, and not only Djangs, but Lamnias and Fristles and Brokelsh and others of the marvelous diffs of Kregen, had reached a dead end in their hopes for Djanduin. The leemsheads were now so bold in their raids that only strongly escorted parties of non-Djangs might venture out onto the white dusty roads, or take cautiously to the air astride their flutduins.

The onslaught of the Gorgrens had, at last and following on the death of Chuktar Naghan Rumferling, burst through a pathway of the Yawfi Suth, and a clever feint southward toward the Wendwath had sent the bulk of the Djanduin army rushing southward. The Gorgrens surged through the land of East Djanduin to reach the Mountains of Mirth. Here they were stopped, not by the army but by those old allies of Djanduin, the Mountains of Mirth and the desolate country at their feet to the east.

You will recall that great period when the events chronicled in the song "The Fetching of Drak na Valka" were being enacted. Somehow, during this time when I struggled with only two hands to hold Djanduin together and to defeat the Gorgrens, I could take no high joy from the enterprise. No song, I thought, would be composed by the skalds of Djanduin to commemorate these wild and skirling events.

Well, I was wrong in that, as you shall hear.

One day when the little band I had gathered together — old soldiers, young men out for adventure, rascals like Khobo the So, one or two diffs from overseas who thought I looked a likely prospect for future plunder — came down into a hollow among tuffa trees and found the remnants of an army unit shattered and burned, I met Kytun Kholin Dom. We had a smart set-to with the Gorgrens — nasty brutes — before they were seen off, and I took pleasure from the way this tall and agile young Djang fought. He roared his joy as my men came running down swiftly into the hollow between the tuffa trees, and his thraxter twinkled merrily in and out, and his shield rang with return blows.

"You are welcome, Dray Prescot!" he yelled at me, and dispatched his man and swung to engage the next. "Lara has told me what a great shaggy graint you are! But, Lahal! You are right welcome!"

"Lahal, Kytun Dom," I shouted, and ran to stand with him back to back and so beat off the last of the Gorgrens. Truly, he is a man among men, Kytun!

We had incredible adventures together and he became a good comrade to whom I could confide much of my story. We understood each other. He was a Dwadjang, and therefore as bonny a fighter as there is on Kregen, and I was apim, and therefore as canny as an Obdjang. We formed a great team.

The years went by and the kings came and went and the Gorgrens moldered sullenly to the east of the Mountains of Mirth. On the day they made their final massive attempt to break through they also did something they had not attempted before, according to Kytun, through all of recorded history.

We were riding our flutduins toward the mountains followed by the advanced aerial wing of our army — oh, yes, by this time we had our own army, and efficient and formidable it was, too — when the merker reached us. We alighted at once.

"I find it impossible to believe, Dray," said Kytun. His coppery hair blazed in the emerald and ruby lights from Antares. His tough, bluffly handsome face with the amber eyes twisted up in deep reflection as he twisted the signal paper. "The Gorgrens, may Djan rot 'em! Sailing across the sea to attack us!"

"The Gorgrens hate the sea, Notor," said old Panjit, the Obdjang Chuktar who had thrown in his lot with us, at Pallan Coper's urgent suggestion. "They have no navy, no marine. They are a nomad people above themselves with pride and greed who wish to sweep us up into their jaws, as they have done Tarnish and Sava."

"I agree, Panjit," said Kytun. "But the signal says their ships are landing men in the Bay of Djanguraj, at the mouth of the River of Wraiths."

"Then the capital is immediately threatened." Panjit gave his fine white whiskers a polishing rub. "We cannot be in two places at once. The army of the east must hold the Mountains of Mirth — but they are too weak, as we well know." He looked at me a moment, wanting me to say something; but I remained silent. Finally he said, "The reserve army should be called out, of course. But they will never stand if the invasion is so close to Djanguraj." Again he rubbed his whiskers. "We will have to return."

Kytun looked at me.

Our officers had gathered, standing in the relaxed yet alert postures of the fighting-man. And very romantic and barbaric they looked, with their flying leathers covered in flying silks and furs, their jewels and their ornaments, their weapons gleaming, the feathers nodding from their helmets. I took heart from their firm bronzed faces, the light of determination in their eyes. The Djangs are a warrior people. They would need all their devotion to me, all their belief in an apim's powers of strategy, for them to follow me now and trust my word.

I said, "We go on to the Mountains of Mirth."

There was a silence.

I can see them now in my mind's eye, as I sit talking into this microphone, here on the world of my birth. Oh, they are a bonny lot, the fighting-men of Djanduin! The brilliant colors of their decorations, their silver and gold sword-mountings, the jewels studding their harness, the meticulously executed designs upon their shields, all the affected trappings a fighting-man acquires during his years of service giving them this wonderful pagan, barbaric look tempered by the discipline of a professional army. The flutduin men are addicted to the pelisse and sabretache and look like savage editions of hussars. Their national weapon, the djangir, is worn by every soldier — aye! — and he knows how to use it to devastating advantage.

The silence hung.

Slowly I turned and glowered on them, one by one. The streaming opaz light from Zim and Genodras flooded down in brilliance all about us upon that windy plain, and the feathers and silks and scarves rustled and fluttered. With a steady slogging tramp of metal-studded sandals the infantry were marching up, as I glared around on my knot of high officers. The joat-mounted cavalry trotted by, every lance aligned, the colors flying.

I waited for one of them to break the silence, but all, every one, lowered his eyelids as my gaze fell upon him. I glared with special ferocity upon Felder Mindner, for he was my Jiktar of flutduins, and he looked away, and slapped his sabretache against his leg, and fidgeted; but he did not speak.

"By Zim-Zair!" I burst out, at last, forced by their sullen silence to speak against my will. "Must I explain everything!"

Kytun — that same K. Kholin Dom, who was a Kov and a good comrade — at last lifted his head, the coppery hair flying, and he said, "Dray — Notor Prescot, Lord of Strombor! We have followed you faithfully and well, in good times and in bad. But now that Djanguraj is attacked from the sea we—"

I would not let him continue. I did not wish him to utter words he would afterward regret.

"Yes! You have vowed to follow me, and I seek nothing from any of you, except the saving of the country!"

This was a lie. Thankfully, it was the last lie I had need of telling my men, my wonderful men, of Djanduin.

And, do not misunderstand me, for there were many girls who marched and rode and flew with us, glorious girls with coppery hair and tawny skins and flashing eyes, girls whose four arms were as deft with sword and djangir as any man's. Girls who, into the bargain, had other, gentler skills.

"You have sworn to serve me as I serve you in freeing our country from the devil Gorgrens and the devil leems-heads! Together, Obdjang, Dwadjang, apim, diff, we will cleanse Djanduin and found for ourselves a new, clean, brave country where our children may live in peace!"

Around us now the army gathered, *my* army, the force I had built up and trained and given spirit, all so that Khokkak the Meddler might glee within my skull.

In the sound of stamping hooves, the snorts of joats, the rustling of flutduin wings, the clink of armor and weapons, that silence came back. It hung there between us like a rashoon of the inner sea, stark and dark and brutal.

I glared at Felder; he is a fine fellow but a blockhead. I glared at the Obdjang Chuktar Panjit, and he rubbed his whiskers and looked away.

Again I looked around the circle of my officers, my trusted comrades, and again they looked away.

And then Kytun stepped forward. He dragged out — not his thraxter but his djangir. He lifted it high.

"I trust Notor Prescot! I believe in him! I, for one, will fly to the Mountains of Mirth and there thrash the Gorgrens, once and for all!" He swung the broad short blade about his head. "Who will follow me and ride with Notor Prescot?"

The spell was broken, the dam breached. The djangirs flashed out, a forest of blades, and they cried, every one, that they would follow me. For, by Djan, was I not Notor Prescot, the man who had sworn he would put their poor abused country back on its feet again?

I stood, looking on them as they shouted and cheered and pledged themselves again, as the great cry was taken up by the massed men beyond, as infantry and cavalry and artillery and flyers all caught the fever, the understanding that this was a new and bright beginning, a fresh compact between themselves and me. And I looked and saw what I had wrought.

In that moment, I now see, I drove Khokkak the Meddler from my brain.

In that moment there on the wind-blowing plain with the acclamations and the pledges of my men ringing in my ears, I sloughed off at last my willful foolishness, my malicious antics. I had decided to become King of Djanduin because I had been bored, on a whim, as something to do to amuse me. Now I saw something I should have seen from the very beginning: that I had been meddling in the affairs of men and women, men and women whose own lives were profoundly affected by my petty games.

Never again with the men of Djanduin could I act the games-master. The country needed a strong hand at the helm. If I could become King of Djanduin, I would do so. Not, this time, just for amusement and to see if I could do it in the time allowed me, but so as to fulfill all the glib pledges I had made, so as really to make of the country a fine and wonderful place in which to live — as we had in Valka!

So we rode and flew and marched to the Mountains of Mirth, and we caught the Gorgrens as they tried to debouch from a high pass. The battle was long and weary, but in the end we overcame and routed them and sent them packing back to East Djanduin. When we had overcome our internal problems and gathered our strength we in our turn would descend from the Mountains of Mirth and drive the cramphs of Gorgrens right out of Djanduin and back over their own borders.

As you know the colors of Djanduin are orange and gray. I had not bothered overmuch about banners and flags, apart from ensuring that every unit flew its identifying guidon or standard. But just before the battle in the high pass of the Mountains of Mirth, in the pass known as the Jaws of Nundji, I had made a flag. I told the women who stitched it that it was to be a large flag, and a noble one, with a heavy gold-bullion fringe, and with golden ropes and tassels, and to the men who turned the staff I told them I wanted a djangir blade mounted atop, proudly, as was fitting.

So, when we fought the Gorgrens in the pass of the Jaws of Nundji, and routed them utterly, my old flag flew over my men. That old flag with its yellow cross on the scarlet field floated high as we charged down. Truly, with Old Superb to fight under, I was totally committed. No longer was I merely playing a political and military game, so as to see if I might make myself king within a stipulated time.

Now, I did not care if I became king or not. Now I decided that Djanduin came first...

You may laugh and mock and call me a sentimental fool. For, of course, you might say, these Djangs were a leaderless bunch, naturally they would accept my decision. But they were hotheaded fighting-men, and they believed their homes were in danger, behind their backs, with their enemies creeping upon their wives and children from the sea. Had you been there on that windswept plain, under the streaming brilliance of the Suns of Scorpio, I do not think you would have dubbed me either an onker or sentimental.

When we were taking an enforced rest after the battle, seeing to our wounded and counting the cost, and I sat in a miserable little tent of hides and pored over the map, in the light of a samphron-oil lamp we had captured from the Gorgrens, the merker came.

His fluttclepper was exhausted. These fast racing birds are built for speed and speed and more speed. He had reached us from Djanduin in record time.

After the Llahals had been made and he had gulped a goblet of wine, he said, "I see my message of warning is not necessary."

"Tell us, man!" Kytun spat out wrathfully, as befitted a Kov kept waiting, although he was a good-hearted fellow as I well know.

"As to that," I said, "the merker will say that the ships were a feint, that they carried straw dummies, that only a small force landed, and straightaway took themselves off when once they had aroused the neighborhood and news had been carried to Djanguraj in all haste, as they could see."

The merker gaped at me.

Then Kytun let out a great bellow of laughter.

"By Zodjuin of the Silver Stux! Is that the way of it?"

"Aye, Kov," said the messenger. He licked his bearded lips where the wine glittered in the lamplight. "It is as the Notor says. The reserve army marched out, and the Gorgrens had gone." He looked at me. "By your leave, Notor, there is more."

I nodded.

"The ships were provided by the leemshead Kov Nath Jagdur. The plan was his. A Gorgren was taken prisoner, and he talked freely."

"By Djan!" said Kytun, leaping up and fairly rocking the tent with the violence of his anger. "One day I will take that false Kov's head from his shoulders."

"The king has sent messengers to the army of the east, to warn them; they began their westward march as soon as news was brought them that the Gorgrens had invaded by sea, difficult though it be to believe such a thing."

"Difficult to believe the Gorgrens would sail the sea, merker, or difficult to believe Chuktar Rogan Kolanier — who is a Zan-Chuktar — would believe it and take his army of the east to the west?"

Kytun chortled at this, and my other officers crowded into the little tent gave vent to their amusement in various picturesque ways. The merker was not discomposed. His light colored eyes remained fastened on me. In his life, I suppose, he was accustomed to delivering messages that would evoke all manner of violent responses in their recipients.

"I think, Notor, both."

I looked at him.

"Your name, merker?"

"If it please you, Notor, I am called Chan of the Wings."

I nodded to him. I knew a messenger did not receive the appellation *of the Wings* lightly.

"The Pallan Coper sent you, I know. Therefore you must be a good man. Is there any other news?"

He had no need to hesitate. "Whatever was the news before, Notor, your victory here today will change everything. Now, perhaps, the food will flow more freely." Then, with a great deal of meaning, he added, "The king will be pleased."

Kytun said, somewhat coarsely, "And the king had better think what best to be done about Chuktar Kolanier! He was completely caught by the wiles of those Opaz-forsaken Gorgrens."

"Like Marshal Grouchy," I said, but softly, for they could not understand that reference.

Then, with a simple directness that took the wind out of my sails, for one, the merker Chan of the Wings, committed himself — and others, besides.

"I am privy to many secrets, Notor. I and my fellow merkers — and we are a not insignificant khand — have been saved from despair by you and your army and your determination to save the country. These things we know, for we carry them. We are sworn to secrecy, but we know." By *khand* he meant the merker's guild, or caste, or brotherhood. They were small in number but, by reason of their calling, influential. A good merker is a great jewel in any man's retinue. "We declare for you, Notor Prescot, as king. Take the throne, and we are with you."

A murmur broke out from my officers. This, as far as they were concerned, was the first anyone had said of Notor Prescot, the Lord of Strombor — who was apim! — ascending the faerling throne in the sacred court of the warrior gods.

I sensed the hand of Pallan Coper in this. The old fox! He wanted someone he could trust on the throne, but he sure as the hot springs in the ice floes wasn't going to sit on that hot seat himself!

It was left to Kytun to spring up, waving wildly, and knock the tent completely over so that his bellow rang out between the mountains, echoing back and forth: "Aye! Notor Prescot, Lord of Strombor! *King of Djanduin!*"

Eleven

Kytun Kholin Dorn

There is little left to tell of that first sojourn of mine in the beautiful, wild and headstrong land of Djanduin. Beautiful — for we would look upon the Mountains of Mirth as their narrow peaks pierced the blue Kregan sky and the snow dazzle would glitter like all the diamonds and sapphires in creation; we could turn and look over the vast expanse of West Djanduin with its fields and forests, its meadows and farms, and we felt the ache in the heart that afflicts a man when he looks upon beauty. Wild — for leem prowled in the uncultivated areas, and great gales would blow up the Tarnish Channel and everyone would shutter their windows and pray the roof tiles stayed on. Headstrong — why, yes, for my Dwadjangs proved irresistible in battle, given a fair chance, and the sight of them surging into battle with their four arms going filled me always with a shivery sense of awe.

The Gorgrens remained for a time in occupation of East Djanduin.

The army of the east, hearing of my own army's success, and knowing that the eastern front was for the moment secure, continued on to the capital. Here, before the current king could make a move to discipline him, Chuktar Rogan Kolanier, who was of the Porlin tan, or House, set his men upon the king's bodyguard and burst into the palace. No one ever did know what happened to that king; but Chuktar R. Porlin Kolanier sat himself on the faerling throne in the sacred court of the warrior gods, and was duly crowned.

You may imagine the indignation of my men.

"The impious yetch!" Kytun bellowed, furious, his face an interesting scarlet, his eyes fairly snapping as he strode up waving the merker's signal. We were camped at the base of the mountains, covering three exits, and our flyer scouts patrolled ceaselessly. "I'll have to take his head from his shoulders, Dray! That is crystal clear."

The merker had this time flown here in a flier, and the voller, a lean stripped one-man craft, openly flew the flag of the Pallan Coper. Coper was no longer Pallan of the Highways. Because he had remained alive when so many of his Obdjang colleagues had been murdered he had found himself pressed upward in the civil service beneath the various kings, and he was now Pallan of the Vollers.

"When you quiet down, Kytun, we must make sure the Gorgrens have really withdrawn from the Valley of the Bantings, for if they have it means they—"

"Dray! Dray! Didn't you hear what I said?"

I looked up and although I do not smile easily I managed to crack out a millimeter of lip movement for Kytun, a great fighter and a good comrade.

"I heard, Kytun. There is a saying: 'Give a man full armor and two shields to ride a fluttclepper.' This Chuktar Kolanier will not last."

He glowered down, sullen with his concern for my dignity. "Agreed, Dray, agreed. But we should march for Djanguraj and place you on the faerling throne!"

I stood up. "Perhaps, Kytun, I would prefer to see you seated there."

Kytun threw back his head and bellowed with laughter, his good humor restored. "Me! The Kov of Uttar Djombey? Why, I have no desire to sit on the throne. It needs an Obdjang or an apim. You, Dray Prescot, you!"

We sent back a noncommittal reply by the merker and his flier shot away, traveling fast and low as a flyer came in from the scouts to report the Valley of the Bantings clear.

I set about rearranging our dispositions. Truth to tell, I was merely marking time, giving this new King Kolanier enough rope to hang himself. I knew — or thought I did — that Ortyg Coper would send me the word when it was time to move.

The banting, by the way, is a cheeky little rock-bird of brilliant coloration, not unlike the English chaffinch in a superficial way; their nests high along the rocky clefts grow greater each season and they fill the valley with their darting wings. They live on lizards and insects and are regarded with great affection by the Djangs.

My own messengers were out in force, and with the Kholin tan solidly behind me, and with the obvious scarcity of Obdjangs either capable or willing to take the throne, I felt it to be a mere matter of waiting until the right time and then of striking hard and surely. I had no wish to gain the throne in the same stupid way of those onkers who would, when I succeeded, become my predecessors, and then of having someone else rise up behind my back. Also, I admit, the whole country was sick and tired of this nonsense. They needed a person at the helm who would direct and control, fairly and justly, giving aid to the weak and yet not penalizing too unfairly the strong and clever, so that the wheels of industry and commerce, of religion and order, might continue to turn.

I, Dray Prescot, had set out to take the throne because I had nothing better to do. Now that I had had my eyes opened by the sheer loyalty, the dependence of my men, I hesitated. What right had I to aspire to another country's throne? Would I do any better for them than any of the other idiots who had grabbed the crown from greed? Perhaps I might; as you know I had had considerable success in Valka, and the Clans of Felschraung and Longuelm had prospered. But — and it was a big but — had all the joy gone from the scheme? Because I might now take the throne, had all the contest gone from the exercise?

With all the force of a millstone running downhill events had taken charge.

I discovered that the Kov of Hyr Khor, this Nath Jagdur, had once been of the Djin tan. When he had been declared leemshead, an outlaw, his tan had rejected him. He had made short work of them, and now he alone remained of the tan, with the exception of a young, crippled girl who had sought protection in North Djanduin with the Bolin tan, and who was now, therefore, behind the enemy lines, in an area dominated by the Gorgrens.

Day by day secret messages of support flowed in. Coper was now working urgently. The treasury was bankrupt. The soldiers received no pay. No ships called. The harvest had been good but the farmers, true to their canny nature, hid most of their produce and sold only a tithe of it in the markets. There were riots in the city. The new king, this Kolanier, caroused in the palace, and sent his men out into the countryside to burn barns and seize hidden food. This food was then brought back to the city and distributed only to those in favor with the king. That meant his army and their dependents. Coper wrote that he felt disaster of a colossal scale could not now be prevented unless I struck soon.

So I had to make up my mind.

I prevaricated.

Oh, yes, I was very far from the Dray Prescot who once would hurl himself unthinkingly into the leem's jaws. Now I pondered long and deeply, and, if I say that in the end I made up my mind to do as Coper and Kytun and our other friends begged me to do, and if that sounds megalomaniac to you, I can ask only for understanding. I am conscious always of that old saw about absolute power corrupting absolutely. I had held power in my hands. If I was corrupt I could blame only myself. That I did not think myself corrupt meant merely that, perhaps, I did not grasp the truth. But, also, I doubt if any of you would care to stand up and say to me, face to face, what you might murmur behind my back.

Is that megalomania?

I try always to treat a man fairly, to give him his just deserts, and to seek for mercy if he is evil, and to heap overpraise on him if he is meritorious.

These are a weakling's ways, I know.

On the day appointed we marched for Djanguraj.

We made a magnificent spectacle.

The flutduins beat the sky with their yellow wings, their sharp black beaks pointed on toward success. The infantry marched in their regulation formations, pastang by pastang, regiment by regiment. The artillery trundled on, drawn by sleek teams of quoffas or calsanys. The joats of the cavalry jingled as they trotted on over the white roads. And, over all the host, which had swollen day by day with fresh and eager men anxious to have an end of the troubles, there floated my old scarlet and yellow flag, Old Superb.

A flier reached us from Coper. The merker was that same Chan of the Wings, whom I had grown to trust.

"Lahal, Notor Prescot — soon to be King of Djanduin!"

"Lahal, Chan of the Wings."

He told me the news even as he handed me the balass box.

"The King, this Kolanier, is dead. The Kov of Hyr Khor, Nath Jagdur, sits on the faerling throne!"

My first thought was one of relief.

I might not need, after all, to march in and fight and place the crown upon my head.

Then — to my surprise — Kytun burst out laughing. He roared. "By Nundji! So the cramph has done it at last!"

The explanation was simple. All the time I had been building my strength, Kov Nath had been doing the same. He had recruited leemsheads, outlaws, wild savages from the distant western islands surrounding Uttar Djombey, criminals, and those who believed he could bring the country out of its troubles. He had bribed Kolanier's guards and subverted his army, that had once been the army of the east. Now, truly, Kov Nath thought he had succeeded. He sat on the throne and his word was law.

But — no more food came into the city, and starvation now stalked the streets of Djanguraj.

Now I saw very clearly, with an appalled vision that summed up that dreadful charisma I possess, that this was no time for my personal relief. Now I *had* to make myself king and save the country of Djanduin.

Megalomania?

We marched for Djanguraj and the faerling throne.

My men and women of the army called me the apim with the yrium.

They had lived so long on promises: promises that they would be paid, their dependents cared for. They had subsisted at times on roots and berries and water from the streams. Some country folk had assisted us, but I had hanged a party of infantry who had burned a farmhouse in search of hidden food. I had issued notes, promissory notes, and very few had ever believed they would be honored.

What right had I to hang men, even if they were soldiers caught looting and raping and burning? In truth, I had not passed sentence, for the court did that; but the court knew my views and they worked to rules and regulations I had set down for all to read who could. For those who could not read a stylor had been appointed to read out to every unit the standing orders under which my army marched into a campaign.

"In Hamal," said Kytun, perplexed at my discomposure over the hangings. "The law gives the next of kin the right to select tortures for the condemned before they are executed."

"I know," I said. There had been a husband, distraught, howling his grief as he mourned over the ruptured bodies of his wife and three daughters. "I know."

Kytun's Kovnate island of Uttar Djombey lay at the extreme southwestern tip of Havilfar. Hamal extended over the whole northeastern corner of the continent. Yet word of the laws of Hamal penetrated even to Uttar Djombey.

Also, Kytun told me as we had fought and campaigned together, his island of Uttar Djombey, which lay off the west coast of Djanduin, as you know, was flanked on the north by an island of equal size. At the west ends the two islands were not above two ulms apart. They trended north and south as they extended eastward so that a large, sheltered sheet of water lay between them. This second island was the home of Kov Nath Jagdur. This was the island of Hyr Khor.

"And a worse nulsh for a neighbor no man could have!"

Judge, then, my mental state when I replied, "You will have a bad neighbor for not very much longer now, Kytun!"

So many of the troubles of the country could be laid directly at Kov Nath Jagdur's door. Through his barbaric assassination of Obdjangs he had stripped the country of those who could guide it and keep it on a safe and level course. My first task, after securing the food supply, must be to strengthen the civil service and bolster the courage of the Obdjangs. Many had left the country, as Coper had told me. This gave me a measure of the Pallan of the Vollers. He had courage, to stay on. I thought of Sinkie, and I determined that nothing could harm them.

If I do not dwell on those last days of the troubles it is, I suppose, because good men fought one another, and died, and as the streaming opaz light of Zim and Genodras drenched the battling armies in color and warmth and light, so the thraxters and the stuxes and the djangirs sucked the life from them and stained the dust with blood.

Old Superb flew over my victorious army.

Truth to tell, the battle was not much of a fight, from a strategic point of view, although there were one or two tactical moves I rather liked, for as soon as the way of it was clearly seen Kov Nath Jagdur's men began to desert him and to come over to our side. I had to use them, of course, but with all of human frailty in me I knew I would never fully trust them, which is a great pity.

Being a bit of a maniac still, and seeing this battle as the outcome of a foolish whim made manifest in destiny, I had dived into the battle myself. The great and impossibly long sword I had taken from Kov Nath at our first encounter at the inn had given me ideas. Without Naghan the Gnat I had done the work myself, with the assistance of a young armorer, Wil of the Bellows, who was handy with a tempering hammer.

At least, memory of our days spent in the smithy around the forge as, stripped to the waist, our bodies running with sweat, our muscles bulging, drinking huge drafts of a much-watered weak wine, we worked the metal in cunning fashion, yes, at least, those memories recur with pleasure.

I took off enough of the blade to bring what was left to the length of the blade of a Krozair longsword. We were scrupulously careful not to impair the temper, for the steel was of fine meld, springy, strong, capable of taking a sharp edge. I rebuilt the handle, and gave it that subtle two-handed Krozair grip. I bound it with silver wire we took from the shattered effects of a Gorgren supply column, looted and burned in the hills. The overly ornate and clumsy quillons were cut back by a fine craftsman, for they had been built snugly into the blade and handle, and I rewound the velvet before them, thinking it a flamboyant touch, but, possibly, a useful one, and I left the lugs before the velvet, for obvious reasons. So it was with a sword not properly a Krozair longsword, and yet with a weapon that had much of the superb quality of that magnificent brand, that I went into action.

As to the balance, Wil of the Bellows and I spent a long time getting the pommel weight just right. The blade balanced perfectly.

Wil had shaken his head, at the beginning, and said, "The great swords of the islands of Djanduin are notorious, Notor. You are cutting this one down—"

"Aye, young Wil. And for a reason."

But he, like them all here, had never heard of the inner sea, the Eye of the World, and a Krozair of Zy meant nothing to them. Well, in various actions, they saw what a Krozair longsword might do in the hands of a Krozair brother skilled in these matters.

"By Zodjuin of the Rainbow, Dray!" yelled Kytun as we pressed the remnants of Kov Nath's army back past the canal of fresh water, over the arcaded bridge, and into the Palazzo of the Four Winds. "You fight almost as well as a normal man with four arms!"

It was an old jest.

Djanguraj is a sprawling, arcaded, windy city with much granite and brick and little marble. The merezo — where the zorca and sleeth race — is one of the finer buildings. The palace contains many courtyards and inner ways, with the sacred court of the warrior gods placed centrally. To reach it we encircled the entire area and with flutduin flyers on patrol and the fliers available also helping to cover escape by air, we pressed on to the central sacred court.

Ortyg Coper had joined us, and he wore armor and carried thraxter, shield, and djangir, but he was not at home in a warrior's garb, and I detailed sturdy Nath ti Jondaria, a Djang who understood that an order from me was to be obeyed until death without a thought or a question in that craggy skull of his, to look out for Coper and to guard him from his own excitement and unskilled desire to be a man among men.

Now we came up against wildly vicious Djangs armed with the great sword of the islands of Djanduin. They were Nath Jagdur's personal bodyguard, men recruited from his own island of Hyr Khor. Against them, and with an unholy zest that infuriated all present, went the great swordsmen from Kytun's island of Uttar Djombey. There was work to be done here for the future.

A merker alighted in a rush of fluttclepper wings and I had to draw back from the forefront of the battle at this vital moment of conquest to deal with problems of handling the city. There were orders to give, and decisions to make, all the pressing demands on a commander in battle that, in truth, were my proper role instead of bashing on with my longsword. I sent a scrabble of merkers into the air and racing on zorcas among the arcaded avenues of the city so as to make absolutely sure of every point within Djanguraj.

Coper had done his work well. Despite my proud boasts I could never have kept the city once I had taken it without his work. The fruits of those labors now bore sweet fruit. The people appeared everywhere, shouting for Notor Prescot, and great crowds surged up the avenues, waving flags of orange and gray, and there were many who waved small copies of Old Superb in their violent excitement.

Coper was hauled out of the line by the scruff of his neck and Nath ti Jondaria, a bluff fellow with a moustache wider than his ears, grinned hugely as he dumped Ortyg Coper down. They are good friends in nature's way, are Obdjang and Dwadjang, but the four-armed Djangs love to exhibit their strengths to the gerbil-faced Obdjangs. We are all human.

"Here, Notor, is the Pallan as you ordered!"

"Thank you, Nath. If you wish to carve yourself some fun in the battle—"

But he was off, running and waving his sword above his head, screeching with sheer joy at being alive.

"Now, Ortyg, we must plan the food supplies. That is the most important item in our plans. The people shout for us now, and for that I thank you with all my heart, but they will change their tune if we cannot feed them."

Ortyg Coper squirmed inside his uncomfortable armor.

"You speak the truth, Dray. And, as Mother Diocaster is my witness, I was never cut out to be a warrior. Now, as to food, there are caches we have uncovered here and there—" And so we went at it, with maps and lists and sending off of merkers with orders to the detachments of the army. Quoffa carts were collected by the hundred, and calsanys with panniers ready prepared. Djanguraj would not starve if I could help it.

The noise of battle sensibly diminished. Coper and his stylors and I worked on in a feverish bustle, for we knew we must instantly show the people that we were not as other conquerors had been, and that we really meant what we said about the welfare of the Djangs of Djanduin.

Presently Chan of the Wings appeared. He was walking. His leather flying gear showed a streak of blood, and he held his djangir in his hand. When he advanced to stand before me at the long tables set up in the court of the Stux of Zodjuin, he looked not so much tired as regretful and resentful of his errand. This was most unlike a merker.

"Well, Chan of the Wings," I said, scribbling notes at the foot of a distribution list — that was for palines, I noticed, having asked to inspect the paline supply position personally — and looking up sharply. "You have a message?"

"Aye, Notor Prescot, whom henceforth men will hail as King of Djanduin. The last remnants of the leemsheads are barricaded within the sacred court. Kov Kytun Kholin Dom pens them there. And the Opaz-forsaken rast of a Kov Nath Jagdur has sent a message—"

Instantly my mind flew back seven years, to the moment when I had appeared by the Star Lords' command in Djanduin, beside the burning inn. And I could hear myself shouting, so as to give a little breathing space, throw a little bafflement into the picture, half-taunting this Nath Jagdur, Kov of Hyr Khor. His men had been hurling stuxes at me, and loosing when they could, and he had been trying to get at me with that damned great sword which now swung at my side. I remembered letting him have a curse and an offer.

"By the Black Chunkrah, Kov Nath! Let you and me settle this between ourselves, like true Horters."

And he had laughed and said he was no Horter.

Neither am I, when it comes down to it. If I had to cut him up or stick him I would do so, fairly or foully.

"I am coming, Chan of the Wings," I said, and rose and clapped my left hand to that great sword of the island of Djanduin that I had cut down into an imitation longsword of the Eye of the World. I strode off toward the sacred court of the warrior gods.

Chan shook his head.

"You seem ever able, Notor, to read a man's mind."

How easy to have said, in the old harsh way, "Believe it!"

But that would have been cheap.

Kytun met me, blood-spattered, angry, alive with his deep humor and his fighting blood aroused and baffled.

"By the blood of Holy Djan-kadjiryon!" he bellowed. "The yetch challenges you, Dray! He challenges you to single combat!"

"He but takes up a challenge issued seven years ago, Kytun." I spoke mildly. I had no wish, now, to fight this wild leem of a rebellious Kov who had made himself king; but I would so do. I would do so for the sake of this new country of mine. For, make no mistake, Djanduin had become a country I counted and honored.

Coper had also pushed up with us, and now he squeaked his own outrage.

"If he kills you, Dray, if he does — why — it is all for nothing, for he will be the rightful king still—"

"I do not think Djanduin would care for that."

"No — we would have to kill him then, ourselves. And the country—" Kytun flicked blood-drops from his sword. "By Djan! This is a sorry business. The challenge should never have been allowed!"

"But it has been, good Kytun, and I accept. Is all prepared?"

"Aye, Dray. It will be as the old laws prescribe. Man against man, and no other man will raise his hand to help either, no matter what the outcome."

So I walked forward between the arcades with the sculptured and painted friezes — fine work but nothing to compare with what I had seen elsewhere on Kregen. Fresh torches were brought and they cast their flickering erratic light down into the sacred court of the warrior gods. Kov Nath sat on the faerling throne. He looked as I had last seen him, save that his once-smooth helmet of copper hair had now grown long and was disarranged. Many dead Djangs lay about the court. I marked them. The night was very dark, and the stars sparkled down with unwonted brilliance.

"Bring torches!" bellowed Kytun.

I went with my people in a kind of procession into the sacred court; the thought occurred to me then: almost as though we marched ceremoniously into the Jikhorkdun where we would perform our bloody rituals.

Still more torches were brought. Their golden light streaked upon the chemzite carvings of the walls, upon the mosaics of the floor, now dabbled in blood, upon the gold and silver and ivory of the faerling throne, and upon the huge and solidly gem-plated hood which rose, high and domed and arching, above. Like a hollow benediction of gold and jewels the sacred hood of the faerling throne rose over the throne itself, both protecting and threatening. As Kov Nath stood up to reveal himself, clad only in a scarlet breechclout, I loosened my longsword and drew it forth.

Kov Nath stepped down the six golden steps and trod upon the mosaic floor. His four hands were empty.

Thinking it a useful ploy to be seen not to have the advantage of armor I started to strip it off, and Wil of the Bellows was there, unstrapping and carefully removing all the dinted pieces from my body. He took my sword. I held out my hand for the weapon.

An old Dwadjang came forward with a wide and shallow balass box. Wil clung on to my sword, his eyes wide and fear filled upon me. The old Djang opened the box. Inside were ranked eight djangirs. The short broad blades of the double-edged swords glittered in the torchlight.

"This is by the customs of the ancients of Djanduin!" he cried out in a reedy voice. "The challenge has been made and accepted. It is man against man and the prize is the crown and the faerling throne!"

In the rustling silence the spit and crackle of the torches sounded loud and ominous. I stood, all manner of thoughts rushing and colliding in my head.

"Come, cramph, the rast men call Notor Prescot! Select your weapons!"

Slowly I drew out two djangirs.

Kov Nath Jagdur laughed with immense scorn. He plunged his four hands in and withdrew four djangirs.

This was the way of it, then! This was the ancient custom! In Djanduin the Djangs fight duels and ritual battles with their national weapon, the djangir.

We faced each other. Two men, alike in so many ways, for had Kov Nath not possessed an extra pair of arms he would have been apim. And — because of a little fad, a weakness, of mine which made me don my old scarlet breechclout on the morning of battle — we both stood naked but for a scarlet loincloth.

He fell into a fighting crouch and then surged up, laughing, gleeful, swinging his arms.

I stand as though mesmerized at those four whirling djangirs.

So he faced me, at the end, Nath Jagdur, Kov of Hyr Khor, who was once of the Djin tan. The torchlight threw two stars of mocking gold into his eyes, and his four arms wove a flickering silver net before my eyes. He leaped for me, and in his four hands the whirling blades swung into a lethal wheel of deadly steel!

Twelve

The fight in the sacred court of the warrior gods

The marvelous world of Kregen is blessed with two suns and seven moons. Usually at night a combination of moons sends down their streaming pinkish rays, sometimes golden, sometimes jade, as seasons change and the mists rise. Sometimes there falls a night in which no moons are visible. There are two suns and seven moons, and each has many names, and the tenth is called Notor Zan, the Tenth Lord, the Lord of Blackness.

The Djangs are ferocious warriors.

Had I my trusted longsword — or a thraxter and shield — or a rapier and main-gauche — for it might perhaps have been too much to ask that I gripped the superb Savanti sword I had left with Delia — I would have gone up against Kov Nath with greater confidence.

As it was, we fought with his national weapon, and he had four arms and he was possessed of great skill. He leaped for me and his arms wove a deadly net of steel. I backed away nimbly, leaping dead bodies, for the court had not been cleared of the corpses. He roared and charged.

"Stand and fight, you nulsh! By Zodjuin of the Storm-clouds! Act like a man, even if you are only apim!"

There had to be a way of taking him. He would not be decoyed so easily as to stumble over a dead man. Djangs are warriors born. I circled, for we were pent between the mystic friezes of the sacred court of the warrior gods, and men clustered in the arcades, watching us by the light of torches.

On those walls frowned down the carved representations of warrior gods, the pantheon of Djanduin. High over the rest rose a giant stele with symbols incised upon it describing the creation of Djanduin out of the primitive miasmas of the Ocean of Doubt. Djan had called forth the land and the land had risen and, lo! that land was Djanduin, blessed among the lands of the world.

Kov Nath flickered his three djangirs most expertly while he kept his left lower blade down and limp, as though out of the play. I might not have four arms, but I recognized the symptom of the ploy he was trying there. As I circled he rushed me in an attempt to finish the thing quickly. I took two djangirs upon my own and skipped aside as the third sliced down past my thigh and only just managed to interpose a hurriedly snatched blade between that last, treacherous, left low blade and my belly. He roared, and stood back, the sweat starting out all over his body.

"Hai! For a cripple you fight passing well!"

I did not reply. Along the walls the sacred carvings seemed to flicker in the torchlight and to march, writhing across the stone. They appeared to me to be marching around, up there, along the friezes, and to be looking down on us as we fought for the faerling throne.

Asshurphaz, Djondalar, Rig, Zodjuin, perhaps the most favored by warriors of the warrior gods, Djan-kadjiryon. All of them were armed, armored, crested, their diamond and ruby eyes gleaming down in the torchlight, and they writhed and rippled there upon the solid stone walls. Nundji was there, escorted by wild leems, railing against the warriors who had jailed him in a leem-hell. Over on the far side the draperies of Mother Diocaster seemed to surge as the torchlight shimmered across the pale alabaster surfaces. The shadows moved.

Kov Nath leaped again and his blades wove a deceptive circle of sparks. I ducked and slid sideways and tried to stick him in the belly. Two djangirs came down with a firm finality and halted my blade, and only a savage kick and lunge saved a third from going through my shoulder.

Those watchful Djangs kept a strict silence at first. But as we leaped and lunged across the mosaics of the floor, hurdling dead bodies, slipping and recovering in the pools of spilled blood, so the fire got to those wild warriors and they began to yell. There were fierce shouts of encouragement for Kov Nath from those of his men who had remained here, until the challenge and acceptance had been confirmed. My men yelled, too. The torches waved in the wide space, curling the streaming golden hair against the darkness of Notor Zan. I knew I was likely to go down into Notor Zan's paunch, and wake up in the Ice Floes of Sicce, if I did not speedily devise a system for sticking a man with four arms who knew how to handle four deadly djangirs with consummate skill.

"You are no Djang, rast; but stand and fight like a man, by Zodjuin of the Glittering Stux!"

As Kov Nath spoke, I leaped with a great fury and so took him high on the upper left shoulder. The morphology of the Djangs is remarkable, for their doubled shoulder blades constructed rather like sliding doors give equal power — well, almost equal power — to their upper and lower arms, and their muscles rope like steel across their backs. I sliced some flesh and the blood spouted. A hoarse shout rose from the assembled warriors and then, out of nowhere, I felt a keen blade slice down my side. I swiveled and lurched away and I felt the blood running down my side; but I did not put a hand to it. There was no time.

Kov Nath bored in, his four blades wheeling with as much ferocity as when we had begun.

"You are a dead nulsh now, Notor Prescot!"

I had discarded the idea of throwing a djangir. I could have done so — as could he — but I think we both realized we had the skill to slip a blade. But the hurling of a djangir was something he could afford better than could I, for he had four.

"Prepare to meet your pagan gods!" he bellowed again, and charged, and the four blades sang and whistled about me. I thought of nothing much thereafter, except a memory of three things — of Zair, of dealing with the savage beasts of Kregen, and of Delia.

I concentrated on cutting him up piece by piece. I would not be clever, or go for the big one. As I had the shorgortz and the Ullgishoa and the boloth, three out of many memorable combats, I would deal with this wild leemshead piece-meal.

He was very quick and very clever and he bored in without allowing me a moment's respite, now that he thought he had me and I was done for. I let him come in and so twisted and leaped far to the side, away from the point of his attack. As I leaped both my djangirs came down onto his upper right arm. I hacked with tremendous force, and, together, the blades struck, cutting and shattering the arm so that the white bone showed bloodily through the skin.

Immediate yells broke out from all around the sacred court. Kov Nath staggered back, looking stupidly at the ruin of his arm. His fingers could no longer hold the djangir and they opened, and the blade — it had some of my blood upon it — slid jangling to the floor.

I did not give him time to recover from the shock.

I came in low, almost bent double, surged up, and hacked across his lower left forearm, taking off the wrist, the hand, and the djangir in a splashing gout of blood.

The Djangs have an astounding agility and an almost superhuman strength. Shock and amazement shattered Kov Nath, but he came back at me with fearful courage and ferocity. I had to hack and slash and slice and fend him off, but, all blood-smeared with his two ruined arms flailing, like some ghastly monster from the deepest hells of Kregen, he pursued me. I backed up and turned and waited. Then, as he lunged with a fearful scream to sink the djangirs in my throat, and I fronted him and smashed them aside, I saw the first faint crack in his psychology, the first chink in his armor of courage.

But he would not give in as easily as that. The stump of his left lower arm battered my body, bruising me around the ribs. I swung away, and as he bellowed and charged to follow I let him have a Krozair of Zy foot-kick. I missed the target, but he screamed and backed away, and I slashed — rather foolishly — at his throat, for I wanted to finish this ghastly business quickly now. His return sliced down my arm, drawing blood and making me grip the djangir tightly, for I thought I'd lost control of my arm then.

He saw that, and the chink in his armor closed. He stood for a moment glaring, his chest heaving, blood and sweat rivering down his magnificent body.

"By Zodjuin of the Stormclouds! You will die now, apim!"

I felt that I might usefully add an observation to the so far one-sided conversation.

I said, "By Vox, you nurdling onker! You have but two hands now! You are less than an apim now! And, by Zim-Zair, you will be less than a dead apim before a mur or two!"

He flinched back.

Oh, yes, he was magnificent, even pathetically smothered with blood, with his two useless arms dangling. But the two he had left still clutched sharp steel, and he made a final enormous effort to bear me down with him. He jumped and roared and the two djangirs lanced for me, one to the eyes, the other to the belly. I parried them both.

He knew then, did Kov Nath Jagdur, that this was his end.

For, marvelous fighter that he was, he recognized that I had not instantly followed the parries with attack. I had held back, poised to destroy him at my pleasure. He saw all that.

He was too fine a fighter not to recognize the truth. He had tried all his tricks, and they had failed him. He knew that I had not riposted through fear of closing with him; he understood I had him at my mercy now, for I had read all his cunning and skill and bested them.

It was in my mind not to kill this man, for I valued him as a fighter and as a man, even if he was a wild leemshead who had brought near-destruction to the country I loved.

"Kov Nath!" I called to him. "I am minded to spare you your life, if you will—"

"No bargain, rast! The Kov of Hyr Khor does not bargain with rasts of apims!"

"It is your own blood."

I spoke as mildly as I could, but he flinched back, seeing that old devil look upon my face. Brutality and war wreak a fearful havoc upon a man.

"Aye, my own blood! And I would shed it all again to rid my country of Obdjang and apim!"

"In that you are an onker, Kov Nath."

"I am the King of Djanduin, cramph!"

"You were, for a short space only. But you brought the country to ruin. I would rather not have your blood on my hands — or any more than there already is." At this I heard the roar of coarse and appreciative laughter from those watching. The Kregan often has a bloody line in jests.

He was bleeding profusely now, and he dropped one of the djangirs to grip the shattered arm. He felt it with great and ghastly disbelief. He glared at me, his coppery hair wild about his face, the silver fillet long since lost.

"What bargain do you offer me — the Kov of Hyr Khor?"

There appeared no strangeness in that the two of us, who were in the midst of so violent a combat, could talk thus.

"If I am to be King of Djanduin, as men say I am, for the good of the country, I would not relish a wild leemshead within the realm."

"That would not be wise, I promise you."

"So you would find a new home, somewhere in Havilfar."

"That I could never do, Notor Prescot."

I did not fail to perceive his change of tone.

I decided to press a trifle. "You are a dead man if we fight again. I can slap you, my two arms against your two. But I see in you some good you cannot see in yourself. Kregen would do ill to lose too many men like you, leemshead though you are."

A growl ran around the packed men watching. I wondered what their reactions truly were, and then forced them out of my mind. Slaying for the sake of slaying is a pastime for the perverted, for the insane, for the kleeshes of two worlds.

He rallied. His blood dropped ever more rapidly upon the mosaics, making their colors blot with a more dreadful stain.

"And if I leave Djanduin, what is to become of my people of Hyr Khor?"

"They will be treated with honor. Hyr Khor is a part of Djanduin. If I am to be king I will not permit one part of Djanduin to set itself above another part."

There might be explanations due to Kytun; he would get them.

Kov Nath sagged back. How near death he was without treatment we did not know, but he would not leave here until he had given his word.

He knew that. That subtle chink in his psychological armor, opened when he recognized he had met a man who could best him — and that man an apim! — widened more as he saw a way out. He forced himself to stand upright, panting now, the blood running, the sweat sparkling redly upon him. He threw the last djangir upon the floor.

"I accept! If I am to leave Djanduin, then it is to you, Dray Prescot, Lord of Strombor, that I pass on the Kovnate of Hyr Khor! To you I bestow Hyr Khor!"

This was perfectly legal, although I fancied the little crippled girl with the Bolinas would have to be seriously consulted. But, too, I saw his cunning ruse. He would hand me his Kovnate of Hyr Khor and with it, he surmised, the enmity of his people, who would seek to revenge him upon me.

I was prepared to accept anything to get this great gory, sweaty man out of here as safely as might be.

"I accept, Nath Jagdur. I take upon myself the title of Kov of Hyr Khor and release you from that burden. Now, I will see to your wounds, and bind you up, and care for you—"

My men were lax.

I do not blame them, for the drama had been compelling, there in the torchlight of the sacred court of the warrior gods, as the warrior gods themselves seemed to parade around the friezes above us. Out of the torchlights flew a stux. I had sensed its flight instantly, like any Krozair brother, and could do nothing.

Straight for the heart of Nath Jagdur, who had been Kov of Hyr Khor and King of Djanduin, flew the stux. The spear penetrated and such was its force it staggered him back and threw him to the ground.

He had time to look up at me, his handsome face drawn with the bitter knowledge of failure. The blood gushed from his mouth and he died.

I heard a chunking meaty *thwunk* from the side, and knew the man who had thrown the stux was dead, also.

Kytun said, "It was that Nundji-lover Cleitar! He could not believe his master had done what he had done. Truly, loyalty and revenge are entwined plants."

After that Coper's people could organize everything. I have learned to live with and to defeat fatigue for long periods, and, truly, I believe, my immersion in the sacred Pool of Baptism in far Aphrasöe confers on me the ability to stay awake and alert long after other people have fallen in stupor. But the tiredness would not be denied now. My wounds were bound up, the court was cleared, the mosaics scrubbed and washed. All through that night of Notor Zan we worked on, and men stumbled away, to collapse with exhaustion, as we started to put Djanduin back on its feet. It had taken me seven years since I had come here. Well, there were three more to go in this enforced prison of time before I would be free.

In those three years we accomplished much. I ordered the coronation to be a serious affair, swiftly done and yet seen to be done. Food was unearthed from its caches. We were blessed by good harvests, in the due time of harvesting for every crop, rotation by rotation. Gradually in the first two years we hauled Djanduin back. Then the army mobilized and we marched up against the Gorgrens. By moves that outfoxed that unpleasant people we swarmed down out of the Mountains of Mirth, defeated three separate armies in three separate battles, and drove the Gorgrens clear back to the Yawfi Suth and the Wendwath. We did not really care if they were sucked down by the bog and quagmires, or if they succumbed to the wiles of the Maidens of the Dreaming Lake, just so long as they left the soil of Djanduin. Once we were back where the frontiers had for so long been placed I was content to halt. We might gather our strength, plan, and arise to strike into Gorgrendrin itself, but that must come later.

I hankered after releasing Herrelldrin from the yoke of the Gorgrens. Turko the Shield would welcome that, for he had spoken so little of his home, out of shame, as I believed. There was no doubt but that the Djangs would follow. For one thing they loved a fight and wished to teach the Gorgrens a sorely needed lesson; and, two, by this time they regarded me as a king who could do no wrong, and would have followed me to the Ice Floes of Sicce if need be. The only pleasure I could take from that was that the country was recovering, people could look up and laugh again, the good days were returning.

As for the Lady Lara, I had with great cunning avoided whatever she might have thought, and the issue was now clearly joined between Felder Mindner and Kytun Dom.

I visited the Kovnate so uncannily thrust upon me by a bleeding man near to death, and found it to be rugged and wild as to country, and even more rugged and wild as to people. Kytun had clapped me on the back and roared out that — by Zodjuin of the Glittering Stux — he had a good neighbor now!

I agreed with him, for I meant to make this gift of a Kovnate into a place to be proud of; but that, too, had to take its turn in the round of days.

On Hyr Khor I was taken to see a marvel of the island, a marvel, indeed, of all of Djanduin, and whose fame had spread eastward to the Shrouded Sea.

This marvel was the Kharoi Stones.

An enormous area covered with the time-shattered wreck of an ancient city, stones tumbled in indescribable confusion, columns, shafts, arcades, walls, towers, hanging gardens now slithered into pyramids to dwarf those of Egypt, channels cumbered with chipped marbles and vast tessellated areas, all smothered with vegetation and the home for wild beasts of many descriptions, this, then, was the eerie place called the Kharoi Stones. I have seen Karnak, and Angkor Wat, and other famed relics of the past on our own Earth, and I have seen other of the ancient monuments of the Sunset People on Kregen; the Kharoi Stones holds a mystery and a deep secret all its own. At this time, as you know, I had not seen the Dam of Days, which controls the tides through the western end of the Grand Canal of the Eye of the World. But I walked among the tumbled masses of the Kharoi Stones and I marveled.

Everywhere was to be seen, sculpted boldly in relief or in the round, the magnificent representation of the Ombor, the mythical flying monster of immense size and fiery heart, who dying is yet reborn, whose breath scorches cities, whose tears water the oceans, whose hearts beat for all humankind, and, as I knew, for whom my enclave in Zenicce had been named.

Coupled with this plethora of ornamentation was the symbol of the double-ax — not the Minoan double-ax but an ax double-bitted yet narrow of blade, eminently suitable for the sweeping blow and the lethal chop from the saddle of a vove.

You may well believe I promised myself much future exploration of the Kharoi Stones.

On a day in Djanguraj after I had been up all night by the light of four of the moons, reading reports, dictating answers and orders to my stylors, planning for the well-being of the country, I met for breakfast by prearrangement with Ortyg Coper and Kytun Dom.

We sat drinking that glorious Kregan tea and eating crisp vosk rashers, and eggs, and finishing with palines from a silver dish. Food, transport, law, education, security, all were now practically back to normal in Djanduin, and I had but a single sennight left of my prison sentence. The Todalpheme had been explicit, and my own calculations confirmed their findings.

Now I said to Ortyg Coper, "Is the realm faring well, Ortyg?"

And he said, "The realm is doing well, Majister, and will do better than it has ever done in the next two years."

"By Djan!" said Kytun in his fierce way. "That is so!"

"I find it extraordinarily strange," said Coper. "I was attacked as often as other Obdjangs by the leemsheads led by Nath Jagdur, and yet my life was spared. Soldiers could never find him or his leemsheads after the attacks; but I did not die. Others of my friends died."

We were silent for a space, remembering. The Obdjangs had been returning to Djanduin and the country really was set fine. Prosperity was just around the corner.

"There was a reason, Ortyg." I looked at him as I spoke.

He munched a paline. "I am alive — Sinkie and I live."

"Yes, Ortyg. And I will tell you why. But, first, let me ask you, Kytun, once more, the question — would you become king of Djanduin?"

He didn't even think. "Not I, by Djan!"

"Would you loyally support Ortyg if he were king?"

Before Kytun could begin to reply Ortyg had reared up, agitatedly brushing his whiskers.

"Now, wait a minute! Here — my dear Majister — I mean — hold on!"

I tried to keep my face composed; it was a struggle.

"I am going on a journey. I cannot avoid it, nor do I wish to do so. I want the country to prosper and to remain fruitful and peaceful. The young men get enough fighting in the eternal games, and the merezo has been enlarged for even bigger and better zorca races. There is nothing now for which I am needed. You,

Ortyg, are the next king of Djanduin, arid Kytun will give you all his loyal help, as he does us both."

Kytun spat out a mouthful of palines, which is a terrible waste.

"You do not have to go, really, Dray! You are King! By Zodjuin of the Rainbow! You can't desert us!"

I sighed. "I feared you would regard this as desertion. But it is a task laid on me. I must go. Ortyg will be—"

"No, Majister." Ortyg Coper stood up, and abruptly he was formal and deadly serious. "No, Majister. I will not be king. But I will stand as regent for the throne."

And with that I had to be content. I would return here, I promised that; but as to when... That, in truth, partly lay in the inscrutable hands of the Star Lords. Had they two hands apiece, I wondered, or four?

Ortyg Coper was fully invested as regent, and Kytun was the first to lift his djangir in loyalty. I was as satisfied as I am ever satisfied about anything, that I had done all that I could do. Everyone knew I was taking a journey laid upon me, and the news traveled that the task was a reward given to me by the Glorious Djan Himself, He whose figure was not to be sculptured upon stone along with the warrior gods of Djanduin. As far as mortal mind and hand could contrive, I left the kingdom of Djanduin, of which I was sovereign, in good heart and good hands, and looking forward to golden days.

The airboat I had bought and had provisioned was a small two-place flier. Over in my island of Hyr Khor I had found a strange and scarcely self-comprehending willingness to help. As their new Kov I was both suspect and welcome, for the old Kov, besides being a violent man, much given to breaking heads, had been impious and a leemshead, and a ravisher of the young girls of the island. I convinced the people of Hyr Khor that although I was no angel, and no simpleton, either, I was prepared to let them make their own lives, saving that they must always remain friends with the people of Uttar Djombey. There was some grumbling, I have no doubt, but on the surface the scheme worked well. So it was to Hyr Khor I went for a last farewell and to collect my flier.

My plan was simple. I would fly from Djanduin, across Gorgrendrin, over the back hills of Migla, and out over the Shrouded Sea to the place where I had last seen Delia. I fancied the Star Lords would permit this.

It was with a light heart I called Remberee to the people of Hyr Khor. They waved their great swords of the islands, and I took off into the morning sunslight.

"Remberee!"

"Remberee, Kov Dray Prescot, King of Djanduin!"

Thirteen

The scorpion

The little flier lanced through the bright clean air of Kregen.

There is a coolness and sweetness about the air of these latitudes of Kregen. Because of that extraordinary width of the temperate zones of Kregen beneath Antares the climate as far south as Djanduin is perfectly suitable for comfortable living, not as hot as, for instance, northern Havilfar, by any means, but nowhere near as cold as the gray waters south of Thothangir. Between the Yawfi Suth and the Wendwath and the back mountains of Migla there lies a broad tract of country, sometimes fertile, sometimes less so, seldom truly inhospitable. The western areas are the ancestral homes of the peoples of Herrelldrin and Sava. The Gorgrens in their aimless meanderings over the vast inner plains had come down to the west and had occupied Sava and Herrelldrin and Tarnish, which lies to the south of the Tarnish Channel. Between the somewhat undefined eastern limits of the Gorgrens' lands and the back hills of Migla lies the country of Yanthur.

It was over this area, in a place where spiny hills made of the landscape a miniature tree bark in appearance, that the flier chose to go wrong.

I cursed.

I was well used to airboats breaking down in Vallia and Zenicce; I had formed the opinion that they were built with some kind of weakness which was obviated in those models built for sale in Havilfar. This was a voller purchased from a Hamalian yard and delivered to express orders of the King of Djanduin. For this airboat to go wrong boded ill for someone.

And that someone was likely to be me.

I touched down in a lonely valley where a narrow fast-running stream poured in a silvery tinkle over sandstone rocks, and where violet and yellow flowers clustered. The lower slopes of the hills on every side were covered with trees, and their crests, too, were tree covered. The voller touched down and skidded wildly across rock and grass and ended up embedded in the low-sweeping branches of the tamiyan trees. The shaking released a cloud of yellow petals that pirouetted in the air and spread, shining in the suns.

I just sat there for a moment, and thought of the journey ahead of me. Until I reached a place where I could hire or buy fresh transport, I must perforce walk. I had walked before to reach Delia; I would do so again.

A laccapin, one of those monstrous flying reptiles of Havilfar, cruised by high above, its tail extended well aft and looking barbed and angry. I was about to climb down from the flier by way of the tamiyan branches, keeping my eyes open for any unwelcome beasts, when I saw the gorgeous gold and scarlet bird come flying into my view, just beyond the edge of the tree branches.

All the time of my enforced exile in Djanduin I had not seen the Gdoinye, the magnificent scarlet-and-golden-feathered hunting bird of the Star Lords. The remarkable bird is the spy and messenger of the Everoinye, and I know that great things are afoot when it heaves in sight.

It perched on a branch and squawked at me.

I rubbed my hand over my chin. This was a period, in Djanduin, when I had shaved carefully, leaving only my fierce old moustache.

I smelled trouble.

"What do you want, bird of ill omen?"

"An onker, Dray Prescot! As ever was!" the bird shrieked in jovial abuse at me.

I prepared to argue my case to the Star Lords through the bird's mediation. "I do not seek to break your interdiction upon me," I said. I spoke firmly, as though I meant business, which I did, Zair knows. "I shall meet my comrades in the voller after they have searched for me, and they will suspect nothing, for this voller will be sunk in the Shrouded Sea." Then I cracked a fist against the wooden-framed hull. "If, that is, I can get the Makki-Grodno beast to working again."

The Gdoinye cackled.

"An onker, Dray Prescot! There is work for you to do—"

I froze.

"No," I said. I spoke calmly. Remember, I had been a king for three Terrestrial years. "No, I cannot work for you until I have seen my friends again."

"You dare not argue with the Star Lords, Dray Prescot."

"I think I shall."

The scarlet and gold raptor ruffled up its feathers and dug its vicious claws into the tamiyan bark.

"To refuse would bring down great wrath on your head."

I had a bow in the voller, along with food and supplies and other weapons. Now I lifted the bow, and with a practiced jerk strung it, for it was the familiar compound reflex bow, and nocked an arrow. I aimed the steel head of the arrow at the Gdoinye.

"Once, a man called Xoltemb, a caravan master, said he might cut down any man who raised a shaft against you."

"Onker."

"If I loose, would the arrow slay you, Gdoinye, or would it merely pass through air? Are you real?"

"There is work for your hands in a place to which you would wish to go. This voller you bought — and others — do you remember Tyr Nath Kynam ti Hippax?"

"I remember," I growled, for the memory was still sore in me. Tyr Nath Kynam had been a valued member of the Djangs who had been rebuilding the country. Coper, who as Pallan of the Vollers, had bought the flier, had been pleased he had secured a brand-new specimen for Nath Kynam, and although it was of the minor sort, it was new and smart. Nath Kynam was short and squat and a dynamo of a man, always working at top speed, always ready to talk energetically, and a good friend. Yet he had personal problems, and was always anxious to have acupuncture needles in him, soothing and calming his restless energy.

Well, the brand-new flier had failed him, or his heart had burst the bonds of mere flesh. He had crashed and been killed. Yes, I would not forget Tyr Nath Kynam ti Hippax.

"I remember Nath Kynam. And Tyr Man Dorga ti Palding, who would have saved him if he could. I do not need you, bird of ill omen, to remind me of my good fortune in true friends on Kregen; so what is this to the Star Lords?"

"A year, Dray Prescot, onker of onkers. A single year is all the Everoinye require of you."

If I knew what the raptor meant I would not allow that awful knowledge to crowd into my brain.

"The Star Lords are so far above you, Dray Prescot, as you perhaps may be above a nit on a calsany. But they have been watching you with an interest you may — or may not — warrant. Beware lest you be cast forth!"

Almost, I let the arrow loose.

But I held it fast and shouted, "By Makki-Grodno's diseased left armpit! Tell me straight, you nurdling yetch!"

"A year, Prescot." The bird stretched those gorgeous pinions wide and with a spring he was airborne. "A single year. Then you may — for a space only — imagine yourself a free man." Then, with what I can only describe as a derisive howl, the raptor winged away into the blue, a scarlet and golden splash of color that rose and darkened into a black blot and so vanished in the suns-glow.

I lowered the bow.

Damned uppity bird!

Sinkie had cried when I bid her and her husband, Ortyg Coper, who was now Regent for the King of Djanduin, Remberee.

Yet she could have no knowledge of what dangers and what terrors I would face upon the beautiful hostile face of Kregen.

No manifestation of a blue scorpion arose before my eyes, no blue radiance engulfed me to suck me into emptiness. Remember, it was a full ten years since I had last experienced the summons of the scorpion. Then the Star Lords had clearly missed their target in time, although they had found it in space, for they had dumped me down by the inn and the crossroads *after* the time I should have been there. We had heard that one of the leemsheads had been hung up in chains on the tree; so all was explained about what I had seen — the repaired roof, the different season. But perhaps the Star Lords were waiting for my violent protestations, which they assumed I must make with such vehement anger. Perhaps if they transmitted me during my burst of rage they were, in some way unknown to me, dislocated in their calculations.

Certainly, I had defeated their purposes before this.

Could it be that a mere mortal man might thwart the Everoinye not merely in an underhand way, as I had done, but in a straight contest of wills? I thought it hardly likely.

"Why do you wait, you puissant Star Lords?" I bellowed out, there beneath the tamiyan trees, perched so ridiculously in my broken-down voller in the land of Yanthur. "Where is your powerful and venomous blue scorpion?"

I thought then to look to see if by chance the white dove of the Savanti might not be circling overhead, watching me, and watching the Gdoinye of the Star Lords, too.

But I saw nothing of the white dove of the Savanti.

This was becoming ludicrous. I had been learning a little of the fliers and their idiosyncrasies. Ever since the time Delia had told me to move the silver boxes so as to bring our runaway flier to the plains of Segesthes I had been fascinated by all vollers. I held the Air Service of Vallia in great esteem. So I thought it prudent before I girded myself up for a long trek to see if I might not be able to fiddle about with the cantankerous voller and get it into the air again.

I stood up in the small two-place flier and rested my hands on the wooden-framed hull. It was a shallow, petal-shaped craft, with a small windshield and a pit filled with flying furs and silks. I was putting my leg over the side to crawl out on a branch of the tamiyan trees, when the blueness came down with such speed and force that I gasped. I felt a giant rushing wind and I struggled for breath. I shouted something, anything, I know not what, and went pitching out and down.

One thing I recall; I hit my head on something extraordinarily hard. So it was that with the bells of Beng-Kishi ringing in my skull and the hovering presence of Notor Zan about me that I was pitched headlong into the next adventurous task I must fulfill for the Star Lords.

Fourteen

Muruaa speaks

Stark naked, weaponless, and with a thump on the head that left me dizzy and half senseless, I struggled to open my eyes to find out where on Kregen I had been flung.

I could hear shrieking and screaming.

That was normal enough.

Also I could hear a strange hissing sizzling, as though a thousand giant vosk steaks fried upon Notor Kanli's forge.

That was odd.

Someone crashed into me and knocked me flat.

The air was warm — very warm. Even as I scrabbled around with those damned bells of Beng-Kishi clamoring in my skull the heat increased with throat-drying speed. I managed to get an eye unglued and peered about on a scene of terror and panic. The rumblings of hell shook the ground. Sulfur stank.

An exquisite girl with long lithe legs ran toward me, screaming. Her clothes were on fire. Her hair blazed terribly. She was apim; soon she would be a burned corpse.

I jumped for her, knocked her down, smashed at the burning clothes, ripping off the coarse gray dress, smothering the blazing hair. She screamed and screamed.

Around me people were running and screaming. Some were on fire. Some had pitchers of water which were soon expended. They ran from a village of mud huts with wooden roofs, and the roofs blazed to the sky. I followed the streaked tracks of the smoke and looked into the sky.

Up there, towering over the world, poured the mouth of hell.

Fire. Fire and flame. Fire and destruction. Burning and smoking and roaring, the volcano pumped out its fiery breath and its destructive vomit and smothered the village in terror and horror. Huge, that volcano, towering, high, and cone-sided, and the lava ran down swiftly in glowing orange and red spuming gouts over everything in its path.

Evilly swirling in wide writhing tentacles from a violent smoky orange through a snarling ruby-red to a pure fiery white, the lava raged downslope and through the village. The heat grew. The noise battered as the lava poured and slipped over the steep edge of an embankment to fall into the blue and placid waters of a lake. Trees burned before they fell to be consumed utterly. The waters roiled near the shore and the waves spread out in wide ripples so that the placid surface grew congested and turbulent in a wide and swiftly growing circle.

Terraces of neat agriculture had been hacked in alternating wide and narrow steps down the flanks of the low surrounding hills. But the monster of fire poured down over everything, and a village was dying and a people was being destroyed — and, as usual, Dray Prescot was there, naked and disoriented, expected to select the right person to save.

The girl was burned, but she was still alive and she would live.

I bent to her.

"Muruaa!" she moaned. "Muruaa!"

"On your feet, girl, and run! Past the slide and into the lake! *Move!*"

She saw my face and she flinched, all burned and naked and in pain. But she staggered to her feet and ran off. I had taken stock of the situation as I saw it. The village was doomed. But below, down the steep slope, lay a sizable town, neatly mud walled and wooden roofed, in a cleft between the low, terraced hills. I could look down and see the peaked roofs of sturm-wood, and the mud-brick walls, the enclosures, and the little backyard chimneys smoking with preparations for one of the many daytime meals of Kregen. The suns were rising in the sky, and they blazed through a crown of smoke. The land lay lit in ghastly orange and lurid vermilion from the fires of the volcano.

The fugitives from the outlying village vanished below. Some staggered, burned; others crawled; but one or two young men lifted the old folk, and in a bunch they disappeared below the brick-wall of a terrace. The girl whose clothes I had wrenched off and whose blazing hair I had put out ran with them. I stood alone.

If I refused to imperil my life? It was the Earth of my birth for me, then, and no mistake.

So, like the puppet I swore I would someday cease from being, I ran. One day, please Zair, I would cut the strings that held me puppet-slave to the Everoinye.

As I ran I studied the landscape. There is much to be learned from the landscape of a people. Here there was no wide aa. I know that is the volcanologists' term. Also I have walked over the uneven lumpy lava fields below Etna, which the locals call sciara, and shuddered at what they hide. But here the ground was fertile and the crops grew lushly, vine and gregarian, paline and many another luxurious plant of Kregen. So the last eruption must have occurred more than, say, a hundred years ago. These people might not know what to do — or what to try to do.

Down in the town the panic was atrocious. Men and women ran from their houses with bundles wobbling on their heads. Calsanys were being prodded along with sticks. Babies were crying. Girls were carrying out cloths with bits of household furniture sticking out, candlesticks, frying pans, grinders, samphron-oil lamps, anything they had thought to snatch up in their panic.

Sulfur and brimstone choked in the air. The congested rumblings and explosions of the volcano battered at reason.

I grabbed a young man whose face showed stark fear. He was babbling incoherently, so I kicked him away and grabbed another man who swung at me, uglily, a stux thrusting forward. He bore a vosk-hide satchel over his shoulder and nothing else, and I suspected he had seized his chance to loot a neighbor's house.

"Listen, dom, and I will not kill you," I told him.

He reacted stupidly. He tried to stick me with the spear.

I took it away from him and poked the point into his sweating belly.

"Who is the chief man of the town, dom? Tell me his name and where I may hope to find him, or your tripes will spill into the road."

He yelled, but he gabbled out what I wanted to know.

"Lart Lykon, the Elten! But he has fled—"

I shook him.

"Toward the jetties — a boat — for the sake of Kuerden the Merciless!"

I threw him from me. Useless to work on these people one at a time. Whatever the Star Lords were up to here, I scarcely thought it had been the saving of that first girl upon the higher slopes where the lava ran and would have engulfed her if she had not burned to death first. Everything was happening with enormous speed. I burst through a packed rabble wailing and clamoring at the jetty. A few boats lay there, small open double-ended craft, and a number had already pushed off. It was perfectly clear that the boats could not carry all the people of the town. It was equally and horribly clear that the lava pouring down so swiftly toward them would fill the narrow valley in which the town huddled, fill the green slot and cover the houses, rise up the terraced hills, pouring all the time through and over the town and into the lake. To jump into the water and swim would help only if one could outrace the lava. This is what many were doing; but soon the water grew too hot for them, so that they boiled.

I found Lart Lykon, the Elten. He was a large, raw-boned man with a hectoring voice, hooded eyes, a massive beard, and golden rings about his fingers and bracelets upon his arms. He wore only a gray shirt and a pair of blue trousers. I took him by the shoulder as he pushed a woman aside and went to step into a boat. He had guards, tough men with stuxes who shouted at me to let the Elten alone, and who thrust at me. I took the first stux and hit the fellow over the head with it. Ash was now falling, raining down in white-hot droplets that stung as they hit flesh. People were screaming everywhere. Yet we were penned into this tiny space of the jetties between the lake-wall and the town.

"Elten," I said, shouting into his ear. "By all you hold holy, you will not run away. There is a way to defeat Muruaa!"

"It cannot be done," he gasped, his eyes rolling. "Muruaa will eat us all, burn us alive!"

Another guard, panicking, tried to thrust his stux into my back, so that I was forced to turn, my left hand grasping the Elten by the shoulder, and take the stux away from the guard. He looked a mean, low-browed fellow — well, maybe I do him an injustice — but I thrust back hard intending to frighten him away. But the press of people forced him on to the stux. He writhed like a fish on a harpoon, and lurched away.

I turned my face on the other guards.

They were relatively primitive people, at least in their relationship with authority. They understood what my face told them long before they heard what I bellowed out.

I lifted my voice and I shouted.

"Listen to me! It is useless to run away. You must do what I say, at once, for if you do not, then you will all be killed, and I along with you."

I dragged up the Elten of the town, and hung him up in the air so that his heels dangled.

"Your Elten will confirm what I say! You must go up past the flanks of the lava flow, behind the houses, along the terraces, back above the town, below the village. You must carry cloths, wetted, over your heads. You must take picks and shovels, and you will do as I bid you. If you do not you will all surely be killed!"

There followed a wild argument; but I held the stux against the side of Lart Lykon, the Elten, and I pressed the cruel and broad head into the swell of his belly. "Tell them to obey, Lykon, or your tripes spill into the dirt!"

He squeaked and then managed a shout as I set him back on his feet.

"Do as this wild leem says! There is a chance! I know, for in my grandfather's time Muruaa showed his anger and the people placated him by sacrifice—"

"You great nurdling onker!" I roared. I shook him so that he rattled internally.

"You will dig a gap in the side of the flow, where it has cooled a little. It will be hard. But if you do it the fire will flow a new way — the way you must know — over the cliff and into the lake beyond the village."

Uproar, chaos, confusion, but out of them I hammered away at the people. I shook Lart Lykon and brandished the stux at some of his guards who attempted to launch a boat and sail away. When they would not stop I hurled the stux and wounded their Deldar; that brought the others directly back up onto the jetty. I seized another stux from the guard's stuxcal and I waved it.

"Forward! Up the slope! Muruaa is merely a pit of fire! And are we not men and women? Dig! *Dig!* Trap Muruaa's vile vomit in the lake!"

The conceit caught them. Anyway, they knew they could not escape. Volcanoes have this nasty habit of forming basins, such as the one in which the town had been slotted, by the collapse of part of the surrounding land in ancient, prehistoric eruptions, and then of filling the basin in the subsequent eruptions. The lake had flowed in to fill any hope of escape: the water boiled near the shore as the stream of lava poured over the town and plunged into the water.

So we snatched up cloths and hides and I organized a water-carrying chain. We went back up the slope, around the fiery lava flow, and we ventured near the outer cooler edges. We dug. We sweated. We were burned. We died, some of us, who were not nimble enough, or who could not stand the heat. But we chopped a gap in the edge of the flow and, not suddenly, but quickly enough to make us skip out of the way, a fresh tentacle of flaming lava broke through, and swung toward the lake on its new course. The flow would not stop in its destructive travel over the town, but enough would now be channeled away so that the slot would not fill. We could find a safe if hot refuge on the higher terraces.

The big man with the tawny mane of hair and the whip-marks on his back who had shouted, first, that he would come with me up the mountain of fire, bellowed now that he would go up higher and break a fresh gap.

"If you desire, Avec," I said. "But the heat up there is worse even than here."

"I care nothing for these cramphs of Orlush. I wish only to spite that yetch Elten Lart."

Out of spite, then, he went up the mountain. I went up with him because I was not absolutely sure I had done all I could do to save the people of this town of Orlush. I had no idea where we were on Kregen. The Star Lords had given me the task of saving someone — perhaps the whole damned town — and until I was satisfied that I had done that, I could not rest.

We were followed by an intrepid band of young men — and some not so young — and we went at the lava flow again. This time the work was immensely more difficult; but we persevered.

When even I was satisfied, and I had struck blow for blow with Avec, driving great swathing layers of flaming lava away to open a new breach and we were all burned and blistered, I shouted halt. Avec dragged a blackened arm across his sweat-grimed forehead, and he smiled at me.

"I do not know who you are, dom; but you are a man!"

"A man like yourself, Avec. I am Dray Prescot."

"And I am Avec Brand, Notor of nothing, Elten of emptiness, Strom of onkers."

"Aye, Avec!" shouted a sinewy young man whose strength as he slewed burning lava had surprised me. "Aye, by Havil the Green! You are Kov of hulus, also!"

"And you, Ilter Monicep, are the Vad of boasters!"

There and then, these two, they would have set to and knocked each other about — there, after the exertions they had so desperately made to save the town.

One thing said had chilled me.

Havil the Green!

Well — I was still in Havilfar.

But — the Green! It was long and long since I had fought so bitterly for

Zairians against Grodnims. Long and long since I had sailed the Eye of the World in my fleet swifter *Zorg.* Yet, still, even after all these seasons when I had talked and befriended and grown accustomed to the Green — even then, to my shame, the old starchy pride of a Krozair of Zy stiffened me up at the hated name of the Green.

"There is a great statue of Havil the Green in Huringa," I said.

Avec looked at me as though I had made some fatuous remark about the time of day.

"I have heard of Huringa — have I not, you onker, Ilter?"

"Huringa?" said Ilter Monicep. We walked down the cut steps in the terrace walls, ready to help up to the higher sanctuary those who needed help. "Huringa? I believe old Naghan the Calsany once said it was a great city in Hyrklana. It was Hyrklana — I think?"

"Yes, Ilter. In Hyrklana."

So that told me that wherever I was, I was not in Hyrklana. It also told me clearly that wherever I was, was firmly in the backwoods. These were simple country people farming the terraced fields pent between the hills and the lake and the volcano. I wanted to know where I was. A year, the Gdoinye had said. I knew, because for the moment the action was over and I had not been caught up in a blue radiance and whirled back to Earth, that I had done what the Star Lords in their beatific wisdom had sent me here to do.

"I am a stranger here," I began.

Avec laughed, and then winced as burned skin caught him at the edge of his mouth.

"We know you are a stranger. Where you came from only Opaz the Vile himself may know. We know everyone in Orlush."

"Aye, Avec," mocked Ilter. "And everyone in Orlush knows you!"

Again I felt a shock of premonitory — what? Not fear, not horror, unease perhaps. Anger certainly.

Opaz — the *Vile?*

Opaz, the invisible embodiment of the dual-spirit, the Invisible Twins, the great and good Opaz? Opaz made manifest by the visible presence of the suns Zim and Genodras the heavens above in Kregen — the suns which in Havilfar are called Far and Havil.

I couldn't stop myself. I was exhausted — as were we all — and I was in a foul temper as may be imagined. I had been a king, and now I was a mere puppet dancing to the tune played by superbeings who refused to treat me seriously.

"Where are we, by the diseased and stinking right eyeball of Makki-Grodno?"

They stared at me, both of them, shaken by my tone.

When they saw my face glowering upon them, they were more mightily shaken still.

Then Avec, with something of a bluster in his voice and manner, said, "Why, in Orlush, of course."

Ilter Monicep regarded me with his dark eyes half veiled, and a pucker to his lips. He had recovered from that instinctive panic, that insubstantial terror, that seems to grip people when I glare at them with purpose. He spoke softly, and yet with meaning.

"You are in Orlush, as this great fambly Avec has said. And Orlush lies in the kingdom of Pwentel, and Pwentel has the great and glorious honor of being part of the Empire of Hamal." He chuckled harshly. Then he said bitterly, "Not a large or important part, for King Rorton Turmeyr whom men call the Splendid, is a frightened king. And Orlush, as you see, is not a great and famous town, for our Elten, Lart Lykon, is a corrupt bladder of vileness."

"You have said it, Ilter, although I shall beat you for calling me a fambly, you clever onker!"

While I digested this information the people of the town secured themselves on the highest terraces, clustering near the irrigation trenches which poured downslope from tier to tier. There are many degrees in the various peerages of Kregen, and I have not detailed them to you except when necessary. Suffice it to say that an Elten is two ranks lower in the hierarchy than a Strom. And I was in Hamal!

Something of what the Gdoinye had said made sense now.

Food had been saved from the disaster and we could eat the portion of the crop that was already ripe. All the rest of the day and the next night we huddled as Muruaa spouted into the air and poured his molten fury down the slopes. In the evening of the third day the fires slackened. Toward the decline of the twin suns — Zim now followed Genodras below the horizon — and with She of the Veils floating smokily between the stars, we saw a cavalcade drop down swiftly through the last level rays of emerald and ruby. It came to rest on the broadest and driest of the terraces encircling a low hill.

Surrounding a large and ornately decorated voller flew a squadron of mirvols, their riders flamboyant with flying silks and furs, with slanted weapons and the glitter of gems and steel.

"That will be Strom Nopac, come to find out what has happened," said Ilter Monicep. From his tone it was perfectly clear he had as little love for Strom Nopac as he had for Elten Lart.

"Who'd be a Notor?" Avec offered as his contribution to the philosophy of the evening. "It'd worry a man's guts out."

We were eating palines, and precious little else we had had, too, and we leaned in the last of the twin suns' glow, resting our elbows on a brick wall and looking down the slopes in the gathering dusk. Men moved urgently about down there, and Elten Lart would no doubt be pushing as hard as he could for help and relief in the disaster. The town showed like a patchwork of roofs protruding from the cooling lava.

Soldiers were climbing the stairs cut in the terrace walls. Zim and Genodras winked from the armor and the weapons.

"I just hope they've brought food," said Ilter, and he belched with a hungry hollow sound.

I remembered the whip-marks upon Avec's broad back, lash-stripes that were newly healed. Avec pushed up from the wall and flexed his arms and then rubbed his hair and nose. "They'll put me back in the Opaz-rotten cells," he said. He sighed. "Well, it was a rouser to be out, if for such a short time."

"They'll flog you again, Avec," said Ilter.

"Ah!" Avec spoke with a crowing kind of pleasure. "But they can't jikaider me! The law doesn't allow that to an Elten, by Krun!"

The soldiers approached.

In the last of the light they looked bulky, powerful, wearing uniforms which to me smacked of the overly ostentatious. I had been in Hamal before, at the Heavenly Mines, and I had no love for the Hamalese — although, Zair knew, Avec and Ilter were shaping up as interesting companions for a fight.

I readied myself in case Avec would put up a fight; but he held his wrists out, together, crossed, and said, "Here I am, boys. Anybody got a bottle of dopa handy?"

One of the soldiers laughed and a Deldar put his hand on Avec's shoulder. "You are Avec Brand the Niltch? You will come with us." Before the Deldar had finished speaking a voice lifted farther back in the shadows beyond the group of soldiers.

"There he is! There is the cramph who wounded two of my guards! Seize him, instantly!"

Ilter Monicep swung before me, so that his body blocked off my instinctive reaction to belt the first soldier over the head with his own stux. The soldiers closed in, their spears pointing for me, deadly in the fading light.

Monicep whispered, swiftly, frantically: "You resist, they'll kill us all!"

Helpless, I was taken, my hands bound. With stuxes prodding my back I was marched down the terraces and flung like a sack of refuse into the bottom of the voller.

Fifteen

Of Avec, Ilter, and ripe fruit

Avec Brand, also, was flung down with me. He was a Niltch. At the time I had no idea what that could be.

The bottom of the voller did not smell as pleasantly as I suspected a voller should smell, although for a man like myself who knows what an eighteenth-century seventy-four's bilges smelled like after eighteen months on blockade, smells are usually merely information clusters. This voller had been carrying gregarians, squishes, and malsidges. I saw no reason, now, to wait before freeing myself.

"Avec!" I said, not loudly, but not whispering, either. "Is your crime so serious?"

I wanted to know if he was just a petty criminal who was always in trouble, or if he had just done one thing wrong.

"Serious?" He chuckled, there, tied up in the malodorous hold of the voller. "Had I not left to go to Sumbakir I would have challenged him earlier, for although I am not a Horter neither am I a slave! Elten Lart is corrupt. I told the cramph what I thought of him, then I threw slursh at him — slursh with best red honey stirred in, too!"

Slursh is a remarkably fine porridge, which may be cooked in a number of different ways according to taste, and is so common on Kregen that if I have not mentioned it previously it is surely for that reason. Slursh and red honey, now — superb.

"Slursh wouldn't hurt him, Avec. Not enough to flog you—"

"I did not trouble to take it out of the pot, Dray."

"Ah!"

"The pot was that cheeky shishi Sosie's, a brave iron pot exceedingly thick and heavy, with the story of Kov Logan na Hirrume and the two Fristle fifis molded around the rim."

"What will they do to you?"

"For thumping a Notor? The Jikhorkdun, for sure. The Strom has jurisdiction, I think. The law is very strict. That rast Lart Lykon must bow to the Strom, as he bows to the king."

"You do not appear to me to be worried, Avec."

"No. Ilter Monicep is a clever lad, schooled, and no more of a fambly than I am. He will get me out. He is my sister's son."

"I had thought, Avec, I might break out soon." I did not wish to enter the Hamalian Jikhorkdun. I moved my wrists and the thongs burst. "About — now."

He could barely see me in the reflected glow of oil lamps shining through the hatchway from the deck above. "You have freed yourself of your bonds? By Krun! That is a deed!"

I reached over in the dimness, found his wrists, said, "Hold steady if they cut, Avec," and jerked his thongs apart.

He rubbed his wrists for a few murs in thoughtful silence. Then he belched. Then he said, "I have read you, Dray, I have read you. You are a paktun. A Hyr-paktun, in all probability."

I have been called a paktun before and, by Zair, I supposed I was and am. A paktun is a name given only to a mercenary who has achieved considerable fame — or notoriety. I would not lie.

"If you think that, Avec, I shall not quarrel with you. Shall we go up?"

"Aye — with all my heart."

We crawled up the ladder cautiously and came out onto the lower deck. Above us the upper deck showed a rectangle of night sky. We crept up there and Avec put the watch to sleep, and we slunk down off the voller. Avec padded ahead of me in the pink-lit darkness. I heard his voice, and an exclamation. From the trees of this terrace two figures tangled together, flailing. Then—

"By Havil the Green, you fambly! You make more noise than a pair of calsanys!"

"Onker! Can't you look where you're going!"

369

I sighed. I had a right pair here — and, instantly, flooding me with nostalgia, warm and wonderful memories of Nath and Zolta, my own two oar-comrades, my two favorite rogues, leaped into my mind.

There was no love of Hamal in my heart. But although these two, Avec and Ilter, might be of Hamal, I did not care about that impediment in them.

I said, "If you shout a little louder you might wake the guards. I don't think they can hear you — yet."

They came closer, dark shadows between the pink shafts of moonshine beneath the trees.

Ilter said, "You are something of a wild leem, Dray Prescot. Avec tells me you burst your bonds, and his. They are regulation thongs, manufactured by the government, to government regulations. It is a marvel."

I almost said, "They were not lesten hide." But I did not. Hostages are given to fortune all too often for my taste. I would not add to the blabbermouths of Kregen.

We had found odd scraps of clothing after we had diverted some of Muruaa's lava, and the night was warm enough, up here in Hamal, although in the Hamalian deserts of the altiplano one finds freezing temperatures almost every night. We walked on in the pink darkness, arguing about what we should do. Rather, they argued, and I listened until we reached the soldiers and their mirvol lines.

Then I said, "I am not of Orlush. I shall take a mirvol and fly out."

They stopped whispering, and turned on me together, saying, "Where will you fly to?" and "I am with you!"

"I welcome you, Avec. I know not, Ilter. Where the flyer takes me, I think."

"He'll take you straight back to the Strom's stables."

"I do not think I would like that."

Avec said, "I left Orlush many seasons ago, and did well. I return for a visit, to see the onkerish son of my dead sister, and Yurncra the Mischievous clutches me in his talons so that the cramph Lart has me flogged and now the Strom will sentence me to the Jikhorkdun. I shall not return to Orlush again."

What Ilter's plans were we never did discover, for we never did ask him. At that moment from beyond the encampment among the trees a soldier appeared bearing a torch which scattered its light upon us. He shouted.

He recognized both Avec and Ilter, for he called their names before my flung stone knocked him down.

Ilter said, "It seems, Uncle, I shall have to accompany you, and that is a fate no well-deserving young man deserves."

The shout would arouse the sleeping camp. We made great speed to select three fine mirvols with full saddlebags still attached, and to release the restraining ropes and hobbles of the others and to beat them into the air. We took off in a veritable welter of wings.

All that night we flew north and east.

The capital of Hamal, Ruathytu, situated on the River Havilthytus lies almost midway between the northern coast and the southern border of the country bounded by the large and impressive River Os, often called He of the Commendable Countenance. Ruathytu is an inland city, situated approximately sixty dwaburs from the eastern coastline. It stands at the junction of the River Mak, known as the Black River, with the River Havilthytus. It was this latter river we followed now, winging through the pink-strewn darkness and seeing the moon's reflection upon the dark and gleaming waters. The Black River is well named, for when it discharges its inky waters into the Havilthytus they run side by side for a surprising number of dwaburs before at last they mingle and merge.

Ilter waved his arm and pointed down. We let our mirvols plane through the sky and came to ground on a yellow bluff above the Black River. Above us two of the lesser moons of Kregen hurtled past, always in a hurry.

"I do not wish to travel all the way to Ruathytu," said Avec, his Kregish thickening a trifle more with the local accent. "But I wish to escape those cramphs on our necks, now we have started. What in Kaerlan the Merciful's name do you want, Ilter?"

"I thought you intended to fly to Ruathytu, the way you were going, by Krun! Had you done so, better to call on Kuerden the Merciless than Kaerlan the Merciful, my onkerish uncle."

"I'll strap you across my knee, nephew! By Krun, I'll—"

I said, "You may fight all you wish. Just give me some idea of a suitable place to find rest and food and I will leave you."

They glared at each other, chests heaving, faces angry and puffed, hands half raised. I was interested to notice that they did not clench their fists or adopt an unarmed-combat discipline posture. They were like two bantam cocks.

"Rest? Food?" Ilter slowly let his hands drop and looked at me. "Where I want to go, of course, is to Dovad, if only this onkerish fambly uncle of mine will allow."

"You ingrate! That your father, my dear sister's husband, is dead! I come to visit you, dwabur after dwabur—"

"My crystal is shattered, oh nit of Nathian girth!"[10]

They really would have gone at each other then, but I stirred my mirvol, and in a fluster of wing-beats shouted down at them, "Where is Dovad, then, dom?"

Ilter leaped into his saddle with such force he almost missed and went slithering over the far side. He caught the pommel and wrenched himself back.

"I'll fly with you, by Krun, and leave this onker to simmer in his own droppings."

"By Krun!" howled Avec. He sprawled up into his saddle somehow, pommel and cantle at the wrong ends, so that he had to fling himself around and grab the flying reins, for the mirvol took an extreme distaste to these antics. The mirvol lowered his head, and his neck, and flicked his wings. Long before Avec could grab on to anything that was fastened, off he spun, up into the air, head over heels, and down on the flat of his broad back.

He yelled.

I was no longer amused. I had seen his back.

I quieted my mirvol and kicked him to close his wings, then hopped off to get to Avec, who lay winded, Ilter's mirvol had responded faster, and when I reached

Avec his nephew was already there, bending over him, lifting his head. I saw Ilter's face.

"I'm all right, Ilter, lad. The beasts aren't trained like they used to be."

"I know, Uncle. Lie still for a moment while I—" and Ilter stopped talking and began to feel his uncle's body. He looked up. "Nothing broken."

"Help me up, lad, for it fair thwacked me, like the kick of a calsany."

Avec had made no outcry. I did not wish to shame him by inquiring about his back, for a man of Kregen is touchy about pain and punishment — stupidly so, sometimes.

We took to the air once again and flew steadily on downstream along the course of the Black River.

Dovad turned out to be a sizable town, located where the river broadened into a lake before plunging on and through a low range of hills, scantily clad with brush and gorse, for they were rocky and looked of fairly recent origin, being sharp-peaked. I saw the way the river plunged over a smooth bulbous edge of land to fall beyond, the white smother of the foot of the falls out of view as we landed.

It seemed sensible to us to remove all signs that these mirvols were military beasts, although the brands on their leathery skins would not easily come out, for obvious reasons. In the end Avec said, "The trouble they will bring is not worth their sale price."

"I agree," said Ilter.

So we took the silks and furs and Avec was about to give his mount a blow to send him into the air when I stopped him.

"Let us take the saddles, if they are not marked, and sell them, and say our flyers perished of a disease."

Ilter said, "The saddles are marked."

"Everything is marked in Hamal, it seems."

We drove the mirvols into the air and soon lost them under the declining rays of She of the Veils as they flew back to Strom Nopac's aerial stables.

Although I had clothes, of a sort, and flying silks and furs to sling over my shoulder, I was still weaponless. It seemed most strange to me that I should walk the face of Kregen without a sword strapped to my side, and yet the very law of this country of Hamal offered a kind of surrogate guarantee of safety. I would find a weapon soon, that I knew.

"We have not come far from Orlush," said Ilter as we waited for the dawn. "They will think to look farther afield than this. And Dovad is a fine large town — almost a smot. I think we would do well to think of new names for ourselves, and after a few days they will forget about us, and we can move on."

"Will they forget, them and their laws?" I said.

Ilter laughed. "Hamal is a large empire. There are many kingdoms and Kovnates. Why, I am told it is four hundred twenty dwaburs from the north coast to He of the Commendable Countenance. If such a distance can be imagined."

Avec scoffed at his nephew. "You know a great deal for a village smith, nephew! Did Nelda the Cane then thwack some learning into your thick skull?"

"Into the other end, Avec, which is more than she ever did for you! And, further, to display my knowledge, earned by much standing up when I could not sit, the empire is three hundred or more dwaburs from the east coast to the Mountains of the West, which have too many names for any one man to remember."

"Aye — and very few men have seen them, by Krun!"

I knew from what Queen Fahia of Hyrklana had told me that the Emperor of Hamal was extending his powers over these distant mountains, and south of the River Os, and, also, that the maniac was trying to invade South Pandahem — all at the same time. With the scale of these operations demanding such enormous resources and manpower, I fancied that Ilter had the right of it. In the event he was proved right. We spent a few days in Dovad using the money from one of the saddlebags, and bought ourselves new outfits, very tasteful, too. When we took the boat down the Black River we felt in our bones we were as free as fluttcleppers.

As Avec said, "The guard who shouted had his money in his saddlebag so he could keep an eye on it during watch. He did us a good turn, after all."

I doubted this, knowing, probably, a little more about soldiers than Avec, despite that they were his countrymen. The money was neatly pouched in mashcera and I felt it would more likely be true to say it was Strom Nopac's, under guard.

We took a boat below the falls and the captain, a cheerful Amith, delighted in keeping his crew hard at it to beat the record for downstream journeys set up only a season ago by a great rival. The boats on the Black River are usually flat-bottomed, wide, with puntlike bows, and three decks. They are brightly painted and kept in tip-top condition. Downstream the Amiths swear they are faster than a hack flyer, although this is generally conceded as just another of the Amith's genial boasts.

Strange folk, the Amith, with the hindquarters and rear body of a totrix, and with an apim's torso and arms rising from the junction of what appear to be two entirely different bodies. What was originally the center pair of legs of the totrix have become what appear to be the lower limbs of an apim. The males are usually black-bearded, and they look undeniably impressive. Many of the females have masses of curly golden hair, which gives them an oddly coquettish air, most strange, as I have said. And when I say strange, I have in mind that Kregen is peopled by many strange races, of which the diffs called Amith are a proud and delightful example. There is a legend which has received wide credence that the Amiths were the original inhabitants of Hamal.

What with the money and what with my two companions, I spent a most agreeable time roaming around central Hamal. The country is undeniably big. It has a larger population per area than many other places — by contrast Segesthes is practically deserted — and I believe all three of us found in this wandering a kind of release from normal cares. For we all knew we would have to get back to work one day.

The year to which I had been sentenced by the Star Lords slowly crept by. Ilter would find himself a job as a smith and do very well. Avec would go back to being a Niltch.

He said to me one day as we waited to board one of the wheeled vehicles plying for public hire in the main street of Hemlad, a fair-sized town out toward the east of Dovad, "You and Ilter should come with me, Dray. I've had myself a holiday that that cramph of an Elten Lart Lykon ruined. I've enjoyed myself, by Krun! But I must get back to work. That onker Naghan needs me at his side."

I was not interested in working for a living if I had money in my pocket. Oh, yes, I'd work, and work like a slave, if I had to. I'd do anything at all — for certain reasons that you know. So I said as the carriage halted before the little crowd waiting to board, "What do you do, anyway, Avec? You never talk about it."

The carriage — usually they have four central wheels, and like the chaldrons of the Heavenly Mines they run on tracks let into the road — lurched ahead. I sat on a wooden-strip seat as Avec paid the fare. He stumbled across a woman with a shopping basket filled with plump ripe shonages, gloriously red, luscious, making my mouth water, and Avec mumbled some apology and flopped into the seat next to me.

The woman glared at him and then solicitously at her shonages; I didn't blame her. We were going to meet Ilter and the first thing I promised myself was to buy a shonage and sink my teeth into it. I remembered them from Huringa.

"What do I do, dom?" Avec chuckled and cocked one leg over the other and so kicked the shonage basket again. The woman tsk-tsked and glared; but Avec bestowed upon her so sweet and gallant a smile that she was forced to lower her eyelids.

I wondered if Avec in his bumbling way had overdone it. In a country so ridden with laws as Hamal the woman might easily stop the carriage and call the Amith drawing it to come and sort out this yetch who kept insulting her and damaging her fruit.

I was interested in knowing what Avec did, for he had never mentioned it, and I suppose I was assumed to understand what Niltch meant.

Avec struggled in his seat to get a wad of cham from his arm-purse. Avec was a great cham-chewer. He was also leaning over toward me as he tried to flick the purse-lid open, but the pesky thing had stuck. His legs were kicking about dangerously.

"I don't mind telling you, dom," he said, and his voice sank. We had forced ourselves not to use each other's names in public, just in case. "But, you know the way the government and the Emperor regard this matter. I'm not a skilled man, as Havil the Green is my witness, although I would wish to be. Now, young Ilter is now." He swore a little more loudly then, and wrestled with the purse. We both hoped no one would have overheard his careless use of the name. The woman was trying to move her basket away, and a shonage looked about to slide off at any minute. I was looking at the shonage, and thinking my tangled thoughts about emperors and their laws and how poor folk could not afford to ride in a voller and sail through the air, and so avoid knocking into old ladies and damaging prime shonages.

Avec rambled on, under his breath, leaning over more and more, struggling with the arm-purse.

"We are all vowed to secrecy, of course. Penalty death. Oh, yes — death! But I will tell you what I can, and hope you will come with me to Sumbakir, and I'll put in a word for you. We'll be safer there, too, for the guards are fierce, by Krun!"

The woman rescued her shonage. I let my breath out. Avec ripped furiously at his arm-purse. He also spoke softly to me as the purse-lid came free.

"You must know, dom, what I do, from what I have already told you, and my name, and where I work."

His thick arm jerked with the violence with which he dragged the purse open, the elbow driving toward me as he told me.

"I build vollers, dom."

My surprise was complete. I could not stop the instinctive start of shock. Avec's solid elbow hit me as I jumped and my body lunged forward in exact time to a corner-turning lurch of the carriage. It threw me forward putting my face and shoulders slap-bang squash into the woman's basket of ripe shonages.

Sixteen

Vollers of Sumbakir

At this time Sumbakir and the voller yards were organized on military lines; instead of foremen and gang-leaders and time-keepers and floor-managers there were Deldars and Hikdars and Jiktars to run the shops. I fitted in well enough with Avec the Niltch to guide me, and Ilter Monicep as a smith was quickly at home in the smithy where the angle irons, brackets, and control rods were produced. Slaves, of course, swarmed everywhere. They wore the common gray slave breechclout, and they did the hard and onerous tasks set them by the slave-masters, who took their orders from the Deldars of Slaves.

Truly, I would not have welcomed such a life. But I think you will fully understand my motives. For most of my life on Kregen I had been cursed by the dark knowledge that at any time a flier might break down and so precipitate me — and those dear to me — into danger. The people of Vallia and Zenicce and Balintol and many other of the places where Hamalian and Hyrklanian vollers were sold lived with this knowledge. A voller was not to be trusted. Yet I knew that within the bounds of Havilfar itself — certainly in Hamal and Hyrklana — airboats were perfectly sound.

The desire to uncover the secret, perhaps to take away with me the knowledge of the construction of vollers, fired me to a determination that made me do things I detested. Even if this meant I would miss the date on which I could fly back to the Shrouded Sea and pick up my life again with Delia and my friends, even this I would do to secure the secret knowledge.

I have some skills as a carpenter and can turn my hand to that trade when necessary, as a ship's officer of a wooden navy must be able to, if he is a tarpaulin lieutenant without prospects. Learning my way about the yards took little time after our arrival, and Deldar Naghan the Triangle took to me, with Avec's coarse comments to spur him on.[11]

The long open sheds resounded with the blows of ax and adz, the *chirr-chirr* of saws, the sliding hiss of planes and the sharp staccato cracks of hammers. I'll admit they built well. The wooden frames were fashioned from seasoned wood, and the Kregans know what there is to know about seasoning and steam bending as about compass timbers. Sometimes the coverings were mere canvas and hide, at others sliced planks produced with extraordinary skill by slaves trained from birth to the work. The timbers were beautifully jointed and glued. As well they were on occasion pinned. Over at Conelawlad, so Naghan the Triangle told me, they built their frames from metal. Ilter said he would stick by that fambly of an uncle of his, for the nurdling onker would as well cut his thumbs off as saw a straight line.

We were a harum-scarum bunch, as I see now, looking back. Under the harsh laws of Hamal we still found time to skylark. The lot of the slaves was far less enviable. They were guarded by the prowling black-and-white-striped forms of the werstings. These four-legged hunting dogs are extraordinarily vicious, and when they draw their lips back from their fangs it is time either to face front with a weapon or to run. But, running, you would be brought down in an instant. The wersting packs kept the slaves under guard, and the guards kept intruders out, and in Sumbakir there in south-central Hamal we built fliers.

Looking at the black and white stripes of the werstings reminded me of Jumnee of Nycresand, that Hikdar of a wersting pack, and on the morning the Kov of Apulad paid us his customary once-a-sennight-visit, I thought of Jumnee and wondered what he was doing now.

This morning the Kov was in a foul temper. This was quite normal. Only once had I seen him come in smiling, and that morning the rumor was that one of the Emperor's daughters had had a miscarriage.

"I run Sumbakir for the glory of the Emperor!" This Ornol ham Feoste, the Kov of Apulad, was fond of declaiming.

He stalked into our shed and everyone straightened up from their tasks and bent their heads, even me, Dray Prescot who was called Chaadur. The four guls the Kov had had whipped last week were back to work, and we all knew that the Kov was out to find fault. Any one of us might find the thongs around his wrists and his shirt stripped down his back, and the Deldar of the Lash laying on.

Ornol ham Feoste stalked between the lines of petal-shaped vollers, for we were working on an order that called for simple four-place fliers at the time. He ran his hand down the wood to test its smoothness, then he would wrench away at joints hoping they would come apart in his hands.

As usual, I did not look at his wife. The Kovneva, however, as usual, looked at me.

The silly woman wore her fine sensil veil swathed across her face so that her large dark eyes could look boldly upon whatever and whoever she wished. Her gown, a gaudy combination of emerald and ruby and diamond stripes sewn against a white soft material spun from the wool of the Methydrian ponsho, clung to her body as she moved. This was scarcely the dress a Hortera would

376

wear to visit a workshop. The custom of elderly Earthwomen never to wear silk out of doors is a strange custom not followed upon Kregen; but this dress was too flamboyant by half.

In her arms she carried a wersting pup. The thing grew bigger week by week, and now the Lady Esme, Kovneva of Apulad, held a thin golden chain in her dainty hand, a chain that fastened to a gem-studded golden collar around the pup's neck.

We were all standing there, and many of the guls were trembling in a thinly controlled way that indicated they were almost beyond control. We were all wondering what the Kov would find fault with this week, for we knew that find fault he would. We stood there, hating the cramph, for in a very real and meaningful way he was the chief blot upon the landscape.

Ornol ham Feoste, Kov of Apulad, broke the joint that young Lenki had just made.

I saw Lenki sway and his hands wring together behind his back. The Kov turned to him quite slowly, and the Kov's face bore a look that chilled the human soul in Lenki.

"You call yourself a gul, rast," said the Kov in a quiet and deadly way. "No Horter would demean himself with you. A slave could do better work than you. And yet I, the Kov, must spend my time seeing you do work for which you are paid well — golden deldys the empire could use better elsewhere."

Lenki had sense enough not to reply.

The Kov gestured to his guards. They were apim, heavy-set fellows in half-armor and close-fitting helmets with the bright plumes of the arbora flaunting from their crests. They were soldiers, as their insignia showed, for it was the habit of the Hamalian government to post regiments from one part of the empire to duty in another and remote part. They seized Lenki.

He yelled, then, a thin shriek of abject fear.

"The joint broke, rast!" The Kov was enjoying this.

There was no excuse. The joint should not have broken, even in the thick and sweating hands of the Kov. We looked after Lenki as he was dragged out, screaming.

Esme, Kovneva of Apulad, lingered as her husband strutted on. She eyed me. I could see the red smudge of her mouth beneath the veil. Her body thrust boldly forward as she snuggled the wersting pup against her bosom. The golden chain jingled.

"Should I ask the Kov to break your joint, Chaadur?"

I said, "Your gracious eminence must do as she pleases. The joint will not break to a bungling clasp."

She flushed.

She had said to me, the week before last, "I am the Kovneva, Chaadur. You would do well not to forget that."

She walked on, swinging her hips. She had taken many lovers from the strong young men working here, soldier, guard, Horter, gul, slave. It was rumored she preferred slaves, for their mouths might be stoppered with least inconvenience.

When the inspection was finished the Kov strode to the wide double-doors which stood open so that the radiance of Far and Havil might strike through. He paused and shouted at us.

"You must work harder! By Hanitcha the Harrower! The Emperor demands more fliers. You will build them, or as Malahak is my witness, it will be the Jikhorkdun for you!"

He strode away, the thraxter swinging at his side, his guards at his heels. Following them strolled Esme, insolent in her power and beauty, with her two maids.

Avec rumbled an oath and said, "The Emperor will have that rast of a Kov in the Jikhorkdun if we do not work!"

Avec had no real idea of what a strike was; one day the minds of the guls might veer to the concept. The guls have no power, no privileges, no ranks. They are free men, not slaves, children of free parents, and they are not Horters, not gentlemen. They are not working people of the tradesmen class nor yet are they of the class of which stylors form the bulk. They are craftsmen, masters at their trades, and without them Kregen — aye, and the Earth — would tumble into ruin.

Soon after that the petal-shaped four-place flier I was helping to build was framed out and her canvas covering sewn on. With Avec and old Ob-eye I helped trundle her out of the double doors and across the yard into the fitting shed.

This was a place I needed to know more about. Here was where the controls and the silver boxes were fitted. The boxes were made up from tin. In a black-walled room at one end of the shed the tin boxes went in with their lids neatly laid beside them, for they were all handmade, and one lid might not fit a different box. They came out from the black-walled room with their lids fastened down and soldered. At the opposite end of the fitting shed stood the red-walled room. The tin boxes went in here just as they did into the black-walled room and came out exactly the same, filled and with the lids soldered. With great care the guls then took a tin from the red room and a tin from the black room and slotted them into the grooves made for them in the voller. Then the controls could be fitted.

As usual, a guard — he was a Rhaclaw — herded us out as soon as we had pushed our flier into the fitting shed. We wet our lips, but the next mealtime lay a few burs ahead yet, and took ourselves off to the stores to draw fresh timber and so begin the construction of the next voller.

Ilter had told me that the silver boxes were made up from sheets of metal beaten to an extraordinary thinness and then passed through a bath of molten tin. Iron or copper, he said, he supposed, were the favorite metals. I was far more interested about what was inside the tins. Those silver boxes intrigued me. The Emperor of Vallia had once ordered a silver box broken open so as to discover the secret of the fliers. In one tin they had found fine grit and sand and earth, packed in tightly to the lid. The other tin had been empty.

That had been some time ago, and the flier had, of course, been ruined. Despite my suggestion that I would pay to open a flier's silver boxes, the Emperor,

Delia's father, had told me that he would not permit it. He knew, he said, what was in the silver boxes: dirt and air. With that I had been content at the time; now I was actually standing in the very place where fliers were made, where the silver boxes were filled!

Let the devils of a Herrelldrin hell take me if I didn't find out the answers now!

Around at the far end of the fitting shed, where I made it my business to wander as though merely dawdling, I had seen piles of dirt and gravel and sand. As unlikely as it had sounded, the Emperor's story must be true — not that I doubted his word in a matter like this even if, and despite my Delia, I would not trust him wholeheartedly.

Dirt and air?

There was a mystery here, by Vox!

On the night I decided it was worth the risk of breaking out of our barracks by the back way and sneaking over to the fitting shed I made a few suitable precautions and then prepared to burglarize a window from the inside. Just as I put the blade of a chisel to the window a knock rattled the door of my cubicle, for the barracks, as I have said, were subdivided into single cubicles. I cursed and slid the chisel up the sleeve of my shirt and flopped onto the three-legged stool by the bed, and bellowed grumpily, "Come in, come in!"

If my plans worked as I envisaged I wanted no one knowing I had broken out and gone prowling. The front door was open, and anyone could go out and come in, but I did not want to be noticed.

It was Ilter. He carried a Jikaida board under his arm and a sturm-wood box of pieces. I dissembled. I owed him a game for I had beaten him soundly the previous evening, and he wanted revenge. We set up the board in deadly silence and ranked our Deldars and set to work. Although he was a fine player and my mind was not fully occupied with the game, I managed to hold him to a Pyrrhic victory. He grimaced and shuffled the pieces up, folding the board. "Next time, Chaadur, I will smite you, hip and thigh!"

When he left the suns were completely gone from the sky and the Maiden with the Many Smiles floated above serenely. I did not bother with the cheap oil lamp in my room but again laid the chisel against the window. I was not too concerned over the delay. Now was probably a better time, anyway.

The door opened swiftly, so swiftly that I only just had time to slide the chisel into my shirtsleeve.

Hikdar Covell ti Heltonlad, as thin faced and hollow eyed as ever, with that suspicious beaky nose of his poking where it was not wanted, pushed that very selfsame nose into my room. He wore his uniform, and his thraxter was drawn. He looked as though he barely repressed an explosion of resentment and malice.

"Are you washed, gul? Are you clean?"

He poked his damned thraxter at me, rather as a schoolmaster pokes little boys with his cane.

I did not take it away from him and clout him over the ears with the flat.

Outside in the corridor shapes moved, and I heard the chink of a sword-blade against a lorica, and so I knew Hikdar Covell had not come alone.

He did not wait for me to answer.

"Up! Up with you, rast! Come with me!" He swirled his short cape, checkered green and black with the gold lace and bullion tassels, swung his sword up over his right shoulder, and pranced out. I heard him complaining to his men. "This place smells like a dopa den of Lower Ruathytu! Drag him out if he does not come—"

I stepped into the corridor.

Six soldiers closed around me.

"Smartly, now," rapped Hikdar Covell. "Here—" and a Deldar at his Hikdar's sword clapped a foul black bag over my head. I let them do all this to me. I let them put my head in a black bag and grab me by the elbows and guide me out of the barracks and into the night. I knew where I was being taken. I knew what their errand was. Also, I knew what I wanted to do. I would make a fine dovetail joint of those two wantings that no cramph of a Kov could break.

Seventeen

Concerning the silver chains of Kovneva Esme

I could hear the shrill ululating call of the night straerlker as we walked past the end of the barrack block and up the winding stone-flagged path to the Kov's villa. The night straerlker, unlike its cousin of the daytime, hunts night-flying insects, whereas the day variant hunts in rocky clefts for scurrying arachnids. The black bag over my head smelled of a scent not unlike chypre, heavy, cloying. That was the favorite scent of Esme, Kovneva of Apulad.

Tripping over a step quite deliberately to let them know I was helpless and had no idea where I was being taken, I took stock of our progress. Up the long flight of steps to the villa, past the guardhouse, around to the side where I heard the soft night breeze rustle in the yellow mushk and I smelled its sweet perfume. That recalled Valka to me, and the high fortress of Esser Rarioch. Then I was pushed roughly through a narrow door for those shoulders of mine brushed against each jamb. Up a long carpeted stair. Then a wait before a door, and the faint sound of a girl's laugh, and a door closing, and then the rustle of soft clothes, and the rough hand on my arm relaxing, and a smaller, softer hand, urging me forward. The door clashed at my back, a harsh sound in what I guessed must be a scented, soft and downy bower. I heard the harsh breathing of a man near my right shoulder, and the creak of his harness as he breathed, and I smelled oiled leather and steel, and so knew a guard stood over the doorway, ready to kill if the Kovneva so ordered.

There was mystery and a haunting terror lurking below the threshold here, if I allowed. A normal man might be forgiven if he trembled at what awaited him. I did not tremble; but I admit I wondered if I had been so clever in allowing myself to be brought here. I had thought it a capital scheme, to further my plans. Now, the doubt occurred. Maybe I should have bashed Hikdar Covell and taken his thraxter, and cut up the guards, and gone my own headstrong way.

But, as you know, I was trying to be clever…

The girl pulling me forward halted and again I heard that soft silver jingling. I had an idea what that was, and if my idea was right I would be less than polite to the Kovneva…

I heard a slithery sound that told me a screen had been pulled across. Probably it was sturm-wood cunningly pierced into a grille, or fabricated from ivory from Chem. I heard a low laugh, and then a hand whipped the black bag away and I had to shut my eyes against the glare of soft samphron-oil lamps.

The Kovneva's voice said, "A great shaggy graint! Yes, Merle, I shall enjoy taming this one!"

"Indeed, yes, my lady," responded a young voice, and yet the voice, although bright, held a note of dullness and despair.

Sound of a slap and a muffled shriek, and then I opened my eyes and I could see again.

I'll give her this, Esme, Kovneva of Apulad; she tried to make of her private bower as sophisticated and luxurious a shrine to love as she imagined the empress' in far Ruathytu's must be. She was a Kovneva, and therefore a very great lady; but her husband the Kov had been personally charged by the Emperor with voller production at Sumbakir, and that meant a dreadful provincial prison sentence for Esme. If I had had any feelings of sympathy for her they hardened as her maidservant, a young apim girl, put a hand to her cheek, which flamed scarlet and angry. Bright tears stood in the eyes of the girl, and her bosom moved beneath the scrap of peach-colored silk which the Kovneva allowed her as her only clothing.

"You need not stand looking like a fambly, Chaadur! You onker! Sit on this cushion and drink this wine."

I sat. The room had been festooned with draping silks and tapestries embroidered with various scenes from the more amorous of the legends of Kregen. I saw many that depicted stories I knew, others that at the time I did not know. Samphron-oil lamps stood upon balass-wood tables. Gilt chairs stood against the walls. The sofa upon which Esme reclined rested on six feet sculpted to look like the pads and claws of zhantils. I thought they might be solid gold and then noticed a claw knocked off and the sturm-wood showing through the gilt. Provincial, provincial…

Another slave, a black girl probably from Xuntal, stood waving an exotic fan of whistling-faerling feathers to keep the air moving and sweet. If there were windows in the room they had been closed and shuttered and concealed by the draperies. Rugs upon the floor were strewn here and there; they were not of Walfarg weave.

A third slave girl brought in the wine. She was a Fristle, a superb little fifi, and I thought of Tilly, my little Fristle fifi of the Jikhorkdun of Huringa, who now waited with Delia and my friends in the airboat — to which I would return, by Zair, to which I would return.

The Fristle girl slave poured the wine. The goblet was glass, of a pale cream color, and twisted in the stem, and of a flat shape. I do not care for twisted glass stems, and I prefer a wineglass — given that one must use different shapes for each different wine or liquor — of a more rotund appearance.

But all these things meant little besides the debased appearance of the three slave girls. They did not wear the gray slave breechclouts. I had heard of this manner of collaring and chaining slaves, girl slaves, the manner known as *nohnam*. They wore scanty silk garments, pale green, peach, lake-blue. Around their necks, their wrists, their ankles, were fastened bands of silver — the collars were high, causing the girls to lift their heads when they wished to let their chins sink in misery. I doubted if the metal was really silver. From the collar ran chains to the wrists and to the ankles, and from ankles to wrists ran more chains, caught up beneath the girls' bodies. As they moved the chains swung.

During my time at the Jikhorkdun in Hyrklana I had heard men talking of taking a delight in chaining and collaring their girl slaves in nohnam. They seemed to think that by debasing a girl they exalted themselves.

Merle, the slave whom Esme had slapped — for no reason apart from the enjoyment of administering the punishment — moved near me as I made no attempt to drink the wine the Fristle girl had poured. I looked at Merle's neck, and wrists, and ankles.

The sores on her wrists and ankles were bad enough, some scabbed over and broken again. She had stuffed a few pitiful scraps of cloth down to try to prevent the chafing. But the sores around her neck were nothing short of disgusting. The collar's friction, which is unavoidable in a metal collar in nohnam, had rubbed the skin away in wide areas, and the scabs had formed, and had been knocked off, and the blood and pus dribbled down. Esme saw my look and belted Merle across her backside with the flexible length of tuffa tree handy, as she spoke most viciously to her.

"Wash your neck, you filthy rast!"

"Yes'm, my Lady," said Merle, and scuttled with jangling chains to a screen across one corner. I heard the sound of splashing water.

The black girl's scabs were not so bad, but she suffered, too. As for the Fristle, her fine and delightfully snuggly fur had been worn away where the fake silver of the nohnam chafed, and the skin showed, red and raw and bleeding.

"These girls are useless, Chaadur! Now when we return to the capital I shall buy slaves who understand the refinements of good breeding and fine manners."

I still had not spoken.

Esme went on talking.

"You are just a gul, Chaadur, at the moment. You are little better than a slave. Now I want you to take the baths of nine — we have a reasonable establishment here, as you will discover — and then I think you and I may talk to our mutual advantage. I can assure you of rapid promotion. I can get you what you desire most in all Havilfar. The Empire of Hamal can be yours for the taking." Then she checked herself, and laughed, and sipped her wine, with the color flooding her cheek. She had overstepped herself. "I mean, of course, that in Hamal under the

Emperor's wise and benign rule you may make your fortune. You can be a Horter, a Notor — there is no reason why you may not be a Kov yourself, one day."

Still I did not say anything but sat on the cushion, which was lumpy and was clearly not stuffed with fine quality feathers. I looked calmly at her, and her slaves, and her tatty little bower.

When I think of the women I have met on Kregen — and only those few whom I had up until now met — who cherished notions not far removed from this Kovneva Esme! The Princess Susheeng, the Princess Natema, Queen Lilah, Kovneva Katrin Rashumin, Queen Fahia, Viridia the Render, oh, yes, and the others, as you know — and do not associate Mayfwy with them — or, come to that, Natema, who was married to my comrade Prince Varden Wanek. When I imagined what they would think of me now I smiled.

I, Dray Prescot, smiled reflectively there in the soft glow from the samphron-oil lamps.

This Esme, this Kovneva, smiled back uncertainly.

"Yes, you see, Chaadur? All you must do is obey me in all things. You can give me so much—" Her moist red lips parted hungrily.

Merle came back. The washing had been painful.

"Why do you not speak, Chaadur?" Then Esme put down my silence to what must have been a not uncommon reaction of a slave, a gul, to this soft blaze of luxury and refinement as they would see it. "This is nothing, Chaadur, to what may be yours in the future if you will but obey me!"

So I said, "It seems to me to be nothing now." I sipped the wine. "And your wine is a dreadful vintage." I poured it upon one of the rugs, a brash affair with a Chunkrah and a Fristle that is not worth commenting on.

"You!" She didn't believe this.

I said, "If you have the key to these girls' chains I will have it and take the chains off. You are a rast and a cramph for chaining them up."

She gaped at me.

Merle and the Fristle fifi gazed at me as though I were mad. I own I am a bit of a maniac; but that is me, Dray Prescot. I wondered what to do with these three slave girls once I had taken the degrading nohnam from them, so that they would not have to sit and stand in that disgusting slavish posture of humiliation. Some people really think girls are not part of the human race!

The black girl put out her hands, as far as the chains would allow, and she said, "I give you the Jikai, dom; but I fear, by Xurrhuk of the Curved Sword, you are a dead apim."

I stood up. "Give me the key, Esme."

She was a Kovneva. She called out, "Bagor! Here! Kill!"

The sliding door slid aside with a screech. The guard appeared, craggy, bulky, clad in armor, ferociously lusting after letting blood. At his appearance all three slave girls screamed and drew back in such a pitiful way that I knew instantly this Bagor had been mistreating them abominably.

"Kill the rast, Bagor!" screamed Esme.

"You," said this Bagor. His bulk was mostly muscle, but there was fat there, too, as I had judged by his breathing when he stood by the outer door. "Outside! The Kovneva will not be pleased for your blood to stain her carpets."

The girls screamed again.

I am not given to talking when action is imminent, but I wanted to give some heart to these three pitiful slave girls, and so I boasted. How my tough warriors of Valka, or my clansmen, or, even, my fighters of Djanduin would have stared at me then. I dared not think what my Krozair brothers would say.

So I said, "I do not care about splattering the cramph of a Kovneva's carpets with your blood, Bagor!"

And I leaped for him, poor onker, and took his thraxter away and cut his legs from under him. He fell asprawl in blood across the tatty carpets. I thunked the hilt down on his head to put him to sleep.

The Kovneva Esme could not speak. She sat there on her couch, her legs drawn up, her gown bedraggled with blood that had splashed it. She looked at me with horrified eyes and she tried to speak, but her fingers dug clawlike into her throat so that she could not utter a word.

I went over to her and ripped the dress about until I found the key. Then I unlocked the fetters and the manacles and took the collars from their necks. I am not a vengeful man. But I did something then, I, perhaps, should not have done.

When I had finished, there lay Esme, the Kovneva of Apulad, collared and chained in nohnam, degraded in her own bower.

Eighteen

Dirt and air

Although Esme appeared paralyzed and unable to cry out, lying there on her blood-spattered carpets with the collar and chains and manacles of nohnam upon her, the previous screaming must soon bring guards. They would not be big, bloated hunks of female-tamers like Bagor. And Bagor was an honorable name in most parts of Kregen.

I picked up the curved dagger he wore in a cheap brass scabbard and held it in my left hand. The thraxter in my right, my old shirt and ragged pair of trousers cut off at the knees, and I was as fully armed and accoutered as I could be, for Bagor carried no shield for this duty of chastising female slaves in chains and of cutting down slaves or guls if they displeased his mistress. What of the laws of Hamal here?

As I did this, Merle snatched up the thin tuffa rod and started hitting Esme. She swung wildly, her body heaving with each blow, her gasps sounding painfully loud. The black girl, Xasha, laughed. I took Merle's arm.

"Do you wish to remain here, Merle?"

She looked at me with deep shock in her eyes, very pitiful to see. She drew in a deep breath and threw the switch away.

"I cannot remain here, Jikai, and live!"

"That is true," said Xasha. "And if we do not leave at once the guards will take us all. Then, after the beatings it will be the Jikhorkdun for us all."

I moved to the door. I heard a soft click from the direction of the couch, and turning to call the girls, I saw the Fristle, Floy, take a long thin dagger from the tray which had slid out from its concealment in the side of the sofa. She lifted the dagger high and the samphron-oil lamps gleamed off the blade and sparkled off the gems set in the hilt.

With a triumphant shriek the Fristle girl buried the dagger in Esme's throat.

Esme choked, coughed, vomited blood, kicked her legs, and then rolled slowly over onto her face.

There was nothing anyone could do for her.

Floy, the Fristle girl, stood, her legs apart, her diaphanous scrap of silk quivering with her own excited body-movements. She whispered, to herself, really, unaware for the moment of any other person.

"Hai," she whispered. "Hai, Jikai!"

Not unmoved, I turned away and with a harsh and intemperate gesture and a few uncouth words bade the girls follow me.

Xasha said, "We would do well to take what jewels and money we can carry, dom. Also, we will need clothes."

I nodded. "Very well. I will stand by the door."

Still panting, her bosom in tumult, Floy circled the contorted body of the Kovneva. She spat upon the corpse. She would have stuck the dagger again and again into that hated form; but I held the dagger and the blood dripped, drop by drop, upon the carpet.

We collected jewels, mostly from the dead person of the Kovneva, and the girls threw clothes about themselves, breechclouts of silk, mashcere blouses, and long cloaks of checkered green and crimson and blue. Out of a habit that I would not break if I could I seized up a scarlet length and wound it around my middle. Bagor's belt held it up, and his scabbard of risslaca scale would be useful if there was climbing to be done.

"This way," said Merle.

We went out past the sliding screen — which was of ivory not from Chem, but from the northern jungles of Havilfar, as one might notice from the whiter color and coarser texture — and down the passageways up which I had been brought, and down to the outer door. Here Merle paused, her finger to her lips in the dwindling light of the Maiden with the Many Smiles. Soon the Twins, the two second moons of Kregen eternally orbiting each other, would be up and throwing down enough light by which to see comfortably. Merle beckoned and we hurried from the door, which we closed, and down a shadowed arcaded way to the first garden of the pools.

"The stables are beyond the Pagoda of the Green Smile," she whispered. "Can you ride a saddle-flyer?"

"Yes."

"So can we all. It is something our mistress thought proper in her girl slaves, her Chail Sheom." She spoke with a bitter savagery, a masochistic anger. The Chail Sheom is the name on Kregen given to these beautiful girl slaves who wear fine silks and pearls and who minister intimately to their mistresses.

"You shall be free, Merle," I said. "You and Xasha and Floy."

We crept toward the aerial stables. Before we crossed the second garden of the pools where the intricately pierced stonework of the Pagoda of the Green Smile stood against the rising of the Twins, we could hear the birds. They rustled and stirred and fluttered their wings. We approached cautiously.

At the barred gate the guards, sleepy, not caring to catch this boring duty, talking desultorily between them, had no notion of our presence. They still could not have known what it was that sent Notor Zan's cavernous paunch encircling them in darkness. I did not kill them. I stepped over their unconscious bodies and called the girls. They ran up, lissome forms in the moons-light.

"You have homes to go to? Places where you will be safe?"

They were surprised, and even though they were still in shock, they were dismayed that I meant what I did.

"You will not desert us now, Jikai?"

Shouts resounded and torches flared in the gardens, beyond the pools, toward the villa.

"If you fly now they will never find you. Go. I have tasks I must do here before I may leave."

Floy in her drugged way said, "If you plan to kill the Kov I will stand with you. Give me back the dagger."

"I do not wish to kill the Kov. He is an onker and a rast. But I have more important work to do." I pushed the gate open and started to untether the nearest fluttrell. He banged his wings and pretended he was asleep; but I woke him up smartly enough and with a whimper he was dragged out.

"Chaadur," said Merle, again. "Will you not fly with us?"

I brought out two more fluttrells before I answered.

"You must fly fast and far, Merle. If you are sure you know where you may go, I will trust in that. And you, Floy, for you are of Havilfar, also, I think." I turned to the beautiful black girl. "But you, Xasha, are from Xuntal, I believe. Where will you fly?"

Her cool appraising eyes rested on me. She put out a finger and touched my upper arm. "I have friends beyond the Mountains of the West, where I lived as a small girl. I shall fly there."

"And I to Hyrklana," said Merle, "for I do not think I can live more in Hamal."

The shouts and the torches passed away beyond the Pagoda of the Green Smile. In a few more murs the searchers would reach the aerial stables. "Floy?" I said.

The Fristle fifi smiled lazily. "Ifilion," she said. "Which is yet a kingdom with its own soul."

Where the River Os marking the southern boundary of Hamal proper bifurcates, so that one arm runs around toward the north and the other arm runs around toward the south, the land between the arms right up to the sea has over the centuries been extended outward in a smooth rounded promontory which faces northwestern Hyrklana. This is the land of Ifilion. Its kingdom has remained independent, and there are whispers that sorcery and magic account for this integrity in the face of Hamalian aggrandizement and empire-building.

"Ifilion is small," I said. "You will do it much honor."

The girls mounted up. They saw I meant what I said. I clapped the birds on their tails and stood back. As they rose into the night sky with that streaming pink moons-shine gleaming upon their pinions, I thought I heard three separate words ghost down from the wind-rush. "Remberee," and, "Remberee," and, yet again for the last time, "Remberee."

"Remberee," I said, but I spoke to myself.

Already I crouched and ran into the shadows beyond the aerial stable wall. Guards were running and torches flared and the shouts were strong and confident now.

"The stables! The cramphs make for the stables!"

The wing-beats of the three fluttrells dwindled and died. The guards burst out past the Pagoda of the Green Smile.

"They fly! See — *they fly!*"

A Hikdar ran up, waving his thraxter, untidy in shadowed pink light.

"After them, you onkers! Mount up and fly!"

In the shadows I gripped the hilt of Bagor's thraxter and I cursed.

Women! Forever talking! And now they had talked so long and so late they had allowed the guards to see them winging away.

Silly girls! Stupid onkerish women!

I had a task to do here for Vallia and for Valka. No longer, if I was successful, would our Air Service have to make do with fractious fliers that broke down at the most inconvenient moments. No longer would I tremble every time Delia or the twins took to the air in a voller. No, by Vox! My job was here, to break into the fitting shed, to find out everything hidden there, everything there was to know about how to build fliers.

And then I must hurry back to the Shrouded Sea and meet the airboat with my friends and clasp Delia in my arms again. That was my duty. But I am grown soft and a weakling, even on Kregen, which is death to weaklings.

Holding the thraxter easily I stepped out into the moons-light and I shouted, high and hard, at the running guards.

"Hold! The first man to try to enter the stables is a dead man! This I promise you, by Havil the Green, whose name be eternally damned!"

Well, it created a stir. I'll say that.

At the time I did not like the Hamalese, as you know. I had not forgotten the way, through their laws, they had tortured young Doyden, and then hanged him, or their underhanded tricks, their dishonest dealings in fliers. They had tried to kill me many times, and failed, and I wanted to be gone from here.[12]

They had not been kind to me in the Heavenly Mines, either.

The guards took little stock of a lone man, armed with a thraxter, without a shield. They charged, a bunch of them, hotly, furiously, instantly. Their very reaction betrayed them.

As they converged on me over the trimmed grass of the garden of the pools outside the aerial stables I slipped into a fighting crouch. That crouch was a little exaggerated, for I wished to fool them. The first, the fleetest, simply held his shield before him and thrust with his thraxter. I slid the blow, pulled the shield down, and stabbed him in the throat over the top band of his lorica. He fell away, choking, splattering gouts of blood, dark in the moons-light.

The next two came in together and I ran at them, leaped between them and chopped the right one's face off, landed, sprang back, and without compunction sliced the other's neck beneath the back helmet rim.

A stux flew past. I deflected a second stux with the thraxter. I dodged about. If I was badly wounded now I'd be done for, for they'd swamp me with numbers.

The stars twinkled above, and the twin moons shone down, in their three-quarter phase so that they shed light enough. I ducked and weaved and shifted, to seize a stux with my left hand as it whistled past and so return it. The Hikdar bellowed. I had not thrown wildly.

"By Krun!" yelled a soldier. "The cramph is a devil!"

"Stand back and shoot him down, comrades!" advised another. This being sound advice the soldiers moved back and I saw men trotting up with crossbows. Time had passed, enough time, I hoped, to give the three girls the opportunity to lose their pursuers in the wide wastes of the night sky of Kregen.

The shadows on the far side of the stables looked inviting. I did not wait but ran instantly for them. As I vanished into the shadows of the trees so the first bolts whickered about my heels. Running away might become addictive. But I had work to do...

If any of those thickheaded guards wondered why I had not myself taken to the air they perhaps believed I did not have the skill or knack of riding a saddle-flyer. Most Havilfarese peoples can fly a bird or a flying animal. But they also employ guards and buy slaves from countries where flying on the back of a monstrous bird smacks of the devil himself.

I ran. They might think of a number of places where I might go. I did not think they would guess I would make for the fitting shed. Whatever story they had pieced together, they would know from Hikdar Covell that it was the gul Chaadur who had caused this trouble, slain the Kovneva, and was now on the run from justice and the laws of Hamal.

The parking areas for fliers which regularly brought in supplies and stores had to be given a wide berth. Most of our food and timber came by quoffa cart, but the fliers which brought in specialized equipment for the yards lay neatly parked and it would be childish to suppose they would not be regarded as my target. So I avoided their dark bulks as they lay, neatly aligned, in their parks.

Guards paced before them, weapons glinting.

Then I heard the first fierce howls.

I knew.

Werstings!

They would pick up my scent at the stables. That was certain sure. The black-and-white-striped devilish forms would come bounding through the pink moons-light, tongues lolling, eyes bright, panting in their eagerness to sink their fangs into me. They were friendly enough to a friend; to the quarry they were death.

Well, I had escaped from the Manhounds of Faol. They were a scary enough bunch, Zair knows. So I ran on swiftly through the shadows and skirted the parked fliers and the cargo carts. Slaves did all this manual labor of unloading and loading and carting. I knew little of it, here in Sumbakir. The fitting shed lifted against the star glitter.

Already the ridge showed a pink icing as the Twins rose higher in the sky. Soon their light would flood down and the shadows would lessen. And shadows were my best friends this night.

The guard had been alerted. The Hamalese with their laws are assured that their lower officers obey their orders and post their sentries, and I have noticed that guards are a mark of a lawful country as well as a lawless; whether one influences the other is hard to say. He peered about, and I caught the gleam of his eyes beneath the rim of his helmet. His thraxter lay in its scabbard. His shield hung over his left shoulder and he grasped his stux as though ready to slay the ghastly minions of Hanitcha the Harrower in the next moment.

Well, he did not have phantom devils of the imagination to face. He faced me, although he did not realize it, Dray Prescot, Krozair of Zy.

I treated him gently. A distracting noise, a quiet leap, and he fell unconscious at my feet. I dragged him in through the double-doors and shut them as quietly as I could. High grilled and fretted skylights in the roof admitted a faint pink glow, enough to make my way between the dark bulks of the waiting fliers. I felt the ghostly atmosphere of this place. Soon with the morning suns the workers would open the doors and begin their daily labors; for the moment the whole space lay silent and deserted and strange.

In the black-walled room I found benches strewn with soldering apparatus, with the fires banked and aglow, piles of empty tins with their lids, and piles of dirt — sand, gravel, grit. I sifted it in my fingers. This was packed tightly into the tins and the lids were fastened. Where from this common dirt could come the magical lifting power of the voller?

I suppose, in all honesty, you who listen to these tapes spinning through the heads must have already guessed. And I too, I confess, shared a premonitory breeze of understanding, and with understanding — rejection.

For — how could it be?

Fliers of the deep-hold, square build called binhoys in Hamal arrived here regularly. The bottom doors were opened and the dirt poured out to form the jealously guarded piles. I had seen binhoys like these flying from the Heavenly Mines. They had been loaded with the broken, crushed, and refined rock the poor devils of slaves had dug from the mountain quarries. As I sifted the dirt in my fingers I think I understood that this dirt had been mixed with the refined rock from the Heavenly Mines; I understood but I did not believe.

389

Just to make sure I slid the chisel down from my sleeve and forced open the lid of a freshly soldered tin. It was as I expected filled with the dirt from the piles about me; but, also, there glittered among the grit and sand and dirt the tiny chips of rock that, I was sure, had come from the Heavenly Mines.

The shadows seemed to move as I padded out of the black-walled room and crossed the fitting shed and entered the red-walled room. Here, except for the absence of the piles of dirt, the scene was the same as the one I had left. This time when I opened a box it was empty. Delia's father knew this. He had not lied. I opened another and then another. All were empty. A small door opened off the red-walled room and I pushed it open and went into the storeroom beyond. The entire space was filled with pottery amphorae, large jars with their pointed ends sunk into the earth. They were stoppered and waxed and sealed and secured with wires.

I smashed the thraxter against one rotund jar and the amphora collapsed and fell in shards. It was empty. But — it *couldn't* be empty! No one was going to go to all the trouble of so securely sealing and wiring the stoppers on empty jars!

A faint sickly sweet odor tasted foul on my tongue, as though some careless onker had left a slice of malsidge to go rotten in the room. I looked about, and there was nothing more I could do. Silver boxes of dirt and silver boxes of air!

Dirt and air!

About to curse a foul Makki-Grodno oath I halted, my hand reaching for my thraxter hilt.

A sound, a slithery, scratchy, furtive sound from the closed double-doors brought me out into the shadows of the shed between the benches. At first I thought the sentry was recovering his senses, although I had thought he would remain unconscious longer than this, for I know to a nicety the value of my blows. Again that scratching and then the left-hand leaf of the doors groaned against its hinges — and I knew.

They can make the most devilish row when they are hunting, the werstings, ululating and shrieking and pounding down the trail after their prey. They can also move silently and swiftly and seize their quarry without warning. The nurdling cramphs almost had me.

The door eased back and the low lean shape of a wersting padded in. His head was down, his ears erect, his tail a bar like a sword. He saw me, standing there in the light from the moons, and he halted, and his companion of the pair sidled in through the half-open door.

Even then, in that moment, I noticed how two instinctive reactions battled to find first expression. Both werstings had found their quarry and now they wished to fling back their heads and howl their success to the night air, and so summon their hunting companions and their masters the Deldars of the Wersting Pack. The other instinct, the one that overcame them, was to put their heads down even lower, bare their fangs, and let their hackles bristle. Yellowy-white those fangs, cruel and sharp. Red the mouth and purplish-red the tongue. Greenish-yellow the eyes, with black pupils rounded and concentrated into complete attention upon me.

Perhaps those two werstings recognized more in me than a soldier of Hamal ever could.

I gave them no chance. Vicious, deadly, cunning, feral, are werstings. A man does ill to run from them. Without a sound I leaped full at them with the brand in my fist upraised.

They reacted with breathy snarls, lifting so as to slash me with their claws as well as attempt to hamstring me and then seize me by the throat. The thraxter slashed into the neck of the right-hand one, a controlled stroke. I followed on without a pause, ducking and avoiding the second's lunge. Now he was howling, shrill ululations that would bring the guards running. I flicked the thraxter at him and he avoided it and sprang. I barely managed to dive flat and roll over and kick him mercilessly in the belly as he flew past. We both sprang up to renew the attack, but I was that fraction faster, and I buried the thraxter in his muscular chest as he scrabbled for me. I had to thrust with massive force to penetrate the plate of gristle beneath the skin; but, shrieking and foaming and attempting to claw at the blade, he died.

I dragged the thraxter free, one foot on the black-and-white-striped corpse. I ran for the double-doors, closed them with a thump, and slotted the thick lenken beam into place in its iron staples. Now let a wersting try to sneak in!

Fresh yells broke from outside. They quieted and I heard a voice, a harsh, intemperate, hectoring voice, the foul-mouthed bellowing voice of Ornol ham Feoste, Kov of Apulad.

"You, Chaadur! We know you are in there! Come out quietly, you kleesh, and obey the law! Or, by Hanitcha the Harrower, we'll break in and tear the beating heart out of you and feed it to the werstings!"

Nineteen

A promise of Jikai

I, Dray Prescot, of Earth and of Kregen, had failed.

Failed miserably. Failed utterly.

The armed guards and soldiers of Kov Ornol surrounded the shed. The ferocious snarls and howls of the werstings resounded through the pink-lit gloom and I could hear their claws scrabbling at the doors. The Kov and his men were convinced they had me trapped in here, and they would no doubt seek to keep the werstings away from my throat so that their famous laws of Hamal could pronounce upon me. What did the law prescribe for the murder of a Kovneva?

Maybe the Jikhorkdun would be too merciful.

I was absolutely certain that Kov Ornol would go to the full rigors the law allowed in his punishment of me before I was hanged.

All this meant nothing.

All I could think of was that I had failed. I knew no more of the secrets of the fliers than when I flew one over Valka and the damned thing broke down.

There had to be some answer, somewhere...

Like a maniac I began to overturn amphorae, smash at silver boxes, run through the shed slicing and slashing with the thraxter, turn over the piles of dirt, slewing it about as we had slewed the fiery vomit of Muruaa. But nothing more was vouchsafed me in understanding of the ways of a voller.

So sure I had been that I would discover the secret here! Deldar Naghan the Triangle had told me that here in Sumbakir we built only small vollers, two- and four-place fliers, sometimes a six-place job for a special order. Over in Conelaw-lad, he said, they built larger vessels. The Air Service had their ships built in a number of yards, some near Ruathytu, the capital itself, some near Hollalalad, others at Malathytu. Maybe, there, I would find the answers I sought...

"Come out, you Kovneva-murdering rast! Come out so that I may plunge my hands into your guts and rip out your evil stinking heart!"

I didn't bother to reply.

If the answer was not here, then here was no place for me.

I thought of Avec Brand the Niltch, and of Ilter Monicep, and I knew I would miss them in the future. They were a right pair, and no mistake. Even though they were Hamalese and swore by Havil the Green, and called Opaz vile, they had been good friends. Now, I must bid them a farewell they would never hear.

The double-doors shuddered as a beam thumped against them. Those doors would stand considerable maltreatment before they would give. There would be time.

"By Hanitcha the Harrower! You yetch, Chaadur! As Malahak is my witness I will hang you by the heels over a slow fire and watch your eyeballs sizzle! You nulsh! Rast! I will carve you into strips for the werstings!"

Still I did not reply. The door shivered and a panel smashed through.

The snarls and howls of the werstings now concentrated into one area, off to one side of the door, and I guessed the Deldars had leashed them up. The Kov wanted to get his own hands on me. The werstings had done their work well. Now in the business of tearing me to shreds the Kov would take over.

The werstings were snapping and screeching in a frenzied way. Kov Ornol yelled viciously. "By Hanitcha the Harrower! Keep those nurdling werstings quiet! I want the nulsh to know what I shall do to him."

The werstings quieted down. I pulled the glowing ashes from a fire where the soldering equipment lay on the benches, and blew upon it, and fed it shavings from the grooves cut for the silver boxes in the flier's control apparatus, which looks not unlike a series of wheels a spider might construct, pivoted and swiveled. In fanning a little blaze, I built the fire. The yells outside, the thumpings on the door, all added a macabre note of chaos to the orderliness within.

I took the fire and spread it in the bottom sections of smashed amphorae like scoops. When the preparations were ready I stood back and surveyed the pink-lit gloom of the place with the red glowing eyes of the fire-crocks positioned by the fliers.

Where could the answer I so eagerly sought be hidden?

There was nothing here. I had to steel myself to that. The door splintered and the holding beam groaned and sagged. A few more murs and it would give. The doors would swing open and the Kov and his soldiers would rush in.

A fight would be a diversion. I had more important tasks to do. I knew from my private calendar that I had a few days left, and that was all, to the time of my disappearance from the voller over the Shrouded Sea.

The flier I had selected, a fast two-place craft with the lean and rakish lines of a racer that had been built, as we knew, to the special orders of a famous voller-racer in Ruathytu, lifted me easily to the roof. I eased in the down-dropping flap of the skylight and its sturm-wood lattice fell free, allowing a flood of pink light from the Twins to illuminate in fuzzy rose and wavering black the interior of the shed. I dropped to the floor again and hopped out of the flier, ran swiftly around the shed tipping the fire-filled amphorae crocks over. Some smoldered; one or two caught at the canvas or hide of the coverings and burst instantly into flames. Back in the two-place voller I rose into the air as the door at last caved in, with a smash, and soldiers leaped into the shed.

They did not see me at first. They saw the flames.

"Fire! Fire!"

After that they would be busy for a while. I shot through the opened skylight and set the controls for up and forward, and raced away into the night.

It had been so easy. If I felt regret, that was as natural as the regret I felt over my failure. And, I was to meet the Kov of Apulad, Ornol ham Feoste, again, as you shall hear…

The Star Lords had given me a year as a second prison sentence on top of the first. I had served my time — eleven years which had taken the space of ten. Now I was free! I was racing through the pink-lit night sky of Kregen for the Shrouded Sea and the airboat and my friends — and Delia!

If they pursued me I did not know then. The racer was swift, a fine craft; I was confident it would have won many important trophy challenges in the fliers' races of Ruathytu. Now, she carried me fast and far toward the southwest, over the River Os, broad and calm far below, over the settled and industrious lands beyond, past the areas in turmoil where the legions of Hamal sought to extend their empire's sway. On and on I flew, and into the daylight, and with a pause to hunt up a little food in one of the pockets of wild country found in even the most densely developed countryside of Kregen, I flashed over Methydria and so came at last to the shores of the Shrouded Sea.

All my regrets were put behind me. To the Ice Floes of Sicce with concerns over vollers for the moment! Ahead, only a day in the future, lay all I cared for or wanted in two worlds. I looked down at the pile of silver boxes I had brought, carefully separated – those from the red-walled room at one end of the voller, those from the black-walled room at the other. I would get around to those in the fullness of time.

No stormclouds, no lightnings, no supernatural phenomena prevented me carrying out my designs. The Star Lords had no objections to my rejoining Delia just after I had tumbled out of the voller in the storm, instead of waiting until I had been transported from the Heavenly Mines. Perhaps the Star Lords were, at least, taking notice of me as a human being and not as a mere puppet to obey their august wills. I did not know. I do know that I rode the little voller high above the Shrouded Sea and watched the storm bursting and roiling far out across the waters, and the feeling I had, that in the storm an airboat flew, with me aboard, chilled and exhilarated me.

Surely, the Star Lords could see that I could be trusted not to do a foolish thing? I would not seek out of overweening pride or curiosity to investigate the storm, to see if I might in fact see myself. I would see only my damn fool self smash the stanchion and tumble overboard, like a veritable coy!

With that seaman's instinct reinforced by my years of wandering the Great Plains of Segesthes I found the island of Shanpo in the Lesser Sharangil Archipelago, the islands black formless splotches against the pink glitter of the water. I swung down. Below me the Kataki were at their evil trade, the aragorn and the slave-masters arrogant in their vileness. Well, their day would come.

With the dawn I took the racer on to the far side of the island. I knew exactly what was going on in that small fishing village on the other shore, right at this minute, right now...

The slaves were rubbing their eyes, I among them, and cursing at the poor quality of the food, and being beaten. An aragorn would be running into the square and yelling and the Katakis would be beating the slaves into cover, and the fishing village would be in the process of being made to look innocent as the airboat flying Old Superb cruised into view.

All that was happening, over the hill, even now, as I waited... I felt my breathing quicken and I cursed and I spoke aloud, wrathfully, to myself.

"By the diseased intestines of Makki-Grodno, you great nurdling onker! Calm down!"

With what emotions I lifted the little racing voller into the morning air and guided her up past the trees and held her there and then — oh, yes! And then—!

That magnificent flier flew into sight, over the trees, picking up speed, heading to make another desperate search for the husband of the Princess Majestrix of Vallia. The flags of scarlet and yellow flew proudly from every staff. I stared up and I swallowed.

"By Zim-Zair!" I said.

I sent the racer up in a swirl of power and the levers were hard over and she fairly stormed through the air. I roared up to the big voller and circled her. I dived beneath her keel and rose on the other side and so turned and planed back, an Immelman of perfect execution, and dived down over the decks. Everyone had turned out. A packed forest of faces stared up at me from the decks. Arms waved, scarves fluttered. I looked over the side.

Yes! Yes — there stood Delia, one hand lifted to her forehead to shield the glow of Zim and Genodras. And — she recognized me! She waved — she waved fiercely, joyfully, triumphantly!

I slammed the little racer for the airboat's deck, for she would fit neatly enough in the broad space, and I landed her and stepped out. With a rib-crunching tackle, Delia clasped me to her and I held her and we stood and stood, fast locked in each other's arms.

"Dray! Dray!" she said at last, drawing back. "We've been looking all over! We've been frantic. And the little voller? And your clothes? And — and—"

They were all there, crowding around, shouting and laughing and welcoming me back. Seg Segutorio, Inch, Turko the Shield, Korf Aighos, Tom ti Vulheim, Naghan the Gnat, Balass the Hawk, and Tilly and Oby — all of them, jumping up and down and trying to get at me, and Delia holding me, holding me! Obquam of Tajkent, the flying Strom, circled around in his excitement — he, so grave and reserved. They made such a racket I could not make myself heard. I held up my left hand, for my right clasped my Delia to me.

They fell silent.

"Dray!" said Delia. "You great shaggy graint! You must tell us all about it — but first, you need a bath. And then we will have tea. And then we can continue on to Migladrin—"

So now they had to know, this early, this brutally.

"A bath and tea," I said. "Oh, my Delia, my Princess Majestrix!" I shouted. Then, loudly, for all to hear "You must go on to Migladrin and do what is necessary there. As for me, my duty to Valka and Vallia now lies elsewhere."

They hung on my words. Delia looked up at me, half frowning. "Now where are you flying off to, Dray Prescot?"

"I have unfinished business in Hamal. I must go to Hamal."

Their reaction should not have surprised me, but it did.

Instantly, all of them, were yelling it out: "Hamal! Hamal! We will go with you to Hamal!"

"Even to the Heavenly Mines?"

"Aye, Dray Prescot, Prince Majister! Even to the Heavenly Mines!"

This was nonsense, of course — but glorious nonsense!

There were things to be done, important things upon Kregen, for the good of Vallia and Valka and Migladrin and for the wishes of the Star Lords. I held Delia close.

"And will you, Dray, really venture to the Heavenly Mines?"

"Aye, for it will be a kind of Jikai."

"Then you will not leave me. I shall, of course, come with you."

I laughed — I, Dray Prescot, laughed.

"As to that, my Delia of Delphond, my Delia of the Blue Mountains, we shall see what we shall see!"

Endnotes

1: Notor: Lord. Prescot has used *notor* a number of times previously in his narrative and I have amended it to *lord*. I feel, though, that *notor* is peculiar to Havilfar and so have used it throughout as Prescot does. *A.B.A.*

2: Prescot has used this oath of the Rapas before and I have deleted it; here it sounds absolutely right. He spells it out and pronounces it with a clearing-of-the-throat sound. *A.B.A.*

3: This is intriguing. It seems to imply that Prescot did fight a leem barehanded before — or possibly after — he had become a Krozair of Zy on the Eye of the World. If so, it is just one more fascinating story lost to us in those tapes, as recounted in *The Suns of Scorpio*. *A.B.A.*

4: db: Dwaburs per bur.

5: See *Swordships of Scorpio,* Chapter Fifteen: "I give an opinion at Careless Repose."

6: At this point occurs another of these annoying breaks in the Tapes from Rio de Janeiro. Prescot has just begun a fresh cassette. There is a sound of a door opening in the background. Then a voice calls in Portuguese: "Dray, my friend. The cars are waiting. Leave those infernal recordings of yours!" And, distantly, there is the sound of a girl laughing. Then follows merely a muddle of noises, and the tape itself is badly creased within the cassette. This has been straightened; but quite clearly Prescot picks up the story after a gap of some time in his sojourn in Huringa in Hyrklana. What is missing we, of course, do not know. However, I think the gladiatorial life was by this time palling on him, and the disappearance of Nath the Arm from the story also offers substance to that theory. *A.B.A.*

7: As a stylor in the warrens of Magdag. See *The Suns of Scorpio*. A.B.A.

8: Town.

9: Flier and flyer. Dray Prescot has made it clear early on by spelling out the two words that by *flier* he means a voller or airboat. By *flyer* he means a man or woman who fly any one of the marvelous winged creatures of Kregen. Also, by *saddle-flyer* he means the bird or animal itself. *A.B.A.*

10: The nit of Earth is the egg of the louse, whereas on Kregen the word *nit is* clearly applied to the louse itself. This is interesting — and the reference to *Nathian* here, clearly, is to Tyr Nath, the Kregen Hercules. *A.B.A.*

11: One of those annoying gaps in the record of the Tapes from Rio de Janeiro occurs immediately after Prescot tells us that he was pitched into the basket of shonages. We have lost all details of his journey to and arrival in Sumbakir, and of the official attitude to him and Avec and Ilter. As, also, excruciatingly, we have lost what happened immediately after he took his fruit-stained face out of the shonages. *A.B.A.*

12: This is lost. *A.B.A.*